Brontë Sisters

Wuthering Heights

&

Villette

This is a FLAME TREE Book

Publisher & Creative Director: Nick Wells
Project Editor: Laura Bulbeck
Editorial Board: Catherine Taylor, Josie Mitchell, Gillian Whitaker
Brontë sisters biographies by Chris McNab & Judith John

FLAME TREE PUBLISHING
6 Melbray Mews, Fulham,
London SW6 3NS, United Kingdom
www.flametreepublishing.com

First published 2017

Copyright © 2017 Flame Tree Publishing Ltd

17 19 21 20 18
1 3 5 7 9 10 8 6 4 2

ISBN: 978-1-78664-550-0

The cover image is created by Flame Tree Studio
Typography based on Octavia Script, Will Sherring and ITC Garamond

A copy of the CIP data for this book is available from the British Library.

Printed and bound in Italy

Foreword by
Alison Case

Brontë Sisters

Wuthering Heights & Villette

FLAME TREE
PUBLISHING

Romantic Fantasy

Contents

Emily Brontë
Wuthering Heights

Charlotte Brontë
Villette

Foreword

IN 1842, two Brontë sisters, Charlotte, 25, and Emily, 23, left their home in remote Yorkshire to travel alone to Brussels. By studying French there, they hoped to qualify themselves to run a school for young ladies with their younger sister Anne. Fortunately for English literature, the school didn't pan out, and the three sisters soon turned to novel writing instead.

For homesick Emily, the trip abroad only confirmed her deep need for her own corner of Yorkshire, and especially for the wild world of the moors that, at Haworth Parsonage, lay at their doorstep. From that love for the landscape, its passionate, rough-edged inhabitants, and the dark stories that swirled around them, she crafted her singular masterpiece, *Wuthering Heights*. Small wonder, then, that novel and landscape have since merged, with many natural features in 'Brontë country' now renamed to highlight their connection to the novel.

What Charlotte found in Brussels proved more momentous for her – a teacher, M. Heger, who recognized something of her genius, and sought to train and cultivate it. Together they brewed that heady excitement of committed teacher and eager pupil that has sometimes led to, and too often been mistaken for, a mighty love. Her last finished novel transforms Brussels into the fictional city of Villette, and M. Heger into the mercurial professor, M. Paul, who takes an interest in the school's lonely English teacher, Lucy Snow.

Wuthering Heights and *Villette* are the strangest of the Brontë sisters' seven novels. These are novels of painful, wrenching passion, passion that tortures the beloved and the self, up to the threshold of madness, and sometimes over it. Both novels, too, flirt with the supernatural, bringing in the exiled ghosts and murdered nuns of Gothic fiction from their conventional locations in remote medieval castles, into the homes of modern-day England or the bourgeois terraces of 'Villette'.

Emily Brontë's heroine Catherine Earnshaw is larger than life: beautiful, privileged, willful, and unapologetically demanding, she seeks love and freedom together at a time when, for women, they were diametrically opposed. Heathcliff, her childhood companion grown into a dark, mysterious lover, is equally scornful of constraint, attacking anyone who comes between him and his love. Between them, they strew the moors with human wreckage, including each other. It is left to the younger generation to make peace with the world, and find a kinder love.

At first glance, Lucy Snow is Catherine's polar opposite: plain, poor, and without a family, she seems to prefer to fade into the woodwork, observing yet unobserved, elusive even as a narrator. Desire, even for friendship, she views as her enemy, threatening her hard-won emotional self-sufficiency. Yet the sheer force of her self-suppression is also a measure of her capacity for passion. Inevitably, it breaks down. *Villette* is a novel of deep psychological complexity, and Lucy Snow remains one of the most intriguing and compelling characters of Victorian fiction.

Enjoy, then, these two novels of passion that do not find their conventional happy ending, and yet triumph, even over death.

Alison Case
english.williams.edu/profile/acase/

Publisher's Note

THE BRONTË SISTERS, though they originally published their works under male pseudonyms, have since earned their places amongst the most beloved of British authors. We include here in this collection two fantastic reads: Emily Brontë's revered work of tortured love, *Wuthering Heights*, and Charlotte Brontë's lesser known but equally passionate story, *Villette*. The wild and dramatic moors in *Wuthering Heights* are the perfect setting for one of the most tempestuous love affairs in literature: that of Catherine and Heathcliff. Although Emily's only novel is the more famous of the two stories in this collection, the neglected *Villette*'s wonderful narrative of repressed and unrequited love rewards repeated readings. It is no wonder that the Brontës' masterpieces have become literary classics.

We have edited the original texts as little as possible, whilst still making choices about how to best present them for full enjoyment and ease of reading. Both of the novels were originally printed in either two or three volumes, and we have identified where these begin, for interest; but the chapter numbers continue to flow chronologically, for clarity. You may note that the start of the second volume in *Wuthering Heights* is not where you might expect it to be in terms of the story (perhaps expecting Volume Two to start with Chapter Eighteen, after the significant passage of time); however we have kept to the original publication. We hope you take great pleasure in either discovering or rediscovering the two stories collected here.

Emily Brontë

Wuthering Heights

Volume One

Chapter One

1801. – I have just returned from a visit to my landlord – the solitary neighbour that I shall be troubled with. This is certainly a beautiful country! In all England, I do not believe that I could have fixed on a situation so completely removed from the stir of society. A perfect misanthropist's heaven: and Mr. Heathcliff and I are such a suitable pair to divide the desolation between us. A capital fellow! He little imagined how my heart warmed towards him when I beheld his black eyes withdraw so suspiciously under their brows, as I rode up, and when his fingers sheltered themselves, with a jealous resolution, still further in his waistcoat, as I announced my name.

"Mr. Heathcliff?" I said.

A nod was the answer.

"Mr. Lockwood, your new tenant, sir. I do myself the honour of calling as soon as possible after my arrival, to express the hope that I have not inconvenienced you by my perseverance in soliciting the occupation of Thrushcross Grange: I heard yesterday you had had some thoughts –"

"Thrushcross Grange is my own, sir," he interrupted, wincing. "I should not allow anyone to inconvenience me, if I could hinder it – walk in!"

The 'walk in' was uttered with closed teeth, and expressed the sentiment, 'Go to the Deuce:' even the gate over which he leant manifested no sympathising movement to the words; and I think that circumstance determined me to accept the invitation: I felt interested in a man who seemed more exaggeratedly reserved than myself.

When he saw my horse's breast fairly pushing the barrier, he did put out his hand to unchain it, and then sullenly preceded me up the causeway, calling, as we entered the court, – "Joseph, take Mr. Lockwood's horse; and bring up some wine."

"Here we have the whole establishment of domestics, I suppose," was the reflection suggested by this compound order. "No wonder the grass grows up between the flags, and cattle are the only hedge-cutters."

Joseph was an elderly, nay, an old man: very old, perhaps, though hale and sinewy. "The Lord help us!" he soliloquised in an undertone of peevish displeasure, while relieving me of my horse: looking, meantime, in my face so sourly that I charitably conjectured he must have need of divine aid to digest his dinner, and his pious ejaculation had no reference to my unexpected advent.

Wuthering Heights is the name of Mr. Heathcliff's dwelling. 'Wuthering' being a significant provincial adjective, descriptive of the atmospheric tumult to which its station is exposed in stormy weather. Pure, bracing ventilation they must have up there at all times, indeed: one may guess the power of the north wind blowing over the edge, by the excessive slant of a few stunted firs at the end of the house; and by a range of gaunt thorns all stretching their limbs one way, as if craving alms of the sun. Happily, the architect had foresight to build it strong: the narrow windows are deeply set in the wall, and the corners defended with large jutting stones.

Before passing the threshold, I paused to admire a quantity of grotesque carving lavished over the front, and especially about the principal door; above which, among a wilderness of crumbling griffins and shameless little boys, I detected the date '1500', and the name 'Hareton Earnshaw'. I would have made a few comments, and requested a short history of the place from the surly owner; but his attitude at the door appeared to demand my speedy entrance, or complete departure, and I had no desire to aggravate his impatience previous to inspecting the penetralium.

One stop brought us into the family sitting-room, without any introductory lobby or passage: they call it here 'the house' pre-eminently. It includes kitchen and parlour, generally; but I believe at Wuthering Heights the kitchen is forced to retreat altogether into another quarter: at least I distinguished a chatter of tongues, and a clatter of culinary utensils, deep within; and I observed no signs of roasting, boiling, or baking, about the huge fireplace; nor any glitter of copper saucepans and tin cullenders on the walls. One end, indeed, reflected splendidly both light and heat from ranks of immense pewter dishes, interspersed with silver jugs and tankards, towering row after row, on a vast oak dresser, to the very roof. The latter had never been under-drawn: its entire anatomy lay bare to an inquiring eye, except where a frame of wood laden with oatcakes and clusters of legs of beef, mutton, and ham, concealed it. Above the chimney were sundry villainous old guns, and a couple of horse-pistols: and, by way of ornament, three gaudily-painted canisters disposed along its ledge. The floor was of smooth, white stone; the chairs, high-backed, primitive structures, painted green: one or two heavy black ones lurking in the shade. In an arch under the dresser reposed a huge, liver-coloured bitch pointer, surrounded by a swarm of squealing puppies; and other dogs haunted other recesses.

The apartment and furniture would have been nothing extraordinary as belonging to a homely, northern farmer, with a stubborn countenance, and stalwart limbs set out to advantage in knee-breeches and gaiters. Such an individual seated in his arm-chair, his mug of ale frothing on the round table before him, is to be seen in any circuit of five or six miles among these hills, if you go at the right time after dinner. But Mr. Heathcliff forms a singular contrast to his abode and style of living. He is a dark-skinned gipsy in aspect, in dress and manners a gentleman: that is, as much a gentleman as many a country squire: rather slovenly, perhaps, yet not looking amiss with his negligence, because he has an erect and handsome figure; and rather morose. Possibly, some people might suspect him of a degree of under-bred pride; I have a sympathetic chord within that tells me it is nothing of the sort: I know, by instinct, his reserve springs from an aversion to showy displays of feeling – to manifestations of mutual kindliness. He'll love and hate equally under cover, and esteem it a species of impertinence to be loved or hated again. No, I'm running on too fast: I bestow my own attributes over-liberally on him. Mr. Heathcliff may have entirely dissimilar reasons for keeping his hand out of the way when he meets a would-be acquaintance, to those which actuate me. Let me hope my constitution is almost peculiar: my dear mother used to say I should never have a comfortable home; and only last summer I proved myself perfectly unworthy of one.

While enjoying a month of fine weather at the sea-coast, I was thrown into the company of a most fascinating creature: a real goddess in my eyes, as long as she took no notice of me. I 'never told my love' vocally; still, if looks have language, the merest idiot might have guessed I was over head and ears: she understood me at last, and looked a return – the sweetest of all imaginable looks. And what did I do? I confess it with shame – shrunk icily into myself, like a snail; at every glance retired colder and farther; till finally the poor innocent was led to doubt her own senses, and, overwhelmed with confusion at her supposed mistake, persuaded her mamma to decamp. By this curious turn of disposition I have gained the reputation of deliberate heartlessness; how undeserved, I alone can appreciate.

I took a seat at the end of the hearthstone opposite that towards which my landlord advanced, and filled up an interval of silence by attempting to caress the canine mother, who had left her nursery, and was sneaking wolfishly to the back of my legs, her lip curled up, and her white teeth watering for a snatch. My caress provoked a long, guttural gnarl.

"You'd better let the dog alone," growled Mr. Heathcliff in unison, checking fiercer demonstrations with a punch of his foot. "She's not accustomed to be spoiled – not kept for a pet." Then, striding to a side door, he shouted again, "Joseph!"

Joseph mumbled indistinctly in the depths of the cellar, but gave no intimation of ascending; so his master dived down to him, leaving me *vis-à-vis* the ruffianly bitch and a pair of grim shaggy sheep-dogs, who shared with her a jealous guardianship over all my movements. Not anxious to come in contact with their fangs, I sat still; but, imagining they would scarcely understand tacit insults, I unfortunately indulged in winking and making faces at the trio, and some turn of my physiognomy so irritated madam, that she suddenly broke into a fury and leapt on my knees. I flung her back, and hastened to interpose the table between us. This proceeding aroused the whole hive: half-a-dozen four-footed fiends, of various sizes and ages, issued from hidden dens to the common centre. I felt my heels and coat-laps peculiar subjects of assault; and parrying off the larger combatants as effectually as I could with the poker, I was constrained to demand, aloud, assistance from some of the household in re-establishing peace.

Mr. Heathcliff and his man climbed the cellar steps with vexatious phlegm: I don't think they moved one second faster than usual, though the hearth was an absolute tempest of worrying and yelping. Happily, an inhabitant of the kitchen made more despatch: a lusty dame, with tucked-up gown, bare arms, and fire-flushed cheeks, rushed into the midst of us flourishing a frying-pan: and used that weapon, and her tongue, to such purpose, that the storm subsided magically, and she only remained, heaving like a sea after a high wind, when her master entered on the scene.

"What the devil is the matter?" he asked, eyeing me in a manner that I could ill endure, after this inhospitable treatment.

"What the devil, indeed!" I muttered. "The herd of possessed swine could have had no worse spirits in them than those animals of yours, sir. You might as well leave a stranger with a brood of tigers!"

"They won't meddle with persons who touch nothing," he remarked, putting the bottle before me, and restoring the displaced table. "The dogs do right to be vigilant. Take a glass of wine?"

"No, thank you."

"Not bitten, are you?"

"If I had been, I would have set my signet on the biter." Heathcliff's countenance relaxed into a grin.

"Come, come," he said, "you are flurried, Mr. Lockwood. Here, take a little wine. Guests are so exceedingly rare in this house that I and my dogs, I am willing to own, hardly know how to receive them. Your health, sir?"

I bowed and returned the pledge; beginning to perceive that it would be foolish to sit sulking for the misbehaviour of a pack of curs; besides, I felt loth to yield the fellow further amusement at my expense; since his humour took that turn. He – probably swayed by prudential consideration of the folly of offending a good tenant – relaxed a little in the laconic style of chipping off his pronouns and auxiliary verbs, and introduced what he supposed would be a subject of interest to me, – a discourse on the advantages and disadvantages of my present place of retirement. I found him very intelligent on the topics we touched; and before I went home, I was encouraged so far as to volunteer another visit tomorrow. He evidently wished no repetition of my intrusion. I shall go, notwithstanding. It is astonishing how sociable I feel myself compared with him.

Chapter Two

YESTERDAY AFTERNOON set in misty and cold. I had half a mind to spend it by my study fire, instead of wading through heath and mud to Wuthering Heights. On coming up from dinner, however, (N.B. – I dine between twelve and one o'clock; the housekeeper, a matronly lady, taken as a fixture along with the house, could not, or would not, comprehend my request that I might be served at five) – on mounting the stairs with this lazy intention, and stepping into the room, I saw a servant-girl on her knees surrounded by brushes and coal-scuttles, and raising an infernal dust as she extinguished the flames with heaps of cinders. This spectacle drove me back immediately; I took my hat, and, after a four-miles' walk, arrived at Heathcliff's garden-gate just in time to escape the first feathery flakes of a snow-shower.

On that bleak hill-top the earth was hard with a black frost, and the air made me shiver through every limb. Being unable to remove the chain, I jumped over, and, running up the flagged causeway bordered with straggling gooseberry-bushes, knocked vainly for admittance, till my knuckles tingled and the dogs howled.

"Wretched inmates!" I ejaculated, mentally, "you deserve perpetual isolation from your species for your churlish inhospitality. At least, I would not keep my doors barred in the day-time. I don't care – I will get in!" So resolved, I grasped the latch and shook it vehemently. Vinegar-faced Joseph projected his head from a round window of the barn.

"What are ye for?" he shouted. "T' maister's down I' t' fowld. Go round by th' end o' t' laith, if ye went to spake to him."

"Is there nobody inside to open the door?" I hallooed, responsively.

"There's nobbut t' missis; and shoo'll not oppen 't an ye mak' yer flaysome dins till neeght."

"Why? Cannot you tell her whom I am, eh, Joseph?"

"Nor-ne me! I'll hae no hend wi't," muttered the head, vanishing.

The snow began to drive thickly. I seized the handle to essay another trial; when a young man without coat, and shouldering a pitchfork, appeared in the yard behind. He hailed me to follow him, and, after marching through a wash-house, and a paved area containing a coal-shed, pump, and pigeon-cot, we at length arrived in the huge, warm, cheerful apartment where I was formerly received. It glowed delightfully in the radiance of an immense fire, compounded of coal, peat, and wood; and near the table, laid for a plentiful evening meal, I was pleased to observe the 'missis', an individual whose existence I had never previously suspected. I bowed and waited, thinking she would bid me take a seat. She looked at me, leaning back in her chair, and remained motionless and mute.

"Rough weather!" I remarked. "I'm afraid, Mrs. Heathcliff, the door must bear the consequence of your servants' leisure attendance: I had hard work to make them hear me."

She never opened her mouth. I stared – she stared also: at any rate, she kept her eyes on me in a cool, regardless manner, exceedingly embarrassing and disagreeable.

"Sit down," said the young man, gruffly. "He'll be in soon."

I obeyed; and hemmed, and called the villain Juno, who deigned, at this second interview, to move the extreme tip of her tail, in token of owning my acquaintance.

"A beautiful animal!" I commenced again. "Do you intend parting with the little ones, madam?"

"They are not mine," said the amiable hostess, more repellingly than Heathcliff himself could have replied.

"Ah, your favourites are among these?" I continued, turning to an obscure cushion full of something like cats.

"A strange choice of favourites!" she observed scornfully.

Unluckily, it was a heap of dead rabbits. I hemmed once more, and drew closer to the hearth, repeating my comment on the wildness of the evening.

"You should not have come out," she said, rising and reaching from the chimney-piece two of the painted canisters.

Her position before was sheltered from the light; now, I had a distinct view of her whole figure and countenance. She was slender, and apparently scarcely past girlhood: an admirable form, and the most exquisite little face that I have ever had the pleasure of beholding; small features, very fair; flaxen ringlets, or rather golden, hanging loose on her delicate neck; and eyes, had they been agreeable in expression, that would have been irresistible: fortunately for my susceptible heart, the only sentiment they evinced hovered between scorn and a kind of desperation, singularly unnatural to be detected there. The canisters were almost out of her reach; I made a motion to aid her; she turned upon me as a miser might turn if anyone attempted to assist him in counting his gold.

"I don't want your help," she snapped; "I can get them for myself."

"I beg your pardon!" I hastened to reply.

"Were you asked to tea?" she demanded, tying an apron over her neat black frock, and standing with a spoonful of the leaf poised over the pot.

"I shall be glad to have a cup," I answered.

"Were you asked?" she repeated.

"No," I said, half smiling. "You are the proper person to ask me."

She flung the tea back, spoon and all, and resumed her chair in a pet; her forehead corrugated, and her red under-lip pushed out, like a child's ready to cry.

Meanwhile, the young man had slung on to his person a decidedly shabby upper garment, and, erecting himself before the blaze, looked down on me from the corner of his eyes, for all the world as if there were some mortal feud unavenged between us. I began to doubt whether he were a servant or not: his dress and speech were both rude, entirely devoid of the superiority observable in Mr. and Mrs. Heathcliff; his thick brown curls were rough and uncultivated, his whiskers encroached bearishly over his cheeks, and his hands were embrowned like those of a common labourer: still his bearing was free, almost haughty, and he showed none of a domestic's assiduity in attending on the lady of the house. In the absence of clear proofs of his condition, I deemed it best to abstain from noticing his curious conduct; and, five minutes afterwards, the entrance of Heathcliff relieved me, in some measure, from my uncomfortable state.

"You see, sir, I am come, according to promise!" I exclaimed, assuming the cheerful; "and I fear I shall be weather-bound for half an hour, if you can afford me shelter during that space."

"Half an hour?" he said, shaking the white flakes from his clothes; "I wonder you should select the thick of a snow-storm to ramble about in. Do you know that you run a risk of being lost in the marshes? People familiar with these moors often miss their road on such evenings; and I can tell you there is no chance of a change at present."

"Perhaps I can get a guide among your lads, and he might stay at the Grange till morning – could you spare me one?"

"No, I could not."

"Oh, indeed! Well, then, I must trust to my own sagacity."

"Umph!"

"Are you going to mak' the tea?" demanded he of the shabby coat, shifting his ferocious gaze from me to the young lady.

"Is *he* to have any?" she asked, appealing to Heathcliff.

"Get it ready, will you?" was the answer, uttered so savagely that I started. The tone in which the words were said revealed a genuine bad nature. I no longer felt inclined to call Heathcliff a capital fellow. When the preparations were finished, he invited me with – "Now, sir, bring forward your chair." And we all, including the rustic youth, drew round the table: an austere silence prevailing while we discussed our meal.

I thought, if I had caused the cloud, it was my duty to make an effort to dispel it. They could not every day sit so grim and taciturn; and it was impossible, however ill-tempered they might be, that the universal scowl they wore was their everyday countenance.

"It is strange," I began, in the interval of swallowing one cup of tea and receiving another – "it is strange how custom can mould our tastes and ideas: many could not imagine the existence of happiness in a life of such complete exile from the world as you spend, Mr. Heathcliff; yet, I'll venture to say, that, surrounded by your family, and with your amiable lady as the presiding genius over your home and heart –"

"My amiable lady!" he interrupted, with an almost diabolical sneer on his face. "Where is she – my amiable lady?"

"Mrs. Heathcliff, your wife, I mean."

"Well, yes – oh, you would intimate that her spirit has taken the post of ministering angel, and guards the fortunes of Wuthering Heights, even when her body is gone. Is that it?"

Perceiving myself in a blunder, I attempted to correct it. I might have seen there was too great a disparity between the ages of the parties to make it likely that they were man and wife. One was about forty: a period of mental vigour at which men seldom cherish the delusion of being married for love by girls: that dream is reserved for the solace of our declining years. The other did not look seventeen.

Then it flashed on me – "The clown at my elbow, who is drinking his tea out of a basin and eating his bread with unwashed hands, may be her husband: Heathcliff junior, of course. Here is the consequence of being buried alive: she has thrown herself away upon that boor from sheer ignorance that better individuals existed! A sad pity – I must beware how I cause her to regret her choice." The last reflection may seem conceited; it was not. My neighbour struck me as bordering on repulsive; I knew, through experience, that I was tolerably attractive.

"Mrs. Heathcliff is my daughter-in-law," said Heathcliff, corroborating my surmise. He turned, as he spoke, a peculiar look in her direction: a look of hatred; unless he has a most perverse set of facial muscles that will not, like those of other people, interpret the language of his soul.

"Ah, certainly – I see now: you are the favoured possessor of the beneficent fairy," I remarked, turning to my neighbour.

This was worse than before: the youth grew crimson, and clenched his fist, with every appearance of a meditated assault. But he seemed to recollect himself presently, and smothered the storm in a brutal curse, muttered on my behalf: which, however, I took care not to notice.

"Unhappy in your conjectures, sir," observed my host; "we neither of us have the privilege of owning your good fairy; her mate is dead. I said she was my daughter-in-law: therefore, she must have married my son."

"And this young man is –"

"Not my son, assuredly."

Heathcliff smiled again, as if it were rather too bold a jest to attribute the paternity of that bear to him.

"My name is Hareton Earnshaw," growled the other; "and I'd counsel you to respect it!"

"I've shown no disrespect," was my reply, laughing internally at the dignity with which he announced himself.

He fixed his eye on me longer than I cared to return the stare, for fear I might be tempted either to box his ears or render my hilarity audible. I began to feel unmistakably out of place in that pleasant family circle. The dismal spiritual atmosphere overcame, and more than neutralised, the glowing physical comforts round me; and I resolved to be cautious how I ventured under those rafters a third time.

The business of eating being concluded, and no one uttering a word of sociable conversation, I approached a window to examine the weather. A sorrowful sight I saw: dark night coming down prematurely, and sky and hills mingled in one bitter whirl of wind and suffocating snow.

"I don't think it possible for me to get home now without a guide," I could not help exclaiming. "The roads will be buried already; and, if they were bare, I could scarcely distinguish a foot in advance."

"Hareton, drive those dozen sheep into the barn porch. They'll be covered if left in the fold all night: and put a plank before them," said Heathcliff.

"How must I do?" I continued, with rising irritation.

There was no reply to my question; and on looking round I saw only Joseph bringing in a pail of porridge for the dogs, and Mrs. Heathcliff leaning over the fire, diverting herself with burning a bundle of matches which had fallen from the chimney-piece as she restored the tea-canister to its place. The former, when he had deposited his burden, took a critical survey of the room, and in cracked tones grated out – "Aw wonder how yah can faishion to stand thear i' idleness un war, when all on 'ems goan out! Bud yah're a nowt, and it's no use talking – yah'll niver mend o'yer ill ways, but goa raight to t' divil, like yer mother afore ye!"

I imagined, for a moment, that this piece of eloquence was addressed to me; and, sufficiently enraged, stepped towards the aged rascal with an intention of kicking him out of the door. Mrs. Heathcliff, however, checked me by her answer.

"You scandalous old hypocrite!" she replied. "Are you not afraid of being carried away bodily, whenever you mention the devil's name? I warn you to refrain from provoking me, or I'll ask your abduction as a special favour! Stop! Look here, Joseph," she continued, taking a long, dark book from a shelf; "I'll show you how far I've progressed in the Black Art: I shall soon be competent to make a clear house of it. The red cow didn't die by chance; and your rheumatism can hardly be reckoned among providential visitations!"

"Oh, wicked, wicked!" gasped the elder; "may the Lord deliver us from evil!"

"No, reprobate! You are a castaway – be off, or I'll hurt you seriously! I'll have you all modelled in wax and clay! And the first who passes the limits I fix shall – I'll not say what he shall be done to – but, you'll see! Go, I'm looking at you!"

The little witch put a mock malignity into her beautiful eyes, and Joseph, trembling with sincere horror, hurried out, praying, and ejaculating 'wicked' as he went. I thought her conduct must be prompted by a species of dreary fun; and, now that we were alone, I endeavoured to interest her in my distress.

"Mrs. Heathcliff," I said earnestly, "you must excuse me for troubling you. I presume, because, with that face, I'm sure you cannot help being good-hearted. Do point out some landmarks by which I may know my way home: I have no more idea how to get there than you would have how to get to London!"

"Take the road you came," she answered, ensconcing herself in a chair, with a candle, and the long book open before her. "It is brief advice, but as sound as I can give."

"Then, if you hear of me being discovered dead in a bog or a pit full of snow, your conscience won't whisper that it is partly your fault?"

"How so? I cannot escort you. They wouldn't let me go to the end of the garden wall."

"*You!* I should be sorry to ask you to cross the threshold, for my convenience, on such a night," I cried. "I want you to tell me my way, not to *show* it: or else to persuade Mr. Heathcliff to give me a guide."

"Who? There is himself, Earnshaw, Zillah, Joseph and I. Which would you have?"

"Are there no boys at the farm?"

"No; those are all."

"Then, it follows that I am compelled to stay."

"That you may settle with your host. I have nothing to do with it."

"I hope it will be a lesson to you to make no more rash journeys on these hills," cried Heathcliff's stern voice from the kitchen entrance. "As to staying here, I don't keep accommodations for visitors: you must share a bed with Hareton or Joseph, if you do."

"I can sleep on a chair in this room," I replied.

"No, no! A stranger is a stranger, be he rich or poor: it will not suit me to permit anyone the range of the place while I am off guard!" said the unmannerly wretch.

With this insult my patience was at an end. I uttered an expression of disgust, and pushed past him into the yard, running against Earnshaw in my haste. It was so dark that I could not see the means of exit; and, as I wandered round, I heard another specimen of their civil behaviour amongst each other. At first the young man appeared about to befriend me.

"I'll go with him as far as the park," he said.

"You'll go with him to hell!" exclaimed his master, or whatever relation he bore. "And who is to look after the horses, eh?"

"A man's life is of more consequence than one evening's neglect of the horses: somebody must go," murmured Mrs. Heathcliff, more kindly than I expected.

"Not at your command!" retorted Hareton. "If you set store on him, you'd better be quiet."

"Then I hope his ghost will haunt you; and I hope Mr. Heathcliff will never get another tenant till the Grange is a ruin," she answered, sharply.

"Hearken, hearken, shoo's cursing on 'em!" muttered Joseph, towards whom I had been steering.

He sat within earshot, milking the cows by the light of a lantern, which I seized unceremoniously, and, calling out that I would send it back on the morrow, rushed to the nearest postern.

"Maister, maister, he's staling t' lanthern!" shouted the ancient, pursuing my retreat. "Hey, Gnasher! Hey, dog! Hey Wolf, holld him, holld him!"

On opening the little door, two hairy monsters flew at my throat, bearing me down, and extinguishing the light; while a mingled guffaw from Heathcliff and Hareton put the copestone on my rage and humiliation. Fortunately, the beasts seemed more bent on stretching their paws, and yawning, and flourishing their tails, than devouring me alive; but they would suffer no resurrection, and I was forced to lie till their malignant masters pleased to deliver me: then, hatless and trembling with wrath, I ordered the miscreants to let me out – on their peril to keep me one minute longer – with several incoherent threats of retaliation that, in their indefinite depth of virulency, smacked of King Lear.

The vehemence of my agitation brought on a copious bleeding at the nose, and still Heathcliff laughed, and still I scolded. I don't know what would have concluded the scene, had there not been one person at hand rather more rational than myself, and more benevolent than my entertainer. This was Zillah, the stout housewife; who at length issued forth to inquire into the nature of the uproar. She thought that some of them had been laying violent hands on me; and, not daring to attack her master, she turned her vocal artillery against the younger scoundrel.

"Well, Mr. Earnshaw," she cried, "I wonder what you'll have agait next? Are we going to murder folk on our very door-stones? I see this house will never do for me – look at t' poor lad, he's fair choking! Wisht, wisht; you mun'n't go on so. Come in, and I'll cure that: there now, hold ye still."

With these words she suddenly splashed a pint of icy water down my neck, and pulled me into the kitchen. Mr. Heathcliff followed, his accidental merriment expiring quickly in his habitual moroseness.

I was sick exceedingly, and dizzy, and faint; and thus compelled perforce to accept lodgings under his roof. He told Zillah to give me a glass of brandy, and then passed on to the inner room; while she condoled with me on my sorry predicament, and having obeyed his orders, whereby I was somewhat revived, ushered me to bed.

Chapter Three

WHILE LEADING the way upstairs, she recommended that I should hide the candle, and not make a noise; for her master had an odd notion about the chamber she would put me in, and never let anybody lodge there willingly. I asked the reason. She did not know, she answered: she had only lived there a year or two; and they had so many queer goings on, she could not begin to be curious.

Too stupefied to be curious myself, I fastened my door and glanced round for the bed. The whole furniture consisted of a chair, a clothes-press, and a large oak case, with squares cut out near the top resembling coach windows. Having approached this structure, I looked inside, and perceived it to be a singular sort of old-fashioned couch, very conveniently designed to obviate the necessity for every member of the family having a room to himself. In fact, it formed a little closet, and the ledge of a window, which it enclosed, served as a table. I slid back the panelled sides, got in with my light, pulled them together again, and felt secure against the vigilance of Heathcliff, and everyone else.

The ledge, where I placed my candle, had a few mildewed books piled up in one corner; and it was covered with writing scratched on the paint. This writing, however, was nothing but a name repeated in all kinds of characters, large and small – *Catherine Earnshaw*, here and there varied to *Catherine Heathcliff*, and then again to *Catherine Linton*.

In vapid listlessness I leant my head against the window, and continued spelling over Catherine Earnshaw – Heathcliff – Linton, till my eyes closed; but they had not rested five minutes when a glare of white letters started from the dark, as vivid as spectres – the air swarmed with Catherines; and rousing myself to dispel the obtrusive name, I discovered my candle-wick reclining on one of the antique volumes, and perfuming the place with an odour of roasted calf-skin. I snuffed it off, and, very ill at ease under the influence of cold and lingering nausea, sat up and spread open the injured tome on my knee. It was a Testament, in lean type, and smelling dreadfully musty: a fly-leaf bore the inscription – 'Catherine Earnshaw, her book', and a date some quarter of a century back. I shut it, and took up another and another, till I had examined all. Catherine's library was select, and its state of dilapidation proved it to have been well used, though not altogether for a legitimate purpose: scarcely one chapter had escaped, a pen-and-ink commentary – at least the appearance of one – covering every morsel of blank that the printer had left. Some were detached sentences; other parts took the form of a regular diary, scrawled in an unformed, childish hand. At the top of an extra page (quite a treasure, probably, when first lighted on) I was greatly amused to behold an excellent caricature of my friend Joseph, – rudely, yet powerfully sketched. An immediate interest kindled within me for the unknown Catherine, and I began forthwith to decipher her faded hieroglyphics.

An awful Sunday, commenced the paragraph beneath. *I wish my father were back again. Hindley is a detestable substitute – his conduct to Heathcliff is atrocious – H. and I are going to rebel – we took our initiatory step this evening.*

All day had been flooding with rain; we could not go to church, so Joseph must needs get up a congregation in the garret; and, while Hindley and his wife basked downstairs before a comfortable fire – doing anything but reading their Bibles, I'll answer for it – Heathcliff, myself, and the unhappy ploughboy were commanded to take our prayer-books, and mount: we were ranged in a row, on a sack of corn, groaning and shivering, and hoping that Joseph would shiver too, so that he might give us a short homily for his own sake. A vain idea! The service lasted precisely three hours; and yet my brother had the face to exclaim, when he saw us descending, "What, done already?" On Sunday evenings we used to be permitted to play, if we did not make much noise; now a mere titter is sufficient to send us into corners.

"You forget you have a master here," says the tyrant. "I'll demolish the first who puts me out of temper! I insist on perfect sobriety and silence. Oh, boy! Was that you? Frances darling, pull his hair as you go by: I heard him snap his fingers." Frances pulled his hair heartily, and then went and seated herself on her husband's knee, and there they were, like two babies, kissing and talking nonsense by the hour – foolish palaver that we should be ashamed of. We made ourselves as snug as our means allowed in the arch of the dresser. I had just fastened our pinafores together, and hung them up for a curtain, when in comes Joseph, on an errand from the stables. He tears down my handiwork, boxes my ears, and croaks:

"T' maister nobbut just buried, and Sabbath not o'ered, und t' sound o' t' gospel still i' yer lugs, and ye darr be laiking! Shame on ye! Sit ye down, ill childer! There's good books eneugh if ye'll read 'em: sit ye down, and think o' yer sowls!"

Saying this, he compelled us so to square our positions that we might receive from the far-off fire a dull ray to show us the text of the lumber he thrust upon us. I could not bear the employment. I took my dingy volume by the scroop, and hurled it into the dog-kennel, vowing I hated a good book. Heathcliff kicked his to the same place. Then there was a hubbub!

"Maister Hindley!" shouted our chaplain. "Maister, coom hither! Miss Cathy's riven th' back off 'Th' Helmet o' Salvation,' un' Heathcliff's pawsed his fit into t' first part o' 'T' Brooad Way to Destruction!' It's fair flaysome that ye let 'em go on this gait. Ech! th' owd man wad ha' laced 'em properly – but he's goan!"

Hindley hurried up from his paradise on the hearth, and seizing one of us by the collar, and the other by the arm, hurled both into the back-kitchen; where, Joseph asseverated, 'owd Nick' would fetch us as sure as we were living: and, so comforted, we each sought a separate nook to await his advent. I reached this book, and a pot of ink from a shelf, and pushed the house-door ajar to give me light, and I have got the time on with writing for twenty minutes; but my companion is impatient, and proposes that we should appropriate the dairywoman's cloak, and have a scamper on the moors, under its shelter. A pleasant suggestion – and then, if the surly old man come in, he may believe his prophecy verified – we cannot be damper, or colder, in the rain than we are here.

* * *

I suppose Catherine fulfilled her project, for the next sentence took up another subject: she waxed lachrymose.

How little did I dream that Hindley would ever make me cry so! She wrote. *My head aches, till I cannot keep it on the pillow; and still I can't give over. Poor Heathcliff! Hindley calls him a vagabond, and won't let him sit with us, nor eat with us any more; and, he says, he and I must not play together, and threatens to turn him out of the house if we break his orders. He has been blaming our father (how dared he?) for treating H. too liberally; and swears he will reduce him to his right place –*

* * *

I began to nod drowsily over the dim page: my eye wandered from manuscript to print. I saw a red ornamented title – 'Seventy Times Seven, and the First of the Seventy-First. A Pious Discourse delivered by the Reverend Jabez Branderham, in the Chapel of Gimmerden Sough.' And while I was, half-consciously, worrying my brain to guess what Jabez Branderham would make of his subject, I sank back in bed, and fell asleep. Alas, for the effects of bad tea and bad temper! What else could it be that made me pass such a terrible night? I don't remember another that I can at all compare with it since I was capable of suffering.

I began to dream, almost before I ceased to be sensible of my locality. I thought it was morning; and I had set out on my way home, with Joseph for a guide. The snow lay yards deep in our road; and, as we floundered on, my companion wearied me with constant reproaches that I had not brought a pilgrim's staff: telling me that I could never get into the house without one, and boastfully flourishing a heavy-headed cudgel, which I understood to be so denominated. For a moment I considered it absurd that I should need such a weapon to gain admittance into my own residence. Then a new idea flashed across me. I was not going there: we were journeying to hear the famous Jabez Branderham preach, from the text – 'Seventy Times Seven'; and either Joseph, the preacher, or I had committed the 'First of the Seventy-First', and were to be publicly exposed and excommunicated.

We came to the chapel. I have passed it really in my walks, twice or thrice; it lies in a hollow, between two hills: an elevated hollow, near a swamp, whose peaty moisture is said to answer all the purposes of embalming on the few corpses deposited there. The roof has been kept whole hitherto; but as the clergyman's stipend is only twenty pounds per annum, and a house with two rooms, threatening speedily to determine into one, no clergyman will undertake the duties of pastor: especially as it is currently reported that his flock would rather let him starve than increase the living by one penny from their own pockets. However, in my dream, Jabez had a full and attentive congregation; and he preached – good God! What a sermon; divided into *four hundred and ninety* parts, each fully equal to an ordinary address from the pulpit, and each discussing a separate sin! Where he searched for them, I cannot tell. He had his private manner of interpreting the phrase, and it seemed necessary the brother should sin different sins on every occasion. They were of the most curious character: odd transgressions that I never imagined previously.

Oh, how weary I grow. How I writhed, and yawned, and nodded, and revived! How I pinched and pricked myself, and rubbed my eyes, and stood up, and sat down again, and nudged Joseph to inform me if he would *ever* have done. I was condemned to hear all out: finally, he reached the *'First of the Seventy-First'*. At that crisis, a sudden inspiration descended on me; I was moved to rise and denounce Jabez Branderham as the sinner of the sin that no Christian need pardon.

"Sir," I exclaimed, "sitting here within these four walls, at one stretch, I have endured and forgiven the four hundred and ninety heads of your discourse. Seventy times seven times have I plucked up my hat and been about to depart – Seventy times seven times have you preposterously forced me to resume my seat. The four hundred and ninety-first is too much. Fellow-martyrs, have at him! Drag him down, and crush him to atoms, that the place which knows him may know him no more!"

"Thou art the Man!" cried Jabez, after a solemn pause, leaning over his cushion. "Seventy times seven times didst thou gapingly contort thy visage – seventy times seven did I take counsel with my soul – lo, this is human weakness: this also may be absolved! The First of the Seventy-First is come. Brethren, execute upon him the judgment written. Such honour have all His saints!"

With that concluding word, the whole assembly, exalting their pilgrim's staves, rushed round me in a body; and I, having no weapon to raise in self-defence, commenced grappling with Joseph, my nearest and most ferocious assailant, for his. In the confluence of the multitude, several clubs crossed; blows, aimed at me, fell on other sconces. Presently the whole chapel resounded with rappings and counter rappings: every man's hand was against his neighbour; and Branderham, unwilling to remain idle, poured forth his zeal in a shower of loud taps on the boards of the pulpit, which responded so smartly that, at last, to my unspeakable relief, they woke me. And what was it that had suggested the tremendous tumult? What had played Jabez's part in the row? Merely the branch of a fir-tree that touched my lattice as the blast wailed by, and rattled its dry cones against the panes! I listened doubtingly an instant; detected the disturber, then turned and dozed, and dreamt again: if possible, still more disagreeably than before.

This time, I remembered I was lying in the oak closet, and I heard distinctly the gusty wind, and the driving of the snow; I heard, also, the fir bough repeat its teasing sound, and ascribed it to the right cause: but it annoyed me so much, that I resolved to silence it, if possible; and, I thought, I rose and endeavoured to unhasp the casement. The hook was soldered into the staple: a circumstance observed by me when awake, but forgotten. "I must stop it, nevertheless!" I muttered, knocking my knuckles through the glass, and stretching an arm out to seize the importunate branch; instead of which, my fingers closed on the fingers of a little, ice-cold hand! The intense horror of nightmare came over me: I tried to draw back my arm, but the hand clung to it, and a most melancholy voice sobbed, "Let me in – let me in!"

"Who are you?" I asked, struggling, meanwhile, to disengage myself.

"Catherine Linton," it replied, shiveringly (why did I think of *Linton*? I had read *Earnshaw* twenty times for Linton) – "I'm come home: I'd lost my way on the moor!" As it spoke, I discerned, obscurely, a child's face looking through the window. Terror made me cruel; and, finding it useless to attempt shaking the creature off, I pulled its wrist on to the broken pane, and rubbed it to and fro till the blood ran down and soaked the bedclothes: still it wailed, "Let me in!" and maintained its tenacious gripe, almost maddening me with fear.

"How can I!" I said at length. "Let *me* go, if you want me to let you in!" The fingers relaxed, I snatched mine through the hole, hurriedly piled the books up in a pyramid against it, and stopped my ears to exclude the lamentable prayer. I seemed to keep them closed above a quarter of an hour; yet, the instant I listened again, there was the doleful cry moaning on!

"Begone!" I shouted. "I'll never let you in, not if you beg for twenty years."

"It is twenty years," mourned the voice: "twenty years. I've been a waif for twenty years!" Thereat began a feeble scratching outside, and the pile of books moved as if thrust forward. I tried to jump up; but could not stir a limb; and so yelled aloud, in a frenzy of fright. To my confusion, I discovered the yell was not ideal: hasty footsteps approached my chamber door; somebody pushed it open, with a vigorous hand, and a light glimmered through the squares at the top of the bed. I sat shuddering yet, and wiping the perspiration from my forehead: the intruder appeared to hesitate, and muttered to himself. At last, he said, in a half-whisper, plainly not expecting an answer, "Is anyone here?" I considered it best to confess my presence; for I knew Heathcliff's accents, and feared he might search further, if I kept quiet. With this intention, I turned and opened the panels. I shall not soon forget the effect my action produced.

Heathcliff stood near the entrance, in his shirt and trousers; with a candle dripping over his fingers, and his face as white as the wall behind him. The first creak of the oak startled him like an electric shock: the light leaped from his hold to a distance of some feet, and his agitation was so extreme, that he could hardly pick it up.

"It is only your guest, sir," I called out, desirous to spare him the humiliation of exposing his cowardice further. "I had the misfortune to scream in my sleep, owing to a frightful nightmare. I'm sorry I disturbed you."

"Oh, God confound you, Mr. Lockwood! I wish you were at the –" commenced my host, setting the candle on a chair, because he found it impossible to hold it steady. "And who showed you up into this room?" he continued, crushing his nails into his palms, and grinding his teeth to subdue the maxillary convulsions. "Who was it? I've a good mind to turn them out of the house this moment!"

"It was your servant Zillah," I replied, flinging myself on to the floor, and rapidly resuming my garments. "I should not care if you did, Mr. Heathcliff; she richly deserves it. I suppose that she wanted to get another proof that the place was haunted, at my expense. Well, it is – swarming with ghosts and goblins! You have reason in shutting it up, I assure you. No one will thank you for a doze in such a den!"

"What do you mean?" asked Heathcliff, "And what are you doing? Lie down and finish out the night, since you *are* here; but, for heaven's sake! Don't repeat that horrid noise: nothing could excuse it, unless you were having your throat cut!"

"If the little fiend had got in at the window, she probably would have strangled me!" I returned. "I'm not going to endure the persecutions of your hospitable ancestors again. Was not the Reverend Jabez Branderham akin to you on the mother's side? And that minx, Catherine Linton, or Earnshaw, or however she was called – she must have been a changeling – wicked little soul! She told me she had been walking the earth these twenty years: a just punishment for her mortal transgressions, I've no doubt!"

Scarcely were these words uttered when I recollected the association of Heathcliff's with Catherine's name in the book, which had completely slipped from my memory, till thus awakened. I blushed at my inconsideration: but, without showing further consciousness of the offence, I hastened to add – "The truth is, sir, I passed the first part of the night in –". Here I stopped afresh – I was about to say "perusing those old volumes," then it would have revealed my knowledge of their written, as well as their printed, contents; so, correcting myself, I went on – "in spelling over the name scratched on that window-ledge. A monotonous occupation, calculated to set me asleep, like counting, or –"

"What *can* you mean by talking in this way to *me*!" thundered Heathcliff with savage vehemence. "How – how *dare* you, under my roof? – God! He's mad to speak so!" And he struck his forehead with rage.

I did not know whether to resent this language or pursue my explanation; but he seemed so powerfully affected that I took pity and proceeded with my dreams; affirming I had never heard the appellation of 'Catherine Linton' before, but reading it often over produced an impression which personified itself when I had no longer my imagination under control. Heathcliff gradually fell back into the shelter of the bed, as I spoke; finally sitting down almost concealed behind it. I guessed, however, by his irregular and intercepted breathing, that he struggled to vanquish an excess of violent emotion. Not liking to show him that I had heard the conflict, I continued my toilette rather noisily, looked at my watch, and soliloquised on the length of the night: "Not three o'clock yet! I could have taken oath it had been six. Time stagnates here: we must surely have retired to rest at eight!"

"Always at nine in winter, and rise at four," said my host, suppressing a groan: and, as I fancied, by the motion of his arm's shadow, dashing a tear from his eyes. "Mr. Lockwood," he added, "you may go into my room: you'll only be in the way, coming downstairs so early: and your childish outcry has sent sleep to the devil for me."

"And for me, too," I replied. "I'll walk in the yard till daylight, and then I'll be off; and you need not dread a repetition of my intrusion. I'm now quite cured of seeking pleasure in society, be it country or town. A sensible man ought to find sufficient company in himself."

"Delightful company!" muttered Heathcliff. "Take the candle, and go where you please. I shall join you directly. Keep out of the yard, though, the dogs are unchained; and the house – Juno mounts sentinel there, and – nay, you can only ramble about the steps and passages. But, away with you! I'll come in two minutes!"

I obeyed, so far as to quit the chamber; when, ignorant where the narrow lobbies led, I stood still, and was witness, involuntarily, to a piece of superstition on the part of my landlord which belied, oddly, his apparent sense. He got on to the bed, and wrenched open the lattice, bursting, as he pulled at it, into an uncontrollable passion of tears. "Come in! Come in!" he sobbed. "Cathy, do come. Oh, do – *once* more! Oh! My heart's darling! Hear me *this* time, Catherine, at last!" The spectre showed a spectre's ordinary caprice: it gave no sign of being; but the snow and wind whirled wildly through, even reaching my station, and blowing out the light.

There was such anguish in the gush of grief that accompanied this raving, that my compassion made me overlook its folly, and I drew off, half angry to have listened at all, and vexed at having related my ridiculous nightmare, since it produced that agony; though *why* was beyond my comprehension. I descended cautiously to the lower regions, and landed in the back-kitchen, where a gleam of fire, raked compactly together, enabled me to rekindle my candle. Nothing was stirring except a brindled, grey cat, which crept from the ashes, and saluted me with a querulous mew.

Two benches, shaped in sections of a circle, nearly enclosed the hearth; on one of these I stretched myself, and Grimalkin mounted the other. We were both of us nodding ere anyone invaded our retreat, and then it was Joseph, shuffling down a wooden ladder that vanished in the roof, through a trap: the ascent to his garret, I suppose. He cast a sinister look at the little flame which I had enticed to play between the ribs, swept the cat from its elevation, and bestowing himself in the vacancy, commenced the operation of stuffing a three-inch pipe with tobacco. My presence in his sanctum was evidently esteemed a piece of impudence too shameful for remark: he silently applied the tube to his lips, folded his arms, and puffed away. I let him enjoy the luxury unannoyed; and after sucking out his last wreath, and heaving a profound sigh, he got up, and departed as solemnly as he came.

A more elastic footstep entered next; and now I opened my mouth for a "good-morning", but closed it again, the salutation unachieved; for Hareton Earnshaw was performing his orison *sotto voce*, in a series of curses directed against every object he touched, while he rummaged a corner for a spade or shovel to dig through the drifts. He glanced over the back of the bench, dilating his nostrils, and thought as little of exchanging civilities with me as with my companion the cat. I guessed, by his preparations, that egress was allowed, and, leaving my hard couch, made a movement to follow him. He noticed this, and thrust at an inner door with the end of his spade, intimating by an inarticulate sound that there was the place where I must go, if I changed my locality.

It opened into the house, where the females were already astir; Zillah urging flakes of flame up the chimney with a colossal bellows; and Mrs. Heathcliff, kneeling on the hearth, reading a book by the aid of the blaze. She held her hand interposed between the furnace-heat and her eyes, and seemed absorbed in her occupation; desisting from it only to chide the servant for covering her with sparks, or to push away a dog, now and then, that snoozled its nose over-forwardly into her face. I was surprised to see Heathcliff there also. He stood by the fire, his back towards me, just finishing a stormy scene with poor Zillah; who ever and anon interrupted her labour to pluck up the corner of her apron, and heave an indignant groan.

"And you, you worthless –" he broke out as I entered, turning to his daughter-in-law, and employing an epithet as harmless as duck, or sheep, but generally represented by a dash – "There you are, at your idle tricks again! The rest of them do earn their bread – you live on my charity! Put your trash away, and find something to do. You shall pay me for the plague of having you eternally in my sight – do you hear, damnable jade?"

"I'll put my trash away, because you can make me if I refuse," answered the young lady, closing her book, and throwing it on a chair. "But I'll not do anything, though you should swear your tongue out, except what I please!"

Heathcliff lifted his hand, and the speaker sprang to a safer distance, obviously acquainted with its weight. Having no desire to be entertained by a cat-and-dog combat, I stepped forward briskly, as if eager to partake the warmth of the hearth, and innocent of any knowledge of the interrupted dispute. Each had enough decorum to suspend further hostilities: Heathcliff placed his fists, out of temptation, in his pockets; Mrs. Heathcliff curled her lip, and walked to a seat far off, where she kept her word by playing the part of a statue during the remainder of my stay. That was not long. I declined joining their breakfast, and, at the first gleam of dawn, took an opportunity of escaping into the free air, now clear, and still, and cold as impalpable ice.

My landlord hallooed for me to stop ere I reached the bottom of the garden, and offered to accompany me across the moor. It was well he did, for the whole hill-back was one billowy, white ocean; the swells and falls not indicating corresponding rises and depressions in the ground: many pits, at least, were filled to a level; and entire ranges of mounds, the refuse of the quarries, blotted from the chart which my yesterday's walk left pictured in my mind. I had remarked on one side of the road, at intervals of six or seven yards, a line of upright stones, continued through the whole length of the barren: these were erected and daubed with lime on purpose to serve as guides in the dark, and also when a fall, like the present, confounded the deep swamps on either hand with the firmer path:

but, excepting a dirty dot pointing up here and there, all traces of their existence had vanished: and my companion found it necessary to warn me frequently to steer to the right or left, when I imagined I was following, correctly, the windings of the road.

We exchanged little conversation, and he halted at the entrance of Thrushcross Park, saying, I could make no error there. Our adieux were limited to a hasty bow, and then I pushed forward, trusting to my own resources; for the porter's lodge is untenanted as yet. The distance from the gate to the grange is two miles; I believe I managed to make it four, what with losing myself among the trees, and sinking up to the neck in snow: a predicament which only those who have experienced it can appreciate. At any rate, whatever were my wanderings, the clock chimed twelve as I entered the house; and that gave exactly an hour for every mile of the usual way from Wuthering Heights.

My human fixture and her satellites rushed to welcome me; exclaiming, tumultuously, they had completely given me up: everybody conjectured that I perished last night; and they were wondering how they must set about the search for my remains. I bid them be quiet, now that they saw me returned, and, benumbed to my very heart, I dragged upstairs; whence, after putting on dry clothes, and pacing to and fro thirty or forty minutes, to restore the animal heat, I adjourned to my study, feeble as a kitten: almost too much so to enjoy the cheerful fire and smoking coffee which the servant had prepared for my refreshment.

Chapter Four

WHAT VAIN WEATHERCOCKS we are! I, who had determined to hold myself independent of all social intercourse, and thanked my stars that, at length, I had lighted on a spot where it was next to impracticable – I, weak wretch, after maintaining till dusk a struggle with low spirits and solitude, was finally compelled to strike my colours; and under pretence of gaining information concerning the necessities of my establishment, I desired Mrs. Dean, when she brought in supper, to sit down while I ate it; hoping sincerely she would prove a regular gossip, and either rouse me to animation or lull me to sleep by her talk.

"You have lived here a considerable time," I commenced; "did you not say sixteen years?"

"Eighteen, sir: I came when the mistress was married, to wait on her; after she died, the master retained me for his housekeeper."

"Indeed."

There ensued a pause. She was not a gossip, I feared; unless about her own affairs, and those could hardly interest me. However, having studied for an interval, with a fist on either knee, and a cloud of meditation over her ruddy countenance, she ejaculated – "Ah, times are greatly changed since then!"

"Yes," I remarked, "you've seen a good many alterations, I suppose?"

"I have: and troubles too," she said.

"Oh, I'll turn the talk on my landlord's family!" I thought to myself. "A good subject to start! And that pretty girl-widow, I should like to know her history: whether she be a native of the country, or, as is more probable, an exotic that the surly *indigenae* will not recognise for kin." With this intention I asked Mrs. Dean why Heathcliff let Thrushcross Grange, and preferred living in a situation and residence so much inferior. "Is he not rich enough to keep the estate in good order?" I inquired.

"Rich, sir!" she returned. "He has nobody knows what money, and every year it increases. Yes, yes, he's rich enough to live in a finer house than this: but he's very near – close-handed; and, if he had meant to flit to Thrushcross Grange, as soon as he heard of a good tenant he could not have borne to miss the chance of getting a few hundreds more. It is strange people should be so greedy, when they are alone in the world!"

"He had a son, it seems?"

"Yes, he had one – he is dead."

"And that young lady, Mrs. Heathcliff, is his widow?"

"Yes."

"Where did she come from originally?"

"Why, sir, she is my late master's daughter: Catherine Linton was her maiden name. I nursed her, poor thing! I did wish Mr. Heathcliff would remove here, and then we might have been together again."

"What! Catherine Linton?" I exclaimed, astonished. But a minute's reflection convinced me it was not my ghostly Catherine. Then," I continued, "my predecessor's name was Linton?"

"It was."

"And who is that Earnshaw: Hareton Earnshaw, who lives with Mr. Heathcliff? Are they relations?"

"No; he is the late Mrs. Linton's nephew."

"The young lady's cousin, then?"

"Yes; and her husband was her cousin also: one on the mother's, the other on the father's side: Heathcliff married Mr. Linton's sister."

"I see the house at Wuthering Heights has 'Earnshaw' carved over the front door. Are they an old family?"

"Very old, sir; and Hareton is the last of them, as our Miss Cathy is of us – I mean, of the Lintons. Have you been to Wuthering Heights? I beg pardon for asking; but I should like to hear how she is!"

"Mrs. Heathcliff? She looked very well, and very handsome; yet, I think, not very happy."

"Oh dear, I don't wonder! And how did you like the master?"

"A rough fellow, rather, Mrs. Dean. Is not that his character?

"Rough as a saw-edge, and hard as whinstone! The less you meddle with him the better."

"He must have had some ups and downs in life to make him such a churl. Do you know anything of his history?"

"It's a cuckoo's, sir – I know all about it: except where he was born, and who were his parents, and how he got his money at first. And Hareton has been cast out like an unfledged dunnock! The unfortunate lad is the only one in all this parish that does not guess how he has been cheated."

"Well, Mrs. Dean, it will be a charitable deed to tell me something of my neighbours: I feel I shall not rest if I go to bed; so be good enough to sit and chat an hour."

"Oh, certainly, sir! I'll just fetch a little sewing, and then I'll sit as long as you please. But you've caught cold: I saw you shivering, and you must have some gruel to drive it out."

The worthy woman bustled off, and I crouched nearer the fire; my head felt hot, and the rest of me chill: moreover, I was excited, almost to a pitch of foolishness, through my nerves and brain. This caused me to feel, not uncomfortable, but rather fearful (as I am still) of serious effects from the incidents of today and yesterday. She returned presently, bringing a smoking basin and a basket of work; and, having placed the former on the hob, drew in her seat, evidently pleased to find me so companionable.

Before I came to live here, she commenced – waiting no farther invitation to her story – I was almost always at Wuthering Heights; because my mother had nursed Mr. Hindley Earnshaw, that was Hareton's father, and I got used to playing with the children: I ran errands too, and helped to make hay, and hung about the farm ready for anything that anybody would set me to. One fine summer morning – it was the beginning of harvest, I remember – Mr. Earnshaw, the old master, came downstairs, dressed for a journey; and, after he had told Joseph what was to be done during the day, he turned to Hindley, and Cathy, and me – for I sat eating my porridge with them – and he said, speaking to his son, "Now, my bonny man, I'm going to Liverpool today, what shall I bring you? You may choose what you like: only let it be little, for I shall walk there and back: sixty miles each way, that is a long spell!" Hindley named a fiddle, and then he asked Miss Cathy; she was hardly six years old, but she could ride any horse in the stable, and she chose a whip. He did not forget me; for he had a kind heart, though he was rather severe sometimes. He promised to bring me a pocketful of apples and pears, and then he kissed his children, said goodbye, and set off.

It seemed a long while to us all – the three days of his absence – and often did little Cathy ask when he would be home. Mrs. Earnshaw expected him by supper-time on the third evening, and she put the meal off hour after hour; there were no signs of his coming, however, and at last the children got tired of running down to the gate to look. Then it grew dark; she would have had them to bed, but they begged sadly to be allowed to stay up; and, just about eleven o'clock, the door-latch was raised quietly, and in stepped the master. He threw himself into a chair, laughing and groaning, and bid them all stand off, for he was nearly killed – he would not have such another walk for the three kingdoms.

"And at the end of it to be flighted to death!" he said, opening his great-coat, which he held bundled up in his arms. "See here, wife! I was never so beaten with anything in my life: but you must e'en take it as a gift of God; though it's as dark almost as if it came from the devil."

We crowded round, and over Miss Cathy's head I had a peep at a dirty, ragged, black-haired child; big enough both to walk and talk: indeed, its face looked older than Catherine's; yet when it was set on its feet, it only stared round, and repeated over and over again some gibberish that nobody could understand. I was frightened, and Mrs. Earnshaw was ready to fling it out of doors: she did fly up, asking how he could fashion to bring that gipsy brat into the house, when they had their own bairns to feed and fend for? What he meant to do with it, and whether he were mad? The master tried to explain the matter; but he was really half dead with fatigue, and all that I could make out, amongst her scolding, was a tale of his seeing it starving, and houseless, and as good as dumb, in the streets of Liverpool, where he picked it up and inquired for its owner. Not a soul knew to whom it belonged, he said; and his money and time being both limited, he thought it better to take it home with him at once, than run into vain expenses there: because he was determined he would not leave it as he found it. Well, the conclusion was, that my mistress grumbled herself calm; and Mr. Earnshaw told me to wash it, and give it clean things, and let it sleep with the children.

Hindley and Cathy contented themselves with looking and listening till peace was restored: then, both began searching their father's pockets for the presents he had promised them. The former was a boy of fourteen, but when he drew out what had been a fiddle, crushed to morsels in the great-coat, he blubbered aloud; and Cathy, when she learned the master had lost her whip in attending on the stranger, showed her humour by grinning and spitting at the stupid little thing; earning for her pains a sound blow from her father, to teach her cleaner manners. They entirely refused to have it in bed with them, or even in their room; and I had no more sense, so I put it on the landing of the stairs, hoping it might be gone on the morrow. By chance, or else attracted by hearing his voice, it crept to Mr. Earnshaw's door, and there he found it on quitting his chamber. Inquiries were made as to how it got there; I was obliged to confess, and in recompense for my cowardice and inhumanity was sent out of the house.

This was Heathcliff's first introduction to the family. On coming back a few days afterwards (for I did not consider my banishment perpetual), I found they had christened him "Heathcliff: it was the name of a son who died in childhood, and it has served him ever since, both for Christian and surname. Miss Cathy and he were now very thick; but Hindley hated him: and to say the truth I did the same; and we plagued and went on with him shamefully: for I wasn't reasonable enough to feel my injustice, and the mistress never put in a word on his behalf when she saw him wronged.

He seemed a sullen, patient child; hardened, perhaps, to ill-treatment: he would stand Hindley's blows without winking or shedding a tear, and my pinches moved him only to draw in a breath and open his eyes, as if he had hurt himself by accident, and nobody was to blame. This endurance made old Earnshaw furious, when he discovered his son persecuting the poor fatherless child, as he called him. He took to Heathcliff strangely, believing all he said (for that matter, he said precious little, and generally the truth), and petting him up far above Cathy, who was too mischievous and wayward for a favourite.

So, from the very beginning, he bred bad feeling in the house; and at Mrs. Earnshaw's death, which happened in less than two years after, the young master had learned to regard his father as an oppressor rather than a friend, and Heathcliff as a usurper of his parent's affections and his privileges; and he grew bitter with brooding over these injuries. I sympathised a while; but when the children fell ill of the measles, and I had to tend them, and take on me the cares of a woman at once, I changed my idea. Heathcliff was dangerously sick; and while he lay at the worst he would have me constantly by his pillow: I suppose he felt I did a good deal for him, and he hadn't wit to guess that I was compelled to do it. However, I will say this, he was the quietest child that ever nurse watched over. The difference between him and the others forced me to be less partial. Cathy and her brother harassed me terribly: he was as uncomplaining as a lamb; though hardness, not gentleness, made him give little trouble.

He got through, and the doctor affirmed it was in a great measure owing to me, and praised me for my care. I was vain of his commendations, and softened towards the being by whose means I earned them, and thus Hindley lost his last ally: still I couldn't dote on Heathcliff, and I wondered often what my master saw to admire so much in the sullen boy; who never, to my recollection, repaid his indulgence by any sign of gratitude. He was not insolent to his benefactor, he was simply insensible; though knowing perfectly the hold he had on his heart, and conscious he had only to speak and all the house would be obliged to bend to his wishes. As an instance, I remember Mr. Earnshaw once bought a couple of colts at the parish fair, and gave the lads each one. Heathcliff took the handsomest, but it soon fell lame, and when he discovered it, he said to Hindley –

"You must exchange horses with me: I don't like mine; and if you won't I shall tell your father of the three thrashings you've given me this week, and show him my arm, which is black to the shoulder." Hindley put out his tongue, and cuffed him over the ears. "You'd better do it at once," he persisted, escaping to the porch (they were in the stable): "you will have to: and if I speak of these blows, you'll get them again with interest."

"Off, dog!" cried Hindley, threatening him with an iron weight used for weighing potatoes and hay.

"Throw it," he replied, standing still, "and then I'll tell how you boasted that you would turn me out of doors as soon as he died, and see whether he will not turn you out directly." Hindley threw it, hitting him on the breast, and down he fell, but staggered up immediately, breathless and white; and, had not I prevented it, he would have gone just so to the master, and got full revenge by letting his condition plead for him, intimating who had caused it.

"Take my colt, Gipsy, then!" said young Earnshaw. "And I pray that he may break your neck: take him, and be damned, you beggarly interloper! And wheedle my father out of all he has: only afterwards show him what you are, imp of Satan. – And take that, I hope he'll kick out your brains!"

Heathcliff had gone to loose the beast, and shift it to his own stall; he was passing behind it, when Hindley finished his speech by knocking him under its feet, and without stopping to examine whether his hopes were fulfilled, ran away as fast as he could. I was surprised to witness how coolly the child gathered himself up, and went on with his intention; exchanging saddles and all, and then sitting down on a bundle of hay to overcome the qualm which the violent blow occasioned, before he entered the house. I persuaded him easily to let me lay the blame of his bruises on the horse: he minded little what tale was told since he had what he wanted. He complained so seldom, indeed, of such stirs as these, that I really thought him not vindictive: I was deceived completely, as you will hear.

Chapter Five

IN THE COURSE of time Mr. Earnshaw began to fail. He had been active and healthy, yet his strength left him suddenly; and when he was confined to the chimney-corner he grew grievously irritable. A nothing vexed him; and suspected slights of his authority nearly threw him into fits. This was especially to be remarked if anyone attempted to impose upon, or domineer over, his favourite: he was painfully jealous lest a word should be spoken amiss to him; seeming to have got into his head the notion that, because he liked Heathcliff, all hated, and longed to do him an ill-turn. It was a disadvantage to the lad; for the kinder among us did not wish to fret the master, so we humoured his partiality; and that humouring was rich nourishment to the child's pride and black tempers. Still it became in a manner necessary; twice, or thrice, Hindley's manifestation of scorn, while his father was near, roused the old man to a fury: he seized his stick to strike him, and shook with rage that he could not do it.

At last, our curate (we had a curate then who made the living answer by teaching the little Lintons and Earnshaws, and farming his bit of land himself) advised that the young man should be sent to college; and Mr. Earnshaw agreed, though with a heavy spirit, for he said – "Hindley was nought, and would never thrive as where he wandered."

I hoped heartily we should have peace now. It hurt me to think the master should be made uncomfortable by his own good deed. I fancied the discontent of age and disease arose from his family disagreements; as he would have it that it did: really, you know, sir, it was in his sinking frame. We might have got on tolerably, notwithstanding, but for two people – Miss Cathy, and Joseph, the servant: you saw him, I daresay, up yonder. He was, and is yet most likely, the wearisomest self-righteous Pharisee that ever ransacked a Bible to rake the promises to himself and fling the curses to his neighbours. By his knack of sermonising and pious discoursing, he contrived to make a great impression on Mr. Earnshaw; and the more feeble the master became, the more influence he gained. He was relentless in worrying him about his soul's concerns, and about ruling his children rigidly. He encouraged him to regard Hindley as a reprobate; and, night after night, he regularly grumbled out a long string of tales against Heathcliff and Catherine: always minding to flatter Earnshaw's weakness by heaping the heaviest blame on the latter.

Certainly she had ways with her such as I never saw a child take up before; and she put all of us past our patience fifty times and oftener in a day: from the hour she came downstairs till the hour she went to bed, we had not a minute's security that she wouldn't be in mischief. Her spirits were always at high-water mark, her tongue always going – singing, laughing, and plaguing everybody who would not do the same. A wild, wicked slip she was – but she had the bonniest eye, the sweetest smile, and lightest foot in the parish: and, after all, I believe she meant no harm; for when once she made you cry in good earnest, it seldom happened that she would not keep you company, and oblige you to be quiet that you might comfort her. She was much too fond of Heathcliff. The greatest punishment we could invent for her was to keep her separate from him: yet she got chided more than any of us on his account. In play, she liked exceedingly to act the little mistress; using her hands freely, and commanding her companions: she did so to me, but I would not bear slapping and ordering; and so I let her know.

Now, Mr. Earnshaw did not understand jokes from his children: he had always been strict and grave with them; and Catherine, on her part, had no idea why her father should be crosser and less patient in his ailing condition than he was in his prime. His peevish reproofs wakened in her a naughty delight to provoke him: she was never so happy as when we were all scolding her at once, and she defying us with her bold, saucy look, and her ready words; turning Joseph's religious curses into ridicule, baiting me, and doing just what her father hated most – showing how her pretended insolence, which he thought real, had more power over Heathcliff than his kindness: how the boy would do *her* bidding in anything, and *his* only when it suited his own inclination. After behaving as badly as possible all day, she sometimes came fondling to make it up at night. "Nay, Cathy," the old man would say, "I cannot love thee, thou'rt worse than thy brother. Go, say thy prayers, child, and ask God's pardon. I doubt thy mother and I must rue that we ever reared thee!" That made her cry, at first; and then being repulsed continually hardened her, and she laughed if I told her to say she was sorry for her faults, and beg to be forgiven.

But the hour came, at last, that ended Mr. Earnshaw's troubles on earth. He died quietly in his chair one October evening, seated by the fire-side. A high wind blustered round the house, and roared in the chimney: it sounded wild and stormy, yet it was not cold, and we were all together – I, a little removed from the hearth, busy at my knitting, and Joseph reading his Bible near the table (for the servants generally sat in the house then, after their work was done). Miss Cathy had been sick, and that made her still; she leant against her father's knee, and Heathcliff was lying on the floor with his head in her lap. I remember the master, before he fell into a doze, stroking her bonny hair – it pleased him rarely to see her gentle – and saying, "Why canst thou not always be a good lass, Cathy?" And she turned her face up to his, and laughed, and answered, "Why cannot you always be a good man, father?" But as soon as she saw him vexed again, she kissed his hand, and said she would sing him to sleep. She began singing very low, till his fingers dropped from hers, and his head sank on his breast. Then I told her to hush, and not stir, for fear she should wake him. We all kept as mute as mice a full half-hour, and should have done so longer, only Joseph, having finished his chapter, got up and said that he must rouse the master for prayers and bed. He stepped forward, and called him by name, and touched his shoulder; but he would not move: so he took the candle and looked at him. I thought there was something wrong as he set down the light; and seizing the children each by an arm, whispered them to "frame upstairs, and make little din – they might pray alone that evening – he had summut to do."

"I shall bid father good-night first," said Catherine, putting her arms round his neck, before we could hinder her. The poor thing discovered her loss directly – she screamed out – "Oh, he's dead, Heathcliff! He's dead!" And they both set up a heart-breaking cry.

I joined my wail to theirs, loud and bitter; but Joseph asked what we could be thinking of to roar in that way over a saint in heaven. He told me to put on my cloak and run to Gimmerton for the doctor and the parson. I could not guess the use that either would be of, then. However, I went, through wind and rain, and brought one, the doctor, back with me; the other said he would come in the morning. Leaving Joseph to explain matters, I ran to the children's room: their door was ajar, I saw they had never lain down, though it was past midnight; but they were calmer, and did not need me to console them. The little souls were comforting each other with better thoughts than I could have hit on: no parson in the world ever pictured heaven so beautifully as they did, in their innocent talk; and, while I sobbed and listened, I could not help wishing we were all there safe together.

Chapter Six

MR. HINDLEY came home to the funeral; and – a thing that amazed us, and set the neighbours gossiping right and left – he brought a wife with him. What she was, and where she was born, he never informed us: probably, she had neither money nor name to recommend her, or he would scarcely have kept the union from his father.

She was not one that would have disturbed the house much on her own account. Every object she saw, the moment she crossed the threshold, appeared to delight her; and every circumstance that took place about her: except the preparing for the burial, and the presence of the mourners. I thought she was half silly, from her behaviour while that went on: she ran into her chamber, and made me come with her, though I should have been dressing the children: and there she sat shivering and clasping her hands, and asking repeatedly – "Are they gone yet?" Then she began describing with hysterical emotion the effect it produced on her to see black; and started, and trembled, and, at last, fell a-weeping – and when I asked what was the matter, answered, she didn't know; but she felt so afraid of dying! I imagined her as little likely to die as myself. She was rather thin, but young, and fresh-complexioned, and her eyes sparkled as bright as diamonds. I did remark, to be sure, that mounting the stairs made her breathe very quick; that the least sudden noise set her all in a quiver, and that she coughed troublesomely sometimes: but I knew nothing of what these symptoms portended, and had no impulse to sympathise with her. We don't in general take to foreigners here, Mr. Lockwood, unless they take to us first.

Young Earnshaw was altered considerably in the three years of his absence. He had grown sparer, and lost his colour, and spoke and dressed quite differently; and, on the very day of his return, he told Joseph and me we must thenceforth quarter ourselves in the back-kitchen, and leave the house for him. Indeed, he would have carpeted and papered a small spare room for a parlour; but his wife expressed such pleasure at the white floor and huge glowing fireplace, at the pewter dishes and delf-case, and dog-kennel, and the wide space there was to move about in where they usually sat, that he thought it unnecessary to her comfort, and so dropped the intention.

She expressed pleasure, too, at finding a sister among her new acquaintance; and she prattled to Catherine, and kissed her, and ran about with her, and gave her quantities of presents, at the beginning. Her affection tired very soon, however, and when she grew peevish, Hindley became tyrannical. A few words from her, evincing a dislike to Heathcliff, were enough to rouse in him all his old hatred of the boy. He drove him from their company to the servants, deprived him of the instructions of the curate, and insisted that he should labour out of doors instead; compelling him to do so as hard as any other lad on the farm.

Heathcliff bore his degradation pretty well at first, because Cathy taught him what she learnt, and worked or played with him in the fields. They both promised fair to grow up as rude as savages; the young master being entirely negligent how they behaved, and what they did, so they kept clear of him. He would not even have seen after their going to church on Sundays, only Joseph and the curate reprimanded his carelessness when they absented themselves; and that reminded him to order Heathcliff a flogging, and Catherine a fast from dinner or supper. But it was one of their chief amusements to run away to the moors in the morning and remain there all day, and the after punishment grew a mere thing to laugh at. The curate might set as many chapters as he pleased for Catherine to get by heart, and Joseph might thrash Heathcliff till his arm ached; they forgot everything the minute they were together again: at least the minute they had contrived some naughty plan of revenge; and many a time I've cried to myself to watch them growing more reckless daily, and I not daring to speak a syllable, for fear of losing the small power I still retained over the unfriended creatures. One Sunday evening, it chanced that they were banished from the sitting-room, for making a noise, or a light offence of the kind; and when I went to call them to supper, I could discover them nowhere. We searched the house, above and below, and the yard and stables; they were invisible: and, at last, Hindley in a passion told us to bolt the doors, and swore nobody should let them in that night. The household went to bed; and I, too, anxious to lie down, opened my lattice and put my head out to hearken, though it rained: determined to admit them in spite of the prohibition, should they return. In a while, I distinguished steps coming up the road, and the light of a lantern glimmered through the gate. I threw a shawl over my head and ran to prevent them from waking Mr. Earnshaw by knocking. There was Heathcliff, by himself: it gave me a start to see him alone.

"Where is Miss Catherine?" I cried hurriedly. "No accident, I hope?"

"At Thrushcross Grange," he answered; "and I would have been there too, but they had not the manners to ask me to stay."

"Well, you will catch it!" I said: "you'll never be content till you're sent about your business. What in the world led you wandering to Thrushcross Grange?"

"Let me get off my wet clothes, and I'll tell you all about it, Nelly," he replied. I bid him beware of rousing the master, and while he undressed and I waited to put out the candle, he continued –

"Cathy and I escaped from the wash-house to have a ramble at liberty, and getting a glimpse of the Grange lights, we thought we would just go and see whether the Lintons passed their Sunday evenings standing shivering in corners, while their father and mother sat eating and drinking, and singing and laughing, and burning their eyes out before the fire. Do you think they do? Or reading sermons, and being catechised by their manservant, and set to learn a column of Scripture names, if they don't answer properly?"

"Probably not," I responded. "They are good children, no doubt, and don't deserve the treatment you receive, for your bad conduct."

"Don't cant, Nelly," he said: "nonsense! We ran from the top of the Heights to the park, without stopping – Catherine completely beaten in the race, because she was barefoot. You'll have to seek for her shoes in the bog tomorrow. We crept through a broken hedge, groped our way up the path, and planted ourselves on a flower-plot under the drawing-room window. The light came from thence; they had not put up the shutters, and the curtains were only half closed. Both of us were able to look in by standing on the basement, and clinging to the ledge, and we saw – ah! It was beautiful – a splendid place carpeted with crimson, and crimson-covered chairs and tables, and a pure white ceiling bordered by gold, a shower of glass-drops hanging in silver chains from the centre, and shimmering with little soft tapers. Old Mr. and Mrs. Linton were not there; Edgar and his sisters had it entirely to themselves. Shouldn't they have been happy? We should have thought ourselves in heaven! And now, guess what your good children were doing? Isabella – I believe she is eleven, a year younger than Cathy – lay screaming at the farther end of the room, shrieking as if witches were running red-hot needles into her. Edgar stood on the hearth weeping silently, and in the middle of the table sat a little dog, shaking its paw and yelping; which, from their mutual accusations, we understood they had nearly pulled in two between them. The idiots! That was their pleasure! To quarrel who should hold a heap of warm hair, and each begin to cry because both, after struggling to get it, refused to take it. We laughed outright at the petted things; we did despise them! When would you catch me wishing to have what Catherine wanted? Or find us by ourselves, seeking entertainment in yelling, and sobbing, and rolling on the ground, divided by the whole room? I'd not exchange, for a thousand lives, my condition here, for Edgar Linton's at Thrushcross Grange – not if I might have the privilege of flinging Joseph off the highest gable, and painting the house-front with Hindley's blood!"

"Hush, hush!" I interrupted. "Still you have not told me, Heathcliff, how Catherine is left behind?"

"I told you we laughed," he answered. "The Lintons heard us, and with one accord they shot like arrows to the door; there was silence, and then a cry, 'Oh, mamma, mamma! Oh, papa! Oh, mamma, come here. Oh, papa, oh!' They really did howl out something in that way. We made frightful noises to terrify them still more, and then we dropped off the ledge, because somebody was drawing the bars, and we felt we had better flee. I had Cathy by the hand, and was urging her on, when all at once she fell down. 'Run, Heathcliff, run!' she whispered. 'They have let the bull-dog loose, and he holds me!' The devil had seized her ankle, Nelly: I heard his abominable snorting. She did not yell out – no! She would have scorned to do it, if she had been spitted on the horns of a mad cow. I did, though: I vociferated curses enough to annihilate any fiend in Christendom; and I got a stone and thrust it between his jaws, and tried with all my might to cram it down his throat. A beast of a servant came up with a lantern, at last, shouting – 'Keep fast, Skulker, keep fast!' He changed his note, however, when he saw Skulker's game. The dog was throttled off; his huge, purple tongue hanging half a foot out of his mouth, and his pendent lips streaming with bloody slaver. The man took Cathy up; she was sick: not from fear, I'm certain, but from pain. He carried her in; I followed, grumbling execrations and vengeance. 'What prey, Robert?' hallooed Linton from the entrance. 'Skulker has caught a little girl, sir,' he replied; 'and there's a lad here,' he added, making a clutch at me, 'who looks an out-and-outer! Very like the robbers were for putting them through the window to open the doors to the gang after all were asleep, that they might murder us at their ease. Hold your tongue, you foul-mouthed thief, you! You shall go to the gallows for this. Mr. Linton, sir, don't lay by your gun.'

"'No, no, Robert,' said the old fool. 'The rascals knew that yesterday was my rent-day: they thought to have me cleverly. Come in; I'll furnish them a reception. There, John, fasten the chain. Give Skulker some water, Jenny. To beard a magistrate in his stronghold, and on the Sabbath, too! Where will their insolence stop? Oh, my dear Mary, look here! Don't be afraid, it is but a boy – yet the villain scowls so plainly in his face; would it not be a kindness to the country to hang him at once, before he shows his nature in acts as well as features?' He pulled me under the chandelier, and Mrs. Linton placed her spectacles on her nose and raised her hands in horror. The cowardly children crept nearer also, Isabella lisping – 'Frightful thing! Put him in the cellar, papa. He's exactly like the son of the fortune-teller that stole my tame pheasant. Isn't he, Edgar?'

"While they examined me, Cathy came round; she heard the last speech, and laughed. Edgar Linton, after an inquisitive stare, collected sufficient wit to recognise her. They see us at church, you know, though we seldom meet them elsewhere. 'That's Miss Earnshaw?' he whispered to his mother, 'and look how Skulker has bitten her – how her foot bleeds!'

"'Miss Earnshaw? Nonsense!' cried the dame; 'Miss Earnshaw scouring the country with a gipsy! And yet, my dear, the child is in mourning – surely it is – and she may be lamed for life!'

"'What culpable carelessness in her brother!' exclaimed Mr. Linton, turning from me to Catherine. 'I've understood from Shielders'" (that was the curate, sir) "'that he lets her grow up in absolute heathenism. But who is this? Where did she pick up this companion? Oho! I declare he is that strange acquisition my late neighbour made, in his journey to Liverpool – a little Lascar, or an American or Spanish castaway.'

"'A wicked boy, at all events,' remarked the old lady, 'and quite unfit for a decent house! Did you notice his language, Linton? I'm shocked that my children should have heard it.'

"I recommenced cursing – don't be angry, Nelly – and so Robert was ordered to take me off. I refused to go without Cathy; he dragged me into the garden, pushed the lantern into my hand, assured me that Mr. Earnshaw should be informed of my behaviour, and, bidding me march directly, secured the door again. The curtains were still looped up at one corner, and I resumed my station as spy; because, if Catherine had wished to return, I intended shattering their great glass panes to a million of fragments, unless they let her out. She sat on the sofa quietly. Mrs. Linton took off the grey cloak of the dairy-maid which we had borrowed for our excursion, shaking her head and expostulating with her, I suppose: she was a young lady, and they made a distinction between her treatment and mine. Then the woman-servant brought a basin of warm water, and washed her feet; and Mr. Linton mixed a tumbler of negus, and Isabella emptied a plateful of cakes into her lap, and Edgar stood gaping at a distance.

Afterwards, they dried and combed her beautiful hair, and gave her a pair of enormous slippers, and wheeled her to the fire; and I left her, as merry as she could be, dividing her food between the little dog and Skulker, whose nose she pinched as he ate; and kindling a spark of spirit in the vacant blue eyes of the Lintons – a dim reflection from her own enchanting face. I saw they were full of stupid admiration; she is so immeasurably superior to them – to everybody on earth, is she not, Nelly?"

"There will more come of this business than you reckon on," I answered, covering him up and extinguishing the light. "You are incurable, Heathcliff; and Mr. Hindley will have to proceed to extremities, see if he won't." My words came truer than I desired. The luckless adventure made Earnshaw furious. And then Mr. Linton, to mend matters, paid us a visit himself on the morrow, and read the young master such a lecture on the road he guided his family, that he was stirred to look about him, in earnest. Heathcliff received no flogging, but he was told that the first word he spoke to Miss Catherine should ensure a dismissal; and Mrs. Earnshaw undertook to keep her sister-in-law in due restraint when she returned home; employing art, not force: with force she would have found it impossible.

Chapter Seven

CATHY STAYED at Thrushcross Grange five weeks: till Christmas. By that time her ankle was thoroughly cured, and her manners much improved. The mistress visited her often in the interval, and commenced her plan of reform by trying to raise her self-respect with fine clothes and flattery, which she took readily; so that, instead of a wild, hatless little savage jumping into the house, and rushing to squeeze us all breathless, there 'lighted from a handsome black pony a very dignified person, with brown ringlets falling from the cover of a feathered beaver, and a long cloth habit, which she was obliged to hold up with both hands that she might sail in. Hindley lifted her from her horse, exclaiming delightedly, "Why, Cathy, you are quite a beauty! I should scarcely have known you: you look like a lady now. Isabella Linton is not to be compared with her, is she, Frances?"

"Isabella has not her natural advantages," replied his wife: "but she must mind and not grow wild again here. Ellen, help Miss Catherine off with her things – stay, dear, you will disarrange your curls – let me untie your hat."

I removed the habit, and there shone forth beneath a grand plaid silk frock, white trousers, and burnished shoes; and, while her eyes sparkled joyfully when the dogs came bounding up to welcome her, she dared hardly touch them lest they should fawn upon her splendid garments. She kissed me gently: I was all flour making the Christmas cake, and it would not have done to give me a hug; and then she looked round for Heathcliff. Mr. and Mrs. Earnshaw watched anxiously their meeting; thinking it would enable them to judge, in some measure, what grounds they had for hoping to succeed in separating the two friends.

Heathcliff was hard to discover, at first. If he were careless, and uncared for, before Catherine's absence, he had been ten times more so since. Nobody but I even did him the kindness to call him a dirty boy, and bid him wash himself, once a week; and children of his age seldom have a natural pleasure in soap and water. Therefore, not to mention his clothes, which had seen three months' service in mire and dust, and his thick uncombed hair, the surface of his face and hands was dismally beclouded. He might well skulk behind the settle, on beholding such a bright, graceful damsel enter the house, instead of a rough-headed counterpart of himself, as he expected. "Is Heathcliff not here?" she demanded, pulling off her gloves, and displaying fingers wonderfully whitened with doing nothing and staying indoors.

"Heathcliff, you may come forward," cried Mr. Hindley, enjoying his discomfiture, and gratified to see what a forbidding young blackguard he would be compelled to present himself. "You may come and wish Miss Catherine welcome, like the other servants."

Cathy, catching a glimpse of her friend in his concealment, flew to embrace him; she bestowed seven or eight kisses on his cheek within the second, and then stopped, and drawing back, burst into a laugh, exclaiming, "Why, how very black and cross you look! And how – how funny and grim! But that's because I'm used to Edgar and Isabella Linton. Well, Heathcliff, have you forgotten me?"

She had some reason to put the question, for shame and pride threw double gloom over his countenance, and kept him immovable.

"Shake hands, Heathcliff," said Mr. Earnshaw, condescendingly; "once in a way that is permitted."

"I shall not," replied the boy, finding his tongue at last; "I shall not stand to be laughed at. I shall not bear it!" And he would have broken from the circle, but Miss Cathy seized him again.

"I did not mean to laugh at you," she said; "I could not hinder myself: Heathcliff, shake hands at least! What are you sulky for? It was only that you looked odd. If you wash your face and brush your hair, it will be all right: but you are so dirty!"

She gazed concernedly at the dusky fingers she held in her own, and also at her dress; which she feared had gained no embellishment from its contact with his.

"You needn't have touched me!" he answered, following her eye and snatching away his hand. "I shall be as dirty as I please: and I like to be dirty, and I will be dirty."

With that he dashed headforemost out of the room, amid the merriment of the master and mistress, and to the serious disturbance of Catherine; who could not comprehend how her remarks should have produced such an exhibition of bad temper.

After playing lady's-maid to the new-comer, and putting my cakes in the oven, and making the house and kitchen cheerful with great fires, befitting Christmas-eve, I prepared to sit down and amuse myself by singing carols, all alone; regardless of Joseph's affirmations that he considered the merry tunes I chose as next door to songs. He had retired to private prayer in his chamber, and Mr. and Mrs. Earnshaw were engaging Missy's attention by sundry gay trifles bought for her to present to the little Lintons, as an acknowledgment of their kindness. They had invited them to spend the morrow at Wuthering Heights, and the invitation had been accepted, on one condition: Mrs. Linton begged that her darlings might be kept carefully apart from that 'naughty swearing boy.'

Under these circumstances I remained solitary. I smelt the rich scent of the heating spices; and admired the shining kitchen utensils, the polished clock, decked in holly, the silver mugs ranged on a tray ready to be filled with mulled ale for supper; and above all, the speckless purity of my particular care – the scoured and well-swept floor. I gave due inward applause to every object, and then I remembered how old Earnshaw used to come in when all was tidied, and call me a cant lass, and slip a shilling into my hand as a Christmas-box; and from that I went on to think of his fondness for Heathcliff, and his dread lest he should suffer neglect after death had removed him: and that naturally led me to consider the poor lad's situation now, and from singing I changed my mind to crying. It struck me soon, however, there would be more sense in endeavouring to repair some of his wrongs than shedding tears over them: I got up and walked into the court to seek him. He was not far; I found him smoothing the glossy coat of the new pony in the stable, and feeding the other beasts, according to custom.

"Make haste, Heathcliff!" I said, "the kitchen is so comfortable; and Joseph is upstairs: make haste, and let me dress you smart before Miss Cathy comes out, and then you can sit together, with the whole hearth to yourselves, and have a long chatter till bedtime."

He proceeded with his task, and never turned his head towards me.

"Come – are you coming?" I continued. "There's a little cake for each of you, nearly enough; and you'll need half-an-hour's donning."

I waited five minutes, but getting no answer left him. Catherine supped with her brother and sister-in-law: Joseph and I joined at an unsociable meal, seasoned with reproofs on one side and sauciness on the other. His cake and cheese remained on the table all night for the fairies. He managed to continue work till nine o'clock, and then marched dumb and dour to his chamber. Cathy sat up late, having a world of things to order for the reception of her new friends: she came into the kitchen once to speak to her old one; but he was gone, and she only stayed to ask what was the matter with him, and then went back. In the morning he rose early; and, as it was a holiday, carried his ill-humour on to the moors; not re-appearing till the family were departed for church. Fasting and reflection seemed to have brought him to a better spirit. He hung about me for a while, and having screwed up his courage, exclaimed abruptly – "Nelly, make me decent, I'm going to be good."

"High time, Heathcliff," I said; "you *have* grieved Catherine: she's sorry she ever came home, I daresay! It looks as if you envied her, because she is more thought of than you."

The notion of *envying* Catherine was incomprehensible to him, but the notion of grieving her he understood clearly enough.

"Did she say she was grieved?" he inquired, looking very serious.

"She cried when I told her you were off again this morning."

"Well, *I* cried last night," he returned, "and I had more reason to cry than she."

"Yes: you had the reason of going to bed with a proud heart and an empty stomach," said I. "Proud people breed sad sorrows for themselves. But, if you be ashamed of your touchiness, you must ask pardon, mind, when she comes in. You must go up and offer to kiss her, and say – you know best what to say; only do it heartily, and not as if you thought her converted into a stranger by her grand dress. And now, though I have dinner to get ready, I'll steal time to arrange you so that Edgar Linton shall look quite a doll beside you: and that he does. You are younger, and yet, I'll be bound, you are taller and twice as broad across the shoulders; you could knock him down in a twinkling; don't you feel that you could?"

Heathcliff's face brightened a moment; then it was overcast afresh, and he sighed.

"But, Nelly, if I knocked him down twenty times, that wouldn't make him less handsome or me more so. I wish I had light hair and a fair skin, and was dressed and behaved as well, and had a chance of being as rich as he will be!"

"And cried for mamma at every turn," I added, "and trembled if a country lad heaved his fist against you, and sat at home all day for a shower of rain. Oh, Heathcliff, you are showing a poor spirit! Come to the glass, and I'll let you see what you should wish. Do you mark those two lines between your eyes; and those thick brows, that, instead of rising arched, sink in the middle; and that couple of black fiends, so deeply buried, who never open their windows boldly, but lurk glinting under them, like devil's spies? Wish and learn to smooth away the surly wrinkles, to raise your lids frankly, and change the fiends to confident, innocent angels, suspecting and doubting nothing, and always seeing friends where they are not sure of foes. Don't get the expression of a vicious cur that appears to know the kicks it gets are its desert, and yet hates all the world, as well as the kicker, for what it suffers."

"In other words, I must wish for Edgar Linton's great blue eyes and even forehead," he replied. "I do – and that won't help me to them."

"A good heart will help you to a bonny face, my lad," I continued, "if you were a regular black; and a bad one will turn the bonniest into something worse than ugly. And now that we've done washing, and combing, and sulking – tell me whether you don't think yourself rather handsome? I'll tell you, I do. You're fit for a prince in disguise. Who knows but your father was Emperor of China, and your mother an Indian queen, each of them able to buy up, with one week's income, Wuthering Heights and Thrushcross Grange together? And you were kidnapped by wicked sailors and brought to England. Were I in your place, I would frame high notions of my birth; and the thoughts of what I was should give me courage and dignity to support the oppressions of a little farmer!"

So I chattered on; and Heathcliff gradually lost his frown and began to look quite pleasant, when all at once our conversation was interrupted by a rumbling sound moving up the road and entering the court. He ran to the window and I to the door, just in time to behold the two Lintons descend from the family carriage, smothered in cloaks and furs, and the Earnshaws dismount from their horses: they often rode to church in winter. Catherine took a hand of each of the children, and brought them into the house and set them before the fire, which quickly put colour into their white faces.

I urged my companion to hasten now and show his amiable humour, and he willingly obeyed; but ill luck would have it that, as he opened the door leading from the kitchen on one side, Hindley opened it on the other. They met, and the master, irritated at seeing him clean and cheerful, or, perhaps, eager to keep his promise to Mrs. Linton, shoved him back with a sudden thrust, and angrily bade Joseph "keep the fellow out of the room – send him into the garret till dinner is over. He'll be cramming his fingers in the tarts and stealing the fruit, if left alone with them a minute."

"Nay, sir," I could not avoid answering, "he'll touch nothing, not he: and I suppose he must have his share of the dainties as well as we."

"He shall have his share of my hand, if I catch him downstairs till dark," cried Hindley. "Begone, you vagabond! What! You are attempting the coxcomb, are you? Wait till I get hold of those elegant locks – see if I won't pull them a bit longer!"

"They are long enough already," observed Master Linton, peeping from the doorway; "I wonder they don't make his head ache. It's like a colt's mane over his eyes!"

He ventured this remark without any intention to insult; but Heathcliff's violent nature was not prepared to endure the appearance of impertinence from one whom he seemed to hate, even then, as a rival. He seized a tureen of hot apple sauce (the first thing that came under his gripe) and dashed it full against the speaker's face and neck; who instantly commenced a lament that brought Isabella and Catherine hurrying to the place. Mr. Earnshaw snatched up the culprit directly and conveyed him to his chamber; where, doubtless, he administered a rough remedy to cool the fit of passion, for he appeared red and breathless. I got the dishcloth, and rather spitefully scrubbed Edgar's nose and mouth, affirming it served him right for meddling. His sister began weeping to go home, and Cathy stood by confounded, blushing for all.

"You should not have spoken to him!" she expostulated with Master Linton. "He was in a bad temper, and now you've spoilt your visit; and he'll be flogged: I hate him to be flogged! I can't eat my dinner. Why did you speak to him, Edgar?"

"I didn't," sobbed the youth, escaping from my hands, and finishing the remainder of the purification with his cambric pocket-handkerchief. "I promised mamma that I wouldn't say one word to him, and I didn't."

"Well, don't cry," replied Catherine, contemptuously; "you're not killed. Don't make more mischief; my brother is coming: be quiet! Hush, Isabella! Has anybody hurt you?"

"There, there, children – to your seats!" cried Hindley, bustling in. "That brute of a lad has warmed me nicely. Next time, Master Edgar, take the law into your own fists – it will give you an appetite!"

The little party recovered its equanimity at sight of the fragrant feast. They were hungry after their ride, and easily consoled, since no real harm had befallen them. Mr. Earnshaw carved bountiful platefuls, and the mistress made them merry with lively talk. I waited behind her chair, and was pained to behold Catherine, with dry eyes and an indifferent air, commence cutting up the wing of a goose before her. "An unfeeling child," I thought to myself; "how lightly she dismisses her old playmate's troubles. I could not have imagined her to be so selfish." She lifted a mouthful to her lips: then she set it down again: her cheeks flushed, and the tears gushed over them. She slipped her fork to the floor, and hastily dived under the cloth to conceal her emotion. I did not call her unfeeling long; for I perceived she was in purgatory throughout the day, and wearying to find an opportunity of getting by herself, or paying a visit to Heathcliff, who had been locked up by the master: as I discovered, on endeavouring to introduce to him a private mess of victuals.

In the evening we had a dance. Cathy begged that he might be liberated then, as Isabella Linton had no partner: her entreaties were vain, and I was appointed to supply the deficiency. We got rid of all gloom in the excitement of the exercise, and our pleasure was increased by the arrival of the Gimmerton band, mustering fifteen strong: a trumpet, a trombone, clarionets, bassoons, French horns, and a bass viol, besides singers. They go the rounds of all the respectable houses, and receive contributions every Christmas, and we esteemed it a first-rate treat to hear them. After the usual carols had been sung, we set them to songs and glees. Mrs. Earnshaw loved the music, and so they gave us plenty.

Catherine loved it too: but she said it sounded sweetest at the top of the steps, and she went up in the dark: I followed. They shut the house door below, never noting our absence, it was so full of people. She made no stay at the stairs'-head, but mounted farther, to the garret where Heathcliff was confined, and called him. He stubbornly declined answering for a while: she persevered, and finally persuaded him to hold communion with her through the boards. I let the poor things converse unmolested, till I supposed the songs were going to cease, and the singers to get some refreshment: then I clambered up the ladder to warn her. Instead of finding her outside, I heard her voice within. The little monkey had crept by the skylight of one garret, along the roof, into the skylight of the other, and it was with the utmost difficulty I could coax her out again. When she did come, Heathcliff came with her, and she insisted that I should take him into the kitchen, as my fellow-servant had gone to a neighbour's, to be removed from the sound of our 'devil's psalmody', as it pleased him to call it. I told them I intended by no means to encourage their tricks: but as the prisoner had never broken his fast since yesterday's dinner, I would wink at his cheating Mr. Hindley that once. He went down: I set him a stool by the fire, and offered him a quantity of good things: but he was sick and could eat little, and my attempts to entertain him were thrown away. He leant his two elbows on his knees, and his chin on his hands and remained rapt in dumb meditation. On my inquiring the subject of his thoughts, he answered gravely – "I'm trying to settle how I shall pay Hindley back. I don't care how long I wait, if I can only do it at last. I hope he will not die before I do!"

"For shame, Heathcliff!" said I. "It is for God to punish wicked people; we should learn to forgive."

"No, God won't have the satisfaction that I shall," he returned. "I only wish I knew the best way! Let me alone, and I'll plan it out: while I'm thinking of that I don't feel pain."

But, Mr. Lockwood, I forget these tales cannot divert you. I'm annoyed how I should dream of chattering on at such a rate; and your gruel cold, and you nodding for bed! I could have told Heathcliff's history, all that you need hear, in half a dozen words.

* * *

Thus interrupting herself, the housekeeper rose, and proceeded to lay aside her sewing; but I felt incapable of moving from the hearth, and I was very far from nodding. "Sit still, Mrs. Dean," I cried; "do sit still another half-hour. You've done just right to tell the story leisurely. That is the method I like; and you must finish it in the same style. I am interested in every character you have mentioned, more or less."

"The clock is on the stroke of eleven, sir."

"No matter – I'm not accustomed to go to bed in the long hours. One or two is early enough for a person who lies till ten."

"You shouldn't lie till ten. There's the very prime of the morning gone long before that time. A person who has not done one-half his day's work by ten o'clock, runs a chance of leaving the other half undone."

"Nevertheless, Mrs. Dean, resume your chair; because tomorrow I intend lengthening the night till afternoon. I prognosticate for myself an obstinate cold, at least."

"I hope not, sir. Well, you must allow me to leap over some three years; during that space Mrs. Earnshaw –"

"No, no, I'll allow nothing of the sort! Are you acquainted with the mood of mind in which, if you were seated alone, and the cat licking its kitten on the rug before you, you would watch the operation so intently that puss's neglect of one ear would put you seriously out of temper?"

"A terribly lazy mood, I should say."

"On the contrary, a tiresomely active one. It is mine, at present; and, therefore, continue minutely. I perceive that people in these regions acquire over people in towns the value that a spider in a dungeon does over a spider in a cottage, to their various occupants; and yet the deepened attraction is not entirely owing to the situation of the looker-on. They *do* live more in earnest, more in themselves, and less in surface, change, and frivolous external things. I could fancy a love for life here almost possible; and I was a fixed unbeliever in any love of a year's standing. One state resembles setting a hungry man down to a single dish, on which he may concentrate his entire appetite and do it justice; the other, introducing him to a table laid out by French cooks: he can perhaps extract as much enjoyment from the whole; but each part is a mere atom in his regard and remembrance."

"Oh! Here we are the same as anywhere else, when you get to know us," observed Mrs. Dean, somewhat puzzled at my speech.

"Excuse me," I responded; "you, my good friend, are a striking evidence against that assertion. Excepting a few provincialisms of slight consequence, you have no marks of the manners which I am habituated to consider as peculiar to your class. I am sure you have thought a great deal more than the generality of servants think. You have been compelled to cultivate your reflective faculties for want of occasions for frittering your life away in silly trifles."

Mrs. Dean laughed.

"I certainly esteem myself a steady, reasonable kind of body," she said; "not exactly from living among the hills and seeing one set of faces, and one series of actions, from year's end to year's end; but I have undergone sharp discipline, which has taught me wisdom; and then, I have read more than you would fancy, Mr. Lockwood. You could not open a book in this library that I have not looked into, and got something out of also: unless it be that range of Greek and Latin, and that of French; and those I know one from another: it is as much as you can expect of a poor man's daughter. However, if I am to follow my story in true gossip's fashion, I had better go on; and instead of leaping three years, I will be content to pass to the next summer – the summer of 1778, that is nearly twenty-three years ago."

Chapter Eight

ON THE MORNING of a fine June day my first bonny little nursling, and the last of the ancient Earnshaw stock, was born. We were busy with the hay in a far-away field, when the girl that usually brought our breakfasts came running an hour too soon across the meadow and up the lane, calling me as she ran.

"Oh, such a grand bairn!" she panted out. "The finest lad that ever breathed! But the doctor says missis must go: he says she's been in a consumption these many months. I heard him tell Mr. Hindley: and now she has nothing to keep her, and she'll be dead before winter. You must come home directly. You're to nurse it, Nelly: to feed it with sugar and milk, and take care of it day and night. I wish I were you, because it will be all yours when there is no missis!"

"But is she very ill?" I asked, flinging down my rake and tying my bonnet.

"I guess she is; yet she looks bravely," replied the girl, "and she talks as if she thought of living to see it grow a man. She's out of her head for joy, it's such a beauty! If I were her I'm certain I should not die: I should get better at the bare sight of it, in spite of Kenneth. I was fairly mad at him. Dame Archer brought the cherub down to master, in the house, and his face just began to light up, when the old croaker steps forward, and says he – 'Earnshaw, it's a blessing your wife has been spared to leave you this son. When she came, I felt convinced we shouldn't keep her long; and now, I must tell you, the winter will probably finish her. Don't take on, and fret about it too much: it can't be helped. And besides, you should have known better than to choose such a rush of a lass!'"

"And what did the master answer?" I inquired.

"I think he swore: but I didn't mind him, I was straining to see the bairn," and she began again to describe it rapturously. I, as zealous as herself, hurried eagerly home to admire, on my part; though I was very sad for Hindley's sake. He had room in his heart only for two idols – his wife and himself: he doted on both, and adored one, and I couldn't conceive how he would bear the loss.

When we got to Wuthering Heights, there he stood at the front door; and, as I passed in, I asked, "How was the baby?"

"Nearly ready to run about, Nell!" he replied, putting on a cheerful smile.

"And the mistress?" I ventured to inquire; "the doctor says she's –"

"Damn the doctor!" he interrupted, reddening. "Frances is quite right: she'll be perfectly well by this time next week. Are you going upstairs? Will you tell her that I'll come, if she'll promise not to talk. I left her because she would not hold her tongue; and she must – tell her Mr. Kenneth says she must be quiet."

I delivered this message to Mrs. Earnshaw; she seemed in flighty spirits, and replied merrily, "I hardly spoke a word, Ellen, and there he has gone out twice, crying. Well, say I promise I won't speak: but that does not bind me not to laugh at him!"

Poor soul! Till within a week of her death that gay heart never failed her; and her husband persisted doggedly, nay, furiously, in affirming her health improved every day. When Kenneth warned him that his medicines were useless at that stage of the malady, and he needn't put him to further expense by attending her, he retorted, "I know you need not – she's well – she does not want any more attendance from you! She never was in a consumption. It was a fever; and it is gone: her pulse is as slow as mine now, and her cheek as cool."

He told his wife the same story, and she seemed to believe him; but one night, while leaning on his shoulder, in the act of saying she thought she should be able to get up tomorrow, a fit of coughing took her – a very slight one – he raised her in his arms; she put her two hands about his neck, her face changed, and she was dead.

As the girl had anticipated, the child Hareton fell wholly into my hands. Mr. Earnshaw, provided he saw him healthy and never heard him cry, was contented, as far as regarded him. For himself, he grew desperate: his sorrow was of that kind that will not lament. He neither wept nor prayed; he cursed and defied: execrated God and man, and gave himself up to reckless dissipation. The servants could not bear his tyrannical and evil conduct long: Joseph and I were the only two that would stay. I had not the heart to leave my charge; and besides, you know, I had been his foster-sister, and excused his behaviour more readily than a stranger would. Joseph remained to hector over tenants and labourers; and because it was his vocation to be where he had plenty of wickedness to reprove.

The master's bad ways and bad companions formed a pretty example for Catherine and Heathcliff. His treatment of the latter was enough to make a fiend of a saint. And, truly, it appeared as if the lad *were* possessed of something diabolical at that period. He delighted to witness Hindley degrading himself past redemption; and became daily more notable for savage sullenness and ferocity. I could not half tell what an infernal house we had. The curate dropped calling, and nobody decent came near us, at last; unless Edgar Linton's visits to Miss Cathy might be an exception. At fifteen she was the queen of the countryside; she had no peer; and she did turn out a haughty, headstrong creature! I own I did not like her, after infancy was past; and I vexed her frequently by trying to bring down her arrogance: she never took an aversion to me, though. She had a wondrous constancy to old attachments: even Heathcliff kept his hold on her affections unalterably; and young Linton, with all his superiority, found it difficult to make an equally deep impression. He was my late master: that is his portrait over the fireplace. It used to hang on one side, and his wife's on the other; but hers has been removed, or else you might see something of what she was. Can you make that out?

Mrs. Dean raised the candle, and I discerned a soft-featured face, exceedingly resembling the young lady at the Heights, but more pensive and amiable in expression. It formed a sweet picture. The long light hair curled slightly on the temples; the eyes were large and serious; the figure almost too graceful. I did not marvel how Catherine Earnshaw could forget her first friend for such an individual. I marvelled much how he, with a mind to correspond with his person, could fancy my idea of Catherine Earnshaw.

"A very agreeable portrait," I observed to the house-keeper. "Is it like?"

"Yes," she answered; "but he looked better when he was animated; that is his everyday countenance: he wanted spirit in general."

Catherine had kept up her acquaintance with the Lintons since her five-weeks' residence among them; and as she had no temptation to show her rough side in their company, and had the sense to be ashamed of being rude where she experienced such invariable courtesy, she imposed unwittingly on the old lady and gentleman by her ingenious cordiality; gained the admiration of Isabella, and the heart and soul of her brother: acquisitions that flattered her from the first – for she was full of ambition – and led her to adopt a double character without exactly intending to deceive any one. In the place where she heard Heathcliff termed a 'vulgar young ruffian,' and 'worse than a brute,' she took care not to act like him; but at home she had small inclination to practise politeness that would only be laughed at, and restrain an unruly nature when it would bring her neither credit nor praise.

Mr. Edgar seldom mustered courage to visit Wuthering Heights openly. He had a terror of Earnshaw's reputation, and shrunk from encountering him; and yet he was always received with our best attempts at civility: the master himself avoided offending him, knowing why he came; and if he could not be gracious, kept out of the way. I rather think his appearance there was distasteful to Catherine; she was not artful, never played the coquette, and had evidently an objection to her two friends meeting at all; for when Heathcliff expressed contempt of Linton in his presence, she could not half coincide, as she did in his absence; and when Linton evinced disgust and antipathy to Heathcliff, she dared not treat his sentiments with indifference, as if depreciation of her playmate were of scarcely any consequence to her. I've had many a laugh at her perplexities and untold troubles, which she vainly strove to hide from my mockery. That sounds ill-natured: but she was so proud it became really impossible to pity her distresses, till she should be chastened into more humility. She did bring herself, finally, to confess, and to confide in me: there was not a soul else that she might fashion into an adviser.

Mr. Hindley had gone from home one afternoon, and Heathcliff presumed to give himself a holiday on the strength of it. He had reached the age of sixteen then, I think, and without having bad features, or being deficient in intellect, he contrived to convey an impression of inward and outward repulsiveness that his present aspect retains no traces of. In the first place, he had by that time lost the benefit of his early education: continual hard work, begun soon and concluded late, had extinguished any curiosity he once possessed in pursuit of knowledge, and any love for books or learning. His childhood's sense of superiority, instilled into him by the favours of old Mr. Earnshaw, was faded away. He struggled long to keep up an equality with Catherine in her studies, and yielded with poignant though silent regret: but he yielded completely; and there was no prevailing on him to take a step in the way of moving upward, when he found he must, necessarily, sink beneath his former level. Then personal appearance sympathised with mental deterioration: he acquired a slouching gait and ignoble look; his naturally reserved disposition was exaggerated into an almost idiotic excess of unsociable moroseness; and he took a grim pleasure, apparently, in exciting the aversion rather than the esteem of his few acquaintance.

Catherine and he were constant companions still at his seasons of respite from labour; but he had ceased to express his fondness for her in words, and recoiled with angry suspicion from her girlish caresses, as if conscious there could be no gratification in lavishing such marks of affection on him. On the before-named occasion he came into the house to announce his intention of doing nothing, while I was assisting Miss Cathy to arrange her dress: she had not reckoned on his taking it into his head to be idle; and imagining she would have the whole place to herself, she managed, by some means, to inform Mr. Edgar of her brother's absence, and was then preparing to receive him.

"Cathy, are you busy this afternoon?" asked Heathcliff. "Are you going anywhere?"

"No, it is raining," she answered.

"Why have you that silk frock on, then?" he said. "Nobody coming here, I hope?"

"Not that I know of," stammered Miss: "but you should be in the field now, Heathcliff. It is an hour past dinnertime: I thought you were gone."

"Hindley does not often free us from his accursed presence," observed the boy. "I'll not work any more today: I'll stay with you."

"Oh, but Joseph will tell," she suggested; "you'd better go!"

"Joseph is loading lime on the further side of Penistone Crags; it will take him till dark, and he'll never know."

So, saying, he lounged to the fire, and sat down. Catherine reflected an instant, with knitted brows – she found it needful to smooth the way for an intrusion. "Isabella and Edgar Linton talked of calling this afternoon," she said, at the conclusion of a minute's silence. "As it rains, I hardly expect them; but they may come, and if they do, you run the risk of being scolded for no good."

"Order Ellen to say you are engaged, Cathy," he persisted; "don't turn me out for those pitiful, silly friends of yours! I'm on the point, sometimes, of complaining that they – but I'll not –"

"That they what?" cried Catherine, gazing at him with a troubled countenance. "Oh, Nelly!" she added petulantly, jerking her head away from my hands, "you've combed my hair quite out of curl! That's enough; let me alone. What are you on the point of complaining about, Heathcliff?"

"Nothing – only look at the almanack on that wall;" he pointed to a framed sheet hanging near the window, and continued, "The crosses are for the evenings you have spent with the Lintons, the dots for those spent with me. Do you see? I've marked every day."

"Yes – very foolish: as if I took notice!" replied Catherine, in a peevish tone. "And where is the sense of that?"

"To show that I *do* take notice," said Heathcliff.

"And should I always be sitting with you?" she demanded, growing more irritated. "What good do I get? What do you talk about? You might be dumb, or a baby, for anything you say to amuse me, or for anything you do, either!"

"You never told me before that I talked too little, or that you disliked my company, Cathy!" exclaimed Heathcliff, in much agitation.

"It's no company at all, when people know nothing and say nothing," she muttered.

Her companion rose up, but he hadn't time to express his feelings further, for a horse's feet were heard on the flags, and having knocked gently, young Linton entered, his face brilliant with delight at the unexpected summon he had received. Doubtless Catherine marked the difference between her friends, as one came in and the other went out. The contrast resembled what you see in exchanging a bleak, hilly, coal country for a beautiful fertile valley; and his voice and greeting were as opposite as his aspect. He had a sweet, low manner of speaking, and pronounced his words as you do: that's less gruff than we talk here, and softer.

"I'm not come too soon, am I?" he said, casting a look at me: I had begun to wipe the plate, and tidy some drawers at the far end in the dresser.

"No," answered Catherine. "What are you doing there, Nelly?"

"My work, Miss," I replied. (Mr. Hindley had given me directions to make a third party in any private visits Linton chose to pay.)

She stepped behind me and whispered crossly, "Take yourself and your dusters off; when company are in the house, servants don't commence scouring and cleaning in the room where they are!"

"It's a good opportunity, now that master is away," I answered aloud: "he hates me to be fidgeting over these things in his presence. I'm sure Mr. Edgar will excuse me."

"I hate you to be fidgeting in *my* presence," exclaimed the young lady imperiously, not allowing her guest time to speak: she had failed to recover her equanimity since the little dispute with Heathcliff.

"I'm sorry for it, Miss Catherine," was my response; and I proceeded assiduously with my occupation.

She, supposing Edgar could not see her, snatched the cloth from my hand, and pinched me, with a prolonged wrench, very spitefully on the arm. I've said I did not love her, and rather relished mortifying her vanity now and then: besides, she hurt me extremely; so I started up from my knees, and screamed out, "Oh, Miss, that's a nasty trick! You have no right to nip me, and I'm not going to bear it."

"I didn't touch you, you lying creature!" cried she, her fingers tingling to repeat the act, and her ears red with rage. She never had power to conceal her passion, it always set her whole complexion in a blaze.

"What's that, then?" I retorted, showing a decided purple witness to refute her.

She stamped her foot, wavered a moment, and then, irresistibly impelled by the naughty spirit within her, slapped me on the cheek: a stinging blow that filled both eyes with water.

"Catherine, love! Catherine!" interposed Linton, greatly shocked at the double fault of falsehood and violence which his idol had committed.

"Leave the room, Ellen!" she repeated, trembling all over.

Little Hareton, who followed me everywhere, and was sitting near me on the floor, at seeing my tears commenced crying himself, and sobbed out complaints against 'wicked aunt Cathy,' which drew her fury on to his unlucky head: she seized his shoulders, and shook him till the poor child waxed livid, and Edgar thoughtlessly laid hold of her hands to deliver him. In an instant one was wrung free, and the astonished young man felt it applied over his own ear in a way that could not be mistaken for jest. He drew back in consternation. I lifted Hareton in my arms, and walked off to the kitchen with him, leaving the door of communication open, for I was curious to watch how they would settle their disagreement. The insulted visitor moved to the spot where he had laid his hat, pale and with a quivering lip.

"That's right!" I said to myself. "Take warning and begone! It's a kindness to let you have a glimpse of her genuine disposition."

"Where are you going?" demanded Catherine, advancing to the door.

He swerved aside, and attempted to pass.

"You must not go!" she exclaimed, energetically.

"I must and shall!" he replied in a subdued voice.

"No," she persisted, grasping the handle; "not yet, Edgar Linton: sit down; you shall not leave me in that temper. I should be miserable all night, and I won't be miserable for you!"

"Can I stay after you have struck me?" asked Linton.

Catherine was mute.

"You've made me afraid and ashamed of you," he continued; "I'll not come here again!"

Her eyes began to glisten and her lids to twinkle.

"And you told a deliberate untruth!" he said.

"I didn't!" she cried, recovering her speech; "I did nothing deliberately. Well, go, if you please – get away! And now I'll cry – I'll cry myself sick!"

She dropped down on her knees by a chair, and set to weeping in serious earnest. Edgar persevered in his resolution as far as the court; there he lingered. I resolved to encourage him.

"Miss is dreadfully wayward, sir," I called out. "As bad as any marred child: you'd better be riding home, or else she will be sick, only to grieve us."

The soft thing looked askance through the window: he possessed the power to depart as much as a cat possesses the power to leave a mouse half killed, or a bird half eaten. Ah, I thought, there will be no saving him: he's doomed, and flies to his fate! And so it was: he turned abruptly, hastened into the house again, shut the door behind him; and when I went in a while after to inform them that Earnshaw had come home rabid drunk, ready to pull the whole place about our ears (his ordinary frame of mind in that condition), I saw the quarrel had merely effected a closer intimacy – had broken the outworks of youthful timidity, and enabled them to forsake the disguise of friendship, and confess themselves lovers.

Intelligence of Mr. Hindley's arrival drove Linton speedily to his horse, and Catherine to her chamber. I went to hide little Hareton, and to take the shot out of the master's fowling-piece, which he was fond of playing with in his insane excitement, to the hazard of the lives of any who provoked, or even attracted his notice too much; and I had hit upon the plan of removing it, that he might do less mischief if he did go the length of firing the gun.

Chapter Nine

HE ENTERED, vociferating oaths dreadful to hear; and caught me in the act of stowing his son away in the kitchen cupboard. Hareton was impressed with a wholesome terror of encountering either his wild beast's fondness or his madman's rage; for in one he ran a chance of being squeezed and kissed to death, and in the other of being flung into the fire, or dashed against the wall; and the poor thing remained perfectly quiet wherever I chose to put him.

"There, I've found it out at last!" cried Hindley, pulling me back by the skin of my neck, like a dog. "By heaven and hell, you've sworn between you to murder that child! I know how it is, now, that he is always out of my way. But, with the help of Satan, I shall make you swallow the carving-knife, Nelly! You needn't laugh; for I've just crammed Kenneth, head-downmost, in the Black-horse marsh; and two is the same as one – and I want to kill some of you: I shall have no rest till I do!"

"But I don't like the carving-knife, Mr. Hindley," I answered; "it has been cutting red herrings. I'd rather be shot, if you please."

"You'd rather be damned!" he said; "and so you shall. No law in England can hinder a man from keeping his house decent, and mine's abominable! Open your mouth." He held the knife in his hand, and pushed its point between my teeth: but, for my part, I was never much afraid of his vagaries. I spat out, and affirmed it tasted detestably – I would not take it on any account.

"Oh!" said he, releasing me, "I see that hideous little villain is not Hareton: I beg your pardon, Nell. If it be, he deserves flaying alive for not running to welcome me, and for screaming as if I were a goblin. Unnatural cub, come hither! I'll teach thee to impose on a good-hearted, deluded father. Now, don't you think the lad would be handsomer cropped? It makes a dog fiercer, and I love something fierce – get me a scissors – something fierce and trim! Besides, it's infernal affectation – devilish conceit it is, to cherish our ears – we're asses enough without them. Hush, child, hush! Well then, it is my darling! Wisht, dry thy eyes – there's a joy; kiss me. What! It won't? Kiss me, Hareton! Damn thee, kiss me! By God, as if I would rear such a monster! As sure as I'm living, I'll break the brat's neck."

Poor Hareton was squalling and kicking in his father's arms with all his might, and redoubled his yells when he carried him upstairs and lifted him over the banister. I cried out that he would frighten the child into fits, and ran to rescue him. As I reached them, Hindley leant forward on the rails to listen to a noise below; almost forgetting what he had in his hands. "Who is that?" he asked, hearing someone approaching the stairs'-foot. I leant forward also, for the purpose of signing to Heathcliff, whose step I recognised, not to come further; and, at the instant when my eye quitted Hareton, he gave a sudden spring, delivered himself from the careless grasp that held him, and fell.

There was scarcely time to experience a thrill of horror before we saw that the little wretch was safe. Heathcliff arrived underneath just at the critical moment; by a natural impulse he arrested his descent, and setting him on his feet, looked up to discover the author of the accident. A miser who has parted with a lucky lottery ticket for five shillings, and finds next day he has lost in the bargain five thousand pounds, could not show a blanker countenance than he did on beholding the figure of Mr. Earnshaw above. It expressed, plainer than words could do, the intensest anguish at having made himself the instrument of thwarting his own revenge. Had it been dark, I daresay he would have tried to remedy the mistake by smashing Hareton's skull on the steps; but, we witnessed his salvation; and I was presently below with my precious charge pressed to my heart. Hindley descended more leisurely, sobered and abashed.

"It is your fault, Ellen," he said; "you should have kept him out of sight: you should have taken him from me! Is he injured anywhere?"

"Injured!" I cried angrily; "if he is not killed, he'll be an idiot! Oh! I wonder his mother does not rise from her grave to see how you use him. You're worse than a heathen – treating your own flesh and blood in that manner!" He attempted to touch the child, who, on finding himself with me, sobbed off his terror directly. At the first finger his father laid on him, however, he shrieked again louder than before, and struggled as if he would go into convulsions.

"You shall not meddle with him!" I continued. "He hates you – they all hate you – that's the truth! A happy family you have; and a pretty state you're come to!"

"I shall come to a prettier, yet, Nelly," laughed the misguided man, recovering his hardness. "At present, convey yourself and him away. And hark you, Heathcliff! Clear you too quite from my reach and hearing. I wouldn't murder you tonight; unless, perhaps, I set the house on fire: but that's as my fancy goes."

While saying this he took a pint bottle of brandy from the dresser, and poured some into a tumbler.

"Nay, don't!" I entreated. "Mr. Hindley, do take warning. Have mercy on this unfortunate boy, if you care nothing for yourself!"

"Anyone will do better for him than I shall," he answered.

"Have mercy on your own soul!" I said, endeavouring to snatch the glass from his hand.

"Not I! On the contrary, I shall have great pleasure in sending it to perdition to punish its Maker," exclaimed the blasphemer. "Here's to its hearty damnation!"

He drank the spirits and impatiently bade us go; terminating his command with a sequel of horrid imprecations too bad to repeat or remember.

"It's a pity he cannot kill himself with drink," observed Heathcliff, muttering an echo of curses back when the door was shut. "He's doing his very utmost; but his constitution defies him. Mr. Kenneth says he would wager his mare that he'll outlive any man on this side Gimmerton, and go to the grave a hoary sinner; unless some happy chance out of the common course befall him."

I went into the kitchen, and sat down to lull my little lamb to sleep. Heathcliff, as I thought, walked through to the barn. It turned out afterwards that he only got as far as the other side the settle, when he flung himself on a bench by the wall, removed from the fire and remained silent.

I was rocking Hareton on my knee, and humming a song that began –

> *It was far in the night, and the bairnies grat,*
> *The mither beneath the mools heard that –*

when Miss Cathy, who had listened to the hubbub from her room, put her head in, and whispered, "Are you alone, Nelly?"

"Yes, Miss," I replied.

She entered and approached the hearth. I, supposing she was going to say something, looked up. The expression of her face seemed disturbed and anxious. Her lips were half asunder, as if she meant to speak, and she drew a breath; but it escaped in a sigh instead of a sentence. I resumed my song; not having forgotten her recent behaviour.

"Where's Heathcliff?" she said, interrupting me.

"About his work in the stable," was my answer.

He did not contradict me; perhaps he had fallen into a doze. There followed another long pause, during which I perceived a drop or two trickle from Catherine's cheek to the flags. Is she sorry for her shameful conduct? I asked myself. That will be a novelty: but she may come to the point – as she will – I shan't help her! No, she felt small trouble regarding any subject, save her own concerns.

"Oh, dear!" she cried at last. "I'm very unhappy!"

"A pity," observed I. "You're hard to please; so many friends and so few cares, and can't make yourself content!"

"Nelly, will you keep a secret for me?" she pursued, kneeling down by me, and lifting her winsome eyes to my face with that sort of look which turns off bad temper, even when one has all the right in the world to indulge it.

"Is it worth keeping?" I inquired, less sulkily.

"Yes, and it worries me, and I must let it out! I want to know what I should do. Today, Edgar Linton has asked me to marry him, and I've given him an answer. Now, before I tell you whether it was a consent or denial, you tell me which it ought to have been."

"Really, Miss Catherine, how can I know?" I replied. "To be sure, considering the exhibition you performed in his presence this afternoon, I might say it would be wise to refuse him: since he asked you after that, he must either be hopelessly stupid or a venturesome fool."

"If you talk so, I won't tell you any more," she returned, peevishly rising to her feet. "I accepted him, Nelly. Be quick, and say whether I was wrong!"

"You accepted him! Then what good is it discussing the matter? You have pledged your word, and cannot retract."

"But say whether I should have done so – do!" she exclaimed in an irritated tone; chafing her hands together, and frowning.

"There are many things to be considered before that question can be answered properly," I said, sententiously. "First and foremost, do you love Mr. Edgar?"

"Who can help it? Of course I do," she answered.

Then I put her through the following catechism: for a girl of twenty-two it was not injudicious.

"Why do you love him, Miss Cathy?"

"Nonsense, I do – that's sufficient."

"By no means; you must say why?"

"Well, because he is handsome, and pleasant to be with."

"Bad!" was my commentary.

"And because he is young and cheerful."

"Bad, still."

"And because he loves me."

"Indifferent, coming there."

"And he will be rich, and I shall like to be the greatest woman of the neighbourhood, and I shall be proud of having such a husband."

"Worst of all. And now, say how you love him?"

"As everybody loves – you're silly, Nelly."

"Not at all – answer."

"I love the ground under his feet, and the air over his head, and everything he touches, and every word he says. I love all his looks, and all his actions, and him entirely and altogether. There now!"

"And why?"

"Nay; you are making a jest of it: it is exceedingly ill-natured! It's no jest to me!" said the young lady, scowling, and turning her face to the fire.

"I'm very far from jesting, Miss Catherine," I replied. "You love Mr. Edgar because he is handsome, and young, and cheerful, and rich, and loves you. The last, however, goes for nothing: you would love him without that, probably; and with it you wouldn't, unless he possessed the four former attractions."

"No, to be sure not: I should only pity him – hate him, perhaps, if he were ugly, and a clown."

"But there are several other handsome, rich young men in the world: handsomer, possibly, and richer than he is. What should hinder you from loving them?"

"If there be any, they are out of my way: I've seen none like Edgar."

"You may see some; and he won't always be handsome, and young, and may not always be rich."

"He is now; and I have only to do with the present. I wish you would speak rationally."

"Well, that settles it: if you have only to do with the present, marry Mr. Linton."

"I don't want your permission for that – I *shall* marry him: and yet you have not told me whether I'm right."

"Perfectly right; if people be right to marry only for the present. And now, let us hear what you are unhappy about. Your brother will be pleased; the old lady and gentleman will not object, I think; you will escape from a disorderly, comfortless home into a wealthy, respectable one; and you love Edgar, and Edgar loves you. All seems smooth and easy: where is the obstacle?"

"*Here*! And *here*!" replied Catherine, striking one hand on her forehead, and the other on her breast: "in whichever place the soul lives. In my soul and in my heart, I'm convinced I'm wrong!"

"That's very strange! I cannot make it out."

"It's my secret. But if you will not mock at me, I'll explain it: I can't do it distinctly; but I'll give you a feeling of how I feel."

She seated herself by me again: her countenance grew sadder and graver, and her clasped hands trembled.

"Nelly, do you never dream queer dreams?" she said, suddenly, after some minutes' reflection.

"Yes, now and then," I answered.

"And so do I. I've dreamt in my life dreams that have stayed with me ever after, and changed my ideas: they've gone through and through me, like wine through water, and altered the colour of my mind. And this is one: I'm going to tell it – but take care not to smile at any part of it."

"Oh! Don't, Miss Catherine!" I cried. "We're dismal enough without conjuring up ghosts and visions to perplex us. Come, come, be merry and like yourself! Look at little Hareton! *He's* dreaming nothing dreary. How sweetly he smiles in his sleep!"

"Yes; and how sweetly his father curses in his solitude! You remember him, I daresay, when he was just such another as that chubby thing: nearly as young and innocent. However, Nelly, I shall oblige you to listen: it's not long; and I've no power to be merry tonight."

"I won't hear it, I won't hear it!" I repeated, hastily.

I was superstitious about dreams then, and am still; and Catherine had an unusual gloom in her aspect, that made me dread something from which I might shape a prophecy, and foresee a fearful catastrophe. She was vexed, but she did not proceed. Apparently taking up another subject, she recommenced in a short time.

"If I were in heaven, Nelly, I should be extremely miserable."

"Because you are not fit to go there," I answered. "All sinners would be miserable in heaven."

"But it is not for that. I dreamt once that I was there."

"I tell you I won't hearken to your dreams, Miss Catherine! I'll go to bed," I interrupted again.

She laughed, and held me down; for I made a motion to leave my chair.

"This is nothing," cried she: "I was only going to say that heaven did not seem to be my home; and I broke my heart with weeping to come back to earth; and the angels were so angry that they flung me out into the middle of the heath on the top of Wuthering Heights; where I woke sobbing for joy. That will do to explain my secret, as well as the other. I've no more business to marry Edgar Linton than I have to be in heaven; and if the wicked man in there had not brought Heathcliff so low, I shouldn't have thought of it. It would degrade me to marry Heathcliff now; so he shall never know how I love him: and that, not because he's handsome, Nelly, but because he's more myself than I am. Whatever our souls are made of, his and mine are the same; and Linton's is as different as a moonbeam from lightning, or frost from fire."

Ere this speech ended I became sensible of Heathcliff's presence. Having noticed a slight movement, I turned my head, and saw him rise from the bench, and steal out noiselessly. He had listened till he heard Catherine say it would degrade her to marry him, and then he stayed to hear no further. My companion, sitting on the ground, was prevented by the back of the settle from remarking his presence or departure; but I started, and bade her hush!

"Why?" she asked, gazing nervously round.

"Joseph is here," I answered, catching opportunely the roll of his cartwheels up the road; "and Heathcliff will come in with him. I'm not sure whether he were not at the door this moment."

"Oh, he couldn't overhear me at the door!" said she. "Give me Hareton, while you get the supper, and when it is ready ask me to sup with you. I want to cheat my uncomfortable conscience, and be convinced that Heathcliff has no notion of these things. He has not, has he? He does not know what being in love is!"

"I see no reason that he should not know, as well as you," I returned; "and if you are his choice, he'll be the most unfortunate creature that ever was born! As soon as you become Mrs. Linton, he loses friend, and love, and all! Have you considered how you'll bear the separation, and how he'll bear to be quite deserted in the world? Because, Miss Catherine –"

"He quite deserted! We separated!" she exclaimed, with an accent of indignation. "Who is to separate us, pray? They'll meet the fate of Milo! Not as long as I live, Ellen: for no mortal creature. Every Linton on the face of the earth might melt into nothing before I could consent to forsake Heathcliff. Oh, that's not what I intend – that's not what I mean! I shouldn't be Mrs. Linton were such a price demanded! He'll be as much to me as he has been all his lifetime. Edgar must shake off his antipathy, and tolerate him, at least. He will, when he learns my true feelings towards him. Nelly, I see now you think me a selfish wretch; but did it never strike you that if Heathcliff and I married, we should be beggars? Whereas, if I marry Linton I can aid Heathcliff to rise, and place him out of my brother's power."

"With your husband's money, Miss Catherine?" I asked. "You'll find him not so pliable as you calculate upon: and, though I'm hardly a judge, I think that's the worst motive you've given yet for being the wife of young Linton."

"It is not," retorted she; "it is the best! The others were the satisfaction of my whims: and for Edgar's sake, too, to satisfy him. This is for the sake of one who comprehends in his person my feelings to Edgar and myself. I cannot express it; but surely you and everybody have a notion that there is or should be an existence of yours beyond you. What were the use of my creation, if I were entirely contained here? My great miseries in this world have been Heathcliff's miseries, and I watched and felt each from the beginning: my great thought in living is himself. If all else perished, and *he* remained, *I* should still continue to be; and if all else remained, and he were annihilated, the universe would turn to a mighty stranger: I should not seem a part of it. My love for Linton is like the foliage in the woods: time will change it, I'm well aware, as winter changes the trees. My love for Heathcliff resembles the eternal rocks beneath: a source of little visible delight, but necessary. Nelly, I *am* Heathcliff! He's always, always in my mind: not as a pleasure, any more than I am always a pleasure to myself, but as my own being. So don't talk of our separation again: it is impracticable; and –"

She paused, and hid her face in the folds of my gown; but I jerked it forcibly away. I was out of patience with her folly!

"If I can make any sense of your nonsense, Miss," I said, "it only goes to convince me that you are ignorant of the duties you undertake in marrying; or else that you are a wicked, unprincipled girl. But trouble me with no more secrets: I'll not promise to keep them."

"You'll keep that?" she asked, eagerly.

"No, I'll not promise," I repeated.

She was about to insist, when the entrance of Joseph finished our conversation; and Catherine removed her seat to a corner, and nursed Hareton, while I made the supper. After it was cooked, my fellow-servant and I began to quarrel who should carry some to Mr. Hindley; and we didn't settle it till all was nearly cold. Then we came to the agreement that we would let him ask, if he wanted any; for we feared particularly to go into his presence when he had been some time alone.

"And how isn't that nowt comed in fro' th' field, be this time? What is he about? Girt idle seeght!" demanded the old man, looking round for Heathcliff.

"I'll call him," I replied. "He's in the barn, I've no doubt."

I went and called, but got no answer. On returning, I whispered to Catherine that he had heard a good part of what she said, I was sure; and told how I saw him quit the kitchen just as she complained of her brother's conduct regarding him. She jumped up in a fine fright, flung Hareton on to the settle, and ran to seek for her friend herself; not taking leisure to consider why she was so flurried, or how her talk would have affected him. She was absent such a while that Joseph proposed we should wait no longer. He cunningly conjectured they were staying away in order to avoid hearing his protracted blessing. They were "ill enough for ony fahl manners," he affirmed. And on their behalf he added that night a special prayer to the usual quarter-of-an-hour's supplication before meat, and would have tacked another to the end of the grace, had not his young mistress broken in upon him with a hurried command that he must run down the road, and, wherever Heathcliff had rambled, find and make him re-enter directly!

"I want to speak to him, and I *must*, before I go upstairs," she said. "And the gate is open: he is somewhere out of hearing; for he would not reply, though I shouted at the top of the fold as loud as I could."

Joseph objected at first; she was too much in earnest, however, to suffer contradiction; and at last he placed his hat on his head, and walked grumbling forth. Meantime, Catherine paced up and down the floor, exclaiming – "I wonder where he is – I wonder where he can be! What did I say, Nelly? I've forgotten. Was he vexed at my bad humour this afternoon? Dear! Tell me what I've said to grieve him? I do wish he'd come. I do wish he would!"

"What a noise for nothing!" I cried, though rather uneasy myself. "What a trifle scares you! It's surely no great cause of alarm that Heathcliff should take a moonlight saunter on the moors, or even lie too sulky to speak to us in the hay-loft. I'll engage he's lurking there. See if I don't ferret him out!"

I departed to renew my search; its result was disappointment, and Joseph's quest ended in the same.

"Yon lad gets war und war!" observed he on re-entering. "He's left th' gate at t' full swing, and Miss's pony has trodden dahn two rigs o' corn, and plottered through, raight o'er into t' meadow! Hahsomdiver, t' maister 'ull play t' devil to-morn, and he'll do weel. He's patience itsseln wi' sich careless, offald craters – patience itsseln he is! Bud he'll not be soa allus – yah's see, all on ye! Yah mun't drive him out of his heead for nowt!"

"Have you found Heathcliff, you ass?" interrupted Catherine. "Have you been looking for him, as I ordered?"

"I sud more likker look for th' horse," he replied. "It 'ud be to more sense. Bud I can look for norther horse nur man of a neeght loike this – as black as t' chimbley! Und Heathcliff's noan t' chap to coom at *my* whistle – happen he'll be less hard o' hearing wi' *ye*!"

It *was* a very dark evening for summer: the clouds appeared inclined to thunder, and I said we had better all sit down; the approaching rain would be certain to bring him home without further trouble. However, Catherine would not be persuaded into tranquillity. She kept wandering to and fro, from the gate to the door, in a state of agitation which permitted no repose; and at length took up a permanent situation on one side of the wall, near the road: where, heedless of my expostulations and the growling thunder, and the great drops that began to plash around her, she remained, calling at intervals, and then listening, and then crying outright. She beat Hareton, or any child, at a good passionate fit of crying.

About midnight, while we still sat up, the storm came rattling over the Heights in full fury. There was a violent wind, as well as thunder, and either one or the other split a tree off at the corner of the building: a huge bough fell across the roof, and knocked down a portion of the east chimney-stack, sending a clatter of stones and soot into the kitchen-fire. We thought a bolt had fallen in the middle of us; and Joseph swung on to his knees, beseeching the Lord to remember the patriarchs Noah and Lot, and, as in former times, spare the righteous, though he smote the ungodly. I felt some sentiment that it must be a judgment on us also. The Jonah, in my mind, was Mr. Earnshaw; and I shook the handle of his den that I might ascertain if he were yet living. He replied audibly enough, in a fashion which made my companion vociferate, more clamorously than before, that a wide distinction might be drawn between saints like himself and sinners like his master. But the uproar passed away in twenty minutes, leaving us all unharmed; excepting Cathy, who got thoroughly drenched for her obstinacy in refusing to take shelter, and standing bonnetless and shawl-less to catch as much water as she could with her hair and clothes. She came in and lay down on the settle, all soaked as she was, turning her face to the back, and putting her hands before it.

"Well, Miss!" I exclaimed, touching her shoulder; "you are not bent on getting your death, are you? Do you know what o'clock it is? Half-past twelve. Come, come to bed! There's no use waiting any longer on that foolish boy: he'll be gone to Gimmerton, and he'll stay there now. He guesses we shouldn't wait for him till this late hour: at least, he guesses that only Mr. Hindley would be up; and he'd rather avoid having the door opened by the master."

"Nay, nay, he's noan at Gimmerton," said Joseph. "I's niver wonder but he's at t' bothom of a bog-hoile. This visitation won't for nowt, and I wod hev' ye to look out, Miss – yah muh be t' next. Thank Hivin for all! All warks togither for gooid to them as is chozzen, and piked out fro' th' rubbidge! Yah knaw whet t' Scripture ses." And he began quoting several texts, referring us to chapters and verses where we might find them.

I, having vainly begged the wilful girl to rise and remove her wet things, left him preaching and her shivering, and betook myself to bed with little Hareton, who slept as fast as if everyone had been sleeping round him. I heard Joseph read on a while afterwards; then I distinguished his slow step on the ladder, and then I dropped asleep.

Coming down somewhat later than usual, I saw, by the sunbeams piercing the chinks of the shutters, Miss Catherine still seated near the fireplace. The house-door was ajar, too; light entered from its unclosed windows; Hindley had come out, and stood on the kitchen hearth, haggard and drowsy.

"What ails you, Cathy?" he was saying when I entered: "you look as dismal as a drowned whelp. Why are you so damp and pale, child?"

"I've been wet," she answered reluctantly, "and I'm cold, that's all."

"Oh, she is naughty!" I cried, perceiving the master to be tolerably sober. "She got steeped in the shower of yesterday evening, and there she has sat the night through, and I couldn't prevail on her to stir."

Mr. Earnshaw stared at us in surprise. "The night through," he repeated. "What kept her up? Not fear of the thunder, surely? That was over hours since."

Neither of us wished to mention Heathcliff's absence, as long as we could conceal it; so I replied, I didn't know how she took it into her head to sit up; and she said nothing. The morning was fresh and cool; I threw back the lattice, and presently the room filled with sweet scents from the garden; but Catherine called peevishly to me, "Ellen, shut the window. I'm starving!" And her teeth chattered as she shrank closer to the almost extinguished embers.

"She's ill," said Hindley, taking her wrist; "I suppose that's the reason she would not go to bed. Damn it! I don't want to be troubled with more sickness here. What took you into the rain?"

"Running after t' lads, as usuald!" croaked Joseph, catching an opportunity from our hesitation to thrust in his evil tongue. "If I war yah, maister, I'd just slam t' boards I' their faces all on 'em, gentle and simple! Never a day ut yah're off, but yon cat o' Linton comes sneaking hither; and Miss Nelly, shoo's a fine lass! Shoo sits watching for ye i' t' kitchen; and as yah're in at one door, he's out at t'other; and, then, wer grand lady goes a-courting of her side! It's bonny behaviour, lurking amang t' fields, after twelve o' t' night, wi' that fahl, flaysome divil of a gipsy, Heathcliff! They think *I'm* blind; but I'm noan: nowt ut t' soart! – I seed young Linton boath coming and going, and I seed *yah*" (directing his discourse to me), "yah gooid fur nowt, slattenly witch! Nip up and bolt into th' house, t' minute yah heard t' maister's horse-fit clatter up t' road."

"Silence, eavesdropper!" cried Catherine; "None of your insolence before me! Edgar Linton came yesterday by chance, Hindley; and it was *I* who told him to be off: because I knew you would not like to have met him as you were."

"You lie, Cathy, no doubt," answered her brother, "and you are a confounded simpleton! But never mind Linton at present: tell me, were you not with Heathcliff last night? Speak the truth, now. You need not be afraid of harming him: though I hate him as much as ever, he did me a good turn a short time since that will make my conscience tender of breaking his neck. To prevent it, I shall send him about his business this very morning; and after he's gone, I'd advise you all to look sharp: I shall only have the more humour for you."

"I never saw Heathcliff last night," answered Catherine, beginning to sob bitterly: "and if you do turn him out of doors, I'll go with him. But, perhaps, you'll never have an opportunity: perhaps, he's gone." Here she burst into uncontrollable grief, and the remainder of her words were inarticulate.

Hindley lavished on her a torrent of scornful abuse, and bade her get to her room immediately, or she shouldn't cry for nothing! I obliged her to obey; and I shall never forget what a scene she acted when we reached her chamber: it terrified me. I thought she was going mad, and I begged Joseph to run for the doctor. It proved the commencement of delirium: Mr. Kenneth, as soon as he saw her, pronounced her dangerously ill; she had a fever. He bled her, and he told me to let her live on whey and water-gruel, and take care she did not throw herself downstairs or out of the window; and then he left: for he had enough to do in the parish, where two or three miles was the ordinary distance between cottage and cottage.

Though I cannot say I made a gentle nurse, and Joseph and the master were no better, and though our patient was as wearisome and headstrong as a patient could be, she weathered it through. Old Mrs. Linton paid us several visits, to be sure, and set things to rights, and scolded and ordered us all; and when Catherine was convalescent, she insisted on conveying her to Thrushcross Grange: for which deliverance we were very grateful. But the poor dame had reason to repent of her kindness: she and her husband both took the fever, and died within a few days of each other.

Our young lady returned to us saucier and more passionate, and haughtier than ever. Heathcliff had never been heard of since the evening of the thunder-storm; and, one day, I had the misfortune, when she had provoked me exceedingly, to lay the blame of his disappearance on her: where indeed it belonged, as she well knew. From that period, for several months, she ceased to hold any communication with me, save in the relation of a mere servant. Joseph fell under a ban also: he would speak his mind, and lecture her all the same as if she were a little girl; and she esteemed herself a woman, and our mistress, and thought that her recent illness gave her a claim to be treated with consideration. Then the doctor had said that she would not bear crossing much; she ought to have her own way; and it was nothing less than murder in her eyes for anyone to presume to stand up and contradict her. From Mr. Earnshaw and his companions she kept aloof; and tutored by Kenneth, and serious threats of a fit that often attended her rages, her brother allowed her whatever she pleased to demand, and generally avoided aggravating her fiery temper. He was rather too indulgent in humouring her caprices; not from affection, but from pride: he wished earnestly to see her bring honour to the family by an alliance with the Lintons, and as long as she let him alone she might trample on us like slaves, for aught he cared! Edgar Linton, as multitudes have been before and will be after him, was infatuated: and believed himself the happiest man alive on the day he led her to Gimmerton Chapel, three years subsequent to his father's death.

Much against my inclination, I was persuaded to leave Wuthering Heights and accompany her here. Little Hareton was nearly five years old, and I had just begun to teach him his letters. We made a sad parting; but Catherine's tears were more powerful than ours. When I refused to go, and when she found her entreaties did not move me, she went lamenting to her husband and brother. The former offered me munificent wages; the latter ordered me to pack up: he wanted no women in the house, he said, now that there was no mistress; and as to Hareton, the curate should take him in hand, by-and-by.

And so I had but one choice left: to do as I was ordered. I told the master he got rid of all decent people only to run to ruin a little faster; I kissed Hareton, said goodbye; and since then he has been a stranger: and it's very queer to think it, but I've no doubt he has completely forgotten all about Ellen Dean, and that he was ever more than all the world to her and she to him!

* * *

At this point of the housekeeper's story she chanced to glance towards the time-piece over the chimney; and was in amazement on seeing the minute-hand measure half-past one. She would not hear of staying a second longer: in truth, I felt rather disposed to defer the sequel of her narrative myself. And now that she is vanished to her rest, and I have meditated for another hour or two, I shall summon courage to go also, in spite of aching laziness of head and limbs.

Chapter Ten

A CHARMING INTRODUCTION to a hermit's life! Four weeks' torture, tossing, and sickness! Oh, these bleak winds and bitter northern skies, and impassable roads, and dilatory country surgeons! And oh, this dearth of the human physiognomy! And, worse than all, the terrible intimation of Kenneth that I need not expect to be out of doors till spring!

Mr. Heathcliff has just honoured me with a call. About seven days ago he sent me a brace of grouse – the last of the season. Scoundrel! He is not altogether guiltless in this illness of mine; and that I had a great mind to tell him. But, alas! How could I offend a man who was charitable enough to sit at my bedside a good hour, and talk on some other subject than pills and draughts, blisters and leeches? This is quite an easy interval. I am too weak to read; yet I feel as if I could enjoy something interesting. Why not have up Mrs. Dean to finish her tale? I can recollect its chief incidents, as far as she had gone. Yes: I remember her hero had run off, and never been heard of for three years; and the heroine was married. I'll ring: she'll be delighted to find me capable of talking cheerfully. Mrs. Dean came.

"It wants twenty minutes, sir, to taking the medicine," she commenced.

"Away, away with it!" I replied; "I desire to have –"

"The doctor says you must drop the powders."

"With all my heart! Don't interrupt me. Come and take your seat here. Keep your fingers from that bitter phalanx of vials. Draw your knitting out of your pocket – that will do – now continue the history of Mr. Heathcliff, from where you left off, to the present day. Did he finish his education on the Continent, and come back a gentleman? Or did he get a sizar's place at college, or escape to America, and earn honours by drawing blood from his foster-country? Or make a fortune more promptly on the English highways?"

"He may have done a little in all these vocations, Mr. Lockwood; but I couldn't give my word for any. I stated before that I didn't know how he gained his money; neither am I aware of the means he took to raise his mind from the savage ignorance into which it was sunk: but, with your leave, I'll proceed in my own fashion, if you think it will amuse and not weary you. Are you feeling better this morning?"

"Much."

"That's good news."

* * *

I got Miss Catherine and myself to Thrushcross Grange; and, to my agreeable disappointment, she behaved infinitely better than I dared to expect. She seemed almost over-fond of Mr. Linton; and even to his sister she showed plenty of affection. They were both very attentive to her comfort, certainly. It was not the thorn bending to the honeysuckles, but the honeysuckles embracing the thorn. There were no mutual concessions: one stood erect, and the others yielded: and who can be ill-natured and bad-tempered when they encounter neither opposition nor indifference? I observed that Mr. Edgar had a deep-rooted fear of ruffling her humour. He concealed it from her; but if ever he heard me answer sharply, or saw any other servant grow cloudy at some imperious order of hers, he would show his trouble by a frown of displeasure that never darkened on his own account. He many a time spoke sternly to me about my pertness; and averred that the stab of a knife could not inflict a worse pang than he suffered at seeing his lady vexed. Not to grieve a kind master, I learned to be less touchy; and, for the space of half a year, the gunpowder lay as harmless as sand, because no fire came near to explode it. Catherine had seasons of gloom and silence now and then: they were respected with sympathising silence by her husband, who ascribed them to an alteration in her constitution, produced by her perilous illness; as she was never subject to depression of spirits before. The return of sunshine was welcomed by answering sunshine from him. I believe I may assert that they were really in possession of deep and growing happiness.

It ended. Well, we *must* be for ourselves in the long run; the mild and generous are only more justly selfish than the domineering; and it ended when circumstances caused each to feel that the one's interest was not the chief consideration in the other's thoughts. On a mellow evening in September, I was coming from the garden with a heavy basket of apples which I had been gathering. It had got dusk, and the moon looked over the high wall of the court, causing undefined shadows to lurk in the corners of the numerous projecting portions of the building. I set my burden on the house-steps by the kitchen-door, and lingered to rest, and drew in a few more breaths of the soft, sweet air; my eyes were on the moon, and my back to the entrance, when I heard a voice behind me say, – "Nelly, is that you?"

It was a deep voice, and foreign in tone; yet there was something in the manner of pronouncing my name which made it sound familiar. I turned about to discover who spoke, fearfully; for the doors were shut, and I had seen nobody on approaching the steps. Something stirred in the porch; and, moving nearer, I distinguished a tall man dressed in dark clothes, with dark face and hair. He leant against the side, and held his fingers on the latch as if intending to open for himself. "Who can it be?" I thought. "Mr. Earnshaw? Oh, no! The voice has no resemblance to his."

"I have waited here an hour," he resumed, while I continued staring; "and the whole of that time all round has been as still as death. I dared not enter. You do not know me? Look, I'm not a stranger!"

A ray fell on his features; the cheeks were sallow, and half covered with black whiskers; the brows lowering, the eyes deep-set and singular. I remembered the eyes.

"What!" I cried, uncertain whether to regard him as a worldly visitor, and I raised my hands in amazement. "What! You come back? Is it really you? Is it?"

"Yes, Heathcliff," he replied, glancing from me up to the windows, which reflected a score of glittering moons, but showed no lights from within. "Are they at home? Where is she? Nelly, you are not glad! You needn't be so disturbed. Is she here? Speak! I want to have one word with her – your mistress. Go, and say some person from Gimmerton desires to see her."

"How will she take it?" I exclaimed. "What will she do? The surprise bewilders me – it will put her out of her head! And you *are* Heathcliff! But altered! Nay, there's no comprehending it. Have you been for a soldier?"

"Go and carry my message," he interrupted, impatiently. "I'm in hell till you do!"

He lifted the latch, and I entered; but when I got to the parlour where Mr. and Mrs. Linton were, I could not persuade myself to proceed. At length I resolved on making an excuse to ask if they would have the candles lighted, and I opened the door.

They sat together in a window whose lattice lay back against the wall, and displayed, beyond the garden trees, and the wild green park, the valley of Gimmerton, with a long line of mist winding nearly to its top (for very soon after you pass the chapel, as you may have noticed, the sough that runs from the marshes joins a beck which follows the bend of the glen). Wuthering Heights rose above this silvery vapour; but our old house was invisible; it rather dips down on the other side. Both the room and its occupants, and the scene they gazed on, looked wondrously peaceful. I shrank reluctantly from performing my errand; and was actually going away leaving it unsaid, after having put my question about the candles, when a sense of my folly compelled me to return, and mutter, "A person from Gimmerton wishes to see you ma'am."

"What does he want?" asked Mrs. Linton.

"I did not question him," I answered.

"Well, close the curtains, Nelly," she said; "and bring up tea. I'll be back again directly."

She quitted the apartment; Mr. Edgar inquired, carelessly, who it was.

"Someone mistress does not expect," I replied. "That Heathcliff – you recollect him, sir – who used to live at Mr. Earnshaw's."

"What! The gipsy – the ploughboy?" he cried. "Why did you not say so to Catherine?"

"Hush! You must not call him by those names, master," I said. "She'd be sadly grieved to hear you. She was nearly heartbroken when he ran off. I guess his return will make a jubilee to her."

Mr. Linton walked to a window on the other side of the room that overlooked the court. He unfastened it, and leant out. I suppose they were below, for he exclaimed quickly: "Don't stand there, love! Bring the person in, if it be anyone particular." Ere long, I heard the click of the latch, and Catherine flew upstairs, breathless and wild; too excited to show gladness: indeed, by her face, you would rather have surmised an awful calamity.

"Oh, Edgar, Edgar!" she panted, flinging her arms round his neck. "Oh, Edgar darling! Heathcliff's come back – he is!" And she tightened her embrace to a squeeze.

"Well, well," cried her husband, crossly, "don't strangle me for that! He never struck me as such a marvellous treasure. There is no need to be frantic!"

"I know you didn't like him," she answered, repressing a little the intensity of her delight. "Yet, for my sake, you must be friends now. Shall I tell him to come up?"

"Here," he said, "into the parlour?"

"Where else?" she asked.

He looked vexed, and suggested the kitchen as a more suitable place for him. Mrs. Linton eyed him with a droll expression – half angry, half laughing at his fastidiousness.

"No," she added, after a while; "I cannot sit in the kitchen. Set two tables here, Ellen: one for your master and Miss Isabella, being gentry; the other for Heathcliff and myself, being of the lower orders. Will that please you, dear? Or must I have a fire lighted elsewhere? If so, give directions. I'll run down and secure my guest. I'm afraid the joy is too great to be real!"

She was about to dart off again; but Edgar arrested her.

"*You* bid him step up," he said, addressing me; "and, Catherine, try to be glad, without being absurd. The whole household need not witness the sight of your welcoming a runaway servant as a brother."

I descended, and found Heathcliff waiting under the porch, evidently anticipating an invitation to enter. He followed my guidance without waste of words, and I ushered him into the presence of the master and mistress, whose flushed cheeks betrayed signs of warm talking. But the lady's glowed with another feeling when her friend appeared at the door: she sprang forward, took both his hands, and led him to Linton; and then she seized Linton's reluctant fingers and crushed them into his. Now, fully revealed by the fire and candlelight, I was amazed, more than ever, to behold the transformation of Heathcliff. He had grown a tall, athletic, well-formed man; beside whom my master seemed quite slender and youth-like. His upright carriage suggested the idea of his having been in the army. His countenance was much older in expression and decision of feature than Mr. Linton's; it looked intelligent, and retained no marks of former degradation. A half-civilised ferocity lurked yet in the depressed brows and eyes full of black fire, but it was subdued; and his manner was even dignified: quite divested of roughness, though stern for grace. My master's surprise equalled or exceeded mine: he remained for a minute at a loss how to address the ploughboy, as he had called him. Heathcliff dropped his slight hand, and stood looking at him coolly till he chose to speak.

"Sit down, sir," he said, at length. "Mrs. Linton, recalling old times, would have me give you a cordial reception; and, of course, I am gratified when anything occurs to please her."

"And I also," answered Heathcliff, "especially if it be anything in which I have a part. I shall stay an hour or two willingly."

He took a seat opposite Catherine, who kept her gaze fixed on him as if she feared he would vanish were she to remove it. He did not raise his to her often: a quick glance now and then sufficed; but it flashed back, each time more confidently, the undisguised delight he drank from hers. They were too much absorbed in their mutual joy to suffer embarrassment. Not so Mr. Edgar: he grew pale with pure annoyance: a feeling that reached its climax when his lady rose, and stepping across the rug, seized Heathcliff's hands again, and laughed like one beside herself.

"I shall think it a dream tomorrow!" she cried. "I shall not be able to believe that I have seen, and touched, and spoken to you once more. And yet, cruel Heathcliff! You don't deserve this welcome. To be absent and silent for three years, and never to think of me!"

"A little more than you have thought of me," he murmured. "I heard of your marriage, Cathy, not long since; and, while waiting in the yard below, I meditated this plan – just to have one glimpse of your face, a stare of surprise, perhaps, and pretended pleasure; afterwards settle my score with Hindley; and then prevent the law by doing execution on myself. Your welcome has put these ideas out of my mind; but beware of meeting me with another aspect next time! Nay, you'll not drive me off again. You were really sorry for me, were you? Well, there was cause. I've fought through a bitter life since I last heard your voice; and you must forgive me, for I struggled only for you!"

"Catherine, unless we are to have cold tea, please to come to the table," interrupted Linton, striving to preserve his ordinary tone, and a due measure of politeness. "Mr. Heathcliff will have a long walk, wherever he may lodge tonight; and I'm thirsty."

She took her post before the urn; and Miss Isabella came, summoned by the bell; then, having handed their chairs forward, I left the room. The meal hardly endured ten minutes. Catherine's cup was never filled: she could neither eat nor drink. Edgar had made a slop in his saucer, and scarcely swallowed a mouthful. Their guest did not protract his stay that evening above an hour longer. I asked, as he departed, if he went to Gimmerton?

"No, to Wuthering Heights," he answered: "Mr. Earnshaw invited me, when I called this morning."

Mr. Earnshaw invited *him*! And *he* called on Mr. Earnshaw! I pondered this sentence painfully, after he was gone. Is he turning out a bit of a hypocrite, and coming into the country to work mischief under a cloak? I mused: I had a presentiment in the bottom of my heart that he had better have remained away.

About the middle of the night, I was wakened from my first nap by Mrs. Linton gliding into my chamber, taking a seat on my bedside, and pulling me by the hair to rouse me.

"I cannot rest, Ellen," she said, by way of apology. "And I want some living creature to keep me company in my happiness! Edgar is sulky, because I'm glad of a thing that does not interest him: he refuses to open his mouth, except to utter pettish, silly speeches; and he affirmed I was cruel and selfish for wishing to talk when he was so sick and sleepy. He always contrives to be sick at the least cross! I gave a few sentences of commendation to Heathcliff, and he, either for a headache or a pang of envy, began to cry: so I got up and left him."

"What use is it praising Heathcliff to him?" I answered. "As lads they had an aversion to each other, and Heathcliff would hate just as much to hear him praised: it's human nature. Let Mr. Linton alone about him, unless you would like an open quarrel between them."

"But does it not show great weakness?" pursued she. "I'm not envious: I never feel hurt at the brightness of Isabella's yellow hair and the whiteness of her skin, at her dainty elegance, and the fondness all the family exhibit for her. Even you, Nelly, if we have a dispute sometimes, you back Isabella at once; and I yield like a foolish mother: I call her a darling, and flatter her into a good temper. It pleases her brother to see us cordial, and that pleases me. But they are very much alike: they are spoiled children, and fancy the world was made for their accommodation; and though I humour both, I think a smart chastisement might improve them all the same."

"You're mistaken, Mrs. Linton," said I. "They humour you: I know what there would be to do if they did not. You can well afford to indulge their passing whims as long as their business is to anticipate all your desires. You may, however, fall out, at last, over something of equal consequence to both sides; and then those you term weak are very capable of being as obstinate as you."

"And then we shall fight to the death, shan't we, Nelly?" she returned, laughing. "No! I tell you, I have such faith in Linton's love, that I believe I might kill him, and he wouldn't wish to retaliate."

I advised her to value him the more for his affection.

"I do," she answered, "but he needn't resort to whining for trifles. It is childish and, instead of melting into tears because I said that Heathcliff was now worthy of anyone's regard, and it would honour the first gentleman in the country to be his friend, he ought to have said it for me, and been delighted from sympathy. He must get accustomed to him, and he may as well like him: considering how Heathcliff has reason to object to him, I'm sure he behaved excellently!"

"What do you think of his going to Wuthering Heights?" I inquired. "He is reformed in every respect, apparently: quite a Christian: offering the right hand of fellowship to his enemies all around!"

"He explained it," she replied. "I wonder as much as you. He said he called to gather information concerning me from you, supposing you resided there still; and Joseph told Hindley, who came out and fell to questioning him of what he had been doing, and how he had been living; and finally, desired him to walk in. There were some persons sitting at cards; Heathcliff joined them; my brother lost some money to him, and, finding him plentifully supplied, he requested that he would come again in the evening: to which he consented. Hindley is too reckless to select his acquaintance prudently: he doesn't trouble himself to reflect on the causes he might have for mistrusting one whom he has basely injured. But Heathcliff affirms his principal reason for resuming a connection with his ancient persecutor is a wish to install himself in quarters at walking distance from the Grange, and an attachment to the house where we lived together; and likewise a hope that I shall have more opportunities of seeing him there than I could have if he settled in Gimmerton. He means to offer liberal payment for permission to lodge at the Heights; and doubtless my brother's covetousness will prompt him to accept the terms: he was always greedy; though what he grasps with one hand he flings away with the other."

"It's a nice place for a young man to fix his dwelling in!" said I. "Have you no fear of the consequences, Mrs. Linton?"

"None for my friend," she replied: "his strong head will keep him from danger; a little for Hindley: but he can't be made morally worse than he is; and I stand between him and bodily harm. The event of this evening has reconciled me to God and humanity! I had risen in angry rebellion against Providence. Oh, I've endured very, very bitter misery, Nelly! If that creature knew how bitter, he'd be ashamed to cloud its removal with idle petulance. It was kindness for him which induced me to bear it alone: had I expressed the agony I frequently felt, he would have been taught to long for its alleviation as ardently as I. However, it's over, and I'll take no revenge on his folly; I can afford to suffer anything hereafter! Should the meanest thing alive slap me on the cheek, I'd not only turn the other, but I'd ask pardon for provoking it; and, as a proof, I'll go make my peace with Edgar instantly. Good-night! I'm an angel!"

In this self-complacent conviction she departed; and the success of her fulfilled resolution was obvious on the morrow: Mr. Linton had not only abjured his peevishness (though his spirits seemed still subdued by Catherine's exuberance of vivacity), but he ventured no objection to her taking Isabella with her to Wuthering Heights in the afternoon; and she rewarded him with such a summer of sweetness and affection in return as made the house a paradise for several days; both master and servants profiting from the perpetual sunshine.

Heathcliff – Mr. Heathcliff I should say in future – used the liberty of visiting at Thrushcross Grange cautiously, at first: he seemed estimating how far its owner would bear his intrusion. Catherine, also, deemed it judicious to moderate her expressions of pleasure in receiving him; and he gradually established his right to be expected. He retained a great deal of the reserve for which his boyhood was remarkable; and that served to repress all startling demonstrations of feeling. My master's uneasiness experienced a lull, and further circumstances diverted it into another channel for a space.

His new source of trouble sprang from the not anticipated misfortune of Isabella Linton evincing a sudden and irresistible attraction towards the tolerated guest. She was at that time a charming young lady of eighteen; infantile in manners, though possessed of keen wit, keen feelings, and a keen temper, too, if irritated. Her brother, who loved her tenderly, was appalled at this fantastic preference. Leaving aside the degradation of an alliance with a nameless man, and the possible fact that his property, in default of heirs male, might pass into such a one's power, he had sense to comprehend Heathcliff's disposition: to know that, though his exterior was altered, his mind was unchangeable and unchanged. And he dreaded that mind: it revolted him: he shrank forebodingly from the idea of committing Isabella to its keeping. He would have recoiled still more had he been aware that her attachment rose unsolicited, and was bestowed where it awakened no reciprocation of sentiment; for the minute he discovered its existence he laid the blame on Heathcliff's deliberate designing.

We had all remarked, during some time, that Miss Linton fretted and pined over something. She grew cross and wearisome; snapping at and teasing Catherine continually, at the imminent risk of exhausting her limited patience. We excused her, to a certain extent, on the plea of ill-health: she was dwindling and fading before our eyes. But one day, when she had been peculiarly wayward, rejecting her breakfast, complaining that the servants did not do what she told them; that the mistress would allow her to be nothing in the house, and Edgar neglected her; that she had caught a cold with the doors being left open, and we let the parlour fire go out on purpose to vex her, with a hundred yet more frivolous accusations, Mrs. Linton peremptorily insisted that she should get to bed; and, having scolded her heartily, threatened to send for the doctor. Mention of Kenneth caused her to exclaim, instantly, that her health was perfect, and it was only Catherine's harshness which made her unhappy.

"How can you say I am harsh, you naughty fondling?" cried the mistress, amazed at the unreasonable assertion. "You are surely losing your reason. When have I been harsh, tell me?"

"Yesterday," sobbed Isabella, "and now!"

"Yesterday!" said her sister-in-law. "On what occasion?"

"In our walk along the moor: you told me to ramble where I pleased, while you sauntered on with Mr. Heathcliff!"

"And that's your notion of harshness?" said Catherine, laughing. "It was no hint that your company was superfluous; we didn't care whether you kept with us or not; I merely thought Heathcliff's talk would have nothing entertaining for your ears."

"Oh, no," wept the young lady; "you wished me away, because you knew I liked to be there!"

"Is she sane?" asked Mrs. Linton, appealing to me. "I'll repeat our conversation, word for word, Isabella; and you point out any charm it could have had for you."

"I don't mind the conversation," she answered: "I wanted to be with –"

"Well?" said Catherine, perceiving her hesitate to complete the sentence.

"With him: and I won't be always sent off!" she continued, kindling up. "You are a dog in the manger, Cathy, and desire no one to be loved but yourself!"

"You are an impertinent little monkey!" exclaimed Mrs. Linton, in surprise. "But I'll not believe this idiocy! It is impossible that you can covet the admiration of Heathcliff – that you consider him an agreeable person! I hope I have misunderstood you, Isabella?"

"No, you have not," said the infatuated girl. "I love him more than ever you loved Edgar, and he might love me, if you would let him!"

"I wouldn't be you for a kingdom, then!" Catherine declared, emphatically: and she seemed to speak sincerely. "Nelly, help me to convince her of her madness. Tell her what Heathcliff is: an unreclaimed creature, without refinement, without cultivation; an arid wilderness of furze and whinstone. I'd as soon put that little canary into the park on a winter's day, as recommend you to bestow your heart on him! It is deplorable ignorance of his character, child, and nothing else, which makes that dream enter your head. Pray, don't imagine that he conceals depths of benevolence and affection beneath a stern exterior! He's not a rough diamond – a pearl-containing oyster of a rustic: he's a fierce, pitiless, wolfish man. I never say to him, "Let this or that enemy alone, because it would be ungenerous or cruel to harm them;" I say, "Let them alone, because *I* should hate them to be wronged:" and he'd crush you like a sparrow's egg, Isabella, if he found you a troublesome charge. I know he couldn't love a Linton; and yet he'd be quite capable of marrying your fortune and expectations: avarice is growing with him a besetting sin. There's my picture: and I'm his friend – so much so, that had he thought seriously to catch you, I should, perhaps, have held my tongue, and let you fall into his trap."

Miss Linton regarded her sister-in-law with indignation.

"For shame! For shame!" she repeated, angrily. "You are worse than twenty foes, you poisonous friend!"

"Ah! You won't believe me, then?" said Catherine. "You think I speak from wicked selfishness?"

"I'm certain you do," retorted Isabella; "and I shudder at you!"

"Good!" cried the other. "Try for yourself, if that be your spirit: I have done, and yield the argument to your saucy insolence."

"And I must suffer for her egotism!" she sobbed, as Mrs. Linton left the room. "All, all is against me: she has blighted my single consolation. But she uttered falsehoods, didn't she? Mr. Heathcliff is not a fiend: he has an honourable soul, and a true one, or how could he remember her?"

"Banish him from your thoughts, Miss," I said. "He's a bird of bad omen: no mate for you. Mrs. Linton spoke strongly, and yet I can't contradict her. She is better acquainted with his heart than I, or anyone besides; and she never would represent him as worse than he is. Honest people don't hide their deeds. How has he been living? How has he got rich? Why is he staying at Wuthering Heights, the house of a man whom he abhors? They say Mr. Earnshaw is worse and worse since he came. They sit up all night together continually, and Hindley has been borrowing money on his land, and does nothing but play and drink: I heard only a week ago – it was Joseph who told me – I met him at Gimmerton: 'Nelly,' he said, 'we's hae a crowner's 'quest enow, at ahr folks'. One on 'em 's a'most getten his finger cut off wi' hauding t' other fro' stickin' hisseln loike a cawlf. That's maister, yeah knaw, 'at 's soa up o' going tuh t' grand 'sizes. He's noan feared o' t' bench o' judges, norther Paul, nur Peter, nur John, nur Matthew, nor noan on 'em, not he! He fair likes – he langs to set his brazened face agean 'em! And yon bonny lad Heathcliff, yah mind, he's a rare 'un. He can girn a laugh as well 's onybody at a raight divil's jest. Does he niver say nowt of his fine living amang us, when he goes to t' Grange? This is t' way on 't: – up at sun-down: dice, brandy, cloised shutters, und can'le-light till next day at noon: then, t'fooil gangs banning und raving to his cham'er, makking dacent fowks dig thur fingers i' thur lugs fur varry shame; un' the knave, why he can caint his brass, un' ate, un' sleep, un' off to his neighbour's to gossip wi' t' wife. I' course, he tells Dame Catherine how her fathur's goold runs into his pocket, and her fathur's son gallops down t' broad road, while he flees afore to oppen t' pikes!' Now, Miss Linton, Joseph is an old rascal, but no liar; and, if his account of Heathcliff's conduct be true, you would never think of desiring such a husband, would you?"

"You are leagued with the rest, Ellen!" she replied. "I'll not listen to your slanders. What malevolence you must have to wish to convince me that there is no happiness in the world!"

Whether she would have got over this fancy if left to herself, or persevered in nursing it perpetually, I cannot say: she had little time to reflect. The day after, there was a justice-meeting at the next town; my master was obliged to attend; and Mr. Heathcliff, aware of his absence, called rather earlier than usual. Catherine and Isabella were sitting in the library, on hostile terms, but silent: the latter alarmed at her recent indiscretion, and the disclosure she had made of her secret feelings in a transient fit of passion; the former, on mature consideration, really offended with her companion; and, if she laughed again at her pertness, inclined to make it no laughing matter to her. She did laugh as she saw Heathcliff pass the window. I was sweeping the hearth, and I noticed a mischievous smile on her lips. Isabella, absorbed in her meditations, or a book, remained till the door opened; and it was too late to attempt an escape, which she would gladly have done had it been practicable.

"Come in, that's right!" exclaimed the mistress, gaily, pulling a chair to the fire. "Here are two people sadly in need of a third to thaw the ice between them; and you are the very one we should both of us choose. Heathcliff, I'm proud to show you, at last, somebody that dotes on you more than myself. I expect you to feel flattered. Nay, it's not Nelly; don't look at her! My poor little sister-in-law is breaking her heart by mere contemplation of your physical and moral beauty. It lies in your own power to be

Edgar's brother! No, no, Isabella, you shan't run off," she continued, arresting, with feigned playfulness, the confounded girl, who had risen indignantly. "We were quarrelling like cats about you, Heathcliff; and I was fairly beaten in protestations of devotion and admiration: and, moreover, I was informed that if I would but have the manners to stand aside, my rival, as she will have herself to be, would shoot a shaft into your soul that would fix you for ever, and send my image into eternal oblivion!"

"Catherine!" said Isabella, calling up her dignity, and disdaining to struggle from the tight grasp that held her, "I'd thank you to adhere to the truth and not slander me, even in joke! Mr. Heathcliff, be kind enough to bid this friend of yours release me: she forgets that you and I are not intimate acquaintances; and what amuses her is painful to me beyond expression."

As the guest answered nothing, but took his seat, and looked thoroughly indifferent what sentiments she cherished concerning him, she turned and whispered an earnest appeal for liberty to her tormentor.

"By no means!" cried Mrs. Linton in answer. "I won't be named a dog in the manger again. You *shall* stay: now then! Heathcliff, why don't you evince satisfaction at my pleasant news? Isabella swears that the love Edgar has for me is nothing to that she entertains for you. I'm sure she made some speech of the kind; did she not, Ellen? And she has fasted ever since the day before yesterday's walk, from sorrow and rage that I despatched her out of your society under the idea of its being unacceptable."

"I think you belie her," said Heathcliff, twisting his chair to face them. "She wishes to be out of my society now, at any rate!"

And he stared hard at the object of discourse, as one might do at a strange repulsive animal: a centipede from the Indies, for instance, which curiosity leads one to examine in spite of the aversion it raises. The poor thing couldn't bear that; she grew white and red in rapid succession, and, while tears beaded her lashes, bent the strength of her small fingers to loosen the firm clutch of Catherine; and perceiving that as fast as she raised one finger off her arm another closed down, and she could not remove the whole together, she began to make use of her nails; and their sharpness presently ornamented the detainer's with crescents of red.

"There's a tigress!" exclaimed Mrs. Linton, setting her free, and shaking her hand with pain. "Begone, for God's sake, and hide your vixen face! How foolish to reveal those talons to him. Can't you fancy the conclusions he'll draw? Look, Heathcliff! They are instruments that will do execution – you must beware of your eyes."

"I'd wrench them off her fingers, if they ever menaced me," he answered, brutally, when the door had closed after her. "But what did you mean by teasing the creature in that manner, Cathy? You were not speaking the truth, were you?"

"I assure you I was," she returned. "She has been dying for your sake several weeks, and raving about you this morning, and pouring forth a deluge of abuse, because I represented your failings in a plain light, for the purpose of mitigating her adoration. But don't notice it further: I wished to punish her sauciness, that's all. I like her too well, my dear Heathcliff, to let you absolutely seize and devour her up."

"And I like her too ill to attempt it," said he, "except in a very ghoulish fashion. You'd hear of odd things if I lived alone with that mawkish, waxen face: the most ordinary would be painting on its white the colours of the rainbow, and turning the blue eyes black, every day or two: they detestably resemble Linton's."

"Delectably!" observed Catherine. "They are dove's eyes – angel's!"

"She's her brother's heir, is she not?" he asked, after a brief silence.

"I should be sorry to think so," returned his companion. "Half a dozen nephews shall erase her title, please heaven! Abstract your mind from the subject at present: you are too prone to covet your neighbour's goods; remember *this* neighbour's goods are mine."

"If they were *mine*, they would be none the less that," said Heathcliff; "but though Isabella Linton may be silly, she is scarcely mad; and, in short, we'll dismiss the matter, as you advise."

From their tongues they did dismiss it; and Catherine, probably, from her thoughts. The other, I felt certain, recalled it often in the course of the evening. I saw him smile to himself – grin rather – and lapse into ominous musing whenever Mrs. Linton had occasion to be absent from the apartment.

I determined to watch his movements. My heart invariably cleaved to the master's, in preference to Catherine's side: with reason I imagined, for he was kind, and trustful, and honourable; and she – she could not be called *opposite*, yet she seemed to allow herself such wide latitude, that I had little faith in her principles, and still less sympathy for her feelings. I wanted something to happen which might have the effect of freeing both Wuthering Heights and the Grange of Mr. Heathcliff quietly; leaving us as we had been prior to his advent. His visits were a continual nightmare to me; and, I suspected, to my master also. His abode at the Heights was an oppression past explaining. I felt that God had forsaken the stray sheep there to its own wicked wanderings, and an evil beast prowled between it and the fold, waiting his time to spring and destroy.

Chapter Eleven

SOMETIMES, while meditating on these things in solitude, I've got up in a sudden terror, and put on my bonnet to go see how all was at the farm. I've persuaded my conscience that it was a duty to warn him how people talked regarding his ways; and then I've recollected his confirmed bad habits, and, hopeless of benefiting him, have flinched from re-entering the dismal house, doubting if I could bear to be taken at my word.

One time I passed the old gate, going out of my way, on a journey to Gimmerton. It was about the period that my narrative has reached: a bright frosty afternoon; the ground bare, and the road hard and dry. I came to a stone where the highway branches off on to the moor at your left hand; a rough sand-pillar, with the letters W. H. cut on its north side, on the east, G., and on the south-west, T.G. It serves as a guide-post to the Grange, the Heights, and village. The sun shone yellow on its grey head, reminding me of summer; and I cannot say why, but all at once a gush of child's sensations flowed into my heart. Hindley and I held it a favourite spot twenty years before. I gazed long at the weather-worn block; and, stooping down, perceived a hole near the bottom still full of snail-shells and pebbles, which we were fond of storing there with more perishable things; and, as fresh as reality, it appeared that I beheld my early playmate seated on the withered turf: his dark, square head bent forward, and his little hand scooping out the earth with a piece of slate. "Poor Hindley!" I exclaimed, involuntarily. I started: my bodily eye was cheated into a momentary belief that the child lifted its face and stared straight into mine! It vanished in a twinkling; but immediately I felt an irresistible yearning to be at the Heights. Superstition urged me to comply with this impulse: supposing he should be dead! I thought – or should die soon! – Supposing it were a sign of death! The nearer I got to the house the more agitated I grew; and on catching sight of it I trembled in every limb. The apparition had outstripped me: it stood looking through the gate. That was my first idea on observing an elf-locked, brown-eyed boy setting his ruddy countenance against the bars. Further reflection suggested this must be Hareton, *my* Hareton, not altered greatly since I left him, ten months since.

"God bless thee, darling!" I cried, forgetting instantaneously my foolish fears. "Hareton, it's Nelly! Nelly, thy nurse."

He retreated out of arm's length, and picked up a large flint.

"I am come to see thy father, Hareton," I added, guessing from the action that Nelly, if she lived in his memory at all, was not recognised as one with me.

He raised his missile to hurl it; I commenced a soothing speech, but could not stay his hand: the stone struck my bonnet; and then ensued, from the stammering lips of the little fellow, a string of curses, which, whether he comprehended them or not, were delivered with practised emphasis, and distorted his baby features into a shocking expression of malignity. You may be certain this grieved more than angered me. Fit to cry, I took an orange from my pocket, and offered it to propitiate him. He hesitated, and then snatched it from my hold; as if he fancied I only intended to tempt and disappoint him. I showed another, keeping it out of his reach.

"Who has taught you those fine words, my bairn?" I inquired. "The curate?"

"Damn the curate, and thee! Gie me that," he replied.

"Tell us where you got your lessons, and you shall have it," said I. "Who's your master?"

"Devil daddy," was his answer.

"And what do you learn from daddy?" I continued.

He jumped at the fruit; I raised it higher. "What does he teach you?" I asked.

"Naught," said he, "but to keep out of his gait. Daddy cannot bide me, because I swear at him."

"Ah! And the devil teaches you to swear at daddy?" I observed.

"Ay – nay," he drawled.

"Who, then?"

"Heathcliff."

I asked if he liked Mr. Heathcliff.

"Ay!" he answered again.

Desiring to have his reasons for liking him, I could only gather the sentences – "I known't: he pays dad back what he gies to me – he curses daddy for cursing me. He says I mun do as I will."

"And the curate does not teach you to read and write, then?" I pursued.

"No, I was told the curate should have his – teeth dashed down his – throat, if he stepped over the threshold – Heathcliff had promised that!"

I put the orange in his hand, and bade him tell his father that a woman called Nelly Dean was waiting to speak with him, by the garden gate. He went up the walk, and entered the house; but, instead of Hindley, Heathcliff appeared on the door-stones; and I turned directly and ran down the road as hard as ever I could race, making no halt till I gained the guide-post, and feeling as scared as if I had raised a goblin. This is not much connected with Miss Isabella's affair: except that it urged me to resolve further on mounting vigilant guard, and doing my utmost to cheek the spread of such bad influence at the Grange: even though I should wake a domestic storm, by thwarting Mrs. Linton's pleasure.

The next time Heathcliff came my young lady chanced to be feeding some pigeons in the court. She had never spoken a word to her sister-in-law for three days; but she had likewise dropped her fretful complaining, and we found it a great comfort. Heathcliff had not the habit of bestowing a single unnecessary civility on Miss Linton, I knew. Now, as soon as he beheld her, his first precaution was to take a sweeping survey of the house-front. I was standing by the kitchen-window, but I drew out of sight. He then stepped across the pavement to her, and said something: she seemed embarrassed, and desirous of getting away; to prevent it, he laid his hand on her arm. She averted her face: he apparently put some question which she had no mind to answer. There was another rapid glance at the house, and supposing himself unseen, the scoundrel had the impudence to embrace her.

"Judas! Traitor!" I ejaculated. "You are a hypocrite, too, are you? A deliberate deceiver."

"Who is, Nelly?" said Catherine's voice at my elbow: I had been over-intent on watching the pair outside to mark her entrance.

"Your worthless friend!" I answered, warmly: "the sneaking rascal yonder. Ah, he has caught a glimpse of us – he is coming in! I wonder will he have the heart to find a plausible excuse for making love to Miss, when he told you he hated her?"

Mrs. Linton saw Isabella tear herself free, and run into the garden; and a minute after, Heathcliff opened the door. I couldn't withhold giving some loose to my indignation; but Catherine angrily insisted on silence, and threatened to order me out of the kitchen, if I dared to be so presumptuous as to put in my insolent tongue.

"To hear you, people might think you were the mistress!" she cried. "You want setting down in your right place! Heathcliff, what are you about, raising this stir? I said you must let Isabella alone! – I beg you will, unless you are tired of being received here, and wish Linton to draw the bolts against you!"

"God forbid that he should try!" answered the black villain. I detested him just then. "God keep him meek and patient! Every day I grow madder after sending him to heaven!"

"Hush!" said Catherine, shutting the inner door. "Don't vex me. Why have you disregarded my request? Did she come across you on purpose?"

"What is it to you?" he growled. "I have a right to kiss her, if she chooses; and you have no right to object. I am not *your* husband: *you* needn't be jealous of me!"

"I'm not jealous of you," replied the mistress; "I'm jealous for you. Clear your face: you shan't scowl at me! If you like Isabella, you shall marry her. But do you like her? Tell the truth, Heathcliff! There, you won't answer. I'm certain you don't."

"And would Mr. Linton approve of his sister marrying that man?" I inquired.

"Mr. Linton should approve," returned my lady, decisively.

"He might spare himself the trouble," said Heathcliff: "I could do as well without his approbation. And as to you, Catherine, I have a mind to speak a few words now, while we are at it. I want you to be aware that I *know* you have treated me infernally – infernally! Do you hear? And if you flatter yourself that I don't perceive it, you are a fool; and if you think I can be consoled by sweet words, you are an idiot: and if you fancy I'll suffer unrevenged, I'll convince you of the contrary, in a very little while! Meantime, thank you for telling me your sister-in-law's secret: I swear I'll make the most of it. And stand you aside!"

"What new phase of his character is this?" exclaimed Mrs. Linton, in amazement. "I've treated you infernally – and you'll take your revenge! How will you take it, ungrateful brute? How have I treated you infernally?"

"I seek no revenge on you," replied Heathcliff, less vehemently. "That's not the plan. The tyrant grinds down his slaves and they don't turn against him; they crush those beneath them. You are welcome to torture me to death for your amusement, only allow me to amuse myself a little in the same style, and refrain from insult as much as you are able. Having levelled my palace, don't erect a hovel and complacently admire your own charity in giving me that for a home. If I imagined you really wished me to marry Isabel, I'd cut my throat!"

"Oh, the evil is that I am *not* jealous, is it?" cried Catherine. "Well, I won't repeat my offer of a wife: it is as bad as offering Satan a lost soul. Your bliss lies, like his, in inflicting misery. You prove it. Edgar is restored from the ill-temper he gave way to at your coming; I begin to be secure and tranquil; and you, restless to know us at peace, appear resolved on exciting a quarrel. Quarrel with Edgar, if you please, Heathcliff, and deceive his sister: you'll hit on exactly the most efficient method of revenging yourself on me."

The conversation ceased. Mrs. Linton sat down by the fire, flushed and gloomy. The spirit which served her was growing intractable: she could neither lay nor control it. He stood on the hearth with folded arms, brooding on his evil thoughts; and in this position I left them to seek the master, who was wondering what kept Catherine below so long.

"Ellen," said he, when I entered, "have you seen your mistress?"

"Yes; she's in the kitchen, sir," I answered. "She's sadly put out by Mr. Heathcliff's behaviour: and, indeed, I do think it's time to arrange his visits on another footing. There's harm in being too soft, and now it's come to this –." And I related the scene in the court, and, as near as I dared, the whole subsequent dispute. I fancied it could not be very prejudicial to Mrs. Linton; unless she made it so afterwards, by assuming the defensive for her guest. Edgar Linton had difficulty in hearing me to the close. His first words revealed that he did not clear his wife of blame.

"This is insufferable!" he exclaimed. "It is disgraceful that she should own him for a friend, and force his company on me! Call me two men out of the hall, Ellen. Catherine shall linger no longer to argue with the low ruffian – I have humoured her enough."

He descended, and bidding the servants wait in the passage, went, followed by me, to the kitchen. Its occupants had recommenced their angry discussion: Mrs. Linton, at least, was scolding with renewed vigour; Heathcliff had moved to the window, and hung his head, somewhat cowed by her violent rating apparently. He saw the master first, and made a hasty motion that she should be silent; which she obeyed, abruptly, on discovering the reason of his intimation.

"How is this?" said Linton, addressing her; "what notion of propriety must you have to remain here, after the language which has been held to you by that blackguard? I suppose, because it is his ordinary talk you think nothing of it: you are habituated to his baseness, and, perhaps, imagine I can get used to it too!"

"Have you been listening at the door, Edgar?" asked the mistress, in a tone particularly calculated to provoke her husband, implying both carelessness and contempt of his irritation. Heathcliff, who had raised his eyes at the former speech, gave a sneering laugh at the latter; on purpose, it seemed, to draw Mr. Linton's attention to him. He succeeded; but Edgar did not mean to entertain him with any high flights of passion.

"I've been so far forbearing with you, sir," he said quietly; "not that I was ignorant of your miserable, degraded character, but I felt you were only partly responsible for that; and Catherine wishing to keep up your acquaintance, I acquiesced – foolishly. Your presence is a moral poison that would contaminate the most virtuous: for that cause, and to prevent worse consequences, I shall deny you hereafter admission into this house, and give notice now that I require your instant departure. Three minutes' delay will render it involuntary and ignominious."

Heathcliff measured the height and breadth of the speaker with an eye full of derision.

"Cathy, this lamb of yours threatens like a bull!" he said. "It is in danger of splitting its skull against my knuckles. By God! Mr. Linton, I'm mortally sorry that you are not worth knocking down!"

My master glanced towards the passage, and signed me to fetch the men: he had no intention of hazarding a personal encounter. I obeyed the hint; but Mrs. Linton, suspecting something, followed; and when I attempted to call them, she pulled me back, slammed the door to, and locked it.

"Fair means!" she said, in answer to her husband's look of angry surprise. "If you have not courage to attack him, make an apology, or allow yourself to be beaten. It will correct you of feigning more valour than you possess. No, I'll swallow the key before you shall get it! I'm delightfully rewarded for my kindness to each! After constant indulgence of one's weak nature, and the other's bad one, I earn for thanks two samples of blind ingratitude, stupid to absurdity! Edgar, I was defending you and yours; and I wish Heathcliff may flog you sick, for daring to think an evil thought of me!"

It did not need the medium of a flogging to produce that effect on the master. He tried to wrest the key from Catherine's grasp, and for safety she flung it into the hottest part of the fire; whereupon Mr. Edgar was taken with a nervous trembling, and his countenance grew deadly pale. For his life he could not avert that excess of emotion: mingled anguish and humiliation overcame him completely. He leant on the back of a chair, and covered his face.

"Oh, heavens! In old days this would win you knighthood!" exclaimed Mrs. Linton. "We are vanquished! We are vanquished! Heathcliff would as soon lift a finger at you as the king would march his army against a colony of mice. Cheer up! You shan't be hurt! Your type is not a lamb, it's a sucking leveret."

"I wish you joy of the milk-blooded coward, Cathy!" said her friend. "I compliment you on your taste. And that is the slavering, shivering thing you preferred to me! I would not strike him with my fist, but I'd kick him with my foot, and experience considerable satisfaction. Is he weeping, or is he going to faint for fear?"

The fellow approached and gave the chair on which Linton rested a push. He'd better have kept his distance: my master quickly sprang erect, and struck him full on the throat a blow that would have levelled a slighter man. It took his breath for a minute; and while he choked, Mr. Linton walked out by the back door into the yard, and from thence to the front entrance.

"There! You've done with coming here," cried Catherine. "Get away, now; he'll return with a brace of pistols and half-a-dozen assistants. If he did overhear us, of course he'd never forgive you. You've played me an ill turn, Heathcliff! But go – make haste! I'd rather see Edgar at bay than you."

"Do you suppose I'm going with that blow burning in my gullet?" he thundered. "By hell, no! I'll crush his ribs in like a rotten hazelnut before I cross the threshold! If I don't floor him now, I shall murder him some time; so, as you value his existence, let me get at him!"

"He is not coming," I interposed, framing a bit of a lie. "There's the coachman and the two gardeners; you'll surely not wait to be thrust into the road by them! Each has a bludgeon; and master will, very likely, be watching from the parlour-windows to see that they fulfil his orders."

The gardeners and coachman were there: but Linton was with them. They had already entered the court. Heathcliff, on the second thoughts, resolved to avoid a struggle against three underlings: he seized the poker, smashed the lock from the inner door, and made his escape as they tramped in.

Mrs. Linton, who was very much excited, bade me accompany her upstairs. She did not know my share in contributing to the disturbance, and I was anxious to keep her in ignorance.

"I'm nearly distracted, Nelly!" she exclaimed, throwing herself on the sofa. "A thousand smiths' hammers are beating in my head! Tell Isabella to shun me; this uproar is owing to her; and should she or anyone else aggravate my anger at present, I shall get wild. And, Nelly, say to Edgar, if you see him again tonight, that I'm in danger of being seriously ill. I wish it may prove true. He has startled and distressed me shockingly! I want to frighten him. Besides, he might come and begin a string of abuse or complainings; I'm certain I should recriminate, and God knows where we should end! Will you do so, my good Nelly? You are aware that I am no way blamable in this matter. What possessed him to turn listener? Heathcliff's talk was outrageous, after you left us; but I could soon have diverted him from Isabella, and the rest meant nothing. Now all is dashed wrong; by the fool's craving to hear evil of self, that haunts some people like a demon! Had Edgar never gathered our conversation, he would never have been the worse for it. Really, when he opened on me in that unreasonable tone of displeasure after I had scolded Heathcliff till I was hoarse for him, I did not care hardly what they did to each other; especially as I felt that, however the scene closed, we should all be driven asunder for nobody knows how long! Well, if I cannot keep Heathcliff for my friend – if Edgar will be mean and jealous, I'll try to break their hearts by breaking my own. That will be a prompt way of finishing all, when I am pushed to extremity! But it's a deed to be reserved for a forlorn hope; I'd not take Linton by surprise with it. To this point he has been discreet in dreading to provoke me; you must represent the peril of quitting that policy, and remind him of my passionate temper, verging, when kindled, on frenzy. I wish you could dismiss that apathy out of that countenance, and look rather more anxious about me."

The stolidity with which I received these instructions was, no doubt, rather exasperating: for they were delivered in perfect sincerity; but I believed a person who could plan the turning of her fits of passion to account, beforehand, might, by exerting her will, manage to control herself tolerably, even while under their influence; and I did not wish to "frighten" her husband, as she said, and multiply his annoyances for the purpose of serving her selfishness. Therefore I said nothing when I met the master coming towards the parlour; but I took the liberty of turning back to listen whether they would resume their quarrel together. He began to speak first.

"Remain where you are, Catherine," he said; without any anger in his voice, but with much sorrowful despondency. "I shall not stay. I am neither come to wrangle nor be reconciled; but I wish just to learn whether, after this evening's events, you intend to continue your intimacy with –"

"Oh, for mercy's sake," interrupted the mistress, stamping her foot, "for mercy's sake, let us hear no more of it now! Your cold blood cannot be worked into a fever: your veins are full of ice-water; but mine are boiling, and the sight of such chillness makes them dance."

"To get rid of me, answer my question," persevered Mr. Linton. "You must answer it; and that violence does not alarm me. I have found that you can be as stoical as anyone, when you please. Will you give up Heathcliff hereafter, or will you give up me? It is impossible for you to be *my* friend and *his* at the same time; and I absolutely *require* to know which you choose."

"I require to be let alone!" exclaimed Catherine, furiously. "I demand it! Don't you see I can scarcely stand? Edgar, you – you leave me!"

She rang the bell till it broke with a twang; I entered leisurely. It was enough to try the temper of a saint, such senseless, wicked rages! There she lay dashing her head against the arm of the sofa, and grinding her teeth, so that you might fancy she would crash them to splinters! Mr. Linton stood looking at her in sudden compunction and fear. He told me to fetch some water. She had no breath for speaking. I brought a glass full; and as she would not drink, I sprinkled it on her face. In a few seconds she stretched herself out stiff, and turned up her eyes, while her cheeks, at once blanched and livid, assumed the aspect of death. Linton looked terrified.

"There is nothing in the world the matter," I whispered. I did not want him to yield, though I could not help being afraid in my heart.

"She has blood on her lips!" he said, shuddering.

"Never mind!" I answered, tartly. And I told him how she had resolved, previous to his coming, on exhibiting a fit of frenzy. I incautiously gave the account aloud, and she heard me; for she started up – her hair flying over her shoulders, her eyes flashing, the muscles of her neck and arms standing out preternaturally. I made up my mind for broken bones, at least; but she only glared about her for an instant, and then rushed from the room. The master directed me to follow; I did, to her chamber-door: she hindered me from going further by securing it against me.

As she never offered to descend to breakfast next morning, I went to ask whether she would have some carried up. "No!" she replied, peremptorily. The same question was repeated at dinner and tea; and again on the morrow after, and received the same answer. Mr. Linton, on his part, spent his time in the library, and did not inquire concerning his wife's occupations. Isabella and he had had an hour's interview, during which he tried to elicit from her some sentiment of proper horror for Heathcliff's advances: but he could make nothing of her evasive replies, and was obliged to close the examination unsatisfactorily; adding, however, a solemn warning, that if she were so insane as to encourage that worthless suitor, it would dissolve all bonds of relationship between herself and him.

Chapter Twelve

WHILE MISS LINTON moped about the park and garden, always silent, and almost always in tears; and her brother shut himself up among books that he never opened – wearying, I guessed, with a continual vague expectation that Catherine, repenting her conduct, would come of her own accord to ask pardon, and seek a reconciliation – and *she* fasted pertinaciously, under the idea, probably, that at every meal Edgar was ready to choke for her absence, and pride alone held him from running to cast himself at her feet; I went about my household duties, convinced that the Grange had but one sensible soul in its walls, and that lodged in my body. I wasted no condolences on Miss, nor any expostulations on my mistress; nor did I pay much attention to the sighs of my master, who yearned to hear his lady's name, since he might not hear her voice. I determined they should come about as they pleased for me; and though it was a tiresomely slow process, I began to rejoice at length in a faint dawn of its progress: as I thought at first.

Mrs. Linton, on the third day, unbarred her door, and having finished the water in her pitcher and decanter, desired a renewed supply, and a basin of gruel, for she believed she was dying. That I set down as a speech meant for Edgar's ears; I believed no such thing, so I kept it to myself and brought her some tea and dry toast. She ate and drank eagerly, and sank back on her pillow again, clenching her hands and groaning. "Oh, I will die," she exclaimed, "since no one cares anything about me. I wish I had not taken that." Then a good while after I heard her murmur, "No, I'll not die – he'd be glad – he does not love me at all – he would never miss me!"

"Did you want anything, ma'am?" I inquired, still preserving my external composure, in spite of her ghastly countenance and strange, exaggerated manner.

"What is that apathetic being doing?" she demanded, pushing the thick entangled locks from her wasted face. "Has he fallen into a lethargy, or is he dead?"

"Neither," replied I; "if you mean Mr. Linton. He's tolerably well, I think, though his studies occupy him rather more than they ought: he is continually among his books, since he has no other society."

I should not have spoken so if I had known her true condition, but I could not get rid of the notion that she acted a part of her disorder.

"Among his books!" she cried, confounded. "And I dying! I on the brink of the grave! My God! Does he know how I'm altered?" continued she, staring at her reflection in a mirror hanging against the opposite wall. "Is that Catherine Linton? He imagines me in a pet – in play, perhaps. Cannot you inform him that it is frightful earnest? Nelly, if it be not too late, as soon as I learn how he feels, I'll choose between these two: either to starve at once – that would be no punishment unless he had a heart – or to recover, and leave the country. Are you speaking the truth about him now? Take care. Is he actually so utterly indifferent for my life?"

"Why, ma'am," I answered, "the master has no idea of your being deranged; and of course he does not fear that you will let yourself die of hunger."

"You think not? Cannot you tell him I will?" she returned. "Persuade him! Speak of your own mind: say you are certain I will!"

"No, you forget, Mrs. Linton," I suggested, "that you have eaten some food with a relish this evening, and tomorrow you will perceive its good effects."

"If I were only sure it would kill him," she interrupted, "I'd kill myself directly! These three awful nights I've never closed my lids – and oh, I've been tormented! I've been haunted, Nelly! But I begin to fancy you don't like me. How strange! I thought, though everybody hated and despised each other, they could not avoid loving me. And they have all turned to enemies in a few hours: they have, I'm positive; the people here. How dreary to meet death, surrounded by their cold faces! Isabella, terrified and repelled, afraid to enter the room, it would be so dreadful to watch Catherine go. And Edgar standing solemnly by to see it over; then offering prayers of thanks to God for restoring peace to his house, and going back to his *books*! What in the name of all that feels has he to do with *books*, when I am dying?"

She could not bear the notion which I had put into her head of Mr. Linton's philosophical resignation. Tossing about, she increased her feverish bewilderment to madness, and tore the pillow with her teeth; then raising herself up all burning, desired that I would open the window. We were in the middle of winter, the wind blew strong from the north-east, and I objected. Both the expressions flitting over her face, and the changes of her moods, began to alarm me terribly; and brought to my recollection her former illness, and the doctor's injunction that she should not be crossed. A minute previously she was violent; now, supported on one arm, and not noticing my refusal to obey her, she seemed to find childish diversion in pulling the feathers from the rents she had just made, and ranging them on the sheet according to their different species: her mind had strayed to other associations.

"That's a turkey's," she murmured to herself; "and this is a wild duck's; and this is a pigeon's. Ah, they put pigeons' feathers in the pillows – no wonder I couldn't die! Let me take care to throw it on the floor when I lie down. And here is a moor-cock's; and this – I should know it among a thousand – it's a lapwing's. Bonny bird; wheeling over our heads in the middle of the moor. It wanted to get to its nest, for the clouds had touched the swells, and it felt rain coming. This feather was picked up from the heath, the bird was not shot: we saw its nest in the winter, full of little skeletons. Heathcliff set a trap over it, and the old ones dared not come. I made him promise he'd never shoot a lapwing after that, and he didn't. Yes, here are more! Did he shoot my lapwings, Nelly? Are they red, any of them? Let me look."

"Give over with that baby-work!" I interrupted, dragging the pillow away, and turning the holes towards the mattress, for she was removing its contents by handfuls. "Lie down and shut your eyes: you're wandering. There's a mess! The down is flying about like snow."

I went here and there collecting it.

"I see in you, Nelly," she continued dreamily, "an aged woman: you have grey hair and bent shoulders. This bed is the fairy cave under Penistone crags, and you are gathering elf-bolts to hurt our heifers; pretending, while I am near, that they are only locks of wool. That's what you'll come to fifty years hence: I know you are not so now. I'm not wandering: you're mistaken, or else I should believe you really *were* that withered hag, and I should think I *was* under Penistone Crags; and I'm conscious it's night, and there are two candles on the table making the black press shine like jet."

"The black press? Where is that?" I asked. "You are talking in your sleep!"

"It's against the wall, as it always is," she replied. "It *does* appear odd – I see a face in it!"

"There's no press in the room, and never was," said I, resuming my seat, and looping up the curtain that I might watch her.

"Don't *you* see that face?" she inquired, gazing earnestly at the mirror.

And say what I could, I was incapable of making her comprehend it to be her own; so I rose and covered it with a shawl.

"It's behind there still!" she pursued, anxiously. "And it stirred. Who is it? I hope it will not come out when you are gone! Oh! Nelly, the room is haunted! I'm afraid of being alone!"

I took her hand in mine, and bid her be composed; for a succession of shudders convulsed her frame, and she would keep straining her gaze towards the glass.

"There's nobody here!" I insisted. "It was *yourself*, Mrs. Linton: you knew it a while since."

"Myself!" she gasped, "and the clock is striking twelve! It's true, then! That's dreadful!"

Her fingers clutched the clothes, and gathered them over her eyes. I attempted to steal to the door with an intention of calling her husband; but I was summoned back by a piercing shriek – the shawl had dropped from the frame.

"Why, what is the matter?" cried I. "Who is coward now? Wake up! That is the glass – the mirror, Mrs. Linton; and you see yourself in it, and there am I too by your side."

Trembling and bewildered, she held me fast, but the horror gradually passed from her countenance; its paleness gave place to a glow of shame.

"Oh, dear! I thought I was at home," she sighed. "I thought I was lying in my chamber at Wuthering Heights. Because I'm weak, my brain got confused, and I screamed unconsciously. Don't say anything; but stay with me. I dread sleeping: my dreams appal me."

"A sound sleep would do you good, ma'am," I answered: "and I hope this suffering will prevent your trying starving again."

"Oh, if I were but in my own bed in the old house!" she went on bitterly, wringing her hands. "And that wind sounding in the firs by the lattice. Do let me feel it – it comes straight down the moor – do let me have one breath!" To pacify her I held the casement ajar a few seconds. A cold blast rushed through; I closed it, and returned to my post. She lay still now, her face bathed in tears. Exhaustion of body had entirely subdued her spirit: our fiery Catherine was no better than a wailing child.

"How long is it since I shut myself in here?" she asked, suddenly reviving.

"It was Monday evening," I replied, "and this is Thursday night, or rather Friday morning, at present."

"What! Of the same week?" she exclaimed. "Only that brief time?"

"Long enough to live on nothing but cold water and ill-temper," observed I.

"Well, it seems a weary number of hours," she muttered doubtfully: "it must be more. I remember being in the parlour after they had quarrelled, and Edgar being cruelly provoking, and me running into this room desperate. As soon as ever I had barred the door, utter blackness overwhelmed me, and I fell on the floor. I couldn't explain to Edgar how certain I felt of having a fit, or going raging mad, if he persisted in teasing me! I had no command of tongue, or brain, and he did not guess my agony, perhaps: it barely left me sense to try to escape from him and his voice. Before I recovered sufficiently to see and hear, it began to be dawn, and, Nelly, I'll tell you what I thought, and what has kept recurring and recurring till I feared for my reason. I thought as I lay there, with my head against that table leg, and my eyes dimly discerning the grey square of the window, that I was enclosed in the oak-panelled bed at home; and my heart ached with some great grief which, just waking, I could not recollect. I pondered, and worried myself to discover what it could be, and, most strangely, the whole last seven years of my life grew a blank! I did not recall that they had been at all. I was a child; my father was just buried, and my misery arose from the separation that Hindley had ordered between me and Heathcliff. I was laid alone, for the first time; and, rousing from a dismal doze after a night of weeping, I lifted my hand to push the panels aside: it struck the table-top! I swept it along the carpet, and then memory burst in: my late anguish was swallowed in a paroxysm of despair. I cannot say why I felt so wildly wretched: it must have been temporary derangement; for there is scarcely cause. But, supposing at twelve years old I had been wrenched from the Heights, and every early association, and my all in all, as Heathcliff was at that time, and been converted at a stroke into Mrs. Linton, the lady of Thrushcross Grange, and the wife of a stranger: an exile, and outcast, thenceforth, from what had been my world. You may fancy a glimpse of the abyss where I grovelled! Shake your head as you will, Nelly, you have helped to unsettle me! You should have spoken to Edgar, indeed you should, and compelled him to leave me quiet! Oh, I'm burning! I wish I were out of doors! I wish I were a girl again, half savage and hardy, and free; and laughing at injuries, not maddening under them! Why am I so changed? Why does my blood rush into a hell of tumult at a few words? I'm sure I should be myself were I once among the heather on those hills. Open the window again wide: fasten it open! Quick, why don't you move?"

"Because I won't give you your death of cold," I answered.

"You won't give me a chance of life, you mean," she said, sullenly. "However, I'm not helpless yet; I'll open it myself."

And sliding from the bed before I could hinder her, she crossed the room, walking very uncertainly, threw it back, and bent out, careless of the frosty air that cut about her shoulders as keen as a knife. I entreated, and finally attempted to force her to retire. But I soon found her delirious strength much surpassed mine (she was delirious, I became convinced by her subsequent actions and ravings). There was no moon, and everything beneath lay in misty darkness: not a light gleamed from any house, far or near all had been extinguished long ago: and those at Wuthering Heights were never visible – still she asserted she caught their shining.

"Look!" she cried eagerly, "that's my room with the candle in it, and the trees swaying before it; and the other candle is in Joseph's garret. Joseph sits up late, doesn't he? He's waiting till I come home that he may lock the gate. Well, he'll wait a while yet. It's a rough journey, and a sad heart to travel it; and we must pass by Gimmerton Kirk to go that journey! We've braved its ghosts often together, and dared each other to stand among the graves and ask them to come. But, Heathcliff, if I dare you now, will you venture? If you do, I'll keep you. I'll not lie there by myself: they may bury me twelve feet deep, and throw the church down over me, but I won't rest till you are with me. I never will!"

She paused, and resumed with a strange smile. "He's considering – he'd rather I'd come to him! Find a way, then! Not through that kirkyard. You are slow! Be content, you always followed me!"

Perceiving it vain to argue against her insanity, I was planning how I could reach something to wrap about her, without quitting my hold of herself (for I could not trust her alone by the gaping lattice), when, to my consternation, I heard the rattle of the door-handle, and Mr. Linton entered. He had only then come from the library; and, in passing through the lobby, had noticed our talking and been attracted by curiosity, or fear, to examine what it signified, at that late hour.

"Oh, sir!" I cried, checking the exclamation risen to his lips at the sight which met him, and the bleak atmosphere of the chamber. "My poor mistress is ill, and she quite masters me: I cannot manage her at all; pray, come and persuade her to go to bed. Forget your anger, for she's hard to guide any way but her own."

"Catherine ill?" he said, hastening to us. "Shut the window, Ellen! Catherine! Why –"

He was silent. The haggardness of Mrs. Linton's appearance smote him speechless, and he could only glance from her to me in horrified astonishment.

"She's been fretting here," I continued, "and eating scarcely anything, and never complaining: she would admit none of us till this evening, and so we couldn't inform you of her state, as we were not aware of it ourselves; but it is nothing."

I felt I uttered my explanations awkwardly; the master frowned. "It is nothing, is it, Ellen Dean?" he said sternly. "You shall account more clearly for keeping me ignorant of this!" And he took his wife in his arms, and looked at her with anguish.

At first she gave him no glance of recognition: he was invisible to her abstracted gaze. The delirium was not fixed, however; having weaned her eyes from contemplating the outer darkness, by degrees she centred her attention on him, and discovered who it was that held her.

"Ah! You are come, are you, Edgar Linton?" she said, with angry animation. "You are one of those things that are ever found when least wanted, and when you are wanted, never! I suppose we shall have plenty of lamentations now – I see we shall – but they can't keep me from my narrow home out yonder: my resting-place, where I'm bound before spring is over! There it is: not among the Lintons, mind, under the chapel-roof, but in the open air, with a head-stone; and you may please yourself whether you go to them or come to me!"

"Catherine, what have you done?" commenced the master. "Am I nothing to you any more? Do you love that wretch Heath—"

"Hush!" cried Mrs. Linton. "Hush, this moment! You mention that name and I end the matter instantly by a spring from the window! What you touch at present you may have; but my soul will be on that hill-top before you lay hands on me again. I don't want you, Edgar: I'm past wanting you. Return to your books. I'm glad you possess a consolation, for all you had in me is gone."

"Her mind wanders, sir," I interposed. "She has been talking nonsense the whole evening; but let her have quiet, and proper attendance, and she'll rally. Hereafter, we must be cautious how we vex her."

"I desire no further advice from you," answered Mr. Linton. "You knew your mistress's nature, and you encouraged me to harass her. And not to give me one hint of how she has been these three days! It was heartless! Months of sickness could not cause such a change!"

I began to defend myself, thinking it too bad to be blamed for another's wicked waywardness. "I knew Mrs. Linton's nature to be headstrong and domineering," cried I: "but I didn't know that you wished to foster her fierce temper! I didn't know that, to humour her, I should wink at Mr. Heathcliff. I performed the duty of a faithful servant in telling you, and I have got a faithful servant's wages! Well, it will teach me to be careful next time. Next time you may gather intelligence for yourself!"

"The next time you bring a tale to me you shall quit my service, Ellen Dean," he replied.

"You'd rather hear nothing about it, I suppose, then, Mr. Linton?" said I. "Heathcliff has your permission to come a-courting to Miss, and to drop in at every opportunity your absence offers, on purpose to poison the mistress against you?"

Confused as Catherine was, her wits were alert at applying our conversation.

"Ah! Nelly has played traitor," she exclaimed, passionately. "Nelly is my hidden enemy. You witch! So you do seek elf-bolts to hurt us! Let me go, and I'll make her rue! I'll make her howl a recantation!"

A maniac's fury kindled under her brows; she struggled desperately to disengage herself from Linton's arms. I felt no inclination to tarry the event; and, resolving to seek medical aid on my own responsibility, I quitted the chamber.

In passing the garden to reach the road, at a place where a bridle hook is driven into the wall, I saw something white moved irregularly, evidently by another agent than the wind. Notwithstanding my hurry, I stayed to examine it, lest ever after I should have the conviction impressed on my imagination that it was a creature of the other world. My surprise and perplexity were great on discovering, by touch more than vision, Miss Isabella's springer, Fanny, suspended by a handkerchief, and nearly at its last gasp. I quickly released the animal, and lifted it into the garden. I had seen it follow its mistress upstairs when she went to bed; and wondered much how it could have got out there, and what mischievous person had treated it so. While untying the knot round the hook, it seemed to me that I repeatedly caught the beat of horses' feet galloping at some distance; but there were such a number of things to occupy my reflections that I hardly gave the circumstance a thought: though it was a strange sound, in that place, at two o'clock in the morning.

Mr. Kenneth was fortunately just issuing from his house to see a patient in the village as I came up the street; and my account of Catherine Linton's malady induced him to accompany me back immediately. He was a plain rough man; and he made no scruple to speak his doubts of her surviving this second attack; unless she were more submissive to his directions than she had shown herself before.

"Nelly Dean," said he, "I can't help fancying there's an extra cause for this. What has there been to do at the Grange? We've odd reports up here. A stout, hearty lass like Catherine does not fall ill for a trifle; and that sort of people should not either. It's hard work bringing them through fevers, and such things. How did it begin?"

"The master will inform you," I answered; "but you are acquainted with the Earnshaws' violent dispositions, and Mrs. Linton caps them all. I may say this; it commenced in a quarrel. She was struck during a tempest of passion with a kind of fit. That's her account, at least: for she flew off in the height of it, and locked herself up. Afterwards, she refused to eat, and now she alternately raves and remains in a half dream; knowing those about her, but having her mind filled with all sorts of strange ideas and illusions."

"Mr. Linton will be sorry?" observed Kenneth, interrogatively.

"Sorry? He'll break his heart should anything happen!" I replied. "Don't alarm him more than necessary."

"Well, I told him to beware," said my companion; "and he must bide the consequences of neglecting my warning! Hasn't he been intimate with Mr. Heathcliff lately?"

"Heathcliff frequently visits at the Grange," answered I, "though more on the strength of the mistress having known him when a boy, than because the master likes his company. At present he's discharged from the trouble of calling; owing to some presumptuous aspirations after Miss Linton which he manifested. I hardly think he'll be taken in again."

"And does Miss Linton turn a cold shoulder on him?" was the doctor's next question.

"I'm not in her confidence," returned I, reluctant to continue the subject.

"No, she's a sly one," he remarked, shaking his head. "She keeps her own counsel! But she's a real little fool. I have it from good authority that last night (and a pretty night it was!) she and Heathcliff were walking in the plantation at the back of your house above two hours; and he pressed her not to go in again, but just mount his horse and away with him! My informant said she could only put him off by pledging her word of honour to be prepared on their first meeting after that: when it was to be he didn't hear; but you urge Mr. Linton to look sharp!"

This news filled me with fresh fears; I outstripped Kenneth, and ran most of the way back. The little dog was yelping in the garden yet. I spared a minute to open the gate for it, but instead of going to the house door, it coursed up and down snuffing the grass, and would have escaped to the road, had I not seized it and conveyed it in with me. On ascending to Isabella's room, my suspicions were confirmed: it was empty. Had I been a few hours sooner Mrs. Linton's illness might have arrested her rash step. But what could be done now? There was a bare possibility of overtaking them if pursued instantly. *I* could not pursue them, however; and I dared not rouse the family, and fill the place with confusion; still less unfold the business to my master, absorbed as he was in his present calamity, and having no heart to spare for a second grief! I saw nothing for it but to hold my tongue, and suffer matters to take their course; and Kenneth being arrived, I went with a badly composed countenance to announce him. Catherine lay in a troubled sleep: her husband had succeeded in soothing the excess of frenzy; he now hung over her pillow, watching every shade and every change of her painfully expressive features.

The doctor, on examining the case for himself, spoke hopefully to him of its having a favourable termination, if we could only preserve around her perfect and constant tranquillity. To me, he signified the threatening danger was not so much death, as permanent alienation of intellect.

I did not close my eyes that night, nor did Mr. Linton: indeed, we never went to bed; and the servants were all up long before the usual hour, moving through the house with stealthy tread, and exchanging whispers as they encountered each other in their vocations. Everyone was active but Miss Isabella; and they began to remark how sound she slept: her brother, too, asked if she had risen, and seemed impatient for her presence, and hurt that she showed so little anxiety for her sister-in-law. I trembled lest he should send me to call her; but I was spared the pain of being the first proclaimant of her flight. One of the maids, a thoughtless girl, who had been on an early errand to Gimmerton, came panting upstairs, open-mouthed, and dashed into the chamber, crying: "Oh, dear, dear! What mun we have next? Master, master, our young lady –"

"Hold your noise!" cried I hastily, enraged at her clamorous manner.

"Speak lower, Mary – what is the matter?" said Mr. Linton. "What ails your young lady?"

"She's gone, she's gone! Yon' Heathcliff's run off wi' her!" gasped the girl.

"That is not true!" exclaimed Linton, rising in agitation. "It cannot be: how has the idea entered your head? Ellen Dean, go and seek her. It is incredible: it cannot be."

As he spoke he took the servant to the door, and then repeated his demand to know her reasons for such an assertion.

"Why, I met on the road a lad that fetches milk here," she stammered, "and he asked whether we weren't in trouble at the Grange. I thought he meant for missis's sickness, so I answered, yes. Then says he, 'There's somebody gone after 'em, I guess?' I stared. He saw I knew nought about it, and he told how a gentleman and lady had stopped to have a horse's shoe fastened at a blacksmith's shop, two miles out of Gimmerton, not very long after midnight! And how the blacksmith's lass had got up to spy who they were: she knew them both directly. And she noticed the man – Heathcliff it was, she felt certain: nob'dy could mistake him, besides – put a sovereign in her father's hand for payment. The lady had a cloak about her face; but having desired a sup of water, while she drank it fell back, and she saw her very plain. Heathcliff held both bridles as they rode on, and they set their faces from the village, and went as fast as the rough roads would let them. The lass said nothing to her father, but she told it all over Gimmerton this morning."

I ran and peeped, for form's sake, into Isabella's room; confirming, when I returned, the servant's statement. Mr. Linton had resumed his seat by the bed; on my re-entrance, he raised his eyes, read the meaning of my blank aspect, and dropped them without giving an order, or uttering a word.

"Are we to try any measures for overtaking and bringing her back?" I inquired. "How should we do?"

"She went of her own accord," answered the master; "she had a right to go if she pleased. Trouble me no more about her. Hereafter she is only my sister in name: not because I disown her, but because she has disowned me."

And that was all he said on the subject: he did not make single inquiry further, or mention her in any way, except directing me to send what property she had in the house to her fresh home, wherever it was, when I knew it.

Chapter Thirteen

FOR TWO MONTHS the fugitives remained absent; in those two months, Mrs. Linton encountered and conquered the worst shock of what was denominated a brain fever. No mother could have nursed an only child more devotedly than Edgar tended her. Day and night he was watching, and patiently enduring all the annoyances that irritable nerves and a shaken reason could inflict; and, though Kenneth remarked that what he saved from the grave would only recompense his care by forming the source of constant future anxiety – in fact, that his health and strength were being sacrificed to preserve a mere ruin of humanity – he knew no limits in gratitude and joy when Catherine's life was declared out of danger; and hour after hour he would sit beside her, tracing the gradual return to bodily health, and flattering his too sanguine hopes with the illusion that her mind would settle back to its right balance also, and she would soon be entirely her former self.

The first time she left her chamber was at the commencement of the following March. Mr. Linton had put on her pillow, in the morning, a handful of golden crocuses; her eye, long stranger to any gleam of pleasure, caught them in waking, and shone delighted as she gathered them eagerly together.

"These are the earliest flowers at the Heights," she exclaimed. "They remind me of soft thaw winds, and warm sunshine, and nearly melted snow. Edgar, is there not a south wind, and is not the snow almost gone?"

"The snow is quite gone down here, darling," replied her husband; "and I only see two white spots on the whole range of moors: the sky is blue, and the larks are singing, and the becks and brooks are all brim full. Catherine, last spring at this time, I was longing to have you under this roof; now, I wish you were a mile or two up those hills: the air blows so sweetly, I feel that it would cure you."

"I shall never be there but once more," said the invalid; "and then you'll leave me, and I shall remain for ever. Next spring you'll long again to have me under this roof, and you'll look back and think you were happy today."

Linton lavished on her the kindest caresses, and tried to cheer her by the fondest words; but, vaguely regarding the flowers, she let the tears collect on her lashes and stream down her cheeks unheeding. We knew she was really better, and, therefore, decided that long confinement to a single place produced much of this despondency, and it might be partially removed by a change of scene. The master told me to light a fire in the many-weeks' deserted parlour, and to set an easy-chair in the sunshine by the window; and then he brought her down, and she sat a long while enjoying the genial heat, and, as we expected, revived by the objects round her: which, though familiar, were free from the dreary associations investing her hated sick chamber. By evening she seemed greatly exhausted; yet no arguments could persuade her to return to that apartment, and I had to arrange the parlour sofa for her bed, till another room could be prepared. To obviate the fatigue of mounting and descending the stairs, we fitted up this, where you lie at present – on the same floor with the parlour; and she was soon strong enough to move from one to the other, leaning on Edgar's arm. Ah, I thought myself, she might recover, so waited on as she was. And there was double cause to desire it, for on her existence depended that of another: we cherished the hope that in a little while Mr. Linton's heart would be gladdened, and his lands secured from a stranger's gripe, by the birth of an heir.

I should mention that Isabella sent to her brother, some six weeks from her departure, a short note, announcing her marriage with Heathcliff. It appeared dry and cold; but at the bottom was dotted in with pencil an obscure apology, and an entreaty for kind remembrance and reconciliation, if her proceeding had offended him: asserting that she could not help it then, and being done, she had now no power to repeal it. Linton did not reply to this, I believe; and, in a fortnight more, I got a long letter, which I considered odd, coming from the pen of a bride just out of the honeymoon. I'll read it: for I keep it yet. Any relic of the dead is precious, if they were valued living.

* * *

Dear Ellen, it begins, –

I came last night to Wuthering Heights, and heard, for the first time, that Catherine has been, and is yet, very ill. I must not write to her, I suppose, and my brother is either too angry or too distressed to answer what I sent him. Still, I must write to somebody, and the only choice left me is you.

Inform Edgar that I'd give the world to see his face again – that my heart returned to Thrushcross Grange in twenty-four hours after I left it, and is there at this moment, full of warm feelings for him, and Catherine! I can't follow it though – (these words are underlined) – they need not expect me, and they may draw what conclusions they please; taking care, however, to lay nothing at the door of my weak will or deficient affection.

The remainder of the letter is for yourself alone. I want to ask you two questions: the first is, – How did you contrive to preserve the common sympathies of human nature when you resided here? I cannot recognise any sentiment which those around share with me.

The second question I have great interest in; it is this – Is Mr. Heathcliff a man? If so, is he mad? And if not, is he a devil? I shan't tell my reasons for making this inquiry; but I beseech you to explain, if you can, what I have married: that is, when you call to see me; and you must call, Ellen, very soon. Don't write, but come, and bring me something from Edgar.

Now, you shall hear how I have been received in my new home, as I am led to imagine the Heights will be. It is to amuse myself that I dwell on such subjects as the lack of external comforts: they never occupy my thoughts, except at the moment when I miss them. I should laugh and dance for joy, if I found their absence was the total of my miseries, and the rest was an unnatural dream!

The sun set behind the Grange as we turned on to the moors; by that, I judged it to be six o'clock; and my companion halted half an hour, to inspect the park, and the gardens, and, probably, the place itself, as well as he could; so it was dark when we dismounted in the paved yard of the farm-house, and your old fellow-servant, Joseph, issued out to receive us by the light of a dip candle. He did it with a courtesy that redounded to his credit. His first act was to elevate his torch to a level with my face, squint malignantly, project his under-lip, and turn away. Then he took the two horses, and led them into the stables; reappearing for the purpose of locking the outer gate, as if we lived in an ancient castle.

Heathcliff stayed to speak to him, and I entered the kitchen – a dingy, untidy hole; I daresay you would not know it, it is so changed since it was in your charge. By the fire stood a ruffianly child, strong in limb and dirty in garb, with a look of Catherine in his eyes and about his mouth.

"This is Edgar's legal nephew," I reflected – "mine in a manner; I must shake hands, and – yes – I must kiss him. It is right to establish a good understanding at the beginning."

I approached, and, attempting to take his chubby fist, said – "How do you do, my dear?"

He replied in a jargon I did not comprehend.

"Shall you and I be friends, Hareton?" was my next essay at conversation.

An oath, and a threat to set Throttler on me if I did not 'frame off' rewarded my perseverance.

"Hey, Throttler, lad!" whispered the little wretch, rousing a half-bred bull-dog from its lair in a corner. "Now, wilt thou be ganging?" he asked authoritatively.

Love for my life urged a compliance; I stepped over the threshold to wait till the others should enter. Mr. Heathcliff was nowhere visible; and Joseph, whom I followed to the stables, and requested to accompany me in, after staring and muttering to himself, screwed up his nose and replied – "Mim! Mim! Mim! Did iver Christian body hear aught like it? Mincing un' munching! How can I tell whet ye say?"

"I say, I wish you to come with me into the house!" I cried, thinking him deaf, yet highly disgusted at his rudeness.

"None o' me! I getten summut else to do," he answered, and continued his work; moving his lantern jaws meanwhile, and surveying my dress and countenance (the former a great deal too fine, but the latter, I'm sure, as sad as he could desire) with sovereign contempt.

I walked round the yard, and through a wicket, to another door, at which I took the liberty of knocking, in hopes some more civil servant might show himself. After a short suspense, it was opened by a tall, gaunt man, without neckerchief, and otherwise extremely slovenly; his features were lost in masses of shaggy hair that hung on his shoulders; and his eyes, too, were like a ghostly Catherine's with all their beauty annihilated.

"What's your business here?" he demanded, grimly. "Who are you?"

"My name was Isabella Linton," I replied. "You've seen me before, sir. I'm lately married to Mr. Heathcliff, and he has brought me here – I suppose, by your permission."

"Is he come back, then?" asked the hermit, glaring like a hungry wolf.

"Yes – we came just now," I said; "but he left me by the kitchen door; and when I would have gone in, your little boy played sentinel over the place, and frightened me off by the help of a bull-dog."

"It's well the hellish villain has kept his word!" growled my future host, searching the darkness beyond me in expectation of discovering Heathcliff; and then he indulged in a soliloquy of execrations, and threats of what he would have done had the 'fiend' deceived him.

I repented having tried this second entrance, and was almost inclined to slip away before he finished cursing, but ere I could execute that intention, he ordered me in, and shut and re-fastened the door. There was a great fire, and that was all the light in the huge apartment, whose floor had grown a uniform grey; and the once brilliant pewter-dishes, which used to attract my gaze when I was a girl, partook of a similar obscurity, created by tarnish and dust. I inquired whether I might call the maid, and be conducted to a bedroom? Mr. Earnshaw vouchsafed no answer. He walked up and down, with his hands in his pockets, apparently quite forgetting my presence; and his abstraction was evidently so deep, and his whole aspect so misanthropical, that I shrank from disturbing him again.

You'll not be surprised, Ellen, at my feeling particularly cheerless, seated in worse than solitude on that inhospitable hearth, and remembering that four miles distant lay my delightful home, containing the only people I loved on earth; and there might as well be the Atlantic to part us, instead of those four miles: I could not overpass them! I questioned with myself – where must I turn for comfort? And – mind you don't tell Edgar, or Catherine – above every sorrow beside, this rose pre-eminent: despair at finding nobody who could or would be my ally against Heathcliff! I had sought shelter at Wuthering Heights, almost gladly, because I was secured by that arrangement from living alone with him; but he knew the people we were coming amongst, and he did not fear their intermeddling.

I sat and thought a doleful time: the clock struck eight, and nine, and still my companion paced to and fro, his head bent on his breast, and perfectly silent, unless a groan or a bitter ejaculation forced itself out at intervals. I listened to detect a woman's voice in the house, and filled the interim with wild regrets and dismal anticipations, which, at last, spoke audibly in irrepressible sighing and weeping. I was not aware how openly I grieved, till Earnshaw halted opposite, in his measured walk, and gave me a stare of newly-awakened surprise. Taking advantage of his recovered attention, I exclaimed – "I'm tired with my journey, and I want to go to bed! Where is the maid-servant? Direct me to her, as she won't come to me!"

"We have none," he answered; "you must wait on yourself!"

"Where must I sleep, then?" I sobbed; I was beyond regarding self-respect, weighed down by fatigue and wretchedness.

"Joseph will show you Heathcliff's chamber," said he; "open that door – he's in there."

I was going to obey, but he suddenly arrested me, and added in the strangest tone – "Be so good as to turn your lock, and draw your bolt – don't omit it!"

"Well!" I said. "But why, Mr. Earnshaw?" I did not relish the notion of deliberately fastening myself in with Heathcliff.

"Look here!" he replied, pulling from his waistcoat a curiously-constructed pistol, having a double-edged spring knife attached to the barrel. "That's a great tempter to a desperate man, is it not? I cannot resist going up with this every night, and trying his door. If once I find it open he's done for; I do it invariably, even though the minute before I have been recalling a hundred reasons that should make me refrain: it is some devil that urges me to thwart my own schemes by killing him. You fight against that devil for love as long as you may; when the time comes, not all the angels in heaven shall save him!"

I surveyed the weapon inquisitively. A hideous notion struck me: how powerful I should be possessing such an instrument! I took it from his hand, and touched the blade. He looked astonished at the expression my face assumed during a brief second: it was not horror, it was covetousness. He snatched the pistol back, jealously; shut the knife, and returned it to its concealment.

"I don't care if you tell him," said he. "Put him on his guard, and watch for him. You know the terms we are on, I see: his danger does not shock you."

"What has Heathcliff done to you?" I asked. "In what has he wronged you, to warrant this appalling hatred? Wouldn't it be wiser to bid him quit the house?"

"No!" thundered Earnshaw; "Should he offer to leave me, he's a dead man: persuade him to attempt it, and you are a murderess! Am I to lose all, without a chance of retrieval? Is Hareton to be a beggar? Oh, damnation! I will have it back; and I'll have his gold too; and then his blood; and hell shall have his soul! It will be ten times blacker with that guest than ever it was before!"

You've acquainted me, Ellen, with your old master's habits. He is clearly on the verge of madness: he was so last night at least. I shuddered to be near him, and thought on the servant's ill-bred moroseness as comparatively agreeable. He now recommenced his moody walk, and I raised the latch, and escaped into the kitchen. Joseph was bending over the fire, peering into a large pan that swung above it; and a wooden bowl of oatmeal stood on the settle close by. The contents of the pan began to boil, and he turned to plunge his hand into the bowl; I conjectured that this preparation was probably for our supper, and, being hungry, I resolved it should be eatable; so, crying out sharply, "I'll make the porridge!" I removed the vessel out of his reach, and proceeded to take off my hat and riding-habit. "Mr. Earnshaw," I continued, "directs me to wait on myself: I will. I'm not going to act the lady among you, for fear I should starve."

"Goood Lord!" he muttered, sitting down, and stroking his ribbed stockings from the knee to the ankle. "If there's to be fresh ortherings – just when I getten used to two maisters, if I mun hev' a mistress set o'er my heead, it's like time to be flitting. I niver did think to see t' day that I mud lave th' owld place – but I doubt it's nigh at hand!"

This lamentation drew no notice from me: I went briskly to work, sighing to remember a period when it would have been all merry fun; but compelled speedily to drive off the remembrance. It racked me to recall past happiness and the greater peril there was of conjuring up its apparition, the quicker the thible ran round, and the faster the handfuls of meal fell into the water. Joseph beheld my style of cookery with growing indignation.

"Thear!" he ejaculated. "Hareton, thou willn't sup thy porridge to-neeght; they'll be naught but lumps as big as my neive. Thear, agean! I'd fling in bowl un' all, if I wer ye! There, pale t' guilp off, un' then ye'll hae done wi' 't. Bang, bang. It's a mercy t' bothom isn't deaved out!"

It was rather a rough mess, I own, when poured into the basins; four had been provided, and a gallon pitcher of new milk was brought from the dairy, which Hareton seized and commenced drinking and spilling from the expansive lip. I expostulated, and desired that he should have his in a mug; affirming that I could not taste the liquid treated so dirtily. The old cynic chose to be vastly offended at this nicety; assuring me, repeatedly, that "the barn was every bit as good" as I, "and every bit as wollsome," and wondering how I could fashion to be so conceited. Meanwhile, the infant ruffian continued sucking; and glowered up at me defyingly, as he slavered into the jug.

"I shall have my supper in another room," I said. "Have you no place you call a parlour?"

"Parlour!" he echoed, sneeringly, "Parlour! Nay, we've noa parlours. If yah dunnut loike wer company, there's maister's; un' if yah dunnut loike maister, there's us."

"Then I shall go upstairs," I answered; "show me a chamber."

I put my basin on a tray, and went myself to fetch some more milk. With great grumblings, the fellow rose, and preceded me in my ascent: we mounted to the garrets; he opened a door, now and then, to look into the apartments we passed.

"Here's a rahm," he said, at last, flinging back a cranky board on hinges. "It's weel eneugh to ate a few porridge in. There's a pack o' corn i' t' corner, thear, meeterly clane; if ye're feared o' muckying yer grand silk cloes, spread yer hankerchir o' t' top on't."

The 'rahm' was a kind of lumber-hole smelling strong of malt and grain; various sacks of which articles were piled around, leaving a wide, bare space in the middle.

"Why, man," I exclaimed, facing him angrily, "this is not a place to sleep in. I wish to see my bed-room."

"Bed-rume!" he repeated, in a tone of mockery. "Yah's see all t' bed-rumes thear is – yon's mine."

He pointed into the second garret, only differing from the first in being more naked about the walls, and having a large, low, curtainless bed, with an indigo-coloured quilt, at one end.

"What do I want with yours?" I retorted. "I suppose Mr. Heathcliff does not lodge at the top of the house, does he?"

"Oh! It's Maister Hathecliff's ye're wanting?" cried he, as if making a new discovery. "Couldn't ye ha' said soa, at onst? Un' then, I mud ha' telled ye, baht all this wark, that's just one ye cannut see – he allas keeps it locked, un' nob'dy iver mells on't but hisseln."

"You've a nice house, Joseph," I could not refrain from observing, "and pleasant inmates; and I think the concentrated essence of all the madness in the world took up its abode in my brain the day I linked my fate with theirs! However, that is not to the present purpose – there are other rooms. For heaven's sake be quick, and let me settle somewhere!"

He made no reply to this adjuration; only plodding doggedly down the wooden steps, and halting, before an apartment which, from that halt and the superior quality of its furniture, I conjectured to be the best one. There was a carpet – a good one, but the pattern was obliterated by dust; a fireplace hung with cut-paper, dropping to pieces; a handsome oak-bedstead with ample crimson curtains of rather expensive material and modern make; but they had evidently experienced rough usage: the vallances hung in festoons, wrenched from their rings, and the *iron rod supporting them was bent in an arc on one side, causing the drapery to trail upon the floor. The chairs were also damaged, many of them severely; and deep indentations deformed the panels of the walls. I was endeavouring to gather resolution for entering and taking possession, when my fool of a guide announced, – "This here is t' maister's." My supper by this time was cold, my appetite gone, and my patience exhausted. I insisted on being provided instantly with a place of refuge, and means of repose.*

"Whear the divil?" began the religious elder. "The Lord bless us! The Lord forgie us! Whear the hell *wold ye gang? Ye marred, wearisome nowt! Ye've seen all but Hareton's bit of a cham'er. There's not another hoile to lig down in i' th' hahse!"*

I was so vexed, I flung my tray and its contents on the ground; and then seated myself at the stairs'-head, hid my face in my hands, and cried.

"Ech! Ech!" exclaimed Joseph. "Weel done, Miss Cathy! Weel done, Miss Cathy! Howsiver, t' maister sall just tum'le o'er them brooken pots; un' then we's hear summut; we's hear how it's to be. Gooid-for-naught madling! Ye desarve pining fro' this to Churstmas, flinging t' precious gifts o'God under fooit i' yer flaysome rages! But I'm mista'en if ye shew yer sperrit lang. Will Hathecliff bide sich bonny ways, think ye? I nobbut wish he may catch ye i' that plisky. I nobbut wish he may."

And so he went on scolding to his den beneath, taking the candle with him; and I remained in the dark. The period of reflection succeeding this silly action compelled me to admit the necessity of smothering my pride and choking my wrath, and bestirring myself to remove its effects. An unexpected aid presently appeared in the shape of Throttler, whom I now recognised as a son of our old Skulker: it had spent its whelphood at the Grange, and was given by my father to Mr. Hindley. I fancy it knew me: it pushed its nose against mine by way of salute, and then hastened to devour the porridge; while I groped from step to step, collecting the shattered earthenware, and drying the spatters of milk from the banister with my pocket-handkerchief. Our labours were scarcely over when I heard Earnshaw's tread in the passage; my assistant tucked in his tail, and pressed to the wall; I stole into the nearest doorway. The dog's endeavour to avoid him was unsuccessful; as I guessed by a scutter downstairs, and a prolonged, piteous yelping. I had better luck: he passed on, entered his chamber, and shut the door. Directly after Joseph came up with Hareton, to put him to bed. I had found shelter in Hareton's room, and the old man, on seeing me, said, – "They's rahm for boath ye un' yer pride, now, I sud think i' the hahse. It's empty; ye may hev' it all to yerseln, un' Him as allus maks a third, i' sich ill company!"

Gladly did I take advantage of this intimation; and the minute I flung myself into a chair, by the fire, I nodded, and slept. My slumber was deep and sweet, though over far too soon. Mr. Heathcliff awoke me; he had just come in, and demanded, in his loving manner, what I was doing there? I told him the cause of my staying up so late – that he had the key of our room in his pocket. The adjective our gave mortal offence. He swore it was not, nor ever should be, mine; and he'd – but I'll not repeat his language, nor describe his habitual conduct: he is ingenious and unresting in seeking to gain my abhorrence! I sometimes wonder at him with an intensity that deadens my fear: yet, I assure you, a tiger or a venomous serpent could not rouse terror in me equal to that which he wakens. He told me of Catherine's illness, and accused my brother of causing it promising that I should be Edgar's proxy in suffering, till he could get hold of him.

I do hate him – I am wretched – I have been a fool! Beware of uttering one breath of this to any one at the Grange. I shall expect you every day – don't disappoint me!

– Isabella.

Chapter Fourteen

AS SOON AS I had perused this epistle I went to the master, and informed him that his sister had arrived at the Heights, and sent me a letter expressing her sorrow for Mrs. Linton's situation, and her ardent desire to see him; with a wish that he would transmit to her, as early as possible, some token of forgiveness by me.

"Forgiveness!" said Linton. "I have nothing to forgive her, Ellen. You may call at Wuthering Heights this afternoon, if you like, and say that I am not angry, but I'm sorry to have lost her; especially as I can never think she'll be happy. It is out of the question my going to see her, however: we are eternally divided; and should she really wish to oblige me, let her persuade the villain she has married to leave the country."

"And you won't write her a little note, sir?" I asked, imploringly.

"No," he answered. "It is needless. My communication with Heathcliff's family shall be as sparing as his with mine. It shall not exist!"

Mr. Edgar's coldness depressed me exceedingly; and all the way from the Grange I puzzled my brains how to put more heart into what he said, when I repeated it; and how to soften his refusal of even a few lines to console Isabella. I daresay she had been on the watch for me since morning: I saw her looking through the lattice as I came up the garden causeway, and I nodded to her; but she drew back, as if afraid of being observed. I entered without knocking. There never was such a dreary, dismal scene as the formerly cheerful house presented! I must confess, that if I had been in the young lady's place, I would, at least, have swept the hearth, and wiped the tables with a duster. But she already partook of the pervading spirit of neglect which encompassed her. Her pretty face was wan and listless; her hair uncurled: some locks hanging lankly down, and some carelessly twisted round her head. Probably she had not touched her dress since yester evening. Hindley was not there. Mr. Heathcliff sat at a table, turning over some papers in his pocket-book; but he rose when I appeared, asked me how I did, quite friendly, and offered me a chair. He was the only thing there that seemed decent; and I thought he never looked better. So much had circumstances altered their positions, that he would certainly have struck a stranger as a born and bred gentleman; and his wife as a thorough little slattern! She came forward eagerly to greet me, and held out one hand to take the expected letter. I shook my head. She wouldn't understand the hint, but followed me to a sideboard, where I went to lay my bonnet, and importuned me in a whisper to give me directly what I had brought. Heathcliff guessed the meaning of her manoeuvres, and said – "If you have got anything for Isabella (as no doubt you have, Nelly), give it to her. You needn't make a secret of it: we have no secrets between us."

"Oh, I have nothing," I replied, thinking it best to speak the truth at once. "My master bid me tell his sister that she must not expect either a letter or a visit from him at present. He sends his love, ma'am, and his wishes for your happiness, and his pardon for the grief you have occasioned; but he thinks that after this time his household and the household here should drop intercommunication, as nothing could come of keeping it up."

Mrs. Heathcliff's lip quivered slightly, and she returned to her seat in the window. Her husband took his stand on the hearthstone, near me, and began to put questions concerning Catherine. I told him as much as I thought proper of her illness, and he extorted from me, by cross-examination, most of the facts connected with its origin. I blamed her, as she deserved, for bringing it all on herself; and ended by hoping that he would follow Mr. Linton's example and avoid future interference with his family, for good or evil.

"Mrs. Linton is now just recovering," I said; "she'll never be like she was, but her life is spared; and if you really have a regard for her, you'll shun crossing her way again: nay, you'll move out of this country entirely; and that you may not regret it, I'll inform you Catherine Linton is as different now from your old friend Catherine Earnshaw, as that young lady is different from me. Her appearance is changed greatly, her character much more so; and the person who is compelled, of necessity, to be her companion, will only sustain his affection hereafter by the remembrance of what she once was, by common humanity, and a sense of duty!"

"That is quite possible," remarked Heathcliff, forcing himself to seem calm: "quite possible that your master should have nothing but common humanity and a sense of duty to fall back upon. But do you imagine that I shall leave Catherine to his *duty* and *humanity*? And can you compare my feelings respecting Catherine to his? Before you leave this house, I must exact a promise from you that you'll get me an interview with her: consent, or refuse, I *will* see her! What do you say?"

"I say, Mr. Heathcliff," I replied, "you must not: you never shall, through my means. Another encounter between you and the master would kill her altogether."

"With your aid that may be avoided," he continued; "and should there be danger of such an event – should he be the cause of adding a single trouble more to her existence – why, I think I shall be justified in going to extremes! I wish you had sincerity enough to tell me whether Catherine would suffer greatly from his loss: the fear that she would restrains me. And there you see the distinction between our feelings: had he been in my place, and I in his, though I hated him with a hatred that turned my life to gall, I never would have raised a hand against him. You may look incredulous, if you please! I never would have banished him from her society as long as she desired his. The moment her regard ceased, I would have torn his heart out, and drunk his blood! But, till then – if you don't believe me, you don't know me – till then, I would have died by inches before I touched a single hair of his head!"

"And yet," I interrupted, "you have no scruples in completely ruining all hopes of her perfect restoration, by thrusting yourself into her remembrance now, when she has nearly forgotten you, and involving her in a new tumult of discord and distress."

"You suppose she has nearly forgotten me?" he said. "Oh, Nelly! You know she has not! You know as well as I do, that for every thought she spends on Linton she spends a thousand on me! At a most miserable period of my life, I had a notion of the kind: it haunted me on my return to the neighbourhood last summer; but only her own assurance could make me admit the horrible idea again. And then, Linton would be nothing, nor Hindley, nor all the dreams that ever I dreamt. Two words would comprehend my future – *death* and *hell*: existence, after losing her, would be hell. Yet I was a fool to fancy for a moment that she valued Edgar Linton's attachment more than mine. If he loved with all the powers of his puny being, he couldn't love as much in eighty years as I could in a day. And Catherine has a heart as deep as I have: the sea could be as readily contained in that horse-trough as her whole affection be monopolised by him. Tush! He is scarcely a degree dearer to her than her dog, or her horse. It is not in him to be loved like me: how can she love in him what he has not?"

"Catherine and Edgar are as fond of each other as any two people can be," cried Isabella, with sudden vivacity. "No one has a right to talk in that manner, and I won't hear my brother depreciated in silence!"

"Your brother is wondrous fond of you too, isn't he?" observed Heathcliff, scornfully. "He turns you adrift on the world with surprising alacrity."

"He is not aware of what I suffer," she replied. "I didn't tell him that."

"You have been telling him something, then: you have written, have you?"

"To say that I was married, I did write – you saw the note."

"And nothing since?"

"No."

"My young lady is looking sadly the worse for her change of condition," I remarked. "Somebody's love comes short in her case, obviously; whose, I may guess; but, perhaps, I shouldn't say."

"I should guess it was her own," said Heathcliff. "She degenerates into a mere slut! She is tired of trying to please me uncommonly early. You'd hardly credit it, but the very morrow of our wedding she was weeping to go home. However, she'll suit this house so much the better for not being over nice, and I'll take care she does not disgrace me by rambling abroad."

"Well, sir," returned I, "I hope you'll consider that Mrs. Heathcliff is accustomed to be looked after and waited on; and that she has been brought up like an only daughter, whom everyone was ready to serve. You must let her have a maid to keep things tidy about her, and you must treat her kindly. Whatever be your notion of Mr. Edgar, you cannot doubt that she has a capacity for strong attachments, or she wouldn't have abandoned the elegancies, and comforts, and friends of her former home, to fix contentedly, in such a wilderness as this, with you."

"She abandoned them under a delusion," he answered; "picturing in me a hero of romance, and expecting unlimited indulgences from my chivalrous devotion. I can hardly regard her in the light of a rational creature, so obstinately has she persisted in forming a fabulous notion of my character and acting on the false impressions she cherished. But, at last, I think she begins to know me: I don't perceive the silly smiles and grimaces that provoked me at first; and the senseless incapability of discerning that I was in earnest when I gave her my opinion of her infatuation and herself. It was a marvellous effort of perspicacity to discover that I did not love her. I believed, at one time, no lessons could teach her that! And yet it is poorly learnt; for this morning she announced, as a piece of appalling intelligence, that I had actually succeeded in making her hate me! A positive labour of Hercules, I assure you! If it be achieved, I have cause to return thanks. Can I trust your assertion, Isabella? Are you sure you hate me? If I let you alone for half a day, won't you come sighing and wheedling to me again? I daresay she would rather I had seemed all tenderness before you: it wounds her vanity to have the truth exposed. But I don't care who knows that the passion was wholly on one side: and I never told her a lie about it. She cannot accuse me of showing one bit of deceitful softness. The first thing she saw me do, on coming out of the Grange, was to hang up her little dog; and when she pleaded for it, the first words I uttered were a wish that I had the hanging of every being belonging to her, except one: possibly she took that exception for herself. But no brutality disgusted her: I suppose she has an innate admiration of it, if only her precious person were secure from injury! Now, was it not the depth of absurdity – of genuine idiocy, for that pitiful, slavish, mean-minded brach to dream that I could love her? Tell your master, Nelly, that I never, in all my life, met with such an abject thing as she is. She even disgraces the name of Linton; and I've sometimes relented, from pure lack of invention, in my experiments on what she could endure, and still creep shamefully cringing back! But tell him, also, to set his fraternal and magisterial heart at ease: that I keep strictly within the limits of the law. I have avoided, up to this period, giving her the slightest right to claim a separation; and, what's more, she'd thank nobody for dividing us. If she desired to go, she might: the nuisance of her presence outweighs the gratification to be derived from tormenting her!"

"Mr. Heathcliff," said I, "this is the talk of a madman; your wife, most likely, is convinced you are mad; and, for that reason, she has borne with you hitherto: but now that you say she may go, she'll doubtless avail herself of the permission. You are not so bewitched, ma'am, are you, as to remain with him of your own accord?"

"Take care, Ellen!" answered Isabella, her eyes sparkling irefully; there was no misdoubting by their expression the full success of her partner's endeavours to make himself detested. "Don't put faith in a single word he speaks. He's a lying fiend! A monster, and not a human being! I've been told I might leave him before; and I've made the attempt, but I dare not repeat it! Only, Ellen, promise you'll not mention a syllable of his infamous conversation to my brother or Catherine. Whatever he may pretend, he wishes to provoke Edgar to desperation: he says he has married me on purpose to obtain power over him; and he shan't obtain it – I'll die first! I just hope, I pray, that he may forget his diabolical prudence and kill me! The single pleasure I can imagine is to die, or to see him dead!"

"There – that will do for the present!" said Heathcliff. "If you are called upon in a court of law, you'll remember her language, Nelly! And take a good look at that countenance: she's near the point which would suit me. No; you're not fit to be your own guardian, Isabella, now; and I, being your legal protector, must retain you in my custody, however distasteful the obligation may be. Go upstairs; I have something to say to Ellen Dean in private. That's not the way: upstairs, I tell you! Why, this is the road upstairs, child!"

He seized, and thrust her from the room; and returned muttering – "I have no pity! I have no pity! The more the worms writhe, the more I yearn to crush out their entrails! It is a moral teething; and I grind with greater energy in proportion to the increase of pain."

"Do you understand what the word pity means?" I said, hastening to resume my bonnet. "Did you ever feel a touch of it in your life?"

"Put that down!" he interrupted, perceiving my intention to depart. "You are not going yet. Come here now, Nelly: I must either persuade or compel you to aid me in fulfilling my determination to see Catherine, and that without delay. I swear that I meditate no harm: I don't desire to cause any disturbance, or to exasperate or insult Mr. Linton; I only wish to hear from herself how she is, and why she has been ill; and to ask if anything that I could do would be of use to her. Last night I was in the Grange garden six hours, and I'll return there tonight; and every night I'll haunt the place, and every day, till I find an opportunity of entering. If Edgar Linton meets me, I shall not hesitate to knock him down, and give him enough to insure his quiescence while I stay. If his servants oppose me, I shall threaten them off with these pistols. But wouldn't it be better to prevent my coming in contact with them, or their master? And you could do it so easily. I'd warn you when I came, and then you might let me in unobserved, as soon as she was alone, and watch till I departed, your conscience quite calm: you would be hindering mischief."

I protested against playing that treacherous part in my employer's house: and, besides, I urged the cruelty and selfishness of his destroying Mrs. Linton's tranquillity for his satisfaction. "The commonest occurrence startles her painfully," I said. "She's all nerves, and she couldn't bear the surprise, I'm positive. Don't persist, sir! Or else I shall be obliged to inform my master of your designs; and he'll take measures to secure his house and its inmates from any such unwarrantable intrusions!"

"In that case I'll take measures to secure you, woman!" exclaimed Heathcliff; "you shall not leave Wuthering Heights till tomorrow morning. It is a foolish story to assert that Catherine could not bear to see me; and as to surprising her, I don't desire it: you must prepare her – ask her if I may come. You say she never mentions my name, and that I am never mentioned to her. To whom should she mention me if I am a forbidden topic in the house? She thinks you are all spies for her husband. Oh, I've no doubt she's in hell among you! I guess by her silence, as much as anything, what she feels. You say she is often restless, and anxious-looking: is that a proof of tranquillity? You talk of her mind being unsettled. How the devil could it be otherwise in her frightful isolation? And that insipid, paltry creature attending her from *duty* and *humanity*! From *pity* and *charity*! He might as well plant an oak in a flower-pot, and expect it to thrive, as imagine he can restore her to vigour in the soil of his shallow cares! Let us settle it at once: will you stay here, and am I to fight my way to Catherine over Linton and his footman? Or will you be my friend, as you have been hitherto, and do what I request? Decide! because there is no reason for my lingering another minute, if you persist in your stubborn ill-nature!"

Well, Mr. Lockwood, I argued and complained, and flatly refused him fifty times; but in the long run he forced me to an agreement. I engaged to carry a letter from him to my mistress; and should she consent, I promised to let him have intelligence of Linton's next absence from home, when he might come, and get in as he was able: I wouldn't be there, and my fellow-servants should be equally out of the way. Was it right or wrong? I fear it was wrong, though expedient. I thought I prevented another explosion by my compliance; and I thought, too, it might create a favourable crisis in Catherine's mental illness: and then I remembered Mr. Edgar's stern rebuke of my carrying tales; and I tried to smooth away all disquietude on the subject, by affirming, with frequent iteration, that that betrayal of trust, if it merited so harsh an appellation, should be the last. Notwithstanding, my journey homeward was sadder than my journey thither; and many misgivings I had, ere I could prevail on myself to put the missive into Mrs. Linton's hand.

But here is Kenneth; I'll go down, and tell him how much better you are. My history is *dree*, as we say, and will serve to while away another morning.

Dree, and dreary! I reflected as the good woman descended to receive the doctor: and not exactly of the kind which I should have chosen to amuse me. But never mind! I'll extract wholesome medicines from Mrs. Dean's bitter herbs; and firstly, let me beware of the fascination that lurks in Catherine Heathcliff's brilliant eyes. I should be in a curious taking if I surrendered my heart to that young person, and the daughter turned out a second edition of the mother.

Volume Two

Chapter Fifteen

ANOTHER WEEK OVER – and I am so many days nearer health, and spring! I have now heard all my neighbour's history, at different sittings, as the housekeeper could spare time from more important occupations. I'll continue it in her own words, only a little condensed. She is, on the whole, a very fair narrator, and I don't think I could improve her style.

In the evening, she said, the evening of my visit to the Heights, I knew, as well as if I saw him, that Mr. Heathcliff was about the place; and I shunned going out, because I still carried his letter in my pocket, and didn't want to be threatened or teased any more. I had made up my mind not to give it till my master went somewhere, as I could not guess how its receipt would affect Catherine. The consequence was, that it did not reach her before the lapse of three days. The fourth was Sunday, and I brought it into her room after the family were gone to church. There was a manservant left to keep the house with me, and we generally made a practice of locking the doors during the hours of service; but on that occasion the weather was so warm and pleasant that I set them wide open, and, to fulfil my engagement, as I knew who would be coming, I told my companion that the mistress wished very much for some oranges, and he must run over to the village and get a few, to be paid for on the morrow. He departed, and I went upstairs.

Mrs. Linton sat in a loose white dress, with a light shawl over her shoulders, in the recess of the open window, as usual. Her thick, long hair had been partly removed at the beginning of her illness, and now she wore it simply combed in its natural tresses over her temples and neck. Her appearance was altered, as I had told Heathcliff; but when she was calm, there seemed unearthly beauty in the change. The flash of her eyes had been succeeded by a dreamy and melancholy softness; they no longer gave the impression of looking at the objects around her: they appeared always to gaze beyond, and far beyond – you would have said out of this world. Then, the paleness of her face – its haggard aspect having vanished as she recovered flesh – and the peculiar expression arising from her mental state, though painfully suggestive of their causes, added to the touching interest which she awakened; and – invariably to me, I know, and to any person who saw her, I should think – refuted more tangible proofs of convalescence, and stamped her as one doomed to decay.

A book lay spread on the sill before her, and the scarcely perceptible wind fluttered its leaves at intervals. I believe Linton had laid it there: for she never endeavoured to divert herself with reading, or occupation of any kind, and he would spend many an hour in trying to entice her attention to some subject which had formerly been her amusement. She was conscious of his aim, and in her better moods endured his efforts placidly, only showing their uselessness by now and then suppressing a wearied sigh, and checking him at last with the saddest of smiles and kisses. At other times, she would turn petulantly away, and hide her face in her hands, or even push him off angrily; and then he took care to let her alone, for he was certain of doing no good.

Gimmerton chapel bells were still ringing; and the full, mellow flow of the beck in the valley came soothingly on the ear. It was a sweet substitute for the yet absent murmur of the summer foliage, which drowned that music about the Grange when the trees were in leaf. At Wuthering Heights it always sounded on quiet days following a great thaw or a season of steady rain. And of Wuthering Heights Catherine was thinking as she listened: that is, if she thought or listened at all; but she had the vague, distant look I mentioned before, which expressed no recognition of material things either by ear or eye.

"There's a letter for you, Mrs. Linton," I said, gently inserting it in one hand that rested on her knee. "You must read it immediately, because it wants an answer. Shall I break the seal?"

"Yes," she answered, without altering the direction of her eyes. I opened it – it was very short. "Now," I continued, "read it." She drew away her hand, and let it fall. I replaced it in her lap, and stood waiting till it should please her to glance down; but that movement was so long delayed that at last I resumed – "Must I read it, ma'am? It is from Mr. Heathcliff."

There was a start and a troubled gleam of recollection, and a struggle to arrange her ideas. She lifted the letter, and seemed to peruse it; and when she came to the signature she sighed: yet still I found she had not gathered its import, for, upon my desiring to hear her reply, she merely pointed to the name, and gazed at me with mournful and questioning eagerness.

"Well, he wishes to see you," said I, guessing her need of an interpreter. "He's in the garden by this time, and impatient to know what answer I shall bring."

As I spoke, I observed a large dog lying on the sunny grass beneath raise its ears as if about to bark, and then smoothing them back, announce, by a wag of the tail, that someone approached whom it did not consider a stranger. Mrs. Linton bent forward, and listened breathlessly. The minute after a step traversed the hall; the open house was too tempting for Heathcliff to resist walking in: most likely he supposed that I was inclined to shirk my promise, and so resolved to trust to his own audacity. With straining eagerness Catherine gazed towards the entrance of her chamber. He did not hit the right room directly: she motioned me to admit him, but he found it out ere I could reach the door, and in a stride or two was at her side, and had her grasped in his arms.

He neither spoke nor loosed his hold for some five minutes, during which period he bestowed more kisses than ever he gave in his life before, I daresay: but then my mistress had kissed him first, and I plainly saw that he could hardly bear, for downright agony, to look into her face! The same conviction had stricken him as me, from the instant he beheld her, that there was no prospect of ultimate recovery there – she was fated, sure to die.

"Oh, Cathy! Oh, my life! How can I bear it?" was the first sentence he uttered, in a tone that did not seek to disguise his despair. And now he stared at her so earnestly that I thought the very intensity of his gaze would bring tears into his eyes; but they burned with anguish: they did not melt.

"What now?" said Catherine, leaning back, and returning his look with a suddenly clouded brow: her humour was a mere vane for constantly varying caprices. "You and Edgar have broken my heart, Heathcliff! And you both come to bewail the deed to me, as if you were the people to be pitied! I shall not pity you, not I. You have killed me – and thriven on it, I think. How strong you are! How many years do you mean to live after I am gone?"

Heathcliff had knelt on one knee to embrace her; he attempted to rise, but she seized his hair, and kept him down.

"I wish I could hold you," she continued, bitterly, "till we were both dead! I shouldn't care what you suffered. I care nothing for your sufferings. Why shouldn't you suffer? I do! Will you forget me? Will you be happy when I am in the earth? Will you say twenty years hence, "That's the grave of Catherine Earnshaw. I loved her long ago, and was wretched to lose her; but it is past. I've loved many others since: my children are dearer to me than she was; and, at death, I shall not rejoice that I am going to her: I shall be sorry that I must leave them!" Will you say so, Heathcliff?"

"Don't torture me till I'm as mad as yourself," cried he, wrenching his head free, and grinding his teeth.

The two, to a cool spectator, made a strange and fearful picture. Well might Catherine deem that heaven would be a land of exile to her, unless with her mortal body she cast away her moral character also. Her present countenance had a wild vindictiveness in its white cheek, and a bloodless lip and scintillating eye; and she retained in her closed fingers a portion of the locks she had been grasping. As to her companion, while raising himself with one hand, he had taken her arm with the other; and so inadequate was his stock of gentleness to the requirements of her condition, that on his letting go I saw four distinct impressions left blue in the colourless skin.

"Are you possessed with a devil," he pursued, savagely, "to talk in that manner to me when you are dying? Do you reflect that all those words will be branded in my memory, and eating deeper eternally after you have left me? You know you lie to say I have killed you: and, Catherine, you know that I could as soon forget you as my existence! Is it not sufficient for your infernal selfishness, that while you are at peace I shall writhe in the torments of hell?"

"I shall not be at peace," moaned Catherine, recalled to a sense of physical weakness by the violent, unequal throbbing of her heart, which beat visibly and audibly under this excess of agitation. She said nothing further till the paroxysm was over; then she continued, more kindly –

"I'm not wishing you greater torment than I have, Heathcliff. I only wish us never to be parted: and should a word of mine distress you hereafter, think I feel the same distress underground, and for my own sake, forgive me! Come here and kneel down again! You never harmed me in your life. Nay, if you nurse anger, that will be worse to remember than my harsh words! Won't you come here again? Do!"

Heathcliff went to the back of her chair, and leant over, but not so far as to let her see his face, which was livid with emotion. She bent round to look at him; he would not permit it: turning abruptly, he walked to the fireplace, where he stood, silent, with his back towards us. Mrs. Linton's glance followed him suspiciously: every movement woke a new sentiment in her. After a pause and a prolonged gaze, she resumed; addressing me in accents of indignant disappointment:

"Oh, you see, Nelly, he would not relent a moment to keep me out of the grave. *That* is how I'm loved! Well, never mind. That is not *my* Heathcliff. I shall love mine yet; and take him with me: he's in my soul. And," added she musingly, "the thing that irks me most is this shattered prison, after all. I'm tired of being enclosed here. I'm wearying to escape into that glorious world, and to be always there: not seeing it dimly through tears, and yearning for it through the walls of an aching heart: but really with it, and in it. Nelly, you think you are better and more fortunate than I; in full health and strength: you are sorry for me – very soon that will be altered. I shall be sorry for *you*. I shall be incomparably beyond and above you all. I *wonder* he won't be near me!" She went on to herself. "I thought he wished it. Heathcliff, dear! You should not be sullen now. Do come to me, Heathcliff."

In her eagerness she rose and supported herself on the arm of the chair. At that earnest appeal he turned to her, looking absolutely desperate. His eyes, wide and wet, at last flashed fiercely on her; his breast heaved convulsively. An instant they held asunder, and then how they met I hardly saw, but Catherine made a spring, and he caught her, and they were locked in an embrace from which I thought my mistress would never be released alive: in fact, to my eyes, she seemed directly insensible. He flung himself into the nearest seat, and on my approaching hurriedly to ascertain if she had fainted, he gnashed at me, and foamed like a mad dog, and gathered her to him with greedy jealousy. I did not feel as if I were in the company of a creature of my own species: it appeared that he would not understand, though I spoke to him; so I stood off, and held my tongue, in great perplexity.

A movement of Catherine's relieved me a little presently: she put up her hand to clasp his neck, and bring her cheek to his as he held her; while he, in return, covering her with frantic caresses, said wildly –

"You teach me now how cruel you've been – cruel and false. *Why* did you despise me? *Why* did you betray your own heart, Cathy? I have not one word of comfort. You deserve this. You have killed yourself. Yes, you may kiss me, and cry; and wring out my kisses and tears: they'll blight you – they'll damn you. You loved me – then what *right* had you to leave me? What right – answer me – for the poor fancy you felt for Linton? Because misery and degradation, and death, and nothing that God or Satan could inflict would have parted us, *you*, of your own will, did it. I have not broken your heart – *you* have broken it; and in breaking it, you have broken mine. So much the worse for me that I am strong. Do I want to live? What kind of living will it be when you – oh, God! Would *you* like to live with your soul in the grave?"

"Let me alone. Let me alone," sobbed Catherine. "If I've done wrong, I'm dying for it. It is enough! You left me too: but I won't upbraid you! I forgive you. Forgive me!"

"It is hard to forgive, and to look at those eyes, and feel those wasted hands," he answered. "Kiss me again; and don't let me see your eyes! I forgive what you have done to me. I love *my* murderer – but *yours*! How can I?"

They were silent – their faces hid against each other, and washed by each other's tears. At least, I suppose the weeping was on both sides; as it seemed Heathcliff could weep on a great occasion like this.

I grew very uncomfortable, meanwhile; for the afternoon wore fast away, the man whom I had sent off returned from his errand, and I could distinguish, by the shine of the western sun up the valley, a concourse thickening outside Gimmerton chapel porch.

"Service is over," I announced. "My master will be here in half an hour."

Heathcliff groaned a curse, and strained Catherine closer: she never moved.

Ere long I perceived a group of the servants passing up the road towards the kitchen wing. Mr. Linton was not far behind; he opened the gate himself and sauntered slowly up, probably enjoying the lovely afternoon that breathed as soft as summer.

"Now he is here," I exclaimed. "For heaven's sake, hurry down! You'll not meet anyone on the front stairs. Do be quick; and stay among the trees till he is fairly in."

"I must go, Cathy," said Heathcliff, seeking to extricate himself from his companion's arms. "But if I live, I'll see you again before you are asleep. I won't stray five yards from your window."

"You must not go!" she answered, holding him as firmly as her strength allowed. "You *shall* not, I tell you."

"For one hour," he pleaded earnestly.

"Not for one minute," she replied.

"I *must* – Linton will be up immediately," persisted the alarmed intruder.

He would have risen, and unfixed her fingers by the act – she clung fast, gasping: there was mad resolution in her face.

"No!" she shrieked. "Oh, don't, don't go. It is the last time! Edgar will not hurt us. Heathcliff, I shall die! I shall die!"

"Damn the fool! There he is," cried Heathcliff, sinking back into his seat. "Hush, my darling! Hush, hush, Catherine! I'll stay. If he shot me so, I'd expire with a blessing on my lips."

And there they were fast again. I heard my master mounting the stairs – the cold sweat ran from my forehead: I was horrified.

"Are you going to listen to her ravings?" I said, passionately. "She does not know what she says. Will you ruin her, because she has not wit to help herself? Get up! You could be free instantly. That is the most diabolical deed that ever you did. We are all done for – master, mistress, and servant."

I wrung my hands, and cried out; and Mr. Linton hastened his step at the noise. In the midst of my agitation, I was sincerely glad to observe that Catherine's arms had fallen relaxed, and her head hung down.

"She's fainted, or dead," I thought: "so much the better. Far better that she should be dead, than lingering a burden and a misery-maker to all about her."

Edgar sprang to his unbidden guest, blanched with astonishment and rage. What he meant to do I cannot tell; however, the other stopped all demonstrations, at once, by placing the lifeless-looking form in his arms.

"Look there!" he said. "Unless you be a fiend, help her first – then you shall speak to me!"

He walked into the parlour, and sat down. Mr. Linton summoned me, and with great difficulty, and after resorting to many means, we managed to restore her to sensation; but she was all bewildered; she sighed, and moaned, and knew nobody. Edgar, in his anxiety for her, forgot her hated friend. I did not. I went, at the earliest opportunity, and besought him to depart; affirming that Catherine was better, and he should hear from me in the morning how she passed the night.

"I shall not refuse to go out of doors," he answered; "but I shall stay in the garden: and, Nelly, mind you keep your word tomorrow. I shall be under those larch-trees. Mind! Or I pay another visit, whether Linton be in or not."

He sent a rapid glance through the half-open door of the chamber, and, ascertaining that what I stated was apparently true, delivered the house of his luckless presence.

Chapter Sixteen

ABOUT TWELVE O'CLOCK that night was born the Catherine you saw at Wuthering Heights: a puny, seven-months' child; and two hours after the mother died, having never recovered sufficient consciousness to miss Heathcliff, or know Edgar. The latter's distraction at his bereavement is a subject too painful to be dwelt on; its after-effects showed how deep the sorrow sunk. A great addition, in my eyes, was his being left without an heir. I bemoaned that, as I gazed on the feeble orphan; and I mentally abused old Linton for (what was only natural partiality) the securing his estate to his own daughter, instead of his son's. An unwelcomed infant it was, poor thing! It might have wailed out of life, and nobody cared a morsel, during those first hours of existence. We redeemed the neglect afterwards; but its beginning was as friendless as its end is likely to be.

Next morning – bright and cheerful out of doors – stole softened in through the blinds of the silent room, and suffused the couch and its occupant with a mellow, tender glow. Edgar Linton had his head laid on the pillow, and his eyes shut. His young and fair features were almost as deathlike as those of the form beside him, and almost as fixed: but *his* was the hush of exhausted anguish, and *hers* of perfect peace. Her brow smooth, her lids closed, her lips wearing the expression of a smile; no angel in heaven could be more beautiful than she appeared. And I partook of the infinite calm in which she lay: my mind was never in a holier frame than while I gazed on that untroubled image of Divine rest. I instinctively echoed the words she had uttered a few hours before: "Incomparably beyond and above us all! Whether still on earth or now in heaven, her spirit is at home with God!"

I don't know if it be a peculiarity in me, but I am seldom otherwise than happy while watching in the chamber of death, should no frenzied or despairing mourner share the duty with me. I see a repose that neither earth nor hell can break, and I feel an assurance of the endless and shadowless hereafter – the Eternity they have entered – where life is boundless in its duration, and love in its sympathy, and joy in its fulness. I noticed on that occasion how much selfishness there is even in a love like Mr. Linton's, when he so regretted Catherine's blessed release! To be sure, one might have doubted, after the wayward and impatient existence she had led, whether she merited a haven of peace at last. One might doubt in seasons of cold reflection; but not then, in the presence of her corpse. It asserted its own tranquillity, which seemed a pledge of equal quiet to its former inhabitant.

Do you believe such people are happy in the other world, sir? I'd give a great deal to know.

I declined answering Mrs. Dean's question, which struck me as something heterodox. She proceeded:

Retracing the course of Catherine Linton, I fear we have no right to think she is; but we'll leave her with her Maker.

The master looked asleep, and I ventured soon after sunrise to quit the room and steal out to the pure refreshing air. The servants thought me gone to shake off the drowsiness of my protracted watch; in reality, my chief motive was seeing Mr. Heathcliff. If he had remained among the larches all night, he would have heard nothing of the stir at the Grange; unless, perhaps, he might catch the gallop of the messenger going to Gimmerton. If he had come nearer, he would probably be aware, from the lights flitting to and fro, and the opening and shutting of the outer doors, that all was not right within. I wished, yet feared, to find him. I felt the terrible news must be told, and I longed to get it over; but how to do it I did not know. He was there – at least, a few yards further in the park; leant against an old ash-tree, his hat off, and his hair soaked with the dew that had gathered on the budded branches, and fell pattering round him. He had been standing a long time in that position, for I saw a pair of ousels passing and repassing scarcely three feet from him, busy in building their nest, and regarding his proximity no more than that of a piece of timber. They flew off at my approach, and he raised his eyes and spoke: – "She's dead!" he said; "I've not waited for you to learn that. Put your handkerchief away – don't snivel before me. Damn you all! She wants none of your tears!"

I was weeping as much for him as her: we do sometimes pity creatures that have none of the feeling either for themselves or others. When I first looked into his face, I perceived that he had got intelligence of the catastrophe; and a foolish notion struck me that his heart was quelled and he prayed, because his lips moved and his gaze was bent on the ground.

"Yes, she's dead!" I answered, checking my sobs and drying my cheeks. "Gone to heaven, I hope; where we may, everyone, join her, if we take due warning and leave our evil ways to follow good!"

"Did *she* take due warning, then?" asked Heathcliff, attempting a sneer. "Did she die like a saint? Come, give me a true history of the event. How did –?"

He endeavoured to pronounce the name, but could not manage it; and compressing his mouth he held a silent combat with his inward agony, defying, meanwhile, my sympathy with an unflinching, ferocious stare. "How did she die?" he resumed, at last – fain, notwithstanding his hardihood, to have a support behind him; for, after the struggle, he trembled, in spite of himself, to his very finger-ends.

"Poor wretch!" I thought; "You have a heart and nerves the same as your brother men! Why should you be anxious to conceal them? Your pride cannot blind God! You tempt him to wring them, till he forces a cry of humiliation."

"Quietly as a lamb!" I answered, aloud. "She drew a sigh, and stretched herself, like a child reviving, and sinking again to sleep; and five minutes after I felt one little pulse at her heart, and nothing more!"

"And – did she ever mention me?" he asked, hesitating, as if he dreaded the answer to his question would introduce details that he could not bear to hear.

"Her senses never returned: she recognised nobody from the time you left her," I said. "She lies with a sweet smile on her face; and her latest ideas wandered back to pleasant early days. Her life closed in a gentle dream – may she wake as kindly in the other world!"

"May she wake in torment!" he cried, with frightful vehemence, stamping his foot, and groaning in a sudden paroxysm of ungovernable passion. "Why, she's a liar to the end! Where is she? Not *there* – not in heaven – not perished – where? Oh! You said you cared nothing for my sufferings! And I pray one prayer – I repeat it till my tongue stiffens – Catherine Earnshaw, may you not rest as long as I am living; you said I killed you – haunt me, then! The murdered *do* haunt their murderers, I believe. I know that ghosts *have* wandered on earth. Be with me always – take any form – drive me mad! Only *do* not leave me in this abyss, where I cannot find you! Oh, God! It is unutterable! I *cannot* live without my life! I *cannot* live without my soul!"

He dashed his head against the knotted trunk; and, lifting up his eyes, howled, not like a man, but like a savage beast being goaded to death with knives and spears. I observed several splashes of blood about the bark of the tree, and his hand and forehead were both stained; probably the scene I witnessed was a repetition of others acted during the night. It hardly moved my compassion – it appalled me: still, I felt reluctant to quit him so. But the moment he recollected himself enough to notice me watching, he thundered a command for me to go, and I obeyed. He was beyond my skill to quiet or console!

Mrs. Linton's funeral was appointed to take place on the Friday following her decease; and till then her coffin remained uncovered, and strewn with flowers and scented leaves, in the great drawing-room. Linton spent his days and nights there, a sleepless guardian; and – a circumstance concealed from all but me – Heathcliff spent his nights, at least, outside, equally a stranger to repose. I held no communication with him: still, I was conscious of his design to enter, if he could; and on the Tuesday, a little after dark, when my master, from sheer fatigue, had been compelled to retire a couple of hours, I went and opened one of the windows; moved by his perseverance to give him a chance of bestowing on the faded image of his idol one final adieu. He did not omit to avail himself of the opportunity, cautiously and briefly; too cautiously to betray his presence by the slightest noise. Indeed, I shouldn't have discovered that he had been there, except for the disarrangement of the drapery about the corpse's face, and for observing on the floor a curl of light hair, fastened with a silver thread; which, on examination, I ascertained to have been taken from a locket hung round Catherine's neck. Heathcliff had opened the trinket and cast out its contents, replacing them by a black lock of his own. I twisted the two, and enclosed them together.

Mr. Earnshaw was, of course, invited to attend the remains of his sister to the grave; he sent no excuse, but he never came; so that, besides her husband, the mourners were wholly composed of tenants and servants. Isabella was not asked.

The place of Catherine's interment, to the surprise of the villagers, was neither in the chapel under the carved monument of the Lintons, nor yet by the tombs of her own relations, outside. It was dug on a green slope in a corner of the kirk-yard, where the wall is so low that heath and bilberry-plants have climbed over it from the moor; and peat-mould almost buries it. Her husband lies in the same spot now; and they have each a simple headstone above, and a plain grey block at their feet, to mark the graves.

Chapter Seventeen

THAT FRIDAY made the last of our fine days for a month. In the evening the weather broke: the wind shifted from south to north-east, and brought rain first, and then sleet and snow. On the morrow one could hardly imagine that there had been three weeks of summer: the primroses and crocuses were hidden under wintry drifts; the larks were silent, the young leaves of the early trees smitten and blackened. And dreary, and chill, and dismal, that morrow did creep over! My master kept his room; I took possession of the lonely parlour, converting it into a nursery: and there I was, sitting with the moaning doll of a child laid on my knee; rocking it to and fro, and watching, meanwhile, the still driving flakes build up the uncurtained window, when the door opened, and some person entered, out of breath and laughing! My anger was greater than my astonishment for a minute. I supposed it one of the maids, and I cried – "Have done! How dare you show your giddiness here; what would Mr. Linton say if he heard you?"

"Excuse me!" answered a familiar voice; "but I know Edgar is in bed, and I cannot stop myself."

With that the speaker came forward to the fire, panting and holding her hand to her side.

"I have run the whole way from Wuthering Heights!" she continued, after a pause; "except where I've flown. I couldn't count the number of falls I've had. Oh, I'm aching all over! Don't be alarmed! There shall be an explanation as soon as I can give it; only just have the goodness to step out and order the carriage to take me on to Gimmerton, and tell a servant to seek up a few clothes in my wardrobe."

The intruder was Mrs. Heathcliff. She certainly seemed in no laughing predicament: her hair streamed on her shoulders, dripping with snow and water; she was dressed in the girlish dress she commonly wore, befitting her age more than her position: a low frock with short sleeves, and nothing on either head or neck. The frock was of light silk, and clung to her with wet, and her feet were protected merely by thin slippers; add to this a deep cut under one ear, which only the cold prevented from bleeding profusely, a white face scratched and bruised, and a frame hardly able to support itself through fatigue; and you may fancy my first fright was not much allayed when I had had leisure to examine her.

"My dear young lady," I exclaimed, "I'll stir nowhere, and hear nothing, till you have removed every article of your clothes, and put on dry things; and certainly you shall not go to Gimmerton tonight, so it is needless to order the carriage."

"Certainly I shall," she said; "walking or riding: yet I've no objection to dress myself decently. And – ah, see how it flows down my neck now! The fire does make it smart."

She insisted on my fulfilling her directions, before she would let me touch her; and not till after the coachman had been instructed to get ready, and a maid set to pack up some necessary attire, did I obtain her consent for binding the wound and helping to change her garments.

"Now, Ellen," she said, when my task was finished and she was seated in an easy-chair on the hearth, with a cup of tea before her, "you sit down opposite me, and put poor Catherine's baby away: I don't like to see it! You mustn't think I care little for Catherine, because I behaved so foolishly on entering: I've cried, too, bitterly – yes, more than anyone else has reason to cry. We parted unreconciled, you remember, and I shan't forgive myself. But, for all that, I was not going to sympathise with him – the brute beast! Oh, give me the poker! This is the last thing of his I have about me:" she slipped the gold ring from her third finger, and threw it on the floor. "I'll smash it!" she continued, striking it with childish spite, "And then I'll burn it!" and she took and dropped the misused article among the coals. "There! He shall buy another, if he gets me back again. He'd be capable of coming to seek me, to tease Edgar. I dare not stay, lest that notion should possess his wicked head! And besides, Edgar has not been kind, has he? And I won't come suing for his assistance; nor will I bring him into more trouble. Necessity compelled me to seek shelter here; though, if I had not learned he was out of the way, I'd have halted at the kitchen, washed my face, warmed myself, got you to bring what I wanted, and departed again to anywhere out of the reach of my accursed – of that incarnate goblin! Ah, he was in such a fury! If he had caught me! It's a pity Earnshaw is not his match in strength: I wouldn't have run till I'd seen him all but demolished, had Hindley been able to do it!"

"Well, don't talk so fast, Miss!" I interrupted; "You'll disorder the handkerchief I have tied round your face, and make the cut bleed again. Drink your tea, and take breath, and give over laughing: laughter is sadly out of place under this roof, and in your condition!"

"An undeniable truth," she replied. "Listen to that child! It maintains a constant wail – send it out of my hearing for an hour; I shan't stay any longer."

I rang the bell, and committed it to a servant's care; and then I inquired what had urged her to escape from Wuthering Heights in such an unlikely plight, and where she meant to go, as she refused remaining with us.

"I ought, and I wished to remain," answered she, "to cheer Edgar and take care of the baby, for two things, and because the Grange is my right home. But I tell you he wouldn't let me! Do you think he could bear to see me grow fat and merry – could bear to think that we were tranquil, and not resolve on poisoning our comfort? Now, I have the satisfaction of being sure that he detests me, to the point of its annoying him seriously to have me within ear-shot or eyesight: I notice, when I enter his presence, the muscles of his countenance are involuntarily distorted into an expression of hatred; partly arising from his knowledge of the good causes I have to feel that sentiment for him, and partly from original aversion. It is strong enough to make me feel pretty certain that he would not chase me over England, supposing I contrived a clear escape; and therefore I must get quite away. I've recovered from my first desire to be killed by him: I'd rather he'd kill himself! He has extinguished my love effectually, and so I'm at my ease. I can recollect yet how I loved him; and can dimly imagine that I could still be loving him, if – no, no! Even if he had doted on me, the devilish nature would have revealed its existence somehow. Catherine had an awfully perverted taste to esteem him so dearly, knowing him so well. Monster! Would that he could be blotted out of creation, and out of my memory!"

"Hush, hush! He's a human being," I said. "Be more charitable: there are worse men than he is yet!"

"He's not a human being," she retorted; "and he has no claim on my charity. I gave him my heart, and he took and pinched it to death, and flung it back to me. People feel with their hearts, Ellen: and since he has destroyed mine, I have not power to feel for him: and I would not, though he groaned from this to his dying day, and wept tears of blood for Catherine! No, indeed, indeed, I wouldn't!" And here Isabella began to cry; but, immediately dashing the water from her lashes, she recommenced. "You asked, what has driven me to flight at last? I was compelled to attempt it, because I had succeeded in rousing his rage a pitch above his malignity. Pulling out the nerves with red hot pincers requires more coolness than knocking on the head. He was worked up to forget the fiendish prudence he boasted of, and proceeded to murderous violence. I experienced pleasure in being able to exasperate him: the sense of pleasure woke my instinct of self-preservation, so I fairly broke free; and if ever I come into his hands again he is welcome to a signal revenge.

"Yesterday, you know, Mr. Earnshaw should have been at the funeral. He kept himself sober for the purpose – tolerably sober: not going to bed mad at six o'clock and getting up drunk at twelve. Consequently, he rose, in suicidal low spirits, as fit for the church as for a dance; and instead, he sat down by the fire and swallowed gin or brandy by tumblerfuls.

"Heathcliff – I shudder to name him! Has been a stranger in the house from last Sunday till today. Whether the angels have fed him, or his kin beneath, I cannot tell; but he has not eaten a meal with us for nearly a week. He has just come home at dawn, and gone upstairs to his chamber; locking himself in – as if anybody dreamt of coveting his company! There he has continued, praying like a

Methodist: only the deity he implored is senseless dust and ashes; and God, when addressed, was curiously confounded with his own black father! After concluding these precious orisons – and they lasted generally till he grew hoarse and his voice was strangled in his throat – he would be off again; always straight down to the Grange! I wonder Edgar did not send for a constable, and give him into custody! For me, grieved as I was about Catherine, it was impossible to avoid regarding this season of deliverance from degrading oppression as a holiday.

"I recovered spirits sufficient to bear Joseph's eternal lectures without weeping, and to move up and down the house less with the foot of a frightened thief than formerly. You wouldn't think that I should cry at anything Joseph could say; but he and Hareton are detestable companions. I'd rather sit with Hindley, and hear his awful talk, than with 't' little maister' and his staunch supporter, that odious old man! When Heathcliff is in, I'm often obliged to seek the kitchen and their society, or starve among the damp uninhabited chambers; when he is not, as was the case this week, I establish a table and chair at one corner of the house fire, and never mind how Mr. Earnshaw may occupy himself; and he does not interfere with my arrangements. He is quieter now than he used to be, if no one provokes him: more sullen and depressed, and less furious. Joseph affirms he's sure he's an altered man: that the Lord has touched his heart, and he is saved 'so as by fire'. I'm puzzled to detect signs of the favourable change: but it is not my business.

"Yester-evening I sat in my nook reading some old books till late on towards twelve. It seemed so dismal to go upstairs, with the wild snow blowing outside, and my thoughts continually reverting to the kirk-yard and the new-made grave! I dared hardly lift my eyes from the page before me, that melancholy scene so instantly usurped its place. Hindley sat opposite, his head leant on his hand; perhaps meditating on the same subject. He had ceased drinking at a point below irrationality, and had neither stirred nor spoken during two or three hours. There was no sound through the house but the moaning wind, which shook the windows every now and then, the faint crackling of the coals, and the click of my snuffers as I removed at intervals the long wick of the candle. Hareton and Joseph were probably fast asleep in bed. It was very, very sad: and while I read I sighed, for it seemed as if all joy had vanished from the world, never to be restored.

"The doleful silence was broken at length by the sound of the kitchen latch: Heathcliff had returned from his watch earlier than usual; owing, I suppose, to the sudden storm. That entrance was fastened, and we heard him coming round to get in by the other. I rose with an irrepressible expression of what I felt on my lips, which induced my companion, who had been staring towards the door, to turn and look at me.

"'I'll keep him out five minutes,' he exclaimed. 'You won't object?'

"'No, you may keep him out the whole night for me,' I answered. 'Do! Put the key in the lock, and draw the bolts.'

"Earnshaw accomplished this ere his guest reached the front; he then came and brought his chair to the other side of my table, leaning over it, and searching in my eyes for a sympathy with the burning hate that gleamed from his: as he both looked and felt like an assassin, he couldn't exactly find that; but he discovered enough to encourage him to speak.

"'You, and I,' he said, 'have each a great debt to settle with the man out yonder! If we were neither of us cowards, we might combine to discharge it. Are you as soft as your brother? Are you willing to endure to the last, and not once attempt a repayment?'

"'I'm weary of enduring now,' I replied; 'and I'd be glad of a retaliation that wouldn't recoil on myself; but treachery and violence are spears pointed at both ends; they wound those who resort to them worse than their enemies.'

"'Treachery and violence are a just return for treachery and violence!' cried Hindley. 'Mrs. Heathcliff, I'll ask you to do nothing; but sit still and be dumb. Tell me now, can you? I'm sure you would have as much pleasure as I in witnessing the conclusion of the fiend's existence; he'll be *your* death unless you overreach him; and he'll be *my* ruin. Damn the hellish villain! He knocks at the door as if he were master here already! Promise to hold your tongue, and before that clock strikes – it wants three minutes of one – you're a free woman!'

"He took the implements which I described to you in my letter from his breast, and would have turned down the candle. I snatched it away, however, and seized his arm.

"'I'll not hold my tongue!' I said; 'you mustn't touch him. Let the door remain shut, and be quiet!'

"'No! I've formed my resolution, and by God I'll execute it!' cried the desperate being. 'I'll do you a kindness in spite of yourself, and Hareton justice! And you needn't trouble your head to screen me; Catherine is gone. Nobody alive would regret me, or be ashamed, though I cut my throat this minute – and it's time to make an end!'

"I might as well have struggled with a bear, or reasoned with a lunatic. The only resource left me was to run to a lattice and warn his intended victim of the fate which awaited him.

"'You'd better seek shelter somewhere else tonight!' I exclaimed, in rather a triumphant tone. 'Mr. Earnshaw has a mind to shoot you, if you persist in endeavouring to enter.'

"'You'd better open the door, you –' he answered, addressing me by some elegant term that I don't care to repeat.

"'I shall not meddle in the matter,' I retorted again. 'Come in and get shot, if you please. I've done my duty.'

"With that I shut the window and returned to my place by the fire; having too small a stock of hypocrisy at my command to pretend any anxiety for the danger that menaced him. Earnshaw swore passionately at me: affirming that I loved the villain yet; and calling me all sorts of names for the base spirit I evinced. And I, in my secret heart (and conscience never reproached me), thought what a blessing it would be for *him* should Heathcliff put him out of misery; and what a blessing for *me* should he send Heathcliff to his right abode! As I sat nursing these reflections, the casement behind me was banged on to the floor by a blow from the latter individual, and his black countenance looked blightingly through. The stanchions stood too close to suffer his shoulders to follow, and I smiled, exulting in my fancied security. His hair and clothes were whitened with snow, and his sharp cannibal teeth, revealed by cold and wrath, gleamed through the dark.

"'Isabella, let me in, or I'll make you repent!' he 'girned', as Joseph calls it.

"'I cannot commit murder,' I replied. 'Mr. Hindley stands sentinel with a knife and loaded pistol.'

"'Let me in by the kitchen door,' he said.

"'Hindley will be there before me,' I answered: 'and that's a poor love of yours that cannot bear a shower of snow! We were left at peace in our beds as long as the summer moon shone, but the moment a blast of winter returns, you must run for shelter! Heathcliff, if I were you, I'd go stretch myself over her grave and die like a faithful dog. The world is surely not worth living in now, is it? You had distinctly impressed on me the idea that Catherine was the whole joy of your life: I can't imagine how you think of surviving her loss.'

"'He's there, is he?' exclaimed my companion, rushing to the gap. 'If I can get my arm out I can hit him!'

"I'm afraid, Ellen, you'll set me down as really wicked; but you don't know all, so don't judge. I wouldn't have aided or abetted an attempt on even *his* life for anything. Wish that he were dead, I must; and therefore I was fearfully disappointed, and unnerved by terror for the consequences of my taunting speech, when he flung himself on Earnshaw's weapon and wrenched it from his grasp.

"The charge exploded, and the knife, in springing back, closed into its owner's wrist. Heathcliff pulled it away by main force, slitting up the flesh as it passed on, and thrust it dripping into his pocket. He then took a stone, struck down the division between two windows, and sprang in. His adversary had fallen senseless with excessive pain and the flow of blood, that gushed from an artery or a large vein. The ruffian kicked and trampled on him, and dashed his head repeatedly against the flags, holding me with one hand, meantime, to prevent me summoning Joseph. He exerted preterhuman self-denial in abstaining from finishing him completely; but getting out of breath, he finally desisted, and dragged the apparently inanimate body on to the settle. There he tore off the sleeve of Earnshaw's coat, and bound up the wound with brutal roughness; spitting and cursing during the operation as energetically as he had kicked before. Being at liberty, I lost no time in seeking the old servant; who, having gathered by degrees the purport of my hasty tale, hurried below, gasping, as he descended the steps two at once.

"'What is ther to do, now? What is ther to do, now?'

"'There's this to do,' thundered Heathcliff, 'that your master's mad; and should he last another month, I'll have him to an asylum. And how the devil did you come to fasten me out, you toothless hound? Don't stand muttering and mumbling there. Come, I'm not going to nurse him. Wash that stuff away; and mind the sparks of your candle – it is more than half brandy!'

"'And so ye've been murthering on him?' exclaimed Joseph, lifting his hands and eyes in horror. 'If iver I seed a seeght loike this! May the Lord –'

"Heathcliff gave him a push on to his knees in the middle of the blood, and flung a towel to him; but instead of proceeding to dry it up, he joined his hands and began a prayer, which excited my laughter from its odd phraseology. I was in the condition of mind to be shocked at nothing: in fact, I was as reckless as some malefactors show themselves at the foot of the gallows.

"'Oh, I forgot you,' said the tyrant. 'You shall do that. Down with you. And you conspire with him against me, do you, viper? There, that is work fit for you!'

"He shook me till my teeth rattled, and pitched me beside Joseph, who steadily concluded his supplications, and then rose, vowing he would set off for the Grange directly. Mr. Linton was a magistrate, and though he had fifty wives dead, he should inquire into this. He was so obstinate in his resolution, that Heathcliff deemed it expedient to compel from my lips a recapitulation of what had taken place; standing over me, heaving with malevolence, as I reluctantly delivered the account in answer to his questions. It required a great deal of labour to satisfy the old man that Heathcliff was not the aggressor; especially with my hardly-wrung replies. However, Mr. Earnshaw soon convinced him that he was alive still; Joseph hastened to administer a dose of spirits, and by their succour his master presently regained motion and consciousness. Heathcliff, aware that his opponent was ignorant of the treatment received while insensible, called him deliriously intoxicated; and said he should not notice his atrocious conduct further, but advised him to get to bed. To my joy, he left us, after giving this judicious counsel, and Hindley stretched himself on the hearthstone. I departed to my own room, marvelling that I had escaped so easily.

"This morning, when I came down, about half an hour before noon, Mr. Earnshaw was sitting by the fire, deadly sick; his evil genius, almost as gaunt and ghastly, leant against the chimney. Neither appeared inclined to dine, and, having waited till all was cold on the table, I commenced alone. Nothing hindered me from eating heartily, and I experienced a certain sense of satisfaction and superiority, as, at intervals, I cast a look towards my silent companions, and felt the comfort of a quiet conscience within me. After I had done, I ventured on the unusual liberty of drawing near the fire, going round Earnshaw's seat, and kneeling in the corner beside him.

"Heathcliff did not glance my way, and I gazed up, and contemplated his features almost as confidently as if they had been turned to stone. His forehead, that I once thought so manly, and that I now think so diabolical, was shaded with a heavy cloud; his basilisk eyes were nearly quenched by sleeplessness, and weeping, perhaps, for the lashes were wet then: his lips devoid of their ferocious sneer, and sealed in an expression of unspeakable sadness. Had it been another, I would have covered my face in the presence of such grief. In *his* case, I was gratified; and, ignoble as it seems to insult a fallen enemy, I couldn't miss this chance of sticking in a dart: his weakness was the only time when I could taste the delight of paying wrong for wrong."

"Fie, fie, Miss!" I interrupted. "One might suppose you had never opened a Bible in your life. If God afflict your enemies, surely that ought to suffice you. It is both mean and presumptuous to add your torture to his!"

"In general I'll allow that it would be, Ellen," she continued; "but what misery laid on Heathcliff could content me, unless I have a hand in it? I'd rather he suffered less, if I might cause his sufferings and he might *know* that I was the cause. Oh, I owe him so much. On only one condition can I hope to forgive him. It is, if I may take an eye for an eye, a tooth for a tooth; for every wrench of agony return a wrench: reduce him to my level. As he was the first to injure, make him the first to implore pardon; and then – why then, Ellen, I might show you some generosity. But it is utterly impossible I can ever be revenged, and therefore I cannot forgive him. Hindley wanted some water, and I handed him a glass, and asked him how he was.

"'Not as ill as I wish,' he replied. 'But leaving out my arm, every inch of me is as sore as if I had been fighting with a legion of imps!'

"'Yes, no wonder,' was my next remark. 'Catherine used to boast that she stood between you and bodily harm: she meant that certain persons would not hurt you for fear of offending her. It's well people don't *really* rise from their grave, or, last night, she might have witnessed a repulsive scene! Are not you bruised, and cut over your chest and shoulders?'

"'I can't say,' he answered, 'but what do you mean? Did he dare to strike me when I was down?'

"'He trampled on and kicked you, and dashed you on the ground,' I whispered. 'And his mouth watered to tear you with his teeth; because he's only half man: not so much, and the rest fiend.'

"Mr. Earnshaw looked up, like me, to the countenance of our mutual foe; who, absorbed in his anguish, seemed insensible to anything around him: the longer he stood, the plainer his reflections revealed their blackness through his features.

"'Oh, if God would but give me strength to strangle him in my last agony, I'd go to hell with joy,' groaned the impatient man, writhing to rise, and sinking back in despair, convinced of his inadequacy for the struggle.

"'Nay, it's enough that he has murdered one of you,' I observed aloud. 'At the Grange, everyone knows your sister would have been living now had it not been for Mr. Heathcliff. After all, it is preferable to be hated than loved by him. When I recollect how happy we were – how happy Catherine was before he came – I'm fit to curse the day.'

"Most likely, Heathcliff noticed more the truth of what was said, than the spirit of the person who said it. His attention was roused, I saw, for his eyes rained down tears among the ashes, and he drew his breath in suffocating sighs. I stared full at him, and laughed scornfully. The clouded windows of hell flashed a moment towards me; the fiend which usually looked out, however, was so dimmed and drowned that I did not fear to hazard another sound of derision.

"'Get up, and begone out of my sight,' said the mourner.

"I guessed he uttered those words, at least, though his voice was hardly intelligible.

"'I beg your pardon,' I replied. 'But I loved Catherine too; and her brother requires attendance, which, for her sake, I shall supply. Now, that she's dead, I see her in Hindley: Hindley has exactly her eyes, if you had not tried to gouge them out, and made them black and red; and her –'

"'Get up, wretched idiot, before I stamp you to death!' he cried, making a movement that caused me to make one also.

"'But then,' I continued, holding myself ready to flee, 'if poor Catherine had trusted you, and assumed the ridiculous, contemptible, degrading title of Mrs. Heathcliff, she would soon have presented a similar picture! *She* wouldn't have borne your abominable behaviour quietly: her detestation and disgust must have found voice.'

"The back of the settle and Earnshaw's person interposed between me and him; so instead of endeavouring to reach me, he snatched a dinner-knife from the table and flung it at my head. It struck beneath my ear, and stopped the sentence I was uttering; but, pulling it out, I sprang to the door and delivered another; which I hope went a little deeper than his missile. The last glimpse I caught of him was a furious rush on his part, checked by the embrace of his host; and both fell locked together on the hearth. In my flight through the kitchen I bid Joseph speed to his master; I knocked over Hareton, who was hanging a litter of puppies from a chair-back in the doorway; and, blessed as a soul escaped from purgatory, I bounded, leaped, and flew down the steep road; then, quitting its windings, shot direct across the moor, rolling over banks, and wading through marshes: precipitating myself, in fact, towards the beacon-light of the Grange. And far rather would I be condemned to a perpetual dwelling in the infernal regions than, even for one night, abide beneath the roof of Wuthering Heights again."

Isabella ceased speaking, and took a drink of tea; then she rose, and bidding me put on her bonnet, and a great shawl I had brought, and turning a deaf ear to my entreaties for her to remain another hour, she stepped on to a chair, kissed Edgar's and Catherine's portraits, bestowed a similar salute on me, and descended to the carriage, accompanied by Fanny, who yelped wild with joy at recovering her mistress. She was driven away, never to revisit this neighbourhood: but a regular correspondence was established between her and my master when things were more settled. I believe her new abode was in the south, near London; there she had a son born a few months subsequent to her escape. He was christened Linton, and, from the first, she reported him to be an ailing, peevish creature.

Mr. Heathcliff, meeting me one day in the village, inquired where she lived. I refused to tell. He remarked that it was not of any moment, only she must beware of coming to her brother: she should not be with him, if he had to keep her himself. Though I would give no information, he discovered, through some of the other servants, both her place of residence and the existence of the child. Still, he didn't molest her: for which forbearance she might thank his aversion, I suppose. He often asked about the infant, when he saw me; and on hearing its name, smiled grimly, and observed: "They wish me to hate it too, do they?"

"I don't think they wish you to know anything about it," I answered.

"But I'll have it," he said, "when I want it. They may reckon on that!"

Fortunately its mother died before the time arrived; some thirteen years after the decease of Catherine, when Linton was twelve, or a little more.

On the day succeeding Isabella's unexpected visit I had no opportunity of speaking to my master: he shunned conversation, and was fit for discussing nothing. When I could get him to listen, I saw it pleased him that his sister had left her husband; whom he abhorred with an intensity which the mildness of his nature would scarcely seem to allow. So deep and sensitive was his aversion, that he refrained from going anywhere where he was likely to see or hear of Heathcliff. Grief, and that together, transformed him into a complete hermit: he threw up his office of magistrate, ceased even to attend church, avoided the village on all occasions, and spent a life of entire seclusion within the limits of his park and grounds; only varied by solitary rambles on the moors, and visits to the grave of his wife, mostly at evening, or early morning before other wanderers were abroad. But he was too good to be thoroughly unhappy long. *He* didn't pray for Catherine's soul to haunt him. Time brought resignation, and a melancholy sweeter than common joy. He recalled her memory with ardent, tender love, and hopeful aspiring to the better world; where he doubted not she was gone.

And he had earthly consolation and affections also. For a few days, I said, he seemed regardless of the puny successor to the departed: that coldness melted as fast as snow in April, and ere the tiny thing could stammer a word or totter a step it wielded a despot's sceptre in his heart. It was named Catherine; but he never called it the name in full, as he had never called the first Catherine short: probably because Heathcliff had a habit of doing so. The little one was always Cathy: it formed to him a distinction from the mother, and yet a connection with her; and his attachment sprang from its relation to her, far more than from its being his own.

I used to draw a comparison between him and Hindley Earnshaw, and perplex myself to explain satisfactorily why their conduct was so opposite in similar circumstances. They had both been fond husbands, and were both attached to their children; and I could not see how they shouldn't both have taken the same road, for good or evil. But, I thought in my mind, Hindley, with apparently the stronger head, has shown himself sadly the worse and the weaker man. When his ship struck, the captain abandoned his post; and the crew, instead of trying to save her, rushed into riot and confusion, leaving no hope for their luckless vessel. Linton, on the contrary, displayed the true courage of a loyal and faithful soul: he trusted God; and God comforted him. One hoped, and the other despaired: they chose their own lots, and were righteously doomed to endure them. But you'll not want to hear my moralising, Mr. Lockwood; you'll judge, as well as I can, all these things: at least, you'll think you will, and that's the same. The end of Earnshaw was what might have been expected; it followed fast on his sister's: there were scarcely six months between them. We, at the Grange, never got a very succinct account of his state preceding it; all that I did learn was on occasion of going to aid in the preparations for the funeral. Mr. Kenneth came to announce the event to my master.

"Well, Nelly," said he, riding into the yard one morning, too early not to alarm me with an instant presentiment of bad news, "it's yours and my turn to go into mourning at present. Who's given us the slip now, do you think?"

"Who?" I asked in a flurry.

"Why, guess!" he returned, dismounting, and slinging his bridle on a hook by the door. "And nip up the corner of your apron: I'm certain you'll need it."

"Not Mr. Heathcliff, surely?" I exclaimed.

"What! Would you have tears for him?" said the doctor. "No, Heathcliff's a tough young fellow: he looks blooming today. I've just seen him. He's rapidly regaining flesh since he lost his better half."

"Who is it, then, Mr. Kenneth?" I repeated impatiently.

"Hindley Earnshaw! Your old friend Hindley," he replied, "and my wicked gossip: though he's been too wild for me this long while. There! I said we should draw water. But cheer up! He died true to his character: drunk as a lord. Poor lad! I'm sorry, too. One can't help missing an old companion: though he had the worst tricks with him that ever man imagined, and has done me many a rascally turn. He's barely twenty-seven, it seems; that's your own age: who would have thought you were born in one year?"

I confess this blow was greater to me than the shock of Mrs. Linton's death: ancient associations lingered round my heart; I sat down in the porch and wept as for a blood relation, desiring Mr. Kenneth to get another servant to introduce him to the master. I could not hinder myself from pondering on the question – "Had he had fair play?" Whatever I did, that idea would bother me: it was so tiresomely pertinacious that I resolved on requesting leave to go to Wuthering Heights, and assist in the last duties to the dead. Mr. Linton was extremely reluctant to consent, but I pleaded eloquently for the friendless condition in which he lay; and I said my old master and foster-brother had a claim on my services as strong as his own. Besides, I reminded him that the child Hareton was his wife's nephew, and, in the absence of nearer kin, he ought to act as its guardian; and he ought to and must inquire how the property was left, and look over the concerns of his brother-in-law. He was unfit for attending to such matters then, but he bid me speak to his lawyer; and at length permitted me to go. His lawyer had been Earnshaw's also: I called at the village, and asked him to accompany me. He shook his head, and advised that Heathcliff should be let alone; affirming, if the truth were known, Hareton would be found little else than a beggar.

"His father died in debt," he said; "the whole property is mortgaged, and the sole chance for the natural heir is to allow him an opportunity of creating some interest in the creditor's heart, that he may be inclined to deal leniently towards him."

When I reached the Heights, I explained that I had come to see everything carried on decently; and Joseph, who appeared in sufficient distress, expressed satisfaction at my presence. Mr. Heathcliff said he did not perceive that I was wanted; but I might stay and order the arrangements for the funeral, if I chose.

"Correctly," he remarked, "that fool's body should be buried at the cross-roads, without ceremony of any kind. I happened to leave him ten minutes yesterday afternoon, and in that interval he fastened the two doors of the house against me, and he has spent the night in drinking himself to death deliberately! We broke in this morning, for we heard him sporting like a horse; and there he was, laid over the settle: flaying and scalping would not have wakened him. I sent for Kenneth, and he came; but not till the beast had changed into carrion: he was both dead and cold, and stark; and so you'll allow it was useless making more stir about him!"

The old servant confirmed this statement, but muttered:

"I'd rayther he'd goan hisseln for t' doctor! I sud ha,' taen tent o' t' maister better nor him – and he warn't deead when I left, naught o' t' soart!"

I insisted on the funeral being respectable. Mr. Heathcliff said I might have my own way there too: only, he desired me to remember that the money for the whole affair came out of his pocket. He maintained a hard, careless deportment, indicative of neither joy nor sorrow: if anything, it expressed a flinty gratification at a piece of difficult work successfully executed. I observed once, indeed, something like exultation in his aspect: it was just when the people were bearing the coffin from the house. He had the hypocrisy to represent a mourner: and previous to following with Hareton, he lifted the unfortunate child on to the table and muttered, with peculiar gusto, "Now, my bonny lad, you are *mine*! And we'll see if one tree won't grow as crooked as another, with the same wind to twist it!" The unsuspecting thing was pleased at this speech: he played with Heathcliff's whiskers, and stroked his cheek; but I divined its meaning, and observed tartly, "That boy must go back with me to Thrushcross Grange, sir. There is nothing in the world less yours than he is!"

"Does Linton say so?" he demanded.

"Of course – he has ordered me to take him," I replied.

"Well," said the scoundrel, "we'll not argue the subject now: but I have a fancy to try my hand at rearing a young one; so intimate to your master that I must supply the place of this with my own, if he attempt to remove it. I don't engage to let Hareton go undisputed; but I'll be pretty sure to make the other come! Remember to tell him."

This hint was enough to bind our hands. I repeated its substance on my return; and Edgar Linton, little interested at the commencement, spoke no more of interfering. I'm not aware that he could have done it to any purpose, had he been ever so willing.

The guest was now the master of Wuthering Heights: he held firm possession, and proved to the attorney – who, in his turn, proved it to Mr. Linton – that Earnshaw had mortgaged every yard of land he owned for cash to supply his mania for gaming; and he, Heathcliff, was the mortgagee. In that manner Hareton, who should now be the first gentleman in the neighbourhood, was reduced to a state of complete dependence on his father's inveterate enemy; and lives in his own house as a servant, deprived of the advantage of wages: quite unable to right himself, because of his friendlessness, and his ignorance that he has been wronged.

Chapter Eighteen

THE TWELVE YEARS, continued Mrs. Dean, following that dismal period were the happiest of my life: my greatest troubles in their passage rose from our little lady's trifling illnesses, which she had to experience in common with all children, rich and poor. For the rest, after the first six months, she grew like a larch, and could walk and talk too, in her own way, before the heath blossomed a second time over Mrs. Linton's dust. She was the most winning thing that ever brought sunshine into a desolate house: a real beauty in face, with the Earnshaws' handsome dark eyes, but the Lintons' fair skin and small features, and yellow curling hair. Her spirit was high, though not rough, and qualified by a heart sensitive and lively to excess in its affections. That capacity for intense attachments reminded me of her mother: still she did not resemble her: for she could be soft and mild as a dove, and she had a gentle voice and pensive expression: her anger was never furious; her love never fierce: it was deep and tender. However, it must be acknowledged, she had faults to foil her gifts. A propensity to be saucy was one; and a perverse will, that indulged children invariably acquire, whether they be good tempered or cross. If a servant chanced to vex her, it was always – "I shall tell papa!" And if he reproved her, even by a look, you would have thought it a heart-breaking business: I don't believe he ever did speak a harsh word to her. He took her education entirely on himself, and made it an amusement. Fortunately, curiosity and a quick intellect made her an apt scholar: she learned rapidly and eagerly, and did honour to his teaching.

Till she reached the age of thirteen she had not once been beyond the range of the park by herself. Mr. Linton would take her with him a mile or so outside, on rare occasions; but he trusted her to no one else. Gimmerton was an unsubstantial name in her ears; the chapel, the only building she had approached or entered, except her own home. Wuthering Heights and Mr. Heathcliff did not exist for her: she was a perfect recluse; and, apparently, perfectly contented. Sometimes, indeed, while surveying the country from her nursery window, she would observe –

"Ellen, how long will it be before I can walk to the top of those hills? I wonder what lies on the other side – is it the sea?"

"No, Miss Cathy," I would answer; "it is hills again, just like these."

"And what are those golden rocks like when you stand under them?" she once asked.

The abrupt descent of Penistone Crags particularly attracted her notice; especially when the setting sun shone on it and the topmost heights, and the whole extent of landscape besides lay in shadow. I explained that they were bare masses of stone, with hardly enough earth in their clefts to nourish a stunted tree.

"And why are they bright so long after it is evening here?" she pursued.

"Because they are a great deal higher up than we are," replied I; "you could not climb them, they are too high and steep. In winter the frost is always there before it comes to us; and deep into summer I have found snow under that black hollow on the north-east side!"

"Oh, you have been on them!" she cried gleefully. "Then I can go, too, when I am a woman. Has papa been, Ellen?"

"Papa would tell you, Miss," I answered, hastily, "that they are not worth the trouble of visiting. The moors, where you ramble with him, are much nicer; and Thrushcross Park is the finest place in the world."

"But I know the park, and I don't know those," she murmured to herself. "And I should delight to look round me from the brow of that tallest point: my little pony Minny shall take me some time."

One of the maids mentioning the Fairy Cave, quite turned her head with a desire to fulfil this project: she teased Mr. Linton about it; and he promised she should have the journey when she got older. But Miss Catherine measured her age by months, and, "Now, am I old enough to go to Penistone Crags?" was the constant question in her mouth. The road thither wound close by Wuthering Heights. Edgar had not the heart to pass it; so she received as constantly the answer, "Not yet, love: not yet."

I said Mrs. Heathcliff lived above a dozen years after quitting her husband. Her family were of a delicate constitution: she and Edgar both lacked the ruddy health that you will generally meet in these parts. What her last illness was, I am not certain: I conjecture, they died of the same thing, a kind of fever, slow at its commencement, but incurable, and rapidly consuming life towards the close. She wrote to inform her brother of the probable conclusion of a four-months' indisposition under which she had suffered, and entreated him to come to her, if possible; for she had much to settle, and she wished to bid him adieu, and deliver Linton safely into his hands. Her hope was that Linton might be left with him, as he had been with her: his father, she would fain convince herself, had no desire to assume the burden of his maintenance or education. My master hesitated not a moment in complying with her request: reluctant as he was to leave home at ordinary calls, he flew to answer this; commanding Catherine to my peculiar vigilance, in his absence, with reiterated orders that she must not wander out of the park, even under my escort he did not calculate on her going unaccompanied.

He was away three weeks. The first day or two my charge sat in a corner of the library, too sad for either reading or playing: in that quiet state she caused me little trouble; but it was succeeded by an interval of impatient, fretful weariness; and being too busy, and too old then, to run up and down amusing her, I hit on a method by which she might entertain herself. I used to send her on her travels round the grounds – now on foot, and now on a pony; indulging her with a patient audience of all her real and imaginary adventures when she returned.

The summer shone in full prime; and she took such a taste for this solitary rambling that she often contrived to remain out from breakfast till tea; and then the evenings were spent in recounting her fanciful tales. I did not fear her breaking bounds; because the gates were generally locked, and I thought she would scarcely venture forth alone, if they had stood wide open. Unluckily, my confidence proved misplaced. Catherine came to me, one morning, at eight o'clock, and said she was that day an Arabian merchant, going to cross the Desert with his caravan; and I must give her plenty of provision for herself and beasts: a horse, and three camels, personated by a large hound and a couple of pointers. I got together good store of dainties, and slung them in a basket on one side of the saddle; and she sprang up as gay as a fairy, sheltered by her wide-brimmed hat and gauze veil from the July sun, and trotted off with a merry laugh, mocking my cautious counsel to avoid galloping, and come back early. The naughty thing never made her appearance at tea. One traveller, the hound, being an old dog and fond of its ease, returned; but neither Cathy, nor the pony, nor the two pointers were visible in any direction: I despatched emissaries down this path, and that path, and at last went wandering in search of her myself. There was a labourer working at a fence round a plantation, on the borders of the grounds. I inquired of him if he had seen our young lady.

"I saw her at morn," he replied: "she would have me to cut her a hazel switch, and then she leapt her Galloway over the hedge yonder, where it is lowest, and galloped out of sight."

You may guess how I felt at hearing this news. It struck me directly she must have started for Penistone Crags. "What will become of her?" I ejaculated, pushing through a gap which the man was repairing, and making straight to the high-road. I walked as if for a wager, mile after mile, till a turn brought me in view of the Heights; but no Catherine could I detect, far or near. The Crags lie about a mile and a half beyond Mr. Heathcliff's place, and that is four from the Grange, so I began to fear night would fall ere I could reach them. "And what if she should have slipped in clambering among them," I reflected, "and been killed, or broken some of her bones?" My suspense was truly painful; and, at first, it gave me delightful relief to observe, in hurrying by the farmhouse, Charlie, the fiercest of the pointers, lying under a window, with swelled head and bleeding ear. I opened the wicket and ran to the door, knocking vehemently for admittance. A woman whom I knew, and who formerly lived at Gimmerton, answered: she had been servant there since the death of Mr. Earnshaw.

"Ah," said she, "you are come a-seeking your little mistress! Don't be frightened. She's here safe: but I'm glad it isn't the master."

"He is not at home then, is he?" I panted, quite breathless with quick walking and alarm.

"No, no," she replied: "both he and Joseph are off, and I think they won't return this hour or more. Step in and rest you a bit."

I entered, and beheld my stray lamb seated on the hearth, rocking herself in a little chair that had been her mother's when a child. Her hat was hung against the wall, and she seemed perfectly at home, laughing and chattering, in the best spirits imaginable, to Hareton – now a great, strong lad of eighteen – who stared at her with considerable curiosity and astonishment: comprehending precious little of the fluent succession of remarks and questions which her tongue never ceased pouring forth.

"Very well, Miss!" I exclaimed, concealing my joy under an angry countenance. "This is your last ride, till papa comes back. I'll not trust you over the threshold again, you naughty, naughty girl!"

"Aha, Ellen!" she cried, gaily, jumping up and running to my side. "I shall have a pretty story to tell tonight; and so you've found me out. Have you ever been here in your life before?"

"Put that hat on, and home at once," said I. "I'm dreadfully grieved at you, Miss Cathy: you've done extremely wrong! It's no use pouting and crying: that won't repay the trouble I've had, scouring the country after you. To think how Mr. Linton charged me to keep you in; and you stealing off so! It shows you are a cunning little fox, and nobody will put faith in you anymore."

"What have I done?" sobbed she, instantly checked. "Papa charged me nothing: he'll not scold me, Ellen – he's never cross, like you!"

"Come, come!" I repeated. "I'll tie the riband. Now, let us have no petulance. Oh, for shame! You thirteen years old, and such a baby!"

This exclamation was caused by her pushing the hat from her head, and retreating to the chimney out of my reach.

"Nay," said the servant, "don't be hard on the bonny lass, Mrs. Dean. We made her stop: she'd fain have ridden forwards, afeard you should be uneasy. Hareton offered to go with her, and I thought he should: it's a wild road over the hills."

Hareton, during the discussion, stood with his hands in his pockets, too awkward to speak; though he looked as if he did not relish my intrusion.

"How long am I to wait?" I continued, disregarding the woman's interference. "It will be dark in ten minutes. Where is the pony, Miss Cathy? And where is Phoenix? I shall leave you, unless you be quick; so please yourself."

"The pony is in the yard," she replied, "and Phoenix is shut in there. He's bitten – and so is Charlie. I was going to tell you all about it; but you are in a bad temper, and don't deserve to hear."

I picked up her hat, and approached to reinstate it; but perceiving that the people of the house took her part, she commenced capering round the room; and on my giving chase, ran like a mouse over and under and behind the furniture, rendering it ridiculous for me to pursue. Hareton and the woman laughed, and she joined them, and waxed more impertinent still; till I cried, in great irritation, – "Well, Miss Cathy, if you were aware whose house this is you'd be glad enough to get out."

"It's *your* father's, isn't it?" said she, turning to Hareton.

"Nay," he replied, looking down, and blushing bashfully.

He could not stand a steady gaze from her eyes, though they were just his own.

"Whose then – your master's?" she asked.

He coloured deeper, with a different feeling, muttered an oath, and turned away.

"Who is his master?" continued the tiresome girl, appealing to me. "He talked about 'our house', and 'our folk'. I thought he had been the owner's son. And he never said Miss: he should have done, shouldn't he, if he's a servant?"

Hareton grew black as a thunder-cloud at this childish speech. I silently shook my questioner, and at last succeeded in equipping her for departure.

"Now, get my horse," she said, addressing her unknown kinsman as she would one of the stable-boys at the Grange. "And you may come with me. I want to see where the goblin-hunter rises in the marsh, and to hear about the *fairishes*, as you call them: but make haste! What's the matter? Get my horse, I say."

"I'll see thee damned before I be *thy* servant!" growled the lad.

"You'll see me *what*!" asked Catherine in surprise.

"Damned – thou saucy witch!" he replied.

"There, Miss Cathy! You see you have got into pretty company," I interposed. "Nice words to be used to a young lady! Pray don't begin to dispute with him. Come, let us seek for Minny ourselves, and begone."

"But, Ellen," cried she, staring fixed in astonishment, "how dare he speak so to me? Mustn't he be made to do as I ask him? You wicked creature, I shall tell papa what you said. Now, then!"

Hareton did not appear to feel this threat; so the tears sprang into her eyes with indignation. "You bring the pony," she exclaimed, turning to the woman, "and let my dog free this moment!"

"Softly, Miss," answered she addressed; "you'll lose nothing by being civil. Though Mr. Hareton, there, be not the master's son, he's your cousin: and I was never hired to serve you."

"*He* my cousin!" cried Cathy, with a scornful laugh.

"Yes, indeed," responded her reprover.

"Oh, Ellen! Don't let them say such things," she pursued in great trouble. "Papa is gone to fetch my cousin from London: my cousin is a gentleman's son. That my –" she stopped, and wept outright; upset at the bare notion of relationship with such a clown.

"Hush, hush!" I whispered; "people can have many cousins and of all sorts, Miss Cathy, without being any the worse for it; only they needn't keep their company, if they be disagreeable and bad."

"He's not – he's not my cousin, Ellen!" she went on, gathering fresh grief from reflection, and flinging herself into my arms for refuge from the idea.

I was much vexed at her and the servant for their mutual revelations; having no doubt of Linton's approaching arrival, communicated by the former, being reported to Mr. Heathcliff; and feeling as confident that Catherine's first thought on her father's return would be to seek an explanation of the latter's assertion concerning her rude-bred kindred. Hareton, recovering from his disgust at being taken for a servant, seemed moved by her distress; and, having fetched the pony round to the door, he took, to propitiate her, a fine crooked-legged terrier whelp from the kennel, and putting it into her hand, bid her whist! For he meant nought. Pausing in her lamentations, she surveyed him with a glance of awe and horror, then burst forth anew.

I could scarcely refrain from smiling at this antipathy to the poor fellow; who was a well-made, athletic youth, good-looking in features, and stout and healthy, but attired in garments befitting his daily occupations of working on the farm and lounging among the moors after rabbits and game. Still, I thought I could detect in his physiognomy a mind owning better qualities than his father ever possessed. Good things lost amid a wilderness of weeds, to be sure, whose rankness far over-topped their neglected growth; yet, notwithstanding, evidence of a wealthy soil, that might yield luxuriant crops under other and favourable circumstances. Mr. Heathcliff, I believe, had not treated him physically ill; thanks to his fearless nature, which offered no temptation to that course of oppression: he had none of the timid susceptibility that would have given zest to ill-treatment, in Heathcliff's judgment. He appeared to have bent his malevolence on making him a brute: he was never taught to read or write; never rebuked for any bad habit which did not annoy his keeper; never led a single step towards virtue, or guarded by a single precept against vice. And from what I heard, Joseph contributed much to his deterioration, by a narrow-minded partiality which prompted him to flatter and pet him, as a boy, because he was the head of the old family. And as he had been in the habit of accusing Catherine

Earnshaw and Heathcliff, when children, of putting the master past his patience, and compelling him to seek solace in drink by what he termed their 'offald ways', so at present he laid the whole burden of Hareton's faults on the shoulders of the usurper of his property. If the lad swore, he wouldn't correct him: nor however culpably he behaved. It gave Joseph satisfaction, apparently, to watch him go the worst lengths: he allowed that the lad was ruined: that his soul was abandoned to perdition; but then he reflected that Heathcliff must answer for it. Hareton's blood would be required at his hands; and there lay immense consolation in that thought. Joseph had instilled into him a pride of name, and of his lineage; he would, had he dared, have fostered hate between him and the present owner of the Heights: but his dread of that owner amounted to superstition; and he confined his feelings regarding him to muttered innuendoes and private comminations. I don't pretend to be intimately acquainted with the mode of living customary in those days at Wuthering Heights: I only speak from hearsay; for I saw little. The villagers affirmed Mr. Heathcliff was *near*, and a cruel hard landlord to his tenants; but the house, inside, had regained its ancient aspect of comfort under female management, and the scenes of riot common in Hindley's time were not now enacted within its walls. The master was too gloomy to seek companionship with any people, good or bad; and he is yet.

This, however, is not making progress with my story. Miss Cathy rejected the peace-offering of the terrier, and demanded her own dogs, Charlie and Phoenix. They came limping and hanging their heads; and we set out for home, sadly out of sorts, every one of us. I could not wring from my little lady how she had spent the day; except that, as I supposed, the goal of her pilgrimage was Penistone Crags; and she arrived without adventure to the gate of the farm-house, when Hareton happened to issue forth, attended by some canine followers, who attacked her train. They had a smart battle, before their owners could separate them: that formed an introduction. Catherine told Hareton who she was, and where she was going; and asked him to show her the way: finally, beguiling him to accompany her. He opened the mysteries of the Fairy Cave, and twenty other queer places. But, being in disgrace, I was not favoured with a description of the interesting objects she saw. I could gather, however, that her guide had been a favourite till she hurt his feelings by addressing him as a servant; and Heathcliff's housekeeper hurt hers by calling him her cousin. Then the language he had held to her rankled in her heart; she who was always 'love', and 'darling', and 'queen', and 'angel', with everybody at the Grange, to be insulted so shockingly by a stranger! She did not comprehend it; and hard work I had to obtain a promise that she would not lay the grievance before her father. I explained how he objected to the whole household at the Heights, and how sorry he would be to find she had been there; but I insisted most on the fact, that if she revealed my negligence of his orders, he would perhaps be so angry that I should have to leave; and Cathy couldn't bear that prospect: she pledged her word, and kept it for my sake. After all, she was a sweet little girl.

Chapter Nineteen

A LETTER, edged with black, announced the day of my master's return. Isabella was dead; and he wrote to bid me get mourning for his daughter, and arrange a room, and other accommodations, for his youthful nephew. Catherine ran wild with joy at the idea of welcoming her father back; and indulged most sanguine anticipations of the innumerable excellencies of her 'real' cousin. The evening of their expected arrival came. Since early morning she had been busy ordering her own small affairs; and now attired in her new black frock – poor thing! Her aunt's death impressed her with no definite sorrow – she obliged me, by constant worrying, to walk with her down through the grounds to meet them.

"Linton is just six months younger than I am," she chattered, as we strolled leisurely over the swells and hollows of mossy turf, under shadow of the trees. "How delightful it will be to have him for a playfellow! Aunt Isabella sent papa a beautiful lock of his hair; it was lighter than mine – more flaxen, and quite as fine. I have it carefully preserved in a little glass box; and I've often thought what a pleasure it would be to see its owner. Oh! I am happy – and papa, dear, dear papa! Come, Ellen, let us run! Come, run."

She ran, and returned and ran again, many times before my sober footsteps reached the gate, and then she seated herself on the grassy bank beside the path, and tried to wait patiently; but that was impossible: she couldn't be still a minute.

"How long they are!" she exclaimed. "Ah, I see, some dust on the road – they are coming! No! When will they be here? May we not go a little way – half a mile, Ellen, only just half a mile? Do say yes: to that clump of birches at the turn!"

I refused staunchly. At length her suspense was ended: the travelling carriage rolled in sight. Miss Cathy shrieked and stretched out her arms as soon as she caught her father's face looking from the window. He descended, nearly as eager as herself; and a considerable interval elapsed ere they had a thought to spare for any but themselves. While they exchanged caresses I took a peep in to see after Linton. He was asleep in a corner, wrapped in a warm, fur-lined cloak, as if it had been winter. A pale, delicate, effeminate boy, who might have been taken for my master's younger brother, so strong was the resemblance: but there was a sickly peevishness in his aspect that Edgar Linton never had. The latter saw me looking; and having shaken hands, advised me to close the door, and leave him undisturbed; for the journey had fatigued him. Cathy would fain have taken one glance, but her father told her to come, and they walked together up the park, while I hastened before to prepare the servants.

"Now, darling," said Mr. Linton, addressing his daughter, as they halted at the bottom of the front steps: "your cousin is not so strong or so merry as you are, and he has lost his mother, remember, a very short time since; therefore, don't expect him to play and run about with you directly. And don't harass him much by talking: let him be quiet this evening, at least, will you?"

"Yes, yes, papa," answered Catherine: "but I do want to see him; and he hasn't once looked out."

The carriage stopped; and the sleeper being roused, was lifted to the ground by his uncle.

"This is your cousin Cathy, Linton," he said, putting their little hands together. "She's fond of you already; and mind you don't grieve her by crying tonight. Try to be cheerful now; the travelling is at an end, and you have nothing to do but rest and amuse yourself as you please."

"Let me go to bed, then," answered the boy, shrinking from Catherine's salute; and he put his fingers to remove incipient tears.

"Come, come, there's a good child," I whispered, leading him in. "You'll make her weep too – see how sorry she is for you!"

I do not know whether it was sorrow for him, but his cousin put on as sad a countenance as himself, and returned to her father. All three entered, and mounted to the library, where tea was laid ready. I proceeded to remove Linton's cap and mantle, and placed him on a chair by the table; but he was no sooner seated than he began to cry afresh. My master inquired what was the matter.

"I can't sit on a chair," sobbed the boy.

"Go to the sofa, then, and Ellen shall bring you some tea," answered his uncle patiently.

He had been greatly tried, during the journey, I felt convinced, by his fretful ailing charge. Linton slowly trailed himself off, and lay down. Cathy carried a footstool and her cup to his side. At first she sat silent; but that could not last: she had resolved to make a pet of her little cousin, as she would have him to be; and she commenced stroking his curls, and kissing his cheek, and offering him tea in her saucer, like a baby. This pleased him, for he was not much better: he dried his eyes, and lightened into a faint smile.

"Oh, he'll do very well," said the master to me, after watching them a minute. "Very well, if we can keep him, Ellen. The company of a child of his own age will instil new spirit into him soon, and by wishing for strength he'll gain it."

"Ay, if we can keep him!" I mused to myself; and sore misgivings came over me that there was slight hope of that. And then, I thought, how ever will that weakling live at Wuthering Heights? Between his father and Hareton, what playmates and instructors they'll be. Our doubts were presently decided – even earlier than I expected. I had just taken the children upstairs, after tea was finished, and seen Linton asleep – he would not suffer me to leave him till that was the case – I had come down, and was standing by the table in the hall, lighting a bedroom candle for Mr. Edgar, when a maid stepped out of the kitchen and informed me that Mr. Heathcliff's servant Joseph was at the door, and wished to speak with the master.

"I shall ask him what he wants first," I said, in considerable trepidation. "A very unlikely hour to be troubling people, and the instant they have returned from a long journey. I don't think the master can see him."

Joseph had advanced through the kitchen as I uttered these words, and now presented himself in the hall. He was donned in his Sunday garments, with his most sanctimonious and sourest face, and, holding his hat in one hand, and his stick in the other, he proceeded to clean his shoes on the mat.

"Good evening, Joseph," I said, coldly. "What business brings you here tonight?"

"It's Maister Linton I mun spake to," he answered, waving me disdainfully aside.

"Mr. Linton is going to bed; unless you have something particular to say, I'm sure he won't hear it now," I continued. "You had better sit down in there, and entrust your message to me."

"Which is his rahm?" pursued the fellow, surveying the range of closed doors.

I perceived he was bent on refusing my mediation, so very reluctantly I went up to the library, and announced the unseasonable visitor, advising that he should be dismissed till next day. Mr. Linton had no time to empower me to do so, for Joseph mounted close at my heels, and, pushing into the apartment, planted himself at the far side of the table, with his two fists clapped on the head of his stick, and began in an elevated tone, as if anticipating opposition –

"Hathecliff has sent me for his lad, and I munn't goa back 'bout him."

Edgar Linton was silent a minute; an expression of exceeding sorrow overcast his features: he would have pitied the child on his own account; but, recalling Isabella's hopes and fears, and anxious wishes for her son, and her commendations of him to his care, he grieved bitterly at the prospect of yielding him up, and searched in his heart how it might be avoided. No plan offered itself: the very exhibition of any desire to keep him would have rendered the claimant more peremptory: there was nothing left but to resign him. However, he was not going to rouse him from his sleep.

"Tell Mr. Heathcliff," he answered calmly, "that his son shall come to Wuthering Heights tomorrow. He is in bed, and too tired to go the distance now. You may also tell him that the mother of Linton desired him to remain under my guardianship; and, at present, his health is very precarious."

"Noa!" said Joseph, giving a thud with his prop on the floor, and assuming an authoritative air. "Noa! That means naught. Hathecliff maks noa 'count o' t' mother, nor ye norther; but he'll heu' his lad; und I mun tak' him – soa now ye knaw!"

"You shall not tonight!" answered Linton decisively. "Walk downstairs at once, and repeat to your master what I have said. Ellen, show him down. Go –"

And, aiding the indignant elder with a lift by the arm, he rid the room of him and closed the door.

"Varrah weell!" shouted Joseph, as he slowly drew off. "To-morn, he's come hisseln, and thrust *him* out, if ye darr!"

Chapter Twenty

TO OBVIATE the danger of this threat being fulfilled, Mr. Linton commissioned me to take the boy home early, on Catherine's pony; and, said he – "As we shall now have no influence over his destiny, good or bad, you must say nothing of where he is gone to my daughter: she cannot associate with him hereafter, and it is better for her to remain in ignorance of his proximity; lest she should be restless, and anxious to visit the Heights. Merely tell her his father sent for him suddenly, and he has been obliged to leave us."

Linton was very reluctant to be roused from his bed at five o'clock, and astonished to be informed that he must prepare for further travelling; but I softened off the matter by stating that he was going to spend some time with his father, Mr. Heathcliff, who wished to see him so much, he did not like to defer the pleasure till he should recover from his late journey.

"My father!" he cried, in strange perplexity. "Mamma never told me I had a father. Where does he live? I'd rather stay with uncle."

"He lives a little distance from the Grange," I replied; "just beyond those hills: not so far, but you may walk over here when you get hearty. And you should be glad to go home, and to see him. You must try to love him, as you did your mother, and then he will love you."

"But why have I not heard of him before?" asked Linton. "Why didn't mamma and he live together, as other people do?"

"He had business to keep him in the north," I answered, "and your mother's health required her to reside in the south."

"And why didn't mamma speak to me about him?" persevered the child. "She often talked of uncle, and I learnt to love him long ago. How am I to love papa? I don't know him."

"Oh, all children love their parents," I said. "Your mother, perhaps, thought you would want to be with him if she mentioned him often to you. Let us make haste. An early ride on such a beautiful morning is much preferable to an hour's more sleep."

"Is *she* to go with us," he demanded, "the little girl I saw yesterday?"

"Not now," replied I.

"Is uncle?" he continued.

"No, I shall be your companion there," I said.

Linton sank back on his pillow and fell into a brown study.

"I won't go without uncle," he cried at length: "I can't tell where you mean to take me."

I attempted to persuade him of the naughtiness of showing reluctance to meet his father; still he obstinately resisted any progress towards dressing, and I had to call for my master's assistance in coaxing him out of bed. The poor thing was finally got off, with several delusive assurances that his absence should be short: that Mr. Edgar and Cathy would visit him, and other promises, equally ill-founded, which I invented and reiterated at intervals throughout the way. The pure heather-scented air, the bright sunshine, and the gentle canter of Minny, relieved his despondency after a while. He began to put questions concerning his new home, and its inhabitants, with greater interest and liveliness.

"Is Wuthering Heights as pleasant a place as Thrushcross Grange?" he inquired, turning to take a last glance into the valley, whence a light mist mounted and formed a fleecy cloud on the skirts of the blue.

"It is not so buried in trees," I replied, "and it is not quite so large, but you can see the country beautifully all round; and the air is healthier for you – fresher and drier. You will, perhaps, think the building old and dark at first; though it is a respectable house: the next best in the neighbourhood.

And you will have such nice rambles on the moors. Hareton Earnshaw – that is, Miss Cathy's other cousin, and so yours in a manner – will show you all the sweetest spots; and you can bring a book in fine weather, and make a green hollow your study; and, now and then, your uncle may join you in a walk: he does, frequently, walk out on the hills."

"And what is my father like?" he asked. "Is he as young and handsome as uncle?"

"He's as young," said I; "but he has black hair and eyes, and looks sterner; and he is taller and bigger altogether. He'll not seem to you so gentle and kind at first, perhaps, because it is not his way: still, mind you, be frank and cordial with him; and naturally he'll be fonder of you than any uncle, for you are his own."

"Black hair and eyes!" mused Linton. "I can't fancy him. Then I am not like him, am I?"

"Not much," I answered: not a morsel, I thought, surveying with regret the white complexion and slim frame of my companion, and his large languid eyes – his mother's eyes, save that, unless a morbid touchiness kindled them a moment, they had not a vestige of her sparkling spirit.

"How strange that he should never come to see mamma and me!" he murmured. "Has he ever seen me? If he has, I must have been a baby. I remember not a single thing about him!"

"Why, Master Linton," said I, "three hundred miles is a great distance; and ten years seem very different in length to a grown-up person compared with what they do to you. It is probable Mr. Heathcliff proposed going from summer to summer, but never found a convenient opportunity; and now it is too late. Don't trouble him with questions on the subject: it will disturb him, for no good."

The boy was fully occupied with his own cogitations for the remainder of the ride, till we halted before the farmhouse garden-gate. I watched to catch his impressions in his countenance. He surveyed the carved front and low-browed lattices, the straggling gooseberry-bushes and crooked firs, with solemn intentness, and then shook his head: his private feelings entirely disapproved of the exterior of his new abode. But he had sense to postpone complaining: there might be compensation within. Before he dismounted, I went and opened the door. It was half-past six; the family had just finished breakfast: the servant was clearing and wiping down the table. Joseph stood by his master's chair telling some tale concerning a lame horse; and Hareton was preparing for the hayfield.

"Hallo, Nelly!" said Mr. Heathcliff, when he saw me. "I feared I should have to come down and fetch my property myself. You've brought it, have you? Let us see what we can make of it."

He got up and strode to the door: Hareton and Joseph followed in gaping curiosity. Poor Linton ran a frightened eye over the faces of the three.

"Sure-ly," said Joseph after a grave inspection, "he's swopped wi' ye, Maister, an' yon's his lass!"

Heathcliff, having stared his son into an ague of confusion, uttered a scornful laugh.

"God! What a beauty! What a lovely, charming thing!" he exclaimed. "Haven't they reared it on snails and sour milk, Nelly? Oh, damn my soul! But that's worse than I expected – and the devil knows I was not sanguine!"

I bid the trembling and bewildered child get down, and enter. He did not thoroughly comprehend the meaning of his father's speech, or whether it were intended for him: indeed, he was not yet certain that the grim, sneering stranger was his father. But he clung to me with growing trepidation; and on Mr. Heathcliff's taking a seat and bidding him 'come hither' he hid his face on my shoulder and wept.

"Tut, tut!" said Heathcliff, stretching out a hand and dragging him roughly between his knees, and then holding up his head by the chin. "None of that nonsense! We're not going to hurt thee, Linton – isn't that thy name? Thou art thy mother's child, entirely! Where is my share in thee, puling chicken?"

He took off the boy's cap and pushed back his thick flaxen curls, felt his slender arms and his small fingers; during which examination Linton ceased crying, and lifted his great blue eyes to inspect the inspector.

"Do you know me?" asked Heathcliff, having satisfied himself that the limbs were all equally frail and feeble.

"No," said Linton, with a gaze of vacant fear.

"You've heard of me, I daresay?"

"No," he replied again.

"No! What a shame of your mother, never to waken your filial regard for me! You are my son, then, I'll tell you; and your mother was a wicked slut to leave you in ignorance of the sort of father you possessed. Now, don't wince, and colour up! Though it is something to see you have not white blood. Be a good lad; and I'll do for you. Nelly, if you be tired you may sit down; if not, get home again. I guess you'll report what you hear and see to the cipher at the Grange; and this thing won't be settled while you linger about it."

"Well," replied I, "I hope you'll be kind to the boy, Mr. Heathcliff, or you'll not keep him long; and he's all you have akin in the wide world, that you will ever know – remember."

"I'll be very kind to him, you needn't fear," he said, laughing. "Only nobody else must be kind to him: I'm jealous of monopolising his affection. And, to begin my kindness, Joseph, bring the lad some breakfast. Hareton, you infernal calf, begone to your work. Yes, Nell," he added, when they had departed, "my son is prospective owner of your place, and I should not wish him to die till I was certain of being his successor. Besides, he's *mine*, and I want the triumph of seeing *my* descendant fairly lord of their estates; my child hiring their children to till their fathers' lands for wages. That is the sole consideration which can make me endure the whelp: I despise him for himself, and hate him for the memories he revives! But that consideration is sufficient: he's as safe with me, and shall be tended as carefully as your master tends his own. I have a room upstairs, furnished for him in handsome style; I've engaged a tutor, also, to come three times a week, from twenty miles' distance, to teach him what he pleases to learn. I've ordered Hareton to obey him: and in fact I've arranged everything with a view to preserve the superior and the gentleman in him, above his associates. I do regret, however, that he so little deserves the trouble: if I wished any blessing in the world, it was to find him a worthy object of pride; and I'm bitterly disappointed with the whey-faced, whining wretch!"

While he was speaking, Joseph returned bearing a basin of milk-porridge, and placed it before Linton: who stirred round the homely mess with a look of aversion, and affirmed he could not eat it. I saw the old man-servant shared largely in his master's scorn of the child; though he was compelled to retain the sentiment in his heart, because Heathcliff plainly meant his underlings to hold him in honour.

"Cannot ate it?" repeated he, peering in Linton's face, and subduing his voice to a whisper, for fear of being overheard. "But Maister Hareton nivir ate naught else, when he wer a little 'un; and what wer gooid enough for him's gooid enough for ye, I's rayther think!"

"I *shan't* eat it!" answered Linton, snappishly. "Take it away."

Joseph snatched up the food indignantly, and brought it to us.

"Is there aught ails th' victuals?" he asked, thrusting the tray under Heathcliff's nose.

"What should ail them?" he said.

"Wah!" answered Joseph, "yon dainty chap says he cannut ate 'em. But I guess it's raight! His mother wer just soa – we wer a'most too mucky to sow t' corn for makking her breead."

"Don't mention his mother to me," said the master, angrily. "Get him something that he can eat, that's all. What is his usual food, Nelly?"

I suggested boiled milk or tea; and the housekeeper received instructions to prepare some. Come, I reflected, his father's selfishness may contribute to his comfort. He perceives his delicate constitution, and the necessity of treating him tolerably. I'll console Mr. Edgar by acquainting him with the turn Heathcliff's humour has taken. Having no excuse for lingering longer, I slipped out, while Linton was engaged in timidly rebuffing the advances of a friendly sheep-dog. But he was too much on the alert to be cheated: as I closed the door, I heard a cry, and a frantic repetition of the words –

"Don't leave me! I'll not stay here! I'll not stay here!"

Then the latch was raised and fell: they did not suffer him to come forth. I mounted Minny, and urged her to a trot; and so my brief guardianship ended.

Chapter Twenty-One

WE HAD SAD WORK with little Cathy that day: she rose in high glee, eager to join her cousin, and such passionate tears and lamentations followed the news of his departure that Edgar himself was obliged to soothe her, by affirming he should come back soon: he added, however, 'if I can get him'; and there were no hopes of that. This promise poorly pacified her; but time was more potent; and though still at intervals she inquired of her father when Linton would return, before she did see him again his features had waxed so dim in her memory that she did not recognise him.

When I chanced to encounter the housekeeper of Wuthering Heights, in paying business visits to Gimmerton, I used to ask how the young master got on; for he lived almost as secluded as Catherine herself, and was never to be seen. I could gather from her that he continued in weak health, and was a tiresome inmate. She said Mr. Heathcliff seemed to dislike him ever longer and worse, though he took some trouble to conceal it: he had an antipathy to the sound of his voice, and could not do at all with his sitting in the same room with him many minutes together. There seldom passed much talk between them: Linton learnt his lessons and spent his evenings in a small apartment they called the parlour: or else lay in bed all day: for he was constantly getting coughs, and colds, and aches, and pains of some sort.

"And I never know such a fainthearted creature," added the woman; "nor one so careful of hisseln. He *will* go on, if I leave the window open a bit late in the evening. Oh! It's killing, a breath of night air! And he must have a fire in the middle of summer; and Joseph's bacca-pipe is poison; and he must always have sweets and dainties, and always milk, milk for ever – heeding naught how the rest of us are pinched in winter; and there he'll sit, wrapped in his furred cloak in his chair by the fire, with some toast and water or other slop on the hob to sip at; and if Hareton, for pity, comes to amuse him – Hareton is not bad-natured, though he's rough – they're sure to part, one swearing and the other crying. I believe the master would relish Earnshaw's thrashing him to a mummy, if he were not his son; and I'm certain he would be fit to turn him out of doors, if he knew half the nursing he gives hisseln. But then he won't go into danger of temptation: he never enters the parlour, and should Linton show those ways in the house where he is, he sends him upstairs directly."

I divined, from this account, that utter lack of sympathy had rendered young Heathcliff selfish and disagreeable, if he were not so originally; and my interest in him, consequently, decayed: though still I was moved with a sense of grief at his lot, and a wish that he had been left with us. Mr. Edgar encouraged me to gain information: he thought a great deal about him, I fancy, and would have run some risk to see him; and he told me once to ask the housekeeper whether he ever came into the village? She said he had only been twice, on horseback, accompanying his father; and both times he pretended to be quite knocked up for three or four days afterwards. That housekeeper left, if I recollect rightly, two years after he came; and another, whom I did not know, was her successor; she lives there still.

Time wore on at the Grange in its former pleasant way till Miss Cathy reached sixteen. On the anniversary of her birth we never manifested any signs of rejoicing, because it was also the anniversary of my late mistress's death. Her father invariably spent that day alone in the library; and walked, at dusk, as far as Gimmerton kirkyard, where he would frequently prolong his stay beyond midnight. Therefore Catherine was thrown on her own resources for amusement. This twentieth of March was a beautiful spring day, and when her father had retired, my young lady came down dressed for going out, and said she asked to have a ramble on the edge of the moor with me: Mr. Linton had given her leave, if we went only a short distance and were back within the hour.

"So make haste, Ellen!" she cried. "I know where I wish to go; where a colony of moor-game are settled: I want to see whether they have made their nests yet."

"That must be a good distance up," I answered; "they don't breed on the edge of the moor."

"No, it's not," she said. "I've gone very near with papa."

I put on my bonnet and sallied out, thinking nothing more of the matter. She bounded before me, and returned to my side, and was off again like a young greyhound; and, at first, I found plenty of entertainment in listening to the larks singing far and near, and enjoying the sweet, warm sunshine; and watching her, my pet and my delight, with her golden ringlets flying loose behind, and her bright cheek, as soft and pure in its bloom as a wild rose, and her eyes radiant with cloudless pleasure. She was a happy creature, and an angel, in those days. It's a pity she could not be content.

"Well," said I, "where are your moor-game, Miss Cathy? We should be at them: the Grange park-fence is a great way off now."

"Oh, a little further – only a little further, Ellen," was her answer, continually. "Climb to that hillock, pass that bank, and by the time you reach the other side I shall have raised the birds."

But there were so many hillocks and banks to climb and pass, that, at length, I began to be weary, and told her we must halt, and retrace our steps. I shouted to her, as she had outstripped me a long way; she either did not hear or did not regard, for she still sprang on, and I was compelled to follow. Finally, she dived into a hollow; and before I came in sight of her again, she was two miles nearer Wuthering Heights than her own home; and I beheld a couple of persons arrest her, one of whom I felt convinced was Mr. Heathcliff himself.

Cathy had been caught in the fact of plundering, or, at least, hunting out the nests of the grouse. The Heights were Heathcliff's land, and he was reproving the poacher.

"I've neither taken any nor found any," she said, as I toiled to them, expanding her hands in corroboration of the statement. "I didn't mean to take them; but papa told me there were quantities up here, and I wished to see the eggs."

Heathcliff glanced at me with an ill-meaning smile, expressing his acquaintance with the party, and, consequently, his malevolence towards it, and demanded who 'papa' was?

"Mr. Linton of Thrushcross Grange," she replied. "I thought you did not know me, or you wouldn't have spoken in that way."

"You suppose papa is highly esteemed and respected, then?" he said, sarcastically.

"And what are you?" inquired Catherine, gazing curiously on the speaker. "That man I've seen before. Is he your son?"

She pointed to Hareton, the other individual, who had gained nothing but increased bulk and strength by the addition of two years to his age: he seemed as awkward and rough as ever.

"Miss Cathy," I interrupted, "it will be three hours instead of one that we are out, presently. We really must go back."

"No, that man is not my son," answered Heathcliff, pushing me aside. "But I have one, and you have seen him before too; and, though your nurse is in a hurry, I think both you and she would be the better for a little rest. Will you just turn this nab of heath, and walk into my house? You'll get home earlier for the ease; and you shall receive a kind welcome."

I whispered Catherine that she mustn't, on any account, accede to the proposal: it was entirely out of the question.

"Why?" she asked, aloud. "I'm tired of running, and the ground is dewy: I can't sit here. Let us go, Ellen. Besides, he says I have seen his son. He's mistaken, I think; but I guess where he lives: at the farmhouse I visited in coming from Penistone Crags. Don't you?"

"I do. Come, Nelly, hold your tongue – it will be a treat for her to look in on us. Hareton, get forwards with the lass. You shall walk with me, Nelly."

"No, she's not going to any such place," I cried, struggling to release my arm, which he had seized: but she was almost at the door-stones already, scampering round the brow at full speed. Her appointed companion did not pretend to escort her: he shied off by the road-side, and vanished.

"Mr. Heathcliff, it's very wrong," I continued: "you know you mean no good. And there she'll see Linton, and all will be told as soon as ever we return; and I shall have the blame."

"I want her to see Linton," he answered; "he's looking better these few days; it's not often he's fit to be seen. And we'll soon persuade her to keep the visit secret: where is the harm of it?"

"The harm of it is, that her father would hate me if he found I suffered her to enter your house; and I am convinced you have a bad design in encouraging her to do so," I replied.

"My design is as honest as possible. I'll inform you of its whole scope," he said. "That the two cousins may fall in love, and get married. I'm acting generously to your master: his young chit has no expectations, and should she second my wishes she'll be provided for at once as joint successor with Linton."

"If Linton died," I answered, "and his life is quite uncertain, Catherine would be the heir."

"No, she would not," he said. "There is no clause in the will to secure it so: his property would go to me; but, to prevent disputes, I desire their union, and am resolved to bring it about."

"And I'm resolved she shall never approach your house with me again," I returned, as we reached the gate, where Miss Cathy waited our coming.

Heathcliff bade me be quiet; and, preceding us up the path, hastened to open the door. My young lady gave him several looks, as if she could not exactly make up her mind what to think of him; but now he smiled when he met her eye, and softened his voice in addressing her; and I was foolish enough to imagine the memory of her mother might disarm him from desiring her injury. Linton stood on the hearth. He had been out walking in the fields, for his cap was on, and he was calling to Joseph to bring him dry shoes. He had grown tall of his age, still wanting some months of sixteen. His features were pretty yet, and his eye and complexion brighter than I remembered them, though with merely temporary lustre borrowed from the salubrious air and genial sun.

"Now, who is that?" asked Mr. Heathcliff, turning to Cathy. "Can you tell?"

"Your son?" she said, having doubtfully surveyed, first one and then the other.

"Yes, yes," answered he: "but is this the only time you have beheld him? Think! Ah! You have a short memory. Linton, don't you recall your cousin, that you used to tease us so with wishing to see?"

"What, Linton!" cried Cathy, kindling into joyful surprise at the name. "Is that little Linton? He's taller than I am! Are you Linton?"

The youth stepped forward, and acknowledged himself: she kissed him fervently, and they gazed with wonder at the change time had wrought in the appearance of each. Catherine had reached her full height; her figure was both plump and slender, elastic as steel, and her whole aspect sparkling with health and spirits. Linton's looks and movements were very languid, and his form extremely slight; but there was a grace in his manner that mitigated these defects, and rendered him not unpleasing. After exchanging numerous marks of fondness with him, his cousin went to Mr. Heathcliff, who lingered by the door, dividing his attention between the objects inside and those that lay without: pretending, that is, to observe the latter, and really noting the former alone.

"And you are my uncle, then!" she cried, reaching up to salute him. "I thought I liked you, though you were cross at first. Why don't you visit at the Grange with Linton? To live all these years such close neighbours, and never see us, is odd: what have you done so for?"

"I visited it once or twice too often before you were born," he answered. "There – damn it! If you have any kisses to spare, give them to Linton: they are thrown away on me."

"Naughty Ellen!" exclaimed Catherine, flying to attack me next with her lavish caresses. "Wicked Ellen! To try to hinder me from entering. But I'll take this walk every morning in future: may I, uncle? And sometimes bring papa. Won't you be glad to see us?"

"Of course," replied the uncle, with a hardly suppressed grimace, resulting from his deep aversion to both the proposed visitors. "But stay," he continued, turning towards the young lady. "Now I think of it, I'd better tell you. Mr. Linton has a prejudice against me: we quarrelled at one time of our lives, with unchristian ferocity; and, if you mention coming here to him, he'll put a veto on your visits altogether.

Therefore, you must not mention it, unless you be careless of seeing your cousin hereafter: you may come, if you will, but you must not mention it."

"Why did you quarrel?" asked Catherine, considerably crestfallen.

"He thought me too poor to wed his sister," answered Heathcliff, "and was grieved that I got her: his pride was hurt, and he'll never forgive it."

"That's wrong!" said the young lady: "some time I'll tell him so. But Linton and I have no share in your quarrel. I'll not come here, then; he shall come to the Grange."

"It will be too far for me," murmured her cousin: "to walk four miles would kill me. No, come here, Miss Catherine, now and then: not every morning, but once or twice a week."

The father launched towards his son a glance of bitter contempt.

"I am afraid, Nelly, I shall lose my labour," he muttered to me. "Miss Catherine, as the ninny calls her, will discover his value, and send him to the devil. Now, if it had been Hareton! – Do you know that, twenty times a day, I covet Hareton, with all his degradation? I'd have loved the lad had he been someone else. But I think he's safe from *her* love. I'll pit him against that paltry creature, unless it bestir itself briskly. We calculate it will scarcely last till it is eighteen. Oh, confound the vapid thing! He's absorbed in drying his feet, and never looks at her. – Linton!"

"Yes, father," answered the boy.

"Have you nothing to show your cousin anywhere about, not even a rabbit or a weasel's nest? Take her into the garden, before you change your shoes; and into the stable to see your horse."

"Wouldn't you rather sit here?" asked Linton, addressing Cathy in a tone which expressed reluctance to move again.

"I don't know," she replied, casting a longing look to the door, and evidently eager to be active.

He kept his seat, and shrank closer to the fire. Heathcliff rose, and went into the kitchen, and from thence to the yard, calling out for Hareton. Hareton responded, and presently the two re-entered. The young man had been washing himself, as was visible by the glow on his cheeks and his wetted hair.

"Oh, I'll ask *you*, uncle," cried Miss Cathy, recollecting the housekeeper's assertion. "That is not my cousin, is he?"

"Yes," he replied, "your mother's nephew. Don't you like him!"

Catherine looked queer.

"Is he not a handsome lad?" he continued.

The uncivil little thing stood on tiptoe, and whispered a sentence in Heathcliff's ear. He laughed; Hareton darkened: I perceived he was very sensitive to suspected slights, and had obviously a dim notion of his inferiority. But his master or guardian chased the frown by exclaiming –

"You'll be the favourite among us, Hareton! She says you are a – what was it? Well, something very flattering. Here! You go with her round the farm. And behave like a gentleman, mind! Don't use any bad words; and don't stare when the young lady is not looking at you, and be ready to hide your face when she is; and, when you speak, say your words slowly, and keep your hands out of your pockets. Be off, and entertain her as nicely as you can."

He watched the couple walking past the window. Earnshaw had his countenance completely averted from his companion. He seemed studying the familiar landscape with a stranger's and an artist's interest. Catherine took a sly look at him, expressing small admiration. She then turned her attention to seeking out objects of amusement for herself, and tripped merrily on, lilting a tune to supply the lack of conversation.

"I've tied his tongue," observed Heathcliff. "He'll not venture a single syllable all the time! Nelly, you recollect me at his age – nay, some years younger. Did I ever look so stupid: so 'gaumless', as Joseph calls it?"

"Worse," I replied, "because more sullen with it."

"I've a pleasure in him," he continued, reflecting aloud. "He has satisfied my expectations. If he were a born fool I should not enjoy it half so much. But he's no fool; and I can sympathise with all his feelings, having felt them myself. I know what he suffers now, for instance, exactly: it is merely a beginning of what he shall suffer, though. And he'll never be able to emerge from his bathos of coarseness and ignorance. I've got him faster than his scoundrel of a father secured me, and lower; for he takes a pride in his brutishness. I've taught him to scorn everything extra-animal as silly and weak. Don't you think Hindley would be proud of his son, if he could see him? Almost as proud as I am of mine. But there's this difference; one is gold put to the use of paving-stones, and the other is tin polished to ape a service of silver. *Mine* has nothing valuable about it; yet I shall have the merit of making it go as far as such poor stuff can go. *His* had first-rate qualities, and they are lost: rendered worse than unavailing. I have nothing to regret; he would have more than any but I are aware of. And the best of it is, Hareton is damnably fond of me! You'll own that I've outmatched Hindley there. If the dead villain could rise from his grave to abuse me for his offspring's wrongs, I should have the fun of seeing the said offspring fight him back again, indignant that he should dare to rail at the one friend he has in the world!"

Heathcliff chuckled a fiendish laugh at the idea. I made no reply, because I saw that he expected none. Meantime, our young companion, who sat too removed from us to hear what was said, began to evince symptoms of uneasiness, probably repenting that he had denied himself the treat of Catherine's society for fear of a little fatigue. His father remarked the restless glances wandering to the window, and the hand irresolutely extended towards his cap.

"Get up, you idle boy!" he exclaimed, with assumed heartiness.

"Away after them! They are just at the corner, by the stand of hives."

Linton gathered his energies, and left the hearth. The lattice was open, and, as he stepped out, I heard Cathy inquiring of her unsociable attendant what was that inscription over the door? Hareton stared up, and scratched his head like a true clown.

"It's some damnable writing," he answered. "I cannot read it."

"Can't read it?" cried Catherine; "I can read it: it's English. But I want to know why it is there."

Linton giggled: the first appearance of mirth he had exhibited.

"He does not know his letters," he said to his cousin. "Could you believe in the existence of such a colossal dunce?"

"Is he all as he should be?" asked Miss Cathy, seriously; "Or is he simple: not right? I've questioned him twice now, and each time he looked so stupid I think he does not understand me. I can hardly understand him, I'm sure!"

Linton repeated his laugh, and glanced at Hareton tauntingly; who certainly did not seem quite clear of comprehension at that moment.

"There's nothing the matter but laziness; is there, Earnshaw?" he said. "My cousin fancies you are an idiot. There you experience the consequence of scorning 'book-larning', as you would say. Have you noticed, Catherine, his frightful Yorkshire pronunciation?"

"Why, where the devil is the use on't?" growled Hareton, more ready in answering his daily companion. He was about to enlarge further, but the two youngsters broke into a noisy fit of merriment: my giddy miss being delighted to discover that she might turn his strange talk to matter of amusement.

"Where is the use of the devil in that sentence?" tittered Linton. "Papa told you not to say any bad words, and you can't open your mouth without one. Do try to behave like a gentleman, now do!"

"If thou weren't more a lass than a lad, I'd fell thee this minute, I would; pitiful lath of a crater!" retorted the angry boor, retreating, while his face burnt with mingled rage and mortification! For he was conscious of being insulted, and embarrassed how to resent it.

Mr. Heathcliff having overheard the conversation, as well as I, smiled when he saw him go; but immediately afterwards cast a look of singular aversion on the flippant pair, who remained chattering in the door-way: the boy finding animation enough while discussing Hareton's faults and deficiencies, and relating anecdotes of his goings on; and the girl relishing his pert and spiteful sayings, without considering the ill-nature they evinced. I began to dislike, more than to compassionate Linton, and to excuse his father in some measure for holding him cheap.

We stayed till afternoon: I could not tear Miss Cathy away sooner; but happily my master had not quitted his apartment, and remained ignorant of our prolonged absence. As we walked home, I would fain have enlightened my charge on the characters of the people we had quitted: but she got it into her head that I was prejudiced against them.

"Aha!" she cried, "you take papa's side, Ellen: you are partial I know; or else you wouldn't have cheated me so many years into the notion that Linton lived a long way from here. I'm really extremely angry; only I'm so pleased I can't show it! But you must hold your tongue about *my* uncle; he's my uncle, remember; and I'll scold papa for quarrelling with him."

And so she ran on, till I relinquished the endeavour to convince her of her mistake. She did not mention the visit that night, because she did not see Mr. Linton. Next day it all came out, sadly to my chagrin; and still I was not altogether sorry: I thought the burden of directing and warning would be more efficiently borne by him than me. But he was too timid in giving satisfactory reasons for his wish that she should shun connection with the household of the Heights, and Catherine liked good reasons for every restraint that harassed her petted will.

"Papa!" she exclaimed, after the morning's salutations, "Guess whom I saw yesterday, in my walk on the moors. Ah, papa, you started! You've not done right, have you, now? I saw – but listen, and you shall hear how I found you out; and Ellen, who is in league with you, and yet pretended to pity me so, when I kept hoping, and was always disappointed about Linton's coming back!"

She gave a faithful account of her excursion and its consequences; and my master, though he cast more than one reproachful look at me, said nothing till she had concluded. Then he drew her to him, and asked if she knew why he had concealed Linton's near neighbourhood from her? Could she think it was to deny her a pleasure that she might harmlessly enjoy?

"It was because you disliked Mr. Heathcliff," she answered.

"Then you believe I care more for my own feelings than yours, Cathy?" he said. "No, it was not because I disliked Mr. Heathcliff, but because Mr. Heathcliff dislikes me; and is a most diabolical man, delighting to wrong and ruin those he hates, if they give him the slightest opportunity. I knew that you could not keep up an acquaintance with your cousin without being brought into contact with him; and I knew he would detest you on my account; so for your own good, and nothing else, I took precautions that you should not see Linton again. I meant to explain this some time as you grew older, and I'm sorry I delayed it."

"But Mr. Heathcliff was quite cordial, papa," observed Catherine, not at all convinced; "and he didn't object to our seeing each other: he said I might come to his house when I pleased; only I must not tell you, because you had quarrelled with him, and would not forgive him for marrying aunt Isabella. And you won't. *You* are the one to be blamed: he is willing to let us be friends, at least; Linton and I; and you are not."

My master, perceiving that she would not take his word for her uncle-in-law's evil disposition, gave a hasty sketch of his conduct to Isabella, and the manner in which Wuthering Heights became his property. He could not bear to discourse long upon the topic; for though he spoke little of it, he still felt the same horror and detestation of his ancient enemy that had occupied his heart ever since Mrs. Linton's death. "She might have been living yet, if it had not been for him!" was his constant bitter reflection; and, in his eyes, Heathcliff seemed a murderer. Miss Cathy – conversant with no bad deeds except her own slight acts of disobedience, injustice, and passion, arising from hot temper and thoughtlessness, and repented of on the day they were committed – was amazed at the blackness of spirit that could brood on and cover revenge for years, and deliberately prosecute its plans without a visitation of remorse. She appeared so deeply impressed and shocked at this new view of human nature – excluded from all her studies and all her ideas till now – that Mr. Edgar deemed it unnecessary to pursue the subject. He merely added: "You will know hereafter, darling, why I wish you to avoid his house and family; now return to your old employments and amusements, and think no more about them."

Catherine kissed her father, and sat down quietly to her lessons for a couple of hours, according to custom; then she accompanied him into the grounds, and the whole day passed as usual: but in the evening, when she had retired to her room, and I went to help her to undress, I found her crying, on her knees by the bedside.

"Oh, fie, silly child!" I exclaimed. "If you had any real griefs you'd be ashamed to waste a tear on this little contrariety. You never had one shadow of substantial sorrow, Miss Catherine. Suppose, for a minute, that master and I were dead, and you were by yourself in the world: how would you feel, then? Compare the present occasion with such an affliction as that, and be thankful for the friends you have, instead of coveting more."

"I'm not crying for myself, Ellen," she answered, "it's for him. He expected to see me again tomorrow, and there he'll be so disappointed: and he'll wait for me, and I shan't come!"

"Nonsense!" said I, "do you imagine he has thought as much of you as you have of him? Hasn't he Hareton for a companion? Not one in a hundred would weep at losing a relation they had just seen twice, for two afternoons. Linton will conjecture how it is, and trouble himself no further about you."

"But may I not write a note to tell him why I cannot come?" she asked, rising to her feet. "And just send those books I promised to lend him? His books are not as nice as mine, and he wanted to have them extremely, when I told him how interesting they were. May I not, Ellen?"

"No, indeed! No, indeed!" replied I with decision. "Then he would write to you, and there'd never be an end of it. No, Miss Catherine, the acquaintance must be dropped entirely: so papa expects, and I shall see that it is done."

"But how can one little note –?" she recommenced, putting on an imploring countenance.

"Silence!" I interrupted. "We'll not begin with your little notes. Get into bed."

She threw at me a very naughty look, so naughty that I would not kiss her good-night at first: I covered her up, and shut her door, in great displeasure; but, repenting half-way, I returned softly, and lo! There was Miss standing at the table with a bit of blank paper before her and a pencil in her hand, which she guiltily slipped out of sight on my entrance.

"You'll get nobody to take that, Catherine," I said, "if you write it; and at present I shall put out your candle."

I set the extinguisher on the flame, receiving as I did so a slap on my hand and a petulant "cross thing!" I then quitted her again, and she drew the bolt in one of her worst, most peevish humours. The letter was finished and forwarded to its destination by a milk-fetcher who came from the village; but that I didn't learn till some time afterwards. Weeks passed on, and Cathy recovered her temper; though she grew wondrous fond of stealing off to corners by herself and often, if I came near her suddenly while reading, she would start and bend over the book, evidently desirous to hide it; and I detected edges of loose paper sticking out beyond the leaves. She also got a trick of coming down early in the morning and lingering about the kitchen, as if she were expecting the arrival of something; and she had a small drawer in a cabinet in the library, which she would trifle over for hours, and whose key she took special care to remove when she left it.

One day, as she inspected this drawer, I observed that the playthings and trinkets which recently formed its contents were transmuted into bits of folded paper. My curiosity and suspicions were roused; I determined to take a peep at her mysterious treasures; so, at night, as soon as she and my master were safe upstairs, I searched, and readily found among my house keys one that would fit the lock. Having opened, I emptied the whole contents into my apron, and took them with me to examine at leisure in my own chamber. Though I could not but suspect, I was still surprised to discover that they were a mass of correspondence – daily almost, it must have been – from Linton Heathcliff: answers to documents forwarded by her. The earlier dated were embarrassed and short; gradually, however, they expanded into copious love-letters, foolish, as the age of the writer rendered natural, yet with touches here and there which I thought were borrowed from a more experienced source. Some of them struck me as singularly odd compounds of ardour and flatness; commencing in strong feeling, and concluding in the affected, wordy style that a schoolboy might use to a fancied, incorporeal sweetheart. Whether they satisfied Cathy I don't know; but they appeared very worthless trash to me. After turning over as many as I thought proper, I tied them in a handkerchief and set them aside, relocking the vacant drawer.

Following her habit, my young lady descended early, and visited the kitchen: I watched her go to the door, on the arrival of a certain little boy; and, while the dairymaid filled his can, she tucked something into his jacket pocket, and plucked something out. I went round by the garden, and laid wait for the messenger; who fought valorously to defend his trust, and we spilt the milk between us; but I succeeded in abstracting the epistle; and, threatening serious consequences if he did not look sharp home, I remained under the wall and perused Miss Cathy's affectionate composition. It was more simple and more eloquent than her cousin's: very pretty and very silly. I shook my head, and went meditating into the house. The day being wet, she could not divert herself with rambling about the park; so, at the conclusion of her morning studies, she resorted to the solace of the drawer. Her father sat reading at the table; and I, on purpose, had sought a bit of work in some unripped fringes of the window-curtain, keeping my eye steadily fixed on her proceedings. Never did any bird flying back to a plundered nest, which it had left brimful of chirping young ones, express more complete despair, in its anguished cries and flutterings, than she by her single "Oh!" and the change that transfigured her late happy countenance. Mr. Linton looked up.

"What is the matter, love? Have you hurt yourself?" he said.

His tone and look assured her *he* had not been the discoverer of the hoard.

"No, papa!" she gasped. "Ellen! Ellen! Come upstairs – I'm sick!"

I obeyed her summons, and accompanied her out.

"Oh, Ellen! You have got them," she commenced immediately, dropping on her knees, when we were enclosed alone. "Oh, give them to me, and I'll never, never do so again! Don't tell papa. You have not told papa, Ellen? Say you have not? I've been exceedingly naughty, but I won't do it any more!"

With a grave severity in my manner I bade her stand up.

"So," I exclaimed, "Miss Catherine, you are tolerably far on, it seems: you may well be ashamed of them! A fine bundle of trash you study in your leisure hours, to be sure: why, it's good enough to be printed! And what do you suppose the master will think when I display it before him? I haven't shown it yet, but you needn't imagine I shall keep your ridiculous secrets. For shame! And you must have led the way in writing such absurdities: he would not have thought of beginning, I'm certain."

"I didn't! I didn't!" sobbed Cathy, fit to break her heart. "I didn't once think of loving him till –"

"*Loving*!" cried I, as scornfully as I could utter the word. "*Loving*! Did anybody ever hear the like! I might just as well talk of loving the miller who comes once a year to buy our corn. Pretty loving, indeed! And both times together you have seen Linton hardly four hours in your life! Now here is the babyish trash. I'm going with it to the library; and we'll see what your father says to such *loving*."

She sprang at her precious epistles, but I hold them above my head; and then she poured out further frantic entreaties that I would burn them – do anything rather than show them. And being really fully as much inclined to laugh as scold – for I esteemed it all girlish vanity – I at length relented in a measure, and asked, – "If I consent to burn them, will you promise faithfully neither to send nor receive a letter again, nor a book (for I perceive you have sent him books), nor locks of hair, nor rings, nor playthings?"

"We don't send playthings," cried Catherine, her pride overcoming her shame.

"Nor anything at all, then, my lady?" I said. "Unless you will, here I go."

"I promise, Ellen!" she cried, catching my dress. "Oh, put them in the fire, do, do!"

But when I proceeded to open a place with the poker the sacrifice was too painful to be borne. She earnestly supplicated that I would spare her one or two.

"One or two, Ellen, to keep for Linton's sake!"

I unknotted the handkerchief, and commenced dropping them in from an angle, and the flame curled up the chimney.

"I will have one, you cruel wretch!" she screamed, darting her hand into the fire, and drawing forth some half-consumed fragments, at the expense of her fingers.

"Very well – and I will have some to exhibit to papa!" I answered, shaking back the rest into the bundle, and turning anew to the door.

She emptied her blackened pieces into the flames, and motioned me to finish the immolation. It was done; I stirred up the ashes, and interred them under a shovelful of coals; and she mutely, and with a sense of intense injury, retired to her private apartment. I descended to tell my master that the young lady's qualm of sickness was almost gone, but I judged it best for her to lie down a while. She wouldn't dine; but she reappeared at tea, pale, and red about the eyes, and marvellously subdued in outward aspect. Next morning I answered the letter by a slip of paper, inscribed, "Master Heathcliff is requested to send no more notes to Miss Linton, as she will not receive them." And, henceforth, the little boy came with vacant pockets.

Chapter Twenty-Two

SUMMER DREW TO AN END, and early autumn: it was past Michaelmas, but the harvest was late that year, and a few of our fields were still uncleared. Mr. Linton and his daughter would frequently walk out among the reapers; at the carrying of the last sheaves they stayed till dusk, and the evening happening to be chill and damp, my master caught a bad cold, that settled obstinately on his lungs, and confined him indoors throughout the whole of the winter, nearly without intermission.

Poor Cathy, frightened from her little romance, had been considerably sadder and duller since its abandonment; and her father insisted on her reading less, and taking more exercise. She had his companionship no longer; I esteemed it a duty to supply its lack, as much as possible, with mine: an inefficient substitute; for I could only spare two or three hours, from my numerous diurnal occupations, to follow her footsteps, and then my society was obviously less desirable than his.

On an afternoon in October, or the beginning of November – a fresh watery afternoon, when the turf and paths were rustling with moist, withered leaves, and the cold blue sky was half hidden by clouds – dark grey streamers, rapidly mounting from the west, and boding abundant rain – I requested my young lady to forego her ramble, because I was certain of showers. She refused; and I unwillingly donned a cloak, and took my umbrella to accompany her on a stroll to the bottom of the park: a formal walk which she generally affected if low-spirited – and that she invariably was when Mr. Edgar had been worse than ordinary, a thing never known from his confession, but guessed both by her and me from his increased silence and the melancholy of his countenance. She went sadly on: there was no running or bounding now, though the chill wind might well have tempted her to race. And often, from the side of my eye, I could detect her raising a hand, and brushing something off her cheek. I gazed round for a means of diverting her thoughts. On one side of the road rose a high, rough bank, where hazels and stunted oaks, with their roots half exposed, held uncertain tenure: the soil was too loose for the latter; and strong winds had blown some nearly horizontal. In summer Miss Catherine delighted to climb along these trunks, and sit in the branches, swinging twenty feet above the ground; and I, pleased with her agility and her light, childish heart, still considered it proper to scold every time I caught her at such an elevation, but so that she knew there was no necessity for descending. From dinner to tea she would lie in her breeze-rocked cradle, doing nothing except singing old songs – my nursery lore – to herself, or watching the birds, joint tenants, feed and entice their young ones to fly: or nestling with closed lids, half thinking, half dreaming, happier than words can express.

"Look, Miss!" I exclaimed, pointing to a nook under the roots of one twisted tree. "Winter is not here yet. There's a little flower up yonder, the last bud from the multitude of bluebells that clouded those turf steps in July with a lilac mist. Will you clamber up, and pluck it to show to papa?" Cathy stared a long time at the lonely blossom trembling in its earthy shelter, and replied, at length – "No, I'll not touch it: but it looks melancholy, does it not, Ellen?"

"Yes," I observed, "about as starved and suckless as you: your cheeks are bloodless; let us take hold of hands and run. You're so low, I daresay I shall keep up with you."

"No," she repeated, and continued sauntering on, pausing at intervals to muse over a bit of moss, or a tuft of blanched grass, or a fungus spreading its bright orange among the heaps of brown foliage; and, ever and anon, her hand was lifted to her averted face.

"Catherine, why are you crying, love?" I asked, approaching and putting my arm over her shoulder. "You mustn't cry because papa has a cold; be thankful it is nothing worse."

She now put no further restraint on her tears; her breath was stifled by sobs.

"Oh, it will be something worse," she said. "And what shall I do when papa and you leave me, and I am by myself? I can't forget your words, Ellen; they are always in my ear. How life will be changed, how dreary the world will be, when papa and you are dead."

"None can tell whether you won't die before us," I replied. "It's wrong to anticipate evil. We'll hope there are years and years to come before any of us go: master is young, and I am strong, and hardly forty-five. My mother lived till eighty, a canty dame to the last. And suppose Mr. Linton were spared till he saw sixty, that would be more years than you have counted, Miss. And would it not be foolish to mourn a calamity above twenty years beforehand?"

"But Aunt Isabella was younger than papa," she remarked, gazing up with timid hope to seek further consolation.

"Aunt Isabella had not you and me to nurse her," I replied. "She wasn't as happy as Master: she hadn't as much to live for. All you need do, is to wait well on your father, and cheer him by letting him see you cheerful; and avoid giving him anxiety on any subject: mind that, Cathy! I'll not disguise but you might kill him if you were wild and reckless, and cherished a foolish, fanciful affection for the son of a person who would be glad to have him in his grave; and allowed him to discover that you fretted over the separation he has judged it expedient to make."

"I fret about nothing on earth except papa's illness," answered my companion. "I care for nothing in comparison with papa. And I'll never – never – oh, never, while I have my senses, do an act or say a word to vex him. I love him better than myself, Ellen; and I know it by this: I pray every night that I may live after him; because I would rather be miserable than that he should be: that proves I love him better than myself."

"Good words," I replied. "But deeds must prove it also; and after he is well, remember you don't forget resolutions formed in the hour of fear."

As we talked, we neared a door that opened on the road; and my young lady, lightening into sunshine again, climbed up and seated herself on the top of the wall, reaching over to gather some hips that bloomed scarlet on the summit branches of the wild-rose trees shadowing the highway side: the lower fruit had disappeared, but only birds could touch the upper, except from Cathy's present station. In stretching to pull them, her hat fell off; and as the door was locked, she proposed scrambling down to recover it. I bid her be cautious lest she got a fall, and she nimbly disappeared. But the return was no such easy matter: the stones were smooth and neatly cemented, and the rose-bushes and black-berry stragglers could yield no assistance in re-ascending. I, like a fool, didn't recollect that, till I heard her laughing and exclaiming – "Ellen! You'll have to fetch the key, or else I must run round to the porter's lodge. I can't scale the ramparts on this side!"

"Stay where you are," I answered; "I have my bundle of keys in my pocket: perhaps I may manage to open it; if not, I'll go."

Catherine amused herself with dancing to and fro before the door, while I tried all the large keys in succession. I had applied the last, and found that none would do; so, repeating my desire that she would remain there, I was about to hurry home as fast as I could, when an approaching sound arrested me. It was the trot of a horse; Cathy's dance stopped also.

"Who is that?" I whispered.

"Ellen, I wish you could open the door," whispered back my companion, anxiously.

"Ho, Miss Linton!" cried a deep voice (the rider's), "I'm glad to meet you. Don't be in haste to enter, for I have an explanation to ask and obtain."

"I shan't speak to you, Mr. Heathcliff," answered Catherine. "Papa says you are a wicked man, and you hate both him and me; and Ellen says the same."

"That is nothing to the purpose," said Heathcliff. (He it was.) "I don't hate my son, I suppose; and it is concerning him that I demand your attention. Yes; you have cause to blush. Two or three months since, were you not in the habit of writing to Linton? Making love in play, eh? You deserved, both of you, flogging for that! You especially, the elder; and less sensitive, as it turns out. I've got your letters, and if you give me any pertness I'll send them to your father. I presume you grew weary of the amusement and dropped it, didn't you? Well, you dropped Linton with it into a Slough of Despond. He was in earnest: in love, really. As true as I live, he's dying for you; breaking his heart at your fickleness: not figuratively, but actually. Though Hareton has made him a standing jest for six weeks, and I have used more serious measures, and attempted to frighten him out of his idiocy, he gets worse daily; and he'll be under the sod before summer, unless you restore him!"

"How can you lie so glaringly to the poor child?" I called from the inside. "Pray ride on! How can you deliberately get up such paltry falsehoods? Miss Cathy, I'll knock the lock off with a stone: you won't believe that vile nonsense. You can feel in yourself it is impossible that a person should die for love of a stranger."

"I was not aware there were eavesdroppers," muttered the detected villain. "Worthy Mrs. Dean, I like you, but I don't like your double-dealing," he added aloud. "How could *you* lie so glaringly as to affirm I hated the 'poor child'? And invent bugbear stories to terrify her from my door-stones? Catherine Linton (the very name warms me), my bonny lass, I shall be from home all this week; go and see if have not spoken truth: do, there's a darling! Just imagine your father in my place, and Linton in yours; then think how you would value your careless lover if he refused to stir a step to comfort you, when your father himself entreated him; and don't, from pure stupidity, fall into the same error. I swear, on my salvation, he's going to his grave, and none but you can save him!"

The lock gave way and I issued out.

"I swear Linton is dying," repeated Heathcliff, looking hard at me. "And grief and disappointment are hastening his death. Nelly, if you won't let her go, you can walk over yourself. But I shall not return till this time next week; and I think your master himself would scarcely object to her visiting her cousin."

"Come in," said I, taking Cathy by the arm and half forcing her to re-enter; for she lingered, viewing with troubled eyes the features of the speaker, too stern to express his inward deceit.

He pushed his horse close, and, bending down, observed – "Miss Catherine, I'll own to you that I have little patience with Linton; and Hareton and Joseph have less. I'll own that he's with a harsh set. He pines for kindness, as well as love; and a kind word from you would be his best medicine. Don't mind Mrs. Dean's cruel cautions; but be generous, and contrive to see him. He dreams of you day and night, and cannot be persuaded that you don't hate him, since you neither write nor call."

I closed the door, and rolled a stone to assist the loosened lock in holding it; and spreading my umbrella, I drew my charge underneath: for the rain began to drive through the moaning branches of the trees, and warned us to avoid delay. Our hurry prevented any comment on the encounter with Heathcliff, as we stretched towards home; but I divined instinctively that Catherine's heart was clouded now in double darkness. Her features were so sad, they did not seem hers: she evidently regarded what she had heard as every syllable true.

The master had retired to rest before we came in. Cathy stole to his room to inquire how he was; he had fallen asleep. She returned, and asked me to sit with her in the library. We took our tea together; and afterwards she lay down on the rug, and told me not to talk, for she was weary. I got a book, and pretended to read. As soon as she supposed me absorbed in my occupation, she recommenced her silent weeping: it appeared, at present, her favourite diversion. I suffered her to enjoy it a while; then I expostulated: deriding and ridiculing all Mr. Heathcliff's assertions about his son, as if I were certain she would coincide. Alas! I hadn't skill to counteract the effect his account had produced: it was just what he intended.

"You may be right, Ellen," she answered; "but I shall never feel at ease till I know. And I must tell Linton it is not my fault that I don't write, and convince him that I shall not change."

What use were anger and protestations against her silly credulity? We parted that night – hostile; but next day beheld me on the road to Wuthering Heights, by the side of my wilful young mistress's pony. I couldn't bear to witness her sorrow: to see her pale, dejected countenance, and heavy eyes: and I yielded, in the faint hope that Linton himself might prove, by his reception of us, how little of the tale was founded on fact.

Chapter Twenty-Three

THE RAINY NIGHT had ushered in a misty morning – half frost, half drizzle – and temporary brooks crossed our path – gurgling from the uplands. My feet were thoroughly wetted; I was cross and low; exactly the humour suited for making the most of these disagreeable things. We entered the farm-house by the kitchen way, to ascertain whether Mr. Heathcliff were really absent: because I put slight faith in his own affirmation.

Joseph seemed sitting in a sort of elysium alone, beside a roaring fire; a quart of ale on the table near him, bristling with large pieces of toasted oat-cake; and his black, short pipe in his mouth. Catherine ran to the hearth to warm herself. I asked if the master was in? My question remained so long unanswered, that I thought the old man had grown deaf, and repeated it louder.

"Na-ay!" he snarled, or rather screamed through his nose. "Na-ay! Yah muh goa back whear yah coom frough."

"Joseph!" cried a peevish voice, simultaneously with me, from the inner room. "How often am I to call you? There are only a few red ashes now. Joseph! Come this moment."

Vigorous puffs, and a resolute stare into the grate, declared he had no ear for this appeal. The housekeeper and Hareton were invisible; one gone on an errand, and the other at his work, probably. We knew Linton's tones, and entered.

"Oh, I hope you'll die in a garret, starved to death!" said the boy, mistaking our approach for that of his negligent attendant.

He stopped on observing his error: his cousin flew to him.

"Is that you, Miss Linton?" he said, raising his head from the arm of the great chair, in which he reclined. "No – don't kiss me: it takes my breath. Dear me! Papa said you would call," continued he, after recovering a little from Catherine's embrace; while she stood by looking very contrite. "Will you shut the door, if you please? You left it open; and those – those *detestable* creatures won't bring coals to the fire. It's so cold!"

I stirred up the cinders, and fetched a scuttleful myself. The invalid complained of being covered with ashes; but he had a tiresome cough, and looked feverish and ill, so I did not rebuke his temper.

"Well, Linton," murmured Catherine, when his corrugated brow relaxed, "are you glad to see me? Can I do you any good?"

"Why didn't you come before?" he asked. "You should have come, instead of writing. It tired me dreadfully writing those long letters. I'd far rather have talked to you. Now, I can neither bear to talk, nor anything else. I wonder where Zillah is! Will you" (looking at me) "step into the kitchen and see?"

I had received no thanks for my other service; and being unwilling to run to and fro at his behest, I replied – "Nobody is out there but Joseph."

"I want to drink," he exclaimed fretfully, turning away. "Zillah is constantly gadding off to Gimmerton since papa went: it's miserable! And I'm obliged to come down here – they resolved never to hear me upstairs."

"Is your father attentive to you, Master Heathcliff?" I asked, perceiving Catherine to be checked in her friendly advances.

"Attentive? He makes them a little more attentive at least," he cried. "The wretches! Do you know, Miss Linton, that brute Hareton laughs at me! I hate him! Indeed, I hate them all: they are odious beings."

Cathy began searching for some water; she lighted on a pitcher in the dresser, filled a tumbler, and brought it. He bid her add a spoonful of wine from a bottle on the table; and having swallowed a small portion, appeared more tranquil, and said she was very kind.

"And are you glad to see me?" asked she, reiterating her former question and pleased to detect the faint dawn of a smile.

"Yes, I am. It's something new to hear a voice like yours!" he replied. "But I have been vexed, because you wouldn't come. And papa swore it was owing to me: he called me a pitiful, shuffling, worthless thing; and said you despised me; and if he had been in my place, he would be more the master of the Grange than your father by this time. But you don't despise me, do you, Miss –?"

"I wish you would say Catherine, or Cathy," interrupted my young lady. "Despise you? No! Next to papa and Ellen, I love you better than anybody living. I don't love Mr. Heathcliff, though; and I dare not come when he returns: will he stay away many days?"

"Not many," answered Linton; "but he goes on to the moors frequently, since the shooting season commenced; and you might spend an hour or two with me in his absence. Do say you will. I think I should not be peevish with you: you'd not provoke me, and you'd always be ready to help me, wouldn't you?"

"Yes," said Catherine, stroking his long soft hair: "if I could only get papa's consent, I'd spend half my time with you. Pretty Linton! I wish you were my brother."

"And then you would like me as well as your father?" observed he, more cheerfully. "But papa says you would love me better than him and all the world, if you were my wife; so I'd rather you were that."

"No, I should never love anybody better than papa," she returned gravely. "And people hate their wives, sometimes; but not their sisters and brothers: and if you were the latter, you would live with us, and papa would be as fond of you as he is of me."

Linton denied that people ever hated their wives; but Cathy affirmed they did, and, in her wisdom, instanced his own father's aversion to her aunt. I endeavoured to stop her thoughtless tongue. I couldn't succeed till everything she knew was out. Master Heathcliff, much irritated, asserted her relation was false.

"Papa told me; and papa does not tell falsehoods," she answered pertly.

"*My* papa scorns yours!" cried Linton. "He calls him a sneaking fool."

"Yours is a wicked man," retorted Catherine; "and you are very naughty to dare to repeat what he says. He must be wicked to have made Aunt Isabella leave him as she did."

"She didn't leave him," said the boy; "you shan't contradict me."

"She did," cried my young lady.

"Well, I'll tell you something!" said Linton. "Your mother hated your father: now then."

"Oh!" exclaimed Catherine, too enraged to continue.

"And she loved mine," added he.

"You little liar! I hate you now!" she panted, and her face grew red with passion.

"She did! She did!" sang Linton, sinking into the recess of his chair, and leaning back his head to enjoy the agitation of the other disputant, who stood behind.

"Hush, Master Heathcliff!" I said; "that's your father's tale, too, I suppose."

"It isn't: you hold your tongue!" he answered. "She did, she did, Catherine! She did, she did!"

Cathy, beside herself, gave the chair a violent push, and caused him to fall against one arm. He was immediately seized by a suffocating cough that soon ended his triumph. It lasted so long that it frightened even me. As to his cousin, she wept with all her might, aghast at the mischief she had done: though she said nothing. I held him till the fit exhausted itself. Then he thrust me away, and leant his head down silently. Catherine quelled her lamentations also, took a seat opposite, and looked solemnly into the fire.

"How do you feel now, Master Heathcliff?" I inquired, after waiting ten minutes.

"I wish *she* felt as I do," he replied: "spiteful, cruel thing! Hareton never touches me: he never struck me in his life. And I was better today: and there –" his voice died in a whimper.

"*I* didn't strike you!" muttered Cathy, chewing her lip to prevent another burst of emotion.

He sighed and moaned like one under great suffering, and kept it up for a quarter of an hour; on purpose to distress his cousin apparently, for whenever he caught a stifled sob from her he put renewed pain and pathos into the inflexions of his voice.

"I'm sorry I hurt you, Linton," she said at length, racked beyond endurance. "But I couldn't have been hurt by that little push, and I had no idea that you could, either: you're not much, are you, Linton? Don't let me go home thinking I've done you harm. Answer! Speak to me."

"I can't speak to you," he murmured; "you've hurt me so that I shall lie awake all night choking with this cough. If you had it you'd know what it was; but *you'll* be comfortably asleep while I'm in agony, and nobody near me. I wonder how you would like to pass those fearful nights!" And he began to wail aloud, for very pity of himself.

"Since you are in the habit of passing dreadful nights," I said, "it won't be Miss who spoils your ease: you'd be the same had she never come. However, she shall not disturb you again; and perhaps you'll get quieter when we leave you."

"Must I go?" asked Catherine dolefully, bending over him. "Do you want me to go, Linton?"

"You can't alter what you've done," he replied pettishly, shrinking from her, "unless you alter it for the worse by teasing me into a fever."

"Well, then, I must go?" she repeated.

"Let me alone, at least," said he; "I can't bear your talking."

She lingered, and resisted my persuasions to departure a tiresome while; but as he neither looked up nor spoke, she finally made a movement to the door, and I followed. We were recalled by a scream. Linton had slid from his seat on to the hearthstone, and lay writhing in the mere perverseness of an indulged plague of a child, determined to be as grievous and harassing as it can. I thoroughly gauged his disposition from his behaviour, and saw at once it would be folly to attempt humouring him. Not so my companion: she ran back in terror, knelt down, and cried, and soothed, and entreated, till he grew quiet from lack of breath: by no means from compunction at distressing her.

"I shall lift him on to the settle," I said, "and he may roll about as he pleases: we can't stop to watch him. I hope you are satisfied, Miss Cathy, that you are not the person to benefit him; and that his condition of health is not occasioned by attachment to you. Now, then, there he is! Come away: as soon as he knows there is nobody by to care for his nonsense, he'll be glad to lie still."

She placed a cushion under his head, and offered him some water; he rejected the latter, and tossed uneasily on the former, as if it were a stone or a block of wood. She tried to put it more comfortably.

"I can't do with that," he said; "it's not high enough."

Catherine brought another to lay above it.

"That's too high," murmured the provoking thing.

"How must I arrange it, then?" she asked despairingly.

He twined himself up to her, as she half knelt by the settle, and converted her shoulder into a support.

"No, that won't do," I said. "You'll be content with the cushion, Master Heathcliff. Miss has wasted too much time on you already: we cannot remain five minutes longer."

"Yes, yes, we can!" replied Cathy. "He's good and patient now. He's beginning to think I shall have far greater misery than he will tonight, if I believe he is the worse for my visit: and then I dare not come again. Tell the truth about it, Linton; for I mustn't come, if I have hurt you."

"You must come, to cure me," he answered. "You ought to come, because you have hurt me: you know you have extremely! I was not as ill when you entered as I am at present – was I?"

"But you've made yourself ill by crying and being in a passion. – I didn't do it all," said his cousin. "However, we'll be friends now. And you want me: you would wish to see me sometimes, really?"

"I told you I did," he replied impatiently. "Sit on the settle and let me lean on your knee. That's as mamma used to do, whole afternoons together. Sit quite still and don't talk: but you may sing a song, if you can sing; or you may say a nice long interesting ballad – one of those you promised to teach me; or a story. I'd rather have a ballad, though: begin."

Catherine repeated the longest she could remember. The employment pleased both mightily. Linton would have another, and after that another, notwithstanding my strenuous objections; and so they went on until the clock struck twelve, and we heard Hareton in the court, returning for his dinner.

"And tomorrow, Catherine, will you be here tomorrow?" asked young Heathcliff, holding her frock as she rose reluctantly.

"No," I answered, "nor next day neither." She, however, gave a different response evidently, for his forehead cleared as she stooped and whispered in his ear.

"You won't go tomorrow, recollect, Miss!" I commenced, when we were out of the house. "You are not dreaming of it, are you?"

She smiled.

"Oh, I'll take good care," I continued: "I'll have that lock mended, and you can escape by no way else."

"I can get over the wall," she said laughing. "The Grange is not a prison, Ellen, and you are not my gaoler. And besides, I'm almost seventeen: I'm a woman. And I'm certain Linton would recover quickly if he had me to look after him. I'm older than he is, you know, and wiser: less childish, am I not? And he'll soon do as I direct him, with some slight coaxing. He's a pretty little darling when he's good. I'd make such a pet of him, if he were mine. We should never quarrel, should we after we were used to each other? Don't you like him, Ellen?"

"Like him!" I exclaimed. "The worst-tempered bit of a sickly slip that ever struggled into its teens. Happily, as Mr. Heathcliff conjectured, he'll not win twenty. I doubt whether he'll see spring, indeed. And small loss to his family whenever he drops off. And lucky it is for us that his father took him: the kinder he was treated, the more tedious and selfish he'd be. I'm glad you have no chance of having him for a husband, Miss Catherine."

My companion waxed serious at hearing this speech. To speak of his death so regardlessly wounded her feelings.

"He's younger than I," she answered, after a protracted pause of meditation, "and he ought to live the longest: he will – he must live as long as I do. He's as strong now as when he first came into the north; I'm positive of that. It's only a cold that ails him, the same as papa has. You say papa will get better, and why shouldn't he?"

"Well, well," I cried, "after all, we needn't trouble ourselves; for listen, Miss – and mind, I'll keep my word – if you attempt going to Wuthering Heights again, with or without me, I shall inform Mr. Linton, and, unless he allow it, the intimacy with your cousin must not be revived."

"It has been revived," muttered Cathy, sulkily.

"Must not be continued, then," I said.

"We'll see," was her reply, and she set off at a gallop, leaving me to toil in the rear.

We both reached home before our dinner-time; my master supposed we had been wandering through the park, and therefore he demanded no explanation of our absence. As soon as I entered I hastened to change my soaked shoes and stockings; but sitting such awhile at the Heights had done the mischief. On the succeeding morning I was laid up, and during three weeks I remained incapacitated for attending to my duties: a calamity never experienced prior to that period, and never, I am thankful to say, since.

My little mistress behaved like an angel in coming to wait on me, and cheer my solitude; the confinement brought me exceedingly low. It is wearisome, to a stirring active body: but few have slighter reasons for complaint than I had. The moment Catherine left Mr. Linton's room she appeared at my bedside. Her day was divided between us; no amusement usurped a minute: she neglected her meals, her studies, and her play; and she was the fondest nurse that ever watched. She must have had a warm heart, when she loved her father so, to give so much to me. I said her days were divided between us; but the master retired early, and I generally needed nothing after six o'clock, thus the evening was her own. Poor thing! I never considered what she did with herself after tea. And though frequently, when she looked in to bid me good-night, I remarked a fresh colour in her cheeks and a pinkness over her slender fingers, instead of fancying the line borrowed from a cold ride across the moors, I laid it to the charge of a hot fire in the library.

Chapter Twenty-Four

AT THE CLOSE of three weeks I was able to quit my chamber and move about the house. And on the first occasion of my sitting up in the evening I asked Catherine to read to me, because my eyes were weak. We were in the library, the master having gone to bed: she consented, rather unwillingly, I fancied; and imagining my sort of books did not suit her, I bid her please herself in the choice of what she perused. She selected one of her own favourites, and got forward steadily about an hour; then came frequent questions.

"Ellen, are not you tired? Hadn't you better lie down now? You'll be sick, keeping up so long, Ellen."

"No, no, dear, I'm not tired," I returned, continually.

Perceiving me immovable, she essayed another method of showing her disrelish for her occupation. It changed to yawning, and stretching, and –

"Ellen, I'm tired."

"Give over then and talk," I answered.

That was worse: she fretted and sighed, and looked at her watch till eight, and finally went to her room, completely overdone with sleep; judging by her peevish, heavy look, and the constant rubbing she inflicted on her eyes. The following night she seemed more impatient still; and on the third from recovering my company she complained of a headache, and left me. I thought her conduct odd; and having remained alone a long while, I resolved on going and inquiring whether she were better, and asking her to come and lie on the sofa, instead of upstairs in the dark. No Catherine could I discover upstairs, and none below. The servants affirmed they had not seen her. I listened at Mr. Edgar's door; all was silence. I returned to her apartment, extinguished my candle, and seated myself in the window.

The moon shone bright; a sprinkling of snow covered the ground, and I reflected that she might, possibly, have taken it into her head to walk about the garden, for refreshment. I did detect a figure creeping along the inner fence of the park; but it was not my young mistress: on its emerging into the light, I recognised one of the grooms. He stood a considerable period, viewing the carriage-road through the grounds; then started off at a brisk pace, as if he had detected something, and reappeared presently, leading Miss's pony; and there she was, just dismounted, and walking by its side. The man took his charge stealthily across the grass towards the stable. Cathy entered by the casement-window of the drawing-room, and glided noiselessly up to where I awaited her. She put the door gently too, slipped off her snowy shoes, untied her hat, and was proceeding, unconscious of my espionage, to lay aside her mantle, when I suddenly rose and revealed myself. The surprise petrified her an instant: she uttered an inarticulate exclamation, and stood fixed.

"My dear Miss Catherine," I began, too vividly impressed by her recent kindness to break into a scold, "where have you been riding out at this hour? And why should you try to deceive me by telling a tale? Where have you been? Speak!"

"To the bottom of the park," she stammered. "I didn't tell a tale."

"And nowhere else?" I demanded.

"No," was the muttered reply.

"Oh, Catherine!" I cried, sorrowfully. "You know you have been doing wrong, or you wouldn't be driven to uttering an untruth to me. That does grieve me. I'd rather be three months ill, than hear you frame a deliberate lie."

She sprang forward, and bursting into tears, threw her arms round my neck.

"Well, Ellen, I'm so afraid of you being angry," she said. "Promise not to be angry, and you shall know the very truth: I hate to hide it."

We sat down in the window-seat; I assured her I would not scold, whatever her secret might be, and I guessed it, of course; so she commenced –

"I've been to Wuthering Heights, Ellen, and I've never missed going a day since you fell ill; except thrice before, and twice after you left your room. I gave Michael books and pictures to prepare Minny every evening, and to put her back in the stable: you mustn't scold him either, mind. I was at the Heights by half-past six, and generally stayed till half-past eight, and then galloped home. It was not to amuse myself that I went: I was often wretched all the time. Now and then I was happy: once in a week perhaps. At first, I expected there would be sad work persuading you to let me keep my word to Linton: for I had engaged to call again next day, when we quitted him; but, as you stayed upstairs on the morrow, I escaped that trouble. While Michael was refastening the lock of the park door in the afternoon, I got possession of the key, and told him how my cousin wished me to visit him, because he was sick, and couldn't come to the Grange; and how papa would object to my going: and then I negotiated with him about the pony. He is fond of reading, and he thinks of leaving soon to get married; so he offered, if I would lend him books out of the library, to do what I wished: but I preferred giving him my own, and that satisfied him better.

"On my second visit Linton seemed in lively spirits; and Zillah (that is their housekeeper) made us a clean room and a good fire, and told us that, as Joseph was out at a prayer-meeting and Hareton Earnshaw was off with his dogs – robbing our woods of pheasants, as I heard afterwards – we might do what we liked. She brought me some warm wine and gingerbread, and appeared exceedingly good-natured, and Linton sat in the arm-chair, and I in the little rocking chair on the hearth-stone, and we laughed and talked so merrily, and found so much to say: we planned where we would go, and what we would do in summer. I needn't repeat that, because you would call it silly.

"One time, however, we were near quarrelling. He said the pleasantest manner of spending a hot July day was lying from morning till evening on a bank of heath in the middle of the moors, with the bees humming dreamily about among the bloom, and the larks singing high up overhead, and the blue sky and bright sun shining steadily and cloudlessly. That was his most perfect idea of heaven's happiness: mine was rocking in a rustling green tree, with a west wind blowing, and bright white clouds flitting rapidly above; and not only larks, but throstles, and blackbirds, and linnets, and cuckoos pouring out music on every side, and the moors seen at a distance, broken into cool dusky dells; but close by great swells of long grass undulating in waves to the breeze; and woods and sounding water, and the whole world awake and wild with joy. He wanted all to lie in an ecstasy of peace; I wanted all to sparkle and dance in a glorious jubilee. I said his heaven would be only half alive; and he said mine would be drunk: I said I should fall asleep in his; and he said he could not breathe in mine, and began to grow very snappish. At last, we agreed to try both, as soon as the right weather came; and then we kissed each other and were friends.

"After sitting still an hour, I looked at the great room with its smooth uncarpeted floor, and thought how nice it would be to play in, if we removed the table; and I asked Linton to call Zillah in to help us, and we'd have a game at blindman's-buff; she should try to catch us: you used to, you know, Ellen. He wouldn't: there was no pleasure in it, he said; but he consented to play at ball with me. We found two in a cupboard, among a heap of old toys, tops, and hoops, and battledores and shuttlecocks. One was marked C., and the other H.; I wished to have the C., because that stood for Catherine, and the H. might be for Heathcliff, his name; but the bran came out of H., and Linton didn't like it. I beat him constantly: and he got cross again, and coughed, and returned to his chair. That night, though, he easily recovered his good humour: he was charmed with two or three pretty songs – *your* songs, Ellen; and when I was obliged to go, he begged and entreated me to come the following evening; and I promised. Minny and I went flying home as light as air; and I dreamt of Wuthering Heights and my sweet, darling cousin, till morning.

"On the morrow I was sad; partly because you were poorly, and partly that I wished my father knew, and approved of my excursions: but it was beautiful moonlight after tea; and, as I rode on, the gloom cleared. I shall have another happy evening, I thought to myself; and what delights me more, my pretty Linton will. I trotted up their garden, and was turning round to the back, when that fellow Earnshaw met me, took my bridle, and bid me go in by the front entrance. He patted Minny's neck, and said she was a bonny beast, and appeared as if he wanted me to speak to him. I only told him to leave my horse alone, or else it would kick him. He answered in his vulgar accent, 'It wouldn't do mitch hurt if it did'; and surveyed its legs with a smile. I was half inclined to make it try; however, he moved off to open the door, and, as he raised the latch, he looked up to the inscription above, and said, with a stupid mixture of awkwardness and elation: 'Miss Catherine! I can read yon, now.'

"'Wonderful,' I exclaimed. 'Pray let us hear you – you *are* grown clever!'

"He spelt, and drawled over by syllables, the name – 'Hareton Earnshaw.'

"'And the figures?' I cried, encouragingly, perceiving that he came to a dead halt.

"'I cannot tell them yet,' he answered.

"'Oh, you dunce!' I said, laughing heartily at his failure.

"The fool stared, with a grin hovering about his lips, and a scowl gathering over his eyes, as if uncertain whether he might not join in my mirth: whether it were not pleasant familiarity, or what it really was, contempt. I settled his doubts, by suddenly retrieving my gravity and desiring him to walk away, for I came to see Linton, not him. He reddened – I saw that by the moonlight – dropped his hand from the latch, and skulked off, a picture of mortified vanity. He imagined himself to be as accomplished as Linton, I suppose, because he could spell his own name; and was marvellously discomfited that I didn't think the same."

"Stop, Miss Catherine, dear!" – I interrupted. "I shall not scold, but I don't like your conduct there. If you had remembered that Hareton was your cousin as much as Master Heathcliff, you would have felt how improper it was to behave in that way. At least, it was praiseworthy ambition for him to desire to be as accomplished as Linton; and probably he did not learn merely to show off: you had made him ashamed of his ignorance before, I have no doubt; and he wished to remedy it and please you. To sneer at his imperfect attempt was very bad breeding. Had you been brought up in his circumstances, would you be less rude? He was as quick and as intelligent a child as ever you were; and I'm hurt that he should be despised now, because that base Heathcliff has treated him so unjustly."

"Well, Ellen, you won't cry about it, will you?" she exclaimed, surprised at my earnestness. "But wait, and you shall hear if he conned his A B C to please me; and if it were worth while being civil to the brute. I entered; Linton was lying on the settle, and half got up to welcome me.

"'I'm ill tonight, Catherine, love,' he said; 'and you must have all the talk, and let me listen. Come, and sit by me. I was sure you wouldn't break your word, and I'll make you promise again, before you go.'

"I knew now that I mustn't tease him, as he was ill; and I spoke softly and put no questions, and avoided irritating him in any way. I had brought some of my nicest books for him: he asked me to read a little of one, and I was about to comply, when Earnshaw burst the door open: having gathered venom with reflection. He advanced direct to us, seized Linton by the arm, and swung him off the seat.

"'Get to thy own room!' he said, in a voice almost inarticulate with passion; and his face looked swelled and furious. 'Take her there if she comes to see thee: thou shalln't keep me out of this. Begone wi' ye both!'

"He swore at us, and left Linton no time to answer, nearly throwing him into the kitchen; and he clenched his fist as I followed, seemingly longing to knock me down. I was afraid for a moment, and I let one volume fall; he kicked it after me, and shut us out. I heard a malignant, crackly laugh by the fire, and turning, beheld that odious Joseph standing rubbing his bony hands, and quivering.

"'I wer sure he'd sarve ye out! He's a grand lad! He's getten t' raight sperrit in him! *He* knaws – ay, he knaws, as weel as I do, who sud be t' maister yonder – ech, ech, ech! He made ye skift properly! Ech, ech, ech!'

"'Where must we go?' I asked of my cousin, disregarding the old wretch's mockery.

"Linton was white and trembling. He was not pretty then, Ellen: oh, no! He looked frightful; for his thin face and large eyes were wrought into an expression of frantic, powerless fury. He grasped the handle of the door, and shook it: it was fastened inside.

"'If you don't let me in, I'll kill you! – If you don't let me in, I'll kill you!' he rather shrieked than said. 'Devil! Devil! – I'll kill you – I'll kill you!'

"Joseph uttered his croaking laugh again.

"'Thear, that's t' father!' he cried. 'That's father! We've allas summut o' either side in us. Niver heed, Hareton, lad – dunnut be 'feard – he cannot get at thee!'

"I took hold of Linton's hands, and tried to pull him away; but he shrieked so shockingly that I dared not proceed. At last his cries were choked by a dreadful fit of coughing; blood gushed from his mouth, and he fell on the ground. I ran into the yard, sick with terror; and called for Zillah, as loud as I could. She soon heard me: she was milking the cows in a shed behind the barn, and hurrying from her work, she inquired what there was to do? I hadn't breath to explain; dragging her in, I looked about for Linton. Earnshaw had come out to examine the mischief he had caused, and he was then conveying the poor thing upstairs. Zillah and I ascended after him; but he stopped me at the top of the steps, and said I shouldn't go in: I must go home. I exclaimed that he had killed Linton, and I *would* enter. Joseph locked the door, and declared I should do 'no sich stuff,' and asked me whether I were 'bahn to be as mad as him'. I stood crying till the housekeeper reappeared. She affirmed he would be better in a bit, but he couldn't do with that shrieking and din; and she took me, and nearly carried me into the house.

"Ellen, I was ready to tear my hair off my head! I sobbed and wept so that my eyes were almost blind; and the ruffian you have such sympathy with stood opposite: presuming every now and then to bid me 'wisht', and denying that it was his fault; and, finally, frightened by my assertions that I would tell papa, and that he should be put in prison and hanged, he commenced blubbering himself, and hurried out to hide his cowardly agitation. Still, I was not rid of him: when at length they compelled me to depart, and I had got some hundred yards off the premises, he suddenly issued from the shadow of the road-side, and checked Minny and took hold of me.

"'Miss Catherine, I'm ill grieved,' he began, 'but it's rayther too bad –'

"I gave him a cut with my whip, thinking perhaps he would murder me. He let go, thundering one of his horrid curses, and I galloped home more than half out of my senses.

"I didn't bid you good-night that evening, and I didn't go to Wuthering Heights the next: I wished to go exceedingly; but I was strangely excited, and dreaded to hear that Linton was dead, sometimes; and sometimes shuddered at the thought of encountering Hareton. On the third day I took courage: at least, I couldn't bear longer suspense, and stole off once more. I went at five o'clock, and walked; fancying I might manage to creep into the house, and up to Linton's room, unobserved. However, the dogs gave notice of my approach. Zillah received me, and saying 'the lad was mending nicely', showed me into a small, tidy, carpeted apartment, where, to my inexpressible joy, I beheld Linton laid on a little sofa, reading one of my books. But he would neither speak to me nor look at me, through a whole hour, Ellen: he has such an unhappy temper. And what quite confounded me, when he did open his mouth, it was to utter the falsehood that I had occasioned the uproar, and Hareton was not to blame! Unable to reply, except passionately, I got up and walked from the room. He sent after me a faint 'Catherine!' He did not reckon on being answered so: but I wouldn't turn back; and the morrow was the second day on which I stayed at home, nearly determined to visit him no more. But it was so miserable going to bed and getting up, and never hearing anything about him, that my resolution melted into air before it was properly formed. It had appeared wrong to take the journey once; now it seemed wrong to refrain. Michael came to ask if he must saddle Minny; I said 'Yes', and considered myself doing a duty as she bore me over the hills. I was forced to pass the front windows to get to the court: it was no use trying to conceal my presence.

"'Young master is in the house,' said Zillah, as she saw me making for the parlour. I went in; Earnshaw was there also, but he quitted the room directly. Linton sat in the great arm-chair half asleep; walking up to the fire, I began in a serious tone, partly meaning it to be true –

"'As you don't like me, Linton, and as you think I come on purpose to hurt you, and pretend that I do so every time, this is our last meeting: let us say goodbye; and tell Mr. Heathcliff that you have no wish to see me, and that he mustn't invent any more falsehoods on the subject.'

"'Sit down and take your hat off, Catherine,' he answered. 'You are so much happier than I am, you ought to be better. Papa talks enough of my defects, and shows enough scorn of me, to make it natural I should doubt myself. I doubt whether I am not altogether as worthless as he calls me, frequently; and then I feel so cross and bitter, I hate everybody! I am worthless, and bad in temper, and bad in spirit, almost always; and, if you choose, you may say goodbye: you'll get rid of an annoyance. Only, Catherine, do me this justice: believe that if I might be as sweet, and as kind, and as good as you are, I would be; as willingly, and more so, than as happy and as healthy. And believe that your kindness has made me love you deeper than if I deserved your love: and though I couldn't, and cannot help showing my nature to you, I regret it and repent it; and shall regret and repent it till I die!'

"I felt he spoke the truth; and I felt I must forgive him: and, though we should quarrel the next moment, I must forgive him again. We were reconciled; but we cried, both of us, the whole time I stayed: not entirely for sorrow; yet I *was* sorry Linton had that distorted nature. He'll never let his friends be at ease, and he'll never be at ease himself! I have always gone to his little parlour, since that night; because his father returned the day after.

"About three times, I think, we have been merry and hopeful, as we were the first evening; the rest of my visits were dreary and troubled: now with his selfishness and spite, and now with his sufferings: but I've learned to endure the former with nearly as little resentment as the latter. Mr. Heathcliff purposely avoids me: I have hardly seen him at all. Last Sunday, indeed, coming earlier than usual, I heard him abusing poor Linton cruelly for his conduct of the night before. I can't tell how he knew of it, unless he listened. Linton had certainly behaved provokingly: however, it was the business of nobody but me, and I interrupted Mr. Heathcliff's lecture by entering and telling him so. He burst into a laugh, and went away, saying he was glad I took that view of the matter. Since then, I've told Linton he must whisper his bitter things. Now, Ellen, you have heard all. I can't be prevented from going to Wuthering Heights, except by inflicting misery on two people; whereas, if you'll only not tell papa, my going need disturb the tranquillity of none. You'll not tell, will you? It will be very heartless, if you do."

"I'll make up my mind on that point by tomorrow, Miss Catherine," I replied. "It requires some study; and so I'll leave you to your rest, and go think it over."

I thought it over aloud, in my master's presence; walking straight from her room to his, and relating the whole story: with the exception of her conversations with her cousin, and any mention of Hareton. Mr. Linton was alarmed and distressed, more than he would acknowledge to me. In the morning, Catherine learnt my betrayal of her confidence, and she learnt also that her secret visits were to end. In vain she wept and writhed against the interdict, and implored her father to have pity on Linton: all she got to comfort her was a promise that he would write and give him leave to come to the Grange when he pleased; but explaining that he must no longer expect to see Catherine at Wuthering Heights. Perhaps, had he been aware of his nephew's disposition and state of health, he would have seen fit to withhold even that slight consolation.

Chapter Twenty-Five

"THESE THINGS happened last winter, sir," said Mrs. Dean; "hardly more than a year ago. Last winter, I did not think, at another twelve months' end, I should be amusing a stranger to the family with relating them! Yet, who knows how long you'll be a stranger? You're too young to rest always contented, living by yourself; and I some way fancy no one could see Catherine Linton and not love her. You smile; but why do you look so lively and interested when I talk about her? And why have you asked me to hang her picture over your fireplace? And why –?"

"Stop, my good friend!" I cried. "It may be very possible that *I* should love her; but would she love me? I doubt it too much to venture my tranquillity by running into temptation: and then my home is not here. I'm of the busy world, and to its arms I must return. Go on. Was Catherine obedient to her father's commands?"

She was, continued the housekeeper. Her affection for him was still the chief sentiment in her heart; and he spoke without anger: he spoke in the deep tenderness of one about to leave his treasure amid perils and foes, where his remembered words would be the only aid that he could bequeath to guide her. He said to me, a few days afterwards, "I wish my nephew would write, Ellen, or call. Tell me, sincerely, what you think of him: is he changed for the better, or is there a prospect of improvement, as he grows a man?"

"He's very delicate, sir," I replied; "and scarcely likely to reach manhood: but this I can say, he does not resemble his father; and if Miss Catherine had the misfortune to marry him, he would not be beyond her control: unless she were extremely and foolishly indulgent. However, master, you'll have plenty of time to get acquainted with him and see whether he would suit her: it wants four years and more to his being of age."

Edgar sighed; and, walking to the window, looked out towards Gimmerton Kirk. It was a misty afternoon, but the February sun shone dimly, and we could just distinguish the two fir-trees in the yard, and the sparely-scattered gravestones.

"I've prayed often," he half soliloquised, "for the approach of what is coming; and now I begin to shrink, and fear it. I thought the memory of the hour I came down that glen a bridegroom would be less sweet than the anticipation that I was soon, in a few months, or, possibly, weeks, to be carried up, and laid in its lonely hollow! Ellen, I've been very happy with my little Cathy: through winter nights and summer days she was a living hope at my side. But I've been as happy musing by myself among those stones, under that old church: lying, through the long June evenings, on the green mound of her mother's grave, and wishing – yearning for the time when I might lie beneath it. What can I do for Cathy? How must I quit her? I'd not care one moment for Linton being Heathcliff's son; nor for his taking her from me, if he could console her for my loss. I'd not care that Heathcliff gained his ends, and triumphed in robbing me of my last blessing! But should Linton be unworthy – only a feeble tool to his father – I cannot abandon her to him! And, hard though it be to crush her buoyant spirit, I must persevere in making her sad while I live, and leaving her solitary when I die. Darling! I'd rather resign her to God, and lay her in the earth before me."

"Resign her to God as it is, sir," I answered, "and if we should lose you – which may He forbid – under His providence, I'll stand her friend and counsellor to the last. Miss Catherine is a good girl: I don't fear that she will go wilfully wrong; and people who do their duty are always finally rewarded."

Spring advanced; yet my master gathered no real strength, though he resumed his walks in the grounds with his daughter. To her inexperienced notions, this itself was a sign of convalescence; and then his cheek was often flushed, and his eyes were bright; she felt sure of his recovering. On her seventeenth birthday, he did not visit the churchyard: it was raining, and I observed – "You'll surely not go out tonight, sir?"

He answered, "No, I'll defer it this year a little longer." He wrote again to Linton, expressing his great desire to see him; and, had the invalid been presentable, I've no doubt his father would have permitted him to come. As it was, being instructed, he returned an answer, intimating that Mr. Heathcliff objected to his calling at the Grange; but his uncle's kind remembrance delighted him, and he hoped to meet him sometimes in his rambles, and personally to petition that his cousin and he might not remain long so utterly divided.

That part of his letter was simple, and probably his own. Heathcliff knew he could plead eloquently for Catherine's company, then.

I do not ask, he said, *that she may visit here; but am I never to see her, because my father forbids me to go to her home, and you forbid her to come to mine? Do, now and then, ride with her towards the Heights; and let us exchange a few words, in your presence! We have done nothing to deserve this separation; and you are not angry with me: you have no reason to dislike me, you allow, yourself. Dear uncle! Send me a kind note tomorrow, and leave to join you anywhere you please, except at Thrushcross Grange. I believe an interview would convince you that my father's character is not mine: he affirms I am more your nephew than his son; and though I have faults which render me unworthy of Catherine, she has excused them, and for her sake, you should also. You inquire after my health – it is better; but while I remain cut off from all hope, and doomed to solitude, or the society of those who never did and never will like me, how can I be cheerful and well?*

Edgar, though he felt for the boy, could not consent to grant his request; because he could not accompany Catherine. He said, in summer, perhaps, they might meet: meantime, he wished him to continue writing at intervals, and engaged to give him what advice and comfort he was able by letter; being well aware of his hard position in his family. Linton complied; and had he been unrestrained, would probably have spoiled all by filling his epistles with complaints and lamentations: but his father kept a sharp watch over him; and, of course, insisted on every line that my master sent being shown; so, instead of penning his peculiar personal sufferings and distresses, the themes constantly uppermost in his thoughts, he harped on the cruel obligation of being held asunder from his friend and love; and gently intimated that Mr. Linton must allow an interview soon, or he should fear he was purposely deceiving him with empty promises.

Cathy was a powerful ally at home; and between them they at length persuaded my master to acquiesce in their having a ride or a walk together about once a week, under my guardianship, and on the moors nearest the Grange: for June found him still declining. Though he had set aside yearly a portion of his income for my young lady's fortune, he had a natural desire that she might retain – or at least return in a short time to – the house of her ancestors; and he considered her only prospect of doing that was by a union with his heir; he had no idea that the latter was failing almost as fast as himself; nor had any one, I believe: no doctor visited the Heights, and no one saw Master Heathcliff to make report of his condition among us. I, for my part, began to fancy my forebodings were false, and that he must be actually rallying, when he mentioned riding and walking on the moors, and seemed so earnest in pursuing his object. I could not picture a father treating a dying child as tyrannically and wickedly as I afterwards learned Heathcliff had treated him, to compel this apparent eagerness: his efforts redoubling the more imminently his avaricious and unfeeling plans were threatened with defeat by death.

Chapter Twenty-Six

SUMMER was already past its prime, when Edgar reluctantly yielded his assent to their entreaties, and Catherine and I set out on our first ride to join her cousin. It was a close, sultry day: devoid of sunshine, but with a sky too dappled and hazy to threaten rain: and our place of meeting had been fixed at the guide-stone, by the cross-roads. On arriving there, however, a little herd-boy, despatched as a messenger, told us that – "Maister Linton wer just o' this side th' Heights: and he'd be mitch obleeged to us to gang on a bit further."

"Then Master Linton has forgot the first injunction of his uncle," I observed: "he bid us keep on the Grange land, and here we are off at once."

"Well, we'll turn our horses' heads round when we reach him," answered my companion; "our excursion shall lie towards home."

But when we reached him, and that was scarcely a quarter of a mile from his own door, we found he had no horse; and we were forced to dismount, and leave ours to graze. He lay on the heath, awaiting our approach, and did not rise till we came within a few yards. Then he walked so feebly, and looked so pale, that I immediately exclaimed, "Why, Master Heathcliff, you are not fit for enjoying a ramble this morning. How ill you do look!"

Catherine surveyed him with grief and astonishment: she changed the ejaculation of joy on her lips to one of alarm; and the congratulation on their long-postponed meeting to an anxious inquiry, whether he were worse than usual?

"No – better – better!" he panted, trembling, and retaining her hand as if he needed its support, while his large blue eyes wandered timidly over her; the hollowness round them transforming to haggard wildness the languid expression they once possessed.

"But you have been worse," persisted his cousin; "worse than when I saw you last; you are thinner, and –"

"I'm tired," he interrupted, hurriedly. "It is too hot for walking, let us rest here. And, in the morning, I often feel sick – papa says I grow so fast."

Badly satisfied, Cathy sat down, and he reclined beside her.

"This is something like your paradise," said she, making an effort at cheerfulness. "You recollect the two days we agreed to spend in the place and way each thought pleasantest? This is nearly yours, only there are clouds; but then they are so soft and mellow: it is nicer than sunshine. Next week, if you can, we'll ride down to the Grange Park, and try mine."

Linton did not appear to remember what she talked of and he had evidently great difficulty in sustaining any kind of conversation. His lack of interest in the subjects she started, and his equal incapacity to contribute to her entertainment, were so obvious that she could not conceal her disappointment. An indefinite alteration had come over his whole person and manner. The pettishness that might be caressed into fondness, had yielded to a listless apathy; there was less of the peevish temper of a child which frets and teases on purpose to be soothed, and more of the self-absorbed moroseness of a confirmed invalid, repelling consolation, and ready to regard the good-humoured mirth of others as an insult. Catherine perceived, as well as I did, that he held it rather a punishment, than a gratification, to endure our company; and she made no scruple of proposing, presently, to depart. That proposal, unexpectedly, roused Linton from his lethargy, and threw him into a strange state of agitation. He glanced fearfully towards the Heights, begging she would remain another half-hour, at least.

"But I think," said Cathy, "you'd be more comfortable at home than sitting here; and I cannot amuse you today, I see, by my tales, and songs, and chatter: you have grown wiser than I, in these six months; you have little taste for my diversions now: or else, if I could amuse you, I'd willingly stay."

"Stay to rest yourself," he replied. "And, Catherine, don't think or say that I'm *very* unwell: it is the heavy weather and heat that make me dull; and I walked about, before you came, a great deal for me. Tell uncle I'm in tolerable health, will you?"

"I'll tell him that *you* say so, Linton. I couldn't affirm that you are," observed my young lady, wondering at his pertinacious assertion of what was evidently an untruth.

"And be here again next Thursday," continued he, shunning her puzzled gaze. "And give him my thanks for permitting you to come – my best thanks, Catherine. And – and, if you *did* meet my father, and he asked you about me, don't lead him to suppose that I've been extremely silent and stupid: don't look sad and downcast, as you are doing – he'll be angry."

"I care nothing for his anger," exclaimed Cathy, imagining she would be its object.

"But I do," said her cousin, shuddering. "*Don't* provoke him against me, Catherine, for he is very hard."

"Is he severe to you, Master Heathcliff?" I inquired. "Has he grown weary of indulgence, and passed from passive to active hatred?"

Linton looked at me, but did not answer; and, after keeping her seat by his side another ten minutes, during which his head fell drowsily on his breast, and he uttered nothing except suppressed moans of exhaustion or pain, Cathy began to seek solace in looking for bilberries, and sharing the produce of her researches with me: she did not offer them to him, for she saw further notice would only weary and annoy.

"Is it half-an-hour now, Ellen?" she whispered in my ear, at last. "I can't tell why we should stay. He's asleep, and papa will be wanting us back."

"Well, we must not leave him asleep," I answered; "wait till he wakes, and be patient. You were mighty eager to set off, but your longing to see poor Linton has soon evaporated!"

"Why did *he* wish to see me?" returned Catherine. "In his crossest humours, formerly, I liked him better than I do in his present curious mood. It's just as if it were a task he was compelled to perform – this interview – for fear his father should scold him. But I'm hardly going to come to give Mr. Heathcliff pleasure; whatever reason he may have for ordering Linton to undergo this penance. And, though I'm glad he's better in health, I'm sorry he's so much less pleasant, and so much less affectionate to me."

"You think *he is* better in health, then?" I said.

"Yes," she answered; "because he always made such a great deal of his sufferings, you know. He is not tolerably well, as he told me to tell papa; but he's better, very likely."

"There you differ with me, Miss Cathy," I remarked; "I should conjecture him to be far worse."

Linton here started from his slumber in bewildered terror, and asked if anyone had called his name.

"No," said Catherine; "unless in dreams. I cannot conceive how you manage to doze out of doors, in the morning."

"I thought I heard my father," he gasped, glancing up to the frowning nab above us. "You are sure nobody spoke?"

"Quite sure," replied his cousin. "Only Ellen and I were disputing concerning your health. Are you truly stronger, Linton, than when we separated in winter? If you be, I'm certain one thing is not stronger – your regard for me: speak – are you?"

The tears gushed from Linton's eyes as he answered, "Yes, yes, I am!" And, still under the spell of the imaginary voice, his gaze wandered up and down to detect its owner.

Cathy rose. "For today we must part," she said. "And I won't conceal that I have been sadly disappointed with our meeting; though I'll mention it to nobody but you: not that I stand in awe of Mr. Heathcliff."

"Hush," murmured Linton; "for God's sake, hush! He's coming." And he clung to Catherine's arm, striving to detain her; but at that announcement she hastily disengaged herself, and whistled to Minny, who obeyed her like a dog.

"I'll be here next Thursday," she cried, springing to the saddle. "Goodbye. Quick, Ellen!"

And so we left him, scarcely conscious of our departure, so absorbed was he in anticipating his father's approach.

Before we reached home, Catherine's displeasure softened into a perplexed sensation of pity and regret, largely blended with vague, uneasy doubts about Linton's actual circumstances, physical and social: in which I partook, though I counselled her not to say much; for a second journey would make us better judges. My master requested an account of our ongoings. His nephew's offering of thanks was duly delivered, Miss Cathy gently touching on the rest: I also threw little light on his inquiries, for I hardly knew what to hide and what to reveal.

Chapter Twenty-Seven

SEVEN DAYS glided away, every one marking its course by the henceforth rapid alteration of Edgar Linton's state. The havoc that months had previously wrought was now emulated by the inroads of hours. Catherine we would fain have deluded yet; but her own quick spirit refused to delude her: it divined in secret, and brooded on the dreadful probability, gradually ripening into certainty. She had not the heart to mention her ride, when Thursday came round; I mentioned it for her, and obtained permission to order her out of doors: for the library, where her father stopped a short time daily – the brief period he could bear to sit up – and his chamber, had become her whole world. She grudged each moment that did not find her bending over his pillow, or seated by his side. Her countenance grew wan with watching and sorrow, and my master gladly dismissed her to what he flattered himself would be a happy change of scene and society; drawing comfort from the hope that she would not now be left entirely alone after his death.

He had a fixed idea, I guessed by several observations he let fall, that, as his nephew resembled him in person, he would resemble him in mind; for Linton's letters bore few or no indications of his defective character. And I, through pardonable weakness, refrained from correcting the error; asking myself what good there would be in disturbing his last moments with information that he had neither power nor opportunity to turn to account.

We deferred our excursion till the afternoon; a golden afternoon of August: every breath from the hills so full of life, that it seemed whoever respired it, though dying, might revive. Catherine's face was just like the landscape – shadows and sunshine flitting over it in rapid succession; but the shadows rested longer, and the sunshine was more transient; and her poor little heart reproached itself for even that passing forgetfulness of its cares.

We discerned Linton watching at the same spot he had selected before. My young mistress alighted, and told me that, as she was resolved to stay a very little while, I had better hold the pony and remain on horseback; but I dissented: I wouldn't risk losing sight of the charge committed to me a minute; so we climbed the slope of heath together. Master Heathcliff received us with greater animation on this occasion: not the animation of high spirits though, nor yet of joy; it looked more like fear.

"It is late!" he said, speaking short and with difficulty. "Is not your father very ill? I thought you wouldn't come."

"*Why* won't you be candid?" cried Catherine, swallowing her greeting. "Why cannot you say at once you don't want me? It is strange, Linton, that for the second time you have brought me here on purpose, apparently to distress us both, and for no reason besides!"

Linton shivered, and glanced at her, half supplicating, half ashamed; but his cousin's patience was not sufficient to endure this enigmatical behaviour.

"My father *is* very ill," she said; "and why am I called from his bedside? Why didn't you send to absolve me from my promise, when you wished I wouldn't keep it? Come! I desire an explanation: playing and trifling are completely banished out of my mind; and I can't dance attendance on your affectations now!"

"My affectations!" he murmured; "What are they? For heaven's sake, Catherine, don't look so angry! Despise me as much as you please; I am a worthless, cowardly wretch: I can't be scorned enough; but I'm too mean for your anger. Hate my father, and spare me for contempt."

"Nonsense!" cried Catherine in a passion. "Foolish, silly boy! And there! He trembles: as if I were really going to touch him! You needn't bespeak contempt, Linton: anybody will have it spontaneously at your service. Get off! I shall return home: it is folly dragging you from the hearth-stone, and pretending – what do we pretend? Let go my frock! If I pitied you for crying and looking so very frightened, you should spurn such pity. Ellen, tell him how disgraceful this conduct is. Rise, and don't degrade yourself into an abject reptile – *don't*!"

With streaming face and an expression of agony, Linton had thrown his nerveless frame along the ground: he seemed convulsed with exquisite terror.

"Oh!" he sobbed, "I cannot bear it! Catherine, Catherine, I'm a traitor, too, and I dare not tell you! But leave me, and I shall be killed! *Dear* Catherine, my life is in your hands: and you have said you loved me, and if you did, it wouldn't harm you. You'll not go, then? Kind, sweet, good Catherine! And perhaps you *will* consent – and he'll let me die with you!"

My young lady, on witnessing his intense anguish, stooped to raise him. The old feeling of indulgent tenderness overcame her vexation, and she grew thoroughly moved and alarmed.

"Consent to what?" she asked. "To stay! Tell me the meaning of this strange talk, and I will. You contradict your own words, and distract me! Be calm and frank, and confess at once all that weighs on your heart. You wouldn't injure me, Linton, would you? You wouldn't let any enemy hurt me, if you could prevent it? I'll believe you are a coward, for yourself, but not a cowardly betrayer of your best friend."

"But my father threatened me," gasped the boy, clasping his attenuated fingers, "and I dread him – I dread him! I *dare* not tell!"

"Oh, well!" said Catherine, with scornful compassion, "keep your secret: *I'm* no coward. Save yourself: I'm not afraid!"

Her magnanimity provoked his tears: he wept wildly, kissing her supporting hands, and yet could not summon courage to speak out. I was cogitating what the mystery might be, and determined Catherine should never suffer to benefit him or anyone else, by my good will; when, hearing a rustle among the ling, I looked up and saw Mr. Heathcliff almost close upon us, descending the Heights. He didn't cast a glance towards my companions, though they were sufficiently near for Linton's sobs to be audible; but hailing me in the almost hearty tone he assumed to none besides, and the sincerity of which I couldn't avoid doubting, he said –

"It is something to see you so near to my house, Nelly. How are you at the Grange? Let us hear. The rumour goes," he added, in a lower tone, "that Edgar Linton is on his death-bed: perhaps they exaggerate his illness?"

"No; my master is dying," I replied: "it is true enough. A sad thing it will be for us all, but a blessing for him!"

"How long will he last, do you think?" he asked.

"I don't know," I said.

"Because," he continued, looking at the two young people, who were fixed under his eye – Linton appeared as if he could not venture to stir or raise his head, and Catherine could not move, on his account – "because that lad yonder seems determined to beat me; and I'd thank his uncle to be quick, and go before him! Hallo! Has the whelp been playing that game long? I *did* give him some lessons about snivelling. Is he pretty lively with Miss Linton generally?"

"Lively? No – he has shown the greatest distress," I answered. "To see him, I should say, that instead of rambling with his sweetheart on the hills, he ought to be in bed, under the hands of a doctor."

"He shall be, in a day or two," muttered Heathcliff. "But first – get up, Linton! Get up!" he shouted. "Don't grovel on the ground there – up, this moment!"

Linton had sunk prostrate again in another paroxysm of helpless fear, caused by his father's glance towards him, I suppose: there was nothing else to produce such humiliation. He made several efforts to obey, but his little strength was annihilated for the time, and he fell back again with a moan. Mr. Heathcliff advanced, and lifted him to lean against a ridge of turf.

"Now," said he, with curbed ferocity, "I'm getting angry and if you don't command that paltry spirit of yours – *damn* you! Get up directly!"

"I will, father," he panted. "Only, let me alone, or I shall faint. I've done as you wished, I'm sure. Catherine will tell you that I – that I – have been cheerful. Ah! Keep by me, Catherine; give me your hand."

"Take mine," said his father; "stand on your feet. There now – she'll lend you her arm: that's right, look at her. You would imagine I was the devil himself, Miss Linton, to excite such horror. Be so kind as to walk home with him, will you? He shudders if I touch him."

"Linton dear!" whispered Catherine, "I can't go to Wuthering Heights: papa has forbidden me. He'll not harm you: why are you so afraid?"

"I can never re-enter that house," he answered. "I'm *not* to re-enter it without you!"

"Stop!" cried his father. "We'll respect Catherine's filial scruples. Nelly, take him in, and I'll follow your advice concerning the doctor, without delay."

"You'll do well," replied I. "But I must remain with my mistress: to mind your son is not my business."

"You are very stiff," said Heathcliff, "I know that: but you'll force me to pinch the baby and make it scream before it moves your charity. Come, then, my hero. Are you willing to return, escorted by me?"

He approached once more, and made as if he would seize the fragile being; but, shrinking back, Linton clung to his cousin, and implored her to accompany him, with a frantic importunity that admitted no denial. However I disapproved, I couldn't hinder her: indeed, how could she have refused him herself? What was filling him with dread we had no means of discerning; but there he was, powerless under its gripe, and any addition seemed capable of shocking him into idiocy. We reached the threshold; Catherine walked in, and I stood waiting till she had conducted the invalid to a chair, expecting her out immediately; when Mr. Heathcliff, pushing me forward, exclaimed – "My house is not stricken with the plague, Nelly; and I have a mind to be hospitable today: sit down, and allow me to shut the door."

He shut and locked it also. I started.

"You shall have tea before you go home," he added. "I am by myself. Hareton is gone with some cattle to the Lees, and Zillah and Joseph are off on a journey of pleasure; and, though I'm used to being alone, I'd rather have some interesting company, if I can get it. Miss Linton, take your seat by *him*. I give you what I have: the present is hardly worth accepting; but I have nothing else to offer. It is Linton, I mean. How she does stare! It's odd what a savage feeling I have to anything that seems afraid of me! Had I been born where laws are less strict and tastes less dainty, I should treat myself to a slow vivisection of those two, as an evening's amusement."

He drew in his breath, struck the table, and swore to himself, "By hell! I hate them."

"I am not afraid of you!" exclaimed Catherine, who could not hear the latter part of his speech. She stepped close up; her black eyes flashing with passion and resolution. "Give me that key: I will have it!" she said. "I wouldn't eat or drink here, if I were starving."

Heathcliff had the key in his hand that remained on the table. He looked up, seized with a sort of surprise at her boldness; or, possibly, reminded, by her voice and glance, of the person from whom she inherited it. She snatched at the instrument, and half succeeded in getting it out of his loosened fingers: but her action recalled him to the present; he recovered it speedily.

"Now, Catherine Linton," he said, "stand off, or I shall knock you down; and, that will make Mrs. Dean mad."

Regardless of this warning, she captured his closed hand and its contents again. "We *will* go!" she repeated, exerting her utmost efforts to cause the iron muscles to relax; and finding that her nails made no impression, she applied her teeth pretty sharply. Heathcliff glanced at me a glance that kept me from interfering a moment. Catherine was too intent on his fingers to notice his face.

He opened them suddenly, and resigned the object of dispute; but, ere she had well secured it, he seized her with the liberated hand, and, pulling her on his knee, administered with the other a shower of terrific slaps on both sides of the head, each sufficient to have fulfilled his threat, had she been able to fall.

At this diabolical violence I rushed on him furiously. "You villain!" I began to cry, "you villain!" A touch on the chest silenced me: I am stout, and soon put out of breath; and, what with that and the rage, I staggered dizzily back and felt ready to suffocate, or to burst a blood-vessel. The scene was over in two minutes; Catherine, released, put her two hands to her temples, and looked just as if she were not sure whether her ears were off or on. She trembled like a reed, poor thing, and leant against the table perfectly bewildered.

"I know how to chastise children, you see," said the scoundrel, grimly, as he stooped to repossess himself of the key, which had dropped to the floor. "Go to Linton now, as I told you; and cry at your ease! I shall be your father, tomorrow – all the father you'll have in a few days – and you shall have plenty of that. You can bear plenty; you're no weakling: you shall have a daily taste, if I catch such a devil of a temper in your eyes again!"

Cathy ran to me instead of Linton, and knelt down and put her burning cheek on my lap, weeping aloud. Her cousin had shrunk into a corner of the settle, as quiet as a mouse, congratulating himself, I dare say, that the correction had alighted on another than him. Mr. Heathcliff, perceiving us all confounded, rose, and expeditiously made the tea himself. The cups and saucers were laid ready. He poured it out, and handed me a cup.

"Wash away your spleen," he said. "And help your own naughty pet and mine. It is not poisoned, though I prepared it. I'm going out to seek your horses."

Our first thought, on his departure, was to force an exit somewhere. We tried the kitchen door, but that was fastened outside: we looked at the windows – they were too narrow for even Cathy's little figure.

"Master Linton," I cried, seeing we were regularly imprisoned, "you know what your diabolical father is after, and you shall tell us, or I'll box your ears, as he has done your cousin's."

"Yes, Linton, you must tell," said Catherine. "It was for your sake I came; and it will be wickedly ungrateful if you refuse."

"Give me some tea, I'm thirsty, and then I'll tell you," he answered. "Mrs. Dean, go away. I don't like you standing over me. Now, Catherine, you are letting your tears fall into my cup. I won't drink that. Give me another." Catherine pushed another to him, and wiped her face. I felt disgusted at the little wretch's composure, since he was no longer in terror for himself. The anguish he had exhibited on the moor subsided as soon as ever he entered Wuthering Heights; so I guessed he had been menaced with an awful visitation of wrath if he failed in decoying us there; and, that accomplished, he had no further immediate fears.

"Papa wants us to be married," he continued, after sipping some of the liquid. "And he knows your papa wouldn't let us marry now; and he's afraid of my dying if we wait; so we are to be married in the morning, and you are to stay here all night; and, if you do as he wishes, you shall return home next day, and take me with you."

"Take you with her, pitiful changeling!" I exclaimed. "*You* marry? Why, the man is mad! Or he thinks us fools, every one. And do you imagine that beautiful young lady, that healthy, hearty girl, will tie herself to a little perishing monkey like you? Are you cherishing the notion that anybody, let alone Miss Catherine Linton, would have you for a husband? You want whipping for bringing us in here at all, with your dastardly puling tricks: and – don't look so silly, now! I've a very good mind to shake you severely, for your contemptible treachery, and your imbecile conceit."

I did give him a slight shaking; but it brought on the cough, and he took to his ordinary resource of moaning and weeping, and Catherine rebuked me.

"Stay all night? No," she said, looking slowly round. "Ellen, I'll burn that door down but I'll get out."

And she would have commenced the execution of her threat directly, but Linton was up in alarm for his dear self again. He clasped her in his two feeble arms sobbing: – "Won't you have me, and save me? Not let me come to the Grange? Oh, darling Catherine! You mustn't go and leave, after all. You *must* obey my father – you *must*!"

"I must obey my own," she replied, "and relieve him from this cruel suspense. The whole night! What would he think? He'll be distressed already. I'll either break or burn a way out of the house. Be quiet! You're in no danger; but if you hinder me – Linton, I love papa better than you!" The mortal terror he felt of Mr. Heathcliff's anger restored to the boy his coward's eloquence. Catherine was near distraught: still, she persisted that she must go home, and tried entreaty in her turn, persuading him to subdue his selfish agony. While they were thus occupied, our jailor re-entered.

"Your beasts have trotted off," he said, "and – now Linton! Snivelling again? What has she been doing to you? Come, come – have done, and get to bed. In a month or two, my lad, you'll be able to pay her back her present tyrannies with a vigorous hand. You're pining for pure love, are you not? Nothing else in the world: and she shall have you! There, to bed! Zillah won't be here tonight; you must undress yourself. Hush! Hold your noise! Once in your own room, I'll not come near you: you needn't fear. By chance, you've managed tolerably. I'll look to the rest."

He spoke these words, holding the door open for his son to pass, and the latter achieved his exit exactly as a spaniel might which suspected the person who attended on it of designing a spiteful squeeze. The lock was re-secured. Heathcliff approached the fire, where my mistress and I stood silent. Catherine looked up, and instinctively raised her hand to her cheek: his neighbourhood revived a painful sensation. Anybody else would have been incapable of regarding the childish act with sternness, but he scowled on her and muttered – "Oh! You are not afraid of me? Your courage is well disguised: you seem damnably afraid!"

"I *am* afraid now," she replied, "because, if I stay, papa will be miserable: and how can I endure making him miserable – when he – when he – Mr. Heathcliff, let *me* go home! I promise to marry Linton: papa would like me to: and I love him. Why should you wish to force me to do what I'll willingly do of myself?"

"Let him dare to force you," I cried. "There's law in the land, thank God! There is; though we be in an out-of-the-way place. I'd inform if he were my own son: and it's felony without benefit of clergy!"

"Silence!" said the ruffian. "To the devil with your clamour! I don't want *you* to speak. Miss Linton, I shall enjoy myself remarkably in thinking your father will be miserable: I shall not sleep for satisfaction. You could have hit on no surer way of fixing your residence under my roof for the next twenty-four hours than informing me that such an event would follow. As to your promise to marry Linton, I'll take care you shall keep it; for you shall not quit this place till it is fulfilled."

"Send Ellen, then, to let papa know I'm safe!" exclaimed Catherine, weeping bitterly. "Or marry me now. Poor papa! Ellen, he'll think we're lost. What shall we do?"

"Not he! He'll think you are tired of waiting on him, and run off for a little amusement," answered Heathcliff. "You cannot deny that you entered my house of your own accord, in contempt of his injunctions to the contrary. And it is quite natural that you should desire amusement at your age; and that you would weary of nursing a sick man, and that man *only* your father. Catherine, his happiest days were over when your days began. He cursed you, I dare say, for coming into the world (I did, at least); and it would just do if he cursed you as *he* went out of it. I'd join him. I don't love you! How should I? Weep away. As far as I can see, it will be your chief diversion hereafter; unless Linton make amends for other losses: and your provident parent appears to fancy he may. His letters of advice and consolation entertained me vastly. In his last he recommended my jewel to be careful of his; and kind to her when he got her. Careful and kind – that's paternal. But Linton requires his whole stock of care and kindness for himself. Linton can play the little tyrant well. He'll undertake to torture any number of cats, if their teeth be drawn and their claws pared. You'll be able to tell his uncle fine tales of his *kindness*, when you get home again, I assure you."

"You're right there!" I said; "Explain your son's character. Show his resemblance to yourself: and then, I hope, Miss Cathy will think twice before she takes the cockatrice!"

"I don't much mind speaking of his amiable qualities now," he answered; "because she must either accept him or remain a prisoner, and you along with her, till your master dies. I can detain you both, quite concealed, here. If you doubt, encourage her to retract her word, and you'll have an opportunity of judging!"

"I'll not retract my word," said Catherine. "I'll marry him within this hour, if I may go to Thrushcross Grange afterwards. Mr. Heathcliff, you're a cruel man, but you're not a fiend; and you won't, from *mere* malice, destroy irrevocably all my happiness. If papa thought I had left him on purpose, and if he died before I returned, could I bear to live? I've given over crying: but I'm going to kneel here, at your knee; and I'll not get up, and I'll not take my eyes from your face till you look back at me! No, don't turn away! *Do look*! You'll see nothing to provoke you. I don't hate you. I'm not angry that you struck me. Have you never loved *anybody* in all your life, uncle? *Never*? Ah! You must look once. I'm so wretched, you can't help being sorry and pitying me."

"Keep your eft's fingers off; and move, or I'll kick you!" cried Heathcliff, brutally repulsing her. "I'd rather be hugged by a snake. How the devil can you dream of fawning on me? I *detest* you!"

He shrugged his shoulders: shook himself, indeed, as if his flesh crept with aversion; and thrust back his chair; while I got up, and opened my mouth, to commence a downright torrent of abuse. But I was rendered dumb in the middle of the first sentence, by a threat that I should be shown into a room by myself the very next syllable I uttered. It was growing dark – we heard a sound of voices at the garden-gate. Our host hurried out instantly: *he* had his wits about him; *we* had not. There was a talk of two or three minutes, and he returned alone.

"I thought it had been your cousin Hareton," I observed to Catherine. "I wish he would arrive! Who knows but he might take our part?"

"It was three servants sent to seek you from the Grange," said Heathcliff, overhearing me. "You should have opened a lattice and called out: but I could swear that chit is glad you didn't. She's glad to be obliged to stay, I'm certain."

At learning the chance we had missed, we both gave vent to our grief without control; and he allowed us to wail on till nine o'clock. Then he bid us go upstairs, through the kitchen, to Zillah's chamber; and I whispered my companion to obey: perhaps we might contrive to get through the window there, or into a garret, and out by its skylight. The window, however, was narrow, like those below, and the garret trap was safe from our attempts; for we were fastened in as before. We neither of us lay down: Catherine took her station by the lattice, and watched anxiously for morning; a deep sigh being the only answer I could obtain to my frequent entreaties that she would try to rest. I seated myself in a chair, and rocked to and fro, passing harsh judgment on my many derelictions of duty; from which, it struck me then, all the misfortunes of my employers sprang. It was not the case, in reality, I am aware; but it was, in my imagination, that dismal night; and I thought Heathcliff himself less guilty than I.

At seven o'clock he came, and inquired if Miss Linton had risen. She ran to the door immediately, and answered, "Yes."

"Here, then," he said, opening it, and pulling her out. I rose to follow, but he turned the lock again. I demanded my release.

"Be patient," he replied; "I'll send up your breakfast in a while."

I thumped on the panels, and rattled the latch angrily and Catherine asked why I was still shut up? He answered, I must try to endure it another hour, and they went away. I endured it two or three hours; at length, I heard a footstep: not Heathcliff's.

"I've brought you something to eat," said a voice; "oppen t' door!"

Complying eagerly, I beheld Hareton, laden with food enough to last me all day.

"Tak' it," he added, thrusting the tray into my hand.

"Stay one minute," I began.

"Nay," cried he, and retired, regardless of any prayers I could pour forth to detain him.

And there I remained enclosed the whole day, and the whole of the next night; and another, and another. Five nights and four days I remained, altogether, seeing nobody but Hareton once every morning; and he was a model of a jailor: surly, and dumb, and deaf to every attempt at moving his sense of justice or compassion.

Chapter Twenty-Eight

ON THE FIFTH MORNING, or rather afternoon, a different step approached – lighter and shorter; and, this time, the person entered the room. It was Zillah; donned in her scarlet shawl, with a black silk bonnet on her head, and a willow-basket swung to her arm.

"Eh, dear! Mrs. Dean!" she exclaimed. "Well! There is a talk about you at Gimmerton. I never thought but you were sunk in the Blackhorse marsh, and missy with you, till master told me you'd been found, and he'd lodged you here! What! And you must have got on an island, sure? And how long were you in the hole? Did master save you, Mrs. Dean? But you're not so thin – you've not been so poorly, have you?"

"Your master is a true scoundrel!" I replied. "But he shall answer for it. He needn't have raised that tale: it shall all be laid bare!"

"What do you mean?" asked Zillah. "It's not his tale: they tell that in the village – about your being lost in the marsh; and I calls to Earnshaw, when I come in – 'Eh, they's queer things, Mr. Hareton, happened since I went off. It's a sad pity of that likely young lass, and cant Nelly Dean.' He stared. I thought he had not heard aught, so I told him the rumour. The master listened, and he just smiled to himself, and said, "If they have been in the marsh, they are out now, Zillah. Nelly Dean is lodged, at this minute, in your room. You can tell her to flit, when you go up; here is the key. The bog-water got into her head, and she would have run home quite flighty; but I fixed her till she came round to her senses. You can bid her go to the Grange at once, if she be able, and carry a message from me, that her young lady will follow in time to attend the squire's funeral.'"

"Mr. Edgar is not dead?" I gasped. "Oh! Zillah, Zillah!"

"No, no; sit you down, my good mistress," she replied; "you're right sickly yet. He's not dead; Doctor Kenneth thinks he may last another day. I met him on the road and asked."

Instead of sitting down, I snatched my outdoor things, and hastened below, for the way was free. On entering the house, I looked about for someone to give information of Catherine. The place was filled with sunshine, and the door stood wide open; but nobody seemed at hand. As I hesitated whether to go off at once, or return and seek my mistress, a slight cough drew my attention to the hearth. Linton lay on the settle, sole tenant, sucking a stick of sugar-candy, and pursuing my movements with apathetic eyes. "Where is Miss Catherine?" I demanded sternly, supposing I could frighten him into giving intelligence, by catching him thus, alone. He sucked on like an innocent.

"Is she gone?" I said.

"No," he replied; "she's upstairs: she's not to go; we won't let her."

"You won't let her, little idiot!" I exclaimed. "Direct me to her room immediately, or I'll make you sing out sharply."

"Papa would make you sing out, if you attempted to get there," he answered. "He says I'm not to be soft with Catherine: she's my wife, and it's shameful that she should wish to leave me. He says she hates me and wants me to die, that she may have my money; but she shan't have it: and she shan't go home! She never shall! – She may cry, and be sick as much as she pleases!"

He resumed his former occupation, closing his lids, as if he meant to drop asleep.

"Master Heathcliff," I resumed, "have you forgotten all Catherine's kindness to you last winter, when you affirmed you loved her, and when she brought you books and sung you songs, and came many a time through wind and snow to see you? She wept to miss one evening, because you would be disappointed; and you felt then that she was a hundred times too good to you: and now you believe the lies your father tells, though you know he detests you both. And you join him against her. That's fine gratitude, is it not?"

The corner of Linton's mouth fell, and he took the sugar-candy from his lips.

"Did she come to Wuthering Heights because she hated you?" I continued. "Think for yourself! As to your money, she does not even know that you will have any. And you say she's sick; and yet you leave her alone, up there in a strange house! You who have felt what it is to be so neglected! You could pity your own sufferings; and she pitied them, too; but you won't pity hers! I shed tears, Master Heathcliff, you see – an elderly woman, and a servant merely – and you, after pretending such affection, and having reason to worship her almost, store every tear you have for yourself, and lie there quite at ease. Ah! You're a heartless, selfish boy!"

"I can't stay with her," he answered crossly. "I'll not stay by myself. She cries so I can't bear it. And she won't give over, though I say I'll call my father. I did call him once, and he threatened to strangle her if she was not quiet; but she began again the instant he left the room, moaning and grieving all night long, though I screamed for vexation that I couldn't sleep."

"Is Mr. Heathcliff out?" I inquired, perceiving that the wretched creature had no power to sympathize with his cousin's mental tortures.

"He's in the court," he replied, "talking to Doctor Kenneth; who says uncle is dying, truly, at last. I'm glad, for I shall be master of the Grange after him. Catherine always spoke of it as her house. It isn't hers! It's mine: papa says everything she has is mine. All her nice books are mine; she offered to give me them, and her pretty birds, and her pony Minny, if I would get the key of our room, and let her out; but I told her she had nothing to give, they were all, all mine. And then she cried, and took a little picture from her neck, and said I should have that; two pictures in a gold case, on one side her mother, and on the other uncle, when they were young. That was yesterday – I said they were mine, too; and tried to get them from her. The spiteful thing wouldn't let me: she pushed me off, and hurt me. I shrieked out – that frightens her – she heard papa coming, and she broke the hinges and divided the case, and gave me her mother's portrait; the other she attempted to hide: but papa asked what was the matter, and I explained it. He took the one I had away, and ordered her to resign hers to me; she refused, and he – he struck her down, and wrenched it off the chain, and crushed it with his foot."

"And were you pleased to see her struck?" I asked: having my designs in encouraging his talk.

"I winked," he answered: "I wink to see my father strike a dog or a horse, he does it so hard. Yet I was glad at first – she deserved punishing for pushing me: but when papa was gone, she made me come to the window and showed me her cheek cut on the inside, against her teeth, and her mouth filling with blood; and then she gathered up the bits of the picture, and went and sat down with her face to the wall, and she has never spoken to me since: and I sometimes think she can't speak for pain. I don't like to think so; but she's a naughty thing for crying continually; and she looks so pale and wild, I'm afraid of her."

"And you can get the key if you choose?" I said.

"Yes, when I am upstairs," he answered; "but I can't walk upstairs now."

"In what apartment is it?" I asked.

"Oh," he cried, "I shan't tell *you* where it is. It is our secret. Nobody, neither Hareton nor Zillah, is to know. There! You've tired me – go away, go away!" And he turned his face on to his arm, and shut his eyes again.

I considered it best to depart without seeing Mr. Heathcliff, and bring a rescue for my young lady from the Grange. On reaching it, the astonishment of my fellow-servants to see me, and their joy also, was intense; and when they heard that their little mistress was safe, two or three were about to hurry up and shout the news at Mr. Edgar's door: but I bespoke the announcement of it myself. How changed I found him, even in those few days! He lay an image of sadness and resignation awaiting his death. Very young he looked: though his actual age was thirty-nine, one would have called him ten years younger, at least. He thought of Catherine; for he murmured her name. I touched his hand, and spoke.

"Catherine is coming, dear master!" I whispered; "She is alive and well; and will be here, I hope, tonight."

I trembled at the first effects of this intelligence: he half rose up, looked eagerly round the apartment, and then sank back in a swoon. As soon as he recovered, I related our compulsory visit, and detention at the Heights. I said Heathcliff forced me to go in: which was not quite true. I uttered as little as possible against Linton; nor did I describe all his father's brutal conduct – my intentions being to add no bitterness, if I could help it, to his already over-flowing cup.

He divined that one of his enemy's purposes was to secure the personal property, as well as the estate, to his son: or rather himself; yet why he did not wait till his decease was a puzzle to my master, because ignorant how nearly he and his nephew would quit the world together. However, he felt that his will had better be altered: instead of leaving Catherine's fortune at her own disposal, he determined to put it in the hands of trustees for her use during life, and for her children, if she had any, after her. By that means, it could not fall to Mr. Heathcliff should Linton die.

Having received his orders, I despatched a man to fetch the attorney, and four more, provided with serviceable weapons, to demand my young lady of her jailor. Both parties were delayed very late. The single servant returned first. He said Mr. Green, the lawyer, was out when he arrived at his house, and he had to wait two hours for his re-entrance; and then Mr. Green told him he had a little business in the village that must be done; but he would be at Thrushcross Grange before morning. The four men came back unaccompanied also. They brought word that Catherine was ill: too ill to quit her room; and Heathcliff would not suffer them to see her. I scolded the stupid fellows well for listening to that tale, which I would not carry to my master; resolving to take a whole bevy up to the Heights, at day-light, and storm it literally, unless the prisoner were quietly surrendered to us. Her father *shall* see her, I vowed, and vowed again, if that devil be killed on his own doorstones in trying to prevent it!

Happily, I was spared the journey and the trouble. I had gone downstairs at three o'clock to fetch a jug of water; and was passing through the hall with it in my hand, when a sharp knock at the front door made me jump. "Oh! It is Green," I said, recollecting myself – "only Green," and I went on, intending to send somebody else to open it; but the knock was repeated: not loud, and still importunately. I put the jug on the banister and hastened to admit him myself. The harvest moon shone clear outside. It was not the attorney. My own sweet little mistress sprang on my neck sobbing, "Ellen, Ellen! Is papa alive?"

"Yes," I cried: "yes, my angel, he is, God be thanked, you are safe with us again!"

She wanted to run, breathless as she was, upstairs to Mr. Linton's room; but I compelled her to sit down on a chair, and made her drink, and washed her pale face, chafing it into a faint colour with my apron. Then I said I must go first, and tell of her arrival; imploring her to say, she should be happy with young Heathcliff. She stared, but soon comprehending why I counselled her to utter the falsehood, she assured me she would not complain.

I couldn't abide to be present at their meeting. I stood outside the chamber-door a quarter of an hour, and hardly ventured near the bed, then. All was composed, however: Catherine's despair was as silent as her father's joy. She supported him calmly, in appearance; and he fixed on her features his raised eyes that seemed dilating with ecstasy.

He died blissfully, Mr. Lockwood: he died so. Kissing her cheek, he murmured, "I am going to her; and you, darling child, shall come to us!" and never stirred or spoke again; but continued that rapt, radiant gaze, till his pulse imperceptibly stopped and his soul departed. None could have noticed the exact minute of his death, it was so entirely without a struggle.

Whether Catherine had spent her tears, or whether the grief were too weighty to let them flow, she sat there dry-eyed till the sun rose: she sat till noon, and would still have remained brooding over that deathbed, but I insisted on her coming away and taking some repose. It was well I succeeded in removing her, for at dinner-time appeared the lawyer, having called at Wuthering Heights to get his instructions how to behave. He had sold himself to Mr. Heathcliff: that was the cause of his delay in obeying my master's summons. Fortunately, no thought of worldly affairs crossed the latter's mind, to disturb him, after his daughter's arrival.

Mr. Green took upon himself to order everything and everybody about the place. He gave all the servants but me, notice to quit. He would have carried his delegated authority to the point of insisting that Edgar Linton should not be buried beside his wife, but in the chapel, with his family. There was the will, however, to hinder that, and my loud protestations against any infringement of its directions. The funeral was hurried over; Catherine, Mrs. Linton Heathcliff now, was suffered to stay at the Grange till her father's corpse had quitted it.

She told me that her anguish had at last spurred Linton to incur the risk of liberating her. She heard the men I sent disputing at the door, and she gathered the sense of Heathcliff's answer. It drove her desperate. Linton who had been conveyed up to the little parlour soon after I left, was terrified into fetching the key before his father re-ascended. He had the cunning to unlock and re-lock the door, without shutting it; and when he should have gone to bed, he begged to sleep with Hareton, and his petition was granted for once. Catherine stole out before break of day. She dared not try the doors lest the dogs should raise an alarm; she visited the empty chambers and examined their windows; and, luckily, lighting on her mother's, she got easily out of its lattice, and on to the ground, by means of the fir-tree close by. Her accomplice suffered for his share in the escape, notwithstanding his timid contrivances.

Chapter Twenty-Nine

THE EVENING after the funeral, my young lady and I were seated in the library; now musing mournfully – one of us despairingly – on our loss, now venturing conjectures as to the gloomy future.

We had just agreed the best destiny which could await Catherine would be a permission to continue resident at the Grange; at least during Linton's life: he being allowed to join her there, and I to remain as housekeeper. That seemed rather too favourable an arrangement to be hoped for; and yet I did hope, and began to cheer up under the prospect of retaining my home and my employment, and, above all, my beloved young mistress; when a servant – one of the discarded ones, not yet departed – rushed hastily in, and said 'that devil Heathcliff' was coming through the court: should he fasten the door in his face?

If we had been mad enough to order that proceeding, we had not time. He made no ceremony of knocking or announcing his name: he was master, and availed himself of the master's privilege to walk straight in, without saying a word. The sound of our informant's voice directed him to the library; he entered and motioning him out, shut the door.

It was the same room into which he had been ushered, as a guest, eighteen years before: the same moon shone through the window; and the same autumn landscape lay outside. We had not yet lighted a candle, but all the apartment was visible, even to the portraits on the wall: the splendid head of Mrs. Linton, and the graceful one of her husband. Heathcliff advanced to the hearth. Time had little altered his person either. There was the same man: his dark face rather sallower and more composed, his frame a stone or two heavier, perhaps, and no other difference. Catherine had risen with an impulse to dash out, when she saw him.

"Stop!" he said, arresting her by the arm. "No more runnings away! Where would you go? I'm come to fetch you home; and I hope you'll be a dutiful daughter and not encourage my son to further disobedience. I was embarrassed how to punish him when I discovered his part in the business: he's such a cobweb, a pinch would annihilate him; but you'll see by his look that he has received his due! I brought him down one evening, the day before yesterday, and just set him in a chair, and never touched him afterwards. I sent Hareton out, and we had the room to ourselves. In two hours, I called Joseph to carry him up again; and since then my presence is as potent on his nerves as a ghost; and I fancy he sees me often, though I am not near. Hareton says he wakes and shrieks in the night by the hour together, and calls you to protect him from me; and, whether you like your precious mate, or not, you must come: he's your concern now; I yield all my interest in him to you."

"Why not let Catherine continue here," I pleaded, "and send Master Linton to her? As you hate them both, you'd not miss them: they can only be a daily plague to your unnatural heart."

"I'm seeking a tenant for the Grange," he answered; "and I want my children about me, to be sure. Besides, that lass owes me her services for her bread. I'm not going to nurture her in luxury and idleness after Linton is gone. Make haste and get ready, now; and don't oblige me to compel you."

"I shall," said Catherine. "Linton is all I have to love in the world, and though you have done what you could to make him hateful to me, and me to him, you cannot make us hate each other. And I defy you to hurt him when I am by, and I defy you to frighten me!"

"You are a boastful champion," replied Heathcliff; "but I don't like you well enough to hurt him: you shall get the full benefit of the torment, as long as it lasts. It is not I who will make him hateful to you – it is his own sweet spirit. He's as bitter as gall at your desertion and its consequences: don't expect thanks for this noble devotion. I heard him draw a pleasant picture to Zillah of what he would do if he were as strong as I: the inclination is there, and his very weakness will sharpen his wits to find a substitute for strength."

"I know he has a bad nature," said Catherine: "he's your son. But I'm glad I've a better, to forgive it; and I know he loves me, and for that reason I love him. Mr. Heathcliff *you* have *nobody* to love you; and, however miserable you make us, we shall still have the revenge of thinking that your cruelty arises from your greater misery. You *are* miserable, are you not? Lonely, like the devil, and envious like him? *Nobody* loves you – *nobody* will cry for you when you die! I wouldn't be you!"

Catherine spoke with a kind of dreary triumph: she seemed to have made up her mind to enter into the spirit of her future family, and draw pleasure from the griefs of her enemies.

"You shall be sorry to be yourself presently," said her father-in-law, "if you stand there another minute. Begone, witch, and get your things!"

She scornfully withdrew. In her absence I began to beg for Zillah's place at the Heights, offering to resign mine to her; but he would suffer it on no account. He bid me be silent; and then, for the first time, allowed himself a glance round the room and a look at the pictures. Having studied Mrs. Linton's, he said – "I shall have that home. Not because I need it, but –" He turned abruptly to the fire, and continued, with what, for lack of a better word, I must call a smile – "I'll tell you what I did yesterday! I got the sexton, who was digging Linton's grave, to remove the earth off her coffin lid, and I opened it. I thought, once, I would have stayed there: when I saw her face again – it is hers yet! – he had hard work to stir me; but he said it would change if the air blew on it, and so I struck one side of the coffin loose, and covered it up: not Linton's side, damn him! I wish he'd been soldered in lead. And I bribed the sexton to pull it away when I'm laid there, and slide mine out too; I'll have it made so: and then by the time Linton gets to us he'll not know which is which!"

"You were very wicked, Mr. Heathcliff!" I exclaimed; "Were you not ashamed to disturb the dead?"

"I disturbed nobody, Nelly," he replied; "and I gave some ease to myself. I shall be a great deal more comfortable now; and you'll have a better chance of keeping me underground, when I get there. Disturbed her? No! She has disturbed me, night and day, through eighteen years – incessantly – remorselessly – till yesternight; and yesternight I was tranquil. I dreamt I was sleeping the last sleep by that sleeper, with my heart stopped and my cheek frozen against hers."

"And if she had been dissolved into earth, or worse, what would you have dreamt of then?" I said.

"Of dissolving with her, and being more happy still!" he answered. "Do you suppose I dread any change of that sort? I expected such a transformation on raising the lid – but I'm better pleased that it should not commence till I share it. Besides, unless I had received a distinct impression of her passionless features, that strange feeling would hardly have been removed. It began oddly. You know I was wild after she died; and eternally, from dawn to dawn, praying her to return to me her spirit! I have a strong faith in ghosts: I have a conviction that they can, and do, exist among us! The day she was buried, there came a fall of snow. In the evening I went to the churchyard. It blew bleak as winter – all round was solitary. I didn't fear that her fool of a husband would wander up the glen so late; and no one else had business to bring them there. Being alone, and conscious two yards of loose earth was the sole barrier between us, I said to myself – 'I'll have her in my arms again! If she be cold, I'll think it is this north wind that chills *me*; and if she be motionless, it is sleep.' I got a spade from the tool-house, and began to delve with all my might – it scraped the coffin; I fell to work with my hands; the wood commenced cracking about the screws; I was on the point of attaining my object, when it seemed that I heard a sigh from someone above, close at the edge of the grave, and bending down. "If I can only get this off," I muttered, "I wish they may shovel in the earth over us both!" and I wrenched at it more desperately still. There was another sigh, close at my ear. I appeared to feel the warm breath of it displacing the sleet-laden wind. I knew no living thing in flesh and blood was by; but, as certainly as you perceive the approach to some substantial body in the dark, though it cannot be discerned, so certainly I felt that Cathy was there: not under me, but on the earth. A sudden sense of relief flowed from my heart through every limb. I relinquished my labour of agony, and turned consoled at once: unspeakably consoled. Her presence was with me: it remained while I re-filled the grave, and led me home. You may laugh, if you will; but I was sure I should see her there. I was sure she was with me, and I could not help talking to her. Having reached the Heights, I rushed eagerly to the door. It was fastened; and, I remember, that accursed Earnshaw and my wife opposed my entrance. I remember stopping to kick the breath out of him, and then hurrying upstairs, to my room and hers. I looked round impatiently – I felt her by me – I could *almost* see her, and yet I *could not*! I ought to have sweat blood then, from the anguish of my yearning – from the fervour of my supplications to have but one glimpse! I had not one. She showed herself, as she often was in life, a devil to me! And, since then, sometimes more and sometimes less, I've been the sport of that intolerable torture! Infernal! Keeping my nerves at such a stretch that, if they had not resembled catgut, they would long ago have relaxed to the feebleness of Linton's. When I sat in the house with Hareton, it seemed that on going out I should meet her; when I walked on the moors I should meet her coming in. When I went from home I hastened to return; she *must* be somewhere at the Heights, I was certain! And when I slept in her chamber – I was beaten out of that. I couldn't lie there; for the moment I closed my eyes, she was either outside the window, or sliding back the panels, or entering the room, or even resting her darling head on the same pillow as she did when a child; and I must open my lids to see. And so I opened and closed them a hundred times a night – to be always disappointed! It racked me! I've often groaned aloud, till that old rascal Joseph no doubt believed that my conscience was playing the fiend inside of me. Now, since I've seen her, I'm pacified – a little. It was a strange way of killing: not by inches, but by fractions of hairbreadths, to beguile me with the spectre of a hope through eighteen years!"

Mr. Heathcliff paused and wiped his forehead; his hair clung to it, wet with perspiration; his eyes were fixed on the red embers of the fire, the brows not contracted, but raised next the temples; diminishing the grim aspect of his countenance, but imparting a peculiar look of trouble, and a painful appearance of mental tension towards one absorbing subject. He only half addressed me, and I maintained silence. I didn't like to hear him talk! After a short period he resumed his meditation on the picture, took it down and leant it against the sofa to contemplate it at better advantage; and while so occupied Catherine entered, announcing that she was ready, when her pony should be saddled.

"Send that over tomorrow," said Heathcliff to me; then turning to her, he added: "You may do without your pony: it is a fine evening, and you'll need no ponies at Wuthering Heights; for what journeys you take, your own feet will serve you. Come along."

"Goodbye, Ellen!" whispered my dear little mistress.

As she kissed me, her lips felt like ice. "Come and see me, Ellen; don't forget."

"Take care you do no such thing, Mrs. Dean!" said her new father. "When I wish to speak to you I'll come here. I want none of your prying at my house!"

He signed her to precede him; and casting back a look that cut my heart, she obeyed. I watched them, from the window, walk down the garden. Heathcliff fixed Catherine's arm under his: though she disputed the act at first evidently; and with rapid strides he hurried her into the alley, whose trees concealed them.

Chapter Thirty

I HAVE PAID A VISIT to the Heights, but I have not seen her since she left: Joseph held the door in his hand when I called to ask after her, and wouldn't let me pass. He said Mrs. Linton was 'thrang', and the master was not in. Zillah has told me something of the way they go on, otherwise I should hardly know who was dead and who living. She thinks Catherine haughty, and does not like her, I can guess by her talk. My young lady asked some aid of her when she first came; but Mr. Heathcliff told her to follow her own business, and let his daughter-in-law look after herself; and Zillah willingly acquiesced, being a narrow-minded, selfish woman. Catherine evinced a child's annoyance at this neglect; repaid it with contempt, and thus enlisted my informant among her enemies, as securely as if she had done her some great wrong. I had a long talk with Zillah about six weeks ago, a little before you came, one day when we foregathered on the moor; and this is what she told me.

"The first thing Mrs. Linton did," she said, "on her arrival at the Heights, was to run upstairs, without even wishing good evening to me and Joseph; she shut herself into Linton's room, and remained till morning. Then, while the master and Earnshaw were at breakfast, she entered the house, and asked all in a quiver if the doctor might be sent for? Her cousin was very ill.

"'We know that!' answered Heathcliff; 'But his life is not worth a farthing, and I won't spend a farthing on him.'

"'But I cannot tell how to do,' she said; 'and if nobody will help me, he'll die!'

"'Walk out of the room,' cried the master, 'and let me never hear a word more about him! None here care what becomes of him; if you do, act the nurse; if you do not, lock him up and leave him.'

"Then she began to bother me, and I said I'd had enough plague with the tiresome thing; we each had our tasks, and hers was to wait on Linton: Mr. Heathcliff bid me leave that labour to her.

"How they managed together, I can't tell. I fancy he fretted a great deal, and moaned hisseln night and day; and she had precious little rest: one could guess by her white face and heavy eyes. She sometimes came into the kitchen all wildered like, and looked as if she would fain beg assistance; but I was not going to disobey the master: I never dare disobey him, Mrs. Dean; and, though I thought it wrong that Kenneth should not be sent for, it was no concern of mine either to advise or complain, and I always refused to meddle. Once or twice, after we had gone to bed, I've happened to open my door again and seen her sitting crying on the stairs'-top; and then I've shut myself in quick, for fear of being moved to interfere. I did pity her then, I'm sure: still I didn't wish to lose my place, you know.

"At last, one night she came boldly into my chamber, and frightened me out of my wits, by saying, "Tell Mr. Heathcliff that his son is dying – I'm sure he is, this time. Get up, instantly, and tell him."

"Having uttered this speech, she vanished again. I lay a quarter of an hour listening and trembling. Nothing stirred – the house was quiet.

"She's mistaken, I said to myself. He's got over it. I needn't disturb them; and I began to doze. But my sleep was marred a second time by a sharp ringing of the bell – the only bell we have, put up on purpose for Linton; and the master called to me to see what was the matter, and inform them that he wouldn't have that noise repeated.

"I delivered Catherine's message. He cursed to himself, and in a few minutes came out with a lighted candle, and proceeded to their room. I followed. Mrs. Heathcliff was seated by the bedside, with her hands folded on her knees. Her father-in-law went up, held the light to Linton's face, looked at him, and touched him; afterwards he turned to her.

"'Now – Catherine,' he said, 'how do you feel?'

"She was dumb.

"'How do you feel, Catherine?' he repeated.

"'He's safe, and I'm free,' she answered: 'I should feel well – but,' she continued, with a bitterness she couldn't conceal, 'you have left me so long to struggle against death alone, that I feel and see only death! I feel like death!'

"And she looked like it, too! I gave her a little wine. Hareton and Joseph, who had been wakened by the ringing and the sound of feet, and heard our talk from outside, now entered. Joseph was fain, I believe, of the lad's removal; Hareton seemed a thought bothered: though he was more taken up with staring at Catherine than thinking of Linton. But the master bid him get off to bed again: we didn't want his help. He afterwards made Joseph remove the body to his chamber, and told me to return to mine, and Mrs. Heathcliff remained by herself.

"In the morning, he sent me to tell her she must come down to breakfast: she had undressed, and appeared going to sleep, and said she was ill; at which I hardly wondered. I informed Mr. Heathcliff, and he replied, 'Well, let her be till after the funeral; and go up now and then to get her what is needful; and, as soon as she seems better, tell me.'"

Cathy stayed upstairs a fortnight, according to Zillah; who visited her twice a day, and would have been rather more friendly, but her attempts at increasing kindness were proudly and promptly repelled.

Heathcliff went up once, to show her Linton's will. He had bequeathed the whole of his, and what had been her, moveable property, to his father: the poor creature was threatened, or coaxed, into that act during her week's absence, when his uncle died. The lands, being a minor, he could not meddle with. However, Mr. Heathcliff has claimed and kept them in his wife's right and his also: I suppose legally; at any rate, Catherine, destitute of cash and friends, cannot disturb his possession.

"Nobody," said Zillah, "ever approached her door, except that once, but I; and nobody asked anything about her. The first occasion of her coming down into the house was on a Sunday afternoon. She had cried out, when I carried up her dinner, that she couldn't bear any longer being in the cold; and I told her the master was going to Thrushcross Grange, and Earnshaw and I needn't hinder her from descending; so, as soon as she heard Heathcliff's horse trot off, she made her appearance, donned in black, and her yellow curls combed back behind her ears as plain as a Quaker: she couldn't comb them out.

"Joseph and I generally go to chapel on Sundays:" the kirk, you know, has no minister now, explained Mrs. Dean; and they call the Methodists' or Baptists' place (I can't say which it is) at Gimmerton, a chapel. "Joseph had gone," she continued, "but I thought proper to bide at home. Young folks are always the better for an elder's over-looking; and Hareton, with all his bashfulness, isn't a model of nice behaviour. I let him know that his cousin would very likely sit with us, and she had been always used to see the Sabbath respected; so he had as good leave his guns and bits of indoor work alone, while she stayed. He coloured up at the news, and cast his eyes over his hands and clothes. The train-oil and gunpowder were shoved out of sight in a minute. I saw he meant to give her his company; and I guessed, by his way, he wanted to be presentable; so, laughing, as I durst not laugh when the master is by, I offered to help him, if he would, and joked at his confusion. He grew sullen, and began to swear.

"Now, Mrs. Dean," Zillah went on, seeing me not pleased by her manner, "you happen think your young lady too fine for Mr. Hareton; and happen you're right: but I own I should love well to bring her pride a peg lower. And what will all her learning and her daintiness do for her, now? She's as poor as you or I: poorer, I'll be bound: you're saying, and I'm doing my little all that road."

Hareton allowed Zillah to give him her aid; and she flattered him into a good humour; so, when Catherine came, half forgetting her former insults, he tried to make himself agreeable, by the housekeeper's account.

"Missis walked in," she said, "as chill as an icicle, and as high as a princess. I got up and offered her my seat in the arm-chair. No, she turned up her nose at my civility. Earnshaw rose, too, and bid her come to the settle, and sit close by the fire: he was sure she was starved.

"'I've been starved a month and more,' she answered, resting on the word as scornful as she could.

"And she got a chair for herself, and placed it at a distance from both of us. Having sat till she was warm, she began to look round, and discovered a number of books on the dresser; she was instantly upon her feet again, stretching to reach them: but they were too high up. Her cousin, after watching her endeavours a while, at last summoned courage to help her; she held her frock, and he filled it with the first that came to hand.

"That was a great advance for the lad. She didn't thank him; still, he felt gratified that she had accepted his assistance, and ventured to stand behind as she examined them, and even to stoop and point out what struck his fancy in certain old pictures which they contained; nor was he daunted by the saucy style in which she jerked the page from his finger: he contented himself with going a bit farther back and looking at her instead of the book. She continued reading, or seeking for something to read. His attention became, by degrees, quite centred in the study of her thick silky curls: her face he couldn't see, and she couldn't see him. And, perhaps, not quite awake to what he did, but attracted like a child to a candle, at last he proceeded from staring to touching; he put out his hand and stroked one curl, as gently as if it were a bird. He might have stuck a knife into her neck, she started round in such a taking.

"'Get away this moment! How dare you touch me? Why are you stopping there?' she cried, in a tone of disgust. 'I can't endure you! I'll go upstairs again, if you come near me.'

"Mr. Hareton recoiled, looking as foolish as he could do: he sat down in the settle very quiet, and she continued turning over her volumes another half hour; finally, Earnshaw crossed over, and whispered to me.

"'Will you ask her to read to us, Zillah? I'm stalled of doing naught; and I do like – I could like to hear her! Dunnot say I wanted it, but ask of yourseln.'

"'Mr. Hareton wishes you would read to us, ma'am,' I said, immediately. 'He'd take it very kind – he'd be much obliged.'

"She frowned; and looking up, answered –

"'Mr. Hareton, and the whole set of you, will be good enough to understand that I reject any pretence at kindness you have the hypocrisy to offer! I despise you, and will have nothing to say to any of you! When I would have given my life for one kind word, even to see one of your faces, you all kept off. But I won't complain to you! I'm driven down here by the cold; not either to amuse you or enjoy your society.'

"'What could I ha' done?' began Earnshaw. 'How was I to blame?'

"'Oh! You are an exception,' answered Mrs. Heathcliff. 'I never missed such a concern as you.'

"'But I offered more than once, and asked,' he said, kindling up at her pertness, 'I asked Mr. Heathcliff to let me wake for you –'

"'Be silent! I'll go out of doors, or anywhere, rather than have your disagreeable voice in my ear!' said my lady.

"Hareton muttered she might go to hell, for him! And unslinging his gun, restrained himself from his Sunday occupations no longer. He talked now, freely enough; and she presently saw fit to retreat to her solitude: but the frost had set in, and, in spite of her pride, she was forced to condescend to our company, more and more. However, I took care there should be no further scorning at my good nature: ever since, I've been as stiff as herself; and she has no lover or liker among us: and she does not deserve one; for, let them say the least word to her, and she'll curl back without respect of anyone. She'll snap at the master himself, and as good as dares him to thrash her; and the more hurt she gets, the more venomous she grows."

At first, on hearing this account from Zillah, I determined to leave my situation, take a cottage, and get Catherine to come and live with me: but Mr. Heathcliff would as soon permit that as he would set up Hareton in an independent house; and I can see no remedy, at present, unless she could marry again; and that scheme it does not come within my province to arrange.

* * *

Thus ended Mrs. Dean's story. Notwithstanding the doctor's prophecy, I am rapidly recovering strength; and though it be only the second week in January, I propose getting out on horseback in a day or two, and riding over to Wuthering Heights, to inform my landlord that I shall spend the next six months in London; and, if he likes, he may look out for another tenant to take the place after October. I would not pass another winter here for much.

Chapter Thirty-One

YESTERDAY WAS BRIGHT, calm, and frosty. I went to the Heights as I proposed: my housekeeper entreated me to bear a little note from her to her young lady, and I did not refuse, for the worthy woman was not conscious of anything odd in her request. The front door stood open, but the jealous gate was fastened, as at my last visit; I knocked and invoked Earnshaw from among the garden-beds; he unchained it, and I entered. The fellow is as handsome a rustic as need be seen. I took particular notice of him this time; but then he does his best apparently to make the least of his advantages.

I asked if Mr. Heathcliff were at home? He answered, No; but he would be in at dinner-time. It was eleven o'clock, and I announced my intention of going in and waiting for him; at which he immediately flung down his tools and accompanied me, in the office of watchdog, not as a substitute for the host.

We entered together; Catherine was there, making herself useful in preparing some vegetables for the approaching meal; she looked more sulky and less spirited than when I had seen her first. She hardly raised her eyes to notice me, and continued her employment with the same disregard to common forms of politeness as before; never returning my bow and good-morning by the slightest acknowledgment.

"She does not seem so amiable," I thought, "as Mrs. Dean would persuade me to believe. She's a beauty, it is true; but not an angel."

Earnshaw surlily bid her remove her things to the kitchen. "Remove them yourself," she said, pushing them from her as soon as she had done; and retiring to a stool by the window, where she began to carve figures of birds and beasts out of the turnip-parings in her lap. I approached her, pretending to desire a view of the garden; and, as I fancied, adroitly dropped Mrs. Dean's note on to her knee, unnoticed by Hareton – but she asked aloud, "What is that?" And chucked it off.

"A letter from your old acquaintance, the housekeeper at the Grange," I answered; annoyed at her exposing my kind deed, and fearful lest it should be imagined a missive of my own. She would gladly have gathered it up at this information, but Hareton beat her; he seized and put it in his waistcoat, saying Mr. Heathcliff should look at it first. Thereat, Catherine silently turned her face from us, and, very stealthily, drew out her pocket-handkerchief and applied it to her eyes; and her cousin, after struggling awhile to keep down his softer feelings, pulled out the letter and flung it on the floor beside her, as ungraciously as he could. Catherine caught and perused it eagerly; then she put a few questions to me concerning the inmates, rational and irrational, of her former home; and gazing towards the hills, murmured in soliloquy:

"I should like to be riding Minny down there! I should like to be climbing up there! Oh! I'm tired – I'm *stalled*, Hareton!" And she leant her pretty head back against the sill, with half a yawn and half a sigh, and lapsed into an aspect of abstracted sadness: neither caring nor knowing whether we remarked her.

"Mrs. Heathcliff," I said, after sitting some time mute, "you are not aware that I am an acquaintance of yours? So intimate that I think it strange you won't come and speak to me. My housekeeper never wearies of talking about and praising you; and she'll be greatly disappointed if I return with no news of or from you, except that you received her letter and said nothing!"

She appeared to wonder at this speech, and asked –

"Does Ellen like you?"

"Yes, very well," I replied, hesitatingly.

"You must tell her," she continued, "that I would answer her letter, but I have no materials for writing: not even a book from which I might tear a leaf."

"No books!" I exclaimed. "How do you contrive to live here without them? If I may take the liberty to inquire. Though provided with a large library, I'm frequently very dull at the Grange; take my books away, and I should be desperate!"

"I was always reading, when I had them," said Catherine; "and Mr. Heathcliff never reads; so he took it into his head to destroy my books. I have not had a glimpse of one for weeks. Only once, I searched through Joseph's store of theology, to his great irritation; and once, Hareton, I came upon a secret stock in your room – some Latin and Greek, and some tales and poetry: all old friends. I brought the last here – and you gathered them, as a magpie gathers silver spoons, for the mere love of stealing! They are of no use to you; or else you concealed them in the bad spirit that, as you cannot enjoy them, nobody else shall. Perhaps *your* envy counselled Mr. Heathcliff to rob me of my treasures? But I've most of them written on my brain and printed in my heart, and you cannot deprive me of those!"

Earnshaw blushed crimson when his cousin made this revelation of his private literary accumulations, and stammered an indignant denial of her accusations.

"Mr. Hareton is desirous of increasing his amount of knowledge," I said, coming to his rescue. "He is not *envious*, but *emulous* of your attainments. He'll be a clever scholar in a few years."

"And he wants me to sink into a dunce, meantime," answered Catherine. "Yes, I hear him trying to spell and read to himself, and pretty blunders he makes! I wish you would repeat Chevy Chase as you did yesterday: it was extremely funny. I heard you; and I heard you turning over the dictionary to seek out the hard words, and then cursing because you couldn't read their explanations!"

The young man evidently thought it too bad that he should be laughed at for his ignorance, and then laughed at for trying to remove it. I had a similar notion; and, remembering Mrs. Dean's anecdote of his first attempt at enlightening the darkness in which he had been reared, I observed – "But, Mrs. Heathcliff, we have each had a commencement, and each stumbled and tottered on the threshold; had our teachers scorned instead of aiding us, we should stumble and totter yet."

"Oh!" she replied, "I don't wish to limit his acquirements: still, he has no right to appropriate what is mine, and make it ridiculous to me with his vile mistakes and mispronunciations! Those books, both prose and verse, are consecrated to me by other associations; and I hate to have them debased and profaned in his mouth! Besides, of all, he has selected my favourite pieces that I love the most to repeat, as if out of deliberate malice."

Hareton's chest heaved in silence a minute: he laboured under a severe sense of mortification and wrath, which it was no easy task to suppress. I rose, and, from a gentlemanly idea of relieving his embarrassment, took up my station in the doorway, surveying the external prospect as I stood. He followed my example, and left the room; but presently reappeared, bearing half a dozen volumes in his hands, which he threw into Catherine's lap, exclaiming, – "Take them! I never want to hear, or read, or think of them again!"

"I won't have them now," she answered. "I shall connect them with you, and hate them."

She opened one that had obviously been often turned over, and read a portion in the drawling tone of a beginner; then laughed, and threw it from her. "And listen," she continued, provokingly, commencing a verse of an old ballad in the same fashion.

But his self-love would endure no further torment: I heard, and not altogether disapprovingly, a manual check given to her saucy tongue. The little wretch had done her utmost to hurt her cousin's sensitive though uncultivated feelings, and a physical argument was the only mode he had of balancing the account, and repaying its effects on the inflictor. He afterwards gathered the books and hurled them on the fire. I read in his countenance what anguish it was to offer that sacrifice to spleen. I fancied that as they consumed, he recalled the pleasure they had already imparted, and the triumph and ever-increasing pleasure he had anticipated from them; and I fancied I guessed the incitement to his secret studies also. He had been content with daily labour and rough animal enjoyments, till Catherine crossed his path. Shame at her scorn, and hope of her approval, were his first prompters to higher pursuits; and instead of guarding him from one and winning him to the other, his endeavours to raise himself had produced just the contrary result.

"Yes that's all the good that such a brute as you can get from them!" cried Catherine, sucking her damaged lip, and watching the conflagration with indignant eyes.

"You'd *better* hold your tongue, now," he answered fiercely.

And his agitation precluded further speech; he advanced hastily to the entrance, where I made way for him to pass. But ere he had crossed the door-stones, Mr. Heathcliff, coming up the causeway, encountered him, and laying hold of his shoulder asked, – "What's to do now, my lad?"

"Naught, naught," he said, and broke away to enjoy his grief and anger in solitude.

Heathcliff gazed after him, and sighed.

"It will be odd if I thwart myself," he muttered, unconscious that I was behind him. "But when I look for his father in his face, I find *her* every day more! How the devil is he so like? I can hardly bear to see him."

He bent his eyes to the ground, and walked moodily in. There was a restless, anxious expression in his countenance. I had never remarked there before; and he looked sparer in person. His daughter-in-law, on perceiving him through the window, immediately escaped to the kitchen, so that I remained alone.

"I'm glad to see you out of doors again, Mr. Lockwood," he said, in reply to my greeting; "from selfish motives partly: I don't think I could readily supply your loss in this desolation. I've wondered more than once what brought you here."

"An idle whim, I fear, sir," was my answer; "or else an idle whim is going to spirit me away. I shall set out for London next week; and I must give you warning that I feel no disposition to retain Thrushcross Grange beyond the twelve months I agreed to rent it. I believe I shall not live there anymore."

"Oh, indeed; you're tired of being banished from the world, are you?" he said. "But if you be coming to plead off paying for a place you won't occupy, your journey is useless: I never relent in exacting my due from any one."

"I'm coming to plead off nothing about it," I exclaimed, considerably irritated. "Should you wish it, I'll settle with you now," and I drew my note-book from my pocket.

"No, no," he replied, coolly; "you'll leave sufficient behind to cover your debts, if you fail to return: I'm not in such a hurry. Sit down and take your dinner with us; a guest that is safe from repeating his visit can generally be made welcome. Catherine! Bring the things in: where are you?"

Catherine reappeared, bearing a tray of knives and forks.

"You may get your dinner with Joseph," muttered Heathcliff, aside, "and remain in the kitchen till he is gone."

She obeyed his directions very punctually: perhaps she had no temptation to transgress. Living among clowns and misanthropists, she probably cannot appreciate a better class of people when she meets them.

With Mr. Heathcliff, grim and saturnine, on the one hand, and Hareton, absolutely dumb, on the other, I made a somewhat cheerless meal, and bade adieu early. I would have departed by the back way, to get a last glimpse of Catherine and annoy old Joseph; but Hareton received orders to lead up my horse, and my host himself escorted me to the door, so I could not fulfil my wish.

"How dreary life gets over in that house!" I reflected, while riding down the road. "What a realisation of something more romantic than a fairy tale it would have been for Mrs. Linton Heathcliff, had she and I struck up an attachment, as her good nurse desired, and migrated together into the stirring atmosphere of the town!"

Chapter Thirty-Two

1802. – This September I was invited to devastate the moors of a friend in the north, and on my journey to his abode, I unexpectedly came within fifteen miles of Gimmerton. The ostler at a roadside public-house was holding a pail of water to refresh my horses, when a cart of very green oats, newly reaped, passed by, and he remarked, – "Yon's frough Gimmerton, nah! They're allas three wick' after other folk wi' ther harvest."

"Gimmerton?" I repeated – my residence in that locality had already grown dim and dreamy. "Ah! I know. How far is it from this?"

"Happen fourteen mile o'er th' hills; and a rough road," he answered.

A sudden impulse seized me to visit Thrushcross Grange. It was scarcely noon, and I conceived that I might as well pass the night under my own roof as in an inn. Besides, I could spare a day easily to arrange matters with my landlord, and thus save myself the trouble of invading the neighbourhood again. Having rested awhile, I directed my servant to inquire the way to the village; and, with great fatigue to our beasts, we managed the distance in some three hours.

I left him there, and proceeded down the valley alone. The grey church looked greyer, and the lonely churchyard lonelier. I distinguished a moor-sheep cropping the short turf on the graves. It was sweet, warm weather – too warm for travelling; but the heat did not hinder me from enjoying the delightful scenery above and below: had I seen it nearer August, I'm sure it would have tempted me to waste a month among its solitudes. In winter nothing more dreary, in summer nothing more divine, than those glens shut in by hills, and those bluff, bold swells of heath.

I reached the Grange before sunset, and knocked for admittance; but the family had retreated into the back premises, I judged, by one thin, blue wreath, curling from the kitchen chimney, and they did not hear. I rode into the court. Under the porch, a girl of nine or ten sat knitting, and an old woman reclined on the housesteps, smoking a meditative pipe.

"Is Mrs. Dean within?" I demanded of the dame.

"Mistress Dean? Nay!" she answered, "she doesn't bide here: shoo's up at th' Heights."

"Are you the housekeeper, then?" I continued.

"Eea, aw keep th' hause," she replied.

"Well, I'm Mr. Lockwood, the master. Are there any rooms to lodge me in, I wonder? I wish to stay all night."

"T' maister!" she cried in astonishment. "Whet, whoiver knew yah wur coming? Yah sud ha' send word. They's nowt norther dry nor mensful abaht t' place: nowt there isn't!"

She threw down her pipe and bustled in, the girl followed, and I entered too; soon perceiving that her report was true, and, moreover, that I had almost upset her wits by my unwelcome apparition, I bade her be composed. I would go out for a walk; and, meantime she must try to prepare a corner of a sitting-room for me to sup in, and a bedroom to sleep in. No sweeping and dusting, only good fire and dry sheets were necessary. She seemed willing to do her best; though she thrust the hearth-brush into the grates in mistake for the poker, and malappropriated several other articles of her craft: but I retired, confiding in her energy for a resting-place against my return. Wuthering Heights was the goal of my proposed excursion. An afterthought brought me back, when I had quitted the court.

"All well at the Heights?" I inquired of the woman.

"Eea, f'r owt ee knaw!" she answered, skurrying away with a pan of hot cinders.

I would have asked why Mrs. Dean had deserted the Grange, but it was impossible to delay her at such a crisis, so I turned away and made my exit, rambling leisurely along, with the glow of a sinking sun behind, and the mild glory of a rising moon in front – one fading, and the other brightening – as I quitted the park, and climbed the stony by-road branching off to Mr. Heathcliff's dwelling. Before I arrived in sight of it, all that remained of day was a beamless amber light along the west: but I could see every pebble on the path, and every blade of grass, by that splendid moon. I had neither to climb the gate nor to knock – it yielded to my hand. That is an improvement, I thought. And I noticed another, by the aid of my nostrils; a fragrance of stocks and wallflowers wafted on the air from amongst the homely fruit-trees.

Both doors and lattices were open; and yet, as is usually the case in a coal-district, a fine red fire illumined the chimney: the comfort which the eye derives from it renders the extra heat endurable. But the house of Wuthering Heights is so large that the inmates have plenty of space for withdrawing out of its influence; and accordingly what inmates there were had stationed themselves not far from one of the windows. I could both see them and hear them talk before I entered, and looked and listened in consequence; being moved thereto by a mingled sense of curiosity and envy, that grew as I lingered.

"Con-*trary*!" said a voice as sweet as a silver bell. "That for the third time, you dunce! I'm not going to tell you again. Recollect, or I'll pull your hair!"

"Contrary, then," answered another, in deep but softened tones. "And now, kiss me, for minding so well."

"No, read it over first correctly, without a single mistake."

The male speaker began to read: he was a young man, respectably dressed and seated at a table, having a book before him. His handsome features glowed with pleasure, and his eyes kept impatiently wandering from the page to a small white hand over his shoulder, which recalled him by a smart slap on the cheek, whenever its owner detected such signs of inattention. Its owner stood behind; her light, shining ringlets blending, at intervals, with his brown looks, as she bent to superintend his studies; and her face – it was lucky he could not see her face, or he would never have been so steady. I could; and I bit my lip in spite, at having thrown away the chance I might have had of doing something besides staring at its smiting beauty.

The task was done, not free from further blunders; but the pupil claimed a reward, and received at least five kisses; which, however, he generously returned. Then they came to the door, and from their conversation I judged they were about to issue out and have a walk on the moors. I supposed I should be condemned in Hareton Earnshaw's heart, if not by his mouth, to the lowest pit in the infernal regions if I showed my unfortunate person in his neighbourhood then; and feeling very mean and malignant, I skulked round to seek refuge in the kitchen. There was unobstructed admittance on that side also; and at the door sat my old friend Nelly Dean, sewing and singing a song; which was often interrupted from within by harsh words of scorn and intolerance, uttered in far from musical accents.

"I'd rayther, by th' haulf, hev' 'em swearing i' my lugs fro'h morn to neeght, nor hearken ye hahsiver!" said the tenant of the kitchen, in answer to an unheard speech of Nelly's. "It's a blazing shame, that I cannot oppen t' blessed Book, but yah set up them glories to sattan, and all t' flaysome wickednesses that iver were born into th' warld! Oh! Ye're a raight nowt; and shoo's another; and that poor lad 'll be lost atween ye. Poor lad!" he added, with a groan; "he's witched: I'm sartin on't. Oh, Lord, judge 'em, for there's norther law nor justice among wer rullers!"

"No! Or we should be sitting in flaming fagots, I suppose," retorted the singer. "But wisht, old man, and read your Bible like a Christian, and never mind me. This is 'Fairy Annie's Wedding' – a bonny tune – it goes to a dance."

Mrs. Dean was about to recommence, when I advanced; and recognising me directly, she jumped to her feet, crying – "Why, bless you, Mr. Lockwood! How could you think of returning in this way? All's shut up at Thrushcross Grange. You should have given us notice!"

"I've arranged to be accommodated there, for as long as I shall stay," I answered. "I depart again tomorrow. And how are you transplanted here, Mrs. Dean? Tell me that."

"Zillah left, and Mr. Heathcliff wished me to come, soon after you went to London, and stay till you returned. But, step in, pray! Have you walked from Gimmerton this evening?"

"From the Grange," I replied; "and while they make me lodging room there, I want to finish my business with your master; because I don't think of having another opportunity in a hurry."

"What business, sir?" said Nelly, conducting me into the house. "He's gone out at present, and won't return soon."

"About the rent," I answered.

"Oh! Then it is with Mrs. Heathcliff you must settle," she observed; "or rather with me. She has not learnt to manage her affairs yet, and I act for her: there's nobody else."

I looked surprised.

"Ah! You have not heard of Heathcliff's death, I see," she continued.

"Heathcliff dead!" I exclaimed, astonished. "How long ago?"

"Three months since: but sit down, and let me take your hat, and I'll tell you all about it. Stop, you have had nothing to eat, have you?"

"I want nothing: I have ordered supper at home. You sit down too. I never dreamt of his dying! Let me hear how it came to pass. You say you don't expect them back for some time – the young people?"

"No – I have to scold them every evening for their late rambles: but they don't care for me. At least, have a drink of our old ale; it will do you good: you seem weary."

She hastened to fetch it before I could refuse, and I heard Joseph asking whether "it warn't a crying scandal that she should have followers at her time of life? And then, to get them jocks out o' t' maister's cellar! He fair shaamed to 'bide still and see it."

She did not stay to retaliate, but re-entered in a minute, bearing a reaming silver pint, whose contents I lauded with becoming earnestness. And afterwards she furnished me with the sequel of Heathcliff's history. He had a 'queer' end, as she expressed it.

I was summoned to Wuthering Heights, within a fortnight of your leaving us, she said; and I obeyed joyfully, for Catherine's sake. My first interview with her grieved and shocked me: she had altered so much since our separation. Mr. Heathcliff did not explain his reasons for taking a new mind about my coming here; he only told me he wanted me, and he was tired of seeing Catherine: I must make the little parlour my sitting-room, and keep her with me. It was enough if he were obliged to see her once or twice a day. She seemed pleased at this arrangement; and, by degrees, I smuggled over a great number of books, and other articles, that had formed her amusement at the Grange; and flattered myself we should get on in tolerable comfort. The delusion did not last long. Catherine, contented at first, in a brief space grew irritable and restless. For one thing, she was forbidden to move out of the garden, and it fretted her sadly to be confined to its narrow bounds as spring drew on; for another, in following the house, I was forced to quit her frequently, and she complained of loneliness: she preferred quarrelling with Joseph in the kitchen to sitting at peace in her solitude. I did not mind their skirmishes: but Hareton was often obliged to seek the kitchen also, when the master wanted to have the house to himself! And though in the beginning she either left it at his approach, or quietly joined in my occupations, and shunned remarking or addressing him – and though he was always as sullen and silent as possible – after a while, she changed her behaviour, and became incapable of letting him alone: talking at him; commenting on his stupidity and idleness; expressing her wonder how he could endure the life he lived – how he could sit a whole evening staring into the fire, and dozing.

"He's just like a dog, is he not, Ellen?" she once observed, "Or a cart-horse? He does his work, eats his food, and sleeps eternally! What a blank, dreary mind he must have! Do you ever dream, Hareton? And, if you do, what is it about? But you can't speak to me!"

Then she looked at him; but he would neither open his mouth nor look again.

"He's, perhaps, dreaming now," she continued. "He twitched his shoulder as Juno twitches hers. Ask him, Ellen."

"Mr. Hareton will ask the master to send you upstairs, if you don't behave!" I said. He had not only twitched his shoulder but clenched his fist, as if tempted to use it.

"I know why Hareton never speaks, when I am in the kitchen," she exclaimed, on another occasion. "He is afraid I shall laugh at him. Ellen, what do you think? He began to teach himself to read once; and, because I laughed, he burned his books, and dropped it: was he not a fool?"

"Were not you naughty?" I said; "Answer me that."

"Perhaps I was," she went on; "but I did not expect him to be so silly. Hareton, if I gave you a book, would you take it now? I'll try!"

She placed one she had been perusing on his hand; he flung it off, and muttered, if she did not give over, he would break her neck.

"Well, I shall put it here," she said, "in the table-drawer; and I'm going to bed."

Then she whispered me to watch whether he touched it, and departed. But he would not come near it; and so I informed her in the morning, to her great disappointment. I saw she was sorry for his persevering sulkiness and indolence: her conscience reproved her for frightening him off improving himself: she had done it effectually. But her ingenuity was at work to remedy the injury: while I ironed, or pursued other such stationary employments as I could not well do in the parlour, she would bring some pleasant volume and read it aloud to me. When Hareton was there, she generally paused in an interesting part, and left the book lying about: that she did repeatedly; but he was as obstinate as a mule, and, instead of snatching at her bait, in wet weather he took to smoking with Joseph; and they sat like automatons, one on each side of the fire, the elder happily too deaf to understand her wicked nonsense, as he would have called it, the younger doing his best to seem to disregard it. On fine evenings the latter followed his shooting expeditions, and Catherine yawned and sighed, and teased me to talk to her, and ran off into the court or garden the moment I began; and, as a last resource, cried, and said she was tired of living: her life was useless.

Mr. Heathcliff, who grew more and more disinclined to society, had almost banished Earnshaw from his apartment. Owing to an accident at the commencement of March, he became for some days a fixture in the kitchen. His gun burst while out on the hills by himself; a splinter cut his arm, and he lost a good deal of blood before he could reach home. The consequence was that, perforce, he was condemned to the fireside and tranquillity, till he made it up again. It suited Catherine to have him there: at any rate, it made her hate her room upstairs more than ever: and she would compel me to find out business below, that she might accompany me.

On Easter Monday, Joseph went to Gimmerton fair with some cattle; and, in the afternoon, I was busy getting up linen in the kitchen. Earnshaw sat, morose as usual, at the chimney corner, and my little mistress was beguiling an idle hour with drawing pictures on the window-panes, varying her amusement by smothered bursts of songs, and whispered ejaculations, and quick glances of annoyance and impatience in the direction of her cousin, who steadfastly smoked, and looked into the grate. At a notice that I could do with her no longer intercepting my light, she removed to the hearthstone. I bestowed little attention on her proceedings, but, presently, I heard her begin – "I've found out, Hareton, that I want – that I'm glad – that I should like you to be my cousin now, if you had not grown so cross to me, and so rough."

Hareton returned no answer.

"Hareton, Hareton, Hareton! Do you hear?" she continued.

"Get off wi' ye!" he growled, with uncompromising gruffness.

"Let me take that pipe," she said, cautiously advancing her hand and abstracting it from his mouth.

Before he could attempt to recover it, it was broken, and behind the fire. He swore at her and seized another.

"Stop," she cried, "you must listen to me first; and I can't speak while those clouds are floating in my face."

"Will you go to the devil!" he exclaimed, ferociously, "And let me be!"

"No," she persisted, "I won't: I can't tell what to do to make you talk to me; and you are determined not to understand. When I call you stupid, I don't mean anything: I don't mean that I despise you. Come, you shall take notice of me, Hareton: you are my cousin, and you shall own me."

"I shall have naught to do wi' you and your mucky pride, and your damned mocking tricks!" he answered. "I'll go to hell, body and soul, before I look sideways after you again. Side out o' t' gate, now, this minute!"

Catherine frowned, and retreated to the window-seat chewing her lip, and endeavouring, by humming an eccentric tune, to conceal a growing tendency to sob.

"You should be friends with your cousin, Mr. Hareton," I interrupted, "since she repents of her sauciness. It would do you a great deal of good: it would make you another man to have her for a companion."

"A companion!" he cried; "When she hates me, and does not think me fit to wipe her shoon! Nay, if it made me a king, I'd not be scorned for seeking her good-will any more."

"It is not I who hate you, it is you who hate me!" wept Cathy, no longer disguising her trouble. "You hate me as much as Mr. Heathcliff does, and more."

"You're a damned liar," began Earnshaw: "why have I made him angry, by taking your part, then, a hundred times? And that when you sneered at and despised me, and – go on plaguing me, and I'll step in yonder, and say you worried me out of the kitchen!"

"I didn't know you took my part," she answered, drying her eyes; "and I was miserable and bitter at everybody; but now I thank you, and beg you to forgive me: what can I do besides?"

She returned to the hearth, and frankly extended her hand. He blackened and scowled like a thunder-cloud, and kept his fists resolutely clenched, and his gaze fixed on the ground. Catherine, by instinct, must have divined it was obdurate perversity, and not dislike, that prompted this dogged conduct; for, after remaining an instant undecided, she stooped and impressed on his cheek a gentle kiss. The little rogue thought I had not seen her, and, drawing back, she took her former station by the window, quite demurely. I shook my head reprovingly, and then she blushed and whispered – "Well! What should I have done, Ellen? He wouldn't shake hands, and he wouldn't look: I must show him some way that I like him – that I want to be friends."

Whether the kiss convinced Hareton, I cannot tell: he was very careful, for some minutes, that his face should not be seen, and when he did raise it, he was sadly puzzled where to turn his eyes.

Catherine employed herself in wrapping a handsome book neatly in white paper, and having tied it with a bit of ribbon, and addressed it to "Mr. Hareton Earnshaw," she desired me to be her ambassadress, and convey the present to its destined recipient.

"And tell him, if he'll take it, I'll come and teach him to read it right," she said; "and, if he refuse it, I'll go upstairs, and never tease him again."

I carried it, and repeated the message; anxiously watched by my employer. Hareton would not open his fingers, so I laid it on his knee. He did not strike it off, either. I returned to my work. Catherine leaned her head and arms on the table, till she heard the slight rustle of the covering being removed; then she stole away, and quietly seated herself beside her cousin. He trembled, and his face glowed: all his rudeness and all his surly harshness had deserted him: he could not summon courage, at first, to utter a syllable in reply to her questioning look, and her murmured petition.

"Say you forgive me, Hareton, do. You can make me so happy by speaking that little word."

He muttered something inaudible.

"And you'll be my friend?" added Catherine, interrogatively.

"Nay, you'll be ashamed of me every day of your life," he answered; "and the more ashamed, the more you know me; and I cannot bide it."

"So you won't be my friend?" she said, smiling as sweet as honey, and creeping close up.

I overheard no further distinguishable talk, but, on looking round again, I perceived two such radiant countenances bent over the page of the accepted book, that I did not doubt the treaty had been ratified on both sides; and the enemies were, thenceforth, sworn allies.

The work they studied was full of costly pictures; and those and their position had charm enough to keep them unmoved till Joseph came home. He, poor man, was perfectly aghast at the spectacle of Catherine seated on the same bench with Hareton Earnshaw, leaning her hand on his shoulder; and confounded at his favourite's endurance of her proximity: it affected him too deeply to allow an observation on the subject that night. His emotion was only revealed by the immense sighs he drew, as he solemnly spread his large Bible on the table, and overlaid it with dirty bank-notes from his pocket-book, the produce of the day's transactions. At length he summoned Hareton from his seat.

"Tak' these in to t' maister, lad," he said, "and bide there. I's gang up to my own rahm. This hoile's neither mensful nor seemly for us: we mun side out and seearch another."

"Come, Catherine," I said, "we must 'side out' too: I've done my ironing. Are you ready to go?"

"It is not eight o'clock!" she answered, rising unwillingly.

"Hareton, I'll leave this book upon the chimney-piece, and I'll bring some more tomorrow."

"Ony books that yah leave, I shall tak' into th' hahse," said Joseph, "and it'll be mitch if yah find 'em agean; soa, yah may plase yerseln!"

Cathy threatened that his library should pay for hers; and, smiling as she passed Hareton, went singing upstairs: lighter of heart, I venture to say, than ever she had been under that roof before; except, perhaps, during her earliest visits to Linton.

The intimacy thus commenced grew rapidly; though it encountered temporary interruptions. Earnshaw was not to be civilized with a wish, and my young lady was no philosopher, and no paragon of patience; but both their minds tending to the same point – one loving and desiring to esteem, and the other loving and desiring to be esteemed – they contrived in the end to reach it.

You see, Mr. Lockwood, it was easy enough to win Mrs. Heathcliff's heart. But now, I'm glad you did not try. The crown of all my wishes will be the union of those two. I shall envy no one on their wedding day: there won't be a happier woman than myself in England!

Chapter Thirty-Three

ON THE MORROW of that Monday, Earnshaw being still unable to follow his ordinary employments, and therefore remaining about the house, I speedily found it would be impracticable to retain my charge beside me, as heretofore. She got downstairs before me, and out into the garden, where she had seen her cousin performing some easy work; and when I went to bid them come to breakfast, I saw she had persuaded him to clear a large space of ground from currant and gooseberry bushes, and they were busy planning together an importation of plants from the Grange.

I was terrified at the devastation which had been accomplished in a brief half-hour; the black-currant trees were the apple of Joseph's eye, and she had just fixed her choice of a flower-bed in the midst of them.

"There! That will be all shown to the master," I exclaimed, "the minute it is discovered. And what excuse have you to offer for taking such liberties with the garden? We shall have a fine explosion on the head of it: see if we don't! Mr. Hareton, I wonder you should have no more wit than to go and make that mess at her bidding!"

"I'd forgotten they were Joseph's," answered Earnshaw, rather puzzled; "but I'll tell him I did it."

We always ate our meals with Mr. Heathcliff. I held the mistress's post in making tea and carving; so I was indispensable at table. Catherine usually sat by me, but today she stole nearer to Hareton; and I presently saw she would have no more discretion in her friendship than she had in her hostility.

"Now, mind you don't talk with and notice your cousin too much," were my whispered instructions as we entered the room. "It will certainly annoy Mr. Heathcliff, and he'll be mad at you both."

"I'm not going to," she answered.

The minute after, she had sidled to him, and was sticking primroses in his plate of porridge.

He dared not speak to her there: he dared hardly look; and yet she went on teasing, till he was twice on the point of being provoked to laugh. I frowned, and then she glanced towards the master: whose mind was occupied on other subjects than his company, as his countenance evinced; and she grew serious for an instant, scrutinizing him with deep gravity. Afterwards she turned, and recommenced her nonsense; at last, Hareton uttered a smothered laugh. Mr. Heathcliff started; his eye rapidly surveyed our faces, Catherine met it with her accustomed look of nervousness and yet defiance, which he abhorred.

"It is well you are out of my reach," he exclaimed. "What fiend possesses you to stare back at me, continually, with those infernal eyes? Down with them! And don't remind me of your existence again. I thought I had cured you of laughing."

"It was me," muttered Hareton.

"What do you say?" demanded the master.

Hareton looked at his plate, and did not repeat the confession. Mr. Heathcliff looked at him a bit, and then silently resumed his breakfast and his interrupted musing. We had nearly finished, and the two young people prudently shifted wider asunder, so I anticipated no further disturbance during that sitting: when Joseph appeared at the door, revealing by his quivering lip and furious eyes that the outrage committed on his precious shrubs was detected. He must have seen Cathy and her cousin about the spot before he examined it, for while his jaws worked like those of a cow chewing its cud, and rendered his speech difficult to understand, he began: –

"I mun hev' my wage, and I mun goa! I *bed* aimed to dee wheare I'd sarved fur sixty year; and I thowt I'd lug my books up into t' garret, and all my bits o' stuff, and they sud hev' t' kitchen to theirsen; for t' sake o' quietness. It wur hard to gie up my awn hearthstun, but I thowt I *could* do that! But nah, shoo's taan my garden fro' me, and by th' heart, maister, I cannot stand it! Yah may bend to th' yoak an ye will – I noan used to 't, and an old man doesn't sooin get used to new barthens. I'd rayther arn my bite an' my sup wi' a hammer in th' road!"

"Now, now, idiot!" interrupted Heathcliff, "cut it short! What's your grievance? I'll interfere in no quarrels between you and Nelly. She may thrust you into the coal-hole for anything I care."

"It's noan Nelly!" answered Joseph. "I sudn't shift for Nelly – nasty ill nowt as shoo is. Thank God! *Shoo* cannot stale t' sowl o' nob'dy! Shoo wer niver soa handsome, but what a body mud look at her 'bout winking. It's yon flaysome, graceless quean, that's witched our lad, wi' her bold een and her forrard ways – till – nay! It fair brusts my heart! He's forgotten all I've done for him, and made on him, and goan and riven up a whole row o' t' grandest currant-trees i' t' garden!" and here he lamented outright; unmanned by a sense of his bitter injuries, and Earnshaw's ingratitude and dangerous condition.

"Is the fool drunk?" asked Mr. Heathcliff. "Hareton, is it you he's finding fault with?"

"I've pulled up two or three bushes," replied the young man; "but I'm going to set 'em again."

"And why have you pulled them up?" said the master.

Catherine wisely put in her tongue.

"We wanted to plant some flowers there," she cried. "I'm the only person to blame, for I wished him to do it."

"And who the devil gave *you* leave to touch a stick about the place?" demanded her father-in-law, much surprised. "And who ordered *you* to obey her?" he added, turning to Hareton.

The latter was speechless; his cousin replied – "You shouldn't grudge a few yards of earth for me to ornament, when you have taken all my land!"

"Your land, insolent slut! You never had any," said Heathcliff.

"And my money," she continued; returning his angry glare, and meantime biting a piece of crust, the remnant of her breakfast.

"Silence!" he exclaimed. "Get done, and begone!"

"And Hareton's land, and his money," pursued the reckless thing. "Hareton and I are friends now; and I shall tell him all about you!"

The master seemed confounded a moment: he grew pale, and rose up, eyeing her all the while, with an expression of mortal hate.

"If you strike me, Hareton will strike you," she said; "so you may as well sit down."

"If Hareton does not turn you out of the room, I'll strike him to hell," thundered Heathcliff. "Damnable witch! Dare you pretend to rouse him against me? Off with her! Do you hear? Fling her into the kitchen! I'll kill her, Ellen Dean, if you let her come into my sight again!"

Hareton tried, under his breath, to persuade her to go.

"Drag her away!" he cried, savagely. "Are you staying to talk?" And he approached to execute his own command.

"He'll not obey you, wicked man, anymore," said Catherine; "and he'll soon detest you as much as I do."

"Wisht! Wisht!" muttered the young man, reproachfully; "I will not hear you speak so to him. Have done."

"But you won't let him strike me?" she cried.

"Come, then," he whispered earnestly.

It was too late: Heathcliff had caught hold of her.

"Now, *you* go!" he said to Earnshaw. "Accursed witch! This time she has provoked me when I could not bear it; and I'll make her repent it for ever!"

He had his hand in her hair; Hareton attempted to release her locks, entreating him not to hurt her that once. Heathcliff's black eyes flashed; he seemed ready to tear Catherine in pieces, and I was just worked up to risk coming to the rescue, when of a sudden his fingers relaxed; he shifted his grasp from her head to her arm, and gazed intently in her face. Then he drew his hand over his eyes, stood a moment to collect himself apparently, and turning anew to Catherine, said, with assumed calmness – "You must learn to avoid putting me in a passion, or I shall really murder you sometime! Go with Mrs. Dean, and keep with her; and confine your insolence to her ears. As to Hareton Earnshaw, if I see him listen to you, I'll send him seeking his bread where he can get it! Your love will make him an outcast and a beggar. Nelly, take her; and leave me, all of you! Leave me!"

I led my young lady out: she was too glad of her escape to resist; the other followed, and Mr. Heathcliff had the room to himself till dinner. I had counselled Catherine to dine upstairs; but, as soon as he perceived her vacant seat, he sent me to call her. He spoke to none of us, ate very little, and went out directly afterwards, intimating that he should not return before evening.

The two new friends established themselves in the house during his absence; where I heard Hareton sternly check his cousin, on her offering a revelation of her father-in-law's conduct to his father. He said he wouldn't suffer a word to be uttered in his disparagement: if he were the devil, it didn't signify; he would stand by him; and he'd rather she would abuse himself, as she used to, than begin on Mr. Heathcliff. Catherine was waxing cross at this; but he found means to make her hold her tongue, by asking how she would like *him* to speak ill of her father? Then she comprehended that Earnshaw took the master's reputation home to himself; and was attached by ties stronger than reason could break – chains, forged by habit, which it would be cruel to attempt to loosen. She showed a good heart, thenceforth, in avoiding both complaints and expressions of antipathy concerning Heathcliff; and confessed to me her sorrow that she had endeavoured to raise a bad spirit between him and Hareton: indeed, I don't believe she has ever breathed a syllable, in the latter's hearing, against her oppressor since.

When this slight disagreement was over, they were friends again, and as busy as possible in their several occupations of pupil and teacher. I came in to sit with them, after I had done my work; and I felt so soothed and comforted to watch them, that I did not notice how time got on. You know, they both appeared in a measure my children: I had long been proud of one; and now, I was sure, the other would be a source of equal satisfaction. His honest, warm, and intelligent nature shook off rapidly the clouds of ignorance and degradation in which it had been bred; and Catherine's sincere commendations acted as a spur to his industry. His brightening mind brightened his features, and added spirit and nobility to their aspect: I could hardly fancy it the same individual I had beheld on the day I discovered my little lady at Wuthering Heights, after her expedition to the Crags. While I admired and they laboured, dusk drew on, and with it returned the master. He came upon us quite unexpectedly, entering by the front way, and had a full view of the whole three, ere we could raise our heads to glance at him. Well, I reflected, there was never a pleasanter, or more harmless sight; and it will be a burning shame to scold them. The red fire-light glowed on their two bonny heads, and revealed their faces animated with the eager interest of children; for, though he was twenty-three and she eighteen, each had so much of novelty to feel and learn, that neither experienced nor evinced the sentiments of sober disenchanted maturity.

They lifted their eyes together, to encounter Mr. Heathcliff: perhaps you have never remarked that their eyes are precisely similar, and they are those of Catherine Earnshaw. The present Catherine has no other likeness to her, except a breadth of forehead, and a certain arch of the nostril that makes her appear rather haughty, whether she will or not. With Hareton the resemblance is carried farther: it is singular at all times, *then* it was particularly striking; because his senses were alert, and his mental faculties wakened to unwonted activity. I suppose this resemblance disarmed Mr. Heathcliff: he walked to the hearth in evident agitation; but it quickly subsided as he looked at the young man: or, I should say, altered its character; for it was there yet. He took the book from his hand, and glanced at the open page, then returned it without any observation; merely signing Catherine away: her companion lingered very little behind her, and I was about to depart also, but he bid me sit still.

"It is a poor conclusion, is it not?" he observed, having brooded awhile on the scene he had just witnessed: "an absurd termination to my violent exertions? I get levers and mattocks to demolish the two houses, and train myself to be capable of working like Hercules, and when everything is ready and in my power, I find the will to lift a slate off either roof has vanished! My old enemies have not beaten me; now would be the precise time to revenge myself on their representatives: I could do it; and none could hinder me. But where is the use? I don't care for striking: I can't take the trouble to raise my hand! That sounds as if I had been labouring the whole time only to exhibit a fine trait of magnanimity. It is far from being the case: I have lost the faculty of enjoying their destruction, and I am too idle to destroy for nothing.

"Nelly, there is a strange change approaching; I'm in its shadow at present. I take so little interest in my daily life that I hardly remember to eat and drink. Those two who have left the room are the only objects which retain a distinct material appearance to me; and that appearance causes me pain, amounting to agony. About *her* I won't speak; and I don't desire to think; but I earnestly wish she were invisible: her presence invokes only maddening sensations. *He* moves me differently: and yet if I could do it without seeming insane, I'd never see him again! You'll perhaps think me rather inclined to become so," he added, making an effort to smile, "if I try to describe the thousand forms of past associations and ideas he awakens or embodies. But you'll not talk of what I tell you; and my mind is so eternally secluded in itself, it is tempting at last to turn it out to another.

"Five minutes ago Hareton seemed a personification of my youth, not a human being; I felt to him in such a variety of ways, that it would have been impossible to have accosted him rationally. In the first place, his startling likeness to Catherine connected him fearfully with her. That, however, which you may suppose the most potent to arrest my imagination, is actually the least: for what is not connected with her to me? And what does not recall her? I cannot look down to this floor, but her features are shaped in the flags! In every cloud, in every tree – filling the air at night, and caught by glimpses in every object by day – I am surrounded with her image! The most ordinary faces of men and women – my own features – mock me with a resemblance. The entire world is a dreadful collection of memoranda that she did exist, and that I have lost her! Well, Hareton's aspect was the ghost of my immortal love; of my wild endeavours to hold my right; my degradation, my pride, my happiness, and my anguish –

"But it is frenzy to repeat these thoughts to you: only it will let you know why, with a reluctance to be always alone, his society is no benefit; rather an aggravation of the constant torment I suffer: and it partly contributes to render me regardless how he and his cousin go on together. I can give them no attention anymore."

"But what do you mean by a *change*, Mr. Heathcliff?" I said, alarmed at his manner: though he was neither in danger of losing his senses, nor dying, according to my judgment: he was quite strong and healthy; and, as to his reason, from childhood he had a delight in dwelling on dark things, and entertaining odd fancies. He might have had a monomania on the subject of his departed idol; but on every other point his wits were as sound as mine.

"I shall not know that till it comes," he said; "I'm only half conscious of it now."

"You have no feeling of illness, have you?" I asked.

"No, Nelly, I have not," he answered.

"Then you are not afraid of death?" I pursued.

"Afraid? No!" he replied. "I have neither a fear, nor a presentiment, nor a hope of death. Why should I? With my hard constitution and temperate mode of living, and unperilous occupations, I ought to, and probably *shall*, remain above ground till there is scarcely a black hair on my head. And yet I cannot continue in this condition! I have to remind myself to breathe – almost to remind my heart to beat! And it is like bending back a stiff spring: it is by compulsion that I do the slightest act not prompted by one thought; and by compulsion that I notice anything alive or dead, which is not associated with one universal idea. I have a single wish, and my whole being and faculties are yearning to attain it. They have yearned towards it so long, and so unwaveringly, that I'm convinced it will be reached – and soon – because it has devoured my existence: I am swallowed up in the anticipation of its fulfilment.

My confessions have not relieved me; but they may account for some otherwise unaccountable phases of humour which I show. O God! It is a long fight; I wish it were over!"

He began to pace the room, muttering terrible things to himself, till I was inclined to believe, as he said Joseph did, that conscience had turned his heart to an earthly hell. I wondered greatly how it would end. Though he seldom before had revealed this state of mind, even by looks, it was his habitual mood, I had no doubt: he asserted it himself; but not a soul, from his general bearing, would have conjectured the fact. You did not when you saw him, Mr. Lockwood: and at the period of which I speak, he was just the same as then; only fonder of continued solitude, and perhaps still more laconic in company.

Chapter Thirty-Four

FOR SOME DAYS after that evening Mr. Heathcliff shunned meeting us at meals; yet he would not consent formally to exclude Hareton and Cathy. He had an aversion to yielding so completely to his feelings, choosing rather to absent himself; and eating once in twenty-four hours seemed sufficient sustenance for him.

One night, after the family were in bed, I heard him go downstairs, and out at the front door. I did not hear him re-enter, and in the morning I found he was still away. We were in April then: the weather was sweet and warm, the grass as green as showers and sun could make it, and the two dwarf apple-trees near the southern wall in full bloom. After breakfast, Catherine insisted on my bringing a chair and sitting with my work under the fir-trees at the end of the house; and she beguiled Hareton, who had perfectly recovered from his accident, to dig and arrange her little garden, which was shifted to that corner by the influence of Joseph's complaints. I was comfortably revelling in the spring fragrance around, and the beautiful soft blue overhead, when my young lady, who had run down near the gate to procure some primrose roots for a border, returned only half laden, and informed us that Mr. Heathcliff was coming in. "And he spoke to me," she added, with a perplexed countenance.

"What did he say?" asked Hareton.

"He told me to begone as fast as I could," she answered. "But he looked so different from his usual look that I stopped a moment to stare at him."

"How?" he inquired.

"Why, almost bright and cheerful. No, *almost* nothing – *very much* excited, and wild, and glad!" she replied.

"Night-walking amuses him, then," I remarked, affecting a careless manner: in reality as surprised as she was, and anxious to ascertain the truth of her statement; for to see the master looking glad would not be an every-day spectacle. I framed an excuse to go in. Heathcliff stood at the open door; he was pale, and he trembled: yet, certainly, he had a strange joyful glitter in his eyes, that altered the aspect of his whole face.

"Will you have some breakfast?" I said. "You must be hungry, rambling about all night!" I wanted to discover where he had been, but I did not like to ask directly.

"No, I'm not hungry," he answered, averting his head, and speaking rather contemptuously, as if he guessed I was trying to divine the occasion of his good humour.

I felt perplexed: I didn't know whether it were not a proper opportunity to offer a bit of admonition.

"I don't think it right to wander out of doors," I observed, "instead of being in bed: it is not wise, at any rate this moist season. I daresay you'll catch a bad cold or a fever: you have something the matter with you now!"

"Nothing but what I can bear," he replied; "and with the greatest pleasure, provided you'll leave me alone: get in, and don't annoy me."

I obeyed: and, in passing, I noticed he breathed as fast as a cat.

"Yes!" I reflected to myself, "we shall have a fit of illness. I cannot conceive what he has been doing."

That noon he sat down to dinner with us, and received a heaped-up plate from my hands, as if he intended to make amends for previous fasting.

"I've neither cold nor fever, Nelly," he remarked, in allusion to my morning's speech; "and I'm ready to do justice to the food you give me."

He took his knife and fork, and was going to commence eating, when the inclination appeared to become suddenly extinct. He laid them on the table, looked eagerly towards the window, then rose and went out. We saw him walking to and fro in the garden while we concluded our meal, and Earnshaw said he'd go and ask why he would not dine: he thought we had grieved him some way.

"Well, is he coming?" cried Catherine, when her cousin returned.

"Nay," he answered; "but he's not angry: he seemed rarely pleased indeed; only I made him impatient by speaking to him twice; and then he bid me be off to you: he wondered how I could want the company of anybody else."

I set his plate to keep warm on the fender; and after an hour or two he re-entered, when the room was clear, in no degree calmer: the same unnatural – it was unnatural – appearance of joy under his black brows; the same bloodless hue, and his teeth visible, now and then, in a kind of smile; his frame shivering, not as one shivers with chill or weakness, but as a tight-stretched cord vibrates – a strong thrilling, rather than trembling.

I will ask what is the matter, I thought; or who should? And I exclaimed – "Have you heard any good news, Mr. Heathcliff? You look uncommonly animated."

"Where should good news come from to me?" he said. "I'm animated with hunger; and, seemingly, I must not eat."

"Your dinner is here," I returned; "why won't you get it?"

"I don't want it now," he muttered, hastily: "I'll wait till supper. And, Nelly, once for all, let me beg you to warn Hareton and the other away from me. I wish to be troubled by nobody: I wish to have this place to myself."

"Is there some new reason for this banishment?" I inquired. "Tell me why you are so queer, Mr. Heathcliff? Where were you last night? I'm not putting the question through idle curiosity, but –"

"You are putting the question through very idle curiosity," he interrupted, with a laugh. "Yet I'll answer it. Last night I was on the threshold of hell. Today, I am within sight of my heaven. I have my eyes on it: hardly three feet to sever me! And now you'd better go! You'll neither see nor hear anything to frighten you, if you refrain from prying."

Having swept the hearth and wiped the table, I departed; more perplexed than ever.

He did not quit the house again that afternoon, and no one intruded on his solitude; till, at eight o'clock, I deemed it proper, though unsummoned, to carry a candle and his supper to him. He was leaning against the ledge of an open lattice, but not looking out: his face was turned to the interior gloom. The fire had smouldered to ashes; the room was filled with the damp, mild air of the cloudy evening; and so still, that not only the murmur of the beck down Gimmerton was distinguishable, but its ripples and its gurgling over the pebbles, or through the large stones which it could not cover. I uttered an ejaculation of discontent at seeing the dismal grate, and commenced shutting the casements, one after another, till I came to his.

"Must I close this?" I asked, in order to rouse him; for he would not stir.

The light flashed on his features as I spoke. Oh, Mr. Lockwood, I cannot express what a terrible start I got by the momentary view! Those deep black eyes! That smile, and ghastly paleness! It appeared to me, not Mr. Heathcliff, but a goblin; and, in my terror, I let the candle bend towards the wall, and it left me in darkness.

"Yes, close it," he replied, in his familiar voice. "There, that is pure awkwardness! Why did you hold the candle horizontally? Be quick, and bring another."

I hurried out in a foolish state of dread, and said to Joseph – "The master wishes you to take him a light and rekindle the fire." For I dared not go in myself again just then.

Joseph rattled some fire into the shovel, and went: but he brought it back immediately, with the supper-tray in his other hand, explaining that Mr. Heathcliff was going to bed, and he wanted nothing to eat till morning. We heard him mount the stairs directly; he did not proceed to his ordinary chamber, but turned into that with the panelled bed: its window, as I mentioned before, is wide enough for anybody to get through; and it struck me that he plotted another midnight excursion, of which he had rather we had no suspicion.

"Is he a ghoul or a vampire?" I mused. I had read of such hideous incarnate demons. And then I set myself to reflect how I had tended him in infancy, and watched him grow to youth, and followed him almost through his whole course; and what absurd nonsense it was to yield to that sense of horror. "But where did he come from, the little dark thing, harboured by a good man to his bane?" muttered Superstition, as I dozed into unconsciousness. And I began, half dreaming, to weary myself with imagining some fit parentage for him; and, repeating my waking meditations, I tracked his existence over again, with grim variations; at last, picturing his death and funeral: of which, all I can remember is, being exceedingly vexed at having the task of dictating an inscription for his monument, and consulting the sexton about it; and, as he had no surname, and we could not tell his age, we were obliged to content ourselves with the single word, 'Heathcliff'. That came true: we were. If you enter the kirkyard, you'll read, on his headstone, only that, and the date of his death.

Dawn restored me to common sense. I rose, and went into the garden, as soon as I could see, to ascertain if there were any footmarks under his window. There were none. "He has stayed at home," I thought, "and he'll be all right today." I prepared breakfast for the household, as was my usual custom, but told Hareton and Catherine to get theirs ere the master came down, for he lay late. They preferred taking it out of doors, under the trees, and I set a little table to accommodate them.

On my re-entrance, I found Mr. Heathcliff below. He and Joseph were conversing about some farming business; he gave clear, minute directions concerning the matter discussed, but he spoke rapidly, and turned his head continually aside, and had the same excited expression, even more exaggerated. When Joseph quitted the room he took his seat in the place he generally chose, and I put a basin of coffee before him. He drew it nearer, and then rested his arms on the table, and looked at the opposite wall, as I supposed, surveying one particular portion, up and down, with glittering, restless eyes, and with such eager interest that he stopped breathing during half a minute together.

"Come now," I exclaimed, pushing some bread against his hand, "eat and drink that, while it is hot: it has been waiting near an hour."

He didn't notice me, and yet he smiled. I'd rather have seen him gnash his teeth than smile so.

"Mr. Heathcliff! Master!" I cried, "Don't, for God's sake, stare as if you saw an unearthly vision."

"Don't, for God's sake, shout so loud," he replied. "Turn round, and tell me, are we by ourselves?"

"Of course," was my answer; "of course we are."

Still, I involuntarily obeyed him, as if I was not quite sure. With a sweep of his hand he cleared a vacant space in front among the breakfast things, and leant forward to gaze more at his ease.

Now, I perceived he was not looking at the wall; for when I regarded him alone, it seemed exactly that he gazed at something within two yards' distance. And whatever it was, it communicated, apparently, both pleasure and pain in exquisite extremes: at least the anguished, yet raptured, expression of his countenance suggested that idea. The fancied object was not fixed, either: his eyes pursued it with unwearied diligence, and, even in speaking to me, were never weaned away. I vainly reminded him of his protracted abstinence from food: if he stirred to touch anything in compliance with my entreaties, if he stretched his hand out to get a piece of bread, his fingers clenched before they reached it, and remained on the table, forgetful of their aim.

I sat, a model of patience, trying to attract his absorbed attention from its engrossing speculation; till he grew irritable, and got up, asking why I would not allow him to have his own time in taking his meals? And saying that on the next occasion I needn't wait: I might set the things down and go. Having uttered these words he left the house, slowly sauntered down the garden path, and disappeared through the gate.

The hours crept anxiously by: another evening came. I did not retire to rest till late, and when I did, I could not sleep. He returned after midnight, and, instead of going to bed, shut himself into the room beneath. I listened, and tossed about, and, finally, dressed and descended. It was too irksome to lie there, harassing my brain with a hundred idle misgivings.

I distinguished Mr. Heathcliff's step, restlessly measuring the floor, and he frequently broke the silence by a deep inspiration, resembling a groan. He muttered detached words also; the only one I could catch was the name of Catherine, coupled with some wild term of endearment or suffering; and spoken as one would speak to a person present; low and earnest, and wrung from the depth of his soul. I had not courage to walk straight into the apartment; but I desired to divert him from his reverie, and therefore fell foul of the kitchen fire, stirred it, and began to scrape the cinders. It drew him forth sooner than I expected. He opened the door immediately, and said – "Nelly, come here – is it morning? Come in with your light."

"It is striking four," I answered. "You want a candle to take upstairs: you might have lit one at this fire."

"No, I don't wish to go upstairs," he said. "Come in, and kindle *me* a fire, and do anything there is to do about the room."

"I must blow the coals red first, before I can carry any," I replied, getting a chair and the bellows.

He roamed to and fro, meantime, in a state approaching distraction; his heavy sighs succeeding each other so thick as to leave no space for common breathing between.

"When day breaks I'll send for Green," he said; "I wish to make some legal inquiries of him while I can bestow a thought on those matters, and while I can act calmly. I have not written my will yet; and how to leave my property I cannot determine. I wish I could annihilate it from the face of the earth."

"I would not talk so, Mr. Heathcliff," I interposed. "Let your will be a while: you'll be spared to repent of your many injustices yet! I never expected that your nerves would be disordered: they are, at present, marvellously so, however; and almost entirely through your own fault. The way you've passed these three last days might knock up a Titan. Do take some food, and some repose. You need only look at yourself in a glass to see how you require both. Your cheeks are hollow, and your eyes blood-shot, like a person starving with hunger and going blind with loss of sleep."

"It is not my fault that I cannot eat or rest," he replied. "I assure you it is through no settled designs. I'll do both, as soon as I possibly can. But you might as well bid a man struggling in the water rest within arms' length of the shore! I must reach it first, and then I'll rest. Well, never mind Mr. Green: as to repenting of my injustices, I've done no injustice, and I repent of nothing. I'm too happy; and yet I'm not happy enough. My soul's bliss kills my body, but does not satisfy itself."

"Happy, master?" I cried. "Strange happiness! If you would hear me without being angry, I might offer some advice that would make you happier."

"What is that?" he asked. "Give it."

"You are aware, Mr. Heathcliff," I said, "that from the time you were thirteen years old you have lived a selfish, unchristian life; and probably hardly had a Bible in your hands during all that period. You must have forgotten the contents of the book, and you may not have space to search it now. Could it be hurtful to send for someone – some minister of any denomination, it does not matter which – to explain it, and show you how very far you have erred from its precepts; and how unfit you will be for its heaven, unless a change takes place before you die?"

"I'm rather obliged than angry, Nelly," he said, "for you remind me of the manner in which I desire to be buried. It is to be carried to the churchyard in the evening. You and Hareton may, if you please, accompany me: and mind, particularly, to notice that the sexton obeys my directions concerning the two coffins! No minister need come; nor need anything be said over me. I tell you I have nearly attained *my* heaven; and that of others is altogether unvalued and uncoveted by me."

"And supposing you persevered in your obstinate fast, and died by that means, and they refused to bury you in the precincts of the kirk?" I said, shocked at his godless indifference. "How would you like it?"

"They won't do that," he replied: "if they did, you must have me removed secretly; and if you neglect it you shall prove, practically, that the dead are not annihilated!"

As soon as he heard the other members of the family stirring he retired to his den, and I breathed freer. But in the afternoon, while Joseph and Hareton were at their work, he came into the kitchen again, and, with a wild look, bid me come and sit in the house: he wanted somebody with him. I declined; telling him plainly that his strange talk and manner frightened me, and I had neither the nerve nor the will to be his companion alone.

"I believe you think me a fiend," he said, with his dismal laugh: "something too horrible to live under a decent roof." Then turning to Catherine, who was there, and who drew behind me at his approach, he added, half sneeringly, – "Will *you* come, chuck? I'll not hurt you. No! To you I've made myself worse than the devil. Well, there is *one* who won't shrink from my company! By God! She's relentless. Oh, damn it! It's unutterably too much for flesh and blood to bear – even mine."

He solicited the society of no one more. At dusk he went into his chamber. Through the whole night, and far into the morning, we heard him groaning and murmuring to himself. Hareton was anxious to enter; but I bid him fetch Mr. Kenneth, and he should go in and see him. When he came, and I requested admittance and tried to open the door, I found it locked; and Heathcliff bid us be damned. He was better, and would be left alone; so the doctor went away.

The following evening was very wet: indeed, it poured down till day-dawn; and, as I took my morning walk round the house, I observed the master's window swinging open, and the rain driving straight in. He cannot be in bed, I thought: those showers would drench him through. He must either be up or out. But I'll make no more ado, I'll go boldly and look.

Having succeeded in obtaining entrance with another key, I ran to unclose the panels, for the chamber was vacant; quickly pushing them aside, I peeped in. Mr. Heathcliff was there – laid on his back. His eyes met mine so keen and fierce, I started; and then he seemed to smile. I could not think him dead: but his face and throat were washed with rain; the bed-clothes dripped, and he was perfectly still. The lattice, flapping to and fro, had grazed one hand that rested on the sill; no blood trickled from the broken skin, and when I put my fingers to it, I could doubt no more: he was dead and stark!

I hasped the window; I combed his black long hair from his forehead; I tried to close his eyes: to extinguish, if possible, that frightful, life-like gaze of exultation before anyone else beheld it. They would not shut: they seemed to sneer at my attempts; and his parted lips and sharp white teeth sneered too! Taken with another fit of cowardice, I cried out for Joseph. Joseph shuffled up and made a noise, but resolutely refused to meddle with him.

"Th' divil's harried off his soul," he cried, "and he may hev' his carcass into t' bargin, for aught I care! Ech! What a wicked 'un he looks, girning at death!" and the old sinner grinned in mockery. I thought he intended to cut a caper round the bed; but suddenly composing himself, he fell on his knees, and raised his hands, and returned thanks that the lawful master and the ancient stock were restored to their rights.

I felt stunned by the awful event; and my memory unavoidably recurred to former times with a sort of oppressive sadness. But poor Hareton, the most wronged, was the only one who really suffered much. He sat by the corpse all night, weeping in bitter earnest. He pressed its hand, and kissed the sarcastic, savage face that everyone else shrank from contemplating; and bemoaned him with that strong grief which springs naturally from a generous heart, though it be tough as tempered steel.

Mr. Kenneth was perplexed to pronounce of what disorder the master died. I concealed the fact of his having swallowed nothing for four days, fearing it might lead to trouble, and then, I am persuaded, he did not abstain on purpose: it was the consequence of his strange illness, not the cause.

We buried him, to the scandal of the whole neighbourhood, as he wished. Earnshaw and I, the sexton, and six men to carry the coffin, comprehended the whole attendance. The six men departed when they had let it down into the grave: we stayed to see it covered. Hareton, with a streaming face, dug green sods, and laid them over the brown mould himself: at present it is as smooth and verdant as its companion mounds – and I hope its tenant sleeps as soundly. But the country folks, if you ask them, would swear on the Bible that he *walks*: there are those who speak to having met him near the church, and on the moor, and even within this house. Idle tales, you'll say, and so say I. Yet that old man by the kitchen fire affirms he has seen two on 'em looking out of his chamber window on every rainy night since his death: – and an odd thing happened to me about a month ago. I was going to the Grange one evening – a dark evening, threatening thunder – and, just at the turn of the Heights, I encountered a little boy with a sheep and two lambs before him; he was crying terribly; and I supposed the lambs were skittish, and would not be guided.

"What is the matter, my little man?" I asked.

"There's Heathcliff and a woman yonder, under t' nab," he blubbered, "un' I darnut pass 'em."

I saw nothing; but neither the sheep nor he would go on so I bid him take the road lower down. He probably raised the phantoms from thinking, as he traversed the moors alone, on the nonsense he had heard his parents and companions repeat. Yet, still, I don't like being out in the dark now; and I don't like being left by myself in this grim house: I cannot help it; I shall be glad when they leave it, and shift to the Grange.

"They are going to the Grange, then?" I said.

"Yes," answered Mrs. Dean, "as soon as they are married, and that will be on New Year's Day."

"And who will live here then?"

"Why, Joseph will take care of the house, and, perhaps, a lad to keep him company. They will live in the kitchen, and the rest will be shut up."

"For the use of such ghosts as choose to inhabit it?" I observed.

"No, Mr. Lockwood," said Nelly, shaking her head. "I believe the dead are at peace: but it is not right to speak of them with levity."

At that moment the garden gate swung to; the ramblers were returning.

"*They* are afraid of nothing," I grumbled, watching their approach through the window. "Together, they would brave Satan and all his legions."

As they stepped on to the door-stones, and halted to take a last look at the moon – or, more correctly, at each other by her light – I felt irresistibly impelled to escape them again; and, pressing a remembrance into the hand of Mrs. Dean, and disregarding her expostulations at my rudeness, I vanished through the kitchen as they opened the house-door; and so should have confirmed Joseph in his opinion of his fellow-servant's gay indiscretions, had he not fortunately recognised me for a respectable character by the sweet ring of a sovereign at his feet.

My walk home was lengthened by a diversion in the direction of the kirk. When beneath its walls, I perceived decay had made progress, even in seven months: many a window showed black gaps deprived of glass; and slates jutted off here and there, beyond the right line of the roof, to be gradually worked off in coming autumn storms.

I sought, and soon discovered, the three headstones on the slope next the moor: the middle one grey, and half buried in the heath; Edgar Linton's only harmonized by the turf and moss creeping up its foot; Heathcliff's still bare.

I lingered round them, under that benign sky: watched the moths fluttering among the heath and harebells, listened to the soft wind breathing through the grass, and wondered how anyone could ever imagine unquiet slumbers for the sleepers in that quiet earth.

Charlotte Brontë

Villette

Volume One

Chapter One
Bretton

MY GODMOTHER lived in a handsome house in the clean and ancient town of Bretton. Her husband's family had been residents there for generations, and bore, indeed, the name of their birthplace – Bretton of Bretton: whether by coincidence, or because some remote ancestor had been a personage of sufficient importance to leave his name to his neighbourhood, I know not.

When I was a girl I went to Bretton about twice a year, and well I liked the visit. The house and its inmates specially suited me. The large peaceful rooms, the well-arranged furniture, the clear wide windows, the balcony outside, looking down on a fine antique street, where Sundays and holidays seemed always to abide – so quiet was its atmosphere, so clean its pavement – these things pleased me well.

One child in a household of grown people is usually made very much of, and in a quiet way I was a good deal taken notice of by Mrs. Bretton, who had been left a widow, with one son, before I knew her; her husband, a physician, having died while she was yet a young and handsome woman.

She was not young, as I remember her, but she was still handsome, tall, well-made, and though dark for an Englishwoman, yet wearing always the clearness of health in her brunette cheek, and its vivacity in a pair of fine, cheerful black eyes. People esteemed it a grievous pity that she had not conferred her complexion on her son, whose eyes were blue – though, even in boyhood, very piercing – and the colour of his long hair such as friends did not venture to specify, except as the sun shone on it, when they called it golden. He inherited the lines of his mother's features, however; also her good teeth, her stature (or the promise of her stature, for he was not yet full-grown), and, what was better, her health without flaw, and her spirits of that tone and equality which are better than a fortune to the possessor.

In the autumn of the year — I was staying at Bretton; my godmother having come in person to claim me of the kinsfolk with whom was at that time fixed my permanent residence. I believe she then plainly saw events coming, whose very shadow I scarce guessed; yet of which the faint suspicion sufficed to impart unsettled sadness, and made me glad to change scene and society.

Time always flowed smoothly for me at my godmother's side; not with tumultuous swiftness, but blandly, like the gliding of a full river through a plain. My visits to her resembled the sojourn of Christian and Hopeful beside a certain pleasant stream, with 'green trees on each bank, and meadows beautified with lilies all the year round'. The charm of variety there was not, nor the excitement of incident; but I liked peace so well, and sought stimulus so little, that when the latter came I almost felt it a disturbance, and wished rather it had still held aloof.

One day a letter was received of which the contents evidently caused Mrs. Bretton surprise and some concern. I thought at first it was from home, and trembled, expecting I know not what disastrous communication: to me, however, no reference was made, and the cloud seemed to pass.

The next day, on my return from a long walk, I found, as I entered my bedroom, an unexpected change. In, addition to my own French bed in its shady recess, appeared in a corner a small crib, draped with white; and in addition to my mahogany chest of drawers, I saw a tiny rosewood chest. I stood still, gazed, and considered.

"Of what are these things the signs and tokens?" I asked. The answer was obvious. "A second guest is coming: Mrs. Bretton expects other visitors."

On descending to dinner, explanations ensued. A little girl, I was told, would shortly be my companion: the daughter of a friend and distant relation of the late Dr. Bretton's. This little girl, it was added, had recently lost her mother; though, indeed, Mrs. Bretton ere long subjoined, the loss was not so great as might at first appear. Mrs. Home (Home it seems was the name) had been a very pretty, but a giddy, careless woman, who had neglected her child, and disappointed and disheartened her husband. So far from congenial had the union proved, that separation at last ensued – separation by mutual consent, not after any legal process. Soon after this event, the lady having over-exerted herself at a ball, caught cold, took a fever, and died after a very brief illness. Her husband, naturally a man of very sensitive feelings, and shocked inexpressibly by too sudden communication of the news, could hardly, it seems, now be persuaded but that some over-severity on his part – some deficiency in patience and indulgence – had contributed to hasten her end. He had brooded over this idea till his spirits were seriously affected; the medical men insisted on travelling being tried as a remedy, and meanwhile Mrs. Bretton had offered to take charge of his little girl. "And I hope," added my godmother in conclusion, "the child will not be like her mamma; as silly and frivolous a little flirt as ever sensible man was weak enough to marry. For," said she, "Mr. Home *is* a sensible man in his way, though not very practical: he is fond of science, and lives half his life in a laboratory trying experiments – a thing his butterfly wife could neither comprehend nor endure; and indeed" confessed my godmother, "I should not have liked it myself."

In answer to a question of mine, she further informed me that her late husband used to say, Mr. Home had derived this scientific turn from a maternal uncle, a French savant; for he came, it seems; of mixed French and Scottish origin, and had connections now living in France, of whom more than one wrote *de* before his name, and called himself noble.

That same evening at nine o'clock, a servant was despatched to meet the coach by which our little visitor was expected. Mrs. Bretton and I sat alone in the drawing-room waiting her coming; John Graham Bretton being absent on a visit to one of his schoolfellows who lived in the country. My godmother read the evening paper while she waited; I sewed. It was a wet night; the rain lashed the panes, and the wind sounded angry and restless.

"Poor child!" said Mrs. Bretton from time to time. "What weather for her journey! I wish she were safe here."

A little before ten the door-bell announced Warren's return. No sooner was the door opened than I ran down into the hall; there lay a trunk and some band-boxes, beside them stood a person like a nurse-girl, and at the foot of the staircase was Warren with a shawled bundle in his arms.

"Is that the child?" I asked.

"Yes, miss."

I would have opened the shawl, and tried to get a peep at the face, but it was hastily turned from me to Warren's shoulder.

"Put me down, please," said a small voice when Warren opened the drawing-room door, "and take off this shawl," continued the speaker, extracting with its minute hand the pin, and with a sort of fastidious haste doffing the clumsy wrapping. The creature which now appeared made a deft attempt to fold the shawl; but the drapery was much too heavy and large to be sustained or wielded by those hands and arms. "Give it to Harriet, please," was then the direction, "and she can put it away." This said, it turned and fixed its eyes on Mrs. Bretton.

"Come here, little dear," said that lady. "Come and let me see if you are cold and damp: come and let me warm you at the fire."

The child advanced promptly. Relieved of her wrapping, she appeared exceedingly tiny; but was a neat, completely-fashioned little figure, light, slight, and straight. Seated on my godmother's ample lap, she looked a mere doll; her neck, delicate as wax, her head of silky curls, increased, I thought, the resemblance.

Mrs. Bretton talked in little fond phrases as she chafed the child's hands, arms, and feet; first she was considered with a wistful gaze, but soon a smile answered her. Mrs. Bretton was not generally a caressing woman: even with her deeply-cherished son, her manner was rarely sentimental, often the reverse; but when the small stranger smiled at her, she kissed it, asking, "What is my little one's name?"

"Missy."

"But besides Missy?"

"Polly, papa calls her."

"Will Polly be content to live with me?"

"Not *always*; but till papa comes home. Papa is gone away." She shook her head expressively.

"He will return to Polly, or send for her."

"Will he, ma'am? Do you know he will?"

"I think so."

"But Harriet thinks not: at least not for a long while. He is ill."

Her eyes filled. She drew her hand from Mrs. Bretton's and made a movement to leave her lap; it was at first resisted, but she said – "Please, I wish to go: I can sit on a stool."

She was allowed to slip down from the knee, and taking a footstool, she carried it to a corner where the shade was deep, and there seated herself. Mrs. Bretton, though a commanding, and in grave matters even a peremptory woman, was often passive in trifles: she allowed the child her way. She said to me, "Take no notice at present." But I did take notice: I watched Polly rest her small elbow on her small knee, her head on her hand; I observed her draw a square inch or two of pocket-handkerchief from the doll-pocket of her doll-skirt, and then I heard her weep. Other children in grief or pain cry aloud, without shame or restraint; but this being wept: the tiniest occasional sniff testified to her emotion. Mrs. Bretton did not hear it: which was quite as well. Ere long, a voice, issuing from the corner, demanded – "May the bell be rung for Harriet!"

I rang; the nurse was summoned and came.

"Harriet, I must be put to bed," said her little mistress. "You must ask where my bed is."

Harriet signified that she had already made that inquiry.

"Ask if you sleep with me, Harriet."

"No, Missy," said the nurse: "you are to share this young lady's room," designating me.

Missy did not leave her seat, but I saw her eyes seek me. After some minutes' silent scrutiny, she emerged from her corner.

"I wish you, ma'am, good night," said she to Mrs. Bretton; but she passed me mute.

"Goodnight, Polly," I said.

"No need to say goodnight, since we sleep in the same chamber," was the reply, with which she vanished from the drawing-room. We heard Harriet propose to carry her upstairs. "No need," was again her answer – "no need, no need:" and her small step toiled wearily up the staircase.

On going to bed an hour afterwards, I found her still wide awake. She had arranged her pillows so as to support her little person in a sitting posture: her hands, placed one within the other, rested quietly on the sheet, with an old-fashioned calm most unchildlike. I abstained from speaking to her for some time, but just before extinguishing the light, I recommended her to lie down.

"By and by," was the answer.

"But you will take cold, Missy."

She took some tiny article of raiment from the chair at her crib side, and with it covered her shoulders. I suffered her to do as she pleased. Listening awhile in the darkness, I was aware that she still wept, – wept under restraint, quietly and cautiously.

On awaking with daylight, a trickling of water caught my ear. Behold! There she was risen and mounted on a stool near the washstand, with pains and difficulty inclining the ewer (which she could not lift) so as to pour its contents into the basin. It was curious to watch her as she washed and dressed, so small, busy, and noiseless. Evidently she was little accustomed to perform her own toilet; and the buttons, strings, hooks and eyes, offered difficulties which she encountered with a perseverance good to witness. She folded her night-dress, she smoothed the drapery of her couch quite neatly;

withdrawing into a corner, where the sweep of the white curtain concealed her, she became still. I half rose, and advanced my head to see how she was occupied. On her knees, with her forehead bent on her hands, I perceived that she was praying.

Her nurse tapped at the door. She started up.

"I am dressed, Harriet," said she; "I have dressed myself, but I do not feel neat. Make me neat!"

"Why did you dress yourself, Missy?"

"Hush! Speak low, Harriet, for fear of waking *the girl*" (meaning me, who now lay with my eyes shut). "I dressed myself to learn, against the time you leave me."

"Do you want me to go?"

"When you are cross, I have many a time wanted you to go, but not now. Tie my sash straight; make my hair smooth, please."

"Your sash is straight enough. What a particular little body you are!"

"It must be tied again. Please to tie it."

"There, then. When I am gone you must get that young lady to dress you."

"On no account."

"Why? She is a very nice young lady. I hope you mean to behave prettily to her, Missy, and not show your airs."

"She shall dress me on no account."

"Comical little thing!"

"You are not passing the comb straight through my hair, Harriet; the line will be crooked."

"Ay, you are ill to please. Does that suit?"

"Pretty well. Where should I go now that I am dressed?"

"I will take you into the breakfast-room."

"Come, then."

They proceeded to the door. She stopped.

"Oh! Harriet, I wish this was papa's house! I don't know these people."

"Be a good child, Missy."

"I am good, but I ache here;" putting her hand to her heart, and moaning while she reiterated, "Papa! Papa!"

I roused myself and started up, to check this scene while it was yet within bounds.

"Say good morning to the young lady," dictated Harriet. She said, "Good morning," and then followed her nurse from the room. Harriet temporarily left that same day, to go to her own friends, who lived in the neighbourhood.

On descending, I found Paulina (the child called herself Polly, but her full name was Paulina Mary) seated at the breakfast-table, by Mrs. Bretton's side; a mug of milk stood before her, a morsel of bread filled her hand, which lay passive on the table-cloth: she was not eating.

"How we shall conciliate this little creature," said Mrs. Bretton to me, "I don't know: she tastes nothing, and by her looks, she has not slept."

I expressed my confidence in the effects of time and kindness.

"If she were to take a fancy to anybody in the house, she would soon settle; but not till then," replied Mrs. Bretton.

Chapter Two
Paulina

SOME DAYS ELAPSED, and it appeared she was not likely to take much of a fancy to anybody in the house. She was not exactly naughty or wilful: she was far from disobedient; but an object less conducive to comfort – to tranquillity even – than she presented, it was scarcely possible to have before one's eyes. She moped: no grown person could have performed that uncheering business better; no furrowed face of adult exile, longing for Europe at Europe's antipodes, ever bore more legibly the signs of home sickness than did her infant visage. She seemed growing old and unearthly. I, Lucy Snowe, plead guiltless of that curse, an overheated and discursive imagination; but whenever, opening a room-door, I found her seated in a corner alone, her head in her pigmy hand, that room seemed to me not inhabited, but haunted.

And again, when of moonlight nights, on waking, I beheld her figure, white and conspicuous in its night-dress, kneeling upright in bed, and praying like some Catholic or Methodist enthusiast – some precocious fanatic or untimely saint – I scarcely know what thoughts I had; but they ran risk of being hardly more rational and healthy than that child's mind must have been.

I seldom caught a word of her prayers, for they were whispered low: sometimes, indeed, they were not whispered at all, but put up unuttered; such rare sentences as reached my ear still bore the burden, "Papa; my dear papa!" This, I perceived, was a one-idea'd nature; betraying that monomaniac tendency I have ever thought the most unfortunate with which man or woman can be cursed.

What might have been the end of this fretting, had it continued unchecked, can only be conjectured: it received, however, a sudden turn.

One afternoon, Mrs. Bretton, coaxing her from her usual station in a corner, had lifted her into the window-seat, and, by way of occupying her attention, told her to watch the passengers and count how many ladies should go down the street in a given time. She had sat listlessly, hardly looking, and not counting, when – my eye being fixed on hers – I witnessed in its iris and pupil a startling transfiguration. These sudden, dangerous natures – *sensitive* as they are called – offer many a curious spectacle to those whom a cooler temperament has secured from participation in their angular vagaries. The fixed and heavy gaze swum, trembled, then glittered in fire; the small, overcast brow cleared; the trivial and dejected features lit up; the sad countenance vanished, and in its place appeared a sudden eagerness, an intense expectancy. "It *is*!" were her words.

Like a bird or a shaft, or any other swift thing, she was gone from the room. How she got the house-door open I cannot tell; probably it might be ajar; perhaps Warren was in the way and obeyed her behest, which would be impetuous enough. I – watching calmly from the window – saw her, in her black frock and tiny braided apron (to pinafores she had an antipathy), dart half the length of the street; and, as I was on the point of turning, and quietly announcing to Mrs. Bretton that the child was run out mad, and ought instantly to be pursued, I saw her caught up, and rapt at once from my cool observation, and from the wondering stare of the passengers. A gentleman had done this good turn, and now, covering her with his cloak, advanced to restore her to the house whence he had seen her issue.

I concluded he would leave her in a servant's charge and withdraw; but he entered: having tarried a little while below, he came upstairs.

His reception immediately explained that he was known to Mrs. Bretton. She recognised him; she greeted him, and yet she was fluttered, surprised, taken unawares. Her look and manner were even expostulatory; and in reply to these, rather than her words, he said, – "I could not help it, madam: I found it impossible to leave the country without seeing with my own eyes how she settled."

"But you will unsettle her."

"I hope not. And how is papa's little Polly?"

This question he addressed to Paulina, as he sat down and placed her gently on the ground before him.

"How is Polly's papa?" was the reply, as she leaned on his knee, and gazed up into his face.

It was not a noisy, not a wordy scene: for that I was thankful; but it was a scene of feeling too brimful, and which, because the cup did not foam up high or furiously overflow, only oppressed one the more. On all occasions of vehement, unrestrained expansion, a sense of disdain or ridicule comes to the weary spectator's relief; whereas I have ever felt most burdensome that sort of sensibility which bends of its own will, a giant slave under the sway of good sense.

Mr. Home was a stern-featured – perhaps I should rather say, a hard-featured man: his forehead was knotty, and his cheekbones were marked and prominent. The character of his face was quite Scotch; but there was feeling in his eye, and emotion in his now agitated countenance. His northern accent in speaking harmonised with his physiognomy. He was at once proud-looking and homely-looking. He laid his hand on the child's uplifted head. She said – "Kiss Polly."

He kissed her. I wished she would utter some hysterical cry, so that I might get relief and be at ease. She made wonderfully little noise: she seemed to have got what she wanted – *all* she wanted, and to be in a trance of content. Neither in mien nor in features was this creature like her sire, and yet she was of his strain: her mind had been filled from his, as the cup from the flagon.

Indisputably, Mr. Home owned manly self-control, however he might secretly feel on some matters. "Polly," he said, looking down on his little girl, "go into the hall; you will see papa's great-coat lying on a chair; put your hand into the pockets, you will find a pocket-handkerchief there; bring it to me."

She obeyed; went and returned deftly and nimbly. He was talking to Mrs. Bretton when she came back, and she waited with the handkerchief in her hand. It was a picture, in its way, to see her, with her tiny stature, and trim, neat shape, standing at his knee. Seeing that he continued to talk, apparently unconscious of her return, she took his hand, opened the unresisting fingers, insinuated into them the handkerchief, and closed them upon it one by one. He still seemed not to see or to feel her; but by-and-by, he lifted her to his knee; she nestled against him, and though neither looked at nor spoke to the other for an hour following, I suppose both were satisfied.

During tea, the minute thing's movements and behaviour gave, as usual, full occupation to the eye. First she directed Warren, as he placed the chairs.

"Put papa's chair here, and mine near it, between papa and Mrs. Bretton: *I* must hand his tea."

She took her own seat, and beckoned with her hand to her father.

"Be near me, as if we were at home, papa."

And again, as she intercepted his cup in passing, and would stir the sugar, and put in the cream herself, "I always did it for you at home; papa: nobody could do it as well, not even your own self."

Throughout the meal she continued her attentions: rather absurd they were. The sugar-tongs were too wide for one of her hands, and she had to use both in wielding them; the weight of the silver cream-ewer, the bread-and-butter plates, the very cup and saucer, tasked her insufficient strength and dexterity; but she would lift this, hand that, and luckily contrived through it all to break nothing. Candidly speaking, I thought her a little busy-body; but her father, blind like other parents, seemed perfectly content to let her wait on him, and even wonderfully soothed by her offices.

"She is my comfort!" he could not help saying to Mrs. Bretton. That lady had her own 'comfort' and nonpareil on a much larger scale, and, for the moment, absent; so she sympathised with his foible.

This second 'comfort' came on the stage in the course of the evening. I knew this day had been fixed for his return, and was aware that Mrs. Bretton had been expecting him through all its hours. We were seated round the fire, after tea, when Graham joined our circle: I should rather say, broke it up

– for, of course, his arrival made a bustle; and then, as Mr. Graham was fasting, there was refreshment to be provided. He and Mr. Home met as old acquaintance; of the little girl he took no notice for a time.

His meal over, and numerous questions from his mother answered, he turned from the table to the hearth. Opposite where he had placed himself was seated Mr. Home, and at his elbow, the child. When I say *child* I use an inappropriate and undescriptive term – a term suggesting any picture rather than that of the demure little person in a mourning frock and white chemisette, that might just have fitted a good-sized doll – perched now on a high chair beside a stand, whereon was her toy work-box of white varnished wood, and holding in her hands a shred of a handkerchief, which she was professing to hem, and at which she bored perseveringly with a needle, that in her fingers seemed almost a skewer, pricking herself ever and anon, marking the cambric with a track of minute red dots; occasionally starting when the perverse weapon – swerving from her control – inflicted a deeper stab than usual; but still silent, diligent, absorbed, womanly.

Graham was at that time a handsome, faithless-looking youth of sixteen. I say faithless-looking, not because he was really of a very perfidious disposition, but because the epithet strikes me as proper to describe the fair, Celtic (not Saxon) character of his good looks; his waved light auburn hair, his supple symmetry, his smile frequent, and destitute neither of fascination nor of subtlety (in no bad sense). A spoiled, whimsical boy he was in those days.

"Mother," he said, after eyeing the little figure before him in silence for some time, and when the temporary absence of Mr. Home from the room relieved him from the half-laughing bashfulness, which was all he knew of timidity – "Mother, I see a young lady in the present society to whom I have not been introduced."

"Mr. Home's little girl, I suppose you mean," said his mother.

"Indeed, ma'am," replied her son, "I consider your expression of the least ceremonious: Miss Home *I* should certainly have said, in venturing to speak of the gentlewoman to whom I allude."

"Now, Graham, I will not have that child teased. Don't flatter yourself that I shall suffer you to make her your butt."

"Miss Home," pursued Graham, undeterred by his mother's remonstrance, "might I have the honour to introduce myself, since no one else seems willing to render you and me that service? Your slave, John Graham Bretton."

She looked at him; he rose and bowed quite gravely. She deliberately put down thimble, scissors, work; descended with precaution from her perch, and curtsying with unspeakable seriousness, said, "How do you do?"

"I have the honour to be in fair health, only in some measure fatigued with a hurried journey. I hope, ma'am, I see you well?"

"Tor-rer-ably well," was the ambitious reply of the little woman and she now essayed to regain her former elevation, but finding this could not be done without some climbing and straining – a sacrifice of decorum not to be thought of – and being utterly disdainful of aid in the presence of a strange young gentleman, she relinquished the high chair for a low stool: towards that low stool Graham drew in his chair.

"I hope, ma'am, the present residence, my mother's house, appears to you a convenient place of abode?"

"Not par-tic-er-er-ly; I want to go home."

"A natural and laudable desire, ma'am; but one which, notwithstanding, I shall do my best to oppose. I reckon on being able to get out of you a little of that precious commodity called amusement, which mamma and Mistress Snowe there fail to yield me."

"I shall have to go with papa soon: I shall not stay long at your mother's."

"Yes, yes; you will stay with me, I am sure. I have a pony on which you shall ride, and no end of books with pictures to show you."

"Are *you* going to live here now?"

"I am. Does that please you? Do you like me?"

"No."

"Why?"

"I think you queer."

"My face, ma'am?"

"Your face and all about you: You have long red hair."

"Auburn hair, if you please: mamma, calls it auburn, or golden, and so do all her friends. But even with my 'long red hair'" (and he waved his mane with a sort of triumph – tawny he himself well knew that it was, and he was proud of the leonine hue), "I cannot possibly be queerer than is your ladyship."

"You call me queer?"

"Certainly."

(After a pause), "I think I shall go to bed."

"A little thing like you ought to have been in bed many hours since; but you probably sat up in the expectation of seeing me?"

"No, indeed."

"You certainly wished to enjoy the pleasure of my society. You knew I was coming home, and would wait to have a look at me."

"I sat up for papa, and not for you."

"Very good, Miss Home. I am going to be a favourite: preferred before papa soon, I daresay."

She wished Mrs. Bretton and myself goodnight; she seemed hesitating whether Graham's deserts entitled him to the same attention, when he caught her up with one hand, and with that one hand held her poised aloft above his head. She saw herself thus lifted up on high, in the glass over the fireplace. The suddenness, the freedom, the disrespect of the action were too much.

"For shame, Mr. Graham!" was her indignant cry, "Put me down!" – and when again on her feet, "I wonder what you would think of me if I were to treat you in that way, lifting you with my hand" (raising that mighty member) "as Warren lifts the little cat."

So saying, she departed.

Chapter Three
The Playmates

MR. HOME stayed two days. During his visit he could not be prevailed on to go out: he sat all day long by the fireside, sometimes silent, sometimes receiving and answering Mrs. Bretton's chat, which was just of the proper sort for a man in his morbid mood – not over-sympathetic, yet not too uncongenial, sensible; and even with a touch of the motherly – she was sufficiently his senior to be permitted this touch.

As to Paulina, the child was at once happy and mute, busy and watchful. Her father frequently lifted her to his knee; she would sit there till she felt or fancied he grew restless; then it was – "Papa, put me down; I shall tire you with my weight."

And the mighty burden slid to the rug, and establishing itself on carpet or stool just at 'papa's' feet, the white work-box and the scarlet-speckled handkerchief came into play. This handkerchief, it seems, was intended as a keepsake for 'papa', and must be finished before his departure; consequently the demand on the sempstress's industry (she accomplished about a score of stitches in half-an-hour) was stringent.

The evening, by restoring Graham to the maternal roof (his days were passed at school), brought us an accession of animation – a quality not diminished by the nature of the scenes pretty sure to be enacted between him and Miss Paulina.

A distant and haughty demeanour had been the result of the indignity put upon her the first evening of his arrival: her usual answer, when he addressed her, was – "I can't attend to you; I have other things to think about." Being implored to state *what* things:

"Business."

Graham would endeavour to seduce her attention by opening his desk and displaying its multifarious contents: seals, bright sticks of wax, pen-knives, with a miscellany of engravings – some of them gaily coloured – which he had amassed from time to time. Nor was this powerful temptation wholly unavailing: her eyes, furtively raised from her work, cast many a peep towards the writing-table, rich in scattered pictures. An etching of a child playing with a Blenheim spaniel happened to flutter to the floor.

"Pretty little dog!" said she, delighted.

Graham prudently took no notice. Ere long, stealing from her corner, she approached to examine the treasure more closely. The dog's great eyes and long ears, and the child's hat and feathers, were irresistible.

"Nice picture!" was her favourable criticism.

"Well – you may have it," said Graham.

She seemed to hesitate. The wish to possess was strong, but to accept would be a compromise of dignity. No. She put it down and turned away.

"You won't have it, then, Polly?"

"I would rather not, thank you."

"Shall I tell you what I will do with the picture if you refuse it?"

She half turned to listen.

"Cut it into strips for lighting the taper."

"No!"

"But I shall."

"Please – don't."

Graham waxed inexorable on hearing the pleading tone; he took the scissors from his mother's work-basket.

"Here goes!" said he, making a menacing flourish. "Right through Fido's head, and splitting little Harry's nose."

"No! *No!* NO!"

"Then come to me. Come quickly, or it is done."

She hesitated, lingered, but complied.

"Now, will you have it?" he asked, as she stood before him.

"Please."

"But I shall want payment."

"How much?"

"A kiss."

"Give the picture first into my hand."

Polly, as she said this, looked rather faithless in her turn. Graham gave it. She absconded a debtor, darted to her father, and took refuge on his knee. Graham rose in mimic wrath and followed. She buried her face in Mr. Home's waistcoat.

"Papa – papa – send him away!"

"I'll not be sent away," said Graham.

With face still averted, she held out her hand to keep him off.

"Then, I shall kiss the hand," said he; but that moment it became a miniature fist, and dealt him payment in a small coin that was not kisses.

Graham – not failing in his way to be as wily as his little playmate – retreated apparently quite discomfited; he flung himself on a sofa, and resting his head against the cushion, lay like one in pain. Polly, finding him silent, presently peeped at him. His eyes and face were covered with his hands. She turned on her father's knee, and gazed at her foe anxiously and long. Graham groaned.

"Papa, what is the matter?" she whispered.

"You had better ask him, Polly."

"Is he hurt?" (groan second.)

"He makes a noise as if he were," said Mr. Home.

"Mother," suggested Graham, feebly, "I think you had better send for the doctor. Oh my eye!" (renewed silence, broken only by sighs from Graham.)

"If I were to become blind –?" suggested this last.

His chastiser could not bear the suggestion. She was beside him directly.

"Let me see your eye: I did not mean to touch it, only your mouth; and I did not think I hit so *very* hard."

Silence answered her. Her features worked, – "I am sorry; I am sorry!"

Then succeeded emotion, faltering; weeping.

"Have done trying that child, Graham," said Mrs. Bretton.

"It is all nonsense, my pet," cried Mr. Home.

And Graham once more snatched her aloft, and she again punished him; and while she pulled his lion's locks, termed him – "The naughtiest, rudest, worst, untruest person that ever was."

* * *

On the morning of Mr. Home's departure, he and his daughter had some conversation in a window-recess by themselves; I heard part of it.

"Couldn't I pack my box and go with you, papa?" she whispered earnestly.

He shook his head.

"Should I be a trouble to you?"

"Yes, Polly."

"Because I am little?"

"Because you are little and tender. It is only great, strong people that should travel. But don't look sad, my little girl; it breaks my heart. Papa, will soon come back to his Polly."

"Indeed, indeed, I am not sad, scarcely at all."

"Polly would be sorry to give papa pain; would she not?"

"Sorrier than sorry."

"Then Polly must be cheerful: not cry at parting; not fret afterwards. She must look forward to meeting again, and try to be happy meanwhile. Can she do this?"

"She will try."

"I see she will. Farewell, then. It is time to go."

"*Now?* – Just *now*?"

"Just now."

She held up quivering lips. Her father sobbed, but she, I remarked, did not. Having put her down, he shook hands with the rest present, and departed.

When the street-door closed, she dropped on her knees at a chair with a cry – "Papa!"

It was low and long; a sort of 'Why hast thou forsaken me?' During an ensuing space of some minutes, I perceived she endured agony. She went through, in that brief interval of her infant life, emotions such as some never feel; it was in her constitution: she would have more of such instants if she lived. Nobody spoke. Mrs. Bretton, being a mother, shed a tear or two. Graham, who was writing, lifted up his eyes and gazed at her. I, Lucy Snowe, was calm.

The little creature, thus left unharassed, did for herself what none other could do – contended with an intolerable feeling; and, ere long, in some degree, repressed it. That day she would accept solace from none; nor the next day: she grew more passive afterwards.

On the third evening, as she sat on the floor, worn and quiet, Graham, coming in, took her up gently, without a word. She did not resist: she rather nestled in his arms, as if weary. When he sat down, she laid her head against him; in a few minutes she slept; he carried her upstairs to bed. I was not surprised that, the next morning, the first thing she demanded was, "Where is Mr. Graham?"

It happened that Graham was not coming to the breakfast-table; he had some exercises to write for that morning's class, and had requested his mother to send a cup of tea into the study. Polly volunteered to carry it: she must be busy about something, look after somebody. The cup was entrusted to her; for, if restless, she was also careful. As the study was opposite the breakfast-room, the doors facing across the passage, my eye followed her.

"What are you doing?" she asked, pausing on the threshold.

"Writing," said Graham.

"Why don't you come to take breakfast with your mamma?"

"Too busy."

"Do you want any breakfast?"

"Of course."

"There, then."

And she deposited the cup on the carpet, like a jailor putting a prisoner's pitcher of water through his cell-door, and retreated. Presently she returned.

"What will you have besides tea – what to eat?"

"Anything good. Bring me something particularly nice; that's a kind little woman."

She came back to Mrs. Bretton.

"Please, ma'am, send your boy something good."

"You shall choose for him, Polly; what shall my boy have?"

She selected a portion of whatever was best on the table; and, ere long, came back with a whispered request for some marmalade, which was not there. Having got it, however, (for Mrs. Bretton refused the pair nothing), Graham was shortly after heard lauding her to the skies; promising that, when he had a house of his own, she should be his housekeeper, and perhaps – if she showed any culinary genius – his cook; and, as she did not return, and I went to look after her, I found Graham and her breakfasting *tête-à-tête* – she standing at his elbow, and sharing his fare: excepting the marmalade, which she delicately refused to touch, lest, I suppose, it should appear that she had procured it as much on her own account as his. She constantly evinced these nice perceptions and delicate instincts.

The league of acquaintanceship thus struck up was not hastily dissolved; on the contrary, it appeared that time and circumstances served rather to cement than loosen it. Ill-assimilated as the two were in age, sex, pursuits, etc., they somehow found a great deal to say to each other. As to Paulina, I observed that her little character never properly came out, except with young Bretton. As she got settled, and accustomed to the house, she proved tractable enough with Mrs. Bretton; but she would sit on a stool at that lady's feet all day long, learning her task, or sewing, or drawing figures with a pencil on a slate, and never kindling once to originality, or showing a single gleam of the peculiarities of her nature. I ceased to watch her under such circumstances: she was not interesting. But the moment Graham's knock sounded of an evening, a change occurred; she was instantly at the head of the staircase. Usually her welcome was a reprimand or a threat.

"You have not wiped your shoes properly on the mat. I shall tell your mamma."

"Little busybody! Are you there?"

"Yes – and you can't reach me: I am higher up than you" (peeping between the rails of the banister; she could not look over them).

"Polly!"

"My dear boy!" (such was one of her terms for him, adopted in imitation of his mother.)

"I am fit to faint with fatigue," declared Graham, leaning against the passage-wall in seeming exhaustion. "Dr. Digby" (the headmaster) "has quite knocked me up with overwork. Just come down and help me to carry up my books."

"Ah! You're cunning!"

"Not at all, Polly – it is positive fact. I'm as weak as a rush. Come down."

"Your eyes are quiet like the cat's, but you'll spring."

"Spring? Nothing of the kind: it isn't in me. Come down."

"Perhaps I may – if you'll promise not to touch – not to snatch me up, and not to whirl me round."

"I? I couldn't do it!" (sinking into a chair.)

"Then put the books down on the first step, and go three yards off"

This being done, she descended warily, and not taking her eyes from the feeble Graham. Of course her approach always galvanized him to new and spasmodic life: the game of romps was sure to be exacted. Sometimes she would be angry; sometimes the matter was allowed to pass smoothly, and we could hear her say as she led him upstairs: "Now, my dear boy, come and take your tea – I am sure you must want something."

It was sufficiently comical to observe her as she sat beside Graham, while he took that meal. In his absence she was a still personage, but with him the most officious, fidgety little body possible. I often wished she would mind herself and be tranquil; but no – herself was forgotten in him: he could not be sufficiently well waited on, nor carefully enough looked after; he was more than the Grand Turk in her estimation. She would gradually assemble the various plates before him, and, when one would suppose all he could possibly desire was within his reach, she would find out something else: "Ma'am," she would whisper to Mrs. Bretton, – "perhaps your son would like a little cake – sweet cake, you know – there is some in there" (pointing to the sideboard cupboard). Mrs. Bretton, as a rule, disapproved of sweet cake at tea, but still the request was urged, – "One little piece – only for him – as he goes to school: girls – such as me and Miss Snowe – don't need treats, but *he* would like it."

Graham did like it very well, and almost always got it. To do him justice, he would have shared his prize with her to whom he owed it; but that was never allowed: to insist, was to ruffle her for the evening. To stand by his knee, and monopolize his talk and notice, was the reward she wanted – not a share of the cake.

With curious readiness did she adapt herself to such themes as interested him. One would have thought the child had no mind or life of her own, but must necessarily live, move, and have her being in another: now that her father was taken from her, she nestled to Graham, and seemed to feel by his feelings: to exist in his existence. She learned the names of all his schoolfellows in a trice: she got by heart their characters as given from his lips: a single description of an individual seemed to suffice. She never forgot, or confused identities: she would talk with him the whole evening about people she had never seen, and appear completely to realise their aspect, manners, and dispositions. Some she learned to mimic: an under-master, who was an aversion of young Bretton's, had, it seems, some peculiarities, which she caught up in a moment from Graham's representation, and rehearsed for his amusement; this, however, Mrs. Bretton disapproved and forbade.

The pair seldom quarrelled; yet once a rupture occurred, in which her feelings received a severe shock.

One day Graham, on the occasion of his birthday, had some friends – lads of his own age – to dine with him. Paulina took much interest in the coming of these friends; she had frequently heard of them; they were amongst those of whom Graham oftenest spoke. After dinner, the young gentlemen were left by themselves in the dining-room, where they soon became very merry and made a good deal of noise. Chancing to pass through the hall, I found Paulina sitting alone on the lowest step of the staircase, her eyes fixed on the glossy panels of the dining-room door, where the reflection of the hall-lamp was shining; her little brow knit in anxious meditation.

"What are you thinking about, Polly?"

"Nothing particular; only I wish that door was clear glass – that I might see through it. The boys seem very cheerful, and I want to go to them: I want to be with Graham, and watch his friends."

"What hinders you from going?"

"I feel afraid: but may I try, do you think? May I knock at the door, and ask to be let in?"

I thought perhaps they might not object to have her as a playmate, and therefore encouraged the attempt.

She knocked – too faintly at first to be heard, but on a second essay the door unclosed; Graham's head appeared; he looked in high spirits, but impatient.

"What do you want, you little monkey?"

"To come to you."

"Do you indeed? As if I would be troubled with you! Away to mamma and Mistress Snowe, and tell them to put you to bed." The auburn head and bright flushed face vanished, – the door shut peremptorily. She was stunned.

"Why does he speak so? He never spoke so before," she said in consternation. "What have I done?"

"Nothing, Polly; but Graham is busy with his school-friends."

"And he likes them better than me! He turns me away now they are here!"

I had some thoughts of consoling her, and of improving the occasion by inculcating some of those maxims of philosophy whereof I had ever a tolerable stock ready for application. She stopped me, however, by putting her fingers in her ears at the first words I uttered, and then lying down on the mat with her face against the flags; nor could either Warren or the cook root her from that position: she was allowed to lie, therefore, till she chose to rise of her own accord.

Graham forgot his impatience the same evening, and would have accosted her as usual when his friends were gone, but she wrenched herself from his hand; her eye quite flashed; she would not bid him goodnight; she would not look in his face. The next day he treated her with indifference, and she grew like a bit of marble. The day after, he teased her to know what was the matter; her lips would not unclose. Of course he could not feel real anger on his side: the match was too unequal in every way; he tried soothing and coaxing. "Why was she so angry? What had he done?" By-and-by tears answered him; he petted her, and they were friends. But she was one on whom such incidents were not lost: I remarked that never after this rebuff did she seek him, or follow him, or in any way solicit his notice. I told her once to carry a book or some other article to Graham when he was shut up in his study.

"I shall wait till he comes out," said she, proudly; "I don't choose to give him the trouble of rising to open the door."

Young Bretton had a favourite pony on which he often rode out; from the window she always watched his departure and return. It was her ambition to be permitted to have a ride round the courtyard on this pony; but far be it from her to ask such a favour. One day she descended to the yard to watch him dismount; as she leaned against the gate, the longing wish for the indulgence of a ride glittered in her eye.

"Come, Polly, will you have a canter?" asked Graham, half carelessly.

I suppose she thought he was *too* careless.

"No, thank you," said she, turning away with the utmost coolness.

"You'd better," pursued he. "You will like it, I am sure."

"Don't think I should care a fig about it," was the response.

"That is not true. You told Lucy Snowe you longed to have a ride."

"Lucy Snowe is a *tatter*-box," I heard her say (her imperfect articulation was the least precocious thing she had about her); and with this; she walked into the house.

Graham, coming in soon after, observed to his mother, "Mamma, I believe that creature is a changeling: she is a perfect cabinet of oddities; but I should be dull without her: she amuses me a great deal more than you or Lucy Snowe."

* * *

"Miss Snowe," said Paulina to me (she had now got into the habit of occasionally chatting with me when we were alone in our room at night), "do you know on what day in the week I like Graham best?"

"How can I possibly know anything so strange? Is there one day out of the seven when he is otherwise than on the other six?"

"To be sure! Can't you see? Don't you know? I find him the most excellent on a Sunday; then we have him the whole day, and he is quiet, and, in the evening, *so* kind."

This observation was not altogether groundless: going to church, etc., kept Graham quiet on the Sunday, and the evening he generally dedicated to a serene, though rather indolent sort of enjoyment by the parlour fireside. He would take possession of the couch, and then he would call Polly.

Graham was a boy not quite as other boys are; all his delight did not lie in action: he was capable of some intervals of contemplation; he could take a pleasure too in reading, nor was his selection of books wholly indiscriminate: there were glimmerings of characteristic preference, and even of instinctive taste in the choice. He rarely, it is true, remarked on what he read, but I have seen him sit and think of it.

Polly, being near him, kneeling on a little cushion or the carpet, a conversation would begin in murmurs, not inaudible, though subdued. I caught a snatch of their tenor now and then; and, in truth, some influence better and finer than that of every day, seemed to soothe Graham at such times into no ungentle mood.

"Have you learned any hymns this week, Polly?"

"I have learned a very pretty one, four verses long. Shall I say it?"

"Speak nicely, then: don't be in a hurry."

The hymn being rehearsed, or rather half-chanted, in a little singing voice, Graham would take exceptions at the manner, and proceed to give a lesson in recitation. She was quick in learning, apt in imitating; and, besides, her pleasure was to please Graham: she proved a ready scholar. To the hymn would succeed some reading – perhaps a chapter in the Bible; correction was seldom required here, for the child could read any simple narrative chapter very well; and, when the subject was such as she could understand and take an interest in, her expression and emphasis were something remarkable. Joseph cast into the pit; the calling of Samuel; Daniel in the lions' den; – these were favourite passages: of the first especially she seemed perfectly to feel the pathos.

"Poor Jacob!" she would sometimes say, with quivering lips. "How he loved his son Joseph! As much," she once added – "as much, Graham, as I love you: if you were to die" (and she re-opened the book, sought the verse, and read), "I should refuse to be comforted, and go down into the grave to you mourning."

With these words she gathered Graham in her little arms, drawing his long-tressed head towards her. The action, I remember, struck me as strangely rash; exciting the feeling one might experience on seeing an animal dangerous by nature, and but half-tamed by art, too heedlessly fondled. Not that I feared Graham would hurt, or very roughly check her; but I thought she ran risk of incurring such a careless, impatient repulse, as would be worse almost to her than a blow. On the whole, however, these demonstrations were borne passively: sometimes even a sort of complacent wonder at her earnest partiality would smile not unkindly in his eyes. Once he said: "You like me almost as well as if you were my little sister, Polly."

"Oh! I *do* like you," said she; "I *do* like you very much."

I was not long allowed the amusement of this study of character. She had scarcely been at Bretton two months, when a letter came from Mr. Home, signifying that he was now settled amongst his maternal kinsfolk on the Continent; that, as England was become wholly distasteful to him, he had no thoughts of returning hither, perhaps, for years; and that he wished his little girl to join him immediately.

"I wonder how she will take this news?" said Mrs. Bretton, when she had read the letter. *I* wondered, too, and I took upon myself to communicate it.

Repairing to the drawing-room – in which calm and decorated apartment she was fond of being alone, and where she could be implicitly trusted, for she fingered nothing, or rather soiled nothing she fingered – I found her seated, like a little Odalisque, on a couch, half shaded by the drooping draperies of the window near. She seemed happy; all her appliances for occupation were about her; the white wood workbox, a shred or two of muslin, an end or two of ribbon collected for conversion into doll-millinery. The doll, duly night-capped and night-gowned, lay in its cradle; she was rocking it to sleep, with an air of the most perfect faith in its possession of sentient and somnolent faculties; her eyes, at the same time, being engaged with a picture-book, which lay open on her lap.

"Miss Snowe," said she in a whisper, "this is a wonderful book. Candace" (the doll, christened by Graham; for, indeed, its begrimed complexion gave it much of an Ethiopian aspect) – "Candace is asleep now, and I may tell you about it; only we must both speak low, lest she should waken. This book was given me by Graham; it tells about distant countries, a long, long way from England, which no traveller can reach without sailing thousands of miles over the sea. Wild men live in these countries, Miss Snowe, who wear clothes different from ours: indeed, some of them wear scarcely any clothes, for the sake of being cool, you know; for they have very hot weather. Here is a picture of thousands gathered in a desolate place – a plain, spread with sand – round a man in black, – a good, *good* Englishman – a missionary, who is preaching to them under a palm-tree." (She showed a little coloured cut to that effect.) "And here are pictures" (she went on) "more stranger" (grammar was occasionally forgotten) "than that. There is the wonderful Great Wall of China; here is a Chinese lady, with a foot littler than mine. There is a wild horse of Tartary; and here, most strange of all – is a land of ice and snow, without green fields, woods, or gardens. In this land, they found some mammoth bones: there are no mammoths now. You don't know what it was; but I can tell you, because Graham told me. A mighty, goblin creature, as high as this room, and as long as the hall; but not a fierce, flesh-eating thing, Graham thinks. He believes, if I met one in a forest, it would not kill me, unless I came quite in its way; when it would trample me down amongst the bushes, as I might tread on a grasshopper in a hayfield without knowing it."

Thus she rambled on.

"Polly," I interrupted, "should you like to travel?"

"Not just yet," was the prudent answer; "but perhaps in twenty years, when I am grown a woman, as tall as Mrs. Bretton, I may travel with Graham. We intend going to Switzerland, and climbing Mount Blanck; and some day we shall sail over to South America, and walk to the top of Kim-kim-borazo."

"But how would you like to travel now, if your papa was with you?"

Her reply – not given till after a pause – evinced one of those unexpected turns of temper peculiar to her.

"Where is the good of talking in that silly way?" said she. "Why do you mention papa? What is papa to you? I was just beginning to be happy, and not think about him so much; and there it will be all to do over again!"

Her lip trembled. I hastened to disclose the fact of a letter having been received, and to mention the directions given that she and Harriet should immediately rejoin this dear papa. "Now, Polly, are you not glad?" I added.

She made no answer. She dropped her book and ceased to rock her doll; she gazed at me with gravity and earnestness.

"Shall not you like to go to papa?"

"Of course," she said at last in that trenchant manner she usually employed in speaking to me; and which was quite different from that she used with Mrs. Bretton, and different again from the one dedicated to Graham. I wished to ascertain more of what she thought but no: she would converse no more. Hastening to Mrs. Bretton, she questioned her, and received the confirmation of my news. The weight and importance of these tidings kept her perfectly serious the whole day. In the evening, at the moment Graham's entrance was heard below, I found her at my side. She began to arrange a locket-ribbon about my neck, she displaced and replaced the comb in my hair; while thus busied, Graham entered.

"Tell him by-and-by," she whispered; "tell him I am going."

In the course of tea-time I made the desired communication. Graham, it chanced, was at that time greatly preoccupied about some school-prize, for which he was competing. The news had to be told twice before it took proper hold of his attention, and even then he dwelt on it but momently.

"Polly going? What a pity! Dear little Mousie, I shall be sorry to lose her: she must come to us again, mamma."

And hastily swallowing his tea, he took a candle and a small table to himself and his books, and was soon buried in study.

'Little Mousie' crept to his side, and lay down on the carpet at his feet, her face to the floor; mute and motionless she kept that post and position till bed-time. Once I saw Graham – wholly unconscious of her proximity – push her with his restless foot. She receded an inch or two. A minute after one little hand stole out from beneath her face, to which it had been pressed, and softly caressed the heedless foot. When summoned by her nurse she rose and departed very obediently, having bid us all a subdued goodnight.

I will not say that I dreaded going to bed, an hour later; yet I certainly went with an unquiet anticipation that I should find that child in no peaceful sleep. The forewarning of my instinct was but fulfilled, when I discovered her, all cold and vigilant, perched like a white bird on the outside of the bed. I scarcely knew how to accost her; she was not to be managed like another child. She, however, accosted me. As I closed the door, and put the light on the dressing-table, she turned to me with these words: "I cannot – *cannot* sleep; and in this way I cannot – *cannot* live!"

I asked what ailed her.

"Dedful miz-er-y!" said she, with her piteous lisp.

"Shall I call Mrs. Bretton?"

"That is downright silly," was her impatient reply; and, indeed, I well knew that if she had heard Mrs. Bretton's foot approach, she would have nestled quiet as a mouse under the bedclothes. Whilst lavishing her eccentricities regardlessly before me – for whom she professed scarcely the semblance of affection – she never showed my godmother one glimpse of her inner self: for her, she was nothing but a docile, somewhat quaint little maiden. I examined her; her cheek was crimson; her dilated eye was both troubled and glowing, and painfully restless: in this state it was obvious she must not be left till morning. I guessed how the case stood.

"Would you like to bid Graham goodnight again?" I asked. "He is not gone to his room yet."

She at once stretched out her little arms to be lifted. Folding a shawl round her, I carried her back to the drawing-room. Graham was just coming out.

"She cannot sleep without seeing and speaking to you once more," I said. "She does not like the thought of leaving you."

"I've spoilt her," said he, taking her from me with good humour, and kissing her little hot face and burning lips. "Polly, you care for me more than for papa, now –"

"I *do* care for you, but you care nothing for me," was her whisper.

She was assured to the contrary, again kissed, restored to me, and I carried her away; but, alas! not soothed.

When I thought she could listen to me, I said – "Paulina, you should not grieve that Graham does not care for you so much as you care for him. It must be so."

Her lifted and questioning eyes asked why.

"Because he is a boy and you are a girl; he is sixteen and you are only six; his nature is strong and gay, and yours is otherwise."

"But I love him so much; he *should* love me a little."

"He does. He is fond of you. You are his favourite."

"Am I Graham's favourite?"

"Yes, more than any little child I know."

The assurance soothed her; she smiled in her anguish.

"But," I continued, "don't fret, and don't expect too much of him, or else he will feel you to be troublesome, and then it is all over."

"All over!" she echoed softly; "then I'll be good. I'll try to be good, Lucy Snowe."

I put her to bed.

"Will he forgive me this one time?" she asked, as I undressed myself. I assured her that he would; that as yet he was by no means alienated; that she had only to be careful for the future.

"There is no future," said she: "I am going. Shall I ever – ever – see him again, after I leave England?"

I returned an encouraging response. The candle being extinguished, a still half-hour elapsed. I thought her asleep, when the little white shape once more lifted itself in the crib, and the small voice asked – "Do you like Graham, Miss Snowe?"

"Like him! Yes, a little."

"Only a little! Do you like him as I do?"

"I think not. No: not as you do."

"Do you like him much?"

"I told you I liked him a little. Where is the use of caring for him so very much: he is full of faults."

"Is he?"

"All boys are."

"More than girls?"

"Very likely. Wise people say it is folly to think anybody perfect; and as to likes and dislikes, we should be friendly to all, and worship none."

"Are you a wise person?"

"I mean to try to be so. Go to sleep."

"I *cannot* go to sleep. Have you no pain just here" (laying her elfish hand on her elfish breast,) "when you think *you* shall have to leave Graham; for *your* home is not here?"

"Surely, Polly," said I, "you should not feel so much pain when you are very soon going to rejoin your father. Have you forgotten him? Do you no longer wish to be his little companion?"

Dead silence succeeded this question.

"Child, lie down and sleep," I urged.

"My bed is cold," said she. "I can't warm it."

I saw the little thing shiver. "Come to me," I said, wishing, yet scarcely hoping, that she would comply: for she was a most strange, capricious, little creature, and especially whimsical with me. She came, however, instantly, like a small ghost gliding over the carpet. I took her in. She was chill: I warmed her in my arms. She trembled nervously; I soothed her. Thus tranquillized and cherished she at last slumbered.

"A very unique child," thought I, as I viewed her sleeping countenance by the fitful moonlight, and cautiously and softly wiped her glittering eyelids and her wet cheeks with my handkerchief. "How will she get through this world, or battle with this life? How will she bear the shocks and repulses, the humiliations and desolations, which books, and my own reason, tell me are prepared for all flesh?"

She departed the next day; trembling like a leaf when she took leave, but exercising self-command.

Chapter Four
Miss Marchmont

ON QUITTING BRETTON, which I did a few weeks after Paulina's departure – little thinking then I was never again to visit it; never more to tread its calm old streets – I betook myself home, having been absent six months. It will be conjectured that I was of course glad to return to the bosom of my kindred. Well! The amiable conjecture does no harm, and may therefore be safely left uncontradicted. Far from saying nay, indeed, I will permit the reader to picture me, for the next eight years, as a bark slumbering through halcyon weather, in a harbour still as glass – the steersman stretched on the little deck, his face up to heaven, his eyes closed: buried, if you will, in a long prayer. A great many women and girls are supposed to pass their lives something in that fashion; why not I with the rest?

Picture me then idle, basking, plump, and happy, stretched on a cushioned deck, warmed with constant sunshine, rocked by breezes indolently soft. However, it cannot be concealed that, in that case, I must somehow have fallen overboard, or that there must have been wreck at last. I too well remember a time – a long time – of cold, of danger, of contention. To this hour, when I have the nightmare, it repeats the rush and saltness of briny waves in my throat, and their icy pressure on my lungs. I even know there was a storm, and that not of one hour nor one day. For many days and nights neither sun nor stars appeared; we cast with our own hands the tackling out of the ship; a heavy tempest lay on us; all hope that we should be saved was taken away. In fine, the ship was lost, the crew perished.

As far as I recollect, I complained to no one about these troubles. Indeed, to whom could I complain? Of Mrs. Bretton I had long lost sight. Impediments, raised by others, had, years ago, come in the way of our intercourse, and cut it off. Besides, time had brought changes for her, too: the handsome property of which she was left guardian for her son, and which had been chiefly invested in some joint-stock undertaking, had melted, it was said, to a fraction of its original amount. Graham, I learned from incidental rumours, had adopted a profession; both he and his mother were gone from Bretton, and were understood to be now in London. Thus, there remained no possibility of dependence on others; to myself alone could I look. I know not that I was of a self-reliant or active nature; but self-reliance and exertion were forced upon me by circumstances, as they are upon thousands besides; and when Miss Marchmont, a maiden lady of our neighbourhood, sent for me, I obeyed her behest, in the hope that she might assign me some task I could undertake.

Miss Marchmont was a woman of fortune, and lived in a handsome residence; but she was a rheumatic cripple, impotent, foot and hand, and had been so for twenty years. She always sat upstairs: her drawing-room adjoined her bed-room. I had often heard of Miss Marchmont, and of her peculiarities (she had the character of being very eccentric), but till now had never seen her. I found her a furrowed, grey-haired woman, grave with solitude, stern with long affliction, irritable also, and perhaps exacting. It seemed that a maid, or rather companion, who had waited on her for some years, was about to be married; and she, hearing of my bereaved lot, had sent for me, with the idea that I might supply this person's place. She made the proposal to me after tea, as she and I sat alone by her fireside.

"It will not be an easy life;" said she candidly, "for I require a good deal of attention, and you will be much confined; yet, perhaps, contrasted with the existence you have lately led, it may appear tolerable."

I reflected. Of course it ought to appear tolerable, I argued inwardly; but somehow, by some strange fatality, it would not. To live here, in this close room, the watcher of suffering – sometimes, perhaps, the butt of temper – through all that was to come of my youth; while all that was gone had passed, to say the least, not blissfully! My heart sunk one moment, then it revived; for though I forced myself to *realise* evils, I think I was too prosaic to *idealise*, and consequently to exaggerate them.

"My doubt is whether I should have strength for the undertaking," I observed.

"That is my own scruple," said she; "for you look a worn-out creature."

So I did. I saw myself in the glass, in my mourning-dress, a faded, hollow-eyed vision. Yet I thought little of the wan spectacle. The blight, I believed, was chiefly external: I still felt life at life's sources.

"What else have you in view – anything?"

"Nothing clear as yet: but I may find something."

"So you imagine: perhaps you are right. Try your own method, then; and if it does not succeed, test mine. The chance I have offered shall be left open to you for three months."

This was kind. I told her so, and expressed my gratitude. While I was speaking, a paroxysm of pain came on. I ministered to her; made the necessary applications, according to her directions, and, by the time she was relieved, a sort of intimacy was already formed between us. I, for my part, had learned from the manner in which she bore this attack, that she was a firm, patient woman (patient under physical pain, though sometimes perhaps excitable under long mental canker); and she, from the good-will with which I succoured her, discovered that she could influence my sympathies (such as they were). She sent for me the next day; for five or six successive days she claimed my company. Closer acquaintance, while it developed both faults and eccentricities, opened, at the same time, a view of a character I could respect. Stern and even morose as she sometimes was, I could wait on her and sit beside her with that calm which always blesses us when we are sensible that our manners, presence, contact, please and soothe the persons we serve. Even when she scolded me – which she did, now and then, very tartly – it was in such a way as did not humiliate, and left no sting; it was rather like an irascible mother rating her daughter, than a harsh mistress lecturing a dependant: lecture, indeed, she could not, though she could occasionally storm. Moreover, a vein of reason ever ran through her passion: she was logical even when fierce. Ere long a growing sense of attachment began to present the thought of staying with her as companion in quite a new light; in another week I had agreed to remain.

Two hot, close rooms thus became my world; and a crippled old woman, my mistress, my friend, my all. Her service was my duty – her pain, my suffering – her relief, my hope – her anger, my punishment – her regard, my reward. I forgot that there were fields, woods, rivers, seas, an ever-changing sky outside the steam-dimmed lattice of this sick chamber; I was almost content to forget it. All within me became narrowed to my lot. Tame and still by habit, disciplined by destiny, I demanded no walks in the fresh air; my appetite needed no more than the tiny messes served for the invalid. In addition, she gave me the originality of her character to study: the steadiness of her virtues, I will add, the power of her passions, to admire; the truth of her feelings to trust. All these things she had, and for these things I clung to her.

For these things I would have crawled on with her for twenty years, if for twenty years longer her life of endurance had been protracted. But another decree was written. It seemed I must be stimulated into action. I must be goaded, driven, stung, forced to energy. My little morsel of human affection, which I prized as if it were a solid pearl, must melt in my fingers and slip thence like a dissolving hailstone. My small adopted duty must be snatched from my easily contented conscience. I had wanted to compromise with Fate: to escape occasional great agonies by submitting to a whole life of privation and small pains. Fate would not so be pacified; nor would Providence sanction this shrinking sloth and cowardly indolence.

One February night – I remember it well – there came a voice near Miss Marchmont's house, heard by every inmate, but translated, perhaps, only by one. After a calm winter, storms were ushering in the spring. I had put Miss Marchmont to bed; I sat at the fireside sewing. The wind was wailing at the windows; it had wailed all day; but, as night deepened, it took a new tone – an accent keen, piercing, almost articulate to the ear; a plaint, piteous and disconsolate to the nerves, trilled in every gust.

"Oh, hush! Hush!" I said in my disturbed mind, dropping my work, and making a vain effort to stop my ears against that subtle, searching cry. I had heard that very voice ere this, and compulsory observation had forced on me a theory as to what it boded. Three times in the course of my life, events had taught me that these strange accents in the storm – this restless, hopeless cry – denote a coming state of the atmosphere unpropitious to life. Epidemic diseases, I believed, were often heralded by a gasping, sobbing, tormented, long-lamenting east wind. Hence, I inferred, arose the legend of the Banshee. I fancied, too, I had noticed – but was not philosopher enough to know whether there was any connection between the circumstances – that we often at the same time hear of disturbed volcanic action in distant parts of the world; of rivers suddenly rushing above their banks; and of strange high tides flowing furiously in on low sea-coasts. "Our globe," I had said to myself, "seems at such periods torn and disordered; the feeble amongst us wither in her distempered breath, rushing hot from steaming volcanoes."

I listened and trembled; Miss Marchmont slept.

About midnight, the storm in one half-hour fell to a dead calm. The fire, which had been burning dead, glowed up vividly. I felt the air change, and become keen. Raising blind and curtain, I looked out, and saw in the stars the keen sparkle of a sharp frost.

Turning away, the object that met my eyes was Miss Marchmont awake, lifting her head from the pillow, and regarding me with unusual earnestness.

"Is it a fine night?" she asked.

I replied in the affirmative.

"I thought so," she said; "for I feel so strong, so well. Raise me. I feel young tonight," she continued: "young, light-hearted, and happy. What if my complaint be about to take a turn, and I am yet destined to enjoy health? It would be a miracle!"

"And these are not the days of miracles," I thought to myself, and wondered to hear her talk so. She went on directing her conversation to the past, and seeming to recall its incidents, scenes, and personages, with singular vividness.

"I love Memory tonight," she said: "I prize her as my best friend. She is just now giving me a deep delight: she is bringing back to my heart, in warm and beautiful life, realities – not mere empty ideas, but what were once realities, and that I long have thought decayed, dissolved, mixed in with grave-mould. I possess just now the hours, the thoughts, the hopes of my youth. I renew the love of my life – its only love – almost its only affection; for I am not a particularly good woman: I am not amiable. Yet I have had my feelings, strong and concentrated; and these feelings had their object; which, in its single self, was dear to me, as to the majority of men and women, are all the unnumbered points on which they dissipate their regard. While I loved, and while I was loved, what an existence I enjoyed! What a glorious year I can recall – how bright it comes back to me! What a living spring – what a warm, glad summer – what soft moonlight, silvering the autumn evenings – what strength of hope under the ice-bound waters and frost-hoar fields of that year's winter! Through that year my heart lived with Frank's heart. O my noble Frank – my faithful Frank – my *good* Frank! So much better than myself – his standard in all things so much higher! This I can now see and say: if few women have suffered as I did in his loss, few have enjoyed what I did in his love. It was a far better kind of love than common; I had no doubts about it or him: it was such a love as honoured, protected, and elevated, no less than it gladdened her to whom it was given. Let me now ask, just at this moment, when my mind is so strangely clear, – let me reflect why it was taken from me? For what crime was I condemned, after twelve months of bliss, to undergo thirty years of sorrow?

"I do not know," she continued after a pause: "I cannot – *cannot* see the reason; yet at this hour I can say with sincerity, what I never tried to say before, Inscrutable God, Thy will be done! And at this moment I can believe that death will restore me to Frank. I never believed it till now."

"He is dead, then?" I inquired in a low voice.

"My dear girl," she said, "one happy Christmas Eve I dressed and decorated myself, expecting my lover, very soon to be my husband, would come that night to visit me. I sat down to wait. Once more I see that moment – I see the snow twilight stealing through the window over which the curtain was not dropped, for I designed to watch him ride up the white walk; I see and feel the soft firelight warming me, playing on my silk dress, and fitfully showing me my own young figure in a glass. I see the moon of a calm winter night, float full, clear, and cold, over the inky mass of shrubbery, and the silvered turf of my grounds. I wait, with some impatience in my pulse, but no doubt in my breast. The flames had died in the fire, but it was a bright mass yet; the moon was mounting high, but she was still visible from the lattice; the clock neared ten; he rarely tarried later than this, but once or twice he had been delayed so long.

"Would he for once fail me? No – not even for once; and now he was coming – and coming fast – to atone for lost time. 'Frank! you furious rider,' I said inwardly, listening gladly, yet anxiously, to his approaching gallop, 'you shall be rebuked for this: I will tell you it is *my* neck you are putting in peril; for whatever is yours is, in a dearer and tenderer sense, mine.' There he was: I saw him; but I think tears were in my eyes, my sight was so confused. I saw the horse; I heard it stamp – I saw at least a mass; I heard a clamour. *Was* it a horse? Or what heavy, dragging thing was it, crossing, strangely dark, the lawn. How could I name that thing in the moonlight before me? Or how could I utter the feeling which rose in my soul?

"I could only run out. A great animal – truly, Frank's black horse – stood trembling, panting, snorting before the door; a man held it, Frank, as I thought.

"'What is the matter?' I demanded. Thomas, my own servant, answered by saying sharply, 'Go into the house, madam.' And then calling to another servant, who came hurrying from the kitchen as if summoned by some instinct, 'Ruth, take missis into the house directly.' But I was kneeling down in the snow, beside something that lay there – something that I had seen dragged along the ground – something that sighed, that groaned on my breast, as I lifted and drew it to me. He was not dead; he was not quite unconscious. I had him carried in; I refused to be ordered about and thrust from him. I was quite collected enough, not only to be my own mistress but the mistress of others. They had begun by trying to treat me like a child, as they always do with people struck by God's hand; but I gave place to none except the surgeon; and when he had done what he could, I took my dying Frank to myself. He had strength to fold me in his arms; he had power to speak my name; he heard me as I prayed over him very softly; he felt me as I tenderly and fondly comforted him.

"'Maria,' he said, 'I am dying in Paradise.' He spent his last breath in faithful words for me. When the dawn of Christmas morning broke, my Frank was with God.

"And that," she went on, "happened thirty years ago. I have suffered since. I doubt if I have made the best use of all my calamities. Soft, amiable natures they would have refined to saintliness; of strong, evil spirits they would have made demons; as for me, I have only been a woe-struck and selfish woman."

"You have done much good," I said; for she was noted for her liberal almsgiving.

"I have not withheld money, you mean, where it could assuage affliction. What of that? It cost me no effort or pang to give. But I think from this day I am about to enter a better frame of mind, to prepare myself for reunion with Frank. You see I still think of Frank more than of God; and unless it be counted that in thus loving the creature so much, so long, and so exclusively, I have not at least blasphemed the Creator, small is my chance of salvation. What do you think, Lucy, of these things? Be my chaplain, and tell me."

This question I could not answer: I had no words. It seemed as if she thought I *had* answered it.

"Very right, my child. We should acknowledge God merciful, but not always for us comprehensible. We should accept our own lot, whatever it be, and try to render happy that of others. Should we not? Well, tomorrow I will begin by trying to make you happy. I will endeavour to do something for you, Lucy: something that will benefit you when I am dead. My head aches now with talking too much; still I am happy. Go to bed. The clock strikes two. How late you sit up; or rather how late I, in my selfishness, keep you up. But go now; have no more anxiety for me; I feel I shall rest well."

She composed herself as if to slumber. I, too, retired to my crib in a closet within her room. The night passed in quietness; quietly her doom must at last have come: peacefully and painlessly: in the morning she was found without life, nearly cold, but all calm and undisturbed. Her previous excitement of spirits and change of mood had been the prelude of a fit; one stroke sufficed to sever the thread of an existence so long fretted by affliction.

Chapter Five
Turning a New Leaf

MY MISTRESS being dead, and I once more alone, I had to look out for a new place. About this time I might be a little – a very little – shaken in nerves. I grant I was not looking well, but, on the contrary, thin, haggard, and hollow-eyed; like a sitter-up at night, like an overwrought servant, or a placeless person in debt. In debt, however, I was not; nor quite poor; for though Miss Marchmont had not had time to benefit me, as, on that last night, she said she intended, yet, after the funeral, my wages were duly paid by her second cousin, the heir, an avaricious-looking man, with pinched nose and narrow temples, who, indeed, I heard long afterwards, turned out a thorough miser: a direct contrast to his generous kinswoman, and a foil to her memory, blessed to this day by the poor and needy. The possessor, then, of fifteen pounds; of health, though worn, not broken, and of a spirit in similar condition; I might still; in comparison with many people, be regarded as occupying an enviable position. An embarrassing one it was, however, at the same time; as I felt with some acuteness on a certain day, of which the corresponding one in the next week was to see my departure from my present abode, while with another I was not provided.

In this dilemma I went, as a last and sole resource, to see and consult an old servant of our family; once my nurse, now housekeeper at a grand mansion not far from Miss Marchmont's. I spent some hours with her; she comforted, but knew not how to advise me. Still all inward darkness, I left her about twilight; a walk of two miles lay before me; it was a clear, frosty night. In spite of my solitude, my poverty, and my perplexity, my heart, nourished and nerved with the vigour of a youth that had not yet counted twenty-three summers, beat light and not feebly. Not feebly, I am sure, or I should have trembled in that lonely walk, which lay through still fields, and passed neither village nor farmhouse, nor cottage: I should have quailed in the absence of moonlight, for it was by the leading of stars only I traced the dim path; I should have quailed still more in the unwonted presence of that which tonight shone in the north, a moving mystery – the Aurora Borealis. But this solemn stranger influenced me otherwise than through my fears. Some new power it seemed to bring. I drew in energy with the keen, low breeze that blew on its path. A bold thought was sent to my mind; my mind was made strong to receive it.

"Leave this wilderness," it was said to me, "and go out hence."

"Where?" was the query.

I had not very far to look; gazing from this country parish in that flat, rich middle of England – I mentally saw within reach what I had never yet beheld with my bodily eyes: I saw London.

The next day I returned to the hall, and asking once more to see the housekeeper, I communicated to her my plan.

Mrs. Barrett was a grave, judicious woman, though she knew little more of the world than myself; but grave and judicious as she was, she did not charge me with being out of my senses; and, indeed, I had a staid manner of my own which ere now had been as good to me as cloak and hood of hodden grey, since under its favour I had been enabled to achieve with impunity, and even approbation, deeds that, if attempted with an excited and unsettled air, would in some minds have stamped me as a dreamer and zealot.

The housekeeper was slowly propounding some difficulties, while she prepared orange-rind for marmalade, when a child ran past the window and came bounding into the room. It was a pretty child, and as it danced, laughing, up to me – for we were not strangers (nor, indeed, was its mother – a young married daughter of the house – a stranger) – I took it on my knee.

Different as were our social positions now, this child's mother and I had been schoolfellows, when I was a girl of ten and she a young lady of sixteen; and I remembered her, good-looking, but dull, in a lower class than mine.

I was admiring the boy's handsome dark eyes, when the mother, young Mrs. Leigh, entered. What a beautiful and kind-looking woman was the good-natured and comely, but unintellectual, girl become! Wifehood and maternity had changed her thus, as I have since seen them change others even less promising than she. Me she had forgotten. I was changed too, though not, I fear, for the better. I made no attempt to recall myself to her memory; why should I? She came for her son to accompany her in a walk, and behind her followed a nurse, carrying an infant. I only mention the incident because, in addressing the nurse, Mrs. Leigh spoke French (very bad French, by the way, and with an incorrigibly bad accent, again forcibly reminding me of our school-days): and I found the woman was a foreigner. The little boy chattered volubly in French too. When the whole party were withdrawn, Mrs. Barrett remarked that her young lady had brought that foreign nurse home with her two years ago, on her return from a Continental excursion; that she was treated almost as well as a governess, and had nothing to do but walk out with the baby and chatter French with Master Charles; "and," added Mrs. Barrett, "she says there are many Englishwomen in foreign families as well placed as she."

I stored up this piece of casual information, as careful housewives store seemingly worthless shreds and fragments for which their prescient minds anticipate a possible use some day. Before I left my old friend, she gave me the address of a respectable old-fashioned inn in the City, which, she said, my uncles used to frequent in former days.

In going to London, I ran less risk and evinced less enterprise than the reader may think. In fact, the distance was only fifty miles. My means would suffice both to take me there, to keep me a few days, and also to bring me back if I found no inducement to stay. I regarded it as a brief holiday, permitted for once to work-weary faculties, rather than as an adventure of life and death. There is nothing like taking all you do at a moderate estimate: it keeps mind and body tranquil; whereas grandiloquent notions are apt to hurry both into fever.

Fifty miles were then a day's journey (for I speak of a time gone by: my hair, which, till a late period, withstood the frosts of time, lies now, at last white, under a white cap, like snow beneath snow). About nine o'clock of a wet February night I reached London.

My reader, I know, is one who would not thank me for an elaborate reproduction of poetic first impressions; and it is well, inasmuch as I had neither time nor mood to cherish such; arriving as I did late, on a dark, raw, and rainy evening, in a Babylon and a wilderness, of which the vastness and the strangeness tried to the utmost any powers of clear thought and steady self-possession with which, in the absence of more brilliant faculties, Nature might have gifted me.

When I left the coach, the strange speech of the cabmen and others waiting round, seemed to me odd as a foreign tongue. I had never before heard the English language chopped up in that way. However, I managed to understand and to be understood, so far as to get myself and trunk safely conveyed to the old inn whereof I had the address. How difficult, how oppressive, how puzzling seemed my flight! In London for the first time; at an inn for the first time; tired with travelling; confused with darkness; palsied with cold; unfurnished with either experience or advice to tell me how to act, and yet – to act obliged.

Into the hands of common sense I confided the matter. Common sense, however, was as chilled and bewildered as all my other faculties, and it was only under the spur of an inexorable necessity that she spasmodically executed her trust. Thus urged, she paid the porter: considering the crisis, I did not blame her too much that she was hugely cheated; she asked the waiter for a room; she timorously called for the chambermaid; what is far more, she bore, without being wholly overcome, a highly supercilious style of demeanour from that young lady, when she appeared.

I recollect this same chambermaid was a pattern of town prettiness and smartness. So trim her waist, her cap, her dress – I wondered how they had all been manufactured. Her speech had an accent which in its mincing glibness seemed to rebuke mine as by authority; her spruce attire flaunted an easy scorn to my plain country garb.

"Well, it can't be helped," I thought, "and then the scene is new, and the circumstances; I shall gain good."

Maintaining a very quiet manner towards this arrogant little maid, and subsequently observing the same towards the parsonic-looking, black-coated, white-neckclothed waiter, I got civility from them ere long. I believe at first they thought I was a servant; but in a little while they changed their minds, and hovered in a doubtful state between patronage and politeness.

I kept up well till I had partaken of some refreshment, warmed myself by a fire, and was fairly shut into my own room; but, as I sat down by the bed and rested my head and arms on the pillow, a terrible oppression overcame me. All at once my position rose on me like a ghost. Anomalous, desolate, almost blank of hope it stood. What was I doing here alone in great London? What should I do on the morrow? What prospects had I in life? What friends had I on, earth? Whence did I come? Whither should I go? What should I do?

I wet the pillow, my arms, and my hair, with rushing tears. A dark interval of most bitter thought followed this burst; but I did not regret the step taken, nor wish to retract it. A strong, vague persuasion that it was better to go forward than backward, and that I *could* go forward – that a way, however narrow and difficult, would in time open – predominated over other feelings: its influence hushed them so far, that at last I became sufficiently tranquil to be able to say my prayers and seek my couch. I had just extinguished my candle and lain down, when a deep, low, mighty tone swung through the night. At first I knew it not; but it was uttered twelve times, and at the twelfth colossal hum and trembling knell, I said: "I lie in the shadow of St. Paul's."

Chapter Six
London

THE NEXT DAY was the first of March, and when I awoke, rose, and opened my curtain, I saw the risen sun struggling through fog. Above my head, above the house-tops, co-elevate almost with the clouds, I saw a solemn, orbed mass, dark blue and dim – *The Dome*. While I looked, my inner self moved; my spirit shook its always-fettered wings half loose; I had a sudden feeling as if I, who never yet truly lived, were at last about to taste life. In that morning my soul grew as fast as Jonah's gourd.

"I did well to come," I said, proceeding to dress with speed and care. "I like the spirit of this great London which I feel around me. Who but a coward would pass his whole life in hamlets; and for ever abandon his faculties to the eating rust of obscurity?"

Being dressed, I went down; not travel-worn and exhausted, but tidy and refreshed. When the waiter came in with my breakfast, I managed to accost him sedately, yet cheerfully; we had ten minutes' discourse, in the course of which we became usefully known to each other.

He was a grey-haired, elderly man; and, it seemed, had lived in his present place twenty years. Having ascertained this, I was sure he must remember my two uncles, Charles and Wilmot, who, fifteen years ago, were frequent visitors here. I mentioned their names; he recalled them perfectly, and with respect. Having intimated my connection, my position in his eyes was henceforth clear, and on a right footing. He said I was like my uncle Charles: I suppose he spoke truth, because Mrs. Barrett was accustomed to say the same thing. A ready and obliging courtesy now replaced his former uncomfortably doubtful manner; henceforth I need no longer be at a loss for a civil answer to a sensible question.

The street on which my little sitting-room window looked was narrow, perfectly quiet, and not dirty: the few passengers were just such as one sees in provincial towns: here was nothing formidable; I felt sure I might venture out alone.

Having breakfasted, out I went. Elation and pleasure were in my heart: to walk alone in London seemed of itself an adventure. Presently I found myself in Paternoster Row – classic ground this. I entered a bookseller's shop, kept by one Jones: I bought a little book – a piece of extravagance I could ill afford; but I thought I would one day give or send it to Mrs. Barrett. Mr. Jones, a dried-in man of business, stood behind his desk: he seemed one of the greatest, and I one of the happiest of beings.

Prodigious was the amount of life I lived that morning. Finding myself before St. Paul's, I went in; I mounted to the dome: I saw thence London, with its river, and its bridges, and its churches; I saw antique Westminster, and the green Temple Gardens, with sun upon them, and a glad, blue sky, of early spring above; and between them and it, not too dense, a cloud of haze.

Descending, I went wandering whither chance might lead, in a still ecstasy of freedom and enjoyment; and I got – I know not how – I got into the heart of city life. I saw and felt London at last: I got into the Strand; I went up Cornhill; I mixed with the life passing along; I dared the perils of crossings. To do this, and to do it utterly alone, gave me, perhaps an irrational, but a real pleasure. Since those days, I have seen the West End, the parks, the fine squares; but I love the city far better. The city seems so much more in earnest: its business, its rush, its roar, are such serious things, sights, and sounds. The city is getting its living – the West End but enjoying its pleasure. At the West End you may be amused, but in the city you are deeply excited.

Faint, at last, and hungry (it was years since I had felt such healthy hunger), I returned, about two o'clock, to my dark, old, and quiet inn. I dined on two dishes – a plain joint and vegetables; both seemed excellent: how much better than the small, dainty messes Miss Marchmont's cook used to send up to my kind, dead mistress and me, and to the discussion of which we could not bring half an appetite between us! Delightfully tired, I lay down, on three chairs for an hour (the room did not boast a sofa). I slept, then I woke and thought for two hours.

My state of mind, and all accompanying circumstances, were just now such as most to favour the adoption of a new, resolute, and daring – perhaps desperate – line of action. I had nothing to lose. Unutterable loathing of a desolate existence past, forbade return. If I failed in what I now designed to undertake, who, save myself, would suffer? If I died far away from – home, I was going to say, but I had no home – from England, then, who would weep?

I might suffer; I was inured to suffering: death itself had not, I thought, those terrors for me which it has for the softly reared. I had, ere this, looked on the thought of death with a quiet eye. Prepared, then, for any consequences, I formed a project.

That same evening I obtained from my friend, the waiter, information respecting, the sailing of vessels for a certain continental port, Boue-Marine. No time, I found, was to be lost: that very night I must take my berth. I might, indeed, have waited till the morning before going on board, but would not run the risk of being too late.

"Better take your berth at once, ma'am," counselled the waiter. I agreed with him, and having discharged my bill, and acknowledged my friend's services at a rate which I now know was princely, and which in his eyes must have seemed absurd – and indeed, while pocketing the cash, he smiled a faint smile which intimated his opinion of the donor's savoir-faire – he proceeded to call a coach. To the driver he also recommended me, giving at the same time an injunction about taking me, I think, to the wharf, and not leaving me to the watermen; which that functionary promised to observe, but failed in keeping his promise: on the contrary, he offered me up as an oblation, served me as a dripping roast, making me alight in the midst of a throng of watermen.

This was an uncomfortable crisis. It was a dark night. The coachman instantly drove off as soon as he had got his fare: the watermen commenced a struggle for me and my trunk. Their oaths I hear at this moment: they shook my philosophy more than did the night, or the isolation, or the strangeness of the scene. One laid hands on my trunk. I looked on and waited quietly; but when another laid hands on me, I spoke up, shook off his touch, stepped at once into a boat, desired austerely that the trunk should be placed beside me – "Just there," – which was instantly done; for the owner of the boat I had chosen became now an ally: I was rowed off.

Black was the river as a torrent of ink; lights glanced on it from the piles of building round, ships rocked on its bosom. They rowed me up to several vessels; I read by lantern-light their names painted in great white letters on a dark ground. *The Ocean, The Phoenix, The Consort, The Dolphin*, were passed in turns; but *The Vivid* was my ship, and it seemed she lay further down.

Down the sable flood we glided, I thought of the Styx, and of Charon rowing some solitary soul to the Land of Shades. Amidst the strange scene, with a chilly wind blowing in my face and midnight clouds dropping rain above my head; with two rude rowers for companions, whose insane oaths still tortured my ear, I asked myself if I was wretched or terrified. I was neither. Often in my life have I been far more so under comparatively safe circumstances. "How is this?" said I. "Methinks I am animated and alert, instead of being depressed and apprehensive?" I could not tell how it was.

The Vivid started out, white and glaring, from the black night at last. – "Here you are!" said the waterman, and instantly demanded six shillings.

"You ask too much," I said. He drew off from the vessel and swore he would not embark me till I paid it. A young man, the steward as I found afterwards, was looking over the ship's side; he grinned a smile in anticipation of the coming contest; to disappoint him, I paid the money. Three times that afternoon I had given crowns where I should have given shillings; but I consoled myself with the reflection, "It is the price of experience."

"They've cheated you!" said the steward exultingly when I got on board. I answered phlegmatically that "I knew it," and went below.

A stout, handsome, and showy woman was in the ladies' cabin. I asked to be shown my berth; she looked hard at me, muttered something about its being unusual for passengers to come on board at that hour, and seemed disposed to be less than civil. What a face she had – so comely – so insolent and so selfish!

"Now that I am on board, I shall certainly stay here," was my answer. "I will trouble you to show me my berth."

She complied, but sullenly. I took off my bonnet, arranged my things, and lay down. Some difficulties had been passed through; a sort of victory was won: my homeless, anchorless, unsupported mind had again leisure for a brief repose. Till *The Vivid* arrived in harbour, no further action would be required of me; but then…. Oh! I could not look forward. Harassed, exhausted, I lay in a half-trance.

The stewardess talked all night; not to me but to the young steward, her son and her very picture. He passed in and out of the cabin continually: they disputed, they quarrelled, they made it up again twenty times in the course of the night. She professed to be writing a letter home – she said to her father; she read passages of it aloud, heeding me no more than a stock – perhaps she believed me asleep. Several of these passages appeared to comprise family secrets, and bore special reference to one 'Charlotte', a younger sister who, from the bearing of the epistle, seemed to be on the brink of perpetrating a romantic and imprudent match; loud was the protest of this elder lady against the distasteful union. The dutiful son laughed his mother's correspondence to scorn. She defended it, and raved at him. They were a strange pair. She might be thirty-nine or forty, and was buxom and blooming as a girl of twenty. Hard, loud, vain and vulgar, her mind and body alike seemed brazen and imperishable. I should think, from her childhood, she must have lived in public stations; and in her youth might very likely have been a barmaid.

Towards morning her discourse ran on a new theme: 'the Watsons', a certain expected family-party of passengers, known to her, it appeared, and by her much esteemed on account of the handsome profit realized in their fees. She said, "It was as good as a little fortune to her whenever this family crossed."

At dawn all were astir, and by sunrise the passengers came on board. Boisterous was the welcome given by the stewardess to the 'Watsons', and great was the bustle made in their honour. They were four in number, two males and two females. Besides them, there was but one other passenger – a young lady, whom a gentlemanly, though languid-looking man escorted. The two groups offered a marked contrast. The Watsons were doubtless rich people, for they had the confidence of conscious wealth in their bearing; the women – youthful both of them, and one perfectly handsome, as far as physical beauty went – were dressed richly, gaily, and absurdly out of character for the circumstances. Their bonnets with bright flowers, their velvet cloaks and silk dresses, seemed better suited for park or promenade than for a damp packet deck. The men were of low stature, plain, fat, and vulgar; the oldest, plainest, greasiest, broadest, I soon found was the husband – the bridegroom I suppose, for she was very young – of the beautiful girl. Deep was my amazement at this discovery; and deeper still when I perceived that, instead of being desperately wretched in such a union, she was gay even to giddiness. "Her laughter," I reflected, "must be the mere frenzy of despair." And even while this thought was crossing my mind, as I stood leaning quiet and solitary against the ship's side, she came tripping up to me, an utter stranger, with a camp-stool in her hand, and smiling a smile of which the levity puzzled and startled me, though it showed a perfect set of perfect teeth, she offered me the accommodation of this piece of furniture. I declined it of course, with all the courtesy I could put into my manner; she danced off heedless and lightsome. She must have been good-natured; but what had made her marry that individual, who was at least as much like an oil-barrel as a man?

The other lady passenger, with the gentleman-companion, was quite a girl, pretty and fair: her simple print dress, untrimmed straw-bonnet and large shawl, gracefully worn, formed a costume plain to quakerism: yet, for her, becoming enough. Before the gentleman quitted her, I observed him throwing a glance of scrutiny over all the passengers, as if to ascertain in what company his charge would be left. With a most dissatisfied air did his eye turn from the ladies with the gay flowers; he looked at me, and then he spoke to his daughter, niece, or whatever she was: she also glanced in my direction, and slightly curled her short, pretty lip. It might be myself, or it might be my homely mourning habit, that elicited this mark of contempt; more likely, both. A bell rang; her father (I afterwards knew that it was her father) kissed her, and returned to land. The packet sailed.

Foreigners say that it is only English girls who can thus be trusted to travel alone, and deep is their wonder at the daring confidence of English parents and guardians. As for the 'jeunes Meess', by some their intrepidity is pronounced masculine and 'inconvenant', others regard them as the passive victims of an educational and theological system which wantonly dispenses with proper 'surveillance'. Whether this particular young lady was of the sort that can the most safely be left unwatched, I do not know: or, rather did not *then* know; but it soon appeared that the dignity of solitude was not to her taste. She paced the deck once or twice backwards and forwards; she looked with a little sour air of disdain at the flaunting silks and velvets, and the bears which thereon danced attendance, and eventually she approached me and spoke.

"Are you fond of a sea-voyage?" was her question.

I explained that my *fondness* for a sea-voyage had yet to undergo the test of experience; I had never made one.

"Oh, how charming!" cried she. "I quite envy you the novelty: first impressions, you know, are so pleasant. Now I have made so many, I quite forget the first: I am quite blasée about the sea and all that."

I could not help smiling.

"Why do you laugh at me?" she inquired, with a frank testiness that pleased me better than her other talk.

"Because you are so young to be blasée about anything."

"I am seventeen" (a little piqued).

"You hardly look sixteen. Do you like travelling alone?"

"Bah! I care nothing about it. I have crossed the Channel ten times, alone; but then I take care never to be long alone: I always make friends."

"You will scarcely make many friends this voyage, I think" (glancing at the Watson-group, who were now laughing and making a great deal of noise on deck).

"Not of those odious men and women," said she: "such people should be steerage passengers. Are you going to school?"

"No."

"Where are you going?"

"I have not the least idea – beyond, at least, the port of Boue-Marine."

She stared, then carelessly ran on:

"I am going to school. Oh, the number of foreign schools I have been at in my life! And yet I am quite an ignoramus. I know nothing – nothing in the world – I assure you; except that I play and dance beautifully, – and French and German of course I know, to speak; but I can't read or write them very well. Do you know they wanted me to translate a page of an easy German book into English the other day, and I couldn't do it. Papa was so mortified: he says it looks as if M. de Bassompierre – my godpapa, who pays all my school-bills – had thrown away all his money. And then, in matters of information – in history, geography, arithmetic, and so on, I am quite a baby; and I write English so badly – such spelling and grammar, they tell me. Into the bargain I have quite forgotten my religion; they call me a Protestant, you know, but really I am not sure whether I am one or not: I don't well know the difference between Romanism and Protestantism. However, I don't in the least care for that. I was a Lutheran once at Bonn – dear Bonn! – charming Bonn! – where there were so many handsome students. Every nice girl in our school had an admirer; they knew our hours for walking out, and almost always passed us on the promenade: 'Schönes Mädchen', we used to hear them say. I was excessively happy at Bonn!"

"And where are you now?" I inquired.

"Oh! At – chose," said she.

Now, Miss Ginevra Fanshawe (such was this young person's name) only substituted this word 'chose' in temporary oblivion of the real name. It was a habit she had: 'chose' came in at every turn in her conversation – the convenient substitute for any missing word in any language she might chance at the time to be speaking. French girls often do the like; from them she had caught the custom. 'Chose', however, I found in this instance, stood for Villette – the great capital of the great kingdom of Labassecour.

"Do you like Villette?" I asked.

"Pretty well. The natives, you know, are intensely stupid and vulgar; but there are some nice English families."

"Are you in a school?"

"Yes."

"A good one?"

"Oh, no! Horrid: but I go out every Sunday, and care nothing about the maîtresses or the professeurs, or the élèves, and send lessons au diable (one daren't say that in English, you know, but it sounds quite right in French); and thus I get on charmingly.... You are laughing at me again?"

"No – I am only smiling at my own thoughts."

"What are they?" (Without waiting for an answer) – "Now, *do* tell me where you are going."

"Where Fate may lead me. My business is to earn a living where I can find it."

"To earn!" (in consternation) "Are you poor, then?"

"As poor as Job."

(After a pause) – "Bah! How unpleasant! But *I* know what it is to be poor: they are poor enough at home – papa and mamma, and all of them. Papa is called Captain Fanshawe; he is an officer on half-pay, but well-descended, and some of our connections are great enough; but my uncle and godpapa De Bassompierre, who lives in France, is the only one that helps us: he educates us girls. I have five sisters and three brothers. By-and-by we are to marry – rather elderly gentlemen, I suppose, with cash: papa and mamma manage that. My sister Augusta is married now to a man much older-looking than papa. Augusta is very beautiful – not in my style – but dark; her husband, Mr. Davies, had the yellow fever in India, and he is still the colour of a guinea; but then he is rich, and Augusta has her carriage and establishment, and we all think she has done perfectly well. Now, this is better than 'earning a living', as you say. By the way, are you clever?"

"No – not at all."

"You can play, sing, speak three or four languages?"

"By no means."

"Still I think you are clever" (a pause and a yawn).

"Shall you be sea-sick?"

"Shall you?"

"Oh, immensely! As soon as ever we get in sight of the sea: I begin, indeed, to feel it already. I shall go below; and won't I order about that fat odious stewardess! *Heureusement je sais faire aller mon monde.*"

Down she went.

It was not long before the other passengers followed her: throughout the afternoon I remained on deck alone. When I recall the tranquil, and even happy mood in which I passed those hours, and remember, at the same time, the position in which I was placed; its hazardous – some would have said its hopeless – character; I feel that, as –

> *Stone walls do not a prison make,*
> *Nor iron bars – a cage,*

so peril, loneliness, an uncertain future, are not oppressive evils, so long as the frame is healthy and the faculties are employed; so long, especially, as Liberty lends us her wings, and Hope guides us by her star.

I was not sick till long after we passed Margate, and deep was the pleasure I drank in with the sea-breeze; divine the delight I drew from the heaving Channel waves, from the sea-birds on their ridges, from the white sails on their dark distance, from the quiet yet beclouded sky, overhanging all. In my reverie, methought I saw the continent of Europe, like a wide dream-land, far away. Sunshine lay on it, making the long coast one line of gold; tiniest tracery of clustered town and snow-gleaming tower, of woods deep massed, of heights serrated, of smooth pasturage and veiny stream, embossed the metal-bright prospect. For background, spread a sky, solemn and dark blue, and – grand with imperial promise, soft with tints of enchantment – strode from north to south a God-bent bow, an arch of hope.

Cancel the whole of that, if you please, reader – or rather let it stand, and draw thence a moral – an alliterative, text-hand copy –

> *Day-dreams are delusions of the demon.*

Becoming excessively sick, I faltered down into the cabin.

Miss Fanshawe's berth chanced to be next mine; and, I am sorry to say, she tormented me with an unsparing selfishness during the whole time of our mutual distress. Nothing could exceed her impatience and fretfulness. The Watsons, who were very sick too, and on whom the stewardess attended with shameless partiality, were stoics compared with her. Many a time since have I noticed, in persons of Ginevra Fanshawe's light, careless temperament, and fair, fragile style of beauty, an entire incapacity to endure: they seem to sour in adversity, like small beer in thunder. The man who takes such a woman for his wife, ought to be prepared to guarantee her an existence all sunshine. Indignant at last with her teasing peevishness, I curtly requested her "to hold her tongue". The rebuff did her good, and it was observable that she liked me no worse for it.

As dark night drew on, the sea roughened: larger waves swayed strong against the vessel's side. It was strange to reflect that blackness and water were round us, and to feel the ship ploughing straight on her pathless way, despite noise, billow, and rising gale. Articles of furniture began to fall about, and it became needful to lash them to their places; the passengers grew sicker than ever; Miss Fanshawe declared, with groans, that she must die.

"Not just yet, honey," said the stewardess. "We're just in port." Accordingly, in another quarter of an hour, a calm fell upon us all; and about midnight the voyage ended.

I was sorry: yes, I was sorry. My resting-time was past; my difficulties – my stringent difficulties – recommenced. When I went on deck, the cold air and black scowl of the night seemed to rebuke me for my presumption in being where I was: the lights of the foreign sea-port town, glimmering round the foreign harbour, met me like unnumbered threatening eyes. Friends came on board to welcome the Watsons; a whole family of friends surrounded and bore away Miss Fanshawe; I – but I dared not for one moment dwell on a comparison of positions.

Yet where should I go? I must go somewhere. Necessity dare not be nice. As I gave the stewardess her fee – and she seemed surprised at receiving a coin of more value than, from such a quarter, her coarse calculations had probably reckoned on – I said, "Be kind enough to direct me to some quiet, respectable inn, where I can go for the night."

She not only gave me the required direction, but called a commissionaire, and bid him take charge of me, and – *not* my trunk, for that was gone to the custom-house.

I followed this man along a rudely-paved street, lit now by a fitful gleam of moonlight; he brought me to the inn. I offered him sixpence, which he refused to take; supposing it not enough, I changed it for a shilling; but this also he declined, speaking rather sharply, in a language to me unknown. A waiter, coming forward into the lamp-lit inn-passage, reminded me, in broken English, that my money was foreign money, not current here. I gave him a sovereign to change. This little matter settled, I asked for a bedroom; supper I could not take: I was still sea-sick and unnerved, and trembling all over. How deeply glad I was when the door of a very small chamber at length closed on me and my exhaustion. Again I might rest: though the cloud of doubt would be as thick tomorrow as ever; the necessity for exertion more urgent, the peril (of destitution) nearer, the conflict (for existence) more severe.

Chapter Seven
Villette

I AWOKE next morning with courage revived and spirits refreshed: physical debility no longer enervated my judgment; my mind felt prompt and clear.

Just as I finished dressing, a tap came to the door: I said, "Come in," expecting the chambermaid, whereas a rough man walked in and said –

"Gif me your keys, Meess."

"Why?" I asked.

"Gif!" said he impatiently; and as he half-snatched them from my hand, he added, "All right! Haf your tronc soon."

Fortunately it did turn out all right: he was from the custom-house. Where to go to get some breakfast I could not tell; but I proceeded, not without hesitation, to descend.

I now observed, what I had not noticed in my extreme weariness last night, viz. that this inn was, in fact, a large hotel; and as I slowly descended the broad staircase, halting on each step (for I was in wonderfully little haste to get down), I gazed at the high ceiling above me, at the painted walls around, at the wide windows which filled the house with light, at the veined marble I trod (for the steps were all of marble, though uncarpeted and not very clean), and contrasting all this with the dimensions of the closet assigned to me as a chamber, with the extreme modesty of its appointments, I fell into a philosophizing mood.

Much I marvelled at the sagacity evinced by waiters and chamber-maids in proportioning the accommodation to the guest. How could inn-servants and ship-stewardesses everywhere tell at a glance that I, for instance, was an individual of no social significance, and little burdened by cash? They *did* know it evidently: I saw quite well that they all, in a moment's calculation, estimated me at about the same fractional value. The fact seemed to me curious and pregnant: I would not disguise from myself what it indicated, yet managed to keep up my spirits pretty well under its pressure.

Having at last landed in a great hall, full of skylight glare, I made my way somehow to what proved to be the coffee-room. It cannot be denied that on entering this room I trembled somewhat; felt uncertain, solitary, wretched; wished to Heaven I knew whether I was doing right or wrong; felt convinced that it was the last, but could not help myself. Acting in the spirit and with the calm of a fatalist, I sat down at a small table, to which a waiter presently brought me some breakfast; and I partook of that meal in a frame of mind not greatly calculated to favour digestion. There were many other people breakfasting at other tables in the room; I should have felt rather more happy if amongst them all I could have seen any women; however, there was not one – all present were men. But nobody seemed to think I was doing anything strange; one or two gentlemen glanced at me occasionally, but none stared obtrusively: I suppose if there was anything eccentric in the business, they accounted for it by this word '*Anglaise!*'

Breakfast over, I must again move – in what direction? "Go to Villette", said an inward voice; prompted doubtless by the recollection of this slight sentence uttered carelessly and at random by Miss Fanshawe, as she bid me goodbye: "I wish you would come to Madame Beck's; she has some marmots whom you might look after; she wants an English gouvernante, or was wanting one two months ago."

Who Madame Beck was, where she lived, I knew not; I had asked, but the question passed unheard: Miss Fanshawe, hurried away by her friends, left it unanswered. I presumed Villette to be her residence – to Villette I would go. The distance was forty miles. I knew I was catching at straws; but in the wide and weltering deep where I found myself, I would have caught at cobwebs. Having inquired about the means of travelling to Villette, and secured a seat in the diligence, I departed on the strength of this outline – this shadow of a project. Before you pronounce on the rashness of the proceeding, reader, look back to the point whence I started; consider the desert I had left, note how little I perilled: mine was the game where the player cannot lose and may win.

Of an artistic temperament, I deny that I am; yet I must possess something of the artist's faculty of making the most of present pleasure: that is to say, when it is of the kind to my taste. I enjoyed that day, though we travelled slowly, though it was cold, though it rained. Somewhat bare, flat, and treeless was the route along which our journey lay; and slimy canals crept, like half-torpid green snakes, beside the road; and formal pollard willows edged level fields, tilled like kitchen-garden beds. The sky, too, was monotonously grey; the atmosphere was stagnant and humid; yet amidst all these deadening influences, my fancy budded fresh and my heart basked in sunshine. These feelings, however, were well kept in check by the secret but ceaseless consciousness of anxiety lying in wait on enjoyment, like a tiger crouched in a jungle. The breathing of that beast of prey was in my ear always; his fierce heart panted close against mine; he never stirred in his lair but I felt him: I knew he waited only for sun-down to bound ravenous from his ambush.

I had hoped we might reach Villette ere night set in, and that thus I might escape the deeper embarrassment which obscurity seems to throw round a first arrival at an unknown bourne; but, what with our slow progress and long stoppages – what with a thick fog and small, dense rain – darkness, that might almost be felt, had settled on the city by the time we gained its suburbs.

I know we passed through a gate where soldiers were stationed – so much I could see by lamplight; then, having left behind us the miry Chaussée, we rattled over a pavement of strangely rough and flinty surface. At a bureau, the diligence stopped, and the passengers alighted. My first business was to get my trunk; a small matter enough, but important to me. Understanding that it was best not to be importunate or over-eager about luggage, but to wait and watch quietly the delivery of other boxes till I saw my own, and then promptly claim and secure it, I stood apart; my eye fixed on that part of the vehicle in which I had seen my little portmanteau safely stowed, and upon which piles of additional bags and boxes were now heaped. One by one, I saw these removed, lowered, and seized on.

I was sure mine ought to be by this time visible: it was not. I had tied on the direction-card with a piece of green ribbon, that I might know it at a glance: not a fringe or fragment of green was perceptible. Every package was removed; every tin-case and brown-paper parcel; the oilcloth cover was lifted; I saw with distinct vision that not an umbrella, cloak, cane, hat-box or band-box remained.

And my portmanteau, with my few clothes and little pocket-book enclasping the remnant of my fifteen pounds, where were they?

I ask this question now, but I could not ask it then. I could say nothing whatever; not possessing a phrase of *speaking* French: and it was French, and French only, the whole world seemed now gabbling around me. *What* should I do? Approaching the conductor, I just laid my hand on his arm, pointed to a trunk, thence to the diligence-roof, and tried to express a question with my eyes. He misunderstood me, seized the trunk indicated, and was about to hoist it on the vehicle.

"Let that alone – will you?" said a voice in good English; then, in correction, "*Qu'est-ce que vous faîtes donc? Cette malle est à moi.*"

But I had heard the Fatherland accents; they rejoiced my heart; I turned: "Sir," said I, appealing to the stranger, without, in my distress, noticing what he was like, "I cannot speak French. May I entreat you to ask this man what he has done with my trunk?"

Without discriminating, for the moment, what sort of face it was to which my eyes were raised and on which they were fixed, I felt in its expression half-surprise at my appeal and half-doubt of the wisdom of interference.

"*Do* ask him; I would do as much for you," said I.

I don't know whether he smiled, but he said in a gentlemanly tone – that is to say, a tone not hard nor terrifying – "What sort of trunk was yours?"

I described it, including in my description the green ribbon. And forthwith he took the conductor under hand, and I felt, through all the storm of French which followed, that he raked him fore and aft. Presently he returned to me.

"The fellow avers he was overloaded, and confesses that he removed your trunk after you saw it put on, and has left it behind at Boue-Marine with other parcels; he has promised, however, to forward it tomorrow; the day after, therefore, you will find it safe at this bureau."

"Thank you," said I: but my heart sank.

Meantime what should I do? Perhaps this English gentleman saw the failure of courage in my face; he inquired kindly, "Have you any friends in this city?"

"No, and I don't know where to go."

There was a little pause, in the course of which, as he turned more fully to the light of a lamp above him, I saw that he was a young, distinguished, and handsome man; he might be a lord, for anything I knew: nature had made him good enough for a prince, I thought. His face was very pleasant; he looked high but not arrogant, manly but not overbearing. I was turning away, in the deep consciousness of all absence of claim to look for further help from such a one as he.

"Was all your money in your trunk?" he asked, stopping me.

How thankful was I to be able to answer with truth – "No. I have enough in my purse" (for I had near twenty francs) "to keep me at a quiet inn till the day after tomorrow; but I am quite a stranger in Villette, and don't know the streets and the inns."

"I can give you the address of such an inn as you want," said he; "and it is not far off: with my direction you will easily find it."

He tore a leaf from his pocket-book, wrote a few words and gave it to me. I *did* think him kind; and as to distrusting him, or his advice, or his address, I should almost as soon have thought of distrusting the Bible. There was goodness in his countenance, and honour in his bright eyes.

"Your shortest way will be to follow the Boulevard and cross the park," he continued; "but it is too late and too dark for a woman to go through the park alone; I will step with you thus far."

He moved on, and I followed him, through the darkness and the small soaking rain. The Boulevard was all deserted, its path miry, the water dripping from its trees; the park was black as midnight. In the double gloom of trees and fog, I could not see my guide; I could only follow his tread. Not the least fear had I: I believe I would have followed that frank tread, through continual night, to the world's end.

"Now," said he, when the park was traversed, "you will go along this broad street till you come to steps; two lamps will show you where they are: these steps you will descend: a narrower street lies below; following that, at the bottom you will find your inn. They speak English there, so your difficulties are now pretty well over. Goodnight."

"Goodnight, sir," said I: "accept my sincerest thanks." And we parted.

The remembrance of his countenance, which I am sure wore a light not unbenignant to the friendless – the sound in my ear of his voice, which spoke a nature chivalric to the needy and feeble, as well as the youthful and fair – were a sort of cordial to me long after. He was a true young English gentleman.

On I went, hurrying fast through a magnificent street and square, with the grandest houses round, and amidst them the huge outline of more than one overbearing pile; which might be palace or church – I could not tell. Just as I passed a portico, two mustachioed men came suddenly from behind the pillars; they were smoking cigars: their dress implied pretensions to the rank of gentlemen, but, poor things! They were very plebeian in soul. They spoke with insolence, and, fast as I walked, they kept pace with me a long way. At last I met a sort of patrol, and my dreaded hunters were turned from the pursuit; but they had driven me beyond my reckoning: when I could collect my faculties, I no longer knew where I was; the staircase I must long since have passed. Puzzled, out of breath, all my pulses throbbing in inevitable agitation, I knew not where to turn. It was terrible to think of again encountering those bearded, sneering simpletons; yet the ground must be retraced, and the steps sought out.

I came at last to an old and worn flight, and, taking it for granted that this must be the one indicated, I descended them. The street into which they led was indeed narrow, but it contained no inn. On I wandered. In a very quiet and comparatively clean and well-paved street, I saw a light burning over the door of a rather large house, loftier by a story than those round it. *This* might be the inn at last. I hastened on: my knees now trembled under me: I was getting quite exhausted.

No inn was this. A brass-plate embellished the great porte-cochère: 'Pensionnat de Demoiselles' was the inscription; and beneath, a name, 'Madame Beck'.

I started. About a hundred thoughts volleyed through my mind in a moment. Yet I planned nothing, and considered nothing: I had not time. Providence said, "Stop here; this is *your* inn." Fate took me in her strong hand; mastered my will; directed my actions: I rang the door-bell.

While I waited, I would not reflect. I fixedly looked at the street-stones, where the door-lamp shone, and counted them and noted their shapes, and the glitter of wet on their angles. I rang again. They opened at last. A bonne in a smart cap stood before me.

"May I see Madame Beck?" I inquired.

I believe if I had spoken French she would not have admitted me; but, as I spoke English, she concluded I was a foreign teacher come on business connected with the pensionnat, and, even at that late hour, she let me in, without a word of reluctance, or a moment of hesitation.

The next moment I sat in a cold, glittering salon, with porcelain stove, unlit, and gilded ornaments, and polished floor. A pendule on the mantel-piece struck nine o'clock.

A quarter of an hour passed. How fast beat every pulse in my frame! How I turned cold and hot by turns! I sat with my eyes fixed on the door – a great white folding-door, with gilt mouldings: I watched to see a leaf move and open. All had been quiet: not a mouse had stirred; the white doors were closed and motionless.

"You ayre Engliss?" said a voice at my elbow. I almost bounded, so unexpected was the sound; so certain had I been of solitude.

No ghost stood beside me, nor anything of spectral aspect; merely a motherly, dumpy little woman, in a large shawl, a wrapping-gown, and a clean, trim nightcap.

I said I was English, and immediately, without further prelude, we fell to a most remarkable conversation. Madame Beck (for Madame Beck it was – she had entered by a little door behind me, and, being shod with the shoes of silence, I had heard neither her entrance nor approach) – Madame Beck had exhausted her command of insular speech when she said, "You ayre Engliss," and she now proceeded to work away volubly in her own tongue. I answered in mine. She partly understood me, but as I did not at all understand her – though we made together an awful clamour (anything like Madame's gift of utterance I had not hitherto heard or imagined) – we achieved little progress. She rang, ere long, for aid; which arrived in the shape of a 'maîtresse', who had been partly educated in an Irish convent, and was esteemed a perfect adept in the English language. A bluff little personage this maîtresse was – Labassecourienne from top to toe: and how she did slaughter the speech of Albion! However, I told her a plain tale, which she translated. I told her how I had left my own country, intent on extending my knowledge, and gaining my bread; how I was ready to turn my hand to any useful thing, provided it was not wrong or degrading; how I would be a child's-nurse, or a lady's-maid, and would not refuse even housework adapted to my strength. Madame heard this; and, questioning her countenance, I almost thought the tale won her ear:

"*Il n'y a que les Anglaises pour ces sortes d'entreprises,*" said she: "*sont-elles donc intrépides ces femmes là!*"

She asked my name, my age; she sat and looked at me – not pityingly, not with interest: never a gleam of sympathy, or a shade of compassion, crossed her countenance during the interview. I felt she was not one to be led an inch by her feelings: grave and considerate, she gazed, consulting her judgment and studying my narrative. A bell rang.

"*Voilà pour la prière du soir!*" said she, and rose. Through her interpreter, she desired me to depart now, and come back on the morrow; but this did not suit me: I could not bear to return to the perils of darkness and the street. With energy, yet with a collected and controlled manner, I said, addressing herself personally, and not the maîtresse: "Be assured, madame, that by instantly securing my services, your interests will be served and not injured: you will find me one who will wish to give, in her labour, a full equivalent for her wages; and if you hire me, it will be better that I should stay here this night: having no acquaintance in Villette, and not possessing the language of the country, how can I secure a lodging?"

"It is true," said she; "but at least you can give a reference?"

"None."

She inquired after my luggage: I told her when it would arrive. She mused. At that moment a man's step was heard in the vestibule, hastily proceeding to the outer door. (I shall go on with this part of my tale as if I had understood all that passed; for though it was then scarce intelligible to me, I heard it translated afterwards).

"Who goes out now?" demanded Madame Beck, listening to the tread.

"M. Paul," replied the teacher. "He came this evening to give a reading to the first class."

"The very man I should at this moment most wish to see. Call him."

The teacher ran to the salon door. M. Paul was summoned. He entered: a small, dark and spare man, in spectacles.

"Mon cousin," began Madame, "I want your opinion. We know your skill in physiognomy; use it now. Read that countenance."

The little man fixed on me his spectacles: A resolute compression of the lips, and gathering of the brow, seemed to say that he meant to see through me, and that a veil would be no veil for him.

"I read it," he pronounced.

"*Et qu'en dites vous?*"

"*Mais – bien des choses*," was the oracular answer.

"Bad or good?"

"Of each kind, without doubt," pursued the diviner.

"May one trust her word?"

"Are you negotiating a matter of importance?"

"She wishes me to engage her as bonne or gouvernante; tells a tale full of integrity, but gives no reference."

"She is a stranger?"

"An Englishwoman, as one may see."

"She speaks French?"

"Not a word."

"She understands it?"

"No."

"One may then speak plainly in her presence?"

"Doubtless."

He gazed steadily. "Do you need her services?"

"I could do with them. You know I am disgusted with Madame Svini."

Still he scrutinized. The judgment, when it at last came, was as indefinite as what had gone before it.

"Engage her. If good predominates in that nature, the action will bring its own reward; if evil – *eh bien! Ma cousine, ce sera toujours une bonne oeuvre*." And with a bow and a '*bon soir*', this vague arbiter of my destiny vanished.

And Madame did engage me that very night – by God's blessing I was spared the necessity of passing forth again into the lonesome, dreary, hostile street.

Chapter Eight
Madame Beck

BEING DELIVERED into the charge of the maîtresse, I was led through a long narrow passage into a foreign kitchen, very clean but very strange. It seemed to contain no means of cooking – neither fireplace nor oven; I did not understand that the great black furnace which filled one corner, was an efficient substitute for these. Surely pride was not already beginning its whispers in my heart; yet I felt a sense of relief when, instead of being left in the kitchen, as I half anticipated, I was led forward to a small inner room termed a 'cabinet'. A cook in a jacket, a short petticoat and sabots, brought my supper: to wit – some meat, nature unknown, served in an odd and acid, but pleasant sauce; some chopped potatoes, made savoury with, I know not what: vinegar and sugar, I think: a tartine, or slice of bread and butter, and a baked pear. Being hungry, I ate and was grateful.

After the '*prière du soir*', Madame herself came to have another look at me. She desired me to follow her upstairs. Through a series of the queerest little dormitories – which, I heard afterwards, had once been nuns' cells: for the premises were in part of ancient date – and through the oratory – a long, low, gloomy room, where a crucifix hung, pale, against the wall, and two tapers kept dim vigils – she conducted me to an apartment where three children were asleep in three tiny beds. A heated stove made the air of this room oppressive; and, to mend matters, it was scented with an odour rather strong than delicate: a perfume, indeed, altogether surprising and unexpected under the circumstances, being like the combination of smoke with some spirituous essence – a smell, in short, of whisky.

Beside a table, on which flared the remnant of a candle guttering to waste in the socket, a coarse woman, heterogeneously clad in a broad striped showy silk dress, and a stuff apron, sat in a chair fast asleep. To complete the picture, and leave no doubt as to the state of matters, a bottle and an empty glass stood at the sleeping beauty's elbow.

Madame contemplated this remarkable tableau with great calm; she neither smiled nor scowled; no impress of anger, disgust, or surprise, ruffled the equality of her grave aspect; she did not even wake the woman! Serenely pointing to a fourth bed, she intimated that it was to be mine; then, having extinguished the candle and substituted for it a night-lamp, she glided through an inner door, which she left ajar – the entrance to her own chamber, a large, well-furnished apartment; as was discernible through the aperture.

My devotions that night were all thanksgiving. Strangely had I been led since morning – unexpectedly had I been provided for. Scarcely could I believe that not forty-eight hours had elapsed since I left London, under no other guardianship than that which protects the passenger-bird – with no prospect but the dubious cloud-tracery of hope.

I was a light sleeper; in the dead of night I suddenly awoke. All was hushed, but a white figure stood in the room – Madame in her night-dress. Moving without perceptible sound, she visited the three children in the three beds; she approached me: I feigned sleep, and she studied me long. A small pantomime ensued, curious enough. I daresay she sat a quarter of an hour on the edge of my bed, gazing at my face. She then drew nearer, bent close over me; slightly raised my cap, and turned back the border so as to expose my hair; she looked at my hand lying on the bedclothes. This done, she turned to the chair where my clothes lay: it was at the foot of the bed. Hearing her touch and lift them, I opened my eyes with precaution, for I own I felt curious to see how far her taste for research would lead her. It led her a good way: every article did she inspect. I divined her motive for this proceeding, viz. the wish to form from the garments a judgment respecting the wearer, her station, means, neatness, etc. The end was not bad, but the means were hardly fair or justifiable. In my dress was a pocket; she fairly turned it inside out: she counted the money in my purse; she opened a little memorandum-book, coolly perused its contents, and took from between the leaves a small plaited lock of Miss Marchmont's grey hair. To a bunch of three keys, being those of my trunk, desk, and work-box, she accorded special attention: with these, indeed, she withdrew a moment to her own room. I softly rose in my bed and followed her with my eye: these keys, reader, were not brought back till they had left on the toilet of the adjoining room the impress of their wards in wax. All being thus done decently and in order, my property was returned to its place, my clothes were carefully refolded. Of what nature were the conclusions deduced from this scrutiny? Were they favourable or otherwise? Vain question. Madame's face of stone (for of stone in its present night aspect it looked: it had been human, and, as I said before, motherly, in the salon) betrayed no response.

Her duty done – I felt that in her eyes this business was a duty – she rose, noiseless as a shadow: she moved towards her own chamber; at the door, she turned, fixing her eye on the heroine of the bottle, who still slept and loudly snored. Mrs. Svini (I presume this was Mrs. Svini, Anglicé or Hibernicé, Sweeny) – Mrs. Sweeny's doom was in Madame Beck's eye – an immutable purpose that eye spoke: Madame's visitations for shortcomings might be slow, but they were sure. All this was very un-English: truly I was in a foreign land.

The morrow made me further acquainted with Mrs. Sweeny. It seems she had introduced herself to her present employer as an English lady in reduced circumstances: a native, indeed, of Middlesex, professing to speak the English tongue with the purest metropolitan accent. Madame – reliant on her own infallible expedients for finding out the truth in time – had a singular intrepidity in hiring service off-hand (as indeed seemed abundantly proved in my own case). She received Mrs. Sweeny as nursery-governess to her three children. I need hardly explain to the reader that this lady was in effect a native of Ireland; her station I do not pretend to fix: she boldly declared that she had "had the bringing-up of the son and daughter of a marquis". I think myself, she might possibly have been a hanger-on, nurse, fosterer, or washerwoman, in some Irish family: she spoke a smothered tongue, curiously overlaid with mincing cockney inflections. By some means or other she had acquired, and now held in possession, a wardrobe of rather suspicious splendour – gowns of stiff and costly silk, fitting her indifferently, and apparently made for other proportions than those they now adorned; caps with real lace borders, and – the chief item in the inventory, the spell by which she struck a certain awe through the household, quelling the otherwise scornfully disposed teachers and servants, and, so long as her broad shoulders *wore* the folds of that majestic drapery, even influencing Madame herself – *a real Indian shawl* – "*un véritable cachemire*", as Madame Beck said, with unmixed reverence and amaze. I feel quite sure that without this 'cachemire' she would not have kept her footing in the pensionnat for two days: by virtue of it, and it only, she maintained the same a month.

But when Mrs. Sweeny knew that I was come to fill her shoes, then it was that she declared herself – then did she rise on Madame Beck in her full power – then come down on me with her concentrated weight. Madame bore this revelation and visitation so well, so stoically, that I for very shame could not support it otherwise than with composure. For one little moment Madame Beck absented herself from the room; ten minutes after, an agent of the police stood in the midst of us. Mrs. Sweeny and her effects were removed. Madame's brow had not been ruffled during the scene – her lips had not dropped one sharply-accented word.

This brisk little affair of the dismissal was all settled before breakfast: order to march given, policeman called, mutineer expelled; 'chambre d'enfans' fumigated and cleansed, windows thrown open, and every trace of the accomplished Mrs. Sweeny – even to the fine essence and spiritual fragrance which gave token so subtle and so fatal of the head and front of her offending – was annihilated from the Rue Fossette: all this, I say, was done between the moment of Madame Beck's issuing like Aurora from her chamber, and that in which she coolly sat down to pour out her first cup of coffee.

About noon, I was summoned to dress Madame. (It appeared my place was to be a hybrid between gouvernante and lady's-maid.) Till noon, she haunted the house in her wrapping-gown, shawl, and soundless slippers. How would the lady-chief of an English school approve this custom?

The dressing of her hair puzzled me; she had plenty of it: auburn, unmixed with grey: though she was forty years old. Seeing my embarrassment, she said, "You have not been a femme-de-chambre in your own country?" And taking the brush from my hand, and setting me aside, not ungently or disrespectfully, she arranged it herself. In performing other offices of the toilet, she half-directed, half-aided me, without the least display of temper or impatience. N.B. – That was the first and last time I was required to dress her. Henceforth, on Rosine, the portress, devolved that duty.

When attired, Madame Beck appeared a personage of a figure rather short and stout, yet still graceful in its own peculiar way; that is, with the grace resulting from proportion of parts. Her complexion was fresh and sanguine, not too rubicund; her eye, blue and serene; her dark silk dress fitted her as a French sempstress alone can make a dress fit; she looked well, though a little bourgeoise; as bourgeoise, indeed, she was. I know not what of harmony pervaded her whole person; and yet her face offered contrast, too: its features were by no means such as are usually seen in conjunction with a complexion of such blended freshness and repose: their outline was stern: her forehead was high but narrow; it expressed capacity and some benevolence, but no expanse; nor did her peaceful yet watchful eye ever know the fire which is kindled in the heart or the softness which flows thence. Her mouth was hard: it could be a little grim; her lips were thin. For sensibility and genius, with all their tenderness and temerity, I felt somehow that Madame would be the right sort of Minos in petticoats.

In the long run, I found she was something else in petticoats too. Her name was Modeste Maria Beck, née Kint: it ought to have been Ignacia. She was a charitable woman, and did a great deal of good. There never was a mistress whose rule was milder. I was told that she never once remonstrated with the intolerable Mrs. Sweeny, despite her tipsiness, disorder, and general neglect; yet Mrs. Sweeny had to go the moment her departure became convenient. I was told, too, that neither masters nor teachers were found fault with in that establishment; yet both masters and teachers were often changed: they vanished and others filled their places, none could well explain how.

The establishment was both a pensionnat and an externat: the externes or day-pupils exceeded one hundred in number; the boarders were about a score. Madame must have possessed high administrative powers: she ruled all these, together with four teachers, eight masters, six servants, and three children, managing at the same time to perfection the pupils' parents and friends; and that without apparent effort; without bustle, fatigue, fever, or any symptom of undue, excitement: occupied she always was – busy, rarely. It is true that Madame had her own system for managing and regulating this mass of machinery; and a very pretty system it was: the reader has seen a specimen of it, in that small affair of turning my pocket inside out, and reading my private memoranda. 'Surveillance', 'espionage', – these were her watchwords.

Still, Madame knew what honesty was, and liked it – that is, when it did not obtrude its clumsy scruples in the way of her will and interest. She had a respect for 'Angleterre;' and as to 'les Anglaises', she would have the women of no other country about her own children, if she could help it.

Often in the evening, after she had been plotting and counter-plotting, spying and receiving the reports of spies all day, she would come up to my room – a trace of real weariness on her brow – and she would sit down and listen while the children said their little prayers to me in English: the Lord's Prayer, and the hymn beginning 'Gentle Jesus', these little Catholics were permitted to repeat at my knee; and, when I had put them to bed, she would talk to me (I soon gained enough French to be able to understand, and even answer her) about England and Englishwomen, and the reasons for what she was pleased to term their superior intelligence, and more real and reliable probity. Very good sense she often showed; very sound opinions she often broached: she seemed to know that keeping girls in distrustful restraint, in blind ignorance, and under a surveillance that left them no moment and no corner for retirement, was not the best way to make them grow up honest and modest women; but she averred that ruinous consequences would ensue if any other method were tried with continental children: they were so accustomed to restraint, that relaxation, however guarded, would be misunderstood and fatally presumed on. She was sick, she would declare, of the means she had to use, but use them she must; and after discoursing, often with dignity and delicacy, to me, she would move away on her 'souliers de silence', and glide ghost-like through the house, watching and spying everywhere, peering through every keyhole, listening behind every door.

After all, Madame's system was not bad – let me do her justice. Nothing could be better than all her arrangements for the physical well-being of her scholars. No minds were overtasked: the lessons were well distributed and made incomparably easy to the learner; there was a liberty of amusement, and a provision for exercise which kept the girls healthy; the food was abundant and good: neither pale nor puny faces were anywhere to be seen in the Rue Fossette. She never grudged a holiday; she allowed plenty of time for sleeping, dressing, washing, eating; her method in all these matters was easy, liberal, salutary, and rational: many an austere English school-mistress would do vastly well to imitate her – and I believe many would be glad to do so, if exacting English parents would let them.

As Madame Beck ruled by espionage, she of course had her staff of spies: she perfectly knew the quality of the tools she used, and while she would not scruple to handle the dirtiest for a dirty occasion – flinging this sort from her like refuse rind, after the orange has been duly squeezed – I have known her fastidious in seeking pure metal for clean uses; and when once a bloodless and rustless instrument was found, she was careful of the prize, keeping it in silk and cotton-wool. Yet, woe be to that man or woman who relied on her one inch beyond the point where it was her interest to be trustworthy: interest was the master-key of Madame's nature – the mainspring of her motives – the alpha and omega of her life. I have seen her *feelings* appealed to, and I have smiled in half-pity, half-scorn at the appellants. None ever gained her ear through that channel, or swayed her purpose by that means. On the contrary, to attempt to touch her heart was the surest way to rouse her antipathy, and to make of her a secret foe. It proved to her that she had no heart to be touched: it reminded her where she was impotent and dead. Never was the distinction between charity and mercy better exemplified than in her. While devoid of sympathy, she had a sufficiency of rational benevolence: she would give in the readiest manner to people she had never seen – rather, however, to classes than to individuals. 'Pour les pauvres', she opened her purse freely – against *the poor man*, as a rule, she kept it closed. In philanthropic schemes for the benefit of society at large she took a cheerful part; no private sorrow touched her: no force or mass of suffering concentrated in one heart had power to pierce hers. Not the agony in Gethsemane, not the death on Calvary, could have wrung from her eyes one tear.

I say again, Madame was a very great and a very capable woman. That school offered her for her powers too limited a sphere; she ought to have swayed a nation: she should have been the leader of a turbulent legislative assembly. Nobody could have browbeaten her, none irritated her nerves, exhausted her patience, or over-reached her astuteness. In her own single person, she could have comprised the duties of a first minister and a superintendent of police. Wise, firm, faithless; secret, crafty, passionless; watchful and inscrutable; acute and insensate – withal perfectly decorous – what more could be desired?

The sensible reader will not suppose that I gained all the knowledge here condensed for his benefit in one month, or in one half-year. No! What I saw at first was the thriving outside of a large and flourishing educational establishment. Here was a great house, full of healthy, lively girls, all well-dressed and many of them handsome, gaining knowledge by a marvellously easy method, without painful exertion or useless waste of spirits; not, perhaps, making very rapid progress in anything; taking it easy, but still always employed, and never oppressed. Here was a corps of teachers and masters, more stringently tasked, as all the real head-labour was to be done by them, in order to save the pupils, yet having their duties so arranged that they relieved each other in quick succession whenever the work was severe: here, in short, was a foreign school; of which the life, movement, and variety made it a complete and most charming contrast to many English institutions of the same kind.

Behind the house was a large garden, and, in summer, the pupils almost lived out of doors amongst the rose-bushes and the fruit-trees. Under the vast and vine-draped berceau, Madame would take her seat on summer afternoons, and send for the classes, in turns, to sit round her and sew and read. Meantime, masters came and went, delivering short and lively lectures, rather than lessons, and the pupils made notes of their instructions, or did *not* make them – just as inclination prompted; secure that, in case of neglect, they could copy the notes of their companions. Besides the regular monthly jours de sortie, the Catholic fête-days brought a succession of holidays all the year round; and sometimes on a bright summer morning, or soft summer evening; the boarders were taken out for a long walk into the country, regaled with gaufres and vin blanc, or new milk and pain bis, or pistolets au beurre (rolls) and coffee. All this seemed very pleasant, and Madame appeared goodness itself; and the teachers not so bad but they might be worse; and the pupils, perhaps, a little noisy and rough, but types of health and glee.

Thus did the view appear, seen through the enchantment of distance; but there came a time when distance was to melt for me – when I was to be called down from my watch-tower of the nursery, whence I had hitherto made my observations, and was to be compelled into closer intercourse with this little world of the Rue Fossette.

I was one day sitting upstairs, as usual, hearing the children their English lessons, and at the same time turning a silk dress for Madame, when she came sauntering into the room with that absorbed air and brow of hard thought she sometimes wore, and which made her look so little genial. Dropping into a seat opposite mine, she remained some minutes silent. Désirée, the eldest girl, was reading to me some little essay of Mrs. Barbauld's, and I was making her translate currently from English to French as she proceeded, by way of ascertaining that she comprehended what she read: Madame listened.

Presently, without preface or prelude, she said, almost in the tone of one making an accusation, "Meess, in England you were a governess?"

"No, Madame," said I smiling, "you are mistaken."

"Is this your first essay at teaching – this attempt with my children?"

I assured her it was. Again she became silent; but looking up, as I took a pin from the cushion, I found myself an object of study: she held me under her eye; she seemed turning me round in her thoughts – measuring my fitness for a purpose, weighing my value in a plan. Madame had, ere this, scrutinized all I had, and I believe she esteemed herself cognizant of much that I was; but from that day, for the space of about a fortnight, she tried me by new tests. She listened at the nursery door when I was shut in with the children; she followed me at a cautious distance when I walked out with them, stealing within ear-shot whenever the trees of park or boulevard afforded a sufficient screen: a strict preliminary process having thus been observed, she made a move forward.

One morning, coming on me abruptly, and with the semblance of hurry, she said she found herself placed in a little dilemma. Mr. Wilson, the English master, had failed to come at his hour, she feared he was ill; the pupils were waiting in classe; there was no one to give a lesson; should I, for once, object to giving a short dictation exercise, just that the pupils might not have it to say they had missed their English lesson?

"In classe, Madame?" I asked.

"Yes, in classe: in the second division."

"Where there are sixty pupils," said I; for I knew the number, and with my usual base habit of cowardice, I shrank into my sloth like a snail into its shell, and alleged incapacity and impracticability as a pretext to escape action. If left to myself, I should infallibly have let this chance slip. Inadventurous, unstirred by impulses of practical ambition, I was capable of sitting twenty years teaching infants the hornbook, turning silk dresses and making children's frocks. Not that true contentment dignified this infatuated resignation: my work had neither charm for my taste, nor hold on my interest; but it seemed to me a great thing to be without heavy anxiety, and relieved from intimate trial: the negation of severe suffering was the nearest approach to happiness I expected to know. Besides, I seemed to hold two lives – the life of thought, and that of reality; and, provided the former was nourished with a sufficiency of the strange necromantic joys of fancy, the privileges of the latter might remain limited to daily bread, hourly work, and a roof of shelter.

"Come," said Madame, as I stooped more busily than ever over the cutting-out of a child's pinafore, "leave that work."

"But Fifine wants it, Madame."

"Fifine must want it, then, for I want *you*."

And as Madame Beck did really want and was resolved to have me – as she had long been dissatisfied with the English master, with his shortcomings in punctuality, and his careless method of tuition – as, too, *she* did not lack resolution and practical activity, whether *I* lacked them or not – she, without more ado, made me relinquish thimble and needle; my hand was taken into hers, and I was conducted downstairs. When we reached the carré, a large square hall between the dwelling-house and the pensionnat, she paused, dropped my hand, faced, and scrutinized me. I was flushed, and tremulous from head to foot: tell it not in Gath, I believe I was crying. In fact, the difficulties before me were far from being wholly imaginary; some of them were real enough; and not the least substantial lay in my want of mastery over the medium through which I should be obliged to teach. I had, indeed, studied French closely since my arrival in Villette; learning its practice by day, and its theory in every leisure moment at night, to as late an hour as the rule of the house would allow candle-light; but I was far from yet being able to trust my powers of correct oral expression.

"*Dîtes donc*," said Madame sternly, "*vous sentez vous réellement trop faible?*"

I might have said "Yes", and gone back to nursery obscurity, and there, perhaps, mouldered for the rest of my life; but looking up at Madame, I saw in her countenance a something that made me think twice ere I decided. At that instant she did not wear a woman's aspect, but rather a man's. Power of a particular kind strongly limned itself in all her traits, and that power was not my kind of power: neither sympathy, nor congeniality, nor submission, were the emotions it awakened. I stood – not soothed, nor won, nor overwhelmed. It seemed as if a challenge of strength between opposing gifts was given, and I suddenly felt all the dishonour of my diffidence – all the pusillanimity of my slackness to aspire.

"Will you," she said, "go backward or forward?" indicating with her hand, first, the small door of communication with the dwelling-house, and then the great double portals of the classes or schoolrooms.

"*En avant*," I said.

"But," pursued she, cooling as I warmed, and continuing the hard look, from very antipathy to which I drew strength and determination, "can you face the classes, or are you over-excited?"

She sneered slightly in saying this: nervous excitability was not much to Madame's taste.

"I am no more excited than this stone," I said, tapping the flag with my toe: "or than you," I added, returning her look.

"*Bon!* But let me tell you these are not quiet, decorous, English girls you are going to encounter. *Ce sont des Labassecouriennes, rondes, franches, brusques, et tant soit peu rebelles.*"

I said: "I know; and I know, too, that though I have studied French hard since I came here, yet I still speak it with far too much hesitation – too little accuracy to be able to command their respect I shall make blunders that will lay me open to the scorn of the most ignorant. Still I mean to give the lesson."

"They always throw over timid teachers," said she.

"I know that too, Madame; I have heard how they rebelled against and persecuted Miss Turner" – a poor friendless English teacher, whom Madame had employed, and lightly discarded; and to whose piteous history I was no stranger.

"*C'est vrai*," said she, coolly. "Miss Turner had no more command over them than a servant from the kitchen would have had. She was weak and wavering; she had neither tact nor intelligence, decision nor dignity. Miss Turner would not do for these girls at all."

I made no reply, but advanced to the closed schoolroom door.

"You will not expect aid from me, or from anyone," said Madame. "That would at once set you down as incompetent for your office."

I opened the door, let her pass with courtesy, and followed her. There were three schoolrooms, all large. That dedicated to the second division, where I was to figure, was considerably the largest, and accommodated an assemblage more numerous, more turbulent, and infinitely more unmanageable than the other two. In after days, when I knew the ground better, I used to think sometimes (if such a comparison may be permitted), that the quiet, polished, tame first division was to the robust, riotous, demonstrative second division, what the English House of Lords is to the House of Commons.

The first glance informed me that many of the pupils were more than girls – quite young women; I knew that some of them were of noble family (as nobility goes in Labassecour), and I was well convinced that not one amongst them was ignorant of my position in Madame's household. As I mounted the estràde (a low platform, raised a step above the flooring), where stood the teacher's chair and desk, I beheld opposite to me a row of eyes and brows that threatened stormy weather – eyes full of an insolent light, and brows hard and unblushing as marble. The continental 'female' is quite a different being to the insular 'female' of the same age and class: I never saw such eyes and brows in England. Madame Beck introduced me in one cool phrase, sailed from the room, and left me alone in my glory.

I shall never forget that first lesson, nor all the under-current of life and character it opened up to me. Then first did I begin rightly to see the wide difference that lies between the novelist's and poet's ideal 'jeune fille' and the said 'jeune fille' as she really is.

It seems that three titled belles in the first row had sat down predetermined that a bonne d'enfants should not give them lessons in English. They knew they had succeeded in expelling obnoxious teachers before now; they knew that Madame would at any time throw overboard a professeur or maitresse who became unpopular with the school – that she never assisted a weak official to retain his place – that if he had not strength to fight, or tact to win his way, down he went: looking at 'Miss Snowe', they promised themselves an easy victory.

Mesdemoiselles Blanche, Virginie, and Angélique opened the campaign by a series of titterings and whisperings; these soon swelled into murmurs and short laughs, which the remoter benches caught up and echoed more loudly. This growing revolt of sixty against one, soon became oppressive enough; my command of French being so limited, and exercised under such cruel constraint.

Could I but have spoken in my own tongue, I felt as if I might have gained a hearing; for, in the first place, though I knew I looked a poor creature, and in many respects actually was so, yet nature had given me a voice that could make itself heard, if lifted in excitement or deepened by emotion. In the second place, while I had no flow, only a hesitating trickle of language, in ordinary circumstances, yet – under stimulus such as was now rife through the mutinous mass – I could, in English, have rolled out readily phrases stigmatizing their proceedings as such proceedings deserved to be stigmatized; and then with some sarcasm, flavoured with contemptuous bitterness for the ringleaders, and relieved with easy banter for the weaker but less knavish followers, it seemed to me that one might possibly get command over this wild herd, and bring them into training, at least. All I could now do was to walk up to Blanche – Mademoiselle de Melcy, a young baronne – the eldest, tallest, handsomest, and most vicious – stand before her desk, take from under her hand her exercise-book, remount the estrade, deliberately read the composition, which I found very stupid, and, as deliberately, and in the face of the whole school, tear the blotted page in two.

This action availed to draw attention and check noise. One girl alone, quite in the background, persevered in the riot with undiminished energy. I looked at her attentively. She had a pale face, hair like night, broad strong eyebrows, decided features, and a dark, mutinous, sinister eye: I noted that she sat close by a little door, which door, I was well aware, opened into a small closet where books were kept. She was standing up for the purpose of conducting her clamour with freer energies. I measured her stature and calculated her strength. She seemed both tall and wiry; but, so the conflict were brief and the attack unexpected, I thought I might manage her.

Advancing up the room, looking as cool and careless as I possibly could, in short, ayant l'air de rien, I slightly pushed the door and found it was ajar. In an instant, and with sharpness, I had turned on her. In another instant she occupied the closet, the door was shut, and the key in my pocket.

It so happened that this girl, Dolores by name, and a Catalonian by race, was the sort of character at once dreaded and hated by all her associates; the act of summary justice above noted proved popular: there was not one present but, in her heart, liked to see it done. They were stilled for a moment; then a smile – not a laugh – passed from desk to desk: then – when I had gravely and tranquilly returned to the estrade, courteously requested silence, and commenced a dictation as if nothing at all had happened – the pens travelled peacefully over the pages, and the remainder of the lesson passed in order and industry.

"*C'est bien*," said Madame Beck, when I came out of class, hot and a little exhausted. "*Ca ira*."

She had been listening and peeping through a spy-hole the whole time.

From that day I ceased to be nursery governess, and became English teacher. Madame raised my salary; but she got thrice the work out of me she had extracted from Mr. Wilson, at half the expense.

Chapter Nine
Isidore

MY TIME was now well and profitably filled up. What with teaching others and studying closely myself, I had hardly a spare moment. It was pleasant. I felt I was getting on; not lying the stagnant prey of mould and rust, but polishing my faculties and whetting them to a keen edge with constant use. Experience of a certain kind lay before me, on no narrow scale. Villette is a cosmopolitan city, and in this school were girls of almost every European nation, and likewise of very varied rank in life. Equality is much practised in Labassecour; though not republican in form, it is nearly so in substance, and at the desks of Madame Beck's establishment the young countess and the young bourgeoise sat side by side. Nor could you always by outward indications decide which was noble and which plebeian; except that, indeed, the latter had often franker and more courteous manners, while the former bore away the bell for a delicately-balanced combination of insolence and deceit. In the former there was often quick French blood mixed with the marsh-phlegm: I regret to say that the effect of this vivacious fluid chiefly appeared in the oilier glibness with which flattery and fiction ran from the tongue, and in a manner lighter and livelier, but quite heartless and insincere.

To do all parties justice, the honest aboriginal Labassecouriennes had an hypocrisy of their own, too; but it was of a coarse order, such as could deceive few. Whenever a lie was necessary for their occasions, they brought it out with a careless ease and breadth altogether untroubled by the rebuke of conscience. Not a soul in Madame Beck's house, from the scullion to the directress herself, but was above being ashamed of a lie; they thought nothing of it: to invent might not be precisely a virtue, but it was the most venial of faults. "*J'ai menti plusieurs fois,*" formed an item of every girl's and woman's monthly confession: the priest heard unshocked, and absolved unreluctant. If they had missed going to mass, or read a chapter of a novel, that was another thing: these were crimes whereof rebuke and penance were the unfailing weed.

While yet but half-conscious of this state of things, and unlearned in its results, I got on in my new sphere very well. After the first few difficult lessons, given amidst peril and on the edge of a moral volcano that rumbled under my feet and sent sparks and hot fumes into my eyes, the eruptive spirit seemed to subside, as far as I was concerned. My mind was a good deal bent on success: I could not bear the thought of being baffled by mere undisciplined disaffection and wanton indocility, in this first attempt to get on in life. Many hours of the night I used to lie awake, thinking what plan I had best adopt to get a reliable hold on these mutineers, to bring this stiff-necked tribe under permanent influence. In the first place, I saw plainly that aid in no shape was to be expected from Madame: her righteous plan was to maintain an unbroken popularity with the pupils, at any and every cost of justice or comfort to the teachers. For a teacher to seek her alliance in any crisis of insubordination was equivalent to securing her own expulsion. In intercourse with her pupils, Madame only took to herself what was pleasant, amiable, and recommendatory; rigidly requiring of her lieutenants sufficiency for every annoying crisis, where to act with adequate promptitude was to be unpopular. Thus, I must look only to myself.

Imprimis – it was clear as the day that this swinish multitude were not to be driven by force. They were to be humoured, borne with very patiently: a courteous though sedate manner impressed them; a very rare flash of raillery did good. Severe or continuous mental application they could not, or would not, bear: heavy demand on the memory, the reason, the attention, they rejected point-blank. Where an English girl of not more than average capacity and docility would quietly take a theme and bind herself to the task of comprehension and mastery, a Labassecourienne would laugh in your face, and throw it back to you with the phrase – *"Dieu, que c'est difficile! Je n'en veux pas. Cela m'ennuie trop."*

A teacher who understood her business would take it back at once, without hesitation, contest, or expostulation – proceed with even exaggerated care to smoothe every difficulty, to reduce it to the level of their understandings, return it to them thus modified, and lay on the lash of sarcasm with unsparing hand. They would feel the sting, perhaps wince a little under it; but they bore no malice against this sort of attack, provided the sneer was not *sour*, but *hearty*, and that it held well up to them, in a clear, light, and bold type, so that she who ran might read, their incapacity, ignorance, and sloth. They would riot for three additional lines to a lesson; but I never knew them rebel against a wound given to their self-respect: the little they had of that quality was trained to be crushed, and it rather liked the pressure of a firm heel than otherwise.

By degrees, as I acquired fluency and freedom in their language, and could make such application of its more nervous idioms as suited their case, the elder and more intelligent girls began rather to like me in their way: I noticed that whenever a pupil had been roused to feel in her soul the stirring of worthy emulation, or the quickening of honest shame, from that date she was won. If I could but once make their (usually large) ears burn under their thick glossy hair, all was comparatively well. By-and-by bouquets began to be laid on my desk in the morning; by way of acknowledgment for this little foreign attention, I used sometimes to walk with a select few during recreation. In the course of conversation it befell once or twice that I made an unpremeditated attempt to rectify some of their singularly distorted notions of principle; especially I expressed my ideas of the evil and baseness of a lie. In an unguarded moment, I chanced to say that, of the two errors; I considered falsehood worse than an occasional lapse in church-attendance. The poor girls were tutored to report in Catholic ears whatever the Protestant teacher said. An edifying consequence ensued. Something – an unseen, an indefinite, a nameless – something stole between myself and these my best pupils: the bouquets continued to be offered, but conversation thenceforth became impracticable. As I paced the alleys or sat in the berceau, a girl never came to my right hand but a teacher, as if by magic, appeared at my left. Also, wonderful to relate, Madame's shoes of silence brought her continually to my back, as quick, as noiseless and unexpected, as some wandering zephyr.

The opinion of my Catholic acquaintance concerning my spiritual prospects was somewhat naïvely expressed to me on one occasion. A pensionnaire, to whom I had rendered some little service, exclaimed one day as she sat beside me: "Mademoiselle, what a pity you are a Protestant!"

"Why, Isabelle?"

"Parceque, quand vous serez morte – vous brûlerez tout de suite dans l'Enfer."

"Croyez-vous?"

"Certainement que j'y crois: tout le monde le sait; et d'ailleurs le prêtre me l'a dit."

Isabelle was an odd, blunt little creature. She added, *sotto voce:* *"Pour assurer votre salut là-haut, on ferait bien de vous brûler toute vive ici-bas."*

I laughed, as, indeed, it was impossible to do otherwise.

* * *

Has the reader forgotten Miss Ginevra Fanshawe? If so, I must be allowed to re-introduce that young lady as a thriving pupil of Madame Beck's; for such she was. On her arrival in the Rue Fossette, two or three days after my sudden settlement there, she encountered me with very little surprise. She must have had good blood in her veins, for never was any duchess more perfectly, radically, unaffectedly nonchalante than she: a weak, transient amaze was all she knew of the sensation of wonder. Most of her other faculties seemed to be in the same flimsy condition: her liking and disliking, her love and hate, were mere cobweb and gossamer; but she had one thing about her that seemed strong and durable enough, and that was – her selfishness.

She was not proud; and – bonne d'enfants as I was – she would forthwith have made of me a sort of friend and confidant. She teased me with a thousand vapid complaints about school-quarrels and household economy: the cookery was not to her taste; the people about her, teachers and pupils, she held to be despicable, because they were foreigners. I bore with her abuse of the Friday's salt fish and hard eggs – with her invective against the soup, the bread, the coffee – with some patience for a time; but at last, wearied by iteration, I turned crusty, and put her to rights: a thing I ought to have done in the very beginning, for a salutary setting down always agreed with her.

Much longer had I to endure her demands on me in the way of work. Her wardrobe, so far as concerned articles of external wear, was well and elegantly supplied; but there were other habiliments not so carefully provided: what she had, needed frequent repair. She hated needle-drudgery herself, and she would bring her hose, etc. to me in heaps, to be mended. A compliance of some weeks threatening to result in the establishment of an intolerable bore – I at last distinctly told her she must make up her mind to mend her own garments. She cried on receiving this information, and accused me of having ceased to be her friend; but I held by my decision, and let the hysterics pass as they could.

Notwithstanding these foibles, and various others needless to mention – but by no means of a refined or elevating character – how pretty she was! How charming she looked, when she came down on a sunny Sunday morning, well-dressed and well-humoured, robed in pale lilac silk, and with her fair long curls reposing on her white shoulders. Sunday was a holiday which she always passed with friends resident in town; and amongst these friends she speedily gave me to understand was one who would fain become something more. By glimpses and hints it was shown me, and by the general buoyancy of her look and manner it was ere long proved, that ardent admiration – perhaps genuine love – was at her command. She called her suitor 'Isidore': this, however, she intimated was not his real name, but one by which it pleased her to baptize him – his own, she hinted, not being 'very pretty'. Once, when she had been bragging about the vehemence of 'Isidore's' attachment, I asked if she loved him in return.

"*Comme cela*," said she: "he is handsome, and he loves me to distraction, so that I am well amused. *Ca suffit.*"

Finding that she carried the thing on longer than, from her very fickle tastes, I had anticipated, I one day took it upon me to make serious inquiries as to whether the gentleman was such as her parents, and especially her uncle – on whom, it appeared, she was dependent – would be likely to approve. She allowed that this was very doubtful, as she did not believe 'Isidore' had much money.

"Do you encourage him?" I asked.

"*Furieusement* sometimes," said she.

"Without being certain that you will be permitted to marry him?"

"Oh, how dowdyish you are! I don't want to be married. I am too young."

"But if he loves you as much as you say, and yet it comes to nothing in the end, he will be made miserable."

"Of course he will break his heart. I should be shocked and disappointed if he didn't."

"I wonder whether this M. Isidore is a fool?" said I.

"He is, about me; but he is wise in other things, *à ce qu'on dit*. Mrs. Cholmondeley considers him extremely clever: she says he will push his way by his talents; all I know is, that he does little more than sigh in my presence, and that I can wind him round my little finger."

Wishing to get a more definite idea of this love-stricken M. Isidore; whose position seemed to me of the least secure, I requested her to favour me with a personal description; but she could not describe: she had neither words nor the power of putting them together so as to make graphic phrases. She even seemed not properly to have noticed him: nothing of his looks, of the changes in his countenance, had touched her heart or dwelt in her memory – that he was "*beau, mais plutôt bel homme que joli garçon*," was all she could assert. My patience would often have failed, and my interest flagged, in listening to her, but for one thing. All the hints she dropped, all the details she gave, went unconsciously to prove, to my thinking, that M. Isidore's homage was offered with great delicacy and respect. I informed her very plainly that I believed him much too good for her, and intimated with equal plainness my impression that she was but a vain coquette. She laughed, shook her curls from her eyes, and danced away as if I had paid her a compliment.

Miss Ginevra's school-studies were little better than nominal; there were but three things she practised in earnest, viz. music, singing, and dancing; also embroidering the fine cambric handkerchiefs which she could not afford to buy ready worked: such mere trifles as lessons in history, geography, grammar, and arithmetic, she left undone, or got others to do for her. Very much of her time was spent in visiting. Madame, aware that her stay at school was now limited to a certain period, which would not be extended whether she made progress or not, allowed her great licence in this particular. Mrs. Cholmondeley – her chaperon – a gay, fashionable lady, invited her whenever she had company at her own house, and sometimes took her to evening-parties at the houses of her acquaintance. Ginevra perfectly approved this mode of procedure: it had but one inconvenience; she was obliged to be well dressed, and she had not money to buy variety of dresses. All her thoughts turned on this difficulty; her whole soul was occupied with expedients for effecting its solution. It was wonderful to witness the activity of her otherwise indolent mind on this point, and to see the much-daring intrepidity to which she was spurred by a sense of necessity, and the wish to shine.

She begged boldly of Mrs. Cholmondeley – boldly, I say: not with an air of reluctant shame, but in this strain:

"My darling Mrs. C., I have nothing in the world fit to wear for your party next week; you *must* give me a book-muslin dress, and then a *ceinture bleu celeste*: *do* – there's an angel! Will you?"

The 'darling Mrs. C.' yielded at first; but finding that applications increased as they were complied with, she was soon obliged, like all Miss Fanshawe's friends, to oppose resistance to encroachment. After a while I heard no more of Mrs. Cholmondeley's presents; but still, visiting went on, and the absolutely necessary dresses continued to be supplied: also many little expensive etc. – gloves, bouquets, even trinkets. These things, contrary to her custom, and even nature – for she was not secretive – were most sedulously kept out of sight for a time; but one evening, when she was going to a large party for which particular care and elegance of costume were demanded, she could not resist coming to my chamber to show herself in all her splendour.

Beautiful she looked: so young, so fresh, and with a delicacy of skin and flexibility of shape altogether English, and not found in the list of continental female charms. Her dress was new, costly, and perfect. I saw at a glance that it lacked none of those finishing details which cost so much, and give to the general effect such an air of tasteful completeness.

I viewed her from top to toe. She turned airily round that I might survey her on all sides. Conscious of her charms, she was in her best humour: her rather small blue eyes sparkled gleefully. She was going to bestow on me a kiss, in her school-girl fashion of showing her delights but I said, "Steady! Let us be steady, and know what we are about, and find out the meaning of our magnificence" – and so put her off at arm's length, to undergo cooler inspection.

"Shall I do?" was her question.

"Do?" said I. "There are different ways of doing; and, by my word, I don't understand yours."

"But how do I look?"

"You look well dressed."

She thought the praise not warm enough, and proceeded to direct attention to the various decorative points of her attire. "Look at this *parure*," said she. "The brooch, the ear-rings, the bracelets: no one in the school has such a set – not Madame herself."

"I see them all." (Pause.) "Did M. de Bassompierre give you those jewels?"

"My uncle knows nothing about them."

"Were they presents from Mrs. Cholmondeley?"

"Not they, indeed. Mrs. Cholmondeley is a mean, stingy creature; she never gives me anything now."

I did not choose to ask any further questions, but turned abruptly away.

"Now, old Crusty – old Diogenes" (these were her familiar terms for me when we disagreed), "what is the matter now?"

"Take yourself away. I have no pleasure in looking at you or your *parure*."

For an instant, she seemed taken by surprise.

"What now, Mother Wisdom? I have not got into debt for it – that is, not for the jewels, nor the gloves, nor the bouquet. My dress is certainly not paid for, but uncle de Bassompierre will pay it in the bill: he never notices items, but just looks at the total; and he is so rich, one need not care about a few guineas more or less."

"Will you go? I want to shut the door…. Ginevra, people may tell you you are very handsome in that ball-attire; but, in *my* eyes, you will never look so pretty as you did in the gingham gown and plain straw bonnet you wore when I first saw you."

"Other people have not your puritanical tastes," was her angry reply. "And, besides, I see no right you have to sermonize me."

"Certainly! I have little right; and you, perhaps, have still less to come flourishing and fluttering into my chamber – a mere jay in borrowed plumes. I have not the least respect for your feathers, Miss Fanshawe; and especially the peacock's eyes you call a *parure*: very pretty things, if you had bought them with money which was your own, and which you could well spare, but not at all pretty under present circumstances."

"*On est là pour Mademoiselle Fanshawe!*" was announced by the portress, and away she tripped.

This semi-mystery of the *parure* was not solved till two or three days afterwards, when she came to make a voluntary confession.

"You need not be sulky with me," she began, "in the idea that I am running somebody, papa or M. de Bassompierre, deeply into debt. I assure you nothing remains unpaid for, but the few dresses I have lately had: all the rest is settled."

"There," I thought, "lies the mystery; considering that they were not given you by Mrs. Cholmondeley, and that your own means are limited to a few shillings, of which I know you to be excessively careful."

"*Ecoutez!*" she went on, drawing near and speaking in her most confidential and coaxing tone; for my 'sulkiness' was inconvenient to her: she liked me to be in a talking and listening mood, even if I only talked to chide and listened to rail. "*Ecoutez, chère grogneuse!* I will tell you all how and about it; and you will then see, not only how right the whole thing is, but how cleverly managed. In the first place, I *must* go out. Papa himself said that he wished me to see something of the world; he particularly remarked to Mrs. Cholmondeley, that, though I was a sweet creature enough, I had rather a bread-and-butter-eating, school-girl air; of which it was his special desire that I should get rid, by an introduction to society here, before I make my regular début in England. Well, then, if I go out, I *must* dress. Mrs. Cholmondeley is turned shabby, and will give nothing more; it would be too hard upon uncle to make him pay for *all* the things I need: *that* you can't deny – *that* agrees with your own preachments. Well, but *somebody* who heard me (quite by chance, I assure you) complaining to Mrs. Cholmondeley of my distressed circumstances, and what straits I was put to for an ornament or two – *somebody*, far from grudging one a present, was quite delighted at the idea of being permitted to offer some trifle. You should have seen what a *blanc-bec* he looked when he first spoke of it: how he hesitated and blushed, and positively trembled from fear of a repulse."

"That will do, Miss Fanshawe. I suppose I am to understand that M. Isidore is the benefactor: that it is from him you have accepted that costly *parure*; that he supplies your bouquets and your gloves?"

"You express yourself so disagreeably," said she, "one hardly knows how to answer; what I mean to say is, that I occasionally allow Isidore the pleasure and honour of expressing his homage by the offer of a trifle."

"It comes to the same thing.... Now, Ginevra, to speak the plain truth, I don't very well understand these matters; but I believe you are doing very wrong – seriously wrong. Perhaps, however, you now feel certain that you will be able to marry M. Isidore; your parents and uncle have given their consent, and, for your part, you love him entirely?"

"*Mais pas du tout!*" (she always had recourse to French when about to say something specially heartless and perverse). "*Je suis sa reine, mais il n'est pas mon roi.*"

"Excuse me, I must believe this language is mere nonsense and coquetry. There is nothing great about you, yet you are above profiting by the good nature and purse of a man to whom you feel absolute indifference. You love M. Isidore far more than you think, or will avow."

"No. I danced with a young officer the other night, whom I love a thousand times more than he. I often wonder why I feel so very cold to Isidore, for everybody says he is handsome, and other ladies admire him; but, somehow, he bores me: let me see now how it is...."

And she seemed to make an effort to reflect. In this I encouraged her.

"Yes!" I said, "Try to get a clear idea of the state of your mind. To me it seems in a great mess – chaotic as a rag-bag."

"It is something in this fashion," she cried out ere long: "the man is too romantic and devoted, and he expects something more of me than I find it convenient to be. He thinks I am perfect: furnished with all sorts of sterling qualities and solid virtues, such as I never had, nor intend to have. Now, one can't help, in his presence, rather trying to justify his good opinion; and it does so tire one to be goody, and to talk sense, – for he really thinks I am sensible. I am far more at my ease with you, old lady – you, you dear crosspatch – who take me at my lowest, and know me to be coquettish, and ignorant, and flirting, and fickle, and silly, and selfish, and all the other sweet things you and I have agreed to be a part of my character."

"This is all very well," I said, making a strenuous effort to preserve that gravity and severity which ran risk of being shaken by this whimsical candour, "but it does not alter that wretched business of the presents. Pack them up, Ginevra, like a good, honest girl, and send them back."

"Indeed, I won't," said she, stoutly.

"Then you are deceiving M. Isidore. It stands to reason that by accepting his presents you give him to understand he will one day receive an equivalent, in your regard..."

"But he won't," she interrupted: "he has his equivalent now, in the pleasure of seeing me wear them – quite enough for him: he is only bourgeois."

This phrase, in its senseless arrogance, quite cured me of the temporary weakness which had made me relax my tone and aspect. She rattled on:

"My present business is to enjoy youth, and not to think of fettering myself, by promise or vow, to this man or that. When first I saw Isidore, I believed he would help me to enjoy it I believed he would be content with my being a pretty girl; and that we should meet and part and flutter about like two butterflies, and be happy. Lo, and behold! I find him at times as grave as a judge, and deep-feeling and thoughtful. Bah! *Les penseurs, les hommes profonds et passionnés ne sont pas à mon goût. Le Colonel Alfred de Hamal suits me far better. Va pour les beaux fats et les jolis fripons! Vive les joies et les plaisirs! A bas les grandes passions et les sévères vertus!*"

She looked for an answer to this tirade. I gave none.

"*J'aime mon beau Colonel,*" she went on: "*je n'aimerai jamais son rival. Je ne serai jamais femme de bourgeois, moi!*"

I now signified that it was imperatively necessary my apartment should be relieved of the honour of her presence: she went away laughing.

Chapter Ten
Dr. John

MADAME BECK was a most consistent character; forbearing with all the world, and tender to no part of it. Her own children drew her into no deviation from the even tenor of her stoic calm. She was solicitous about her family, vigilant for their interests and physical well-being; but she never seemed to know the wish to take her little children upon her lap, to press their rosy lips with her own, to gather them in a genial embrace, to shower on them softly the benignant caress, the loving word.

I have watched her sometimes sitting in the garden, viewing the little bees afar off, as they walked in a distant alley with Trinette, their *bonne*; in her mien spoke care and prudence. I know she often pondered anxiously what she called 'leur avenir'; but if the youngest, a puny and delicate but engaging child, chancing to spy her, broke from its nurse, and toddling down the walk, came all eager and laughing and panting to clasp her knee, Madame would just calmly put out one hand, so as to prevent inconvenient concussion from the child's sudden onset: *"Prends garde, mon enfant!"* she would say unmoved, patiently permit it to stand near her a few moments, and then, without smile or kiss, or endearing syllable, rise and lead it back to Trinette.

Her demeanour to the eldest girl was equally characteristic in another way. This was a vicious child. *"Quelle peste que cette Désirée! Quel poison que cet enfant là!"* were the expressions dedicated to her, alike in kitchen and in schoolroom. Amongst her other endowments she boasted an exquisite skill in the art of provocation, sometimes driving her *bonne* and the servants almost wild. She would steal to their attics, open their drawers and boxes, wantonly tear their best caps and soil their best shawls; she would watch her opportunity to get at the buffet of the salle-à-manger, where she would smash articles of porcelain or glass – or to the cupboard of the storeroom, where she would plunder the preserves, drink the sweet wine, break jars and bottles, and so contrive as to throw the onus of suspicion on the cook and the kitchen-maid. All this when Madame saw, and of which when she received report, her sole observation, uttered with matchless serenity, was: *"Désirée a besoin d'une surveillance toute particulière."*

Accordingly she kept this promising olive-branch a good deal at her side. Never once, I believe, did she tell her faithfully of her faults, explain the evil of such habits, and show the results which must thence ensue. Surveillance must work the whole cure. It failed of course. Désirée was kept in some measure from the servants, but she teased and pillaged her mamma instead. Whatever belonging to Madame's work-table or toilet she could lay her hands on, she stole and hid. Madame saw all this, but she still pretended not to see: she had not rectitude of soul to confront the child with her vices. When an article disappeared whose value rendered restitution necessary, she would profess to think that Désirée had taken it away in play, and beg her to restore it. Désirée was not to be so cheated: she had learned to bring falsehood to the aid of theft, and would deny having touched the brooch, ring, or scissors. Carrying on the hollow system, the mother would calmly assume an air of belief, and afterwards ceaselessly watch and dog the child till she tracked her: to her hiding-places – some hole in the garden-wall – some chink or cranny in garret or out-house. This done, Madame would send Désirée out for a walk with her bonne, and profit by her absence to rob the robber. Désirée proved herself the true daughter of her astute parent, by never suffering either her countenance or manner to betray the least sign of mortification on discovering the loss.

The second child, Fifine, was said to be like its dead father. Certainly, though the mother had given it her healthy frame, her blue eye and ruddy cheek, not from her was derived its moral being. It was an honest, gleeful little soul: a passionate, warm-tempered, bustling creature it was too, and of the sort likely to blunder often into perils and difficulties. One day it bethought itself to fall from top to bottom of a steep flight of stone steps; and when Madame, hearing the noise (she always heard every noise), issued from the salle-à-manger and picked it up, she said quietly, – "*Cet enfant a un os cassé.*"

At first we hoped this was not the case. It was, however, but too true: one little plump arm hung powerless.

"Let Meess" (meaning me) "take her," said Madame; "*et qu'on aille tout de suite chercher un fiacre.*"

In a *fiacre* she promptly, but with admirable coolness and self-possession, departed to fetch a surgeon.

It appeared she did not find the family-surgeon at home; but that mattered not: she sought until she laid her hand on a substitute to her mind, and brought him back with her. Meantime I had cut the child's sleeve from its arm, undressed and put it to bed.

We none of us, I suppose (by *we* I mean the bonne, the cook, the portress, and myself, all which personages were now gathered in the small and heated chamber), looked very scrutinizingly at the new doctor when he came into the room. I, at least, was taken up with endeavouring to soothe Fifine; whose cries (for she had good lungs) were appalling to hear. These cries redoubled in intensity as the stranger approached her bed; when he took her up, "Let alone!" she cried passionately, in her broken English (for she spoke English as did the other children). "I will not you: I will Dr. Pillule!"

"And Dr. Pillule is my very good friend," was the answer, in perfect English; "but he is busy at a place three leagues off, and I am come in his stead. So now, when we get a little calmer, we must commence business; and we will soon have that unlucky little arm bandaged and in right order."

Hereupon he called for a glass of eau sucrée, fed her with some teaspoonfuls of the sweet liquid (Fifine was a frank gourmande; anybody could win her heart through her palate), promised her more when the operation should be over, and promptly went to work. Some assistance being needed, he demanded it of the cook, a robust, strong-armed woman; but she, the portress, and the nurse instantly fled. I did not like to touch that small, tortured limb, but thinking there was no alternative, my hand was already extended to do what was requisite. I was anticipated; Madame Beck had put out her own hand: hers was steady while mine trembled.

"*Ça vaudra mieux,*" said the doctor, turning from me to her.

He showed wisdom in his choice. Mine would have been feigned stoicism, forced fortitude. Hers was neither forced nor feigned.

"*Merci, Madame; très bien, fort bien!*" said the operator when he had finished. "*Voilà un sang-froid bien opportun, et qui vaut mille élans de sensibilité déplacée.*"

He was pleased with her firmness, she with his compliment. It was likely, too, that his whole general appearance, his voice, mien, and manner, wrought impressions in his favour. Indeed, when you looked well at him, and when a lamp was brought in – for it was evening and now waxing dusk – you saw that, unless Madame Beck had been less than woman, it could not well be otherwise. This young doctor (he *was* young) had no common aspect. His stature looked imposingly tall in that little chamber, and amidst that group of Dutch-made women; his profile was clear, fine and expressive: perhaps his eye glanced from face to face rather too vividly, too quickly, and too often; but it had a most pleasant character, and so had his mouth; his chin was full, cleft, Grecian, and perfect. As to his smile, one could not in a hurry make up one's mind as to the descriptive epithet it merited; there was something in it that pleased, but something too that brought surging up into the mind all one's foibles and weak points: all that could lay one open to a laugh. Yet Fifine liked this doubtful smile, and thought the owner genial: much as he had hurt her, she held out her hand to bid him a friendly goodnight. He patted the little hand kindly, and then he and Madame went downstairs together; she talking in her highest tide of spirits and volubility, he listening with an air of good-natured amenity, dashed with that unconscious roguish archness I find it difficult to describe.

I noticed that though he spoke French well, he spoke English better; he had, too, an English complexion, eyes, and form. I noticed more. As he passed me in leaving the room, turning his face in my direction one moment – not to address me, but to speak to Madame, yet so standing, that I almost necessarily looked up at him – a recollection which had been struggling to form in my memory, since the first moment I heard his voice, started up perfected. This was the very gentleman to whom I had spoken at the bureau; who had helped me in the matter of the trunk; who had been my guide through the dark, wet park. Listening, as he passed down the long vestibule out into the street, I recognised his very tread: it was the same firm and equal stride I had followed under the dripping trees.

* * *

It was to be concluded that this young surgeon-physician's first visit to the Rue Fossette would be the last. The respectable Dr. Pillule being expected home the next day, there appeared no reason why his temporary substitute should again represent him; but the Fates had written their decree to the contrary.

Dr. Pillule had been summoned to see a rich old hypochondriac at the antique university town of Bouquin-Moisi, and upon his prescribing change of air and travel as remedies, he was retained to accompany the timid patient on a tour of some weeks; it but remained, therefore, for the new doctor to continue his attendance at the Rue Fossette.

I often saw him when he came; for Madame would not trust the little invalid to Trinette, but required me to spend much of my time in the nursery. I think he was skilful. Fifine recovered rapidly under his care, yet even her convalescence did not hasten his dismissal. Destiny and Madame Beck seemed in league, and both had ruled that he should make deliberate acquaintance with the vestibule, the private staircase and upper chambers of the Rue Fossette.

No sooner did Fifine emerge from his hands than Désirée declared herself ill. That possessed child had a genius for simulation, and captivated by the attentions and indulgences of a sick-room, she came to the conclusion that an illness would perfectly accommodate her tastes, and took her bed accordingly. She acted well, and her mother still better; for while the whole case was transparent to Madame Beck as the day, she treated it with an astonishingly well-assured air of gravity and good faith.

What surprised me was that Dr. John (so the young Englishman had taught Fifine to call him, and we all took from her the habit of addressing him by this name, till it became an established custom, and he was known by no other in the Rue Fossette) – that Dr. John consented tacitly to adopt Madame's tactics, and to fall in with her manoeuvres. He betrayed, indeed, a period of comic doubt, cast one or two rapid glances from the child to the mother, indulged in an interval of self-consultation, but finally resigned himself with a good grace to play his part in the farce. Désirée ate like a raven, gambolled day and night in her bed, pitched tents with the sheets and blankets, lounged like a Turk amidst pillows and bolsters, diverted herself with throwing her shoes at her bonne and grimacing at her sisters – over-flowed, in short, with unmerited health and evil spirits; only languishing when her mamma and the physician paid their diurnal visit. Madame Beck, I knew, was glad, at any price, to have her daughter in bed out of the way of mischief; but I wondered that Dr. John did not tire of the business.

Every day, on this mere pretext of a motive, he gave punctual attendance; Madame always received him with the same empressement, the same sunshine for himself, the same admirably counterfeited air of concern for her child. Dr. John wrote harmless prescriptions for the patient, and viewed her mother with a shrewdly sparkling eye. Madame caught his rallying looks without resenting them – she had too much good sense for that. Supple as the young doctor seemed, one could not despise him – this pliant part was evidently not adopted in the design to curry favour with his employer: while he liked his office at the pensionnat, and lingered strangely about the Rue Fossette, he was independent, almost careless in his carriage there; and yet, too, he was often thoughtful and preoccupied.

It was not perhaps my business to observe the mystery of his bearing, or search out its origin or aim; but, placed as I was, I could hardly help it. He laid himself open to my observation, according to my presence in the room just that degree of notice and consequence a person of my exterior habitually expects: that is to say, about what is given to unobtrusive articles of furniture, chairs of ordinary joiner's work, and carpets of no striking pattern. Often, while waiting for Madame, he would muse, smile, watch, or listen like a man who thinks himself alone. I, meantime, was free to puzzle over his countenance and movements, and wonder what could be the meaning of that peculiar interest and attachment – all mixed up with doubt and strangeness, and inexplicably ruled by some presiding spell – which wedded him to this demi-convent, secluded in the built-up core of a capital. He, I believe, never remembered that I had eyes in my head, much less a brain behind them.

Nor would he ever have found this out, but that one day, while he sat in the sunshine and I was observing the colouring of his hair, whiskers, and complexion – the whole being of such a tone as a strong light brings out with somewhat perilous force (indeed I recollect I was driven to compare his beamy head in my thoughts to that of the 'golden image' which Nebuchadnezzar the king had set up), an idea new, sudden, and startling, riveted my attention with an over-mastering strength and power of attraction. I know not to this day how I looked at him: the force of surprise, and also of conviction, made me forget myself; and I only recovered wonted consciousness when I saw that his notice was arrested, and that it had caught my movement in a clear little oval mirror fixed in the side of the window recess – by the aid of which reflector Madame often secretly spied persons walking in the garden below. Though of so gay and sanguine a temperament, he was not without a certain nervous sensitiveness which made him ill at ease under a direct, inquiring gaze. On surprising me thus, he turned and said, in a tone which, though courteous, had just so much dryness in it as to mark a shade of annoyance, as well as to give to what was said the character of rebuke, "Mademoiselle does not spare me: I am not vain enough to fancy that it is my merits which attract her attention; it must then be some defect. Dare I ask – what?"

I was confounded, as the reader may suppose, yet not with an irrecoverable confusion; being conscious that it was from no emotion of incautious admiration, nor yet in a spirit of unjustifiable inquisitiveness, that I had incurred this reproof. I might have cleared myself on the spot, but would not. I did not speak. I was not in the habit of speaking to him. Suffering him, then, to think what he chose and accuse me of what he would, I resumed some work I had dropped, and kept my head bent over it during the remainder of his stay. There is a perverse mood of the mind which is rather soothed than irritated by misconstruction; and in quarters where we can never be rightly known, we take pleasure, I think, in being consummately ignored. What honest man, on being casually taken for a housebreaker, does not feel rather tickled than vexed at the mistake?

Chapter Eleven
The Portress's Cabinet

IT WAS SUMMER and very hot. Georgette, the youngest of Madame Beck's children, took a fever. Désirée, suddenly cured of her ailments, was, together with Fifine, packed off to Bonne-Maman, in the country, by way of precaution against infection. Medical aid was now really needed, and Madame, choosing to ignore the return of Dr. Pillule, who had been at home a week, conjured his English rival to continue his visits. One or two of the pensionnaires complained of headache, and in other respects seemed slightly to participate in Georgette's ailment. "Now, at last," I thought, "Dr. Pillule must be recalled: the prudent directress will never venture to permit the attendance of so young a man on the pupils."

The directress was very prudent, but she could also be intrepidly venturous. She actually introduced Dr. John to the school-division of the premises, and established him in attendance on the proud and handsome Blanche de Melcy, and the vain, flirting Angélique, her friend. Dr. John, I thought, testified a certain gratification at this mark of confidence; and if discretion of bearing could have justified the step, it would by him have been amply justified. Here, however, in this land of convents and confessionals, such a presence as his was not to be suffered with impunity in a 'pensionnat de demoiselles'. The school gossiped, the kitchen whispered, the town caught the rumour, parents wrote letters and paid visits of remonstrance. Madame, had she been weak, would now have been lost: a dozen rival educational houses were ready to improve this false step – if false step it were – to her ruin; but Madame was not weak, and little Jesuit though she might be, yet I clapped the hands of my heart, and with its voice cried "brava!" as I watched her able bearing, her skilled management, her temper and her firmness on this occasion.

She met the alarmed parents with a good-humoured, easy grace for nobody matched her in, I know not whether to say the possession or the assumption of a certain '*rondeur et franchise de bonne femme*'; which on various occasions gained the point aimed at with instant and complete success, where severe gravity and serious reasoning would probably have failed.

"*Ce pauvre Docteur Jean!*" she would say, chuckling and rubbing joyously her fat little white hands; "*Ce cher jeune homme! Le meilleur créature du monde!*" and go on to explain how she happened to be employing him for her own children, who were so fond of him they would scream themselves into fits at the thought of another doctor; how, where she had confidence for her own, she thought it natural to repose trust for others, and *au reste*, it was only the most temporary expedient in the world; Blanche and Angélique had the migraine; Dr. John had written a prescription; *voilà tout!*

The parents' mouths were closed. Blanche and Angélique saved her all remaining trouble by chanting loud duets in their physician's praise; the other pupils echoed them, unanimously declaring that when they were ill they would have Dr. John and nobody else; and Madame laughed, and the parents laughed too. The Labassecouriens must have a large organ of philoprogenitiveness: at least the indulgence of offspring is carried by them to excessive lengths; the law of most households being the children's will. Madame now got credit for having acted on this occasion in a spirit of motherly partiality: she came off with flying colours; people liked her as a directress better than ever.

To this day I never fully understood why she thus risked her interest for the sake of Dr. John. What people said, of course I know well: the whole house – pupils, teachers, servants included – affirmed that she was going to marry him. So they had settled it; difference of age seemed to make no obstacle in their eyes: it was to be so.

It must be admitted that appearances did not wholly discountenance this idea; Madame seemed so bent on retaining his services, so oblivious of her former protégé, Pillule. She made, too, such a point of personally receiving his visits, and was so unfailingly cheerful, blithe, and benignant in her manner to him. Moreover, she paid, about this time, marked attention to dress: the morning dishabille, the nightcap and shawl, were discarded; Dr. John's early visits always found her with auburn braids all nicely arranged, silk dress trimly fitted on, neat laced brodequins in lieu of slippers: in short the whole toilette complete as a model, and fresh as a flower. I scarcely think, however, that her intention in this went further than just to show a very handsome man that she was not quite a plain woman; and plain she was not. Without beauty of feature or elegance of form, she pleased. Without youth and its gay graces, she cheered. One never tired of seeing her: she was never monotonous, or insipid, or colourless, or flat. Her unfaded hair, her eye with its temperate blue light, her cheek with its wholesome fruit-like bloom – these things pleased in moderation, but with constancy.

Had she, indeed, floating visions of adopting Dr. John as a husband, taking him to her well-furnished home, endowing him with her savings, which were said to amount to a moderate competency, and making him comfortable for the rest of his life? Did Dr. John suspect her of such visions? I have met him coming out of her presence with a mischievous half-smile about his lips, and in his eyes a look as of masculine vanity elate and tickled. With all his good looks and good-nature, he was not perfect; he must have been very imperfect if he roguishly encouraged aims he never intended to be successful. But did he not intend them to be successful? People said he had no money, that he was wholly dependent upon his profession. Madame – though perhaps some fourteen years his senior – was yet the sort of woman never to grow old, never to wither, never to break down. They certainly were on good terms. *He* perhaps was not in love; but how many people ever *do* love, or at least marry for love, in this world. We waited the end.

For what *he* waited, I do not know, nor for what he watched; but the peculiarity of his manner, his expectant, vigilant, absorbed, eager look, never wore off: it rather intensified. He had never been quite within the compass of my penetration, and I think he ranged farther and farther beyond it.

One morning little Georgette had been more feverish and consequently more peevish; she was crying, and would not be pacified. I thought a particular draught ordered, disagreed with her, and I doubted whether it ought to be continued; I waited impatiently for the doctor's coming in order to consult him.

The door-bell rang, he was admitted; I felt sure of this, for I heard his voice addressing the portress. It was his custom to mount straight to the nursery, taking about three degrees of the staircase at once, and coming upon us like a cheerful surprise. Five minutes elapsed – ten – and I saw and heard nothing of him. What could he be doing? Possibly waiting in the corridor below. Little Georgette still piped her plaintive wail, appealing to me by her familiar term, "Minnie, Minnie, me very poorly!" till my heart ached. I descended to ascertain why he did not come. The corridor was empty. Whither was he vanished? Was he with Madame in the salle-à-manger? Impossible: I had left her but a short time since, dressing in her own chamber. I listened. Three pupils were just then hard at work practising in three proximate rooms – the dining-room and the greater and lesser drawing-rooms, between which and the corridor there was but the portress's cabinet communicating with the salons, and intended originally for a boudoir. Farther off, at a fourth instrument in the oratory, a whole class of a dozen or more were taking a singing lesson, and just then joining in a 'barcarole' (I think they called it), whereof I yet remember these words 'fraîchë', 'brisë', and 'Venisë'. Under these circumstances, what could I hear? A great deal, certainly; had it only been to the purpose.

Yes; I heard a giddy treble laugh in the above-mentioned little cabinet, close by the door of which I stood – that door half-unclosed; a man's voice in a soft, deep, pleading tone, uttered some words, whereof I only caught the adjuration, "For God's sake!" Then, after a second's pause, forth issued Dr. John, his eye full shining, but not with either joy or triumph; his fair English cheek high-coloured; a baffled, tortured, anxious, and yet a tender meaning on his brow.

The open door served me as a screen; but had I been full in his way, I believe he would have passed without seeing me. Some mortification, some strong vexation had hold of his soul: or rather, to write my impressions now as I received them at the time I should say some sorrow, some sense of injustice. I did not so much think his pride was hurt, as that his affections had been wounded – cruelly wounded, it seemed to me. But who was the torturer? What being in that house had him so much in her power? Madame I believed to be in her chamber; the room whence he had stepped was dedicated to the portress's sole use; and she, Rosine Matou, an unprincipled though pretty little French grisette, airy, fickle, dressy, vain, and mercenary – it was not, surely, to *her* hand he owed the ordeal through which he seemed to have passed?

But while I pondered, her voice, clear, though somewhat sharp, broke out in a lightsome French song, trilling through the door still ajar: I glanced in, doubting my senses. There at the table she sat in a smart dress of 'jaconas rose', trimming a tiny blond cap: not a living thing save herself was in the room, except indeed some gold fish in a glass globe, some flowers in pots, and a broad July sunbeam.

Here was a problem: but I must go upstairs to ask about the medicine.

Dr. John sat in a chair at Georgette's bedside; Madame stood before him; the little patient had been examined and soothed, and now lay composed in her crib. Madame Beck, as I entered, was discussing the physician's own health, remarking on some real or fancied change in his looks, charging him with over-work, and recommending rest and change of air. He listened good-naturedly, but with laughing indifference, telling her that she was '*trop bonne*', and that he felt perfectly well. Madame appealed to me – Dr. John following her movement with a slow glance which seemed to express languid surprise at reference being made to a quarter so insignificant.

"What do you think, Miss Lucie?" asked Madame. "Is he not paler and thinner?"

It was very seldom that I uttered more than monosyllables in Dr. John's presence; he was the kind of person with whom I was likely ever to remain the neutral, passive thing he thought me. Now, however, I took licence to answer in a phrase: and a phrase I purposely made quite significant.

"He looks ill at this moment; but perhaps it is owing to some temporary cause: Dr. John may have been vexed or harassed." I cannot tell how he took this speech, as I never sought his face for information. Georgette here began to ask me in her broken English if she might have a glass of *eau sucrée*. I answered her in English. For the first time, I fancy, he noticed that I spoke his language; hitherto he had always taken me for a foreigner, addressing me as 'Mademoiselle', and giving in French the requisite directions about the children's treatment. He seemed on the point of making a remark; but thinking better of it, held his tongue.

Madame recommenced advising him; he shook his head, laughing, rose and bid her good morning, with courtesy, but still with the regardless air of one whom too much unsolicited attention was surfeiting and spoiling.

When he was gone, Madame dropped into the chair he had just left; she rested her chin in her hand; all that was animated and amiable vanished from her face: she looked stony and stern, almost mortified and morose. She sighed; a single, but a deep sigh. A loud bell rang for morning-school. She got up; as she passed a dressing-table with a glass upon it, she looked at her reflected image. One single white hair streaked her nut-brown tresses; she plucked it out with a shudder. In the full summer daylight, her face, though it still had the colour, could plainly be seen to have lost the texture of youth; and then, where were youth's contours? Ah, Madame! Wise as you were, even *you* knew weakness. Never had I pitied Madame before, but my heart softened towards her, when she turned darkly from the glass. A calamity had come upon her. That hag Disappointment was greeting her with a grisly 'All-hail', and her soul rejected the intimacy.

But Rosine! My bewilderment there surpasses description. I embraced five opportunities of passing her cabinet that day, with a view to contemplating her charms, and finding out the secret of their influence. She was pretty, young, and wore a well-made dress. All very good points, and, I suppose, amply sufficient to account, in any philosophic mind, for any amount of agony and distraction in a young man, like Dr. John. Still, I could not help forming half a wish that the said doctor were my brother; or at least that he had a sister or a mother who would kindly sermonize him. I say *half* a wish; I broke it, and flung it away before it became a whole one, discovering in good time its exquisite folly. "Somebody," I argued, "might as well sermonize Madame about her young physician: and what good would that do?"

I believe Madame sermonized herself. She did not behave weakly, or make herself in any shape ridiculous. It is true she had neither strong feelings to overcome, nor tender feelings by which to be miserably pained. It is true likewise that she had an important avocation, a real business to fill her time, divert her thoughts, and divide her interest. It is especially true that she possessed a genuine good sense which is not given to all women nor to all men; and by dint of these combined advantages she behaved wisely – she behaved well. Brava! Once more, Madame Beck. I saw you matched against an Apollyon of a predilection; you fought a good fight, and you overcame!

Chapter Twelve
The Casket

BEHIND THE HOUSE at the Rue Fossette there was a garden – large, considering that it lay in the heart of a city, and to my recollection at this day it seems pleasant: but time, like distance, lends to certain scenes an influence so softening; and where all is stone around, blank wall and hot pavement, how precious seems one shrub, how lovely an enclosed and planted spot of ground!

There went a tradition that Madame Beck's house had in old days been a convent. That in years gone by – how long gone by I cannot tell, but I think some centuries – before the city had over-spread this quarter, and when it was tilled ground and avenue, and such deep and leafy seclusion as ought to embosom a religious house – that something had happened on this site which, rousing fear and inflicting horror, had left to the place the inheritance of a ghost-story. A vague tale went of a black and white nun, sometimes, on some night or nights of the year, seen in some part of this vicinage. The ghost must have been built out some ages ago, for there were houses all round now; but certain convent-relics, in the shape of old and huge fruit-trees, yet consecrated the spot; and, at the foot of one – a Methuselah of a pear-tree, dead, all but a few boughs which still faithfully renewed their perfumed snow in spring, and their honey-sweet pendants in autumn – you saw, in scraping away the mossy earth between the half-bared roots, a glimpse of slab, smooth, hard, and black. The legend went, unconfirmed and unaccredited, but still propagated, that this was the portal of a vault, imprisoning deep beneath that ground, on whose surface grass grew and flowers bloomed, the bones of a girl whom a monkish conclave of the drear middle ages had here buried alive for some sin against her vow. Her shadow it was that tremblers had feared, through long generations after her poor frame was dust; her black robe and white veil that, for timid eyes, moonlight and shade had mocked, as they fluctuated in the night-wind through the garden-thicket.

Independently of romantic rubbish, however, that old garden had its charms. On summer mornings I used to rise early, to enjoy them alone; on summer evenings, to linger solitary, to keep tryst with the rising moon, or taste one kiss of the evening breeze, or fancy rather than feel the freshness of dew descending. The turf was verdant, the gravelled walks were white; sun-bright nasturtiums clustered beautiful about the roots of the doddered orchard giants. There was a large berceau, above which spread the shade of an acacia; there was a smaller, more sequestered bower, nestled in the vines which ran all along a high and grey wall, and gathered their tendrils in a knot of beauty, and hung their clusters in loving profusion about the favoured spot where jasmine and ivy met and married them.

Doubtless at high noon, in the broad, vulgar middle of the day, when Madame Beck's large school turned out rampant, and externes and pensionnaires were spread abroad, vying with the denizens of the boys' college close at hand, in the brazen exercise of their lungs and limbs – doubtless *then* the garden was a trite, trodden-down place enough. But at sunset or the hour of *salut*, when the externes were gone home, and the boarders quiet at their studies; pleasant was it then to stray down the peaceful alleys, and hear the bells of St. Jean Baptiste peal out with their sweet, soft, exalted sound.

I was walking thus one evening, and had been detained farther within the verge of twilight than usual, by the still-deepening calm, the mellow coolness, the fragrant breathing with which flowers no sunshine could win now answered the persuasion of the dew. I saw by a light in the oratory window that the Catholic household were then gathered to evening prayer – a rite, from attendance on which, I now and then, as a Protestant, exempted myself.

"One moment longer," whispered solitude and the summer moon, "stay with us: all is truly quiet now; for another quarter of an hour your presence will not be missed: the day's heat and bustle have tired you; enjoy these precious minutes."

The windowless backs of houses built in this garden, and in particular the whole of one side, was skirted by the rear of a long line of premises – being the boarding-houses of the neighbouring college. This rear, however, was all blank stone, with the exception of certain attic loopholes high up, opening from the sleeping-rooms of the women-servants, and also one casement in a lower story said to mark the chamber or study of a master. But, though thus secure, an alley, which ran parallel with the very high wall on that side the garden, was forbidden to be entered by the pupils. It was called indeed 'l'allée défendue', and any girl setting foot there would have rendered herself liable to as severe a penalty as the mild rules of Madame Beck's establishment permitted. Teachers might indeed go there with impunity; but as the walk was narrow, and the neglected shrubs were grown very thick and close on each side, weaving overhead a roof of branch and leaf which the sun's rays penetrated but in rare chequers, this alley was seldom entered even during day, and after dusk was carefully shunned.

From the first I was tempted to make an exception to this rule of avoidance: the seclusion, the very gloom of the walk attracted me. For a long time the fear of seeming singular scared me away; but by degrees, as people became accustomed to me and my habits, and to such shades of peculiarity as were engrained in my nature – shades, certainly not striking enough to interest, and perhaps not prominent enough to offend, but born in and with me, and no more to be parted with than my identity – by slow degrees I became a frequenter of this strait and narrow path. I made myself gardener of some tintless flowers that grew between its closely-ranked shrubs; I cleared away the relics of past autumns, choking up a rustic seat at the far end. Borrowing of Goton, the cuisinière, a pail of water and a scrubbing-brush, I made this seat clean. Madame saw me at work and smiled approbation: whether sincerely or not I don't know; but she *seemed* sincere.

"*Voyez-vous*," cried she, "*comme elle est propre, cette demoiselle Lucie? Vous aimez donc cette allée*, Meess?"

"Yes," I said, "it is quiet and shady."

"*C'est juste*," cried she with an air of *bonté*; and she kindly recommended me to confine myself to it as much as I chose, saying, that as I was not charged with the surveillance, I need not trouble myself to walk with the pupils: only I might permit her children to come there, to talk English with me.

On the night in question, I was sitting on the hidden seat reclaimed from fungi and mould, listening to what seemed the far-off sounds of the city. Far off, in truth, they were not: this school was in the city's centre; hence, it was but five minutes' walk to the park, scarce ten to buildings of palatial splendour. Quite near were wide streets brightly lit, teeming at this moment with life: carriages were rolling through them to balls or to the opera. The same hour which tolled curfew for our convent, which extinguished each lamp, and dropped the curtain round each couch, rang for the gay city about us the summons to festal enjoyment. Of this contrast I thought not, however: gay instincts my nature had few; ball or opera I had never seen; and though often I had heard them described, and even wished to see them, it was not the wish of one who hopes to partake a pleasure if she could only reach it – who feels fitted to shine in some bright distant sphere, could she but thither win her way; it was no yearning to attain, no hunger to taste; only the calm desire to look on a new thing.

A moon was in the sky, not a full moon, but a young crescent. I saw her through a space in the boughs overhead. She and the stars, visible beside her, were no strangers where all else was strange: my childhood knew them. I had seen that golden sign with the dark globe in its curve leaning back on azure, beside an old thorn at the top of an old field, in Old England, in long past days, just as it now leaned back beside a stately spire in this continental capital.

Oh, my childhood! I had feelings: passive as I lived, little as I spoke, cold as I looked, when I thought of past days, I *could* feel. About the present, it was better to be stoical; about the future – such a future as mine – to be dead. And in catalepsy and a dead trance, I studiously held the quick of my nature.

At that time, I well remember whatever could excite – certain accidents of the weather, for instance, were almost dreaded by me, because they woke the being I was always lulling, and stirred up a craving cry I could not satisfy. One night a thunder-storm broke; a sort of hurricane shook us in our beds: the Catholics rose in panic and prayed to their saints. As for me, the tempest took hold of me with tyranny: I was roughly roused and obliged to live. I got up and dressed myself, and creeping outside the casement close by my bed, sat on its ledge, with my feet on the roof of a lower adjoining building. It was wet, it was wild, it was pitch-dark. Within the dormitory they gathered round the night-lamp in consternation, praying loud. I could not go in: too resistless was the delight of staying with the wild hour, black and full of thunder, pealing out such an ode as language never delivered to man – too terribly glorious, the spectacle of clouds, split and pierced by white and blinding bolts.

I did long, achingly, then and for four and twenty hours afterwards, for something to fetch me out of my present existence, and lead me upwards and onwards. This longing, and all of a similar kind, it was necessary to knock on the head; which I did, figuratively, after the manner of Jael to Sisera, driving a nail through their temples. Unlike Sisera, they did not die: they were but transiently stunned, and at intervals would turn on the nail with a rebellious wrench: then did the temples bleed, and the brain thrill to its core.

Tonight, I was not so mutinous, nor so miserable. My Sisera lay quiet in the tent, slumbering; and if his pain ached through his slumbers, something like an angel – the ideal – knelt near, dropping balm on the soothed temples, holding before the sealed eyes a magic glass, of which the sweet, solemn visions were repeated in dreams, and shedding a reflex from her moonlight wings and robe over the transfixed sleeper, over the tent threshold, over all the landscape lying without. Jael, the stern woman; sat apart, relenting somewhat over her captive; but more prone to dwell on the faithful expectation of Heber coming home. By which words I mean that the cool peace and dewy sweetness of the night filled me with a mood of hope: not hope on any definite point, but a general sense of encouragement and heart-ease.

Should not such a mood, so sweet, so tranquil, so unwonted, have been the harbinger of good? Alas, no good came of it! Presently the rude Real burst coarsely in – all evil grovelling and repellent as she too often is.

Amid the intense stillness of that pile of stone overlooking the walk, the trees, the high wall, I heard a sound; a casement [all the windows here are casements, opening on hinges] creaked. Ere I had time to look up and mark where, in which story, or by whom unclosed, a tree overhead shook, as if struck by a missile; some object dropped prone at my feet.

Nine was striking by St. Jean Baptiste's clock; day was fading, but it was not dark: the crescent moon aided little, but the deep gilding of that point in heaven where the sun beamed last, and the crystalline clearness of a wide space above, sustained the summer twilight; even in my dark walk I could, by approaching an opening, have managed to read print of a small type. Easy was it to see then that the missile was a box, a small box of white and coloured ivory; its loose lid opened in my hand; violets lay within, violets smothering a closely folded bit of pink paper, a note, superscribed, *'Pour la robe grise'*. I wore indeed a dress of French grey.

Good. Was this a billet-doux? A thing I had heard of, but hitherto had not had the honour of seeing or handling. Was it this sort of commodity I held between my finger and thumb at this moment?

Scarcely: I did not dream it for a moment. Suitor or admirer my very thoughts had not conceived. All the teachers had dreams of some lover; one (but she was naturally of a credulous turn) believed in a future husband. All the pupils above fourteen knew of some prospective bridegroom; two or three were already affianced by their parents, and had been so from childhood: but into the realm of feelings and hopes which such prospects open, my speculations, far less my presumptions, had never once had warrant to intrude. If the other teachers went into town, or took a walk on the boulevards, or only attended mass, they were very certain (according to the accounts brought back) to meet with some individual of the 'opposite sex', whose rapt, earnest gaze assured them of their power to strike and to attract. I can't say that my experience tallied with theirs, in this respect. I went to church and I took walks, and am very well convinced that nobody minded me. There was not a girl or woman in the Rue Fossette who could not, and did not testify to having received an admiring beam from our young doctor's blue eyes at one time or other. I am obliged, however humbling it may sound, to except myself: as far as I was concerned, those blue eyes were guiltless, and calm as the sky, to whose tint theirs seemed akin. So it came to pass that I heard the others talk, wondered often at their gaiety, security, and self-satisfaction, but did not trouble myself to look up and gaze along the path they seemed so certain of treading. This then was no billet-doux; and it was in settled conviction to the contrary that I quietly opened it. Thus it ran – I translate:

> *Angel of my dreams! A thousand, thousand thanks for the promise kept: scarcely did I venture to hope its fulfilment. I believed you, indeed, to be half in jest; and then you seemed to think the enterprise beset with such danger – the hour so untimely, the alley so strictly secluded – often, you said, haunted by that dragon, the English teacher –* 'une véritable bégueule Britannique à ce que vous dites – espèce de monstre, brusque et rude comme un vieux caporal de grenadiers, et revêche comme une religieuse' *(the reader will excuse my modesty in allowing this flattering sketch of my amiable self to retain the slight veil of the original tongue). You are aware,* went on this precious effusion, *that little Gustave, on account of his illness, has been removed to a master's chamber – that favoured chamber, whose lattice overlooks your prison-ground. There, I, the best uncle in the world, am admitted to visit him. How tremblingly I approached the window and glanced into your Eden – an Eden for me, though a desert for you! – how I feared to behold vacancy, or the dragon aforesaid! How my heart palpitated with delight when, through apertures in the envious boughs, I at once caught the gleam of your graceful straw-hat, and the waving of your grey dress – dress that I should recognise amongst a thousand. But why, my angel, will you not look up? Cruel, to deny me one ray of those adorable eyes! – How a single glance would have revived me! I write this in fiery haste; while the physician examines Gustave, I snatch an opportunity to enclose it in a small casket, together with a bouquet of flowers, the sweetest that blow – yet less sweet than thee, my Peri – my all-charming!*
>
> *Ever thine – thou well knowest whom!*

"I wish I did know whom," was my comment; and the wish bore even closer reference to the person addressed in this choice document, than to the writer thereof. Perhaps it was from the fiancé of one of the engaged pupils; and, in that case, there was no great harm done or intended – only a small irregularity. Several of the girls, the majority, indeed, had brothers or cousins at the neighbouring college. But 'la robe grise, le chapeau de paille,' here surely was a clue – a very confusing one. The straw-hat was an ordinary garden head-screen, common to a score besides myself. The grey dress hardly gave more definite indication. Madame Beck herself ordinarily wore a grey dress just now; another teacher, and three of the pensionnaires, had had grey dresses purchased of the same shade and fabric as mine: it was a sort of every-day wear which happened at that time to be in vogue.

Meanwhile, as I pondered, I knew I must go in. Lights, moving in the dormitory, announced that prayers were over, and the pupils going to bed. Another half-hour and all doors would be locked – all lights extinguished. The front door yet stood open, to admit into the heated house the coolness of the summer night; from the portress's cabinet close by shone a lamp, showing the long vestibule with the two-leaved drawing-room doors on one side, the great street-door closing the vista.

All at once, quick rang the bell – quick, but not loud – a cautious tinkle – a sort of warning metal whisper. Rosine darted from her cabinet and ran to open. The person she admitted stood with her two minutes in parley: there seemed a demur, a delay. Rosine came to the garden door, lamp in hand; she stood on the steps, lifting her lamp, looking round vaguely.

"*Quel conte!*" she cried, with a coquettish laugh. "*Personne n'y a été.*"

"Let me pass," pleaded a voice I knew: "I ask but five minutes;" and a familiar shape, tall and grand (as we of the Rue Fossette all thought it), issued from the house, and strode down amongst the beds and walks. It was sacrilege – the intrusion of a man into that spot, at that hour; but he knew himself privileged, and perhaps he trusted to the friendly night. He wandered down the alleys, looking on this side and on that – he was lost in the shrubs, trampling flowers and breaking branches in his search – he penetrated at last the 'forbidden walk'. There I met him, like some ghost, I suppose.

"Dr. John! It is found."

He did not ask by whom, for with his quick eye he perceived that I held it in my hand.

"Do not betray her," he said, looking at me as if I were indeed a dragon.

"Were I ever so disposed to treachery, I cannot betray what I do not know," was my answer. "Read the note, and you will see how little it reveals."

"Perhaps you have read it," I thought to myself; and yet I could not believe he wrote it: that could hardly be his style: besides, I was fool enough to think there would be a degree of hardship in his calling me such names. His own look vindicated him; he grew hot, and coloured as he read.

"This is indeed too much: this is cruel, this is humiliating," were the words that fell from him.

I thought it *was* cruel, when I saw his countenance so moved. No matter whether he was to blame or not; somebody, it seemed to me, must be more to blame.

"What shall you do about it?" he inquired of me. "Shall you tell Madame Beck what you have found, and cause a stir – an esclandre?"

I thought I ought to tell, and said so; adding that I did not believe there would be either stir or esclandre: Madame was much too prudent to make a noise about an affair of that sort connected with her establishment.

He stood looking down and meditating. He was both too proud and too honourable to entreat my secrecy on a point which duty evidently commanded me to communicate. I wished to do right, yet loathed to grieve or injure him. Just then Rosine glanced out through the open door; she could not see us, though between the trees I could plainly see her: her dress was grey, like mine. This circumstance, taken in connection with prior transactions, suggested to me that perhaps the case, however deplorable, was one in which I was under no obligation whatever to concern myself. Accordingly, I said, – "If you can assure me that none of Madame Beck's pupils are implicated in this business, I shall be very happy to stand aloof from all interference. Take the casket, the bouquet, and the billet; for my part, I gladly forget the whole affair."

"Look there!" he whispered suddenly, as his hand closed on what I offered, and at the same time he pointed through the boughs.

I looked. Behold Madame, in shawl, wrapping-gown, and slippers, softly descending the steps, and stealing like a cat round the garden: in two minutes she would have been upon Dr. John. If *she* were like a cat, however, *he*, quite as much, resembled a leopard: nothing could be lighter than his tread when he chose. He watched, and as she turned a corner, he took the garden at two noiseless bounds. She reappeared, and he was gone. Rosine helped him, instantly interposing the door between him and his huntress. I, too, might have got away, but I preferred to meet Madame openly.

Though it was my frequent and well-known custom to spend twilight in the garden, yet, never till now, had I remained so late. Full sure was I that Madame had missed – was come in search of me, and designed now to pounce on the defaulter unawares. I expected a reprimand. No. Madame was all goodness. She tendered not even a remonstrance; she testified no shade of surprise. With that consummate tact of hers, in which I believe she was never surpassed by living thing, she even professed merely to have issued forth to taste '*la brise du soir*'.

"*Quelle belle nuit!*" cried she, looking up at the stars – the moon was now gone down behind the broad tower of Jean Baptiste. "*Qu'il fait bon? Que l'air est frais!*"

And, instead of sending me in, she detained me to take a few turns with her down the principal alley. When at last we both re-entered, she leaned affably on my shoulder by way of support in mounting the front-door steps; at parting, her cheek was presented to my lips, and "*Bon soir*, my *bonne amie; dormez bien!*" was her kindly adieu for the night.

I caught myself smiling as I lay awake and thoughtful on my couch – smiling at Madame. The unction, the suavity of her behaviour offered, for one who knew her, a sure token that suspicion of some kind was busy in her brain. From some aperture or summit of observation, through parted bough or open window, she had doubtless caught a glimpse, remote or near, deceptive or instructive, of that night's transactions. Finely accomplished as she was in the art of surveillance, it was next to impossible that a casket could be thrown into her garden, or an interloper could cross her walks to seek it, without that she, in shaken branch, passing shade, unwonted footfall, or stilly murmur (and though Dr. John had spoken very low in the few words he dropped me, yet the hum of his man's voice pervaded, I thought, the whole conventual ground) – without, I say, that she should have caught intimation of things extraordinary transpiring on her premises. *What* things, she might by no means see, or at that time be able to discover; but a delicious little ravelled plot lay tempting her to disentanglement; and in the midst, folded round and round in cobwebs, had she not secured 'Meess Lucie' clumsily involved, like the foolish fly she was?

Chapter Thirteen
A Sneeze out of Season

I HAD OCCASION to smile – nay, to laugh, at Madame again, within the space of four and twenty hours after the little scene treated of in the last chapter.

Villette owns a climate as variable, though not so humid, as that of any English town. A night of high wind followed upon that soft sunset, and all the next day was one of dry storm – dark, beclouded, yet rainless – the streets were dim with sand and dust, whirled from the boulevards. I know not that even lovely weather would have tempted me to spend the evening-time of study and recreation where I had spent it yesterday. My alley, and, indeed, all the walks and shrubs in the garden, had acquired a new, but not a pleasant interest; their seclusion was now become precarious; their calm – insecure. That casement which rained billets, had vulgarized the once dear nook it overlooked; and elsewhere, the eyes of the flowers had gained vision, and the knots in the tree-boles listened like secret ears. Some plants there were, indeed, trodden down by Dr. John in his search, and his hasty and heedless progress, which I wished to prop up, water, and revive; some footmarks, too, he had left on the beds: but these, in spite of the strong wind, I found a moment's leisure to efface very early in the morning, ere common eyes had discovered them. With a pensive sort of content, I sat down to my desk and my German, while the pupils settled to their evening lessons; and the other teachers took up their needlework.

The scene of the 'etude du soir' was always the refectory, a much smaller apartment than any of the three classes or schoolrooms; for here none, save the boarders, were ever admitted, and these numbered only a score. Two lamps hung from the ceiling over the two tables; these were lit at dusk, and their kindling was the signal for school-books being set aside, a grave demeanour assumed, general silence enforced, and then commenced 'la lecture pieuse'. This said 'lecture pieuse' was, I soon found, mainly designed as a wholesome mortification of the Intellect, a useful humiliation of the Reason; and such a dose for Common Sense as she might digest at her leisure, and thrive on as she best could.

The book brought out (it was never changed, but when finished, recommenced) was a venerable volume, old as the hills – grey as the Hôtel de Ville.

I would have given two francs for the chance of getting that book once into my hands, turning over the sacred yellow leaves, ascertaining the title, and perusing with my own eyes the enormous figments which, as an unworthy heretic, it was only permitted me to drink in with my bewildered ears. This book contained legends of the saints. Good God! (I speak the words reverently) What legends they were. What gasconading rascals those saints must have been, if they first boasted these exploits or invented these miracles. These legends, however, were no more than monkish extravagances, over which one laughed inwardly; there were, besides, priestly matters, and the priestcraft of the book was far worse than its monkery. The ears burned on each side of my head as I listened, perforce, to tales of moral martyrdom inflicted by Rome; the dread boasts of confessors, who had wickedly abused their office, trampling to deep degradation high-born ladies, making of countesses and princesses the most tormented slaves under the sun. Stories like that of Conrad and Elizabeth of Hungary, recurred again and again, with all its dreadful viciousness, sickening tyranny and black impiety: tales that were nightmares of oppression, privation, and agony.

I sat out this 'lecture pieuse' for some nights as well as I could, and as quietly too; only once breaking off the points of my scissors by involuntarily sticking them somewhat deep in the worm-eaten board of the table before me. But, at last, it made me so burning hot, and my temples, and my heart, and my wrist throbbed so fast, and my sleep afterwards was so broken with excitement, that I could sit no longer. Prudence recommended henceforward a swift clearance of my person from the place, the moment that guilty old book was brought out. No Mause Headrigg ever felt a stronger call to take up her testimony against Sergeant Bothwell, than I – to speak my mind in this matter of the popish 'lecture pieuse'. However, I did manage somehow to curb and rein in; and though always, as soon as Rosine came to light the lamps, I shot from the room quickly, yet also I did it quietly; seizing that vantage moment given by the little bustle before the dead silence, and vanishing whilst the boarders put their books away.

When I vanished – it was into darkness; candles were not allowed to be carried about, and the teacher who forsook the refectory, had only the unlit hall, schoolroom, or bedroom, as a refuge. In winter I sought the long classes, and paced them fast to keep myself warm – fortunate if the moon shone, and if there were only stars, soon reconciled to their dim gleam, or even to the total eclipse of their absence. In summer it was never quite dark, and then I went upstairs to my own quarter of the long dormitory, opened my own casement (that chamber was lit by five casements large as great doors), and leaning out, looked forth upon the city beyond the garden, and listened to band-music from the park or the palace-square, thinking meantime my own thoughts, living my own life, in my own still, shadow-world.

This evening, fugitive as usual before the Pope and his works, I mounted the staircase, approached the dormitory, and quietly opened the door, which was always kept carefully shut, and which, like every other door in this house, revolved noiselessly on well-oiled hinges. Before I *saw*, I *felt* that life was in the great room, usually void: not that there was either stir or breath, or rustle of sound, but Vacuum lacked, Solitude was not at home. All the white beds – the 'lits d'ange', as they were poetically termed – lay visible at a glance; all were empty: no sleeper reposed therein. The sound of a drawer cautiously slid out struck my ear; stepping a little to one side, my vision took a free range, unimpeded by falling curtains. I now commanded my own bed and my own toilet, with a locked work-box upon it, and locked drawers underneath.

Very good. A dumpy, motherly little body, in decent shawl and the cleanest of possible nightcaps, stood before this toilet, hard at work apparently doing me the kindness of 'tidying out' the 'meuble'. Open stood the lid of the work-box, open the top drawer; duly and impartially was each succeeding drawer opened in turn: not an article of their contents but was lifted and unfolded, not a paper but was glanced over, not a little box but was unlidded; and beautiful was the adroitness, exemplary the care with which the search was accomplished. Madame wrought at it like a true star, 'unhasting yet unresting'. I will not deny that it was with a secret glee I watched her. Had I been a gentleman I believe Madame would have found favour in my eyes, she was so handy, neat, thorough in all she did: some people's movements provoke the soul by their loose awkwardness, hers – satisfied by their trim compactness. I stood, in short, fascinated; but it was necessary to make an effort to break this spell a retreat must be beaten. The searcher might have turned and caught me; there would have been nothing for it then but a scene, and she and I would have had to come all at once, with a sudden clash, to a thorough knowledge of each other: down would have gone conventionalities, away swept disguises, and *I* should have looked into her eyes, and she into mine – we should have known that we could work together no more, and parted in this life for ever.

Where was the use of tempting such a catastrophe? I was not angry, and had no wish in the world to leave her. I could hardly get another employer whose yoke would be so light and so easy of carriage; and truly I liked Madame for her capital sense, whatever I might think of her principles: as to her system, it did me no harm; she might work me with it to her heart's content: nothing would come of the operation. Loverless and inexpectant of love, I was as safe from spies in my heart-poverty, as the beggar from thieves in his destitution of purse. I turned, then, and fled; descending the stairs with progress as swift and soundless as that of the spider, which at the same instant ran down the bannister.

How I laughed when I reached the schoolroom. I knew now she had certainly seen Dr. John in the garden; I knew what her thoughts were. The spectacle of a suspicious nature so far misled by its own inventions, tickled me much. Yet as the laugh died, a kind of wrath smote me, and then bitterness followed: it was the rock struck, and Meribah's waters gushing out. I never had felt so strange and contradictory an inward tumult as I felt for an hour that evening: soreness and laughter, and fire, and grief, shared my heart between them. I cried hot tears: not because Madame mistrusted me – I did not care twopence for her mistrust – but for other reasons. Complicated, disquieting thoughts broke up the whole repose of my nature. However, that turmoil subsided: next day I was again Lucy Snowe.

On revisiting my drawers, I found them all securely locked; the closest subsequent examination could not discover change or apparent disturbance in the position of one object. My few dresses were folded as I had left them; a certain little bunch of white violets that had once been silently presented to me by a stranger (a stranger to me, for we had never exchanged words), and which I had dried and kept for its sweet perfume between the folds of my best dress, lay there unstirred; my black silk scarf, my lace chemisette and collars, were unrumpled. Had she creased one solitary article, I own I should have felt much greater difficulty in forgiving her; but finding all straight and orderly, I said, "Let bygones be bygones. I am unharmed: why should I bear malice?"

* * *

A thing there was which puzzled myself, and I sought in my brain a key to that riddle almost as sedulously as Madame had sought a guide to useful knowledge in my toilet drawers. How was it that Dr. John, if he had not been accessory to the dropping of that casket into the garden, should have known that it *was* dropped, and appeared so promptly on the spot to seek it? So strong was the wish to clear up this point that I began to entertain this daring suggestion: "Why may I not, in case I should ever have the opportunity, ask Dr. John himself to explain this coincidence?"

And so long as Dr. John was absent, I really believed I had courage to test him with such a question.

Little Georgette was now convalescent; and her physician accordingly made his visits very rare: indeed, he would have ceased them altogether, had not Madame insisted on his giving an occasional call till the child should be quite well.

She came into the nursery one evening just after I had listened to Georgette's lisped and broken prayer, and had put her to bed. Taking the little one's hand, she said, "*Cette enfant a toujours un peu de fièvre.*" And presently afterwards, looking at me with a quicker glance than was habitual to her quiet eye, "*Le Docteur John l'a-t-il vue dernièrement? Non, n'est-ce pas?*"

Of course she knew this better than any other person in the house. "Well," she continued, "I am going out, *pour faire quelques courses en fiacre.* I shall call on Dr. John, and send him to the child. I will that he sees her this evening; her cheeks are flushed, her pulse is quick; *you* will receive him – for my part, I shall be from home."

Now the child was well enough, only warm with the warmth of July; it was scarcely less needful to send for a priest to administer extreme unction than for a doctor to prescribe a dose; also Madame rarely made 'courses', as she called them, in the evening: moreover, this was the first time she had chosen to absent herself on the occasion of a visit from Dr. John. The whole arrangement indicated some plan; this I saw, but without the least anxiety. "Ha ha! Madame," laughed Light-heart the Beggar, "your crafty wits are on the wrong tack."

She departed, attired very smartly, in a shawl of price, and a certain chapeau vert tendre – hazardous, as to its tint, for any complexion less fresh than her own, but, to her, not unbecoming. I wondered what she intended: whether she really would send Dr. John or not; or whether indeed he would come: he might be engaged.

Madame had charged me not to let Georgette sleep till the doctor came; I had therefore sufficient occupation in telling her nursery tales and palavering the little language for her benefit. I affected Georgette; she was a sensitive and a loving child: to hold her in my lap, or carry her in my arms, was to me a treat. Tonight she would have me lay my head on the pillow of her crib; she even put her little arms round my neck. Her clasp, and the nestling action with which she pressed her cheek to mine, made me almost cry with a tender pain. Feeling of no kind abounded in that house; this pure little drop from a pure little source was too sweet: it penetrated deep, and subdued the heart, and sent a gush to the eyes. Half an hour or an hour passed; Georgette murmured in her soft lisp that she was growing sleepy. 'And you *shall* sleep,' thought I, 'malgré maman and médecin, if they are not here in ten minutes.'

Hark! There was the ring, and there the tread, astonishing the staircase by the fleetness with which it left the steps behind. Rosine introduced Dr. John, and, with a freedom of manner not altogether peculiar to herself, but characteristic of the domestics of Villette generally, she stayed to hear what he had to say. Madame's presence would have awed her back to her own realm of the vestibule and the cabinet – for mine, or that of any other teacher or pupil, she cared not a jot. Smart, trim and pert, she stood, a hand in each pocket of her gay grisette apron, eyeing Dr. John with no more fear or shyness than if he had been a picture instead of a living gentleman.

"*Le marmot n'a rien, nest-ce pas?*" said she, indicating Georgette with a jerk of her chin.

"*Pas beaucoup,*" was the answer, as the doctor hastily scribbled with his pencil some harmless prescription.

"*Eh bien!*" pursued Rosine, approaching him quite near, while he put up his pencil. "And the box – did you get it? Monsieur went off like a coup-de-vent the other night; I had not time to ask him."

"I found it: yes."

"And who threw it, then?" continued Rosine, speaking quite freely the very words I should so much have wished to say, but had no address or courage to bring it out: how short some people make the road to a point which, for others, seems unattainable!

"That may be my secret," rejoined Dr. John briefly, but with no sort of hauteur: he seemed quite to understand the Rosine or grisette character.

"*Mais enfin,*" continued she, nothing abashed, "monsieur knew it was thrown, since he came to seek it – how did he know?"

"I was attending a little patient in the college near," said he, "and saw it dropped out of his chamber window, and so came to pick it up."

How simple the whole explanation! The note had alluded to a physician as then examining 'Gustave'.

"*Ah ça!*" pursued Rosine; "*Il n'y a donc rien là-dessous: pas de mystère, pas d'amourette, par exemple?*"

"*Pas plus que sur ma main,*" responded the doctor, showing his palm.

"*Quel dommage!*" responded the grisette: "*Et moi – à qui tout cela commençait à donner des idées.*"

"*Vraiment! Vous en êtes pour vos frais,*" was the doctor's cool rejoinder.

She pouted. The doctor could not help laughing at the sort of *moue* she made: when he laughed, he had something peculiarly good-natured and genial in his look. I saw his hand incline to his pocket.

"How many times have you opened the door for me within this last month?" he asked.

"Monsieur ought to have kept count of that," said Rosine, quite readily.

"As if I had not something better to do!" rejoined he; but I saw him give her a piece of gold, which she took unscrupulously, and then danced off to answer the door-bell, ringing just now every five minutes, as the various servants came to fetch the half-boarders.

The reader must not think too hardly of Rosine; on the whole, she was not a bad sort of person, and had no idea there could be any disgrace in grasping at whatever she could get, or any effrontery in chattering like a pie to the best gentleman in Christendom.

I had learnt something from the above scene besides what concerned the ivory box: viz., that not on the robe de jaconas, pink or grey, nor yet on the frilled and pocketed apron, lay the blame of breaking Dr. John's heart: these items of array were obviously guiltless as Georgette's little blue tunic. So much the better. But who then was the culprit? What was the ground – what the origin – what the perfect explanation of the whole business? Some points had been cleared, but how many yet remained obscure as night!

"However," I said to myself, "it is no affair of yours"; and turning from the face on which I had been unconsciously dwelling with a questioning gaze, I looked through the window which commanded the garden below. Dr. John, meantime, standing by the bed-side, was slowly drawing on his gloves and watching his little patient, as her eyes closed and her rosy lips parted in coming sleep. I waited till he should depart as usual, with a quick bow and scarce articulate 'goodnight'. Just as he took his hat, my eyes, fixed on the tall houses bounding the garden, saw the one lattice, already commemorated, cautiously open; forth from the aperture projected a hand and a white handkerchief; both waved. I know not whether the signal was answered from some viewless quarter of our own dwelling; but immediately after there fluttered from the lattice a falling object, white and light – billet the second, of course.

"There!" I ejaculated involuntarily.

"Where?" asked Dr. John with energy, making direct for the window. "What, is it?"

"They have gone and done it again," was my reply. "A handkerchief waved and something fell:" and I pointed to the lattice, now closed and looking hypocritically blank.

"Go, at once; pick it up and bring it here," was his prompt direction; adding, "Nobody will take notice of *you: I* should be seen."

Straight I went. After some little search, I found a folded paper, lodged on the lower branch of a shrub; I seized and brought it direct to Dr. John. This time, I believe not even Rosine saw me.

He instantly tore the billet into small pieces, without reading it. "It is not in the least *her* fault, you must remember," he said, looking at me.

"*Whose* fault?" I asked. "*Who* is it?"

"You don't yet know, then?"

"Not in the least."

"Have you no guess?"

"None."

"If I knew you better, I might be tempted to risk some confidence, and thus secure you as guardian over a most innocent and excellent, but somewhat inexperienced being."

"As a duenna?" I asked.

"Yes," said he abstractedly. "What snares are round her!" he added, musingly: and now, certainly for the first time, he examined my face, anxious, doubtless, to see if any kindly expression there, would warrant him in recommending to my care and indulgence some ethereal creature, against whom powers of darkness were plotting. I felt no particular vocation to undertake the surveillance of ethereal creatures; but recalling the scene at the bureau, it seemed to me that I owed *him* a good turn: if I *could* help him then I would, and it lay not with me to decide how. With as little reluctance as might be, I intimated that "I was willing to do what I could towards taking care of any person in whom he might be interested."

"I am no farther interested than as a spectator," said he, with a modesty, admirable, as I thought, to witness. "I happen to be acquainted with the rather worthless character of the person, who, from the house opposite, has now twice invaded the sanctity of this place; I have also met in society the object at whom these vulgar attempts are aimed. Her exquisite superiority and innate refinement ought, one would think, to scare impertinence from her very idea. It is not so, however; and innocent, unsuspicious as she is, I would guard her from evil if I could. In person, however, I can do nothing; I cannot come near her" – he paused.

"Well, I am willing to help you," said I, "only tell me how." And busily, in my own mind, I ran over the list of our inmates, seeking this paragon, this pearl of great price, this gem without flaw. "It must be Madame," I concluded. "*She* only, amongst us all, has the art even to *seem* superior: but as to being unsuspicious, inexperienced, etc., Dr. John need not distract himself about that. However, this is just his whim, and I will not contradict him; he shall be humoured: his angel shall be an angel."

"Just notify the quarter to which my care is to be directed," I continued gravely: chuckling, however, to myself over the thought of being set to chaperon Madame Beck or any of her pupils. Now Dr. John had a fine set of nerves, and he at once felt by instinct, what no more coarsely constituted mind would have detected; namely, that I was a little amused at him. The colour rose to his cheek; with half a smile he turned and took his hat – he was going. My heart smote me.

"I will – I will help you," said I eagerly. "I will do what you wish. I will watch over your angel; I will take care of her, only tell me who she is."

"But you *must* know," said he then with earnestness, yet speaking very low. "So spotless, so good, so unspeakably beautiful! Impossible that one house should contain two like her. I allude, of course –"

Here the latch of Madame Beck's chamber-door (opening into the nursery) gave a sudden click, as if the hand holding it had been slightly convulsed; there was the suppressed explosion of an irrepressible sneeze. These little accidents will happen to the best of us. Madame – excellent woman! – was then on duty. She had come home quietly, stolen upstairs on tip-toe; she was in her chamber. If she had not sneezed, she would have heard all, and so should I; but that unlucky sternutation routed Dr. John. While he stood aghast, she came forward alert, composed, in the best yet most tranquil spirits: no novice to her habits but would have thought she had just come in, and scouted the idea of her ear having been glued to the key-hole for at least ten minutes. She affected to sneeze again, declared she was 'enrhumée', and then proceeded volubly to recount her 'courses en fiacre'. The prayer-bell rang, and I left her with the doctor.

Chapter Fourteen
The Fête

AS SOON AS Georgette was well, Madame sent her away into the country. I was sorry; I loved the child, and her loss made me poorer than before. But I must not complain. I lived in a house full of robust life; I might have had companions, and I chose solitude. Each of the teachers in turn made me overtures of special intimacy; I tried them all. One I found to be an honest woman, but a narrow thinker, a coarse feeler, and an egotist. The second was a Parisienne, externally refined – at heart, corrupt – without a creed, without a principle, without an affection: having penetrated the outward crust of decorum in this character, you found a slough beneath. She had a wonderful passion for presents; and, in this point, the third teacher – a person otherwise characterless and insignificant – closely resembled her. This last-named had also one other distinctive property – that of avarice. In her reigned the love of money for its own sake. The sight of a piece of gold would bring into her eyes a green glisten, singular to witness. She once, as a mark of high favour, took me upstairs, and, opening a secret door, showed me a hoard – a mass of coarse, large coin – about fifteen guineas, in five-franc pieces. She loved this hoard as a bird loves its eggs. These were her savings. She would come and talk to me about them with an infatuated and persevering dotage, strange to behold in a person not yet twenty-five.

The Parisienne, on the other hand, was prodigal and profligate (in disposition, that is: as to action, I do not know). That latter quality showed its snake-head to me but once, peeping out very cautiously. A curious kind of reptile it seemed, judging from the glimpse I got; its novelty whetted my curiosity: if it would have come out boldly, perhaps I might philosophically have stood my ground, and coolly surveyed the long thing from forked tongue to scaly tail-tip; but it merely rustled in the leaves of a bad novel; and, on encountering a hasty and ill-advised demonstration of wrath, recoiled and vanished, hissing. She hated me from that day.

This Parisienne was always in debt; her salary being anticipated, not only in dress, but in perfumes, cosmetics, confectionery, and condiments. What a cold, callous epicure she was in all things! I see her now. Thin in face and figure, sallow in complexion, regular in features, with perfect teeth, lips like a thread, a large, prominent chin, a well-opened, but frozen eye, of light at once craving and ingrate. She mortally hated work, and loved what she called pleasure; being an insipid, heartless, brainless dissipation of time.

Madame Beck knew this woman's character perfectly well. She once talked to me about her, with an odd mixture of discrimination, indifference, and antipathy. I asked why she kept her in the establishment. She answered plainly, "because it suited her interest to do so"; and pointed out a fact I had already noticed, namely, that Mademoiselle St. Pierre possessed, in an almost unique degree, the power of keeping order amongst her undisciplined ranks of scholars. A certain petrifying influence accompanied and surrounded her: without passion, noise, or violence, she held them in check as a breezeless frost-air might still a brawling stream. She was of little use as far as communication of knowledge went, but for strict surveillance and maintenance of rules she was invaluable. *"Je sais bien qu'elle n'a pas de principes, ni, peut-être, de moeurs,"* admitted Madame frankly; but added with philosophy, *"son maintien en classe est toujours convenable et rempli même d'une certaine dignité: c'est tout ce qu'il faut. Ni les élèves ni les parents ne regardent plus loin; ni, par conséquent, moi non plus."*

* * *

A strange, frolicsome, noisy little world was this school: great pains were taken to hide chains with flowers: a subtle essence of Romanism pervaded every arrangement: large sensual indulgence (so to speak) was permitted by way of counterpoise to jealous spiritual restraint. Each mind was being reared in slavery; but, to prevent reflection from dwelling on this fact, every pretext for physical recreation was seized and made the most of. There, as elsewhere, the Church strove to bring up her children robust in body, feeble in soul, fat, ruddy, hale, joyous, ignorant, unthinking, unquestioning. "Eat, drink, and live!" she says. "Look after your bodies; leave your souls to me. I hold their cure – guide their course: I guarantee their final fate." A bargain, in which every true Catholic deems himself a gainer. Lucifer just offers the same terms: "All this power will I give thee, and the glory of it; for that is delivered unto me, and to whomsoever I will I give it. If thou, therefore, wilt worship me, all shall be thine!"

About this time – in the ripest glow of summer – Madame Beck's house became as merry a place as a school could well be. All day long the broad folding-doors and the two-leaved casements stood wide open: settled sunshine seemed naturalized in the atmosphere; clouds were far off, sailing away beyond sea, resting, no doubt, round islands such as England – that dear land of mists – but withdrawn wholly from the drier continent. We lived far more in the garden than under a roof: classes were held, and meals partaken of, in the *grand berceau*. Moreover, there was a note of holiday preparation, which almost turned freedom into licence. The autumnal long vacation was but two months distant; but before that, a great day – an important ceremony – none other than the fête of Madame – awaited celebration.

The conduct of this fête devolved chiefly on Mademoiselle St. Pierre: Madame herself being supposed to stand aloof, disinterestedly unconscious of what might be going forward in her honour. Especially, she never knew, never in the least suspected, that a subscription was annually levied on the whole school for the purchase of a handsome present. The polite tact of the reader will please to leave out of the account a brief, secret consultation on this point in Madame's own chamber.

"What will you have this year?" was asked by her Parisian lieutenant.

"Oh, no matter! Let it alone. Let the poor children keep their francs," And Madame looked benign and modest.

The St. Pierre would here protrude her chin; she knew Madame by heart; she always called her airs of *bonté – des grimaces*. She never even professed to respect them one instant.

"*Vite!*" she would say coldly. "Name the article. Shall it be jewellery or porcelain, haberdashery or silver?"

."*Eh bien! Deux ou trois cuillers, et autant de fourchettes en argent.*"

And the result was a handsome case, containing 300 francs worth of plate.

The programme of the fête-day's proceedings comprised: Presentation of plate, collation in the garden, dramatic performance (with pupils and teachers for actors), a dance and supper. Very gorgeous seemed the effect of the whole to me, as I well remember. Zélie St. Pierre understood these things and managed them ably.

The play was the main point; a month's previous drilling being there required. The choice, too, of the actors required knowledge and care; then came lessons in elocution, in attitude, and then the fatigue of countless rehearsals. For all this, as may well be supposed, St. Pierre did not suffice: other management, other accomplishments than hers were requisite here. They were supplied in the person of a master – M. Paul Emanuel, professor of literature. It was never my lot to be present at the histrionic lessons of M. Paul, but I often saw him as he crossed the carré (a square hall between the dwelling-house and school-house). I heard him, too, in the warm evenings, lecturing with open doors, and his name, with anecdotes of him, resounded in one's ears from all sides. Especially our former acquaintance, Miss Ginevra Fanshawe, – who had been selected to take a prominent part in the play – used, in bestowing upon me a large portion of her leisure, to lard her discourse with frequent allusions to his sayings and doings. She esteemed him hideously plain, and used to profess herself frightened almost into hysterics at the sound of his step or voice. A dark little man he certainly was; pungent and austere. Even to me he seemed a harsh apparition, with his close-shorn, black head, his broad, sallow brow, his thin cheek, his wide and quivering nostril, his thorough glance, and hurried bearing. Irritable he was; one heard that, as he apostrophized with vehemence the awkward squad under his orders. Sometimes he would break out on these raw amateur actresses with a passion of impatience at their falseness of conception, their coldness of emotion, their feebleness of delivery. "*Ecoutez!*" he would cry; and then his voice rang through the premises like a trumpet; and when, mimicking it, came the small pipe of a Ginevra, a Mathilde, or a Blanche, one understood why a hollow groan of scorn, or a fierce hiss of rage, rewarded the tame echo.

"*Vous n'êtes donc que des poupées,*" I heard him thunder. "*Vous n'avez pas de passions – vous autres. Vous ne sentez donc rien? Votre chair est de neige, votre sang de glace! Moi, je veux que tout cela s'allume, qu'il ait une vie, une âme!*"

Vain resolve! And when he at last found it *was* vain, he suddenly broke the whole business down. Hitherto he had been teaching them a grand tragedy; he tore the tragedy in morsels, and came next day with a compact little comic trifle. To this they took more kindly; he presently knocked it all into their smooth round pates.

Mademoiselle St. Pierre always presided at M. Emanuel's lessons, and I was told that the polish of her manner, her seeming attention, her tact and grace, impressed that gentleman very favourably. She had, indeed, the art of pleasing, for a given time, whom she would; but the feeling would not last: in an hour it was dried like dew, vanished like gossamer.

The day preceding Madame's fête was as much a holiday as the fête itself. It was devoted to clearing out, cleaning, arranging and decorating the three schoolrooms. All within-doors was the gayest bustle; neither upstairs nor down could a quiet, isolated person find rest for the sole of her foot; accordingly, for my part, I took refuge in the garden. The whole day did I wander or sit there alone, finding warmth in the sun, shelter among the trees, and a sort of companionship in my own thoughts. I well remember that I exchanged but two sentences that day with any living being: not that I felt solitary; I was glad to be quiet. For a looker-on, it sufficed to pass through the rooms once or twice, observe what changes were being wrought, how a green-room and a dressing-room were being contrived, a little stage with scenery erected, how M. Paul Emanuel, in conjunction with Mademoiselle St. Pierre, was directing all, and how an eager band of pupils, amongst them Ginevra Fanshawe, were working gaily under his control.

The great day arrived. The sun rose hot and unclouded, and hot and unclouded it burned on till evening. All the doors and all the windows were set open, which gave a pleasant sense of summer freedom – and freedom the most complete seemed indeed the order of the day. Teachers and pupils descended to breakfast in dressing-gowns and curl-papers: anticipating 'avec délices' the toilette of the evening, they seemed to take a pleasure in indulging that forenoon in a luxury of slovenliness; like aldermen fasting in preparation for a feast. About nine o'clock a.m., an important functionary, the coiffeur, arrived. Sacrilegious to state, he fixed his head-quarters in the oratory, and there, in presence of *bénitier*, candle, and crucifix, solemnised the mysteries of his art. Each girl was summoned in turn to pass through his hands; emerging from them with head as smooth as a shell, intersected by faultless white lines, and wreathed about with Grecian plaits that shone as if lacquered. I took my turn with the rest, and could hardly believe what the glass said when I applied to it for information afterwards; the lavished garlandry of woven brown hair amazed me – I feared it was not all my own, and it required several convincing pulls to give assurance to the contrary. I then acknowledged in the coiffeur a first-rate artist – one who certainly made the most of indifferent materials.

The oratory closed, the dormitory became the scene of ablutions, arrayings and bedizenings curiously elaborate. To me it was, and ever must be an enigma, how they contrived to spend so much time in doing so little. The operation seemed close, intricate, prolonged: the result simple. A clear white muslin dress, a blue sash (the Virgin's colours), a pair of white, or straw-colour kid gloves – such was the gala uniform, to the assumption whereof that houseful of teachers and pupils devoted three mortal hours. But though simple, it must be allowed the array was perfect – perfect in fashion, fit, and freshness; every head being also dressed with exquisite nicety, and a certain compact taste – suiting the full, firm comeliness of

Labassecourien contours, though too stiff for any more flowing and flexible style of beauty – the general effect was, on the whole, commendable.

In beholding this diaphanous and snowy mass, I well remember feeling myself to be a mere shadowy spot on a field of light; the courage was not in me to put on a transparent white dress: something thin I must wear – the weather and rooms being too hot to give substantial fabrics sufferance, so I had sought through a dozen shops till I lit upon a crape-like material of purple-grey – the colour, in short, of dun mist, lying on a moor in bloom. My tailleuse had kindly made it as well as she could: because, as she judiciously observed, it was '*si triste – si pen voyant*', care in the fashion was the more imperative: it was well she took this view of the matter, for I, had no flower, no jewel to relieve it: and, what was more, I had no natural rose of complexion.

We become oblivious of these deficiencies in the uniform routine of daily drudgery, but they *will* force upon us their unwelcome blank on those bright occasions when beauty should shine.

However, in this same gown of shadow, I felt at home and at ease; an advantage I should not have enjoyed in anything more brilliant or striking. Madame Beck, too, kept me in countenance; her dress was almost as quiet as mine, except that she wore a bracelet, and a large brooch bright with gold and fine stones. We chanced to meet on the stairs, and she gave me a nod and smile of approbation. Not that she thought I was looking well – a point unlikely to engage her interest – but she considered me dressed '*convenablement*', '*décemment*', and *la Convenance et la Décence* were the two calm deities of Madame's worship. She even paused, laid on my shoulder her gloved hand, holding an embroidered and perfumed handkerchief, and confided to my ear a sarcasm on the other teachers (whom she had just been complimenting to their faces). "Nothing so absurd," she said, "as for *des femmes mûres* 'to dress themselves like girls of fifteen' – *quant à la. St. Pierre, elle a l'air d'une vieille coquette qui fait l'ingénue*."

Being dressed at least a couple of hours before anybody else, I felt a pleasure in betaking myself – not to the garden, where servants were busy propping up long tables, placing seats, and spreading cloths in readiness for the collation but to the schoolrooms, now empty, quiet, cool, and clean; their walls fresh stained, their planked floors fresh scoured and scarce dry; flowers fresh gathered adorning the recesses in pots, and draperies, fresh hung, beautifying the great windows.

Withdrawing to the first classe, a smaller and neater room than the others, and taking from the glazed bookcase, of which I kept the key, a volume whose title promised some interest, I sat down to read. The glass-door of this classe, or schoolroom, opened into the large berceau; acacia-boughs caressed its panes, as they stretched across to meet a rose-bush blooming by the opposite lintel: in this rose-bush bees murmured busy and happy. I commenced reading. Just as the stilly hum, the embowering shade, the warm, lonely calm of my retreat were beginning to steal meaning from the page, vision from my eyes, and to lure me along the track of reverie, down into some deep dell of dreamland – just then, the sharpest ring of the street-door bell to which that much-tried instrument had ever thrilled, snatched me back to consciousness.

Now the bell had been ringing all the morning, as workmen, or servants, or coiffeurs, or tailleuses, went and came on their several errands. Moreover, there was good reason to expect it would ring all the afternoon, since about one hundred externes were yet to arrive in carriages or fiacres: nor could it be expected to rest during the evening, when parents and friends would gather thronging to the play. Under these circumstances, a ring – even a sharp ring – was a matter of course: yet this particular peal had an accent of its own, which chased my dream, and startled my book from my knee.

I was stooping to pick up this last, when – firm, fast, straight – right on through vestibule – along corridor, across carré, through first division, second division, grand salle – strode a step, quick, regular, intent. The closed door of the first classe – my sanctuary – offered no obstacle; it burst open, and a paletôt and a bonnet grec filled the void; also two eyes first vaguely struck upon, and then hungrily dived into me.

"*C'est cela!*" said a voice. "*Je la connais: c'est l'Anglaise. Tant pis. Toute Anglaise, et, par conséquent, toute bégueule qu'elle soit – elle fera mon affaire, ou je saurai pourquoi.*"

Then, with a certain stern politeness (I suppose he thought I had not caught the drift of his previous uncivil mutterings), and in a jargon the most execrable that ever was heard, "Meess —, play you must: I am planted there."

"What can I do for you, M. Paul Emanuel?" I inquired: for M. Paul Emanuel it was, and in a state of no little excitement.

"Play you must. I will not have you shrink, or frown, or make the prude. I read your skull that night you came; I see your *moyens*: play you can; play you must."

"But how, M. Paul? What do you mean?"

"There is no time to be lost," he went on, now speaking in French; "and let us thrust to the wall all reluctance, all excuses, all *minauderies*. You must take a part."

"In the vaudeville?"

"In the vaudeville. You have said it."

I gasped, horror-struck. *What* did the little man mean?

"Listen!" he said. "The case shall be stated, and you shall then answer me Yes, or No; and according to your answer shall I ever after estimate you."

The scarce-suppressed impetus of a most irritable nature glowed in his cheek, fed with sharp shafts his glances, a nature – the injudicious, the mawkish, the hesitating, the sullen, the affected, above all, the unyielding, might quickly render violent and implacable. Silence and attention was the best balm to apply: I listened.

"The whole matter is going to fail," he began. "Louise Vanderkelkov has fallen ill – at least so her ridiculous mother asserts; for my part, I feel sure she might play if she would: it is only good-will that lacks. She was charged with a rôle, as you know, or do *not* know – it is equal: without that *rôle* the play is stopped. There are now but a few hours in which to learn it: not a girl in this school would hear reason, and accept the task. Forsooth, it is not an interesting, not an amiable, part; their vile *amour-propre* – that base quality of which women have so much – would revolt from it. Englishwomen are either the best or the worst of their sex. *Dieu sait que je les déteste comme la peste, ordinairement*" (this between his recreant teeth). "I apply to an Englishwoman to rescue me. What is her answer – Yes, or No?"

A thousand objections rushed into my mind. The foreign language, the limited time, the public display…Inclination recoiled, Ability faltered, Self-respect (that 'vile quality') trembled. "*Non, non, non!*" said all these; but looking up at M. Paul, and seeing in his vexed, fiery, and searching eye, a sort of appeal behind all its menace, my lips dropped the word '*oui*'. For a moment his rigid countenance relaxed with a quiver of content: quickly bent up again, however, he went on, –

"*Vite à l'ouvrage!* Here is the book; here is your rôle: read." And I read. He did not commend; at some passages he scowled and stamped. He gave me a lesson: I diligently imitated. It was a disagreeable part – a man's – an empty-headed fop's. One could put into it neither heart nor soul: I hated it. The play – a mere trifle – ran chiefly on the efforts of a brace of rivals to gain the hand of a fair coquette. One lover was called the 'Ours', a good and gallant but unpolished man, a sort of diamond in the rough; the other was a butterfly, a talker, and a traitor: and I was to be the butterfly, talker, and traitor.

I did my best – which was bad, I know: it provoked M. Paul; he fumed. Putting both hands to the work, I endeavoured to do better than my best; I presume he gave me credit for good intentions; he professed to be partially content. "*Ça ira!*" he cried; and as voices began sounding from the garden, and white dresses fluttering among the trees, he added: "You must withdraw: you must be alone to learn this. Come with me."

Without being allowed time or power to deliberate, I found myself in the same breath convoyed along as in a species of whirlwind, upstairs, up two pair of stairs, nay, actually up three (for this fiery little man seemed as by instinct to know his way everywhere); to the solitary and lofty attic was I borne, put in and locked in, the key being in the door, and that key he took with him and vanished.

The attic was no pleasant place: I believe he did not know how unpleasant it was, or he never would have locked me in with so little ceremony. In this summer weather, it was hot as Africa; as in winter, it was always cold as Greenland. Boxes and lumber filled it; old dresses draped its unstained wall – cobwebs its unswept ceiling. Well was it known to be tenanted by rats, by black beetles, and by cockroaches – nay, rumour affirmed that the ghostly Nun of the garden had once been seen here. A partial darkness obscured one end, across which, as for deeper mystery, an old russet curtain was drawn, by way of screen to a sombre band of winter cloaks, pendent each from its pin, like a malefactor from his gibbet. From amongst these cloaks, and behind that curtain, the Nun was said to issue. I did not believe this, nor was I troubled by apprehension thereof; but I saw a very dark and large rat, with a long tail, come gliding out from that squalid alcove; and, moreover, my eye fell on many a black-beetle, dotting the floor. These objects discomposed me more, perhaps, than it would be wise to say, as also did the dust, lumber, and stifling heat of the place. The last inconvenience would soon have become intolerable, had I not found means to open and prop up the skylight, thus admitting some freshness. Underneath this aperture I pushed a large empty chest, and having mounted upon it a smaller box, and wiped from both the dust, I gathered my dress (my best, the reader must remember, and therefore a legitimate object of care) fastidiously around me, ascended this species of extempore throne, and being seated, commenced the acquisition of my task; while I learned, not forgetting to keep a sharp look-out on the black-beetles and cockroaches, of which, more even, I believe, than of the rats, I sat in mortal dread.

My impression at first was that I had undertaken what it really was impossible to perform, and I simply resolved to do my best and be resigned to fail. I soon found, however, that one part in so short a piece was not more than memory could master at a few hours' notice. I learned and learned on, first in a whisper, and then aloud. Perfectly secure from human audience, I acted my part before the garret-vermin. Entering into its emptiness, frivolity, and falsehood, with a spirit inspired by scorn and impatience, I took my revenge on this 'fat', by making him as fatuitous as I possibly could.

In this exercise the afternoon passed: day began to glide into evening; and I, who had eaten nothing since breakfast, grew excessively hungry. Now I thought of the collation, which doubtless they were just then devouring in the garden far below. (I had seen in the vestibule a basketful of small pâtés à la crème, than which nothing in the whole range of cookery seemed to me better). A pâté, or a square of cake, it seemed to me would come very àpropos; and as my relish for those dainties increased, it began to appear somewhat hard that I should pass my holiday, fasting and in prison. Remote as was the attic from the street-door and vestibule, yet the ever-tinkling bell was faintly audible here; and also the ceaseless roll of wheels, on the tormented pavement. I knew that the house and garden were thronged, and that all was gay and glad below; here it began to grow dusk: the beetles were fading from my sight; I trembled lest they should steal on me a march, mount my throne unseen, and, unsuspected, invade my skirts. Impatient and apprehensive, I recommenced the rehearsal of my part merely to kill time. Just as I was concluding, the long-delayed rattle of the key in the lock came to my ear – no unwelcome sound. M. Paul (I could just see through the dusk that it *was* M. Paul, for light enough still lingered to show the velvet blackness of his close-shorn head, and the sallow ivory of his brow) looked in.

"*Brava!*" cried he, holding the door open and remaining at the threshold. "*J'ai tout entendu. C'est assez bien. Encore!*"

A moment I hesitated.

"*Encore!*" said he sternly. "*Et point de grimaces! A bas la timidité!*"

Again I went through the part, but not half so well as I had spoken it alone.

"*Enfin, elle sait*," said he, half dissatisfied, "and one cannot be fastidious or exacting under the circumstances." Then he added, "You may yet have twenty minutes for preparation: au revoir!" And he was going.

"*Monsieur*," I called out, taking courage.

"*Eh bien! Qu'est-ce que c'est, Mademoiselle?*"

"*J'ai bien faim.*"

"*Comment, vous avez faim! Et la collation?*"

"I know nothing about it. I have not seen it, shut up here."

"*Ah! C'est vrai,*" cried he.

In a moment my throne was abdicated, the attic evacuated; an inverse repetition of the impetus which had brought me up into the attic, instantly took me down – down – down to the very kitchen. I thought I should have gone to the cellar. The cook was imperatively ordered to produce food, and I, as imperatively, was commanded to eat. To my great joy this food was limited to coffee and cake: I had feared wine and sweets, which I did not like. How he guessed that I should like a petit pâté à la crême I cannot tell; but he went out and procured me one from some quarter. With considerable willingness I ate and drank, keeping the petit pâté till the last, as a bonne bouche. M. Paul superintended my repast, and almost forced upon me more than I could swallow.

"A la bonne heure," he cried, when I signified that I really could take no more, and, with uplifted hands, implored to be spared the additional roll on which he had just spread butter. "You will set me down as a species of tyrant and Bluebeard, starving women in a garret; whereas, after all, I am no such thing. Now, Mademoiselle, do you feel courage and strength to appear?"

I said, I thought I did; though, in truth, I was perfectly confused, and could hardly tell how I felt: but this little man was of the order of beings who must not be opposed, unless you possessed an all-dominant force sufficient to crush him at once.

"Come then," said he, offering his hand.

I gave him mine, and he set off with a rapid walk, which obliged me to run at his side in order to keep pace. In the carré he stopped a moment: it was lit with large lamps; the wide doors of the classes were open, and so were the equally wide garden-doors; orange-trees in tubs, and tall flowers in pots, ornamented these portals on each side; groups of ladies and gentlemen in evening-dress stood and walked amongst the flowers. Within, the long vista of the school-rooms presented a thronging, undulating, murmuring, waving, streaming multitude, all rose, and blue, and half translucent white. There were lustres burning overhead; far off there was a stage, a solemn green curtain, a row of footlights.

"*Nest-ce pas que c'est beau?*" demanded my companion.

I should have said it was, but my heart got up into my throat. M. Paul discovered this, and gave me a side-scowl and a little shake for my pains.

"I will do my best, but I wish it was over," said I; then I asked: "Are we to walk through that crowd?"

"By no means: I manage matters better: we pass through the garden – here."

In an instant we were out of doors: the cool, calm night revived me somewhat. It was moonless, but the reflex from the many glowing windows lit the court brightly, and even the alleys – dimly. Heaven was cloudless, and grand with the quiver of its living fires. How soft are the nights of the Continent! How bland, balmy, safe! No sea-fog; no chilling damp: mistless as noon, and fresh as morning.

Having crossed court and garden, we reached the glass door of the first classe. It stood open, like all other doors that night; we passed, and then I was ushered into a small cabinet, dividing the first classe from the grand salle. This cabinet dazzled me, it was so full of light: it deafened me, it was clamorous with voices: it stifled me, it was so hot, choking, thronged.

"*De l'ordre! Du silence!*" cried M. Paul. "Is this chaos?" he demanded; and there was a hush. With a dozen words, and as many gestures, he turned out half the persons present, and obliged the remnant to fall into rank. Those left were all in costume: they were the performers, and this was the green-room. M. Paul introduced me. All stared and some tittered. It was a surprise: they had not expected the Englishwoman would play in a vaudeville. Ginevra Fanshawe, beautifully dressed for her part, and looking fascinatingly pretty, turned on me a pair of eyes as round as beads. In the highest spirit, unperturbed by fear or bashfulness, delighted indeed at the thought of shining off before hundreds – my entrance seemed to transfix her with amazement in the midst of her joy. She would have exclaimed, but M. Paul held her and all the rest in check.

Having surveyed and criticized the whole troop, he turned to me.

"You, too, must be dressed for your part."

"Dressed – dressed like a man!" exclaimed Zélie St. Pierre, darting forwards; adding with officiousness, "I will dress her myself."

To be dressed like a man did not please, and would not suit me. I had consented to take a man's name and part; as to his dress – *halte là!* No. I would keep my own dress, come what might. M. Paul might storm, might rage: I would keep my own dress. I said so, with a voice as resolute in intent, as it was low, and perhaps unsteady in utterance.

He did not immediately storm or rage, as I fully thought he would; he stood silent. But Zélie again interposed.

"She will make a capital petit-maître. Here are the garments, all – all complete: somewhat too large, but – I will arrange all that. Come, *chère amie – belle Anglaise!*"

And she sneered, for I was not 'belle'. She seized my hand, she was drawing me away. M. Paul stood impassable – neutral.

"You must not resist," pursued St. Pierre – for resist I did. "You will spoil all, destroy the mirth of the piece, the enjoyment of the company, sacrifice everything to your amour-propre. This would be too bad – monsieur will never permit this?"

She sought his eye. I watched, likewise, for a glance. He gave her one, and then he gave me one. "Stop!" he said slowly, arresting St. Pierre, who continued her efforts to drag me after her. Everybody awaited the decision. He was not angry, not irritated; I perceived that, and took heart.

"You do not like these clothes?" he asked, pointing to the masculine vestments.

"I don't object to some of them, but I won't have them all."

"How must it be, then? How accept a man's part, and go on the stage dressed as a woman? This is an amateur affair, it is true – a vaudeville de pensionnat; certain modifications I might sanction, yet something you must have to announce you as of the nobler sex."

"And I will, Monsieur; but it must be arranged in my own way: nobody must meddle; the things must not be forced upon me. Just let me dress myself."

Monsieur, without another word, took the costume from St. Pierre, gave it to me, and permitted me to pass into the dressing-room. Once alone, I grew calm, and collectedly went to work. Retaining my woman's garb without the slightest retrenchment, I merely assumed, in addition, a little vest, a collar, and cravat, and a paletôt of small dimensions; the whole being the costume of a brother of one of the pupils. Having loosened my hair out of its braids, made up the long back-hair close, and brushed the front hair to one side, I took my hat and gloves in my hand and came out. M. Paul was waiting, and so were the others. He looked at me. "That may pass in a pensionnat," he pronounced. Then added, not unkindly, "*Courage, mon ami! Un peu de sangfroid – un peu d'aplomb, M. Lucien, et tout ira bien.*"

St. Pierre sneered again, in her cold snaky manner.

I was irritable, because excited, and I could not help turning upon her and saying, that if she were not a lady and I a gentleman, I should feel disposed to call her out.

"After the play, after the play," said M. Paul. "I will then divide my pair of pistols between you, and we will settle the dispute according to form: it will only be the old quarrel of France and England."

But now the moment approached for the performance to commence. M. Paul, setting us before him, harangued us briefly, like a general addressing soldiers about to charge. I don't know what he said, except that he recommended each to penetrate herself with a sense of her personal insignificance. God knows I thought this advice superfluous for some of us. A bell tinkled. I and two more were ushered on to the stage. The bell tinkled again. I had to speak the very first words.

"Do not look at the crowd, nor think of it," whispered M. Paul in my ear. "Imagine yourself in the garret, acting to the rats."

He vanished. The curtain drew up – shrivelled to the ceiling: the bright lights, the long room, the gay throng, burst upon us. I thought of the black-beetles, the old boxes, the worm-eaten bureau. I said my say badly; but I said it. That first speech was the difficulty; it revealed to me this fact, that it was not the crowd I feared so much as my own voice. Foreigners and strangers, the crowd were nothing to me. Nor did I think of them. When my tongue once got free, and my voice took its true pitch, and found its natural tone, I thought of nothing but the personage I represented – and of M. Paul, who was listening, watching, prompting in the side-scenes.

By-and-by, feeling the right power come – the spring demanded gush and rise inwardly – I became sufficiently composed to notice my fellow-actors. Some of them played very well; especially Ginevra Fanshawe, who had to coquette between two suitors, and managed admirably: in fact she was in her element. I observed that she once or twice threw a certain marked fondness and pointed partiality into her manner towards me – the fop. With such emphasis and animation did she favour me, such glances did she dart out into the listening and applauding crowd, that to me – who knew her – it presently became evident she was acting *at* someone; and I followed her eye, her smile, her gesture, and ere long discovered that she had at least singled out a handsome and distinguished aim for her shafts; full in the path of those arrows – taller than other spectators, and therefore more sure to receive them – stood, in attitude quiet but intent, a well-known form – that of Dr. John.

The spectacle seemed somehow suggestive. There was language in Dr. John's look, though I cannot tell what he said; it animated me: I drew out of it a history; I put my idea into the part I performed; I threw it into my wooing of Ginevra. In the 'Ours', or sincere lover, I saw Dr. John. Did I pity him, as erst? No, I hardened my heart, rivalled and out-rivalled him. I knew myself but a fop, but where *he* was outcast *I* could please. Now I know I acted as if wishful and resolute to win and conquer. Ginevra seconded me; between us we half-changed the nature of the rôle, gilding it from top to toe. Between the acts M. Paul told us he knew not what possessed us, and half expostulated. "*C'est peut-être plus beau que votre modèle*," said he, "*mais ce n'est pas juste*." I know not what possessed me either; but somehow, my longing was to eclipse the 'Ours', i.e., Dr. John. Ginevra was tender; how could I be otherwise than chivalric? Retaining the letter, I recklessly altered the spirit of the rôle. Without heart, without interest, I could not play it at all. It must be played – in went the yearned-for seasoning – thus favoured, I played it with relish.

What I felt that night, and what I did, I no more expected to feel and do, than to be lifted in a trance to the seventh heaven. Cold, reluctant, apprehensive, I had accepted a part to please another: ere long, warming, becoming interested, taking courage, I acted to please myself. Yet the next day, when I thought it over, I quite disapproved of these amateur performances; and though glad that I had obliged M. Paul, and tried my own strength for once, I took a firm resolution, never to be drawn into a similar affair. A keen relish for dramatic expression had revealed itself as part of my nature; to cherish and exercise this new-found faculty might gift me with a world of delight, but it would not do for a mere looker-on at life: the strength and longing must be put by; and I put them by, and fastened them in with the lock of a resolution which neither Time nor Temptation has since picked.

No sooner was the play over, and *well* over, than the choleric and arbitrary M. Paul underwent a metamorphosis. His hour of managerial responsibility past, he at once laid aside his magisterial austerity; in a moment he stood amongst us, vivacious, kind, and social, shook hands with us all round, thanked us separately, and announced his determination that each of us should in turn be his partner in the coming ball. On his claiming my promise, I told him I did not dance. "For once I must," was the answer; and if I had not slipped aside and kept out of his way, he would have compelled me to this second performance. But I had acted enough for one evening; it was time I retired into myself and my ordinary life. My dun-coloured dress did well enough under a paletôt on the stage, but would not suit a waltz or a quadrille. Withdrawing to a quiet nook, whence unobserved I could observe – the ball, its splendours and its pleasures, passed before me as a spectacle.

Again Ginevra Fanshawe was the belle, the fairest and the gayest present; she was selected to open the ball: very lovely she looked, very gracefully she danced, very joyously she smiled. Such scenes were her triumphs – she was the child of pleasure. Work or suffering found her listless and dejected, powerless and repining; but gaiety expanded her butterfly's wings, lit up their gold-dust and bright spots, made her flash like a gem, and flush like a flower. At all ordinary diet and plain beverage she would pout; but she fed on creams and ices like a humming-bird on honey-paste: sweet wine was her element, and sweet cake her daily bread. Ginevra lived her full life in a ball-room; elsewhere she drooped dispirited.

Think not, reader, that she thus bloomed and sparkled for the mere sake of M. Paul, her partner, or that she lavished her best graces that night for the edification of her companions only, or for that of the parents and grand-parents, who filled the carré, and lined the ball-room; under circumstances so insipid and limited, with motives so chilly and vapid, Ginevra would scarce have deigned to walk one quadrille, and weariness and fretfulness would have replaced animation and good-humour, but she knew of a leaven in the otherwise heavy festal mass which lighted the whole; she tasted a condiment which gave it zest; she perceived reasons justifying the display of her choicest attractions.

In the ball-room, indeed, not a single male spectator was to be seen who was not married and a father – M. Paul excepted – that gentleman, too, being the sole creature of his sex permitted to lead out a pupil to the dance; and this exceptional part was allowed him, partly as a matter of old-established custom (for he was a kinsman of Madame Beck's, and high in her confidence), partly because he would always have his own way and do as he pleased, and partly because – wilful, passionate, partial, as he might be – he was the soul of honour, and might be trusted with a regiment of the fairest and purest; in perfect security that under his leadership they would come to no harm. Many of the girls – it may be noted in parenthesis – were not pure-minded at all, very much otherwise; but they no more dare betray their natural coarseness in M. Paul's presence, than they dare tread purposely on his corns, laugh in his face during a stormy apostrophe, or speak above their breath while some crisis of irritability was covering his human visage with the mask of an intelligent tiger. M. Paul, then, might dance with whom he would – and woe be to the interference which put him out of step.

Others there were admitted as spectators – with (seeming) reluctance, through prayers, by influence, under restriction, by special and difficult exercise of Madame Beck's gracious good-nature, and whom she all the evening – with her own personal surveillance – kept far aloof at the remotest, drearest, coldest, darkest side of the carré – a small, forlorn band of *'jeunes gens'*; these being all of the best families, grown-up sons of mothers present, and whose sisters were pupils in the school. That whole evening was Madame on duty beside these *'jeunes gens'* – attentive to them as a mother, but strict with them as a dragon. There was a sort of cordon stretched before them, which they wearied her with prayers to be permitted to pass, and just to revive themselves by one dance with that *'belle blonde'*, or that *'jolie brune'*, or *'cette jeune fille magnifique aux cheveux noirs comme le jais'*.

"*Taisez-vous!*" Madame would reply, heroically and inexorably. "*Vous ne passerez pas à moins que ce ne soit sur mon cadavre, et vous ne danserez qu'avec la nonnette du jardin*" (alluding to the legend). And she majestically walked to and fro along their disconsolate and impatient line, like a little Bonaparte in a mouse-coloured silk gown.

Madame knew something of the world; Madame knew much of human nature. I don't think that another directress in Villette would have dared to admit a *'jeune homme'* within her walls; but Madame knew that by granting such admission, on an occasion like the present, a bold stroke might be struck, and a great point gained.

In the first place, the parents were made accomplices to the deed, for it was only through their mediation it was brought about. Secondly: the admission of these rattlesnakes, so fascinating and so dangerous, served to draw out Madame precisely in her strongest character – that of a first-rate surveillante. Thirdly: their presence furnished a most piquant ingredient to the entertainment: the pupils knew it, and saw it, and the view of such golden apples shining afar off, animated them with a spirit no other circumstance could have kindled. The children's pleasure spread to the parents; life and mirth circulated quickly round the ball-room; the *'jeunes gens'* themselves, though restrained, were amused: for Madame never permitted them to feel dull – and thus Madame Beck's fête annually ensured a success unknown to the fête of any other directress in the land.

I observed that Dr. John was at first permitted to walk at large through the classes: there was about him a manly, responsible look, that redeemed his youth, and half-expiated his beauty; but as soon as the ball began, Madame ran up to him.

"Come, Wolf; come," said she, laughing: "you wear sheep's clothing, but you must quit the fold notwithstanding. Come; I have a fine menagerie of twenty here in the carré: let me place you amongst my collection."

"But first suffer me to have one dance with one pupil of my choice."

"Have you the face to ask such a thing? It is madness: it is impiety. *Sortez, sortez, au plus vite.*"

She drove him before her, and soon had him enclosed within the cordon.

Ginevra being, I suppose, tired with dancing, sought me out in my retreat. She threw herself on the bench beside me, and (a demonstration I could very well have dispensed with) cast her arms round my neck.

"Lucy Snowe! Lucy Snowe!" she cried in a somewhat sobbing voice, half hysterical.

"What in the world is the matter?" I drily said.

"How do I look – how do I look tonight?" she demanded.

"As usual," said I; "preposterously vain."

"Caustic creature! You never have a kind word for me; but in spite of you, and all other envious detractors, I know I am beautiful; I feel it, I see it – for there is a great looking-glass in the dressing-room, where I can view my shape from head to foot. Will you go with me now, and let us two stand before it?"

"I will, Miss Fanshawe: you shall be humoured even to the top of your bent."

The dressing-room was very near, and we stepped in. Putting her arm through mine, she drew me to the mirror. Without resistance remonstrance, or remark, I stood and let her self-love have its feast and triumph: curious to see how much it could swallow – whether it was possible it could feed to satiety – whether any whisper of consideration for others could penetrate her heart, and moderate its vainglorious exultation.

Not at all. She turned me and herself round; she viewed us both on all sides; she smiled, she waved her curls, she retouched her sash, she spread her dress, and finally, letting go my arm, and curtseying with mock respect, she said: "I would not be you for a kingdom."

The remark was too naïve to rouse anger; I merely said: "Very good."

"And what would *you* give to be *me*?" she inquired.

"Not a bad sixpence – strange as it may sound," I replied. "You are but a poor creature."

"You don't think so in your heart."

"No; for in my heart you have not the outline of a place: I only occasionally turn you over in my brain."

"Well, but," said she, in an expostulatory tone, "just listen to the difference of our positions, and then see how happy am I, and how miserable are you."

"Go on; I listen."

"In the first place: I am the daughter of a gentleman of family, and though my father is not rich, I have expectations from an uncle. Then, I am just eighteen, the finest age possible. I have had a continental education, and though I can't spell, I have abundant accomplishments. I *am* pretty; *you* can't deny that; I may have as many admirers as I choose. This very night I have been breaking the hearts of two gentlemen, and it is the dying look I had from one of them just now, which puts me in such spirits. I do so like to watch them turn red and pale, and scowl and dart fiery glances at each other, and languishing ones at me. There is *me* – happy *me*; now for *you*, poor soul!

"I suppose you are nobody's daughter, since you took care of little children when you first came to Villette: you have no relations; you can't call yourself young at twenty-three; you have no attractive accomplishments – no beauty. As to admirers, you hardly know what they are; you can't even talk on the subject: you sit dumb when the other teachers quote their conquests. I believe you never were in love, and never will be: you don't know the feeling, and so much the better, for though you might have your own heart broken, no living heart will you ever break. Isn't it all true?"

"A good deal of it is true as gospel, and shrewd besides. There must be good in you, Ginevra, to speak so honestly; that snake, Zélie St. Pierre, could not utter what you have uttered. Still, Miss Fanshawe, hapless as I am, according to your showing, sixpence I would not give to purchase you, body and soul."

"Just because I am not clever, and that is all *you* think of. Nobody in the world but you cares for cleverness."

"On the contrary, I consider you *are* clever, in your way – very smart indeed. But you were talking of breaking hearts – that edifying amusement into the merits of which I don't quite enter; pray on whom does your vanity lead you to think you have done execution tonight?"

She approached her lips to my ear – "Isidore and Alfred de Hamal are both here," she whispered.

"Oh! They are? I should like to see them."

"There's a dear creature! Your curiosity is roused at last. Follow me, I will point them out."

She proudly led the way – "But you cannot see them well from the classes," said she, turning, "Madame keeps them too far off. Let us cross the garden, enter by the corridor, and get close to them behind: we shall be scolded if we are seen, but never mind."

For once, I did not mind. Through the garden we went – penetrated into the corridor by a quiet private entrance, and approaching the carré, yet keeping in the corridor shade, commanded a near view of the band of '*jeunes gens*'.

I believe I could have picked out the conquering de Hamal even undirected. He was a straight-nosed, very correct-featured little dandy. I say *little* dandy, though he was not beneath the middle standard in stature; but his lineaments were small, and so were his hands and feet; and he was pretty and smooth, and as trim as a doll: so nicely dressed, so nicely curled, so booted and gloved and cravated – he was charming indeed. I said so. "What, a dear personage!" cried I, and commended Ginevra's taste warmly; and asked her what she thought de Hamal might have done with the precious fragments of that heart she had broken – whether he kept them in a scent-vial, and conserved them in otto of roses? I observed, too, with deep rapture of approbation, that the colonel's hands were scarce larger than Miss Fanshawe's own, and suggested that this circumstance might be convenient, as he could wear her gloves at a pinch. On his dear curls, I told her I doated: and as to his low, Grecian brow, and exquisite classic headpiece, I confessed I had no language to do such perfections justice.

"And if he were your lover?" suggested the cruelly exultant Ginevra.

"Oh! Heavens, what bliss!" said I; "but do not be inhuman, Miss Fanshawe: to put such thoughts into my head is like showing poor outcast Cain a far glimpse of Paradise."

"You like him, then?"

"As I like sweets, and jams, and comfits, and conservatory flowers."

Ginevra admired my taste, for all these things were her adoration; she could then readily credit that they were mine too.

"Now for Isidore," I went on. I own I felt still more curious to see him than his rival; but Ginevra was absorbed in the latter.

"Alfred was admitted here tonight," said she, "through the influence of his aunt, Madame la Baronne de Dorlodot; and now, having seen him, can you not understand why I have been in such spirits all the evening, and acted so well, and danced with such life, and why I am now happy as a queen? *Dieu! Dieu!* It was such good fun to glance first at him and then at the other, and madden them both."

"But that other – where is he? Show me Isidore."

"I don't like."

"Why not?"

"I am ashamed of him."

"For what reason?"

"Because – because" (in a whisper) "he has such – such whiskers, orange – red – there now!"

"The murder is out," I subjoined. "Never mind, show him all the same; I engage not to faint."

She looked round. Just then an English voice spoke behind her and me.

"You are both standing in a draught; you must leave this corridor."

"There is no draught, Dr. John," said I, turning.

"She takes cold so easily," he pursued, looking at Ginevra with extreme kindness. "She is delicate; she must be cared for: fetch her a shawl."

"Permit me to judge for myself," said Miss Fanshawe, with hauteur. "I want no shawl."

"Your dress is thin, you have been dancing, you are heated."

"Always preaching," retorted she; "always coddling and admonishing."

The answer Dr. John would have given did not come; that his heart was hurt became evident in his eye; darkened, and saddened, and pained, he turned a little aside, but was patient. I knew where there were plenty of shawls near at hand; I ran and fetched one.

"She shall wear this, if I have strength to make her," said I, folding it well round her muslin dress, covering carefully her neck and her arms. "Is that Isidore?" I asked, in a somewhat fierce whisper.

She pushed up her lip, smiled, and nodded.

"Is *that* Isidore?" I repeated, giving her a shake: I could have given her a dozen.

"*C'est lui-même*," said she. "How coarse he is, compared with the Colonel-Count! And then – *oh ciel!* – the whiskers!"

Dr. John now passed on.

"The Colonel-Count!" I echoed. "The doll – the puppet – the manikin – the poor inferior creature! A mere lackey for Dr. John his valet, his foot-boy! Is it possible that fine generous gentleman – handsome as a vision – offers you his honourable hand and gallant heart, and promises to protect your flimsy person and feckless mind through the storms and struggles of life – and you hang back – you scorn, you sting, you torture him! Have you power to do this? Who gave you that power? Where is it? Does it lie all in your beauty – your pink and white complexion, and your yellow hair? Does this bind his soul at your feet, and bend his neck under your yoke? Does this purchase for you his affection, his tenderness, his thoughts, his hopes, his interest, his noble, cordial love – and will you not have it? Do you scorn it? You are only dissembling: you are not in earnest: you love him; you long for him; but you trifle with his heart to make him more surely yours?"

"Bah! How you run on! I don't understand half you have said."

I had got her out into the garden ere this. I now set her down on a seat and told her she should not stir till she had avowed which she meant in the end to accept – the man or the monkey.

"Him you call the man," said she, "is bourgeois, sandy-haired, and answers to the name of John! – *Cela suffit: je n'en veux pas.* Colonel de Hamal is a gentleman of excellent connections, perfect manners, sweet appearance, with pale interesting face, and hair and eyes like an Italian. Then too he is the most delightful company possible – a man quite in my way; not sensible and serious like the other; but one with whom I can talk on equal terms – who does not plague and bore, and harass me with depths, and heights, and passions, and talents for which I have no taste. There now. Don't hold me so fast."

I slackened my grasp, and she darted off. I did not care to pursue her.

Somehow I could not avoid returning once more in the direction of the corridor to get another glimpse of Dr. John; but I met him on the garden-steps, standing where the light from a window fell broad. His well-proportioned figure was not to be mistaken, for I doubt whether there was another in that assemblage his equal. He carried his hat in his hand; his uncovered head, his face and fine brow were most handsome and manly. *His* features were not delicate, not slight like those of a woman, nor were they cold, frivolous, and feeble; though well cut, they were not so chiselled, so frittered away, as to lose in expression or significance what they gained in unmeaning symmetry. Much feeling spoke in them at times, and more sat silent in his eye. Such at least were my thoughts of him: to me he seemed all this. An inexpressible sense of wonder occupied me, as I looked at this man, and reflected that *he* could not be slighted.

It was not my intention to approach or address him in the garden, our terms of acquaintance not warranting such a step; I had only meant to view him in the crowd – myself unseen: coming upon him thus alone, I withdrew. But he was looking out for me, or rather for her who had been with me: therefore he descended the steps, and followed me down the alley.

"You know Miss Fanshawe? I have often wished to ask whether you knew her," said he.

"Yes: I know her."

"Intimately?"

"Quite as intimately as I wish."

"What have you done with her now?"

"Am I her keeper?" I felt inclined to ask; but I simply answered, "I have shaken her well, and would have shaken her better, but she escaped out of my hands and ran away."

"Would you favour me," he asked, "by watching over her this one evening, and observing that she does nothing imprudent – does not, for instance, run out into the night-air immediately after dancing?"

"I may, perhaps, look after her a little; since you wish it; but she likes her own way too well to submit readily to control."

"She is so young, so thoroughly artless," said he.

"To me she is an enigma," I responded.

"Is she?" he asked – much interested. "How?"

"It would be difficult to say how – difficult, at least, to tell *you* how."

"And why me?"

"I wonder she is not better pleased that you are so much her friend."

"But she has not the slightest idea how much I *am* her friend. That is precisely the point I cannot teach her. May I inquire did she ever speak of me to you?"

"Under the name of 'Isidore' she has talked about you often; but I must add that it is only within the last ten minutes I have discovered that you and 'Isidore' are identical. It is only, Dr. John, within that brief space of time I have learned that Ginevra Fanshawe is the person, under this roof, in whom you have long been interested – that she is the magnet which attracts you to the Rue Fossette, that for her sake you venture into this garden, and seek out caskets dropped by rivals."

"You know all?"

"I know so much."

"For more than a year I have been accustomed to meet her in society. Mrs. Cholmondeley, her friend, is an acquaintance of mine; thus I see her every Sunday. But you observed that under the name of 'Isidore' she often spoke of me: may I – without inviting you to a breach of confidence – inquire what was the tone, what the feeling of her remarks? I feel somewhat anxious to know, being a little tormented with uncertainty as to how I stand with her."

"Oh, she varies: she shifts and changes like the wind."

"Still, you can gather some general idea –?"

"I can," thought I, "but it would not do to communicate that general idea to you. Besides, if I said she did not love you, I know you would not believe me."

"You are silent," he pursued. "I suppose you have no good news to impart. No matter. If she feels for me positive coldness and aversion, it is a sign I do not deserve her."

"Do you doubt yourself? Do you consider yourself the inferior of Colonel de Hamal?"

"I love Miss Fanshawe far more than de Hamal loves any human being, and would care for and guard her better than he. Respecting de Hamal, I fear she is under an illusion; the man's character is known to me, all his antecedents, all his scrapes. He is not worthy of your beautiful young friend."

"My 'beautiful young friend' ought to know that, and to know or feel who is worthy of her," said I. "If her beauty or her brains will not serve her so far, she merits the sharp lesson of experience."

"Are you not a little severe?"

"I am excessively severe – more severe than I choose to show you. You should hear the strictures with which I favour my 'beautiful young friend', only that you would be unutterably shocked at my want of tender considerateness for her delicate nature."

"She is so lovely, one cannot but be loving towards her. You – every woman older than herself, must feel for such a simple, innocent, girlish fairy a sort of motherly or elder-sisterly fondness. Graceful angel! Does not your heart yearn towards her when she pours into your ear her pure, childlike confidences? How you are privileged!" And he sighed.

"I cut short these confidences somewhat abruptly now and then," said I. "But excuse me, Dr. John, may I change the theme for one instant? What a god-like person is that de Hamal! What a nose on his face – perfect! Model one in putty or clay, you could not make a better or straighter, or neater; and then, such classic lips and chin – and his bearing – sublime."

"De Hamal is an unutterable puppy, besides being a very white-livered hero."

"You, Dr. John, and every man of a less-refined mould than he, must feel for him a sort of admiring affection, such as Mars and the coarser deities may be supposed to have borne the young, graceful Apollo."

"An unprincipled, gambling little jackanapes!" said Dr. John curtly, "whom, with one hand, I could lift up by the waistband any day, and lay low in the kennel if I liked."

"The sweet seraph!" said I. "What a cruel idea! Are you not a little severe, Dr. John?"

And now I paused. For the second time that night I was going beyond myself – venturing out of what I looked on as my natural habits – speaking in an unpremeditated, impulsive strain, which startled me strangely when I halted to reflect. On rising that morning, had I anticipated that before night I should have acted the part of a gay lover in a vaudeville; and an hour after, frankly discussed with Dr. John the question of his hapless suit, and rallied him on his illusions? I had no more presaged such feats than I had looked forward to an ascent in a balloon, or a voyage to Cape Horn.

The Doctor and I, having paced down the walk, were now returning; the reflex from the window again lit his face: he smiled, but his eye was melancholy. How I wished that he could feel heart's-ease! How I grieved that he brooded over pain, and pain from such a cause! He, with his great advantages, *he* to love in vain! I did not then know that the pensiveness of reverse is the best phase for some minds; nor did I reflect that some herbs, 'though scentless when entire, yield fragrance when they're bruised'.

"Do not be sorrowful, do not grieve," I broke out. "If there is in Ginevra one spark of worthiness of your affection, she will – she *must* feel devotion in return. Be cheerful, be hopeful, Dr. John. Who should hope, if not you?"

In return for this speech I got – what, it must be supposed, I deserved – a look of surprise: I thought also of some disapprobation. We parted, and I went into the house very chill. The clocks struck and the bells tolled midnight; people were leaving fast: the fête was over; the lamps were fading. In another hour all the dwelling-house, and all the pensionnat, were dark and hushed. I too was in bed, but not asleep. To me it was not easy to sleep after a day of such excitement.

Chapter Fifteen
The Long Vacation

FOLLOWING Madame Beck's fête, with its three preceding weeks of relaxation, its brief twelve hours' burst of hilarity and dissipation, and its one subsequent day of utter languor, came a period of reaction; two months of real application, of close, hard study. These two months, being the last of the 'année scolaire', were indeed the only genuine working months in the year. To them was procrastinated – into them concentrated, alike by professors, mistresses, and pupils – the main burden of preparation for the examinations preceding the distribution of prizes. Candidates for rewards had then to work in good earnest; masters and teachers had to set their shoulders to the wheel, to urge on the backward, and diligently aid and train the more promising. A showy demonstration – a telling exhibition – must be got up for public view, and all means were fair to this end.

I scarcely noted how the other teachers went to work; I had my own business to mind; and *my* task was not the least onerous, being to imbue some ninety sets of brains with a due tincture of what they considered a most complicated and difficult science, that of the English language; and to drill ninety tongues in what, for them, was an almost impossible pronunciation – the lisping and hissing dentals of the Isles.

The examination-day arrived. Awful day! Prepared for with anxious care, dressed for with silent despatch – nothing vaporous or fluttering now – no white gauze or azure streamers; the grave, close, compact was the order of the toilette. It seemed to me that I was this day, especially doomed – the main burden and trial falling on me alone of all the female teachers. The others were not expected to examine in the studies they taught; the professor of literature, M. Paul, taking upon himself this duty. He, this school autocrat, gathered all and sundry reins into the hollow of his one hand; he irefully rejected any colleague; he would not have help. Madame herself, who evidently rather wished to undertake the examination in geography – her favourite study, which she taught well – was forced to succumb, and be subordinate to her despotic kinsman's direction. The whole staff of instructors, male and female, he set aside, and stood on the examiner's estrade alone. It irked him that he was forced to make one exception to this rule. He could not manage English: he was obliged to leave that branch of education in the English teacher's hands; which he did, not without a flash of naïve jealousy.

A constant crusade against the 'amour-propre' of every human being but himself, was the crotchet of this able, but fiery and grasping little man. He had a strong relish for public representation in his own person, but an extreme abhorrence of the like display in any other. He quelled, he kept down when he could; and when he could not, he fumed like a bottled storm.

On the evening preceding the examination-day, I was walking in the garden, as were the other teachers and all the boarders. M. Emanuel joined me in the 'allée défendue'; his cigar was at his lips; his paletôt – a most characteristic garment of no particular shape – hung dark and menacing; the tassel of his bonnet grec sternly shadowed his left temple; his black whiskers curled like those of a wrathful cat; his blue eye had a cloud in its glitter.

"*Ainsi*," he began, abruptly fronting and arresting me, "*vous allez trôner comme une reine; demain – trôner à mes côtés? Sans doute vous savourez d'avance les délices de l'autorité. Je crois voir en je ne sais quoi de rayonnante, petite ambitieuse!*"

Now the fact was, he happened to be entirely mistaken. I did not – could not – estimate the admiration or the good opinion of tomorrow's audience at the same rate he did. Had that audience numbered as many personal friends and acquaintance for me as for him, I know not how it might have been: I speak of the case as it stood. On me school-triumphs shed but a cold lustre. I had wondered – and I wondered now – how it was that for him they seemed to shine as with hearth-warmth and hearth-glow. *He* cared for them perhaps too much; *I*, probably, too little. However, I had my own fancies as well as he. I liked, for instance, to see M. Emanuel jealous; it lit up his nature, and woke his spirit; it threw all sorts of queer lights and shadows over his dun face, and into his violet-azure eyes (he used to say that his black hair and blue eyes were '*une de ses beautés*'). There was a relish in his anger; it was artless, earnest, quite unreasonable, but never hypocritical. I uttered no disclaimer then of the complacency he attributed to me; I merely asked where the English examination came in – whether at the commencement or close of the day?

"I hesitate," said he, "whether at the very beginning, before many persons are come, and when your aspiring nature will not be gratified by a large audience, or quite at the close, when everybody is tired, and only a jaded and worn-out attention will be at your service."

"*Que vous êtes dur, Monsieur!*" I said, affecting dejection.

"One ought to be 'dur' with you. You are one of those beings who must be *kept down*. I know you! I know you! Other people in this house see you pass, and think that a colourless shadow has gone by. As for me, I scrutinized your face once, and it sufficed."

"You are satisfied that you understand me?"

Without answering directly, he went on, "Were you not gratified when you succeeded in that vaudeville? I watched you and saw a passionate ardour for triumph in your physiognomy. What fire shot into the glance! Not mere light, but flame: *je me tiens pour averti*."

"What feeling I had on that occasion, Monsieur – and pardon me, if I say, you immensely exaggerate both its quality and quantity – was quite abstract. I did not care for the vaudeville. I hated the part you assigned me. I had not the slightest sympathy with the audience below the stage. They are good people, doubtless, but do I know them? Are they anything to me? Can I care for being brought before their view again tomorrow? Will the examination be anything but a task to me – a task I wish well over?"

"Shall I take it out of your hands?"

"With all my heart; if you do not fear failure."

"But I should fail. I only know three phrases of English, and a few words: *par exemple, de sonn, de mone, de stares – est-ce bien dit?* My opinion is that it would be better to give up the thing altogether: to have no English examination, eh?"

"If Madame consents, I consent."

"Heartily?"

"Very heartily."

He smoked his cigar in silence. He turned suddenly.

"*Donnez-moi la main*," said he, and the spite and jealousy melted out of his face, and a generous kindliness shone there instead.

"Come, we will not be rivals, we will be friends," he pursued. "The examination shall take place, and I will choose a good moment; and instead of vexing and hindering, as I felt half-inclined ten minutes ago – for I have my malevolent moods: I always had from childhood – I will aid you sincerely. After all, you are solitary and a stranger, and have your way to make and your bread to earn; it may be well that you should become known. We will be friends: do you agree?"

"Out of my heart, Monsieur. I am glad of a friend. I like that better than a triumph."

"*Pauvrette?*" said he, and turned away and left the alley.

The examination passed over well; M. Paul was as good as his word, and did his best to make my part easy. The next day came the distribution of prizes; that also passed; the school broke up; the pupils went home, and now began the long vacation.

That vacation! Shall I ever forget it? I think not. Madame Beck went, the first day of the holidays, to join her children at the sea-side; all the three teachers had parents or friends with whom they took refuge; every professor quitted the city; some went to Paris, some to Boue-Marine; M. Paul set forth on a pilgrimage to Rome; the house was left quite empty, but for me, a servant, and a poor deformed and imbecile pupil, a sort of crétin, whom her stepmother in a distant province would not allow to return home.

My heart almost died within me; miserable longings strained its chords. How long were the September days! How silent, how lifeless! How vast and void seemed the desolate premises! How gloomy the forsaken garden – grey now with the dust of a town summer departed. Looking forward at the commencement of those eight weeks, I hardly knew how I was to live to the end. My spirits had long been gradually sinking; now that the prop of employment was withdrawn, they went down fast. Even to look forward was not to hope: the dumb future spoke no comfort, offered no promise, gave no inducement to bear present evil in reliance on future good. A sorrowful indifference to existence often pressed on me – a despairing resignation to reach betimes the end of all things earthly. Alas! When I had full leisure to look on life as life must be looked on by such as me, I found it but a hopeless desert: tawny sands, with no green fields, no palm-tree, no well in view. The hopes which are dear to youth, which bear it up and lead it on, I knew not and dared not know. If they knocked at my heart sometimes, an inhospitable bar to admission must be inwardly drawn. When they turned away thus rejected, tears sad enough sometimes flowed: but it could not be helped: I dared not give such guests lodging. So mortally did I fear the sin and weakness of presumption.

Religious reader, you will preach to me a long sermon about what I have just written, and so will you, moralist: and you, stern sage: you, stoic, will frown; you, cynic, sneer; you, epicure, laugh. Well, each and all, take it your own way. I accept the sermon, frown, sneer, and laugh; perhaps you are all right: and perhaps, circumstanced like me, you would have been, like me, wrong. The first month was, indeed, a long, black, heavy month to me.

The crétin did not seem unhappy. I did my best to feed her well and keep her warm, and she only asked food and sunshine, or when that lacked, fire. Her weak faculties approved of inertion: her brain, her eyes, her ears, her heart slept content; they could not wake to work, so lethargy was their Paradise.

Three weeks of that vacation were hot, fair, and dry, but the fourth and fifth were tempestuous and wet. I do not know why that change in the atmosphere made a cruel impression on me, why the raging storm and beating rain crushed me with a deadlier paralysis than I had experienced while the air had remained serene; but so it was; and my nervous system could hardly support what it had for many days and nights to undergo in that huge empty house. How I used to pray to Heaven for consolation and support! With what dread force the conviction would grasp me that Fate was my permanent foe, never to be conciliated. I did not, in my heart, arraign the mercy or justice of God for this; I concluded it to be a part of his great plan that some must deeply suffer while they live, and I thrilled in the certainty that of this number, I was one.

It was some relief when an aunt of the crétin, a kind old woman, came one day, and took away my strange, deformed companion. The hapless creature had been at times a heavy charge; I could not take her out beyond the garden, and I could not leave her a minute alone: for her poor mind, like her body, was warped: its propensity was to evil. A vague bent to mischief, an aimless malevolence, made constant vigilance indispensable. As she very rarely spoke, and would sit for hours together moping and mowing, and distorting her features with indescribable grimaces, it was more like being prisoned with some strange tameless animal, than associating with a human being. Then there were personal attentions to be rendered which required the nerve of a hospital nurse; my resolution was so tried, it sometimes fell dead-sick. These duties should not have fallen on me; a servant, now absent, had rendered them hitherto, and in the hurry of holiday departure, no substitute to fill this office had been provided. This tax and trial were by no means the least I have known in life. Still, menial and distasteful as they were, my mental pain was far more wasting and wearing. Attendance on the crétin deprived me often of the power and inclination to swallow a meal, and sent me faint to the fresh air, and the well or fountain in the court; but this duty never wrung my heart, or brimmed my eyes, or scalded my cheek with tears hot as molten metal.

The crétin being gone, I was free to walk out. At first I lacked courage to venture very far from the Rue Fossette, but by degrees I sought the city gates, and passed them, and then went wandering away far along chaussées, through fields, beyond cemeteries, Catholic and Protestant, beyond farmsteads, to lanes and little woods, and I know not where. A goad thrust me on, a fever forbade me to rest; a want of companionship maintainèd in my soul the cravings of a most deadly famine. I often walked all day, through the burning noon and the arid afternoon, and the dusk evening, and came back with moonrise.

While wandering in solitude, I would sometimes picture the present probable position of others, my acquaintance. There was Madame Beck at a cheerful watering-place with her children, her mother, and a whole troop of friends who had sought the same scene of relaxation. Zélie St. Pierre was at Paris, with her relatives; the other teachers were at their homes. There was Ginevra Fanshawe, whom certain of her connections had carried on a pleasant tour southward. Ginevra seemed to me the happiest. She was on the route of beautiful scenery; these September suns shone for her on fertile plains, where harvest and vintage matured under their mellow beam. These gold and crystal moons rose on her vision over blue horizons waved in mounted lines.

But all this was nothing; I too felt those autumn suns and saw those harvest moons, and I almost wished to be covered in with earth and turf, deep out of their influence; for I could not live in their light, nor make them comrades, nor yield them affection. But Ginevra had a kind of spirit with her, empowered to give constant strength and comfort, to gladden daylight and embalm darkness; the best of the good genii that guard humanity curtained her with his wings, and canopied her head with his bending form. By True Love was Ginevra followed: never could she be alone. Was she insensible to this presence? It seemed to me impossible: I could not realize such deadness. I imagined her grateful in secret, loving now with reserve; but purposing one day to show how much she loved: I pictured her faithful hero half conscious of her coy fondness, and comforted by that consciousness: I conceived an electric chord of sympathy between them, a fine chain of mutual understanding, sustaining union through a separation of a hundred leagues – carrying, across mound and hollow, communication by prayer and wish. Ginevra gradually became with me a sort of heroine. One day, perceiving this growing illusion, I said, "I really believe my nerves are getting overstretched: my mind has suffered somewhat too much a malady is growing upon it – what shall I do? How shall I keep well?"

Indeed there was no way to keep well under the circumstances. At last a day and night of peculiarly agonizing depression were succeeded by physical illness, I took perforce to my bed. About this time the Indian summer closed and the equinoctial storms began; and for nine dark and wet days, of which the hours rushed on all turbulent, deaf, dishevelled – bewildered with sounding hurricane – I lay in a strange fever of the nerves and blood. Sleep went quite away. I used to rise in the night, look round for her, beseech her earnestly to return. A rattle of the window, a cry of the blast only replied – Sleep never came!

I err. She came once, but in anger. Impatient of my importunity she brought with her an avenging dream. By the clock of St. Jean Baptiste, that dream remained scarce fifteen minutes – a brief space, but sufficing to wring my whole frame with unknown anguish; to confer a nameless experience that had the hue, the mien, the terror, the very tone of a visitation from eternity. Between twelve and one that night a cup was forced to my lips, black, strong, strange, drawn from no well, but filled up seething from a bottomless and boundless sea. Suffering, brewed in temporal or calculable measure, and mixed for mortal lips, tastes not as this suffering tasted. Having drank and woke, I thought all was over: the end come and past by. Trembling fearfully – as consciousness returned – ready to cry out on some fellow-creature to help me, only that I knew no fellow-creature was near enough to catch the wild summons – Goton in her far distant attic could not hear – I rose on my knees in bed. Some fearful hours went over me: indescribably was I torn, racked and oppressed in mind. Amidst the horrors of that dream I think the worst lay here. Methought the well-loved dead, who had loved *me* well in life, met me elsewhere, alienated: galled was my inmost spirit with an unutterable sense of despair about the future. Motive there was none why I should try to recover or wish to live; and yet quite unendurable was the pitiless and haughty voice in which Death challenged me to engage his unknown terrors. When I tried to pray I could only utter these words: "From my youth up Thy terrors have I suffered with a troubled mind."

Most true was it.

On bringing me my tea next morning Goton urged me to call in a doctor. I would not: I thought no doctor could cure me.

One evening – and I was not delirious: I was in my sane mind, I got up – I dressed myself, weak and shaking. The solitude and the stillness of the long dormitory could not be borne any longer; the ghastly white beds were turning into spectres – the coronal of each became a death's-head, huge and sun-bleached – dead dreams of an elder world and mightier race lay frozen in their wide gaping eyeholes. That evening more firmly than ever fastened into my soul the conviction that Fate was of stone, and Hope a false idol – blind, bloodless, and of granite core. I felt, too, that the trial God had appointed me was gaining its climax, and must now be turned by my own hands, hot, feeble, trembling as they were. It rained still, and blew; but with more clemency, I thought, than it had poured and raged all day. Twilight was falling, and I deemed its influence pitiful; from the lattice I saw coming night-clouds trailing low like banners drooping. It seemed to me that at this hour there was affection and sorrow in Heaven above for all pain suffered on earth beneath; the weight of my dreadful dream became alleviated – that insufferable thought of being no more loved – no more owned, half-yielded to hope of the contrary – I was sure this hope would shine clearer if I got out from under this house-roof, which was crushing as the slab of a tomb, and went outside the city to a certain quiet hill, a long way distant in the fields. Covered with a cloak (I could not be delirious, for I had sense and recollection to put on warm clothing), forth I set. The bells of a church arrested me in passing; they seemed to call me in to the salut, and I went in. Any solemn rite, any spectacle of sincere worship, any opening for appeal to God was as welcome to me then as bread to one in extremity of want. I knelt down with others on the stone pavement. It was an old solemn church, its pervading gloom not gilded but purpled by light shed through stained glass.

Few worshippers were assembled, and, the salut over, half of them departed. I discovered soon that those left remained to confess. I did not stir. Carefully every door of the church was shut; a holy quiet sank upon, and a solemn shade gathered about us. After a space, breathless and spent in prayer, a penitent approached the confessional. I watched. She whispered her avowal; her shrift was whispered back; she returned consoled. Another went, and another. A pale lady, kneeling near me, said in a low, kind voice: "Go you now, I am not quite prepared."

Mechanically obedient, I rose and went. I knew what I was about; my mind had run over the intent with lightning-speed. To take this step could not make me more wretched than I was; it might soothe me.

The priest within the confessional never turned his eyes to regard me; he only quietly inclined his ear to my lips. He might be a good man, but this duty had become to him a sort of form: he went through it with the phlegm of custom. I hesitated; of the formula of confession I was ignorant: instead of commencing, then, with the prelude usual, I said: *"Mon père, je suis Protestante."*

He directly turned. He was not a native priest: of that class, the cast of physiognomy is, almost invariably, grovelling: I saw by his profile and brow he was a Frenchman; though grey and advanced in years, he did not, I think, lack feeling or intelligence. He inquired, not unkindly, why, being a Protestant, I came to him?

I said I was perishing for a word of advice or an accent of comfort. I had been living for some weeks quite alone; I had been ill; I had a pressure of affliction on my mind of which it would hardly any longer endure the weight.

"Was it a sin, a crime?" he inquired, somewhat startled. I reassured him on this point, and, as well as I could, I showed him the mere outline of my experience.

He looked thoughtful, surprised, puzzled. "You take me unawares," said he. "I have not had such a case as yours before: ordinarily we know our routine, and are prepared; but this makes a great break in the common course of confession. I am hardly furnished with counsel fitting the circumstances."

Of course, I had not expected he would be; but the mere relief of communication in an ear which was human and sentient, yet consecrated – the mere pouring out of some portion of long accumulating, long pent-up pain into a vessel whence it could not be again diffused – had done me good. I was already solaced.

"Must I go, father?" I asked of him as he sat silent.

"My daughter," he said kindly – and I am sure he was a kind man: he had a compassionate eye – "for the present you had better go: but I assure you your words have struck me. Confession, like other things, is apt to become formal and trivial with habit. You have come and poured your heart out; a thing seldom done. I would fain think your case over, and take it with me to my oratory. Were you of our faith I should know what to say – a mind so tossed can find repose but in the bosom of retreat, and the punctual practice of piety. The world, it is well known, has no satisfaction for that class of natures. Holy men have bidden penitents like you to hasten their path upward by penance, self-denial, and difficult good works. Tears are given them here for meat and drink – bread of affliction and waters of affliction – their recompence comes hereafter. It is my own conviction that these impressions under which you are smarting are messengers from God to bring you back to the true Church. You were made for our faith: depend upon it our faith alone could heal and help you – Protestantism is altogether too dry, cold, prosaic for you. The further I look into this matter, the more plainly I see it is entirely out of the common order of things. On no account would I lose sight of you. Go, my daughter, for the present; but return to me again."

I rose and thanked him. I was withdrawing when he signed me to return.

"You must not come to this church," said he: "I see you are ill, and this church is too cold; you must come to my house: I live –" (and he gave me his address). "Be there tomorrow morning at ten."

In reply to this appointment, I only bowed; and pulling down my veil, and gathering round me my cloak, I glided away.

Did I, do you suppose, reader, contemplate venturing again within that worthy priest's reach? As soon should I have thought of walking into a Babylonish furnace. That priest had arms which could influence me: he was naturally kind, with a sentimental French kindness, to whose softness I knew myself not wholly impervious. Without respecting some sorts of affection, there was hardly any sort having a fibre of root in reality, which I could rely on my force wholly to withstand. Had I gone to him, he would have shown me all that was tender, and comforting, and gentle, in the honest Popish superstition. Then he would have tried to kindle, blow and stir up in me the zeal of good works. I know not how it would all have ended. We all think ourselves strong in some points; we all know ourselves weak in many; the probabilities are that had I visited Numero 10, Rue des Mages, at the hour and day appointed, I might just now, instead of writing this heretic narrative, be counting my beads in the cell of a certain Carmelite convent on the Boulevard of Crécy, in Villette. There was something of Fénélon about that benign old priest; and whatever most of his brethren may be, and whatever I may think of his Church and creed (and I like neither), of himself I must ever retain a grateful recollection. He was kind when I needed kindness; he did me good. May Heaven bless him!

Twilight had passed into night, and the lamps were lit in the streets ere I issued from that sombre church. To turn back was now become possible to me; the wild longing to breathe this October wind on the little hill far without the city walls had ceased to be an imperative impulse, and was softened into a wish with which Reason could cope: she put it down, and I turned, as I thought, to the Rue Fossette. But I had become involved in a part of the city with which I was not familiar; it was the old part, and full of narrow streets of picturesque, ancient, and mouldering houses. I was much too weak to be very collected, and I was still too careless of my own welfare and safety to be cautious; I grew embarrassed; I got immeshed in a network of turns unknown. I was lost and had no resolution to ask guidance of any passenger.

If the storm had lulled a little at sunset, it made up now for lost time. Strong and horizontal thundered the current of the wind from north-west to south-east; it brought rain like spray, and sometimes a sharp hail, like shot: it was cold and pierced me to the vitals. I bent my head to meet it, but it beat me back. My heart did not fail at all in this conflict; I only wished that I had wings and could ascend the gale, spread and repose my pinions on its strength, career in its course, sweep where it swept. While wishing this, I suddenly felt colder where before I was cold, and more powerless where before I was weak. I tried to reach the porch of a great building near, but the mass of frontage and the giant spire turned black and vanished from my eyes. Instead of sinking on the steps as I intended, I seemed to pitch headlong down an abyss. I remember no more.

Volume Two

Chapter Sixteen
Auld Lang Syne

WHERE MY SOUL went during that swoon I cannot tell. Whatever she saw, or wherever she travelled in her trance on that strange night she kept her own secret; never whispering a word to Memory, and baffling imagination by an indissoluble silence. She may have gone upward, and come in sight of her eternal home, hoping for leave to rest now, and deeming that her painful union with matter was at last dissolved. While she so deemed, an angel may have warned her away from heaven's threshold, and, guiding her weeping down, have bound her, once more, all shuddering and unwilling, to that poor frame, cold and wasted, of whose companionship she was grown more than weary.

I know she re-entered her prison with pain, with reluctance, with a moan and a long shiver. The divorced mates, Spirit and Substance, were hard to re-unite: they greeted each other, not in an embrace, but a racking sort of struggle. The returning sense of sight came upon me, red, as if it swam in blood; suspended hearing rushed back loud, like thunder; consciousness revived in fear: I sat up appalled, wondering into what region, amongst what strange beings I was waking. At first I knew nothing I looked on: a wall was not a wall – a lamp not a lamp. I should have understood what we call a ghost, as well as I did the commonest object: which is another way of intimating that all my eye rested on struck it as spectral. But the faculties soon settled each in his place; the life-machine presently resumed its wonted and regular working.

Still, I knew not where I was; only in time I saw I had been removed from the spot where I fell: I lay on no portico-step; night and tempest were excluded by walls, windows, and ceiling. Into some house I had been carried – but what house?

I could only think of the pensionnat in the Rue Fossette. Still half-dreaming, I tried hard to discover in what room they had put me; whether the great dormitory, or one of the little dormitories. I was puzzled, because I could not make the glimpses of furniture I saw accord with my knowledge of any of these apartments. The empty white beds were wanting, and the long line of large windows. "Surely," thought I, "it is not to Madame Beck's own chamber they have carried me!" And here my eye fell on an easy-chair covered with blue damask. Other seats, cushioned to match, dawned on me by degrees; and at last I took in the complete fact of a pleasant parlour, with a wood fire on a clear-shining hearth, a carpet where arabesques of bright blue relieved a ground of shaded fawn; pale walls over which a slight but endless garland of azure forget-me-nots ran mazed and bewildered amongst myriad gold leaves and tendrils. A gilded mirror filled up the space between two windows, curtained amply with blue damask. In this mirror I saw myself laid, not in bed, but on a sofa. I looked spectral; my eyes larger and more hollow, my hair darker than was natural, by contrast with my thin and ashen face. It was obvious, not only from the furniture, but from the position of windows, doors, and fireplace, that this was an unknown room in an unknown house.

Hardly less plain was it that my brain was not yet settled; for, as I gazed at the blue arm-chair, it appeared to grow familiar; so did a certain scroll-couch, and not less so the round centre-table, with a blue-covering, bordered with autumn-tinted foliage; and, above all, two little footstools with worked covers, and a small ebony-framed chair, of which the seat and back were also worked with groups of brilliant flowers on a dark ground.

Struck with these things, I explored further. Strange to say, old acquaintance were all about me, and 'auld lang syne' smiled out of every nook. There were two oval miniatures over the mantel-piece, of which I knew by heart the pearls about the high and powdered 'heads'; the velvets circling the white throats; the swell of the full muslin kerchiefs: the pattern of the lace sleeve-ruffles. Upon the mantel-shelf there were two china vases, some relics of a diminutive tea-service, as smooth as enamel and as thin as egg-shell, and a white centre ornament, a classic group in alabaster, preserved under glass. Of all these things I could have told the peculiarities, numbered the flaws or cracks, like any clairvoyante. Above all, there was a pair of handscreens, with elaborate pencil-drawings finished like line engravings; these, my very eyes ached at beholding again, recalling hours when they had followed, stroke by stroke and touch by touch, a tedious, feeble, finical, school-girl pencil held in these fingers, now so skeleton-like.

Where was I? Not only in what spot of the world, but in what year of our Lord? For all these objects were of past days, and of a distant country. Ten years ago I bade them goodbye; since my fourteenth year they and I had never met. I gasped audibly, "Where am I?"

A shape hitherto unnoticed, stirred, rose, came forward: a shape inharmonious with the environment, serving only to complicate the riddle further. This was no more than a sort of native bonne, in a common-place bonne's cap and print-dress. She spoke neither French nor English, and I could get no intelligence from her, not understanding her phrases of dialect. But she bathed my temples and forehead with some cool and perfumed water, and then she heightened the cushion on which I reclined, made signs that I was not to speak, and resumed her post at the foot of the sofa.

She was busy knitting; her eyes thus drawn from me, I could gaze on her without interruption. I did mightily wonder how she came there, or what she could have to do among the scenes, or with the days of my girlhood. Still more I marvelled what those scenes and days could now have to do with me.

Too weak to scrutinize thoroughly the mystery, I tried to settle it by saying it was a mistake, a dream, a fever-fit; and yet I knew there could be no mistake, and that I was not sleeping, and I believed I was sane. I wished the room had not been so well lighted, that I might not so clearly have seen the little pictures, the ornaments, the screens, the worked chair. All these objects, as well as the blue-damask furniture, were, in fact, precisely the same, in every minutest detail, with those I so well remembered, and with which I had been so thoroughly intimate, in the drawing-room of my godmother's house at Bretton. Methought the apartment only was changed, being of different proportions and dimensions.

I thought of Bedreddin Hassan, transported in his sleep from Cairo to the gates of Damascus. Had a Genius stooped his dark wing down the storm to whose stress I had succumbed, and gathering me from the church-steps, and 'rising high into the air', as the eastern tale said, had he borne me over land and ocean, and laid me quietly down beside a hearth of Old England? But no; I knew the fire of that hearth burned before its Lares no more – it went out long ago, and the household gods had been carried elsewhere.

The bonne turned again to survey me, and seeing my eyes wide open, and, I suppose, deeming their expression perturbed and excited, she put down her knitting. I saw her busied for a moment at a little stand; she poured out water, and measured drops from a phial: glass in hand, she approached me. What dark-tinged draught might she now be offering? What Genii-elixir or Magi-distillation?

It was too late to inquire – I had swallowed it passively, and at once. A tide of quiet thought now came gently caressing my brain; softer and softer rose the flow, with tepid undulations smoother than balm. The pain of weakness left my limbs, my muscles slept. I lost power to move; but, losing at the same time wish, it was no privation. That kind bonne placed a screen between me and the lamp; I saw her rise to do this, but do not remember seeing her resume her place: in the interval between the two acts, I 'fell on sleep'.

* * *

At waking, lo! All was again changed. The light of high day surrounded me; not, indeed, a warm, summer light, but the leaden gloom of raw and blustering autumn. I felt sure now that I was in the pensionnat – sure by the beating rain on the casement; sure by the 'wuther' of wind amongst trees, denoting a garden outside; sure by the chill, the whiteness, the solitude, amidst which I lay. I say *whiteness* – for the dimity curtains, dropped before a French bed, bounded my view.

I lifted them; I looked out. My eye, prepared to take in the range of a long, large, and whitewashed chamber, blinked baffled, on encountering the limited area of a small cabinet – a cabinet with seagreen walls; also, instead of five wide and naked windows, there was one high lattice, shaded with muslin festoons: instead of two dozen little stands of painted wood, each holding a basin and an ewer, there was a toilette-table dressed, like a lady for a ball, in a white robe over a pink skirt; a polished and large glass crowned, and a pretty pin-cushion frilled with lace, adorned it. This toilette, together with a small, low, green and white chintz arm-chair, a washstand topped with a marble slab, and supplied with utensils of pale greenware, sufficiently furnished the tiny chamber.

Reader; I felt alarmed! Why? You will ask. What was there in this simple and somewhat pretty sleeping-closet to startle the most timid? Merely this – these articles of furniture could not be real, solid arm-chairs, looking-glasses, and washstands – they must be the ghosts of such articles; or, if this were denied as too wild an hypothesis – and, confounded as I was, I *did* deny it – there remained but to conclude that I had myself passed into an abnormal state of mind; in short, that I was very ill and delirious: and even then, mine was the strangest figment with which delirium had ever harassed a victim.

I knew – I was obliged to know – the green chintz of that little chair; the little snug chair itself, the carved, shining-black, foliated frame of that glass; the smooth, milky-green of the china vessels on the stand; the very stand too, with its top of grey marble, splintered at one corner; – all these I was compelled to recognise and to hail, as last night I had, perforce, recognised and hailed the rosewood, the drapery, the porcelain, of the drawing-room.

Bretton! Bretton! And ten years ago shone reflected in that mirror. And why did Bretton and my fourteenth year haunt me thus? Why, if they came at all, did they not return complete? Why hovered before my distempered vision the mere furniture, while the rooms and the locality were gone? As to that pincushion made of crimson satin, ornamented with gold beads and frilled with thread-lace, I had the same right to know it as to know the screens – I had made it myself. Rising with a start from the bed, I took the cushion in my hand and examined it. There was the cipher 'L.L.B.' formed in gold beds, and surrounded with an oval wreath embroidered in white silk. These were the initials of my godmother's name – Lonisa Lucy Bretton.

"Am I in England? Am I at Bretton?" I muttered; and hastily pulling up the blind with which the lattice was shrouded, I looked out to try and discover *where* I was; half-prepared to meet the calm, old, handsome buildings and clean grey pavement of St. Ann's Street, and to see at the end the towers of the minster: or, if otherwise, fully expectant of a town view somewhere, a rue in Villette, if not a street in a pleasant and ancient English city.

I looked, on the contrary, through a frame of leafage, clustering round the high lattice, and forth thence to a grassy mead-like level, a lawn-terrace with trees rising from the lower ground beyond – high forest-trees, such as I had not seen for many a day. They were now groaning under the gale of October, and between their trunks I traced the line of an avenue, where yellow leaves lay in heaps and drifts, or were whirled singly before the sweeping west wind. Whatever landscape might lie further must have been flat, and these tall beeches shut it out. The place seemed secluded, and was to me quite strange: I did not know it at all.

Once more I lay down. My bed stood in a little alcove; on turning my face to the wall, the room with its bewildering accompaniments became excluded. Excluded? No! For as I arranged my position in this hope, behold, on the green space between the divided and looped-up curtains, hung a broad, gilded picture-frame enclosing a portrait. It was drawn – well drawn, though but a sketch – in water-colours; a head, a boy's head, fresh, life-like, speaking, and animated. It seemed a youth of sixteen, fair-complexioned, with sanguine health in his cheek; hair long, not dark, and with a sunny sheen;

penetrating eyes, an arch mouth, and a gay smile. On the whole a most pleasant face to look at, especially for those claiming a right to that youth's affections – parents, for instance, or sisters. Any romantic little school-girl might almost have loved it in its frame. Those eyes looked as if when somewhat older they would flash a lightning-response to love: I cannot tell whether they kept in store the steady-beaming shine of faith. For whatever sentiment met him in form too facile, his lips menaced, beautifully but surely, caprice and light esteem.

Striving to take each new discovery as quietly as I could, I whispered to myself –

"Ah! That portrait used to hang in the breakfast-room, over the mantel-piece: somewhat too high, as I thought. I well remember how I used to mount a music-stool for the purpose of unhooking it, holding it in my hand, and searching into those bonny wells of eyes, whose glance under their hazel lashes seemed like a pencilled laugh; and well I liked to note the colouring of the cheek, and the expression of the mouth." I hardly believed fancy could improve on the curve of that mouth, or of the chin; even *my* ignorance knew that both were beautiful, and pondered perplexed over this doubt: "How it was that what charmed so much, could at the same time so keenly pain?" Once, by way of test, I took little Missy Home, and, lifting her in my arms, told her to look at the picture.

"Do you like it, Polly?" I asked. She never answered, but gazed long, and at last a darkness went trembling through her sensitive eye, as she said, "Put me down." So I put her down, saying to myself: "The child feels it too."

All these things do I now think over, adding, "He had his faults, yet scarce ever was a finer nature; liberal, suave, impressible." My reflections closed in an audibly pronounced word, "Graham!"

"Graham!" echoed a sudden voice at the bedside. "Do you want Graham?"

I looked. The plot was but thickening; the wonder but culminating. If it was strange to see that well-remembered pictured form on the wall, still stranger was it to turn and behold the equally well-remembered living form opposite – a woman, a lady, most real and substantial, tall, well-attired, wearing widow's silk, and such a cap as best became her matron and motherly braids of hair. Hers, too, was a good face; too marked, perhaps, now for beauty, but not for sense or character. She was little changed; something sterner, something more robust – but she was my godmother: still the distinct vision of Mrs. Bretton.

I kept quiet, yet internally *I* was much agitated: my pulse fluttered, and the blood left my cheek, which turned cold.

"Madam, where am I?" I inquired.

"In a very safe asylum; well protected for the present; make your mind quite easy till you get a little better; you look ill this morning."

"I am so entirely bewildered, I do not know whether I can trust my senses at all, or whether they are misleading me in every particular: but you speak English, do you not, madam?"

"I should think you might hear that: it would puzzle me to hold a long discourse in French."

"You do not come from England?"

"I am lately arrived thence. Have you been long in this country? You seem to know my son?"

"Do, I, madam? Perhaps I do. Your son – the picture there?"

"That is his portrait as a youth. While looking at it, you pronounced his name."

"Graham Bretton?"

She nodded.

"I speak to Mrs. Bretton, formerly of Bretton, —shire?"

"Quite right; and you, I am told, are an English teacher in a foreign school here: my son recognised you as such."

"How was I found, madam, and by whom?"

"My son shall tell you that by-and-by," said she; "but at present you are too confused and weak for conversation: try to eat some breakfast, and then sleep."

Notwithstanding all I had undergone – the bodily fatigue, the perturbation of spirits, the exposure to weather – it seemed that I was better: the fever, the real malady which had oppressed my frame, was abating; for, whereas during the last nine days I had taken no solid food, and suffered from continual thirst, this morning, on breakfast being offered, I experienced a craving for nourishment: an inward faintness which caused me eagerly to taste the tea this lady offered, and to eat the morsel of dry toast she allowed in accompaniment. It was only a morsel, but it sufficed; keeping up my strength till some two or three hours afterwards, when the bonne brought me a little cup of broth and a biscuit.

As evening began to darken, and the ceaseless blast still blew wild and cold, and the rain streamed on, deluge-like, I grew weary – very weary of my bed. The room, though pretty, was small: I felt it confining: I longed for a change. The increasing chill and gathering gloom, too, depressed me; I wanted to see – to feel firelight. Besides, I kept thinking of the son of that tall matron: when should I see him? Certainly not till I left my room.

At last the bonne came to make my bed for the night. She prepared to wrap me in a blanket and place me in the little chintz chair; but, declining these attentions, I proceeded to dress myself.

The business was just achieved, and I was sitting down to take breath, when Mrs. Bretton once more appeared.

"Dressed!" she exclaimed, smiling with that smile I so well knew – a pleasant smile, though not soft. "You are quite better then? Quite strong – eh?"

She spoke to me so much as of old she used to speak that I almost fancied she was beginning to know me. There was the same sort of patronage in her voice and manner that, as a girl, I had always experienced from her – a patronage I yielded to and even liked; it was not founded on conventional grounds of superior wealth or station (in the last particular there had never been any inequality; her degree was mine); but on natural reasons of physical advantage: it was the shelter the tree gives the herb. I put a request without further ceremony.

"Do let me go downstairs, madam; I am so cold and dull here."

"I desire nothing better, if you are strong enough to bear the change," was her reply. "Come then; here is an arm." And she offered me hers: I took it, and we descended one flight of carpeted steps to a landing where a tall door, standing open, gave admission into the blue-damask room. How pleasant it was in its air of perfect domestic comfort! How warm in its amber lamp-light and vermilion fire-flush! To render the picture perfect, tea stood ready on the table – an English tea, whereof the whole shining service glanced at me familiarly; from the solid silver urn, of antique pattern, and the massive pot of the same metal, to the thin porcelain cups, dark with purple and gilding. I knew the very seed-cake of peculiar form, baked in a peculiar mould, which always had a place on the tea-table at Bretton. Graham liked it, and there it was as of yore – set before Graham's plate with the silver knife and fork beside it. Graham was then expected to tea: Graham was now, perhaps, in the house; ere many minutes I might see him.

"Sit down – sit down," said my conductress, as my step faltered a little in passing to the hearth. She seated me on the sofa, but I soon passed behind it, saying the fire was too hot; in its shade I found another seat which suited me better. Mrs. Bretton was never wont to make a fuss about any person or anything; without remonstrance she suffered me to have my own way. She made the tea, and she took up the newspaper. I liked to watch every action of my godmother; all her movements were so young: she must have been now above fifty, yet neither her sinews nor her spirit seemed yet touched by the rust of age. Though portly, she was alert, and though serene, she was at times impetuous – good health and an excellent temperament kept her green as in her spring.

While she read, I perceived she listened – listened for her son. She was not the woman ever to confess herself uneasy, but there was yet no lull in the weather, and if Graham were out in that hoarse wind – roaring still unsatisfied – I well knew his mother's heart would be out with him.

"Ten minutes behind his time," said she, looking at her watch; then, in another minute, a lifting of her eyes from the page, and a slight inclination of her head towards the door, denoted that she heard some sound. Presently her brow cleared; and then even my ear, less practised, caught the iron clash of a gate swung to, steps on gravel, lastly the door-bell. He was come. His mother filled the teapot from the urn, she drew nearer the hearth the stuffed and cushioned blue chair – her own chair by right, but I saw there was one who might with impunity usurp it. And when that *one* came up the stairs – which he soon did, after, I suppose, some such attention to the toilet as the wild and wet night rendered necessary, and strode straight in –

"Is it you, Graham?" said his mother, hiding a glad smile and speaking curtly.

"Who else should it be, mamma?" demanded the Unpunctual, possessing himself irreverently of the abdicated throne.

"Don't you deserve cold tea, for being late?"

"I shall not get my deserts, for the urn sings cheerily."

"Wheel yourself to the table, lazy boy: no seat will serve you but mine; if you had one spark of a sense of propriety, you would always leave that chair for the Old Lady."

"So I should; only the dear Old Lady persists in leaving it for me. How is your patient, mamma?"

"Will she come forward and speak for herself?" said Mrs. Bretton, turning to my corner; and at this invitation, forward I came. Graham courteously rose up to greet me. He stood tall on the hearth, a figure justifying his mother's unconcealed pride.

"So you are come down," said he; "you must be better then – much better. I scarcely expected we should meet thus, or here. I was alarmed last night, and if I had not been forced to hurry away to a dying patient, I certainly would not have left you; but my mother herself is something of a doctress, and Martha an excellent nurse. I saw the case was a fainting-fit, not necessarily dangerous. What brought it on, I have yet to learn, and all particulars; meantime, I trust you really do feel better?"

"Much better," I said calmly. "Much better, I thank you, Dr. John."

For, reader, this tall young man – this darling son – this host of mine – this Graham Bretton, *was* Dr. John: he, and no other; and, what is more, I ascertained this identity scarcely with surprise. What is more, when I heard Graham's step on the stairs, I knew what manner of figure would enter, and for whose aspect to prepare my eyes. The discovery was not of today, its dawn had penetrated my perceptions long since. Of course I remembered young Bretton well; and though ten years (from sixteen to twenty-six) may greatly change the boy as they mature him to the man, yet they could bring no such utter difference as would suffice wholly to blind my eyes, or baffle my memory. Dr. John Graham Bretton retained still an affinity to the youth of sixteen: he had his eyes; he had some of his features; to wit, all the excellently-moulded lower half of the face; I found him out soon. I first recognised him on that occasion, noted several chapters back, when my unguardedly-fixed attention had drawn on me the mortification of an implied rebuke. Subsequent observation confirmed, in every point, that early surmise. I traced in the gesture, the port, and the habits of his manhood, all his boy's promise. I heard in his now deep tones the accent of former days. Certain turns of phrase, peculiar to him of old, were peculiar to him still; and so was many a trick of eye and lip, many a smile, many a sudden ray levelled from the irid, under his well-charactered brow.

To *say* anything on the subject, to *hint* at my discovery, had not suited my habits of thought, or assimilated with my system of feeling. On the contrary, I had preferred to keep the matter to myself. I liked entering his presence covered with a cloud he had not seen through, while he stood before me under a ray of special illumination which shone all partial over his head, trembled about his feet, and cast light no farther.

Well I knew that to him it could make little difference, were I to come forward and announce, "This is Lucy Snowe!" So I kept back in my teacher's place; and as he never asked my name, so I never gave it. He heard me called 'Miss', and 'Miss Lucy'; he never heard the surname, 'Snowe'. As to spontaneous recognition – though I, perhaps, was still less changed than he – the idea never approached his mind, and why should I suggest it?

During tea, Dr. John was kind, as it was his nature to be; that meal over, and the tray carried out, he made a cosy arrangement of the cushions in a corner of the sofa, and obliged me to settle amongst them. He and his mother also drew to the fire, and ere we had sat ten minutes, I caught the eye of the latter fastened steadily upon me. Women are certainly quicker in some things than men.

"Well," she exclaimed, presently, "I have seldom seen a stronger likeness! Graham, have you observed it?"

"Observed what? What ails the Old Lady now? How you stare, mamma! One would think you had an attack of second sight."

"Tell me, Graham, of whom does that young lady remind you?" pointing to me.

"Mamma, you put her out of countenance. I often tell you abruptness is your fault; remember, too, that to you she is a stranger, and does not know your ways."

"Now, when she looks down; now, when she turns sideways, who is she like, Graham?"

"Indeed, mamma, since you propound the riddle, I think you ought to solve it!"

"And you have known her some time, you say – ever since you first began to attend the school in the Rue Fossette: yet you never mentioned to me that singular resemblance!"

"I could not mention a thing of which I never thought, and which I do not now acknowledge. What *can* you mean?"

"Stupid boy! Look at her."

Graham did look: but this was not to be endured; I saw how it must end, so I thought it best to anticipate.

"Dr. John," I said, "has had so much to do and think of, since he and I shook hands at our last parting in St. Ann's Street, that, while I readily found out Mr. Graham Bretton, some months ago, it never occurred to me as possible that he should recognise Lucy Snowe."

"Lucy Snowe! I thought so! I knew it!" cried Mrs. Bretton. And she at once stepped across the hearth and kissed me. Some ladies would, perhaps, have made a great bustle upon such a discovery without being particularly glad of it; but it was not my godmother's habit to make a bustle, and she preferred all sentimental demonstrations in bas-relief. So she and I got over the surprise with few words and a single salute; yet I daresay she was pleased, and I know I was. While we renewed old acquaintance, Graham, sitting opposite, silently disposed of his paroxysm of astonishment.

"Mamma calls me a stupid boy, and I think I am so," at length he said; "for, upon my honour, often as I have seen you, I never once suspected this fact: and yet I perceive it all now. Lucy Snowe! To be sure! I recollect her perfectly, and there she sits; not a doubt of it. But," he added, "you surely have not known me as an old acquaintance all this time, and never mentioned it."

"That I have," was my answer.

Dr. John commented not. I supposed he regarded my silence as eccentric, but he was indulgent in refraining from censure. I daresay, too, he would have deemed it impertinent to have interrogated me very closely, to have asked me the why and wherefore of my reserve; and, though he might feel a little curious, the importance of the case was by no means such as to tempt curiosity to infringe on discretion.

For my part, I just ventured to inquire whether he remembered the circumstance of my once looking at him very fixedly; for the slight annoyance he had betrayed on that occasion still lingered sore on my mind.

"I think I do!" said he: "I think I was even cross with you."

"You considered me a little bold; perhaps?" I inquired.

"Not at all. Only, shy and retiring as your general manner was, I wondered what personal or facial enormity in me proved so magnetic to your usually averted eyes."

"You see how it was now?"

"Perfectly."

And here Mrs. Bretton broke in with many, many questions about past times; and for her satisfaction I had to recur to gone-by troubles, to explain causes of seeming estrangement, to touch on single-handed conflict with Life, with Death, with Grief, with Fate. Dr. John listened, saying little. He and she then told me of changes they had known: even with them all had not gone smoothly, and fortune had retrenched her once abundant gifts. But so courageous a mother, with such a champion in her son, was well fitted to fight a good fight with the world, and to prevail ultimately. Dr. John himself was one of those on whose birth benign planets have certainly smiled. Adversity might set against him her most sullen front: he was the man to beat her down with smiles. Strong and cheerful, and firm and courteous; not rash, yet valiant; he was the aspirant to woo Destiny herself, and to win from her stone eyeballs a beam almost loving.

In the profession he had adopted, his success was now quite decided. Within the last three months he had taken this house (a small château, they told me, about half a league without the Porte de Crécy); this country site being chosen for the sake of his mother's health, with which town air did not now agree. Hither he had invited Mrs. Bretton, and she, on leaving England, had brought with her such residue furniture of the former St. Ann's Street mansion as she had thought fit to keep unsold. Hence my bewilderment at the phantoms of chairs, and the wraiths of looking-glasses, tea-urns, and teacups.

As the clock struck eleven, Dr. John stopped his mother.

"Miss Snowe must retire now," he said; "she is beginning to look very pale. Tomorrow I will venture to put some questions respecting the cause of her loss of health. She is much changed, indeed, since last July, when I saw her enact with no little spirit the part of a very killing fine gentleman. As to last night's catastrophe, I am sure thereby hangs a tale, but we will inquire no further this evening. Goodnight, Miss Lucy."

And so he kindly led me to the door, and holding a wax-candle, lighted me up the one flight of stairs.

When I had said my prayers, and when I was undressed and laid down, I felt that I still had friends. Friends, not professing vehement attachment, not offering the tender solace of well-matched and congenial relationship; on whom, therefore, but moderate demand of affection was to be made, of whom but moderate expectation formed; but towards whom my heart softened instinctively, and yearned with an importunate gratitude, which I entreated Reason betimes to check.

"Do not let me think of them too often, too much, too fondly," I implored: "let me be content with a temperate draught of this living stream: let me not run athirst, and apply passionately to its welcome waters: let me not imagine in them a sweeter taste than earth's fountains know. Oh! Would to God I may be enabled to feel enough sustained by an occasional, amicable intercourse, rare, brief, unengrossing and tranquil: quite tranquil!"

Still repeating this word, I turned to my pillow; and *still* repeating it, I steeped that pillow with tears.

Chapter Seventeen
La Terrasse

THESE STRUGGLES with the natural character, the strong native bent of the heart, may seem futile and fruitless, but in the end they do good. They tend, however slightly, to give the actions, the conduct, that turn which Reason approves, and which Feeling, perhaps, too often opposes: they certainly make a difference in the general tenour of a life, and enable it to be better regulated, more equable, quieter on the surface; and it is on the surface only the common gaze will fall. As to what lies below, leave that with God. Man, your equal, weak as you, and not fit to be your judge, may be shut out thence: take it to your Maker – show Him the secrets of the spirit He gave – ask Him how you are to bear the pains He has appointed – kneel in His presence, and pray with faith for light in darkness, for strength in piteous weakness, for patience in extreme need. Certainly, at some hour, though perhaps not *your* hour, the waiting waters will stir; in *some* shape, though perhaps not the shape you dreamed, which your heart loved, and for which it bled, the healing herald will descend, the cripple and the blind, and the dumb, and the possessed will be led to bathe. Herald, come quickly! Thousands lie round the pool, weeping and despairing, to see it, through slow years, stagnant. Long are the 'times' of Heaven: the orbits of angel messengers seem wide to mortal vision; they may enring ages: the cycle of one departure and return may clasp unnumbered generations; and dust, kindling to brief suffering life, and through pain, passing back to dust, may meanwhile perish out of memory again, and yet again. To how many maimed and mourning millions is the first and sole angel visitant, him easterns call Azrael!

I tried to get up next morning, but while I was dressing, and at intervals drinking cold water from the carafe on my washstand, with design to brace up that trembling weakness which made dressing so difficult, in came Mrs. Bretton.

"Here is an absurdity!" was her morning accost. "Not so," she added, and dealing with me at once in her own brusque, energetic fashion – that fashion which I used formerly to enjoy seeing applied to her son, and by him vigorously resisted – in two minutes she consigned me captive to the French bed.

"There you lie till afternoon," said she. "My boy left orders before he went out that such should be the case, and I can assure you my son is master and must be obeyed. Presently you shall have breakfast."

Presently she brought that meal – brought it with her own active hands – not leaving me to servants. She seated herself on the bed while I ate. Now it is not everybody, even amongst our respected friends and esteemed acquaintance, whom we like to have near us, whom we like to watch us, to wait on us, to approach us with the proximity of a nurse to a patient. It is not every friend whose eye is a light in a sick room, whose presence is there a solace: but all this was Mrs. Bretton to me; all this she had ever been. Food or drink never pleased me so well as when it came through her hands. I do not remember the occasion when her entrance into a room had not made that room cheerier. Our natures own predilections and antipathies alike strange. There are people from whom we secretly shrink, whom we would personally avoid, though reason confesses that they are good people: there are others with faults of temper, etc., evident enough, beside whom we live content, as if the air about them did us good. My godmother's lively black eye and clear brunette cheek, her warm, prompt hand, her self-reliant mood, her decided bearing, were all beneficial to me as the atmosphere of some salubrious climate. Her son used to call her 'the old lady'; it filled me with pleasant wonder to note how the alacrity and power of five-and-twenty still breathed from her and around her.

"I would bring my work here," she said, as she took from me the emptied teacup, "and sit with you the whole day, if that overbearing John Graham had not put his veto upon such a proceeding.

'Now, mamma,' he said, when he went out, 'take notice, you are not to knock up your god-daughter with gossip,' and he particularly desired me to keep close to my own quarters, and spare you my fine company. He says, Lucy, he thinks you have had a nervous fever, judging from your look, – is that so?"

I replied that I did not quite know what my ailment had been, but that I had certainly suffered a good deal especially in mind. Further, on this subject, I did not consider it advisable to dwell, for the details of what I had undergone belonged to a portion of my existence in which I never expected my godmother to take a share. Into what a new region would such a confidence have led that hale, serene nature! The difference between her and me might be figured by that between the stately ship cruising safe on smooth seas, with its full complement of crew, a captain gay and brave, and venturous and provident; and the life-boat, which most days of the year lies dry and solitary in an old, dark boat-house, only putting to sea when the billows run high in rough weather, when cloud encounters water, when danger and death divide between them the rule of the great deep. No, the *Louisa Bretton* never was out of harbour on such a night, and in such a scene: her crew could not conceive it; so the half-drowned life-boat man keeps his own counsel, and spins no yarns.

She left me, and I lay in bed content: it was good of Graham to remember me before he went out.

My day was lonely, but the prospect of coming evening abridged and cheered it. Then, too, I felt weak, and rest seemed welcome; and after the morning hours were gone by, – those hours which always bring, even to the necessarily unoccupied, a sense of business to be done, of tasks waiting fulfilment, a vague impression of obligation to be employed – when this stirring time was past, and the silent descent of afternoon hushed housemaid steps on the stairs and in the chambers, I then passed into a dreamy mood, not unpleasant.

My calm little room seemed somehow like a cave in the sea. There was no colour about it, except that white and pale green, suggestive of foam and deep water; the blanched cornice was adorned with shell-shaped ornaments, and there were white mouldings like dolphins in the ceiling-angles. Even that one touch of colour visible in the red satin pincushion bore affinity to coral; even that dark, shining glass might have mirrored a mermaid. When I closed my eyes, I heard a gale, subsiding at last, bearing upon the house-front like a settling swell upon a rock-base. I heard it drawn and withdrawn far, far off, like a tide retiring from a shore of the upper world – a world so high above that the rush of its largest waves, the dash of its fiercest breakers, could sound down in this submarine home, only like murmurs and a lullaby.

Amidst these dreams came evening, and then Martha brought a light; with her aid I was quickly dressed, and stronger now than in the morning, I made my way down to the blue saloon unassisted.

Dr. John, it appears, had concluded his round of professional calls earlier than usual; his form was the first object that met my eyes as I entered the parlour; he stood in that window-recess opposite the door, reading the close type of a newspaper by such dull light as closing day yet gave. The fire shone clear, but the lamp stood on the table unlit, and tea was not yet brought up.

As to Mrs. Bretton, my active godmother – who, I afterwards found, had been out in the open air all day – lay half-reclined in her deep-cushioned chair, actually lost in a nap. Her son seeing me, came forward. I noticed that he trod carefully, not to wake the sleeper; he also spoke low: his mellow voice never had any sharpness in it; modulated as at present, it was calculated rather to soothe than startle slumber.

"This is a quiet little château," he observed, after inviting me to sit near the casement. "I don't know whether you may have noticed it in your walks: though, indeed, from the chaussée it is not visible; just a mile beyond the Porte de Crécy, you turn down a lane which soon becomes an avenue, and that leads you on, through meadow and shade, to the very door of this house. It is not a modern place, but built somewhat in the old style of the Basse-Ville. It is rather a manoir than a château; they call it 'La Terrasse', because its front rises from a broad turfed walk, whence steps lead down a grassy slope to the avenue. See yonder! The moon rises: she looks well through the tree-boles."

Where, indeed, does the moon not look well? What is the scene, confined or expansive, which her orb does not hallow? Rosy or fiery, she mounted now above a not distant bank; even while we watched her flushed ascent, she cleared to gold, and in very brief space, floated up stainless into a now calm sky. Did moonlight soften or sadden Dr. Bretton? Did it touch him with romance? I think it did. Albeit of no sighing mood, he sighed in watching it: sighed to himself quietly. No need to ponder the cause or the course of that sigh; I knew it was wakened by beauty; I knew it pursued Ginevra. Knowing this, the idea pressed upon me that it was in some sort my duty to speak the name he meditated. Of course he was ready for the subject: I saw in his countenance a teeming plenitude of comment, question and interest; a pressure of language and sentiment, only checked, I thought, by sense of embarrassment how to begin. To spare him this embarrassment was my best, indeed my sole use. I had but to utter the idol's name, and love's tender litany would flow out. I had just found a fitting phrase, "You know that Miss Fanshawe is gone on a tour with the Cholmondeleys," and was opening my lips to speak to it, when he scattered my plans by introducing another theme.

"The first thing this morning," said he, putting his sentiment in his pocket, turning from the moon, and sitting down, "I went to the Rue Fossette, and told the cuisinière that you were safe and in good hands. Do you know that I actually found that she had not yet discovered your absence from the house: she thought you safe in the great dormitory. With what care you must have been waited on!"

"Oh! All that is very conceivable," said I. "Goton could do nothing for me but bring me a little tisane and a crust of bread, and I had rejected both so often during the past week, that the good woman got tired of useless journeys from the dwelling-house kitchen to the school-dormitory, and only came once a day at noon to make my bed. I believe, however, that she is a good-natured creature, and would have been delighted to cook me côtelettes de mouton, if I could have eaten them."

"What did Madame Beck mean by leaving you alone?"

"Madame Beck could not foresee that I should fall ill."

"Your nervous system bore a good share of the suffering?"

"I am not quite sure what my nervous system is, but I was dreadfully low-spirited."

"Which disables me from helping you by pill or potion. Medicine can give nobody good spirits. My art halts at the threshold of Hypochondria: she just looks in and sees a chamber of torture, but can neither say nor do much. Cheerful society would be of use; you should be as little alone as possible; you should take plenty of exercise."

Acquiescence and a pause followed these remarks. They sounded all right, I thought, and bore the safe sanction of custom, and the well-worn stamp of use.

"Miss Snowe," recommended Dr. John – my health, nervous system included, being now, somewhat to my relief, discussed and done with – "is it permitted me to ask what your religion is? Are you a Catholic?"

I looked up in some surprise – "A Catholic? No! Why suggest such an idea?"

"The manner in which you were consigned to me last night made me doubt."

"I consigned to you? But, indeed, I forget. It yet remains for me to learn how I fell into your hands."

"Why, under circumstances that puzzled me. I had been in attendance all day yesterday on a case of singularly interesting and critical character; the disease being rare, and its treatment doubtful: I saw a similar and still finer case in a hospital in Paris; but that will not interest you. At last a mitigation of the patient's most urgent symptoms (acute pain is one of its accompaniments) liberated me, and I set out homeward. My shortest way lay through the Basse-Ville, and as the night was excessively dark, wild, and wet, I took it. In riding past an old church belonging to a community of Béguines, I saw by a lamp burning over the porch or deep arch of the entrance, a priest lifting some object in his arms. The lamp was bright enough to reveal the priest's features clearly, and I recognised him; he was a man I have often met by the sick beds of both rich and poor: and chiefly the latter. He is, I think, a good old man, far better than most of his class in this country; superior, indeed, in every way, better informed, as well as more devoted to duty. Our eyes met; he called on me to stop: what he supported was a woman, fainting or dying. I alighted.

"'This person is one of your countrywomen,' he said: 'save her, if she is not dead.'

"My countrywoman, on examination, turned out to be the English teacher at Madame Beck's pensionnat. She was perfectly unconscious, perfectly bloodless, and nearly cold.

"'What does it all mean?' was my inquiry.

"He communicated a curious account; that you had been to him that evening at confessional; that your exhausted and suffering appearance, coupled with some things you had said –"

"Things I had said? I wonder what things!"

"Awful crimes, no doubt; but he did not tell me what: there, you know, the seal of the confessional checked his garrulity, and my curiosity. Your confidences, however, had not made an enemy of the good father; it seems he was so struck, and felt so sorry that you should be out on such a night alone, that he had esteemed it a Christian duty to watch you when you quitted the church, and so to manage as not to lose sight of you, till you should have reached home. Perhaps the worthy man might, half unconsciously, have blent in this proceeding some little of the subtlety of his class: it might have been his resolve to learn the locality of your home – did you impart that in your confession?"

"I did not: on the contrary, I carefully avoided the shadow of any indication: and as to my confession, Dr. John, I suppose you will think me mad for taking such a step, but I could not help it: I suppose it was all the fault of what you call my 'nervous system'. I cannot put the case into words, but my days and nights were grown intolerable: a cruel sense of desolation pained my mind: a feeling that would make its way, rush out, or kill me – like (and this you will understand, Dr. John) the current which passes through the heart, and which, if aneurism or any other morbid cause obstructs its natural channels, seeks abnormal outlet. I wanted companionship, I wanted friendship, I wanted counsel. I could find none of these in closet or chamber, so I went and sought them in church and confessional. As to what I said, it was no confidence, no narrative. I have done nothing wrong: my life has not been active enough for any dark deed, either of romance or reality: all I poured out was a dreary, desperate complaint."

"Lucy, you ought to travel for about six months: why, your calm nature is growing quite excitable! Confound Madame Beck! Has the little buxom widow no bowels, to condemn her best teacher to solitary confinement?"

"It was not Madame Beck's fault," said I; "it is no living being's fault, and I won't hear anyone blamed."

"Who is in the wrong, then, Lucy?"

"Me – Dr. John – me; and a great abstraction on whose wide shoulders I like to lay the mountains of blame they were sculptured to bear: me and Fate."

"'Me' must take better care in future," said Dr. John – smiling, I suppose, at my bad grammar.

"Change of air – change of scene; those are my prescriptions," pursued the practical young doctor. "But to return to our muttons, Lucy. As yet, Père Silas, with all his tact (they say he is a Jesuit), is no wiser than you choose him to be; for, instead of returning to the Rue Fossette, your fevered wanderings – there must have been high fever –"

"No, Dr. John: the fever took its turn that night – now, don't make out that I was delirious, for I know differently."

"Good! You were as collected as myself at this moment, no doubt. Your wanderings had taken an opposite direction to the pensionnat. Near the Béguinage, amidst the stress of flood and gust, and in the perplexity of darkness, you had swooned and fallen. The priest came to your succour, and the physician, as we have seen, supervened. Between us we procured a fiacre and brought you here. Père Silas, old as he is, would carry you upstairs, and lay you on that couch himself. He would certainly have remained with you till suspended animation had been restored: and so should I, but, at that juncture, a hurried messenger arrived from the dying patient I had scarcely left – the last duties were called for – the physician's last visit and the priest's last rite; extreme unction could not be deferred. Père Silas and myself departed together, my mother was spending the evening abroad; we gave you in charge to Martha, leaving directions, which it seems she followed successfully. Now, are you a Catholic?"

"Not yet," said I, with a smile. "And never let Père Silas know where I live, or he will try to convert me; but give him my best and truest thanks when you see him, and if ever I get rich I will send him money for his charities. See, Dr. John, your mother wakes; you ought to ring for tea."

Which he did; and, as Mrs. Bretton sat up – astonished and indignant at herself for the indulgence to which she had succumbed, and fully prepared to deny that she had slept at all – her son came gaily to the attack.

"Hushaby, mamma! Sleep again. You look the picture of innocence in your slumbers."

"My slumbers, John Graham! What are you talking about? You know I never *do* sleep by day: it was the slightest doze possible."

"Exactly! A seraph's gentle lapse – a fairy's dream. Mamma, under such circumstances, you always remind me of Titania."

"That is because you, yourself, are so like Bottom."

"Miss Snowe – did you ever hear anything like mamma's wit? She is a most sprightly woman of her size and age."

"Keep your compliments to yourself, sir, and do not neglect your own size: which seems to me a good deal on the increase. Lucy, has he not rather the air of an incipient John Bull? He used to be slender as an eel, and now I fancy in him a sort of heavy dragoon bent – a beef-eater tendency. Graham, take notice! If you grow fat I disown you."

"As if you could not sooner disown your own personality! I am indispensable to the old lady's happiness, Lucy. She would pine away in green and yellow melancholy if she had not my six feet of iniquity to scold. It keeps her lively – it maintains the wholesome ferment of her spirits."

The two were now standing opposite to each other, one on each side the fire-place; their words were not very fond, but their mutual looks atoned for verbal deficiencies. At least, the best treasure of Mrs. Bretton's life was certainly casketed in her son's bosom; her dearest pulse throbbed in his heart. As to him, of course another love shared his feelings with filial love, and, no doubt, as the new passion was the latest born, so he assigned it in his emotions Benjamin's portion. Ginevra! Ginevra! Did Mrs. Bretton yet know at whose feet her own young idol had laid his homage? Would she approve that choice? I could not tell; but I could well guess that if she knew Miss Fanshawe's conduct towards Graham: her alternations between coldness and coaxing, and repulse and allurement; if she could at all suspect the pain with which she had tried him; if she could have seen, as I had seen, his fine spirits subdued and harassed, his inferior preferred before him, his subordinate made the instrument of his humiliation – *then* Mrs. Bretton would have pronounced Ginevra imbecile, or perverted, or both. Well – I thought so too.

That second evening passed as sweetly as the first – *more* sweetly indeed: we enjoyed a smoother interchange of thought; old troubles were not reverted to, acquaintance was better cemented; I felt happier, easier, more at home. That night – instead of crying myself asleep – I went down to dreamland by a pathway bordered with pleasant thoughts.

Chapter Eighteen
We Quarrel

DURING THE FIRST DAYS of my stay at the Terrace, Graham never took a seat near me, or in his frequent pacing of the room approached the quarter where I sat, or looked pre-occupied, or more grave than usual, but I thought of Miss Fanshawe and expected her name to leap from his lips. I kept my ear and mind in perpetual readiness for the tender theme; my patience was ordered to be permanently under arms, and my sympathy desired to keep its cornucopia replenished and ready for outpouring. At last, and after a little inward struggle, which I saw and respected, he one day launched into the topic. It was introduced delicately; anonymously as it were.

"Your friend is spending her vacation in travelling, I hear?"

"Friend, forsooth!" thought I to myself: but it would not do to contradict; he must have his own way; I must own the soft impeachment: friend let it be. Still, by way of experiment, I could not help asking whom he meant?

He had taken a seat at my work-table; he now laid hands on a reel of thread which he proceeded recklessly to unwind.

"Ginevra – Miss Fanshawe, has accompanied the Cholmondeleys on a tour through the south of France?"

"She has."

"Do you and she correspond?"

"It will astonish you to hear that I never once thought of making application for that privilege."

"You have seen letters of her writing?"

"Yes; several to her uncle."

"They will not be deficient in wit and naïveté; there is so much sparkle, and so little art in her soul?"

"She writes comprehensively enough when she writes to M. de Bassompierre: he who runs may read." (In fact, Ginevra's epistles to her wealthy kinsman were commonly business documents, unequivocal applications for cash.)

"And her handwriting? It must be pretty, light, ladylike, I should think?"

It was, and I said so.

"I verily believe that all she does is well done," said Dr. John; and as I seemed in no hurry to chime in with this remark, he added "You, who know her, could you name a point in which she is deficient?"

"She does several things very well." ("Flirtation amongst the rest," subjoined I, in thought.)

"When do you suppose she will return to town?" he soon inquired.

"Pardon me, Dr. John, I must explain. You honour me too much in ascribing to me a degree of intimacy with Miss Fanshawe I have not the felicity to enjoy. I have never been the depositary of her plans and secrets. You will find her particular friends in another sphere than mine: amongst the Cholmondeleys, for instance."

He actually thought I was stung with a kind of jealous pain similar to his own!

"Excuse her," he said; "judge her indulgently; the glitter of fashion misleads her, but she will soon find out that these people are hollow, and will return to you with augmented attachment and confirmed trust. I know something of the Cholmondeleys: superficial, showy, selfish people; depend on it, at heart Ginevra values you beyond a score of such."

"You are very kind," I said briefly.

A disclaimer of the sentiments attributed to me burned on my lips, but I extinguished the flame. I submitted to be looked upon as the humiliated, cast-off, and now pining confidante of the distinguished Miss Fanshawe: but, reader, it was a hard submission.

"Yet, you see," continued Graham, "while I comfort *you*, I cannot take the same consolation to myself; I cannot hope she will do me justice. De Hamal is most worthless, yet I fear he pleases her: wretched delusion!"

My patience really gave way, and without notice: all at once. I suppose illness and weakness had worn it and made it brittle.

"Dr. Bretton," I broke out, "there is no delusion like your own. On all points but one you are a man, frank, healthful, right-thinking, clear-sighted: on this exceptional point you are but a slave. I declare, where Miss Fanshawe is concerned, you merit no respect; nor have you mine."

I got up, and left the room very much excited.

This little scene took place in the morning; I had to meet him again in the evening, and then I saw I had done mischief. He was not made of common clay, not put together out of vulgar materials; while the outlines of his nature had been shaped with breadth and vigour, the details embraced workmanship of almost feminine delicacy: finer, much finer, than you could be prepared to meet with; than you could believe inherent in him, even after years of acquaintance. Indeed, till some over-sharp contact with his nerves had betrayed, by its effects, their acute sensibility, this elaborate construction must be ignored; and the more especially because the sympathetic faculty was not prominent in him: to feel, and to seize quickly another's feelings, are separate properties; a few constructions possess both, some neither. Dr. John had the one in exquisite perfection; and because I have admitted that he was not endowed with the other in equal degree, the reader will considerately refrain from passing to an extreme, and pronouncing him unsympathising, unfeeling: on the contrary, he was a kind, generous man. Make your need known, his hand was open. Put your grief into words, he turned no deaf ear. Expect refinements of perception, miracles of intuition, and realize disappointment. This night, when Dr. John entered the room, and met the evening lamp, I saw well and at one glance his whole mechanism.

To one who had named him 'slave', and, on any point, banned him from respect, he must now have peculiar feelings. That the epithet was well applied, and the ban just, might be; he put forth no denial that it was so: his mind even candidly revolved that unmanning possibility. He sought in this accusation the cause of that ill-success which had got so galling a hold on his mental peace: Amid the worry of a self-condemnatory soliloquy, his demeanour seemed grave, perhaps cold, both to me and his mother. And yet there was no bad feeling, no malice, no rancour, no littleness in his countenance, beautiful with a man's best beauty, even in its depression. When I placed his chair at the table, which I hastened to do, anticipating the servant, and when I handed him his tea, which I did with trembling care, he said: "Thank you, Lucy," in as kindly a tone of his full pleasant voice as ever my ear welcomed.

For my part, there was only one plan to be pursued; I must expiate my culpable vehemence, or I must not sleep that night. This would not do at all; I could not stand it: I made no pretence of capacity to wage war on this footing. School solitude, conventual silence and stagnation, anything seemed preferable to living embroiled with Dr. John. As to Ginevra, she might take the silver wings of a dove, or any other fowl that flies, and mount straight up to the highest place, among the highest stars, where her lover's highest flight of fancy chose to fix the constellation of her charms: never more be it mine to dispute the arrangement. Long I tried to catch his eye. Again and again that eye just met mine; but, having nothing to say, it withdrew, and I was baffled. After tea, he sat, sad and quiet, reading a book. I wished I could have dared to go and sit near him, but it seemed that if I ventured to take that step, he would infallibly evince hostility and indignation. I longed to speak out, and I dared not whisper. His mother left the room; then, moved by insupportable regret, I just murmured the words "Dr. Bretton".

He looked up from his book; his eyes were not cold or malevolent, his mouth was not cynical; he was ready and willing to hear what I might have to say: his spirit was of vintage too mellow and generous to sour in one thunder-clap.

"Dr. Bretton, forgive my hasty words: *do, do* forgive them."

He smiled that moment I spoke. "Perhaps I deserved them, Lucy. If you don't respect me, I am sure it is because I am not respectable. I fear, I am an awkward fool: I must manage badly in some way, for where I wish to please, it seems I don't please."

"Of that you cannot be sure; and even if such be the case, is it the fault of your character, or of another's perceptions? But now, let me unsay what I said in anger. In one thing, and in all things, I deeply respect you. If you think scarcely enough of yourself, and too much of others, what is that but an excellence?"

"Can I think too much of Ginevra?"

"*I* believe you may; *you* believe you can't. Let us agree to differ. Let me be pardoned; that is what I ask."

"Do you think I cherish ill-will for one warm word?"

"I see you do not and cannot; but just say, 'Lucy, I forgive you!' Say that, to ease me of the heart-ache."

"Put away your heart-ache, as I will put away mine; for you wounded me a little, Lucy. Now, when the pain is gone, I more than forgive: I feel grateful, as to a sincere well-wisher."

"I *am* your sincere well-wisher: you are right."

Thus our quarrel ended.

Reader, if in the course of this work, you find that my opinion of Dr. John undergoes modification, excuse the seeming inconsistency. I give the feeling as at the time I felt it; I describe the view of character as it appeared when discovered.

He showed the fineness of his nature by being kinder to me after that misunderstanding than before. Nay, the very incident which, by my theory, must in some degree estrange me and him, changed, indeed, somewhat our relations; but not in the sense I painfully anticipated. An invisible, but a cold something, very slight, very transparent, but very chill: a sort of screen of ice had hitherto, all through our two lives, glazed the medium through which we exchanged intercourse. Those few warm words, though only warm with anger, breathed on that frail frost-work of reserve; about this time, it gave note of dissolution. I think from that day, so long as we continued friends, he never in discourse stood on topics of ceremony with me. He seemed to know that if he would but talk about himself, and about that in which he was most interested, my expectation would always be answered, my wish always satisfied. It follows, as a matter of course, that I continued to hear much of 'Ginevra'.

'Ginevra!' He thought her so fair, so good; he spoke so lovingly of her charms, her sweetness, her innocence, that, in spite of my plain prose knowledge of the reality, a kind of reflected glow began to settle on her idea, even for me. Still, reader, I am free to confess, that he often talked nonsense; but I strove to be unfailingly patient with him. I had had my lesson: I had learned how severe for me was the pain of crossing, or grieving, or disappointing him. In a strange and new sense, I grew most selfish, and quite powerless to deny myself the delight of indulging his mood, and being pliant to his will. He still seemed to me most absurd when he obstinately doubted, and desponded about his power to win in the end Miss Fanshawe's preference. The fancy became rooted in my own mind more stubbornly than ever, that she was only coquetting to goad him, and that, at heart, she coveted everyone of his words and looks. Sometimes he harassed me, in spite of my resolution to bear and hear; in the midst of the indescribable gall-honey pleasure of thus bearing and hearing, he struck so on the flint of what firmness I owned, that it emitted fire once and again. I chanced to assert one day, with a view to stilling his impatience, that in my own mind, I felt positive Miss Fanshawe *must* intend eventually to accept him.

"Positive! It was easy to say so, but had I any grounds for such assurance?"

"The best grounds."

"Now, Lucy, *do* tell me what!"

"You know them as well as I; and, knowing them, Dr. John, it really amazes me that you should not repose the frankest confidence in her fidelity. To doubt, under the circumstances, is almost to insult."

"Now you are beginning to speak fast and to breathe short; but speak a little faster and breathe a little shorter, till you have given an explanation – a full explanation: I must have it."

"You shall, Dr. John. In some cases, you are a lavish, generous man: you are a worshipper ever ready with the votive offering should Père Silas ever convert *you*, you will give him abundance of alms for his poor, you will supply his altar with tapers, and the shrine of your favourite saint you will do your best to enrich: Ginevra, Dr. John –"

"Hush!" said he, "don't go on."

"Hush, I will *not*: and go on I *will*: Ginevra has had her hands filled from your hands more times than I can count. You have sought for her the costliest flowers; you have busied your brain in devising gifts the most delicate: such, one would have thought, as only a woman could have imagined; and in addition, Miss Fanshawe owns a set of ornaments, to purchase which your generosity must have verged on extravagance."

The modesty Ginevra herself had never evinced in this matter, now flushed all over the face of her admirer.

"Nonsense!" he said, destructively snipping a skein of silk with my scissors. "I offered them to please myself: I felt she did me a favour in accepting them."

"She did more than a favour, Dr. John: she pledged her very honour that she would make you some return; and if she cannot pay you in affection, she ought to hand out a business-like equivalent, in the shape of some rouleaux of gold pieces."

"But you don't understand her; she is far too disinterested to care for my gifts, and too simple-minded to know their value."

I laughed out: I had heard her adjudge to every jewel its price; and well I knew money-embarrassment, money-schemes; money's worth, and endeavours to realise supplies, had, young as she was, furnished the most frequent, and the favourite stimulus of her thoughts for years.

He pursued. "You should have seen her whenever I have laid on her lap some trifle; so cool, so unmoved: no eagerness to take, not even pleasure in contemplating. Just from amiable reluctance to grieve me, she would permit the bouquet to lie beside her, and perhaps consent to bear it away. Or, if I achieved the fastening of a bracelet on her ivory arm, however pretty the trinket might be (and I always carefully chose what seemed to *me* pretty, and what of course was not valueless), the glitter never dazzled her bright eyes: she would hardly cast one look on my gift."

"Then, of course, not valuing it, she would unloose, and return it to you?"

"No; for such a repulse she was too good-natured. She would consent to seem to forget what I had done, and retain the offering with lady-like quiet and easy oblivion. Under such circumstances, how can a man build on acceptance of his presents as a favourable symptom? For my part, were I to offer her all I have, and she to take it, such is her incapacity to be swayed by sordid considerations, I should not venture to believe the transaction advanced me one step."

"Dr. John," I began, "Love is blind"; but just then a blue subtle ray sped sideways from Dr. John's eye: it reminded me of old days, it reminded me of his picture: it half led me to think that part, at least, of his professed persuasion of Miss Fanshawe's naïveté was assumed; it led me dubiously to conjecture that perhaps, in spite of his passion for her beauty, his appreciation of her foibles might possibly be less mistaken, more clear-sighted, than from his general language was presumable. After all it might be only a chance look, or at best the token of a merely momentary impression. Chance or intentional real or imaginary, it closed the conversation.

Chapter Nineteen
The Cleopatra

MY STAY at La Terrasse was prolonged a fortnight beyond the close of the vacation. Mrs. Bretton's kind management procured me this respite. Her son having one day delivered the dictum that "Lucy was not yet strong enough to go back to that den of a pensionnat", she at once drove over to the Rue Fossette, had an interview with the directress, and procured the indulgence, on the plea of prolonged rest and change being necessary to perfect recovery. Hereupon, however, followed an attention I could very well have dispensed with, viz – a polite call from Madame Beck.

That lady – one fine day – actually came out in a fiacre as far as the château. I suppose she had resolved within herself to see what manner of place Dr. John inhabited. Apparently, the pleasant site and neat interior surpassed her expectations; she eulogized all she saw, pronounced the blue salon '*une pièce magnifique*', profusely congratulated me on the acquisition of friends, '*tellement dignes, aimables, et respectables*', turned also a neat compliment in my favour, and, upon Dr. John coming in, ran up to him with the utmost buoyancy, opening at the same time such a fire of rapid language, all sparkling with felicitations and protestations about his château, – '*madame sa mère, la digne châtelaine*': also his looks; which, indeed, were very flourishing, and at the moment additionally embellished by the good-natured but amused smile with which he always listened to Madame's fluent and florid French. In short, Madame shone in her very best phase that day, and came in and went out quite a living catherine-wheel of compliments, delight, and affability. Half purposely, and half to ask some question about school-business, I followed her to the carriage, and looked in after she was seated and the door closed. In that brief fraction of time what a change had been wrought! An instant ago, all sparkles and jests, she now sat sterner than a judge and graver than a sage. Strange little woman!

I went back and teased Dr. John about Madame's devotion to him. How he laughed! What fun shone in his eyes as he recalled some of her fine speeches, and repeated them, imitating her voluble delivery! He had an acute sense of humour, and was the finest company in the world – when he could forget Miss Fanshawe.

* * *

To 'sit in sunshine calm and sweet' is said to be excellent for weak people; it gives them vital force. When little Georgette Beck was recovering from her illness, I used to take her in my arms and walk with her in the garden by the hour together, beneath a certain wall hung with grapes, which the Southern sun was ripening: that sun cherished her little pale frame quite as effectually as it mellowed and swelled the clustering fruit.

There are human tempers, bland, glowing, and genial, within whose influence it is as good for the poor in spirit to live, as it is for the feeble in frame to bask in the glow of noon. Of the number of these choice natures were certainly both Dr. Bretton's and his mother's. They liked to communicate happiness, as some like to occasion misery: they did it instinctively; without fuss, and apparently with little consciousness; the means to give pleasure rose spontaneously in their minds. Every day while I stayed with them, some little plan was proposed which resulted in beneficial enjoyment. Fully occupied as was Dr. John's time, he still made it in his way to accompany us in each brief excursion. I can hardly tell how he managed his engagements; they were numerous, yet by dint of system, he classed them in an order which left him a daily period of liberty. I often saw him hard-worked, yet seldom over-driven, and never irritated, confused, or oppressed. What he did was accomplished with the ease and grace of all-sufficing strength; with the bountiful cheerfulness of high and unbroken energies. Under his guidance I saw, in that one happy fortnight, more of Villette, its environs, and its inhabitants, than I had seen in the whole eight months of my previous residence. He took me to places of interest in the town, of whose names I had not before so much as heard; with willingness and spirit he communicated much noteworthy information. He never seemed to think it a trouble to talk to me, and, I am sure, it was never a task to me to listen. It was not his way to treat subjects coldly and vaguely; he rarely generalized, never prosed. He seemed to like nice details almost as much as I liked them myself: he seemed observant of character: and not superficially observant, either. These points gave the quality of interest to his discourse; and the fact of his speaking direct from his own resources, and not borrowing or stealing from books – here a dry fact, and there a trite phrase, and elsewhere a hackneyed opinion – ensured a freshness, as welcome as it was rare. Before my eyes, too, his disposition seemed to unfold another phase; to pass to a fresh day: to rise in new and nobler dawn.

His mother possessed a good development of benevolence, but he owned a better and larger. I found, on accompanying him to the Basse-Ville – the poor and crowded quarter of the city – that his errands there were as much those of the philanthropist as the physician. I understood presently that cheerfully, habitually, and in single-minded unconsciousness of any special merit distinguishing his deeds – he was achieving, amongst a very wretched population, a world of active good. The lower orders liked him well; his poor, patients in the hospitals welcomed him with a sort of enthusiasm.

But stop – I must not, from the faithful narrator, degenerate into the partial eulogist. Well, full well, do I know that Dr. John was not perfect, any more than I am perfect. Human fallibility leavened him throughout: there was no hour, and scarcely a moment of the time I spent with him that in act or speech, or look, he did not betray something that was not of a god. A god could not have the cruel vanity of Dr. John, nor his sometime levity. No immortal could have resembled him in his occasional temporary oblivion of all but the present – in his passing passion for that present; shown not coarsely, by devoting it to material indulgence, but selfishly, by extracting from it whatever it could yield of nutriment to his masculine self-love: his delight was to feed that ravenous sentiment, without thought of the price of provender, or care for the cost of keeping it sleek and high-pampered.

The reader is requested to note a seeming contradiction in the two views which have been given of Graham Bretton – the public and private – the out-door and the in-door view. In the first, the public, he is shown oblivious of self; as modest in the display of his energies, as earnest in their exercise. In the second, the fireside picture, there is expressed consciousness of what he has and what he is; pleasure in homage, some recklessness in exciting, some vanity in receiving the same. Both portraits are correct.

It was hardly possible to oblige Dr. John quietly and in secret. When you thought that the fabrication of some trifle dedicated to his use had been achieved unnoticed, and that, like other men, he would use it when placed ready for his use, and never ask whence it came, he amazed you by a smilingly-uttered observation or two, proving that his eye had been on the work from commencement to close: that he had noted the design, traced its progress, and marked its completion. It pleased him to be thus served, and he let his pleasure beam in his eye and play about his mouth.

This would have been all very well, if he had not added to such kindly and unobtrusive evidence a certain wilfulness in discharging what he called debts. When his mother worked for him, he paid her by showering about her his bright animal spirits, with even more affluence than his gay, taunting, teasing, loving wont. If Lucy Snowe were discovered to have put her hand to such work, he planned, in recompence, some pleasant recreation.

I often felt amazed at his perfect knowledge of Villette; a knowledge not merely confined to its open streets, but penetrating to all its galleries, salles, and cabinets: of every door which shut in an object worth seeing, of every museum, of every hall, sacred to art or science, he seemed to possess the

'Open! Sesame'. I never had a head for science, but an ignorant, blind, fond instinct inclined me to art. I liked to visit the picture-galleries, and I dearly liked to be left there alone. In company, a wretched idiosyncracy forbade me to see much or to feel anything. In unfamiliar company, where it was necessary to maintain a flow of talk on the subjects in presence, half an hour would knock me up, with a combined pressure of physical lassitude and entire mental incapacity. I never yet saw the well-reared child, much less the educated adult, who could not put me to shame, by the sustained intelligence of its demeanour under the ordeal of a conversable, sociable visitation of pictures, historical sights or buildings, or any lions of public interest. Dr. Bretton was a cicerone after my own heart; he would take me betimes, ere the galleries were filled, leave me there for two or three hours, and call for me when his own engagements were discharged. Meantime, I was happy; happy, not always in admiring, but in examining, questioning, and forming conclusions. In the commencement of these visits, there was some misunderstanding and consequent struggle between Will and Power. The former faculty exacted approbation of that which it was considered orthodox to admire; the latter groaned forth its utter inability to pay the tax; it was then self-sneered at, spurred up, goaded on to refine its taste, and whet its zest. The more it was chidden, however, the more it wouldn't praise. Discovering gradually that a wonderful sense of fatigue resulted from these conscientious efforts, I began to reflect whether I might not dispense with that great labour, and concluded eventually that I might, and so sank supine into a luxury of calm before ninety-nine out of a hundred of the exhibited frames.

It seemed to me that an original and good picture was just as scarce as an original and good book; nor did I, in the end, tremble to say to myself, standing before certain chef-d'oeuvres bearing great names, "These are not a whit like nature. Nature's daylight never had that colour: never was made so turbid, either by storm or cloud, as it is laid out there, under a sky of indigo: and that indigo is not ether; and those dark weeds plastered upon it are not trees." Several very well executed and complacent-looking fat women struck me as by no means the goddesses they appeared to consider themselves. Many scores of marvellously-finished little Flemish pictures, and also of sketches, excellent for fashion-books displaying varied costumes in the handsomest materials, gave evidence of laudable industry whimsically applied. And yet there were fragments of truth here and there which satisfied the conscience, and gleams of light that cheered the vision. Nature's power here broke through in a mountain snow-storm; and there her glory in a sunny southern day. An expression in this portrait proved clear insight into character; a face in that historical painting, by its vivid filial likeness, startlingly reminded you that genius gave it birth. These exceptions I loved: they grew dear as friends.

One day, at a quiet early hour, I found myself nearly alone in a certain gallery, wherein one particular picture of portentous size, set up in the best light, having a cordon of protection stretched before it, and a cushioned bench duly set in front for the accommodation of worshipping connoisseurs, who, having gazed themselves off their feet, might be fain to complete the business sitting: this picture, I say, seemed to consider itself the queen of the collection.

It represented a woman, considerably larger, I thought, than the life. I calculated that this lady, put into a scale of magnitude, suitable for the reception of a commodity of bulk, would infallibly turn from fourteen to sixteen stone. She was, indeed, extremely well fed: very much butcher's meat – to say nothing of bread, vegetables, and liquids – must she have consumed to attain that breadth and height, that wealth of muscle, that affluence of flesh. She lay half-reclined on a couch: why, it would be difficult to say; broad daylight blazed round her; she appeared in hearty health, strong enough to do the work of two plain cooks; she could not plead a weak spine; she ought to have been standing, or at least sitting bolt upright. She had no business to lounge away the noon on a sofa. She ought likewise to have worn decent garments; a gown covering her properly, which was not the case: out of abundance of material – seven-and-twenty yards, I should say, of drapery – she managed to make inefficient raiment. Then, for the wretched untidiness surrounding her, there could be no excuse. Pots and pans – perhaps I ought to say vases and goblets – were rolled here and there on the foreground; a perfect rubbish of flowers was mixed amongst them, and an absurd and disorderly mass of curtain upholstery smothered the couch and cumbered the floor. On referring to the catalogue, I found that this notable production bore the name *Cleopatra*.

Well, I was sitting wondering at it (as the bench was there, I thought I might as well take advantage of its accommodation), and thinking that while some of the details – as roses, gold cups, jewels, etc., were very prettily painted, it was on the whole an enormous piece of claptrap; the room, almost vacant when I entered, began to fill. Scarcely noticing this circumstance (as, indeed, it did not matter to me) I retained my seat; rather to rest myself than with a view to studying this huge, dark-complexioned gipsy-queen; of whom, indeed, I soon tired, and betook myself for refreshment to the contemplation of some exquisite little pictures of still life: wild-flowers, wild-fruit, mossy woodnests, casketing eggs that looked like pearls seen through clear green sea-water; all hung modestly beneath that coarse and preposterous canvas.

Suddenly a light tap visited my shoulder. Starting, turning, I met a face bent to encounter mine; a frowning, almost a shocked face it was.

"*Que faites-vous ici?*" said a voice.

"*Mais, Monsieur, je m'amuse.*"

"*Vous vous amusez! Et à quoi, s'il vous plait? Mais d'abord, faites-moi le plaisir de vous lever; prenez mon bras, et allons de l'autre côté.*"

I did precisely as I was bid. M. Paul Emanuel (it was he) returned from Rome, and now a travelled man, was not likely to be less tolerant of insubordination now, than before this added distinction laurelled his temples.

"Permit me to conduct you to your party," said he, as we crossed the room.

"I have no party."

"You are not alone?"

"Yes, Monsieur."

"Did you come here unaccompanied?"

"No, Monsieur. Dr. Bretton brought me here."

"Dr. Bretton and Madame his mother, of course?"

"No; only Dr. Bretton."

"And he told you to look at *that* picture?"

"By no means; I found it out for myself."

M. Paul's hair was shorn close as raven down, or I think it would have bristled on his head. Beginning now to perceive his drift, I had a certain pleasure in keeping cool, and working him up.

"Astounding insular audacity!" cried the Professor. "*Singulières femmes que ces Anglaises!*"

"What is the matter, Monsieur?"

"Matter! How dare you, a young person, sit coolly down, with the self-possession of a garçon, and look at *that* picture?"

"It is a very ugly picture, but I cannot at all see why I should not look at it."

"Bon! Bon! Speak no more of it. But you ought not to be here alone."

"If, however, I have no society – no *party*, as you say? And then, what does it signify whether I am alone, or accompanied? Nobody meddles with me."

"*Taisez-vous, et asseyez-vous là – là!*" – setting down a chair with emphasis in a particularly dull corner, before a series of most specially dreary 'cadres'.

"*Mais, Monsieur?*"

"*Mais, Mademoiselle, asseyez-vous, et ne bougez pas – entendez-vous? – jusqu'à ce qu'on vienne vous chercher, ou que je vous donne la permission.*"

"*Quel triste coin!*" cried I, "*Et quelles laids tableaux!*"

And 'laids', indeed, they were; being a set of four, denominated in the catalogue '*La vie d'une femme*.' They were painted rather in a remarkable style – flat, dead, pale, and formal. The first represented a 'Jeune Fille', coming out of a church-door, a missal in her hand, her dress very prim, her eyes cast down, her mouth pursed up – the image of a most villanous little precocious she-hypocrite. The second, a 'Mariée', with a long white veil, kneeling at a prie-dieu in her chamber, holding her hands plastered together, finger to finger, and showing the whites of her eyes in a most exasperating manner. The third, a 'Jeune Mère', hanging disconsolate over a clayey and puffy baby with a face like an unwholesome full moon. The fourth, a 'Veuve', being a black woman, holding by the hand a black little girl, and the twain studiously surveying an elegant French monument, set up in a corner of some Père la Chaise. All these four 'Anges' were grim and grey as burglars, and cold and vapid as ghosts. What women to live with! Insincere, ill-humoured, bloodless, brainless nonentities! As bad in their way as the indolent gipsy-giantess, the Cleopatra, in hers.

It was impossible to keep one's attention long confined to these master-pieces, and so, by degrees, I veered round, and surveyed the gallery.

A perfect crowd of spectators was by this time gathered round the Lioness, from whose vicinage I had been banished; nearly half this crowd were ladies, but M. Paul afterwards told me, these were 'des dames', and it was quite proper for them to contemplate what no 'demoiselle' ought to glance at. I assured him plainly I could not agree in this doctrine, and did not see the sense of it; whereupon, with his usual absolutism, he merely requested my silence, and also, in the same breath, denounced my mingled rashness and ignorance. A more despotic little man than M. Paul never filled a professor's chair. I noticed, by the way, that he looked at the picture himself quite at his ease, and for a very long while: he did not, however, neglect to glance from time to time my way, in order, I suppose, to make sure that I was obeying orders, and not breaking bounds. By-and-by, he again accosted me.

"Had I not been ill?" he wished to know: "he understood I had."

"Yes, but I was now quite well."

"Where had I spent the vacation?"

"Chiefly in the Rue Fossette; partly with Madame Bretton."

"He had heard that I was left alone in the Rue Fossette; was that so?"

"Not quite alone: Marie Broc" (the crétin) "was with me."

He shrugged his shoulders; varied and contradictory expressions played rapidly over his countenance. Marie Broc was well known to M. Paul; he never gave a lesson in the third division (containing the least advanced pupils), that she did not occasion in him a sharp conflict between antagonistic impressions. Her personal appearance, her repulsive manners, her often unmanageable disposition, irritated his temper, and inspired him with strong antipathy; a feeling he was too apt to conceive when his taste was offended or his will thwarted. On the other hand, her misfortunes constituted a strong claim on his forbearance and compassion – such a claim as it was not in his nature to deny; hence resulted almost daily drawn battles between impatience and disgust on the one hand, pity and a sense of justice on the other; in which, to his credit be it said, it was very seldom that the former feelings prevailed: when they did, however, M. Paul showed a phase of character which had its terrors. His passions were strong, his aversions and attachments alike vivid; the force he exerted in holding both in check by no means mitigated an observer's sense of their vehemence. With such tendencies, it may well be supposed he often excited in ordinary minds fear and dislike; yet it was an error to fear him: nothing drove him so nearly frantic as the tremor of an apprehensive and distrustful spirit; nothing soothed him like confidence tempered with gentleness. To evince these sentiments, however, required a thorough comprehension of his nature; and his nature was of an order rarely comprehended.

"How did you get on with Marie Broc?" he asked, after some minutes' silence.

"Monsieur, I did my best; but it was terrible to be alone with her!"

"You have, then, a weak heart! You lack courage; and, perhaps, charity. Yours are not the qualities which might constitute a Sister of Mercy."

[He was a religious little man, in his way: the self-denying and self-sacrificing part of the Catholic religion commanded the homage of his soul.]

"I don't know, indeed: I took as good care of her as I could; but when her aunt came to fetch her away, it was a great relief."

"Ah! You are an egotist. There are women who have nursed hospitals-full of similar unfortunates. You could not do that?"

"Could Monsieur do it himself?"

"Women who are worthy the name ought infinitely to surpass; our coarse, fallible, self-indulgent sex, in the power to perform such duties."

"I washed her, I kept her clean, I fed her, I tried to amuse her; but she made mouths at me instead of speaking."

"You think you did great things?"

"No; but as great as I *could* do."

"Then limited are your powers, for in tending one idiot you fell sick."

"Not with that, Monsieur; I had a nervous fever: my mind was ill."

"*Vraiment! Vous valez peu de chose.* You are not cast in an heroic mould; your courage will not avail to sustain you in solitude; it merely gives you the temerity to gaze with sang-froid at pictures of Cleopatra."

It would have been easy to show anger at the teasing, hostile tone of the little man. I had never been angry with him yet, however, and had no present disposition to begin.

"Cleopatra!" I repeated, quietly. "Monsieur, too, has been looking at Cleopatra; what does he think of her?"

"*Cela ne vaut rien,*" he responded. "*Une femme superbe – une taille d'impératrice, des formes de Junon, mais une personne dont je ne voudrais ni pour femme, ni pour fille, ni pour soeur. Aussi vous ne jeterez plus un seul coup d'oeil de sa côté.*"

"But I have looked at her a great many times while Monsieur has been talking: I can see her quite well from this corner."

"Turn to the wall and study your four pictures of a woman's life."

"Excuse me, M. Paul; they are too hideous: but if you admire them, allow me to vacate my seat and leave you to their contemplation."

"Mademoiselle," he said, grimacing a half-smile, or what he intended for a smile, though it was but a grim and hurried manifestation. "You nurslings of Protestantism astonish me. You unguarded Englishwomen walk calmly amidst red-hot ploughshares and escape burning. I believe, if some of you were thrown into Nebuchadnezzar's hottest furnace you would issue forth untraversed by the smell of fire."

"Will Monsieur have the goodness to move an inch to one side?"

"How! At what are you gazing now? You are not recognising an acquaintance amongst that group of *jeunes gens*?"

"I think so – yes, I see there a person I know."

In fact, I had caught a glimpse of a head too pretty to belong to any other than the redoubted Colonel de Hamal. What a very finished, highly polished little pate it was! What a figure, so trim and natty! What womanish feet and hands! How daintily he held a glass to one of his optics! With what admiration he gazed upon the Cleopatra! And then, how engagingly he tittered and whispered a friend at his elbow! Oh, the man of sense! Oh, the refined gentleman of superior taste and tact! I observed him for about ten minutes, and perceived that he was exceedingly taken with this dusk and portly Venus of the Nile. So much was I interested in his bearing, so absorbed in divining his character by his looks and movements, I temporarily forgot M. Paul; in the interim a group came between that gentleman and me; or possibly his scruples might have received another and worse shock from my present abstraction, causing him to withdraw voluntarily: at any rate, when I again looked round, he was gone.

My eye, pursuant of the search, met not him, but another and dissimilar figure, well seen amidst the crowd, for the height as well as the port lent each its distinction. This way came Dr. John, in visage, in shape, in hue, as unlike the dark, acerb, and caustic little professor, as the fruit of the Hesperides might be unlike the sloe in the wild thicket; as the high-couraged but tractable Arabian is unlike the rude and stubborn 'sheltie'. He was looking for me, but had not yet explored the corner where the schoolmaster had just put me. I remained quiet; yet another minute I would watch.

He approached de Hamal; he paused near him; I thought he had a pleasure in looking over his head; Dr. Bretton, too, gazed on the Cleopatra. I doubt if it were to his taste: he did not simper like the little Count; his mouth looked fastidious, his eye cool; without demonstration he stepped aside, leaving room for others to approach. I saw now that he was waiting, and, rising, I joined him.

We took one turn round the gallery; with Graham it was very pleasant to take such a turn. I always liked dearly to hear what he had to say about either pictures or books; because without pretending to be a connoisseur, he always spoke his thought, and that was sure to be fresh: very often it was also just and pithy. It was pleasant also to tell him some things he did not know – he listened so kindly, so teachably; unformalized by scruples lest so to bend his bright handsome head, to gather a woman's rather obscure and stammering explanation, should imperil the dignity of his manhood. And when he communicated information in return, it was with a lucid intelligence that left all his words clear graven on the memory; no explanation of his giving, no fact of his narrating, did I ever forget.

As we left the gallery, I asked him what he thought of the Cleopatra (after making him laugh by telling him how Professor Emanuel had sent me to the right about, and taking him to see the sweet series of pictures recommended to my attention.)

"Pooh!" said he. "My mother is a better-looking woman. I heard some French fops, yonder, designating her as '*le type du voluptueux*'; if so, I can only say, 'le voluptueux' is little to my liking. Compare that mulatto with Ginevra!"

Chapter Twenty
The Concert

ONE MORNING, Mrs. Bretton, coming promptly into my room, desired me to open my drawers and show her my dresses; which I did, without a word.

"That will do," said she, when she had turned them over. "You must have a new one."

She went out. She returned presently with a dressmaker. She had me measured. "I mean," said she, "to follow my own taste, and to have my own way in this little matter."

Two days after came home – a pink dress!

"That is not for me," I said, hurriedly, feeling that I would almost as soon clothe myself in the costume of a Chinese lady of rank.

"We shall see whether it is for you or not," rejoined my godmother, adding with her resistless decision: "Mark my words. You will wear it this very evening."

I thought I should not; I thought no human force should avail to put me into it. A pink dress! I knew it not. It knew not me. I had not proved it.

My godmother went on to decree that I was to go with her and Graham to a concert that same night: which concert, she explained, was a grand affair to be held in the large salle, or hall, of the principal musical society. The most advanced of the pupils of the Conservatoire were to perform: it was to be followed by a lottery 'au bénéfice des pauvres'; and to crown all, the King, Queen, and Prince of Labassecour were to be present. Graham, in sending tickets, had enjoined attention to costume as a compliment due to royalty: he also recommended punctual readiness by seven o'clock.

About six, I was ushered upstairs. Without any force at all, I found myself led and influenced by another's will, unconsulted, unpersuaded, quietly overruled. In short, the pink dress went on, softened by some drapery of black lace. I was pronounced to be en grande tenue, and requested to look in the glass. I did so with some fear and trembling; with more fear and trembling, I turned away. Seven o'clock struck; Dr. Bretton was come; my godmother and I went down. *She* was clad in brown velvet; as I walked in her shadow, how I envied her those folds of grave, dark majesty! Graham stood in the drawing-room doorway.

"I *do* hope he will not think I have been decking myself out to draw attention," was my uneasy aspiration.

"Here, Lucy, are some flowers," said he, giving me a bouquet. He took no further notice of my dress than was conveyed in a kind smile and satisfied nod, which calmed at once my sense of shame and fear of ridicule. For the rest; the dress was made with extreme simplicity, guiltless of flounce or furbelow; it was but the light fabric and bright tint which scared me, and since Graham found in it nothing absurd, my own eye consented soon to become reconciled.

I suppose people who go every night to places of public amusement, can hardly enter into the fresh gala feeling with which an opera or a concert is enjoyed by those for whom it is a rarity: I am not sure that I expected great pleasure from the concert, having but a very vague notion of its nature, but I liked the drive there well. The snug comfort of the close carriage on a cold though fine night, the pleasure of setting out with companions so cheerful and friendly, the sight of the stars glinting fitfully through the trees as we rolled along the avenue; then the freer burst of the night-sky when we issued forth to the open chaussée, the passage through the city gates, the lights there burning, the guards there posted, the pretence of inspection, to which we there submitted, and which amused us so much – all these small matters had for me, in their novelty, a peculiarly exhilarating charm. How much of it lay in the atmosphere of friendship diffused about me, I know not: Dr. John and his mother were both in their finest mood, contending animatedly with each other the whole way, and as frankly kind to me as if I had been of their kin.

Our way lay through some of the best streets of Villette, streets brightly lit, and far more lively now than at high noon. How brilliant seemed the shops! How glad, gay, and abundant flowed the tide of life along the broad pavement! While I looked, the thought of the Rue Fossette came across me – of the walled-in garden and school-house, and of the dark, vast 'classes', where, as at this very hour, it was my wont to wander all solitary, gazing at the stars through the high, blindless windows, and listening to the distant voice of the reader in the refectory, monotonously exercised upon the 'lecture pieuse'. Thus must I soon again listen and wander; and this shadow of the future stole with timely sobriety across the radiant present.

By this time we had got into a current of carriages all tending in one direction, and soon the front of a great illuminated building blazed before us. Of what I should see within this building, I had, as before intimated, but an imperfect idea; for no place of public entertainment had it ever been my lot to enter yet.

We alighted under a portico where there was a great bustle and a great crowd, but I do not distinctly remember further details, until I found myself mounting a majestic staircase wide and easy of ascent, deeply and softly carpeted with crimson, leading up to great doors closed solemnly, and whose panels were also crimson-clothed.

I hardly noticed by what magic these doors were made to roll back – Dr. John managed these points; roll back they did, however, and within was disclosed a hall – grand, wide, and high, whose sweeping circular walls, and domed hollow ceiling, seemed to me all dead gold (thus with nice art was it stained), relieved by cornicing, fluting, and garlandry, either bright, like gold burnished, or snow-white, like alabaster, or white and gold mingled in wreaths of gilded leaves and spotless lilies: wherever drapery hung, wherever carpets were spread, or cushions placed, the sole colour employed was deep crimson. Pendent from the dome, flamed a mass that dazzled me – a mass, I thought, of rock-crystal, sparkling with facets, streaming with drops, ablaze with stars, and gorgeously tinged with dews of gems dissolved, or fragments of rainbows shivered. It was only the chandelier, reader, but for me it seemed the work of eastern genii: I almost looked to see if a huge, dark, cloudy hand – that of the Slave of the Lamp – were not hovering in the lustrous and perfumed atmosphere of the cupola, guarding its wondrous treasure.

We moved on – I was not at all conscious whither – but at some turn we suddenly encountered another party approaching from the opposite direction. I just now see that group, as it flashed – upon me for one moment. A handsome middle-aged lady in dark velvet; a gentleman who might be her son – the best face, the finest figure, I thought, I had ever seen; a third person in a pink dress and black lace mantle.

I noted them all – the third person as well as the other two – and for the fraction of a moment believed them all strangers, thus receiving an impartial impression of their appearance. But the impression was hardly felt and not fixed, before the consciousness that I faced a great mirror, filling a compartment between two pillars, dispelled it: the party was our own party. Thus for the first, and perhaps only time in my life, I enjoyed the 'giftie' of seeing myself as others see me. No need to dwell on the result. It brought a jar of discord, a pang of regret; it was not flattering, yet, after all, I ought to be thankful; it might have been worse.

At last, we were seated in places commanding a good general view of that vast and dazzling, but warm and cheerful hall. Already it was filled, and filled with a splendid assemblage. I do not know that the women were very beautiful, but their dresses were so perfect; and foreigners, even such as are ungraceful in domestic privacy, seem to posses the art of appearing graceful in public: however blunt and boisterous those every-day and home movements connected with peignoir and papillotes, there is a slide, a bend, a carriage of the head and arms, a mien of the mouth and eyes, kept nicely in reserve for gala use – always brought out with the grande toilette, and duly put on with the 'parure'.

Some fine forms there were here and there, models of a peculiar style of beauty; a style, I think, never seen in England; a solid, firm-set, sculptural style. These shapes have no angles: a caryatid in marble is almost as flexible; a Phidian goddess is not more perfect in a certain still and stately sort. They have such features as the Dutch painters give to their madonnas: low-country classic features, regular but round, straight but stolid; and for their depth of expressionless calm, of passionless peace, a polar snow-field could alone offer a type. Women of this order need no ornament, and they seldom wear any; the smooth hair, closely braided, supplies a sufficient contrast to the smoother cheek and brow; the dress cannot be too simple; the rounded arm and perfect neck require neither bracelet nor chain.

With one of these beauties I once had the honour and rapture to be perfectly acquainted: the inert force of the deep, settled love she bore herself, was wonderful; it could only be surpassed by her proud impotency to care for any other living thing. Of blood, her cool veins conducted no flow; placid lymph filled and almost obstructed her arteries.

Such a Juno as I have described sat full in our view – a sort of mark for all eyes, and quite conscious that so she was, but proof to the magnetic influence of gaze or glance: cold, rounded, blonde, and beauteous as the white column, capitalled with gilding, which rose at her side.

Observing that Dr. John's attention was much drawn towards her, I entreated him in a low voice "for the love of heaven to shield well his heart. You need not fall in love with *that* lady," I said, "because, I tell you beforehand, you might die at her feet, and she would not love you again."

"Very well," said he, "and how do you know that the spectacle of her grand insensibility might not with me be the strongest stimulus to homage? The sting of desperation is, I think, a wonderful irritant to my emotions: but" (shrugging his shoulders) "you know nothing about these things; I'll address myself to my mother. Mamma, I'm in a dangerous way."

"As if that interested me!" said Mrs. Bretton.

"Alas! The cruelty of my lot!" responded her son. "Never man had a more unsentimental mother than mine: she never seems to think that such a calamity can befall her as a daughter-in-law."

"If I don't, it is not for want of having that same calamity held over my head: you have threatened me with it for the last ten years. 'Mamma, I am going to be married soon!' was the cry before you were well out of jackets."

"But, mother, one of these days it will be realized. All of a sudden, when you think you are most secure, I shall go forth like Jacob or Esau, or any other patriarch, and take me a wife: perhaps of these which are of the daughters of the land."

"At your peril, John Graham! That is all."

"This mother of mine means me to be an old bachelor. What a jealous old lady it is! But now just look at that splendid creature in the pale blue satin dress, and hair of paler brown, with 'reflets satinés' as those of her robe. Would you not feel proud, mamma, if I were to bring that goddess home some day, and introduce her to you as Mrs. Bretton, junior?"

"You will bring no goddess to La Terrasse: that little château will not contain two mistresses; especially if the second be of the height, bulk, and circumference of that mighty doll in wood and wax, and kid and satin."

"Mamma, she would fill your blue chair so admirably!"

"Fill my chair? I defy the foreign usurper! A rueful chair should it be for her: but hush, John Graham! Hold your tongue, and use your eyes."

During the above skirmish, the hall, which, I had thought, seemed full at the entrance, continued to admit party after party, until the semicircle before the stage presented one dense mass of heads, sloping from floor to ceiling. The stage, too, or rather the wide temporary platform, larger than any stage, desert half an hour since, was now overflowing with life; round two grand pianos, placed about the centre, a white flock of young girls, the pupils of the Conservatoire, had noiselessly poured. I had noticed their gathering, while Graham and his mother were engaged in discussing the belle in blue satin, and had watched with interest the process of arraying and marshalling them. Two gentlemen, in each of whom I recognised an acquaintance, officered this virgin troop. One, an artistic-looking man, bearded, and with long hair, was a noted pianiste, and also the first music-teacher in Villette; he attended twice a week at Madame Beck's pensionnat, to give lessons to the few pupils whose parents were rich enough to allow their daughters the privilege of his instructions; his name was M. Josef Emanuel, and he was half-brother to M. Paul: which potent personage was now visible in the person of the second gentleman.

M. Paul amused me; I smiled to myself as I watched him, he seemed so thoroughly in his element – standing conspicuous in presence of a wide and grand assemblage, arranging, restraining, over-aweing about one hundred young ladies. He was, too, so perfectly in earnest – so energetic, so intent, and, above all, so absolute: and yet what business had he there? What had he to do with music or the Conservatoire – he who could hardly distinguish one note from another? I knew that it was his love of display and authority which had brought him there – a love not offensive, only because so naive. It presently became obvious that his brother, M. Josef, was as much under his control as were the girls themselves. Never was such a little hawk of a man as that M. Paul! Ere long, some noted singers and musicians dawned upon the platform: as these stars rose, the comet-like professor set. Insufferable to him were all notorieties and celebrities: where he could not outshine, he fled.

And now all was prepared: but one compartment of the hall waited to be filled – a compartment covered with crimson, like the grand staircase and doors, furnished with stuffed and cushioned benches, ranged on each side of two regal chairs, placed solemnly under a canopy.

A signal was given, the doors rolled back, the assembly stood up, the orchestra burst out, and, to the welcome of a choral burst, enter the King, the Queen, the Court of Labassecour.

Till then, I had never set eyes on living king or queen; it may consequently be conjectured how I strained my powers of vision to take in these specimens of European royalty. By whomsoever majesty is beheld for the first time, there will always be experienced a vague surprise bordering on disappointment, that the same does not appear seated, en permanence, on a throne, bonneted with a crown, and furnished, as to the hand, with a sceptre. Looking out for a king and queen, and seeing only a middle-aged soldier and a rather young lady, I felt half cheated, half pleased.

Well do I recall that King – a man of fifty, a little bowed, a little grey: there was no face in all that assembly which resembled his. I had never read, never been told anything of his nature or his habits; and at first the strong hieroglyphics graven as with iron stylet on his brow, round his eyes, beside his mouth, puzzled and baffled instinct. Ere long, however, if I did not know, at least I felt, the meaning of those characters written without hand. There sat a silent sufferer – a nervous, melancholy man. Those eyes had looked on the visits of a certain ghost – had long waited the comings and goings of that strangest spectre, Hypochondria. Perhaps he saw her now on that stage, over against him, amidst all that brilliant throng. Hypochondria has that wont, to rise in the midst of thousands – dark as Doom, pale as Malady, and well-nigh strong as Death. Her comrade and victim thinks to be happy one moment – "Not so," says she; "I come." And she freezes the blood in his heart, and beclouds the light in his eye.

Some might say it was the foreign crown pressing the King's brows which bent them to that peculiar and painful fold; some might quote the effects of early bereavement. Something there might be of both these; but these are embittered by that darkest foe of humanity – constitutional melancholy. The Queen, his wife, knew this: it seemed to me, the reflection of her husband's grief lay, a subduing shadow, on her own benignant face. A mild, thoughtful, graceful woman that princess seemed; not beautiful, not at all like the women of solid charms and marble feelings described a page or two since. Hers was a somewhat slender shape; her features, though distinguished enough, were too suggestive of reigning dynasties and royal lines to give unqualified pleasure. The expression clothing that profile was agreeable in the present instance; but you could not avoid connecting it with remembered effigies, where similar lines appeared, under phase ignoble; feeble, or sensual, or cunning, as the case might be. The Queen's eye, however, was her own; and pity, goodness, sweet sympathy, blessed it with divinest light. She moved no sovereign, but a lady – kind, loving, elegant. Her little son, the Prince of Labassecour, and young Duc de Dindonneau, accompanied her: he leaned on his mother's knee; and, ever and anon, in the course of that evening, I saw her observant of the monarch at her side, conscious of his beclouded abstraction, and desirous to rouse him from it by drawing his attention to their son. She often bent her head to listen to the boy's remarks, and would then smilingly repeat them to his sire. The moody King started, listened, smiled, but invariably relapsed as soon as his good angel ceased speaking. Full mournful and significant was that spectacle! Not the less so because, both for the aristocracy and the honest bourgeoisie of Labassecour, its peculiarity seemed to be wholly invisible: I could not discover that one soul present was either struck or touched.

With the King and Queen had entered their court, comprising two or three foreign ambassadors; and with them came the elite of the foreigners then resident in Villette. These took possession of the crimson benches; the ladies were seated; most of the men remained standing: their sable rank, lining the background, looked like a dark foil to the splendour displayed in front. Nor was this splendour without varying light and shade and gradation: the middle distance was filled with matrons in velvets and satins, in plumes and gems; the benches in the foreground, to the Queen's right hand, seemed devoted exclusively to young girls, the flower – perhaps, I should rather say, the bud – of Villette aristocracy. Here were no jewels, no head-dresses, no velvet pile or silken sheen purity, simplicity, and aërial grace reigned in that virgin band. Young heads simply braided, and fair forms (I was going to write *sylph* forms, but that would have been quite untrue: several of these 'jeunes filles', who had not numbered more than sixteen or seventeen years, boasted contours as robust and solid as those of a stout Englishwoman of five-and-twenty) – fair forms robed in white, or pale rose, or placid blue, suggested thoughts of heaven and angels. I knew a couple, at least, of these 'rose et blanche' specimens of humanity. Here was a pair of Madame Beck's late pupils – Mesdemoiselles Mathilde and Angélique: pupils who, during their last year at school, ought to have been in the first class, but whose brains never got them beyond the second division. In English, they had been under my own charge, and hard work it was to get them to translate rationally a page of *The Vicar of Wakefield*. Also during three months I had one of them for my vis-à-vis at table, and the quantity of household bread, butter, and stewed fruit, she would habitually consume at 'second déjeuner' was a real world's wonder – to be exceeded only by the fact of her actually pocketing slices she could not eat. Here be truths – wholesome truths, too.

I knew another of these seraphs – the prettiest, or, at any rate, the least demure and hypocritical looking of the lot: she was seated by the daughter of an English peer, also an honest, though haughty-looking girl: both had entered in the suite of the British embassy. She (*i.e.* my acquaintance) had a slight, pliant figure, not at all like the forms of the foreign damsels: her hair, too, was not close-braided, like a shell or a skull-cap of satin; it looked *like* hair, and waved from her head, long, curled, and flowing. She chatted away volubly, and seemed full of a light-headed sort of satisfaction with herself and her position. I did not look at Dr. Bretton; but I knew that he, too, saw Ginevra Fanshawe: he had become so quiet, he answered so briefly his mother's remarks, he so often suppressed a sigh. Why should he sigh? He had confessed a taste for the pursuit of love under difficulties; here was full gratification for that taste. His lady-love beamed upon him from a sphere above his own: he could not come near her; he was not certain that he could win from her a look. I watched to see if she would so far favour him. Our seat was not far from the crimson benches; we must inevitably be seen thence, by eyes so quick and roving as Miss Fanshawe's, and very soon those optics of hers were upon us: at least, upon Dr. and Mrs. Bretton. I kept rather in the shade and out of sight, not wishing to be immediately recognised: she looked quite steadily at Dr. John, and then she raised a glass to examine his mother; a minute or two afterwards she laughingly whispered her neighbour; upon the performance commencing, her rambling attention was attracted to the platform.

On the concert I need not dwell; the reader would not care to have my impressions thereanent: and, indeed, it would not be worth while to record them, as they were the impressions of an ignorance crasse. The young ladies of the Conservatoire, being very much frightened, made rather a tremulous exhibition on the two grand pianos. M. Josef Emanuel stood by them while they played; but he had not the tact or influence of his kinsman, who, under similar circumstances, would certainly have *compelled* pupils of his to demean themselves with heroism and self-possession. M. Paul would have placed the hysteric débutantes between two fires – terror of the audience, and terror of himself – and would have inspired them with the courage of desperation, by making the latter terror incomparably the greater: M. Josef could not do this.

Following the white muslin pianistes, came a fine, full-grown, sulky lady in white satin. She sang. Her singing just affected me like the tricks of a conjuror: I wondered how she did it – how she made her voice run up and down, and cut such marvellous capers; but a simple Scotch melody, played by a rude street minstrel, has often moved me more deeply.

Afterwards stepped forth a gentleman, who, bending his body a good deal in the direction of the King and Queen, and frequently approaching his white-gloved hand to the region of his heart, vented a bitter outcry against a certain 'fausse Isabelle'. I thought he seemed especially to solicit the Queen's sympathy; but, unless I am egregiously mistaken, her Majesty lent her attention rather with the calm of courtesy than the earnestness of interest. This gentleman's state of mind was very harrowing, and I was glad when he wound up his musical exposition of the same.

Some rousing choruses struck me as the best part of the evening's entertainment. There were present deputies from all the best provincial choral societies; genuine, barrel-shaped, native Labassecouriens. These worthies gave voice without mincing the matter their hearty exertions had at least this good result – the ear drank thence a satisfying sense of power.

Through the whole performance – timid instrumental duets, conceited vocal solos, sonorous, brass-lunged choruses – my attention gave but one eye and one ear to the stage, the other being permanently retained in the service of Dr. Bretton: I could not forget him, nor cease to question how he was feeling, what he was thinking, whether he was amused or the contrary. At last he spoke.

"And how do you like it all, Lucy? You are very quiet," he said, in his own cheerful tone.

"I am quiet," I said, "because I am so very, *very* much interested: not merely with the music, but with everything about me."

He then proceeded to make some further remarks, with so much equanimity and composure that I began to think he had really not seen what I had seen, and I whispered – "Miss Fanshawe is here: have you noticed her?"

"Oh, yes! And I observed that you noticed her too."

"Is she come with Mrs. Cholmondeley, do you think?"

"Mrs. Cholmondeley is there with a very grand party. Yes; Ginevra was in *her* train; and Mrs. Cholmondeley was in Lady – – 's train, who was in the Queen's train. If this were not one of the compact little minor European courts, whose very formalities are little more imposing than familiarities, and whose gala grandeur is but homeliness in Sunday array, it would sound all very fine."

"Ginevra saw you, I think?"

"So do I think so. I have had my eye on her several times since you withdrew yours; and I have had the honour of witnessing a little spectacle which you were spared."

I did not ask what; I waited voluntary information, which was presently given.

"Miss Fanshawe," he said, "has a companion with her – a lady of rank. I happen to know Lady Sara by sight; her noble mother has called me in professionally. She is a proud girl, but not in the least insolent, and I doubt whether Ginevra will have gained ground in her estimation by making a butt of her neighbours."

"What neighbours?"

"Merely myself and my mother. As to me it is all very natural: nothing, I suppose, can be fairer game than the young bourgeois doctor; but my mother! I never saw her ridiculed before. Do you know, the curling lip, and sarcastically levelled glass thus directed, gave me a most curious sensation?"

"Think nothing of it, Dr. John: it is not worth while. If Ginevra were in a giddy mood, as she is eminently tonight, she would make no scruple of laughing at that mild, pensive Queen, or that melancholy King. She is not actuated by malevolence, but sheer, heedless folly. To a feather-brained school-girl nothing is sacred."

"But you forget: I have not been accustomed to look on Miss Fanshawe in the light of a feather-brained school-girl. Was she not my divinity – the angel of my career?"

"Hem! There was your mistake."

"To speak the honest truth, without any false rant or assumed romance, there actually was a moment, six months ago, when I thought her divine. Do you remember our conversation about the presents? I was not quite open with you in discussing that subject: the warmth with which you took it up amused me. By way of having the full benefit of your lights, I allowed you to think me more in the dark than I really was. It was that test of the presents which first proved Ginevra mortal. Still her beauty retained its fascination: three days – three hours ago, I was very much her slave. As she passed me tonight, triumphant in beauty, my emotions did her homage; but for one luckless sneer, I should yet be the humblest of her servants. She might have scoffed at *me*, and, while wounding, she would not soon have alienated me: through myself, she could not in ten years have done what, in a moment, she has done through my mother."

He held his peace awhile. Never before had I seen so much fire, and so little sunshine in Dr. John's blue eye as just now.

"Lucy," he recommenced, "look well at my mother, and say, without fear or favour, in what light she now appears to you."

"As she always does – an English, middle-class gentlewoman; well, though gravely dressed, habitually independent of pretence, constitutionally composed and cheerful."

"So she seems to me – bless her! The merry may laugh *with* mamma, but the weak only will laugh *at* her. She shall not be ridiculed, with my consent, at least; nor without my – my scorn – my antipathy – my –"

He stopped: and it was time – for he was getting excited – more it seemed than the occasion warranted. I did not then know that he had witnessed double cause for dissatisfaction with Miss Fanshawe. The glow of his complexion, the expansion of his nostril, the bold curve which disdain gave his well-cut under lip, showed him in a new and striking phase. Yet the rare passion of the constitutionally suave and serene, is not a pleasant spectacle; nor did I like the sort of vindictive thrill which passed through his strong young frame.

"Do I frighten you, Lucy?" he asked.

"I cannot tell why you are so very angry."

"For this reason," he muttered in my ear. "Ginevra is neither a pure angel, nor a pure-minded woman."

"Nonsense! You exaggerate: she has no great harm in her."

"Too much for me. *I* can see where *you* are blind. Now dismiss the subject. Let me amuse myself by teasing mamma: I will assert that she is flagging. Mamma, pray rouse yourself."

"John, I will certainly rouse you if you are not better conducted. Will you and Lucy be silent, that I may hear the singing?"

They were then thundering in a chorus, under cover of which all the previous dialogue had taken place.

"*You* hear the singing, mamma! Now, I will wager my studs, which are genuine, against your paste brooch –"

"My paste brooch, Graham? Profane boy! You know that it is a stone of value."

"Oh! That is one of your superstitions: you were cheated in the business."

"I am cheated in fewer things than you imagine. How do you happen to be acquainted with young ladies of the court, John? I have observed two of them pay you no small attention during the last half-hour."

"I wish you would not observe them."

"Why not? Because one of them satirically levels her eyeglass at me? She is a pretty, silly girl: but are you apprehensive that her titter will discomfit the old lady?"

"The sensible, admirable old lady! Mother, you are better to me than ten wives yet."

"Don't be demonstrative, John, or I shall faint, and you will have to carry me out; and if that burden were laid upon you, you would reverse your last speech, and exclaim, 'Mother, ten wives could hardly be worse to me than you are!'"

* * *

The concert over, the Lottery 'au bénéfice des pauvres' came next: the interval between was one of general relaxation, and the pleasantest imaginable stir and commotion. The white flock was cleared from the platform; a busy throng of gentlemen crowded it instead, making arrangements for the drawing; and amongst these – the busiest of all – re-appeared that certain well-known form, not tall but active, alive with the energy and movement of three tall men. How M. Paul did work! How he issued directions, and, at the same time, set his own shoulder to the wheel! Half-a-dozen assistants were at his beck to remove the pianos, etc.; no matter, he must add to their strength his own. The redundancy of his alertness was half-vexing, half-ludicrous: in my mind I both disapproved and derided most of this fuss. Yet, in the midst of prejudice and annoyance, I could not, while watching, avoid perceiving a certain not disagreeable naïveté in all he did and said; nor could I be blind to certain vigorous characteristics of his physiognomy, rendered conspicuous now by the contrast with a throng of tamer faces: the deep, intent keenness of his eye, the power of his forehead, pale, broad, and full – the mobility of his most flexible mouth. He lacked the calm of force, but its movement and its fire he signally possessed.

Meantime the whole hall was in a stir; most people rose and remained standing, for a change; some walked about, all talked and laughed. The crimson compartment presented a peculiarly animated scene. The long cloud of gentlemen, breaking into fragments, mixed with the rainbow line of ladies; two or three officer-like men approached the King and conversed with him. The Queen, leaving her chair, glided along the rank of young ladies, who all stood up as she passed; and to each in turn I saw her vouchsafe some token of kindness – a gracious word, look or smile. To the two pretty English girls, Lady Sara and Ginevra Fanshawe, she addressed several sentences; as she left them, both, and especially the latter, seemed to glow all over with gratification. They were afterwards accosted by several ladies, and a little circle of gentlemen gathered round them; amongst these – the nearest to Ginevra – stood the Count de Hamal.

"This room is stiflingly hot," said Dr. Bretton, rising with sudden impatience. "Lucy – mother – will you come a moment to the fresh air?"

"Go with him, Lucy," said Mrs. Bretton. "I would rather keep my seat."

Willingly would I have kept mine also, but Graham's desire must take precedence of my own; I accompanied him.

We found the night-air keen; or at least I did: he did not seem to feel it; but it was very still, and the star-sown sky spread cloudless. I was wrapped in a fur shawl. We took some turns on the pavement; in passing under a lamp, Graham encountered my eye.

"You look pensive, Lucy: is it on my account?"

"I was only fearing that you were grieved."

"Not at all: so be of good cheer – as I am. Whenever I die, Lucy, my persuasion is that it will not be of heart-complaint. I may be stung, I may seem to droop for a time, but no pain or malady of sentiment has yet gone through my whole system. You have always seen me cheerful at home?"

"Generally."

"I am glad she laughed at my mother. I would not give the old lady for a dozen beauties. That sneer did me all the good in the world. Thank you, Miss Fanshawe!" And he lifted his hat from his waved locks, and made a mock reverence.

"Yes," he said, "I thank her. She has made me feel that nine parts in ten of my heart have always been sound as a bell, and the tenth bled from a mere puncture: a lancet-prick that will heal in a trice."

"You are angry just now, heated and indignant; you will think and feel differently tomorrow."

"*I* heated and indignant! You don't know me. On the contrary, the heat is gone: I am as cool as the night – which, by the way, may be too cool for you. We will go back."

"Dr. John, this is a sudden change."

"Not it: or if it be, there are good reasons for it – two good reasons: I have told you one. But now let us re-enter."

We did not easily regain our seats; the lottery was begun, and all was excited confusion; crowds blocked the sort of corridor along which we had to pass: it was necessary to pause for a time. Happening to glance round – indeed I half fancied I heard my name pronounced – I saw quite near, the ubiquitous, the inevitable M. Paul. He was looking at me gravely and intently: at me, or rather at my pink dress – sardonic comment on which gleamed in his eye. Now it was his habit to indulge in strictures on the dress, both of the teachers and pupils, at Madame Beck's – a habit which the former, at least, held to be an offensive impertinence: as yet I had not suffered from it – my sombre daily attire not being calculated to attract notice. I was in no mood to permit any new encroachment tonight: rather than accept his banter, I would ignore his presence, and accordingly steadily turned my face to the sleeve of Dr. John's coat; finding in that same black sleeve a prospect more redolent of pleasure and comfort, more genial, more friendly, I thought, than was offered by the dark little Professor's unlovely visage. Dr. John seemed unconsciously to sanction the preference by looking down and saying in his kind voice, "Ay, keep close to my side, Lucy: these crowding burghers are no respecters of persons."

I could not, however, be true to myself. Yielding to some influence, mesmeric or otherwise – an influence unwelcome, displeasing, but effective – I again glanced round to see if M. Paul was gone. No, there he stood on the same spot, looking still, but with a changed eye; he had penetrated my thought, and read my wish to shun him. The mocking but not ill-humoured gaze was turned to a swarthy frown, and when I bowed, with a view to conciliation, I got only the stiffest and sternest of nods in return.

"Whom have you made angry, Lucy?" whispered Dr. Bretton, smiling. "Who is that savage-looking friend of yours?"

"One of the professors at Madame Beck's: a very cross little man."

"He looks mighty cross just now: what have you done to him? What is it all about? Ah, Lucy, Lucy! Tell me the meaning of this."

"No mystery, I assure you. M. Emanuel is very exigeant, and because I looked at your coat-sleeve, instead of curtseying and dipping to him, he thinks I have failed in respect."

"The little –" began Dr. John: I know not what more he would have added, for at that moment I was nearly thrown down amongst the feet of the crowd. M. Paul had rudely pushed past, and was elbowing his way with such utter disregard to the convenience and security of all around, that a very uncomfortable pressure was the consequence.

"I think he is what he himself would call 'méchant,'" said Dr. Bretton. I thought so, too.

Slowly and with difficulty we made our way along the passage, and at last regained our seats. The drawing of the lottery lasted nearly an hour; it was an animating and amusing scene; and as we each held tickets, we shared in the alternations of hope and fear raised by each turn of the wheel. Two little girls, of five and six years old, drew the numbers: and the prizes were duly proclaimed from the platform. These prizes were numerous, though of small value. It so fell out that Dr. John and I each gained one: mine was a cigar-case, his a lady's head-dress – a most airy sort of blue and silver turban, with a streamer of plumage on one side, like a snowy cloud. He was excessively anxious to make an exchange; but I could not be brought to hear reason, and to this day I keep my cigar-case: it serves, when I look at it, to remind me of old times, and one happy evening.

Dr. John, for his part, held his turban at arm's length between his finger and thumb, and looked at it with a mixture of reverence and embarrassment highly provocative of laughter. The contemplation over, he was about coolly to deposit the delicate fabric on the ground between his feet; he seemed to have no shadow of an idea of the treatment or stowage it ought to receive: if his mother had not come to the rescue, I think he would finally have crushed it under his arm like an opera-hat; she restored it to the band-box whence it had issued.

Graham was quite cheerful all the evening, and his cheerfulness seemed natural and unforced. His demeanour, his look, is not easily described; there was something in it peculiar, and, in its way, original. I read in it no common mastery of the passions, and a fund of deep and healthy strength which, without any exhausting effort, bore down Disappointment and extracted her fang. His manner, now, reminded me of qualities I had noticed in him when professionally engaged amongst the poor, the guilty, and the suffering, in the Basse-Ville: he looked at once determined, enduring, and sweet-tempered. Who could help liking him? *He* betrayed no weakness which harassed all your feelings with considerations as to how its faltering must be propped; from *him* broke no irritability which startled calm and quenched mirth; *his* lips let fall no caustic that burned to the bone; *his* eye shot no morose shafts that went cold, and rusty, and venomed through your heart: beside him was rest and refuge – around him, fostering sunshine.

And yet he had neither forgiven nor forgotten Miss Fanshawe. Once angered, I doubt if Dr. Bretton were to be soon propitiated – once alienated, whether he were ever to be reclaimed. He looked at her more than once; not stealthily or humbly, but with a movement of hardy, open observation. De Hamal was now a fixture beside her; Mrs. Cholmondeley sat near, and they and she were wholly absorbed in the discourse, mirth, and excitement, with which the crimson seats were as much astir as any plebeian part of the hall. In the course of some apparently animated discussion, Ginevra once or twice lifted her hand and arm; a handsome bracelet gleamed upon the latter. I saw that its gleam flickered in Dr. John's eye – quickening therein a derisive, ireful sparkle; he laughed:

"I think," he said, "I will lay my turban on my wonted altar of offerings; there, at any rate, it would be certain to find favour: no grisette has a more facile faculty of acceptance. Strange! For after all, I know she is a girl of family."

"But you don't know her education, Dr. John," said I. "Tossed about all her life from one foreign school to another, she may justly proffer the plea of ignorance in extenuation of most of her faults. And then, from what she says, I believe her father and mother were brought up much as she has been brought up."

"I always understood she had no fortune; and once I had pleasure in the thought," said he.

"She tells me," I answered, "that they are poor at home; she always speaks quite candidly on such points: you never find her lying, as these foreigners will often lie. Her parents have a large family: they occupy such a station and possess such connections as, in their opinion, demand display; stringent necessity of circumstances and inherent thoughtlessness of disposition combined, have engendered reckless unscrupulousness as to how they obtain the means of sustaining a good appearance. This is the state of things, and the only state of things, she has seen from childhood upwards."

"I believe it – and I thought to mould her to something better: but, Lucy, to speak the plain truth, I have felt a new thing tonight, in looking at her and de Hamal. I felt it before noticing the impertinence directed at my mother. I saw a look interchanged between them immediately after their entrance, which threw a most unwelcome light on my mind."

"How do you mean? You have been long aware of the flirtation they keep up?"

"Ay, flirtation! That might be an innocent girlish wile to lure on the true lover; but what I refer to was not flirtation: it was a look marking mutual and secret understanding – it was neither girlish nor innocent. No woman, were she as beautiful as Aphrodite, who could give or receive such a glance, shall ever be sought in marriage by me: I would rather wed a paysanne in a short petticoat and high cap – and be sure that she was honest."

I could not help smiling. I felt sure he now exaggerated the case: Ginevra, I was certain, was honest enough, with all her giddiness. I told him so. He shook his head, and said he would not be the man to trust her with his honour.

"The only thing," said I, "with which you may safely trust her. She would unscrupulously damage a husband's purse and property, recklessly try his patience and temper: I don't think she would breathe, or let another breathe, on his honour."

"You are becoming her advocate," said he. "Do you wish me to resume my old chains?"

"No: I am glad to see you free, and trust that free you will long remain. Yet be, at the same time, just."

"I am so: just as Rhadamanthus, Lucy. When once I am thoroughly estranged, I cannot help being severe. But look! The King and Queen are rising. I like that Queen: she has a sweet countenance. Mamma, too, is excessively tired; we shall never get the old lady home if we stay longer."

"I tired, John?" cried Mrs. Bretton, looking at least as animated and as wide-awake as her son. "I would undertake to sit you out yet: leave us both here till morning, and we should see which would look the most jaded by sunrise."

"I should not like to try the experiment; for, in truth, mamma, you are the most unfading of evergreens and the freshest of matrons. It must then be on the plea of your son's delicate nerves and fragile constitution that I found a petition for our speedy adjournment."

"Indolent young man! You wish you were in bed, no doubt; and I suppose you must be humoured. There is Lucy, too, looking quite done up. For shame, Lucy! At your age, a week of evenings-out would not have made me a shade paler. Come away, both of you; and you may laugh at the old lady as much as you please, but, for my part, I shall take charge of the bandbox and turban."

Which she did accordingly. I offered to relieve her, but was shaken off with kindly contempt: my godmother opined that I had enough to do to take care of myself. Not standing on ceremony now, in the midst of the gay 'confusion worse confounded' succeeding to the King and Queen's departure, Mrs. Bretton preceded us, and promptly made us a lane through the crowd. Graham followed, apostrophizing his mother as the most flourishing grisette it had ever been his good fortune to see charged with carriage of a bandbox; he also desired me to mark her affection for the sky-blue turban, and announced his conviction that she intended one day to wear it.

The night was now very cold and very dark, but with little delay we found the carriage. Soon we were packed in it, as warm and as snug as at a fire-side; and the drive home was, I think, still pleasanter than the drive to the concert. Pleasant it was, even though the coachman – having spent in the shop of a 'marchand de vin' a portion of the time we passed at the concert – drove us along the dark and solitary chaussée far past the turn leading down to La Terrasse; we, who were occupied in talking and laughing, not noticing the aberration till, at last, Mrs. Bretton intimated that, though she had always thought the château a retired spot, she did not know it was situated at the world's end, as she declared seemed now to be the case, for she believed we had been an hour and a half en route, and had not yet taken the turn down the avenue.

Then Graham looked out, and perceiving only dim-spread fields, with unfamiliar rows of pollards and limes ranged along their else invisible sunk-fences, began to conjecture how matters were, and calling a halt and descending, he mounted the box and took the reins himself. Thanks to him, we arrived safe at home about an hour and a half beyond our time.

Martha had not forgotten us; a cheerful fire was burning, and a neat supper spread in the dining-room: we were glad of both. The winter dawn was actually breaking before we gained our chambers. I took off my pink dress and lace mantle with happier feelings than I had experienced in putting them on. Not all, perhaps, who had shone brightly arrayed at that concert could say the same; for not all had been satisfied with friendship – with its calm comfort and modest hope.

Chapter Twenty-One
Reaction

Yet three days, and then I must go back to the pensionnat. I almost numbered the moments of these days upon the clock; fain would I have retarded their flight; but they glided by while I watched them: they were already gone while I yet feared their departure.

"Lucy will not leave us today," said Mrs. Bretton, coaxingly at breakfast; "she knows we can procure a second respite."

"I would not ask for one if I might have it for a word," said I. "I long to get the goodbye over, and to be settled in the Rue Fossette again. I must go this morning: I must go directly; my trunk is packed and corded."

It appeared; however, that my going depended upon Graham; he had said he would accompany me, and it so fell out that he was engaged all day, and only returned home at dusk. Then ensued a little combat of words. Mrs. Bretton and her son pressed me to remain one night more. I could have cried, so irritated and eager was I to be gone. I longed to leave them as the criminal on the scaffold longs for the axe to descend: that is, I wished the pang over. How much I wished it, they could not tell. On these points, mine was a state of mind out of their experience.

It was dark when Dr. John handed me from the carriage at Madame Beck's door. The lamp above was lit; it rained a November drizzle, as it had rained all day: the lamplight gleamed on the wet pavement. Just such a night was it as that on which, not a year ago, I had first stopped at this very threshold; just similar was the scene. I remembered the very shapes of the paving-stones which I had noted with idle eye, while, with a thick-beating heart, I waited the unclosing of that door at which I stood – a solitary and a suppliant. On that night, too, I had briefly met him who now stood with me. Had I ever reminded him of that rencontre, or explained it? I had not, nor ever felt the inclination to do so: it was a pleasant thought, laid by in my own mind, and best kept there.

Graham rung the bell. The door was instantly opened, for it was just that period of the evening when the half-boarders took their departure – consequently, Rosine was on the alert.

"Don't come in," said I to him; but he stepped a moment into the well-lighted vestibule. I had not wished him to see that 'the water stood in my eyes', for his was too kind a nature ever to be needlessly shown such signs of sorrow. He always wished to heal – to relieve – when, physician as he was, neither cure nor alleviation were, perhaps, in his power.

"Keep up your courage, Lucy. Think of my mother and myself as true friends. We will not forget you."

"Nor will I forget you, Dr. John."

My trunk was now brought in. We had shaken hands; he had turned to go, but he was not satisfied: he had not done or said enough to content his generous impulses.

"Lucy," – stepping after me – "shall you feel very solitary here?"

"At first I shall."

"Well, my mother will soon call to see you; and, meantime, I'll tell you what I'll do. I'll write – just any cheerful nonsense that comes into my head – shall I?"

"Good, gallant heart!" thought I to myself; but I shook my head, smiling, and said, "Never think of it: impose on yourself no such task. *You* write to *me*! – You'll not have time."

"Oh! I will find or make time. Goodbye!"

He was gone. The heavy door crashed to: the axe had fallen – the pang was experienced.

Allowing myself no time to think or feel – swallowing tears as if they had been wine – I passed to Madame's sitting-room to pay the necessary visit of ceremony and respect. She received me with perfectly well-acted cordiality – was even demonstrative, though brief, in her welcome. In ten minutes I was dismissed. From the salle-à-manger I proceeded to the refectory, where pupils and teachers were now assembled for evening study: again I had a welcome, and one not, I think, quite hollow. That over, I was free to repair to the dormitory.

"And will Graham really write?" I questioned, as I sank tired on the edge of the bed.

Reason, coming stealthily up to me through the twilight of that long, dim chamber, whispered sedately – "He may write once. So kind is his nature, it may stimulate him for once to make the effort. But it *cannot* be continued – it *may* not be repeated. Great were that folly which should build on such a promise – insane that credulity which should mistake the transitory rain-pool, holding in its hollow one draught, for the perennial spring yielding the supply of seasons."

I bent my head: I sat thinking an hour longer. Reason still whispered me, laying on my shoulder a withered hand, and frostily touching my ear with the chill blue lips of eld.

"If," muttered she, "if he *should* write, what then? Do you meditate pleasure in replying? Ah, fool! I warn you! Brief be your answer. Hope no delight of heart – no indulgence of intellect: grant no expansion to feeling – give holiday to no single faculty: dally with no friendly exchange: foster no genial intercommunion...."

"But I have talked to Graham and you did not chide," I pleaded.

"No," said she, "I needed not. Talk for you is good discipline. You converse imperfectly. While you speak, there can be no oblivion of inferiority – no encouragement to delusion: pain, privation, penury stamp your language...."

"But," I again broke in, "where the bodily presence is weak and the speech contemptible, surely there cannot be error in making written language the medium of better utterance than faltering lips can achieve?"

Reason only answered, "At your peril you cherish that idea, or suffer its influence to animate any writing of yours!"

"But if I feel, may I *never* express?"

"*Never!*" declared Reason.

I groaned under her bitter sternness. Never – never – oh, hard word! This hag, this Reason, would not let me look up, or smile, or hope: she could not rest unless I were altogether crushed, cowed, broken-in, and broken-down. According to her, I was born only to work for a piece of bread, to await the pains of death, and steadily through all life to despond. Reason might be right; yet no wonder we are glad at times to defy her, to rush from under her rod and give a truant hour to Imagination – *her* soft, bright foe, *our* sweet Help, our divine Hope. We shall and must break bounds at intervals, despite the terrible revenge that awaits our return. Reason is vindictive as a devil: for me she was always envenomed as a step-mother. If I have obeyed her it has chiefly been with the obedience of fear, not of love. Long ago I should have died of her ill-usage her stint, her chill, her barren board, her icy bed, her savage, ceaseless blows; but for that kinder Power who holds my secret and sworn allegiance. Often has Reason turned me out by night, in mid-winter, on cold snow, flinging for sustenance the gnawed bone dogs had forsaken: sternly has she vowed her stores held nothing more for me – harshly denied my right to ask better things.... Then, looking up, have I seen in the sky a head amidst circling stars, of which the midmost and the brightest lent a ray sympathetic and attent. A spirit, softer and better than Human Reason, has descended with quiet flight to the waste – bringing all round her a sphere of air borrowed of eternal summer; bringing perfume of flowers which cannot fade – fragrance of trees whose fruit is life; bringing breezes pure from a world whose day needs no sun to lighten it. My hunger has this good angel appeased with food, sweet and strange, gathered amongst gleaning angels, garnering their dew-white harvest in the first fresh hour of a heavenly day; tenderly has she assuaged the insufferable fears which weep away life itself – kindly given rest to deadly weariness – generously lent hope and impulse to paralyzed despair. Divine, compassionate, succourable influence! When I bend the knee to other than God, it shall be at thy white and winged feet, beautiful on mountain or on plain. Temples have been reared to the Sun – altars dedicated to the Moon. Oh, greater glory! To thee neither hands build, nor lips consecrate: but hearts, through ages, are faithful to thy worship. A dwelling thou hast, too wide for walls, too high for dome – a temple whose floors are space – rites whose mysteries transpire in presence, to the kindling, the harmony of worlds!

Sovereign complete! Thou hadst, for endurance, thy great army of martyrs; for achievement, thy chosen band of worthies. Deity unquestioned, thine essence foils decay!

This daughter of Heaven remembered me tonight; she saw me weep, and she came with comfort: "Sleep," she said. "Sleep, sweetly – I gild thy dreams!"

She kept her word, and watched me through a night's rest; but at dawn Reason relieved the guard. I awoke with a sort of start; the rain was dashing against the panes, and the wind uttering a peevish cry at intervals; the night-lamp was dying on the black circular stand in the middle of the dormitory: day had already broken. How I pity those whom mental pain stuns instead of rousing! This morning the pang of waking snatched me out of bed like a hand with a giant's gripe. How quickly I dressed in the cold of the raw dawn! How deeply I drank of the ice-cold water in my carafe! This was always my cordial, to which, like other dram-drinkers, I had eager recourse when unsettled by chagrin.

Ere long the bell rang its réveillée to the whole school. Being dressed, I descended alone to the refectory, where the stove was lit and the air was warm; through the rest of the house it was cold, with the nipping severity of a continental winter: though now but the beginning of November, a north wind had thus early brought a wintry blight over Europe: I remember the black stoves pleased me little when I first came; but now I began to associate with them a sense of comfort, and liked them, as in England we like a fireside.

Sitting down before this dark comforter, I presently fell into a deep argument with myself on life and its chances, on destiny and her decrees. My mind, calmer and stronger now than last night, made for itself some imperious rules, prohibiting under deadly penalties all weak retrospect of happiness past; commanding a patient journeying through the wilderness of the present, enjoining a reliance on faith – a watching of the cloud and pillar which subdue while they guide, and awe while they illumine – hushing the impulse to fond idolatry, checking the longing out-look for a far-off promised land whose rivers are, perhaps, never to be, reached save in dying dreams, whose sweet pastures are to be viewed but from the desolate and sepulchral summit of a Nebo.

By degrees, a composite feeling of blended strength and pain wound itself wirily round my heart, sustained, or at least restrained, its throbbings, and made me fit for the day's work. I lifted my head.

As I said before, I was sitting near the stove, let into the wall beneath the refectory and the carré, and thus sufficing to heat both apartments. Piercing the same wall, and close beside the stove, was a window, looking also into the carré; as I looked up a cap-tassel, a brow, two eyes, filled a pane of that window; the fixed gaze of those two eyes hit right against my own glance: they were watching me. I had not till that moment known that tears were on my cheek, but I felt them now.

This was a strange house, where no corner was sacred from intrusion, where not a tear could be shed, nor a thought pondered, but a spy was at hand to note and to divine. And this new, this out-door, this male spy, what business had brought him to the premises at this unwonted hour? What possible right had he to intrude on me thus? No other professor would have dared to cross the carré before the class-bell rang. M. Emanuel took no account of hours nor of claims: there was some book of reference in the first-class library which he had occasion to consult; he had come to seek it: on his way he passed the refectory. It was very much his habit to wear eyes before, behind, and on each side of him: he had seen me through the little window – he now opened the refectory door, and there he stood.

"*Mademoiselle, vous êtes triste.*"

"*Monsieur, j'en ai bien le droit.*"

"*Vous êtes malade de coeur et d'humeur,*" he pursued. "You are at once mournful and mutinous. I see on your cheek two tears which I know are hot as two sparks, and salt as two crystals of the sea. While I speak you eye me strangely. Shall I tell you of what I am reminded while watching you?"

"Monsieur, I shall be called away to prayers shortly; my time for conversation is very scant and brief at this hour – excuse –"

"I excuse everything," he interrupted; "my mood is so meek, neither rebuff nor, perhaps, insult could ruffle it. You remind me, then, of a young she wild creature, new caught, untamed, viewing with a mixture of fire and fear the first entrance of the breaker-in."

Unwarrantable accost! – Rash and rude if addressed to a pupil; to a teacher inadmissible. He thought to provoke a warm reply; I had seen him vex the passionate to explosion before now. In me his malice should find no gratification; I sat silent.

"You look," said he, "like one who would snatch at a draught of sweet poison, and spurn wholesome bitters with disgust."

"Indeed, I never liked bitters; nor do I believe them wholesome. And to whatever is sweet, be it poison or food, you cannot, at least, deny its own delicious quality – sweetness. Better, perhaps, to die quickly a pleasant death, than drag on long a charmless life."

"Yet," said he, "you should take your bitter dose duly and daily, if I had the power to administer it; and, as to the well-beloved poison, I would, perhaps, break the very cup which held it."

I sharply turned my head away, partly because his presence utterly displeased me, and partly because I wished to shun questions: lest, in my present mood, the effort of answering should overmaster self-command.

"Come," said he, more softly, "tell me the truth – you grieve at being parted from friends – is it not so?"

The insinuating softness was not more acceptable than the inquisitorial curiosity. I was silent. He came into the room, sat down on the bench about two yards from me, and persevered long, and, for him, patiently, in attempts to draw me into conversation – attempts necessarily unavailing, because I *could* not talk. At last I entreated to be let alone. In uttering the request, my voice faltered, my head sank on my arms and the table. I wept bitterly, though quietly. He sat a while longer. I did not look up nor speak, till the closing door and his retreating step told me that he was gone. These tears proved a relief.

I had time to bathe my eyes before breakfast, and I suppose I appeared at that meal as serene as any other person: not, however, quite as jocund-looking as the young lady who placed herself in the seat opposite mine, fixed on me a pair of somewhat small eyes twinkling gleefully, and frankly stretched across the table a white hand to be shaken. Miss Fanshawe's travels, gaieties, and flirtations agreed with her mightily; she had become quite plump, her cheeks looked as round as apples. I had seen her last in elegant evening attire. I don't know that she looked less charming now in her school-dress, a kind of careless peignoir of a dark-blue material, dimly and dingily plaided with black. I even think this dusky wrapper gave her charms a triumph; enhancing by contrast the fairness of her skin, the freshness of her bloom, the golden beauty of her tresses.

"I am glad you are come back, Timon," said she. Timon was one of her dozen names for me. "You don't know how often I have wanted you in this dismal hole."

"Oh, have you? Then, of course, if you wanted me, you have something for me to do: stockings to mend, perhaps." I never gave Ginevra a minute's or a farthing's credit for disinterestedness.

"Crabbed and crusty as ever!" said she. "I expected as much: it would not be you if you did not snub one. But now, come, grand-mother, I hope you like coffee as much, and pistolets as little as ever: are you disposed to barter?"

"Take your own way."

This way consisted in a habit she had of making me convenient. She did not like the morning cup of coffee; its school brewage not being strong or sweet enough to suit her palate; and she had an excellent appetite, like any other healthy school-girl, for the morning pistolets or rolls, which were new-baked and very good, and of which a certain allowance was served to each. This allowance being more than I needed, I gave half to Ginevra; never varying in my preference, though many others used to covet the superfluity; and she in return would sometimes give me a portion of her coffee. This morning I was glad of the draught; hunger I had none, and with thirst I was parched. I don't know why I chose to give my bread rather to Ginevra than to another; nor why, if two had to share the convenience of one drinking-vessel, as sometimes happened – for instance, when we took a long walk into the country, and halted for refreshment at a farm – I always contrived that she should be my convive, and rather liked to let her take the lion's share, whether of the white beer, the sweet wine, or the new milk: so it was, however, and she knew it; and, therefore, while we wrangled daily, we were never alienated.

After breakfast my custom was to withdraw to the first classe, and sit and read, or think (oftenest the latter) there alone, till the nine-o'clock bell threw open all doors, admitted the gathered rush of externes and demi-pensionnaires, and gave the signal for entrance on that bustle and business to which, till five p.m., there was no relax.

I was just seated this morning, when a tap came to the door.

"Pardon, Mademoiselle," said a pensionnaire, entering gently; and having taken from her desk some necessary book or paper, she withdrew on tip-toe, murmuring as she passed me, "*Que mademoiselle est appliquée!*"

Appliquée, indeed! The means of application were spread before me, but I was doing nothing; and had done nothing, and meant to do nothing. Thus does the world give us credit for merits we have not. Madame Beck herself deemed me a regular bas-bleu, and often and solemnly used to warn me not to study too much, lest 'the blood should all go to my head'. Indeed, everybody in the Rue Fossette held a superstition that 'Meess Lucie' was learned; with the notable exception of M. Emanuel, who, by means peculiar to himself, and quite inscrutable to me, had obtained a not inaccurate inkling of my real qualifications, and used to take quiet opportunities of chuckling in my ear his malign glee over their scant measure. For my part, I never troubled myself about this penury. I dearly like to think my own thoughts; I had great pleasure in reading a few books, but not many: preferring always those on whose style or sentiment the writer's individual nature was plainly stamped; flagging inevitably over characterless books, however clever and meritorious: perceiving well that, as far as my own mind was concerned, God had limited its powers and, its action – thankful, I trust, for the gift bestowed, but unambitious of higher endowments, not restlessly eager after higher culture.

The polite pupil was scarcely gone, when, unceremoniously, without tap, in burst a second intruder. Had I been blind I should have known who this was. A constitutional reserve of manner had by this time told with wholesome and, for me, commodious effect, on the manners of my co-inmates; rarely did I now suffer from rude or intrusive treatment. When I first came, it would happen once and again that a blunt German would clap me on the shoulder, and ask me to run a race; or a riotous Labassecourienne seize me by the arm and drag me towards the playground: urgent proposals to take a swing at the 'Pas de Géant', or to join in a certain romping hide-and-seek game called 'Un, deux, trois,' were formerly also of hourly occurrence; but all these little attentions had ceased some time ago – ceased, too, without my finding it necessary to be at the trouble of point-blank cutting them short. I had now no familiar demonstration to dread or endure, save from one quarter; and as that was English I could bear it. Ginevra Fanshawe made no scruple of – at times – catching me as I was crossing the carré, whirling me round in a compulsory waltz, and heartily enjoying the mental and physical discomfiture her proceeding induced. Ginevra Fanshawe it was who now broke in upon 'my learned leisure'. She carried a huge music-book under her arm.

"Go to your practising," said I to her at once: "away with you to the little salon!"

"Not till I have had a talk with you, chère amie. I know where you have been spending your vacation, and how you have commenced sacrificing to the graces, and enjoying life like any other belle. I saw you at the concert the other night, dressed, actually, like anybody else. Who is your tailleuse?"

"Tittle-tattle: how prettily it begins! My tailleuse! – A fiddlestick! Come, sheer off, Ginevra. I really don't want your company."

"But when I want yours so much, ange farouche, what does a little reluctance on your part signify? Dieu merci! We know how to manoeuvre with our gifted compatriote – the learned 'ourse Britannique'. And so, Ourson, you know Isidore?"

"I know John Bretton."

"Oh, hush!" (putting her fingers in her ears) "You crack my tympanums with your rude Anglicisms. But, how is our well-beloved John? Do tell me about him. The poor man must be in a sad way. What did he say to my behaviour the other night? Wasn't I cruel?"

"Do you think I noticed you?"

"It was a delightful evening. Oh, that divine de Hamal! And then to watch the other sulking and dying in the distance; and the old lady – my future mamma-in-law! But I am afraid I and Lady Sara were a little rude in quizzing her."

"Lady Sara never quizzed her at all; and for what *you* did, don't make yourself in the least uneasy: Mrs. Bretton will survive *your* sneer."

"She may: old ladies are tough; but that poor son of hers! Do tell me what he said: I saw he was terribly cut up."

"He said you looked as if at heart you were already Madame de Hamal."

"Did he?" she cried with delight. "He noticed that? How charming! I thought he would be mad with jealousy.

"Ginevra, have you seriously done with Dr. Bretton? Do you want him to give you up?"

"Oh! You know he *can't* do that: but wasn't he mad?"

"Quite mad," I assented; "as mad as a March hare."

"Well, and how *ever* did you get him home?"

"How *ever*, indeed! Have you no pity on his poor mother and me? Fancy us holding him tight down in the carriage, and he raving between us, fit to drive everybody delirious. The very coachman went wrong, somehow, and we lost our way."

"You don't say so? You are laughing at me. Now, Lucy Snowe –"

"I assure you it is fact – and fact, also, that Dr. Bretton would *not* stay in the carriage: he broke from us, and *would* ride outside."

"And afterwards?"

"Afterwards – when he *did* reach home – the scene transcends description."

"Oh, but describe it – you know it is such fun!"

"Fun for *you*, Miss Fanshawe? But" (with stern gravity) "you know the proverb – 'What is sport to one may be death to another.'"

"Go on, there's a darling Timon."

"Conscientiously, I cannot, unless you assure me you have some heart."

"I have – such an immensity, you don't know!"

"Good! In that case, you will be able to conceive Dr. Graham Bretton rejecting his supper in the first instance – the chicken, the sweetbread prepared for his refreshment, left on the table untouched. Then – but it is of no use dwelling at length on the harrowing details. Suffice it to say, that never, in the most stormy fits and moments of his infancy, had his mother such work to tuck the sheets about him as she had that night."

"He wouldn't lie still?"

"He wouldn't lie still: there it was. The sheets might be tucked in, but the thing was to keep them tucked in."

"And what did he say?"

"Say! Can't you imagine him demanding his divine Ginevra, anathematizing that demon, de Hamal – raving about golden locks, blue eyes, white arms, glittering bracelets?"

"No, did he? He saw the bracelet?"

"Saw the bracelet? Yes, as plain as I saw it: and, perhaps, for the first time, he saw also the brand-mark with which its pressure has encircled your arm. Ginevra" (rising, and changing my tone), "come, we will have an end of this. Go away to your practising."

And I opened the door.

"But you have not told me all."

"You had better not wait until I *do* tell you all. Such extra communicativeness could give you no pleasure. March!"

"Cross thing!" said she; but she obeyed: and, indeed, the first classe was my territory, and she could not there legally resist a notice of quittance from me.

Yet, to speak the truth, never had I been less dissatisfied with her than I was then. There was pleasure in thinking of the contrast between the reality and my description – to remember Dr. John enjoying the drive home, eating his supper with relish, and retiring to rest with Christian composure. It was only when I saw him really unhappy that I felt really vexed with the fair, frail cause of his suffering.

* * *

A fortnight passed; I was getting once more inured to the harness of school, and lapsing from the passionate pain of change to the palsy of custom. One afternoon, in crossing the carré, on my way to the first classe, where I was expected to assist at a lesson of 'style and literature', I saw, standing by one of the long and large windows, Rosine, the portress. Her attitude, as usual, was quite nonchalante. She always 'stood at ease'; one of her hands rested in her apron-pocket, the other at this moment held to her eyes a letter, whereof Mademoiselle coolly perused the address, and deliberately studied the seal.

A letter! The shape of a letter similar to that had haunted my brain in its very core for seven days past. I had dreamed of a letter last night. Strong magnetism drew me to that letter now; yet, whether I should have ventured to demand of Rosine so much as a glance at that white envelope, with the spot of red wax in the middle, I know not. No; I think I should have sneaked past in terror of a rebuff from Disappointment: my heart throbbed now as if I already heard the tramp of her approach. Nervous mistake! It was the rapid step of the Professor of Literature measuring the corridor. I fled before him. Could I but be seated quietly at my desk before his arrival, with the class under my orders all in disciplined readiness, he would, perhaps, exempt me from notice; but, if caught lingering in the carré, I should be sure to come in for a special harangue. I had time to get seated, to enforce perfect silence, to take out my work, and to commence it amidst the profoundest and best trained hush, ere M. Emanuel entered with his vehement burst of latch and panel, and his deep, redundant bow, prophetic of choler.

As usual he broke upon us like a clap of thunder; but instead of flashing lightning-wise from the door to the estrade, his career halted midway at my desk. Setting his face towards me and the window, his back to the pupils and the room, he gave me a look – such a look as might have licensed me to stand straight up and demand what he meant – a look of scowling distrust.

"Voilà! Pour vous," said he, drawing his hand from his waist-coat, and placing on my desk a letter – the very letter I had seen in Rosine's hand – the letter whose face of enamelled white and single Cyclop's-eye of vermilion-red had printed themselves so clear and perfect on the retina of an inward vision. I knew it, I felt it to be the letter of my hope, the fruition of my wish, the release from my doubt, the ransom from my terror. This letter M. Paul, with his unwarrantably interfering habits, had taken from the portress, and now delivered it himself.

I might have been angry, but had not a second for the sensation. Yes: I held in my hand not a slight note, but an envelope, which must, at least, contain a sheet: it felt not flimsy, but firm, substantial, satisfying. And here was the direction, 'Miss Lucy Snowe', in a clean, clear, equal, decided hand; and here was the seal, round, full, deftly dropped by untremulous fingers, stamped with the well-cut impress of initials, 'J.G.B.' I experienced a happy feeling – a glad emotion which went warm to my heart, and ran lively through all my veins. For once a hope was realized. I held in my hand a morsel of real solid joy: not a dream, not an image of the brain, not one of those shadowy chances imagination pictures, and on which humanity starves but cannot live; not a mess of that manna I drearily eulogized awhile ago – which, indeed, at first melts on the lips with an unspeakable and preternatural sweetness, but which, in the end, our souls full surely loathe; longing deliriously for natural and earth-grown food, wildly praying Heaven's Spirits to reclaim their own spirit-dew and essence – an aliment divine, but for mortals deadly. It was neither sweet hail nor small coriander-seed – neither slight wafer, nor luscious honey, I had lighted on; it was the wild, savoury mess of the hunter, nourishing and salubrious meat, forest-fed or desert-reared, fresh, healthful, and life-sustaining. It was what the old dying patriarch demanded of his son Esau, promising in requital the blessing of his last breath. It was a godsend; and I inwardly thanked the God who had vouchsafed it. Outwardly I only thanked man, crying, "Thank you, thank you, Monsieur!"

Monsieur curled his lip, gave me a vicious glance of the eye, and strode to his estrade. M. Paul was not at all a good little man, though he had good points.

Did I read my letter there and then? Did I consume the venison at once and with haste, as if Esau's shaft flew every day?

I knew better. The cover with its address – the seal, with its three clear letters – was bounty and abundance for the present. I stole from the room, I procured the key of the great dormitory, which was kept locked by day. I went to my bureau; with a sort of haste and trembling lest Madame should creep upstairs and spy me, I opened a drawer, unlocked a box, and took out a case, and – having feasted my eyes with one more look, and approached the seal with a mixture of awe and shame and delight, to my lips – I folded the untasted treasure, yet all fair and inviolate, in silver paper, committed it to the case, shut up box and drawer, reclosed, relocked the dormitory, and returned to class, feeling as if fairy tales were true, and fairy gifts no dream. Strange, sweet insanity! And this letter, the source of my joy, I had not yet read: did not yet know the number of its lines.

When I re-entered the schoolroom, behold M. Paul raging like a pestilence! Some pupil had not spoken audibly or distinctly enough to suit his ear and taste, and now she and others were weeping, and he was raving from his estrade, almost livid. Curious to mention, as I appeared, he fell on me.

"Was I the mistress of these girls? Did I profess to teach them the conduct befitting ladies? – And did I permit and, he doubted not, encourage them to strangle their mother-tongue in their throats, to mince and mash it between their teeth, as if they had some base cause to be ashamed of the words they uttered? Was this modesty? He knew better. It was a vile pseudo sentiment – the offspring or the forerunner of evil. Rather than submit to this mopping and mowing, this mincing and grimacing, this, grinding of a noble tongue, this general affectation and sickening stubbornness of the pupils of the first class, he would throw them up for a set of insupportable petites maîtresses, and confine himself to teaching the ABC to the babies of the third division."

What could I say to all this? Really nothing; and I hoped he would allow me to be silent. The storm recommenced.

"Every answer to his queries was then refused? It seemed to be considered in *that* place – that conceited boudoir of a first classe, with its pretentious book-cases, its green-baized desks, its rubbish of flower-stands, its trash of framed pictures and maps, and its foreign surveillante, forsooth! – It seemed to be the fashion to think *there* that the Professor of Literature was not worthy of a reply! These were new ideas; imported, he did not doubt, straight from 'la Grande Bretagne': they savoured of island insolence and arrogance."

Lull the second – the girls, not one of whom was ever known to weep a tear for the rebukes of any other master, now all melting like snow-statues before the intemperate heat of M. Emanuel: I not yet much shaken, sitting down, and venturing to resume my work.

Something – either in my continued silence or in the movement of my hand, stitching – transported M. Emanuel beyond the last boundary of patience; he actually sprang from his estrade. The stove stood near my desk, he attacked it; the little iron door was nearly dashed from its hinges, the fuel was made to fly.

"*Est-ce que vous avez l'intention de m'insulter?*" said he to me, in a low, furious voice, as he thus outraged, under pretence of arranging the fire.

It was time to soothe him a little if possible.

"Mais, Monsieur," said I, "I would not insult you for the world. I remember too well that you once said we should be friends."

I did not intend my voice to falter, but it did: more, I think, through the agitation of late delight than in any spasm of present fear. Still there certainly was something in M. Paul's anger – a kind of passion of emotion – that specially tended to draw tears. I was not unhappy, nor much afraid, yet I wept.

"*Allons, allons!*" said he presently, looking round and seeing the deluge universal. "Decidedly I am a monster and a ruffian. I have only one pocket-handkerchief," he added, "but if I had twenty, I would offer you each one. Your teacher shall be your representative. Here, Miss Lucy."

And he took forth and held out to me a clean silk handkerchief. Now a person who did not know M. Paul, who was unused to him and his impulses, would naturally have bungled at this offer – declined accepting the same – et cetera. But I too plainly felt this would never do: the slightest hesitation would have been fatal to the incipient treaty of peace. I rose and met the handkerchief half-way, received it with decorum, wiped therewith my eyes, and, resuming my seat, and retaining the flag of truce in my hand and on my lap, took especial care during the remainder of the lesson to touch neither needle nor thimble, scissors nor muslin. Many a jealous glance did M. Paul cast at these implements; he hated them mortally, considering sewing a source of distraction from the attention due to himself. A very eloquent lesson he gave, and very kind and friendly was he to the close. Ere he had done, the clouds were dispersed and the sun shining out – tears were exchanged for smiles.

In quitting the room he paused once more at my desk.

"And your letter?" said he, this time not quite fiercely.

"I have not yet read it, Monsieur."

"Ah! It is too good to read at once; you save it, as, when I was a boy, I used to save a peach whose bloom was very ripe?"

The guess came so near the truth, I could not prevent a suddenly-rising warmth in my face from revealing as much.

"You promise yourself a pleasant moment," said he, "in reading that letter; you will open it when alone – *n'est-ce pas*? Ah! A smile answers. Well, well! One should not be too harsh; '*la jeunesse n'a qu'un temps.*'"

"Monsieur, Monsieur!" I cried, or rather whispered after him, as he turned to go, "do not leave me under a mistake. This is merely a friend's letter. Without reading it, I can vouch for that."

"*Je conçois, je conçois: on sait ce que c'est qu'un ami. Bonjour, Mademoiselle!*"

"But, Monsieur, here is your handkerchief."

"Keep it, keep it, till the letter is read, then bring it me; I shall read the billet's tenor in your eyes."

When he was gone, the pupils having already poured out of the schoolroom into the berceau, and thence into the garden and court to take their customary recreation before the five-o'clock dinner, I stood a moment thinking, and absently twisting the handkerchief round my arm. For some reason – gladdened, I think, by a sudden return of the golden glimmer of childhood, roused by an unwonted renewal of its buoyancy, made merry by the liberty of the closing hour, and, above all, solaced at heart by the joyous consciousness of that treasure in the case, box, drawer upstairs, – I fell to playing with the handkerchief as if it were a ball, casting it into the air and catching it – as it fell. The game was stopped by another hand than mine – a hand emerging from a paletôt-sleeve and stretched over my shoulder; it caught the extemporised plaything and bore it away with these sullen words:

"*Je vois bien que vous vous moquez de moi et de mes effets.*"

Really that little man was dreadful: a mere sprite of caprice and, ubiquity: one never knew either his whim or his whereabout.

Chapter Twenty-Two
The Letter

WHEN ALL WAS STILL in the house; when dinner was over and the noisy recreation-hour past; when darkness had set in, and the quiet lamp of study was lit in the refectory; when the externes were gone home, the clashing door and clamorous bell hushed for the evening; when Madame was safely settled in the salle-à-manger in company with her mother and some friends; I then glided to the kitchen, begged a bougie for one half-hour for a particular occasion, found acceptance of my petition at the hands of my friend Goton, who answered, "*Mais certainement, chou-chou, vous en aurez deux, si vous voulez;*" and, light in hand, I mounted noiseless to the dormitory.

Great was my chagrin to find in that apartment a pupil gone to bed indisposed, – greater when I recognised, amid the muslin nightcap borders, the 'figure chiffonnée' of Mistress Ginevra Fanshawe; supine at this moment, it is true – but certain to wake and overwhelm me with chatter when the interruption would be least acceptable: indeed, as I watched her, a slight twinkling of the eyelids warned me that the present appearance of repose might be but a ruse, assumed to cover sly vigilance over 'Timon's' movements; she was not to be trusted. And I had so wished to be alone, just to read my precious letter in peace.

Well, I must go to the classes. Having sought and found my prize in its casket, I descended. Ill-luck pursued me. The classes were undergoing sweeping and purification by candle-light, according to hebdomadal custom: benches were piled on desks, the air was dim with dust, damp coffee-grounds (used by Labassecourien housemaids instead of tea-leaves) darkened the floor; all was hopeless confusion. Baffled, but not beaten, I withdrew, bent as resolutely as ever on finding solitude *somewhere*.

Taking a key whereof I knew the repository, I mounted three staircases in succession, reached a dark, narrow, silent landing, opened a worm-eaten door, and dived into the deep, black, cold garret. Here none would follow me – none interrupt – not Madame herself. I shut the garret-door; I placed my light on a doddered and mouldy chest of drawers; I put on a shawl, for the air was ice-cold; I took my letter; trembling with sweet impatience, I broke its seal.

"Will it be long – will it be short?" thought I, passing my hand across my eyes to dissipate the silvery dimness of a suave, south-wind shower.

It was long.

"Will it be cool? – Will it be kind?"

It was kind.

To my checked, bridled, disciplined expectation, it seemed very kind: to my longing and famished thought it seemed, perhaps, kinder than it was.

So little had I hoped, so much had I feared; there was a fulness of delight in this taste of fruition – such, perhaps, as many a human being passes through life without ever knowing. The poor English teacher in the frosty garret, reading by a dim candle guttering in the wintry air, a letter simply good-natured – nothing more; though that good-nature then seemed to me godlike – was happier than most queens in palaces.

Of course, happiness of such shallow origin could be but brief; yet, while it lasted it was genuine and exquisite: a bubble – but a sweet bubble – of real honey-dew. Dr. John had written to me at length; he had written to me with pleasure; he had written with benignant mood, dwelling with sunny satisfaction on scenes that had passed before his eyes and mine, – on places we had visited together – on conversations we had held – on all the little subject-matter, in short, of the last few halcyon weeks. But the cordial core of the delight was, a conviction the blithe, genial language generously imparted, that it had been poured out not merely to content *me* – but to gratify *himself.* A gratification he might never more desire, never more seek – an hypothesis in every point of view approaching the certain; but *that* concerned the future. This present moment had no pain, no blot, no want; full, pure, perfect, it deeply blessed me. A passing seraph seemed to have rested beside me, leaned towards my heart, and reposed on its throb a softening, cooling, healing, hallowing wing. Dr. John, you pained me afterwards: forgiven be every ill – freely forgiven – for the sake of that one dear remembered good!

Are there wicked things, not human, which envy human bliss? Are there evil influences haunting the air, and poisoning it for man? What was near me?

Something in that vast solitary garret sounded strangely. Most surely and certainly I heard, as it seemed, a stealthy foot on that floor: a sort of gliding out from the direction of the black recess haunted by the malefactor cloaks. I turned: my light was dim; the room was long – but as I live! I saw in the middle of that ghostly chamber a figure all black and white; the skirts straight, narrow, black; the head bandaged, veiled, white.

Say what you will, reader – tell me I was nervous or mad; affirm that I was unsettled by the excitement of that letter; declare that I dreamed; this I vow – I saw there – in that room – on that night – an image like – a *nun.*

I cried out; I sickened. Had the shape approached me I might have swooned. It receded: I made for the door. How I descended all the stairs I know not. By instinct I shunned the refectory, and shaped my course to Madame's sitting-room: I burst in. I said –

"There is something in the grenier; I have been there: I saw something. Go and look at it, all of you!"

I said, "All of you"; for the room seemed to me full of people, though in truth there were but four present: Madame Beck; her mother, Madame Kint, who was out of health, and now staying with her on a visit; her brother, M. Victor Kint, and another gentleman, who, when I entered the room, was conversing with the old lady, and had his back towards the door.

My mortal fear and faintness must have made me deadly pale. I felt cold and shaking. They all rose in consternation; they surrounded me. I urged them to go to the grenier; the sight of the gentlemen did me good and gave me courage: it seemed as if there were some help and hope, with men at hand. I turned to the door, beckoning them to follow. They wanted to stop me, but I said they must come this way: they must see what I had seen – something strange, standing in the middle of the garret. And, now, I remembered my letter, left on the drawers with the light. This precious letter! Flesh or spirit must be defied for its sake. I flew upstairs, hastening the faster as I knew I was followed: they were obliged to come.

Lo! When I reached the garret-door, all within was dark as a pit: the light was out. Happily someone – Madame, I think, with her usual calm sense – had brought a lamp from the room; speedily, therefore, as they came up, a ray pierced the opaque blackness. There stood the bougie quenched on the drawers; but where was the letter? And I looked for *that* now, and not for the nun.

"My letter! My letter!" I panted and plained, almost beside myself. I groped on the floor, wringing my hands wildly. Cruel, cruel doom! To have my bit of comfort preternaturally snatched from me, ere I had well tasted its virtue!

I don't know what the others were doing; I could not watch them: they asked me questions I did not answer; they ransacked all corners; they prattled about this and that disarrangement of cloaks, a breach or crack in the sky-light – I know not what. "Something or somebody has been here," was sagely averred.

"Oh! They have taken my letter!" cried the grovelling, groping, monomaniac.

"What letter, Lucy? My dear girl, what letter?" asked a known voice in my ear. Could I believe that ear? No: and I looked up. Could I trust my eyes? Had I recognised the tone? Did I now look on the face of the writer of that very letter? Was this gentleman near me in this dim garret, John Graham – Dr. Bretton himself?

Yes: it was. He had been called in that very evening to prescribe for some access of illness in old Madame Kint; he was the second gentleman present in the salle-à-manger when I entered.

"Was it *my* letter, Lucy?"

"Your own: yours – the letter you wrote to me. I had come here to read it quietly. I could not find another spot where it was possible to have it to myself. I had saved it all day – never opened it till this evening: it was scarcely glanced over: I *cannot bear* to lose it. Oh, my letter!"

"Hush! Don't cry and distress yourself so cruelly. What is it worth? Hush! Come out of this cold room; they are going to send for the police now to examine further: we need not stay here – come, we will go down."

A warm hand, taking my cold fingers, led me down to a room where there was a fire. Dr. John and I sat before the stove. He talked to me and soothed me with unutterable goodness, promising me twenty letters for the one lost. If there are words and wrongs like knives, whose deep-inflicted lacerations never heal – cutting injuries and insults of serrated and poison-dripping edge – so, too, there are consolations of tone too fine for the ear not fondly and forever to retain their echo: caressing kindnesses – loved, lingered over through a whole life, recalled with unfaded tenderness, and answering the call with undimmed shine, out of that raven cloud foreshadowing Death himself. I have been told since that Dr. Bretton was not nearly so perfect as I thought him: that his actual character lacked the depth, height, compass, and endurance it possessed in my creed. I don't know: he was as good to me as the well is to the parched wayfarer – as the sun to the shivering jailbird. I remember him heroic. Heroic at this moment will I hold him to be.

He asked me, smiling, why I cared for his letter so very much. I thought, but did not say, that I prized it like the blood in my veins. I only answered that I had so few letters to care for.

"I am sure you did not read it," said he; "or you would think nothing of it!"

"I read it, but only once. I want to read it again. I am sorry it is lost." And I could not help weeping afresh.

"Lucy, Lucy, my poor little god-sister (if there be such a relationship), here – *here* is your letter. Why is it not better worth such tears, and such tenderly exaggerating faith?"

Curious, characteristic manoeuvre! His quick eye had seen the letter on the floor where I sought it; his hand, as quick, had snatched it up. He had hidden it in his waistcoat pocket. If my trouble had wrought with a whit less stress and reality, I doubt whether he would ever have acknowledged or restored it. Tears of temperature one degree cooler than those I shed would only have amused Dr. John.

Pleasure at regaining made me forget merited reproach for the teasing torment; my joy was great; it could not be concealed: yet I think it broke out more in countenance than language. I said little.

"Are you satisfied now?" asked Dr. John.

I replied that I was – satisfied and happy.

"Well then," he proceeded, "how do you feel physically? Are you growing calmer? Not much: for you tremble like a leaf still."

It seemed to me, however, that I was sufficiently calm: at least I felt no longer terrified. I expressed myself composed.

"You are able, consequently, to tell me what you saw? Your account was quite vague, do you know? You looked white as the wall; but you only spoke of 'something', not defining *what*. Was it a man? Was it an animal? What was it?"

"I never will tell exactly what I saw," said I, "unless someone else sees it too, and then I will give corroborative testimony; but otherwise, I shall be discredited and accused of dreaming."

"Tell me," said Dr. Bretton; "I will hear it in my professional character: I look on you now from a professional point of view, and I read, perhaps, all you would conceal – in your eye, which is curiously vivid and restless: in your cheek, which the blood has forsaken; in your hand, which you cannot steady. Come, Lucy, speak and tell me."

"You would laugh –?"

"If you don't tell me you shall have no more letters."

"You are laughing now."

"I will again take away that single epistle: being mine, I think I have a right to reclaim it."

I felt raillery in his words: it made me grave and quiet; but I folded up the letter and covered it from sight.

"You may hide it, but I can possess it any moment I choose. You don't know my skill in sleight of hand; I might practise as a conjuror if I liked. Mamma says sometimes, too, that I have a harmonizing property of tongue and eye; but you never saw that in me – did you, Lucy?"

"Indeed – indeed – when you were a mere boy I used to see both: far more then than now – for now you are strong, and strength dispenses with subtlety. But still, – Dr. John, you have what they call in this country 'un air fin', that nobody can mistake. Madame Beck saw it, and –"

"And liked it," said he, laughing, "because she has it herself. But, Lucy, give me that letter – you don't really care for it."

To this provocative speech I made no answer. Graham in mirthful mood must not be humoured too far. Just now there was a new sort of smile playing about his lips – very sweet, but it grieved me somehow – a new sort of light sparkling in his eyes: not hostile, but not reassuring. I rose to go – I bid him goodnight a little sadly.

His sensitiveness – that peculiar, apprehensive, detective faculty of his – felt in a moment the unspoken complaint – the scarce-thought reproach. He asked quietly if I was offended. I shook my head as implying a negative.

"Permit me, then, to speak a little seriously to you before you go. You are in a highly nervous state. I feel sure from what is apparent in your look and manner, however well controlled, that whilst alone this evening in that dismal, perishing sepulchral garret – that dungeon under the leads, smelling of damp and mould, rank with phthisis and catarrh: a place you never ought to enter – that you saw, or *thought* you saw, some appearance peculiarly calculated to impress the imagination. I know that you *are* not, nor ever were, subject to material terrors, fears of robbers, etc. – I am not so sure that a visitation, bearing a spectral character, would not shake your very mind. Be calm now. This is all a matter of the nerves, I see: but just specify the vision."

"You will tell nobody?"

"Nobody – most certainly. You may trust me as implicitly as you did Père Silas. Indeed, the doctor is perhaps the safer confessor of the two, though he has not grey hair."

"You will not laugh?"

"Perhaps I may, to do you good: but not in scorn. Lucy, I feel as a friend towards you, though your timid nature is slow to trust."

He now looked like a friend: that indescribable smile and sparkle were gone; those formidable arched curves of lip, nostril, eyebrow, were depressed; repose marked his attitude – attention sobered his aspect. Won to confidence, I told him exactly what I had seen: ere now I had narrated to him the legend of the house – whiling away with that narrative an hour of a certain mild October afternoon, when he and I rode through Bois l'Etang.

He sat and thought, and while he thought, we heard them all coming downstairs.

"Are they going to interrupt?" said he, glancing at the door with an annoyed expression.

"They will not come here," I answered; for we were in the little salon where Madame never sat in the evening, and where it was by mere chance that heat was still lingering in the stove. They passed the door and went on to the salle-à-manger.

"Now," he pursued, "they will talk about thieves, burglars, and so on: let them do so – mind you say nothing, and keep your resolution of describing your nun to nobody. She may appear to you again: don't start."

"You think then," I said, with secret horror, "she came out of my brain, and is now gone in there, and may glide out again at an hour and a day when I look not for her?"

"I think it a case of spectral illusion: I fear, following on and resulting from long-continued mental conflict."

"Oh, Doctor John – I shudder at the thought of being liable to such an illusion! It seemed so real. Is there no cure? – No preventive?"

"Happiness is the cure – a cheerful mind the preventive: cultivate both."

No mockery in this world ever sounds to me so hollow as that of being told to *cultivate* happiness. What does such advice mean? Happiness is not a potato, to be planted in mould, and tilled with manure. Happiness is a glory shining far down upon us out of Heaven. She is a divine dew which the soul, on certain of its summer mornings, feels dropping upon it from the amaranth bloom and golden fruitage of Paradise.

"Cultivate happiness!" I said briefly to the doctor: "do *you* cultivate happiness? How do you manage?"

"I am a cheerful fellow by nature: and then ill-luck has never dogged me. Adversity gave me and my mother one passing scowl and brush, but we defied her, or rather laughed at her, and she went by."

"There is no cultivation in all this."

"I do not give way to melancholy."

"Yes: I have seen you subdued by that feeling."

"About Ginevra Fanshawe – eh?"

"Did she not sometimes make you miserable?"

"Pooh! Stuff! Nonsense! You see I am better now."

If a laughing eye with a lively light, and a face bright with beaming and healthy energy, could attest that he was better, better he certainly was.

"You do not look much amiss, or greatly out of condition," I allowed.

"And why, Lucy, can't you look and feel as I do – buoyant, courageous, and fit to defy all the nuns and flirts in Christendom? I would give gold on the spot just to see you snap your fingers. Try the manoeuvre."

"If I were to bring Miss Fanshawe into your presence just now?"

"I vow, Lucy, she should not move me: or, she should move me but by one thing – true, yes, and passionate love. I would accord forgiveness at no less a price."

"Indeed! A smile of hers would have been a fortune to you a while since."

"Transformed, Lucy: transformed! Remember, you once called me a slave! But I am a free man now!"

He stood up: in the port of his head, the carriage of his figure, in his beaming eye and mien, there revealed itself a liberty which was more than ease – a mood which was disdain of his past bondage.

"Miss Fanshawe," he pursued, "has led me through a phase of feeling which is over: I have entered another condition, and am now much disposed to exact love for love – passion for passion – and good measure of it, too."

"Ah, Doctor! Doctor! You said it was your nature to pursue Love under difficulties – to be charmed by a proud insensibility!".

He laughed, and answered, "My nature varies: the mood of one hour is sometimes the mockery of the next. Well, Lucy" (drawing on his gloves), "will the Nun come again tonight, think you?"

"I don't think she will."

"Give her my compliments, if she does – Dr. John's compliments – and entreat her to have the goodness to wait a visit from him. Lucy, was she a pretty nun? Had she a pretty face? You have not told me that yet; and *that* is the really important point."

"She had a white cloth over her face," said I, "but her eyes glittered."

"Confusion to her goblin trappings!" cried he, irreverently: "but at least she had handsome eyes – bright and soft."

"Cold and fixed," was the reply.

"No, no, we'll none of her: she shall not haunt you, Lucy. Give her that shake of the hand, if she comes again. Will she stand *that*, do you think?"

I thought it too kind and cordial for a ghost to stand: and so was the smile which matched it, and accompanied his "Goodnight."

* * *

And had there been anything in the garret? What did they discover? I believe, on the closest examination, their discoveries amounted to very little. They talked, at first, of the cloaks being disturbed; but Madame Beck told me afterwards she thought they hung much as usual: and as for the broken pane in the skylight, she affirmed that aperture was rarely without one or more panes broken or cracked: and besides, a heavy hail-storm had fallen a few days ago. Madame questioned me very closely as to what I had seen, but I only described an obscure figure clothed in black: I took care not to breathe the word 'nun', certain that this word would at once suggest to her mind an idea of romance and unreality. She charged me to say nothing on the subject to any servant, pupil, or teacher, and highly commended my discretion in coming to her private salle-à-manger, instead of carrying the tale of horror to the school refectory. Thus the subject dropped. I was left secretly and sadly to wonder, in my own mind, whether that strange thing was of this world, or of a realm beyond the grave; or whether indeed it was only the child of malady, and I of that malady the prey.

Chapter Twenty-Three
Vashti

TO WONDER SADLY, did I say? No: a new influence began to act upon my life, and sadness, for a certain space, was held at bay. Conceive a dell, deep-hollowed in forest secrecy; it lies in dimness and mist: its turf is dank, its herbage pale and humid. A storm or an axe makes a wide gap amongst the oak-trees; the breeze sweeps in; the sun looks down; the sad, cold dell becomes a deep cup of lustre; high summer pours her blue glory and her golden light out of that beauteous sky, which till now the starved hollow never saw.

A new creed became mine – a belief in happiness.

It was three weeks since the adventure of the garret, and I possessed in that case, box, drawer upstairs, casketed with that first letter, four companions like to it, traced by the same firm pen, sealed with the same clear seal, full of the same vital comfort. Vital comfort it seemed to me then: I read them in after years; they were kind letters enough – pleasing letters, because composed by one well pleased; in the two last there were three or four closing lines half-gay, half-tender, 'by *feeling* touched, but not subdued.' Time, dear reader, mellowed them to a beverage of this mild quality; but when I first tasted their elixir, fresh from the fount so honoured, it seemed juice of a divine vintage: a draught which Hebe might fill, and the very gods approve.

Does the reader, remembering what was said some pages back, care to ask how I answered these letters: whether under the dry, stinting check of Reason, or according to the full, liberal impulse of Feeling?

To speak truth, I compromised matters; I served two masters: I bowed down in the houses of Rimmon, and lifted the heart at another shrine. I wrote to these letters two answers – one for my own relief, the other for Graham's perusal.

To begin with: Feeling and I turned Reason out of doors, drew against her bar and bolt, then we sat down, spread our paper, dipped in the ink an eager pen, and, with deep enjoyment, poured out our sincere heart. When we had done – when two sheets were covered with the language of a strongly-adherent affection, a rooted and active gratitude – (once, for all, in this parenthesis, I disclaim, with the utmost scorn, every sneaking suspicion of what are called 'warmer feelings': women do not entertain these 'warmer feelings' where, from the commencement, through the whole progress of an acquaintance, they have never once been cheated of the conviction that, to do so would be to commit a mortal absurdity: nobody ever launches into Love unless he has seen or dreamed the rising of Hope's star over Love's troubled waters) – when, then, I had given expression to a closely-clinging and deeply-honouring attachment – an attachment that wanted to attract to itself and take to its own lot all that was painful in the destiny of its object; that would, if it could, have absorbed and conducted away all storms and lightnings from an existence viewed with a passion of solicitude – then, just at that moment, the doors of my heart would shake, bolt and bar would yield, Reason would leap in vigorous and revengeful, snatch the full sheets, read, sneer, erase, tear up, re-write, fold, seal, direct, and send a terse, curt missive of a page. She did right.

I did not live on letters only: I was visited, I was looked after; once a week I was taken out to La Terrasse; always I was made much of. Dr. Bretton failed not to tell me *why* he was so kind: "To keep away the nun," he said; "he was determined to dispute with her her prey. He had taken," he declared, "a thorough dislike to her, chiefly on account of that white face-cloth, and those cold grey eyes: the moment he heard of those odious particulars," he affirmed, "consummate disgust had incited him to oppose her; he was determined to try whether he or she was the cleverest, and he only wished she would once more look in upon me when he was present": but *that* she never did. In short, he regarded me scientifically in the light of a patient, and at once exercised his professional skill, and gratified his natural benevolence, by a course of cordial and attentive treatment.

One evening, the first in December, I was walking by myself in the carré; it was six o'clock; the classe-doors were closed; but within, the pupils, rampant in the licence of evening recreation, were counterfeiting a miniature chaos. The carré was quite dark, except a red light shining under and about the stove; the wide glass-doors and the long windows were frosted over; a crystal sparkle of starlight, here and there spangling this blanched winter veil, and breaking with scattered brilliance the paleness of its embroidery, proved it a clear night, though moonless. That I should dare to remain thus alone in darkness, showed that my nerves were regaining a healthy tone: I thought of the nun, but hardly feared her; though the staircase was behind me, leading up, through blind, black night, from landing to landing, to the haunted grenier. Yet I own my heart quaked, my pulse leaped, when I suddenly heard breathing and rustling, and turning, saw in the deep shadow of the steps a deeper shadow still – a shape that moved and descended. It paused a while at the classe-door, and then it glided before me. Simultaneously came a clangor of the distant door-bell. Life-like sounds bring life-like feelings: this shape was too round and low for my gaunt nun: it was only Madame Beck on duty.

"*Mademoiselle Lucy!*" cried Rosine, bursting in, lamp in hand, from the corridor, "*On est là pour vous au salon.*"

Madame saw me, I saw Madame, Rosine saw us both: there was no mutual recognition. I made straight for the salon. There I found what I own I anticipated I should find – Dr. Bretton; but he was in evening-dress.

"The carriage is at the door," said he; "my mother has sent it to take you to the theatre; she was going herself, but an arrival has prevented her: she immediately said, 'Take Lucy in my place.' Will you go?"

"Just now? I am not dressed," cried I, glancing despairingly at my dark merino.

"You have half an hour to dress. I should have given you notice, but I only determined on going since five o'clock, when I heard there was to be a genuine regale in the presence of a great actress."

And he mentioned a name that thrilled me – a name that, in those days, could thrill Europe. It is hushed now: its once restless echoes are all still; she who bore it went years ago to her rest: night and oblivion long since closed above her; but *then* her day – a day of Sirius – stood at its full height, light and fervour.

"I'll go; I will be ready in ten minutes," I vowed. And away I flew, never once checked, reader, by the thought which perhaps at this moment checks you: namely, that to go anywhere with Graham and without Mrs. Bretton could be objectionable. I could not have conceived, much less have expressed to Graham, such thought – such scruple – without risk of exciting a tyrannous self-contempt: of kindling an inward fire of shame so quenchless, and so devouring, that I think it would soon have licked up the very life in my veins. Besides, my godmother, knowing her son, and knowing me, would as soon have thought of chaperoning a sister with a brother, as of keeping anxious guard over our incomings and outgoings.

The present was no occasion for showy array; my dun mist crape would suffice, and I sought the same in the great oak-wardrobe in the dormitory, where hung no less than forty dresses. But there had been changes and reforms, and some innovating hand had pruned this same crowded wardrobe, and carried divers garments to the grenier – my crape amongst the rest. I must fetch it. I got the key, and went aloft fearless, almost thoughtless. I unlocked the door, I plunged in. The reader may believe it or not, but when I thus suddenly entered, that garret was not wholly dark as it should have been: from one point there shone a solemn light, like a star, but broader. So plainly it shone, that it revealed the deep alcove with a portion of the tarnished scarlet curtain drawn over it. Instantly, silently, before my eyes, it vanished; so did the curtain and alcove: all that end of the garret became black as night. I ventured no research; I had not time nor will; snatching my dress, which hung on the wall, happily near the door, I rushed out, relocked the door with convulsed haste, and darted downwards to the dormitory.

But I trembled too much to dress myself: impossible to arrange hair or fasten hooks-and-eyes with such fingers, so I called Rosine and bribed her to help me. Rosine liked a bribe, so she did her best, smoothed and plaited my hair as well as a coiffeur would have done, placed the lace collar mathematically straight, tied the neck-ribbon accurately – in short, did her work like the neat-handed Phillis she could be when she chose. Having given me my handkerchief and gloves, she took the candle and lighted me downstairs. After all, I had forgotten my shawl; she ran back to fetch it; and I stood with Dr. John in the vestibule, waiting.

"What is this, Lucy?" said he, looking down at me narrowly. "Here is the old excitement. Ha! The nun again?"

But I utterly denied the charge: I was vexed to be suspected of a second illusion. He was sceptical.

"She has been, as sure as I live," said he; "her figure crossing your eyes leaves on them a peculiar gleam and expression not to be mistaken."

"She has *not* been," I persisted: for, indeed, I could deny her apparition with truth.

"The old symptoms are there," he affirmed: "a particular pale, and what the Scotch call a 'raised' look."

He was so obstinate, I thought it better to tell him what I really *had* seen. Of course with him it was held to be another effect of the same cause: it was all optical illusion – nervous malady, and so on. Not one bit did I believe him; but I dared not contradict: doctors are so self-opinionated, so immovable in their dry, materialist views.

Rosine brought the shawl, and I was bundled into the carriage.

* * *

The theatre was full – crammed to its roof: royal and noble were there: palace and hotel had emptied their inmates into those tiers so thronged and so hushed. Deeply did I feel myself privileged in having a place before that stage; I longed to see a being of whose powers I had heard reports which made me conceive peculiar anticipations. I wondered if she would justify her renown: with strange curiosity, with feelings severe and austere, yet of riveted interest, I waited. She was a study of such nature as had not encountered my eyes yet: a great and new planet she was: but in what shape? I waited her rising.

She rose at nine that December night: above the horizon I saw her come. She could shine yet with pale grandeur and steady might; but that star verged already on its judgment-day. Seen near, it was a chaos – hollow, half-consumed: an orb perished or perishing – half lava, half glow.

I had heard this woman termed 'plain', and I expected bony harshness and grimness – something large, angular, sallow. What I saw was the shadow of a royal Vashti: a queen, fair as the day once, turned pale now like twilight, and wasted like wax in flame.

For awhile – a long while – I thought it was only a woman, though an unique woman, who moved in might and grace before this multitude. By-and-by I recognised my mistake. Behold! I found upon her something neither of woman nor of man: in each of her eyes sat a devil. These evil forces bore her through the tragedy, kept up her feeble strength – for she was but a frail creature; and as the action rose and the stir deepened, how wildly they shook her with their passions of the pit! They wrote *hell* on her straight, haughty brow. They tuned her voice to the note of torment. They writhed her regal face to a demoniac mask. Hate and Murder and Madness incarnate she stood.

It was a marvellous sight: a mighty revelation.

It was a spectacle low, horrible, immoral.

Swordsmen thrust through, and dying in their blood on the arena sand; bulls goring horses disembowelled, made a meeker vision for the public – a milder condiment for a people's palate – than

Vashti torn by seven devils: devils which cried sore and rent the tenement they haunted, but still refused to be exorcised.

Suffering had struck that stage empress; and she stood before her audience neither yielding to, nor enduring, nor, in finite measure, resenting it: she stood locked in struggle, rigid in resistance. She stood, not dressed, but draped in pale antique folds, long and regular like sculpture. A background and entourage and flooring of deepest crimson threw her out, white like alabaster – like silver: rather, be it said, like Death.

Where was the artist of the Cleopatra? Let him come and sit down and study this different vision. Let him seek here the mighty brawn, the muscle, the abounding blood, the full-fed flesh he worshipped: let all materialists draw nigh and look on.

I have said that she does not *resent* her grief. No; the weakness of that word would make it a lie. To her, what hurts becomes immediately embodied: she looks on it as a thing that can be attacked, worried down, torn in shreds. Scarcely a substance herself, she grapples to conflict with abstractions. Before calamity she is a tigress; she rends her woes, shivers them in convulsed abhorrence. Pain, for her, has no result in good: tears water no harvest of wisdom: on sickness, on death itself, she looks with the eye of a rebel. Wicked, perhaps, she is, but also she is strong; and her strength has conquered Beauty, has overcome Grace, and bound both at her side, captives peerlessly fair, and docile as fair. Even in the uttermost frenzy of energy is each maenad movement royally, imperially, incedingly upborne. Her hair, flying loose in revel or war, is still an angel's hair, and glorious under a halo. Fallen, insurgent, banished, she remembers the heaven where she rebelled. Heaven's light, following her exile, pierces its confines, and discloses their forlorn remoteness.

Place now the Cleopatra, or any other slug, before her as an obstacle, and see her cut through the pulpy mass as the scimitar of Saladin clove the down cushion. Let Paul Peter Rubens wake from the dead, let him rise out of his cerements, and bring into this presence all the army of his fat women; the magian power or prophet-virtue gifting that slight rod of Moses, could, at one waft, release and re-mingle a sea spell-parted, whelming the heavy host with the down-rush of overthrown sea-ramparts.

Vashti was not good, I was told; and I have said she did not look good: though a spirit, she was a spirit out of Tophet. Well, if so much of unholy force can arise from below, may not an equal efflux of sacred essence descend one day from above?

What thought Dr. Graham of this being?

For long intervals I forgot to look how he demeaned himself, or to question what he thought. The strong magnetism of genius drew my heart out of its wonted orbit; the sunflower turned from the south to a fierce light, not solar – a rushing, red, cometary light – hot on vision and to sensation. I had seen acting before, but never anything like this: never anything which astonished Hope and hushed Desire; which outstripped Impulse and paled Conception; which, instead of merely irritating imagination with the thought of what *might* be done, at the same time fevering the nerves because it was *not* done, disclosed power like a deep, swollen winter river, thundering in cataract, and bearing the soul, like a leaf, on the steep and steely sweep of its descent.

Miss Fanshawe, with her usual ripeness of judgment, pronounced Dr. Bretton a serious, impassioned man, too grave and too impressible. Not in such light did I ever see him: no such faults could I lay to his charge. His natural attitude was not the meditative, nor his natural mood the sentimental; *impressionable* he was as dimpling water, but, almost as water, *unimpressible:* the breeze, the sun, moved him – metal could not grave, nor fire brand.

Dr. John *could* think and think well, but he was rather a man of action than of thought; he *could* feel, and feel vividly in his way, but his heart had no chord for enthusiasm: to bright, soft, sweet influences his eyes and lips gave bright, soft, sweet welcome, beautiful to see as dyes of rose and silver, pearl and purple, imbuing summer clouds; for what belonged to storm, what was wild and intense, dangerous, sudden, and flaming, he had no sympathy, and held with it no communion. When I took time and regained inclination to glance at him, it amused and enlightened me to discover that he was watching that sinister and sovereign Vashti, not with wonder, nor worship, nor yet dismay, but simply with intense curiosity. Her agony did not pain him, her wild moan – worse than a shriek – did not much move him; her fury revolted him somewhat, but not to the point of horror. Cool young Briton! The pale cliffs of his own England do not look down on the tides of the Channel more calmly than he watched the Pythian inspiration of that night.

Looking at his face, I longed to know his exact opinions, and at last I put a question tending to elicit them. At the sound of my voice he awoke as if out of a dream; for he had been thinking, and very intently thinking, his own thoughts, after his own manner. "How did he like Vashti?" I wished to know.

"Hm-m-m," was the first scarce articulate but expressive answer; and then such a strange smile went wandering round his lips, a smile so critical, so almost callous! I suppose that for natures of that order his sympathies *were* callous. In a few terse phrases he told me his opinion of, and feeling towards, the actress: he judged her as a woman, not an artist: it was a branding judgment.

That night was already marked in my book of life, not with white, but with a deep-red cross. But I had not done with it yet; and other memoranda were destined to be set down in characters of tint indelible.

Towards midnight, when the deepening tragedy blackened to the death-scene, and all held their breath, and even Graham bit his under-lip, and knit his brow, and sat still and struck – when the whole theatre was hushed, when the vision of all eyes centred in one point, when all ears listened towards one quarter – nothing being seen but the white form sunk on a seat, quivering in conflict with her last, her worst-hated, her visibly-conquering foe – nothing heard but her throes, her gaspings, breathing yet of mutiny, panting still defiance; when, as it seemed, an inordinate will, convulsing a perishing mortal frame, bent it to battle with doom and death, fought every inch of ground, sold every drop of blood, resisted to the latest the rape of every faculty, *would* see, *would* hear, *would* breathe, *would* live, up to, within, well-nigh *beyond* the moment when death says to all sense and all being – "Thus far and no farther!" –

Just then a stir, pregnant with omen, rustled behind the scenes – feet ran, voices spoke. What was it? Demanded the whole house. A flame, a smell of smoke replied.

"Fire!" rang through the gallery. "Fire!" was repeated, re-echoed, yelled forth: and then, and faster than pen can set it down, came panic, rushing, crushing – a blind, selfish, cruel chaos.

And Dr. John? Reader, I see him yet, with his look of comely courage and cordial calm.

"Lucy will sit still, I know," said he, glancing down at me with the same serene goodness, the same repose of firmness that I have seen in him when sitting at his side amid the secure peace of his mother's hearth. Yes, thus adjured, I think I would have sat still under a rocking crag: but, indeed, to sit still in actual circumstances was my instinct; and at the price of my very life, I would not have moved to give him trouble, thwart his will, or make demands on his attention. We were in the stalls, and for a few minutes there was a most terrible, ruthless pressure about us.

"How terrified are the women!" said he; "But if the men were not almost equally so, order might be maintained. This is a sorry scene: I see fifty selfish brutes at this moment, each of whom, if I were near, I could conscientiously knock down. I see some women braver than some men. There is one yonder – Good God!"

While Graham was speaking, a young girl who had been very quietly and steadily clinging to a gentleman before us, was suddenly struck from her protector's arms by a big, butcherly intruder, and hurled under the feet of the crowd. Scarce two seconds lasted her disappearance. Graham rushed forwards; he and the gentleman, a powerful man though grey-haired, united their strength to thrust back the throng; her head and long hair fell back over his shoulder: she seemed unconscious.

"Trust her with me; I am a medical man," said Dr. John.

"If you have no lady with you, be it so," was the answer. "Hold her, and I will force a passage: we must get her to the air."

"I have a lady," said Graham; "but she will be neither hindrance nor incumbrance."

He summoned me with his eye: we were separated. Resolute, however, to rejoin him, I penetrated the living barrier, creeping under where I could not get between or over.

"Fasten on me, and don't leave go," he said; and I obeyed him.

Our pioneer proved strong and adroit; he opened the dense mass like a wedge; with patience and toil he at last bored through the flesh-and-blood rock – so solid, hot, and suffocating – and brought us to the fresh, freezing night.

"You are an Englishman!" said he, turning shortly on Dr. Bretton, when we got into the street.

"An Englishman. And I speak to a countryman?" was the reply.

"Right. Be good enough to stand here two minutes, whilst I find my carriage."

"Papa, I am not hurt," said a girlish voice; "am I with papa?"

"You are with a friend, and your father is close at hand."

"Tell him I am not hurt, except just in my shoulder. Oh, my shoulder! They trod just here."

"Dislocation, perhaps!" muttered the Doctor: "let us hope there is no worse injury done. Lucy, lend a hand one instant."

And I assisted while he made some arrangement of drapery and position for the ease of his suffering burden. She suppressed a moan, and lay in his arms quietly and patiently.

"She is very light," said Graham, "like a child!" and he asked in my ear, "Is she a child, Lucy? Did you notice her age?"

"I am not a child – I am a person of seventeen," responded the patient, demurely and with dignity. Then, directly after: "Tell papa to come; I get anxious."

The carriage drove up; her father relieved Graham; but in the exchange from one bearer to another she was hurt, and moaned again.

"My darling!" said the father, tenderly; then turning to Graham, "You said, sir, you are a medical man?"

"I am: Dr. Bretton, of La Terrasse."

"Good. Will you step into my carriage?"

"My own carriage is here: I will seek it, and accompany you."

"Be pleased, then, to follow us." And he named his address: "The Hôtel Crécy, in the Rue Crécy."

We followed; the carriage drove fast; myself and Graham were silent. This seemed like an adventure.

Some little time being lost in seeking our own equipage, we reached the hotel perhaps about ten minutes after these strangers. It was an hotel in the foreign sense: a collection of dwelling-houses, not an inn – a vast, lofty pile, with a huge arch to its street-door, leading through a vaulted covered way, into a square all built round.

We alighted, passed up a wide, handsome public staircase, and stopped at Numéro 2 on the second landing; the first floor comprising the abode of I know not what 'prince Russe', as Graham informed me. On ringing the bell at a second great door, we were admitted to a suite of very handsome apartments. Announced by a servant in livery, we entered a drawing-room whose hearth glowed with an English fire, and whose walls gleamed with foreign mirrors. Near the hearth appeared a little group: a slight form sunk in a deep arm-chair, one or two women busy about it, the iron-grey gentleman anxiously looking on.

"Where is Harriet? I wish Harriet would come to me," said the girlish voice, faintly.

"Where is Mrs. Hurst?" demanded the gentleman impatiently and somewhat sternly of the man-servant who had admitted us.

"I am sorry to say she is gone out of town, sir; my young lady gave her leave till tomorrow."

"Yes – I did – I did. She is gone to see her sister; I said she might go: I remember now," interposed the young lady; "but I am so sorry, for Manon and Louison cannot understand a word I say, and they hurt me without meaning to do so."

Dr. John and the gentleman now interchanged greetings; and while they passed a few minutes in consultation, I approached the easy-chair, and seeing what the faint and sinking girl wished to have done, I did it for her.

I was still occupied in the arrangement, when Graham drew near; he was no less skilled in surgery than medicine, and, on examination, found that no further advice than his own was necessary to the treatment of the present case. He ordered her to be carried to her chamber, and whispered to me: "Go with the women, Lucy; they seem but dull; you can at least direct their movements, and thus spare her some pain. She must be touched very tenderly."

The chamber was a room shadowy with pale-blue hangings, vaporous with curtainings and veilings of muslin; the bed seemed to me like snow-drift and mist – spotless, soft, and gauzy. Making the women stand apart, I undressed their mistress, without their well-meaning but clumsy aid. I was not in a sufficiently collected mood to note with separate distinctness every detail of the attire I removed, but I received a general impression of refinement, delicacy, and perfect personal cultivation; which, in a period of after-thought, offered in my reflections a singular contrast to notes retained of Miss Ginevra Fanshawe's appointments.

The girl was herself a small, delicate creature, but made like a model. As I folded back her plentiful yet fine hair, so shining and soft, and so exquisitely tended, I had under my observation a young, pale, weary, but high-bred face. The brow was smooth and clear; the eyebrows were distinct, but soft, and melting to a mere trace at the temples; the eyes were a rich gift of nature – fine and full, large, deep, seeming to hold dominion over the slighter subordinate features – capable, probably, of much significance at another hour and under other circumstances than the present, but now languid and suffering. Her skin was perfectly fair, the neck and hands veined finely like the petals of a flower; a thin glazing of the ice of pride polished this delicate exterior, and her lip wore a curl – I doubt not inherent and unconscious, but which, if I had seen it first with the accompaniments of health and state, would have struck me as unwarranted, and proving in the little lady a quite mistaken view of life and her own consequence.

Her demeanour under the Doctor's hands at first excited a smile; it was not puerile – rather, on the whole, patient and firm – but yet, once or twice she addressed him with suddenness and sharpness, saying that he hurt her, and must contrive to give her less pain; I saw her large eyes, too, settle on his face like the solemn eyes of some pretty, wondering child. I know not whether Graham felt this examination: if he did, he was cautious not to check or discomfort it by any retaliatory look. I think he performed his work with extreme care and gentleness, sparing her what pain he could; and she acknowledged as much, when he had done, by the words: "Thank you, Doctor, and goodnight," very gratefully pronounced as she uttered them, however, it was with a repetition of the serious, direct gaze, I thought, peculiar in its gravity and intentness.

The injuries, it seems, were not dangerous: an assurance which her father received with a smile that almost made one his friend – it was so glad and gratified. He now expressed his obligations to Graham with as much earnestness as was befitting an Englishman addressing one who has served him, but is yet a stranger; he also begged him to call the next day.

"Papa," said a voice from the veiled couch, "thank the lady, too; is she there?"

I opened the curtain with a smile, and looked in at her. She lay now at comparative ease; she looked pretty, though pale; her face was delicately designed, and if at first sight it appeared proud, I believe custom might prove it to be soft.

"I thank the lady very sincerely," said her father: "I fancy she has been very good to my child. I think we scarcely dare tell Mrs. Hurst who has been her substitute and done her work; she will feel at once ashamed and jealous."

And thus, in the most friendly spirit, parting greetings were interchanged; and refreshment having been hospitably offered, but by us, as it was late, refused, we withdrew from the Hôtel Crécy.

On our way back we repassed the theatre. All was silence and darkness: the roaring, rushing crowd all vanished and gone – the damps, as well as the incipient fire, extinct and forgotten. Next morning's papers explained that it was but some loose drapery on which a spark had fallen, and which had blazed up and been quenched in a moment.

Chapter Twenty-Four
M. de Bassompierre

THOSE WHO LIVE in retirement, whose lives have fallen amid the seclusion of schools or of other walled-in and guarded dwellings, are liable to be suddenly and for a long while dropped out of the memory of their friends, the denizens of a freer world. Unaccountably, perhaps, and close upon some space of unusually frequent intercourse – some congeries of rather exciting little circumstances, whose natural sequel would rather seem to be the quickening than the suspension of communication – there falls a stilly pause, a wordless silence, a long blank of oblivion. Unbroken always is this blank; alike entire and unexplained. The letter, the message once frequent, are cut off; the visit, formerly periodical, ceases to occur; the book, paper, or other token that indicated remembrance, comes no more.

Always there are excellent reasons for these lapses, if the hermit but knew them. Though he is stagnant in his cell, his connections without are whirling in the very vortex of life. That void interval which passes for him so slowly that the very clocks seem at a stand, and the wingless hours plod by in the likeness of tired tramps prone to rest at milestones – that same interval, perhaps, teems with events, and pants with hurry for his friends.

The hermit – if he be a sensible hermit – will swallow his own thoughts, and lock up his own emotions during these weeks of inward winter. He will know that Destiny designed him to imitate, on occasion, the dormouse, and he will be conformable: make a tidy ball of himself, creep into a hole of life's wall, and submit decently to the drift which blows in and soon blocks him up, preserving him in ice for the season.

Let him say, "It is quite right: it ought to be so, since so it is." And, perhaps, one day his snow-sepulchre will open, spring's softness will return, the sun and south-wind will reach him; the budding of hedges, and carolling of birds, and singing of liberated streams, will call him to kindly resurrection. *Perhaps* this may be the case, perhaps not: the frost may get into his heart and never thaw more; when spring comes, a crow or a pie may pick out of the wall only his dormouse-bones. Well, even in that case, all will be right: it is to be supposed he knew from the first he was mortal, and must one day go the way of all flesh, "As well soon as syne."

Following that eventful evening at the theatre, came for me seven weeks as bare as seven sheets of blank paper: no word was written on one of them; not a visit, not a token.

About the middle of that time I entertained fancies that something had happened to my friends at La Terrasse. The mid-blank is always a beclouded point for the solitary: his nerves ache with the strain of long expectancy; the doubts hitherto repelled gather now to a mass and – strong in accumulation – roll back upon him with a force which savours of vindictiveness. Night, too, becomes an unkindly time, and sleep and his nature cannot agree: strange starts and struggles harass his couch: the sinister band of bad dreams, with horror of calamity, and sick dread of entire desertion at their head, join the league against him. Poor wretch! He does his best to bear up, but he is a poor, pallid, wasting wretch, despite that best.

Towards the last of these long seven weeks I admitted, what through the other six I had jealously excluded – the conviction that these blanks were inevitable: the result of circumstances, the fiat of fate, a part of my life's lot and – above all – a matter about whose origin no question must ever be asked, for whose painful sequence no murmur ever uttered. Of course I did not blame myself for suffering: I thank God I had a truer sense of justice than to fall into any imbecile extravagance of self-accusation;

and as to blaming others for silence, in my reason I well knew them blameless, and in my heart acknowledged them so: but it was a rough and heavy road to travel, and I longed for better days.

I tried different expedients to sustain and fill existence: I commenced an elaborate piece of lace-work, I studied German pretty hard, I undertook a course of regular reading of the driest and thickest books in the library; in all my efforts I was as orthodox as I knew how to be. Was there error somewhere? Very likely. I only know the result was as if I had gnawed a file to satisfy hunger, or drank brine to quench thirst.

My hour of torment was the post-hour. Unfortunately, I knew it too well, and tried as vainly as assiduously to cheat myself of that knowledge; dreading the rack of expectation, and the sick collapse of disappointment which daily preceded and followed upon that well-recognised ring.

I suppose animals kept in cages, and so scantily fed as to be always upon the verge of famine, await their food as I awaited a letter. Oh! – To speak truth, and drop that tone of a false calm which long to sustain, outwears nature's endurance – I underwent in those seven weeks bitter fears and pains, strange inward trials, miserable defections of hope, intolerable encroachments of despair. This last came so near me sometimes that her breath went right through me. I used to feel it like a baleful air or sigh, penetrate deep, and make motion pause at my heart, or proceed only under unspeakable oppression. The letter – the well-beloved letter – would not come; and it was all of sweetness in life I had to look for.

In the very extremity of want, I had recourse again, and yet again, to the little packet in the case – the five letters. How splendid that month seemed whose skies had beheld the rising of these five stars! It was always at night I visited them, and not daring to ask every evening for a candle in the kitchen, I bought a wax taper and matches to light it, and at the study-hour stole up to the dormitory and feasted on my crust from the Barmecide's loaf. It did not nourish me: I pined on it, and got as thin as a shadow: otherwise I was not ill.

Reading there somewhat late one evening, and feeling that the power to read was leaving me – for the letters from incessant perusal were losing all sap and significance: my gold was withering to leaves before my eyes, and I was sorrowing over the disillusion – suddenly a quick tripping foot ran up the stairs. I knew Ginevra Fanshawe's step: she had dined in town that afternoon; she was now returned, and would come here to replace her shawl, etc. in the wardrobe.

Yes: in she came, dressed in bright silk, with her shawl falling from her shoulders, and her curls, half-uncurled in the damp of night, drooping careless and heavy upon her neck. I had hardly time to recasket my treasures and lock them up when she was at my side; her humour seemed none of the best.

"It has been a stupid evening: they are stupid people," she began.

"Who? Mrs. Cholmondeley? I thought you always found her house charming?"

"I have not been to Mrs. Cholmondeley's."

"Indeed! Have you made new acquaintance?"

"My uncle de Bassompierre is come."

"Your uncle de Bassompierre! Are you not glad? – I thought he was a favourite."

"You thought wrong: the man is odious; I hate him."

"Because he is a foreigner? Or for what other reason of equal weight?"

"He is not a foreigner. The man is English enough, goodness knows; and had an English name till three or four years ago; but his mother was a foreigner, a de Bassompierre, and some of her family are dead and have left him estates, a title, and this name: he is quite a great man now."

"Do you hate him for that reason?"

"Don't I know what mamma says about him? He is not my own uncle, but married mamma's sister. Mamma detests him; she says he killed aunt Ginevra with unkindness: he looks like a bear. Such a dismal evening!" she went on. "I'll go no more to his big hotel. Fancy me walking into a room alone, and a great man fifty years old coming forwards, and after a few minutes' conversation actually turning his back upon me, and then abruptly going out of the room. Such odd ways! I daresay his conscience smote him, for they all say at home I am the picture of aunt Ginevra. Mamma often declares the likeness is quite ridiculous."

"Were you the only visitor?"

"The only visitor? Yes; then there was missy, my cousin: little spoiled, pampered thing."

"M. de Bassompierre has a daughter?"

"Yes, yes: don't tease one with questions. Oh, dear! I am so tired."

She yawned. Throwing herself without ceremony on my bed she added, "It seems Mademoiselle was nearly crushed to a jelly in a hubbub at the theatre some weeks ago."

"Ah! Indeed. And they live at a large hotel in the Rue Crécy?"

"Justement. How do *you* know?"

"I have been there."

"Oh, you have? Really! You go everywhere in these days. I suppose Mother Bretton took you. She and Esculapius have the *entrée* of the de Bassompierre apartments: it seems 'my son John' attended missy on the occasion of her accident – Accident? Bah! All affectation! I don't think she was squeezed more than she richly deserves for her airs. And now there is quite an intimacy struck up: I heard something about 'auld lang syne', and what not. Oh, how stupid they all were!"

"*All!* You said you were the only visitor."

"Did I? You see one forgets to particularise an old woman and her boy."

"Dr. and Mrs. Bretton were at M. de Bassompierre's this evening?"

"Ay, ay! As large as life; and missy played the hostess. What a conceited doll it is!"

Soured and listless, Miss Fanshawe was beginning to disclose the causes of her prostrate condition. There had been a retrenchment of incense, a diversion or a total withholding of homage and attention coquetry had failed of effect, vanity had undergone mortification. She lay fuming in the vapours.

"Is Miss de Bassompierre quite well now?" I asked.

"As well as you or I, no doubt; but she is an affected little thing, and gave herself invalid airs to attract medical notice. And to see the old dowager making her recline on a couch, and 'my son John' prohibiting excitement, etcetera – faugh! The scene was quite sickening."

"It would not have been so if the object of attention had been changed: if you had taken Miss de Bassompierre's place."

"Indeed! I hate 'my son John!'"

"'My son John!' – Whom do you indicate by that name? Dr. Bretton's mother never calls him so."

"Then she ought. A clownish, bearish John he is."

"You violate the truth in saying so; and as the whole of my patience is now spun off the distaff, I peremptorily desire you to rise from that bed, and vacate this room."

"Passionate thing! Your face is the colour of a coquelicot. I wonder what always makes you so mighty testy *à l'endroit du gros Jean?* 'John Anderson, my Joe, John!' Oh, the distinguished name!"

Thrilling with exasperation, to which it would have been sheer folly to have given vent – for there was no contending with that unsubstantial feather, that mealy-winged moth – I extinguished my taper, locked my bureau, and left her, since she would not leave me. Small-beer as she was, she had turned insufferably acid.

The morrow was Thursday and a half-holiday. Breakfast was over; I had withdrawn to the first classe. The dreaded hour, the post-hour, was nearing, and I sat waiting it, much as a ghost-seer might wait his spectre. Less than ever was a letter probable; still, strive as I would, I could not forget that it was possible. As the moments lessened, a restlessness and fear almost beyond the average assailed me. It was a day of winter east wind, and I had now for some time entered into that dreary fellowship with the winds and their changes, so little known, so incomprehensible to the healthy. The north and east owned a terrific influence, making all pain more poignant, all sorrow sadder. The south could calm, the west sometimes cheer: unless, indeed, they brought on their wings the burden of thunder-clouds, under the weight and warmth of which all energy died.

Bitter and dark as was this January day, I remember leaving the classe, and running down without bonnet to the bottom of the long garden, and then lingering amongst the stripped shrubs, in the forlorn hope that the postman's ring might occur while I was out of hearing, and I might thus be spared the thrill which some particular nerve or nerves, almost gnawed through with the unremitting tooth of a fixed idea, were becoming wholly unfit to support. I lingered as long as I dared without fear of attracting attention by my absence. I muffled my head in my apron, and stopped my ears in terror of the torturing clang, sure to be followed by such blank silence, such barren vacuum for me. At last I ventured to re-enter the first classe, where, as it was not yet nine o'clock, no pupils had been admitted. The first thing seen was a white object on my black desk, a white, flat object. The post had, indeed, arrived; by me unheard. Rosine had visited my cell, and, like some angel, had left behind her a bright token of her presence. That shining thing on the desk was indeed a letter, a real letter; I saw so much at the distance of three yards, and as I had but one correspondent on earth, from that one it must come. He remembered me yet. How deep a pulse of gratitude sent new life through my heart.

Drawing near, bending and looking on the letter, in trembling but almost certain hope of seeing a known hand, it was my lot to find, on the contrary, an autograph for the moment deemed unknown – a pale female scrawl, instead of a firm, masculine character. I then thought fate was *too* hard for me, and I said, audibly, "This is cruel."

But I got over that pain also. Life is still life, whatever its pangs: our eyes and ears and their use remain with us, though the prospect of what pleases be wholly withdrawn, and the sound of what consoles be quite silenced.

I opened the billet: by this time I had recognised its handwriting as perfectly familiar. It was dated 'La Terrasse,' and it ran thus:

> *Dear Lucy,*
>
> *It occurs to me to inquire what you have been doing with yourself for the last month or two? Not that I suspect you would have the least difficulty in giving an account of your proceedings. I daresay you have been just as busy and as happy as ourselves at La Terrasse. As to Graham, his professional connection extends daily: he is so much sought after, so much engaged, that I tell him he will grow quite conceited. Like a right good mother, as I am, I do my best to keep him down: no flattery does he get from me, as you know. And yet, Lucy, he is a fine fellow: his mother's heart dances at the sight of him. After being hurried here and there the whole day, and passing the ordeal of fifty sorts of tempers, and combating a hundred caprices, and sometimes witnessing cruel sufferings – perhaps, occasionally, as I tell him, inflicting them – at night he still comes home to me in such kindly, pleasant mood, that really, I seem to live in a sort of moral antipodes, and on these January evenings my day rises when other people's night sets in.*
>
> *Still he needs keeping in order, and correcting, and repressing, and I do him that good service; but the boy is so elastic there is no such thing as vexing him thoroughly. When I think I have at last driven him to the sullens, he turns on me with jokes for retaliation: but you know him and all his iniquities, and I am but an elderly simpleton to make him the subject of this epistle.*
>
> *As for me, I have had my old Bretton agent here on a visit, and have been plunged overhead and ears in business matters. I do so wish to regain for Graham at least some part of what his father left him. He laughs to scorn my anxiety on this point, bidding me look and see how he can provide for himself and me too, and asking what the old lady can possibly want that she has not; hinting about sky-blue turbans; accusing me of an ambition to wear diamonds, keep livery servants, have an hotel, and lead the fashion amongst the English clan in Villette.*

Talking of sky-blue turbans, I wish you had been with us the other evening. He had come in really tired, and after I had given him his tea, he threw himself into my chair with his customary presumption. To my great delight, he dropped asleep. (You know how he teases me about being drowsy; I, who never, by any chance, close an eye by daylight.) While he slept, I thought he looked very bonny, Lucy: fool as I am to be so proud of him; but who can help it? Show me his peer. Look where I will, I see nothing like him in Villette. Well, I took it into my head to play him a trick: so I brought out the sky-blue turban, and handling it with gingerly precaution, I managed to invest his brows with this grand adornment. I assure you it did not at all misbecome him; he looked quite Eastern, except that he is so fair. Nobody, however, can accuse him of having red hair now – it is genuine chestnut – a dark, glossy chestnut; and when I put my large cashmere about him, there was as fine a young bey, dey, or pacha improvised as you would wish to see.

It was good entertainment; but only half-enjoyed, since I was alone: you should have been there.

In due time my lord awoke: the looking-glass above the fireplace soon intimated to him his plight: as you may imagine, I now live under threat and dread of vengeance.

But to come to the gist of my letter. I know Thursday is a half-holiday in the Rue Fossette: be ready, then, by five in the afternoon, at which hour I will send the carriage to take you out to La Terrasse. Be sure to come: you may meet some old acquaintance. Goodbye, my wise, dear, grave little god-daughter.

Very truly yours,
Louisa Bretton.

Now, a letter like that sets one to rights! I might still be sad after reading that letter, but I was more composed; not exactly cheered, perhaps, but relieved. My friends, at least, were well and happy: no accident had occurred to Graham; no illness had seized his mother – calamities that had so long been my dream and thought. Their feelings for me too were – as they had been. Yet, how strange it was to look on Mrs. Bretton's seven weeks and contrast them with my seven weeks! Also, how very wise it is in people placed in an exceptional position to hold their tongues and not rashly declare how such position galls them! The world can understand well enough the process of perishing for want of food: perhaps few persons can enter into or follow out that of going mad from solitary confinement. They see the long-buried prisoner disinterred, a maniac or an idiot! – How his senses left him – how his nerves, first inflamed, underwent nameless agony, and then sunk to palsy – is a subject too intricate for examination, too abstract for popular comprehension. Speak of it! You might almost as well stand up in an European market-place, and propound dark sayings in that language and mood wherein Nebuchadnezzar, the imperial hypochondriac, communed with his baffled Chaldeans. And long, long may the minds to whom such themes are no mystery – by whom their bearings are sympathetically seized – be few in number, and rare of rencounter. Long may it be generally thought that physical privations alone merit compassion, and that the rest is a figment. When the world was younger and haler than now, moral trials were a deeper mystery still: perhaps in all the land of Israel there was but one Saul – certainly but one David to soothe or comprehend him.

The keen, still cold of the morning was succeeded, later in the day, by a sharp breathing from Russian wastes: the cold zone sighed over the temperate zone, and froze it fast. A heavy firmament, dull, and thick with snow, sailed up from the north, and settled over expectant Europe. Towards afternoon began the descent. I feared no carriage would come, the white tempest raged so dense and wild. But trust my godmother! Once having asked, she would have her guest. About six o'clock I was lifted from the carriage over the already blocked-up front steps of the château, and put in at the door of La Terrasse.

Running through the vestibule, and upstairs to the drawing-room, there I found Mrs. Bretton – a summer-day in her own person. Had I been twice as cold as I was, her kind kiss and cordial clasp would have warmed me. Inured now for so long a time to rooms with bare boards, black benches, desks, and stoves, the blue saloon seemed to me gorgeous. In its Christmas-like fire alone there was a clear and crimson splendour which quite dazzled me.

When my godmother had held my hand for a little while, and chatted with me, and scolded me for having become thinner than when she last saw me, she professed to discover that the snow-wind had disordered my hair, and sent me upstairs to make it neat and remove my shawl.

Repairing to my own little sea-green room, there also I found a bright fire, and candles too were lit: a tall waxlight stood on each side the great looking glass; but between the candles, and before the glass, appeared something dressing itself – an airy, fairy thing – small, slight, white – a winter spirit.

I declare, for one moment I thought of Graham and his spectral illusions. With distrustful eye I noted the details of this new vision. It wore white, sprinkled slightly with drops of scarlet; its girdle was red; it had something in its hair leafy, yet shining – a little wreath with an evergreen gloss. Spectral or not, here truly was nothing frightful, and I advanced.

Turning quick upon me, a large eye, under long lashes, flashed over me, the intruder: the lashes were as dark as long, and they softened with their pencilling the orb they guarded.

"Ah! You are come!" she breathed out, in a soft, quiet voice, and she smiled slowly, and gazed intently.

I knew her now. Having only once seen that sort of face, with that cast of fine and delicate featuring, I could not but know her.

"Miss de Bassompierre," I pronounced.

"No," was the reply, "not Miss de Bassompierre for *you!*" I did not inquire who then she might be, but waited voluntary information.

"You are changed, but still you are yourself," she said, approaching nearer. "I remember you well – your countenance, the colour of your hair, the outline of your face…."

I had moved to the fire, and she stood opposite, and gazed into me; and as she gazed, her face became gradually more and more expressive of thought and feeling, till at last a dimness quenched her clear vision.

"It makes me almost cry to look so far back," said she: "but as to being sorry, or sentimental, don't think it: on the contrary, I am quite pleased and glad."

Interested, yet altogether at fault, I knew not what to say. At last I stammered, "I think I never met you till that night, some weeks ago, when you were hurt…?"

She smiled. "You have forgotten then that I have sat on your knee, been lifted in your arms, even shared your pillow? You no longer remember the night when I came crying, like a naughty little child as I was, to your bedside, and you took me in. You have no memory for the comfort and protection by which you soothed an acute distress? Go back to Bretton. Remember Mr. Home."

At last I saw it all. "And you are little Polly?"

"I am Paulina Mary Home de Bassompierre."

How time can change! Little Polly wore in her pale, small features, her fairy symmetry, her varying expression, a certain promise of interest and grace; but Paulina Mary was become beautiful – not with the beauty that strikes the eye like a rose – orbed, ruddy, and replete; not with the plump, and pink, and flaxen attributes of her blond cousin Ginevra; but her seventeen years had brought her a refined and tender charm which did not lie in complexion, though hers was fair and clear; nor in outline, though her features were sweet, and her limbs perfectly turned; but, I think, rather in a subdued glow from the soul outward. This was not an opaque vase, of material however costly, but a lamp chastely lucent, guarding from extinction, yet not hiding from worship, a flame vital and vestal. In speaking of her attractions, I would not exaggerate language; but, indeed, they seemed to me very real and engaging. What though all was on a small scale, it was the perfume which gave this white violet distinction, and made it superior to the broadest camelia – the fullest dahlia that ever bloomed.

"Ah! And you remember the old time at Bretton?"

"Better," said she, "better, perhaps, than you. I remember it with minute distinctness: not only the time, but the days of the time, and the hours of the days."

"You must have forgotten some things?"

"Very little, I imagine."

"You were then a little creature of quick feelings: you must, long ere this, have outgrown the impressions with which joy and grief, affection and bereavement, stamped your mind ten years ago."

"You think I have forgotten whom I liked, and in what degree I liked them when a child?"

"The sharpness must be gone – the point, the poignancy – the deep imprint must be softened away and effaced?"

"I have a good memory for those days."

She looked as if she had. Her eyes were the eyes of one who can remember; one whose childhood does not fade like a dream, nor whose youth vanish like a sunbeam. She would not take life, loosely and incoherently, in parts, and let one season slip as she entered on another: she would retain and add; often review from the commencement, and so grow in harmony and consistency as she grew in years. Still I could not quite admit the conviction that *all* the pictures which now crowded upon me were vivid and visible to her. Her fond attachments, her sports and contests with a well-loved playmate, the patient, true devotion of her child's heart, her fears, her delicate reserves, her little trials, the last piercing pain of separation.... I retraced these things, and shook my head incredulous. She persisted. "The child of seven years lives yet in the girl of seventeen," said she.

"You used to be excessively fond of Mrs. Bretton," I remarked, intending to test her. She set me right at once.

"Not *excessively* fond," said she; "I liked her: I respected her as I should do now: she seems to me very little altered."

"She is not much changed," I assented.

We were silent a few minutes. Glancing round the room she said, "There are several things here that used to be at Bretton! I remember that pincushion and that looking-glass."

Evidently she was not deceived in her estimate of her own memory; not, at least, so far.

"You think, then, you would have known Mrs. Bretton?" I went on.

"I perfectly remembered her; the turn of her features, her olive complexion, and black hair, her height, her walk, her voice."

"Dr. Bretton, of course," I pursued, "would be out of the question: and, indeed, as I saw your first interview with him, I am aware that he appeared to you as a stranger."

"That first night I was puzzled," she answered.

"How did the recognition between him and your father come about?"

"They exchanged cards. The names Graham Bretton and Home de Bassompierre gave rise to questions and explanations. That was on the second day; but before then I was beginning to know something."

"How – know something?"

"Why," she said, "how strange it is that most people seem so slow to feel the truth – not to see, but *feel*! When Dr. Bretton had visited me a few times, and sat near and talked to me; when I had observed the look in his eyes, the expression about his mouth, the form of his chin, the carriage of his head, and all that we *do* observe in persons who approach us – how could I avoid being led by association to think of Graham Bretton? Graham was slighter than he, and not grown so tall, and had a smoother face, and longer and lighter hair, and spoke – not so deeply – more like a girl; but yet *he* is Graham, just as *I* am little Polly, or you are Lucy Snowe."

I thought the same, but I wondered to find my thoughts hers: there are certain things in which we so rarely meet with our double that it seems a miracle when that chance befalls.

"You and Graham were once playmates."

"And do you remember that?" she questioned in her turn.

"No doubt he will remember it also," said I.

"I have not asked him: few things would surprise me so much as to find that he did. I suppose his disposition is still gay and careless?"

"Was it so formerly? Did it so strike you? Do you thus remember him?"

"I scarcely remember him in any other light. Sometimes he was studious; sometimes he was merry: but whether busy with his books or disposed for play, it was chiefly the books or game he thought of; not much heeding those with whom he read or amused himself."

"Yet to you he was partial."

"Partial to me? Oh, no! He had other playmates – his school-fellows; I was of little consequence to him, except on Sundays: yes, he was kind on Sundays. I remember walking with him hand-in-hand to St. Mary's, and his finding the places in my prayer-book; and how good and still he was on Sunday evenings! So mild for such a proud, lively boy; so patient with all my blunders in reading; and so wonderfully to be depended on, for he never spent those evenings from home: I had a constant fear that he would accept some invitation and forsake us; but he never did, nor seemed ever to wish to do it. Thus, of course, it can be no more. I suppose Sunday will now be Dr. Bretton's dining-out day...?"

"Children, come down!" here called Mrs. Bretton from below. Paulina would still have lingered, but I inclined to descend: we went down.

Chapter Twenty-Five
The Little Countess

❧

CHEERFUL as my godmother naturally was, and entertaining as, for our sakes, she made a point of being, there was no true enjoyment that evening at La Terrasse, till, through the wild howl of the winter-night, were heard the signal sounds of arrival. How often, while women and girls sit warm at snug fire-sides, their hearts and imaginations are doomed to divorce from the comfort surrounding their persons, forced out by night to wander through dark ways, to dare stress of weather, to contend with the snow-blast, to wait at lonely gates and stiles in wildest storms, watching and listening to see and hear the father, the son, the husband coming home.

Father and son came at last to the château: for the Count de Bassompierre that night accompanied Dr. Bretton. I know not which of our trio heard the horses first; the asperity, the violence of the weather warranted our running down into the hall to meet and greet the two riders as they came in; but they warned us to keep our distance: both were white – two mountains of snow; and indeed Mrs. Bretton, seeing their condition, ordered them instantly to the kitchen; prohibiting them, at their peril, from setting foot on her carpeted staircase till they had severally put off that mask of Old Christmas they now affected. Into the kitchen, however, we could not help following them: it was a large old Dutch kitchen, picturesque and pleasant. The little white Countess danced in a circle about her equally white sire, clapping her hands and crying, "Papa, papa, you look like an enormous Polar bear."

The bear shook himself, and the little sprite fled far from the frozen shower. Back she came, however, laughing, and eager to aid in removing the arctic disguise. The Count, at last issuing from his dreadnought, threatened to overwhelm her with it as with an avalanche.

"Come, then," said she, bending to invite the fall, and when it was playfully advanced above her head, bounding out of reach like some little chamois.

Her movements had the supple softness, the velvet grace of a kitten; her laugh was clearer than the ring of silver and crystal; as she took her sire's cold hands and rubbed them, and stood on tiptoe to reach his lips for a kiss, there seemed to shine round her a halo of loving delight. The grave and reverend seignor looked down on her as men *do* look on what is the apple of their eye.

"Mrs. Bretton," said he: "what am I to do with this daughter or daughterling of mine? She neither grows in wisdom nor in stature. Don't you find her pretty nearly as much the child as she was ten years ago?"

"She cannot be more the child than this great boy of mine," said Mrs. Bretton, who was in conflict with her son about some change of dress she deemed advisable, and which he resisted. He stood leaning against the Dutch dresser, laughing and keeping her at arm's length.

"Come, mamma," said he, "by way of compromise, and to secure for us inward as well as outward warmth, let us have a Christmas wassail-cup, and toast Old England here, on the hearth."

So, while the Count stood by the fire, and Paulina Mary still danced to and fro – happy in the liberty of the wide hall-like kitchen – Mrs. Bretton herself instructed Martha to spice and heat the wassail-bowl, and, pouring the draught into a Bretton flagon, it was served round, reaming hot, by means of a small silver vessel, which I recognised as Graham's christening-cup.

"Here's to Auld Lang Syne!" said the Count; holding the glancing cup on high. Then, looking at Mrs. Bretton. –

> *"We twa ha' paidlet i' the burn*
> *Fra morning sun till dine,*
> *But seas between us braid ha' roared*
> *Sin' auld lane syne.*
> *"And surely ye'll be your pint-stoup,*
> *And surely I'll be mine;*
> *And we'll taste a cup o' kindness yet*
> *For auld lang syne."*

"Scotch! Scotch!" cried Paulina; "Papa is talking Scotch; and Scotch he is, partly. We are Home and de Bassompierre, Caledonian and Gallic."

"And is that a Scotch reel you are dancing, you Highland fairy?" asked her father. "Mrs. Bretton, there will be a green ring growing up in the middle of your kitchen shortly. I would not answer for her being quite cannie: she is a strange little mortal."

"Tell Lucy to dance with me, papa; there is Lucy Snowe."

Mr. Home (there was still quite as much about him of plain Mr. Home as of proud Count de Bassompierre) held his hand out to me, saying kindly, "he remembered me well; and, even had his own memory been less trustworthy, my name was so often on his daughter's lips, and he had listened to so many long tales about me, I should seem like an old acquaintance."

Everyone now had tasted the wassail-cup except Paulina, whose pas de fée, ou de fantaisie, nobody thought of interrupting to offer so profanatory a draught; but she was not to be overlooked, nor baulked of her mortal privileges.

"Let me taste," said she to Graham, as he was putting the cup on the shelf of the dresser out of her reach.

Mrs. Bretton and Mr. Home were now engaged in conversation. Dr. John had not been unobservant of the fairy's dance; he had watched it, and he had liked it. To say nothing of the softness and beauty of the movements, eminently grateful to his grace-loving eye, that ease in his mother's house charmed him, for it set *him* at ease: again she seemed a child for him – again, almost his playmate. I wondered how he would speak to her; I had not yet seen him address her; his first words proved that the old days of 'little Polly' had been recalled to his mind by this evening's child-like light-heartedness.

"Your ladyship wishes for the tankard?"

"I think I said so. I think I intimated as much."

"Couldn't consent to a step of the kind on any account. Sorry for it, but couldn't do it."

"Why? I am quite well now: it can't break my collar-bone again, or dislocate my shoulder. Is it wine?"

"No; nor dew."

"I don't want dew; I don't like dew: but what is it?"

"Ale – strong ale – old October; brewed, perhaps, when I was born."

"It must be curious: is it good?"

"Excessively good."

And he took it down, administered to himself a second dose of this mighty elixir, expressed in his mischievous eyes extreme contentment with the same, and solemnly replaced the cup on the shelf.

"I should like a little," said Paulina, looking up; "I never had any 'old October': is it sweet?"

"Perilously sweet," said Graham.

She continued to look up exactly with the countenance of a child that longs for some prohibited dainty. At last the Doctor relented, took it down, and indulged himself in the gratification of letting her taste from his hand; his eyes, always expressive in the revelation of pleasurable feelings, luminously and smilingly avowed that it *was* a gratification; and he prolonged it by so regulating the position of the cup that only a drop at a time could reach the rosy, sipping lips by which its brim was courted.

"A little more – a little more," said she, petulantly touching his hand with the forefinger, to make him incline the cup more generously and yieldingly. "It smells of spice and sugar, but I can't taste it; your wrist is so stiff, and you are so stingy."

He indulged her, whispering, however, with gravity: "Don't tell my mother or Lucy; they wouldn't approve."

"Nor do I," said she, passing into another tone and manner as soon as she had fairly assayed the beverage, just as if it had acted upon her like some disenchanting draught, undoing the work of a wizard: "I find it anything but sweet; it is bitter and hot, and takes away my breath. Your old October was only desirable while forbidden. Thank you, no more."

And, with a slight bend – careless, but as graceful as her dance – she glided from him and rejoined her father.

I think she had spoken truth: the child of seven was in the girl of seventeen.

Graham looked after her a little baffled, a little puzzled; his eye was on her a good deal during the rest of the evening, but she did not seem to notice him.

As we ascended to the drawing-room for tea, she took her father's arm: her natural place seemed to be at his side; her eyes and her ears were dedicated to him. He and Mrs. Bretton were the chief talkers of our little party, and Paulina was their best listener, attending closely to all that was said, prompting the repetition of this or that trait or adventure.

"And where were you at such a time, papa? And what did you say then? And tell Mrs. Bretton what happened on that occasion." Thus she drew him out.

She did not again yield to any effervescence of glee; the infantine sparkle was exhaled for the night: she was soft, thoughtful, and docile. It was pretty to see her bid goodnight; her manner to Graham was touched with dignity: in her very slight smile and quiet bow spoke the Countess, and Graham could not but look grave, and bend responsive. I saw he hardly knew how to blend together in his ideas the dancing fairy and delicate dame.

Next day, when we were all assembled round the breakfast-table, shivering and fresh from the morning's chill ablutions, Mrs. Bretton pronounced a decree that nobody, who was not forced by dire necessity, should quit her house that day.

Indeed, egress seemed next to impossible; the drift darkened the lower panes of the casement, and, on looking out, one saw the sky and air vexed and dim, the wind and snow in angry conflict. There was no fall now, but what had already descended was torn up from the earth, whirled round by brief shrieking gusts, and cast into a hundred fantastic forms.

The Countess seconded Mrs. Bretton.

"Papa shall not go out," said she, placing a seat for herself beside her father's arm-chair. "I will look after him. You won't go into town, will you, papa?"

"Ay, and no," was the answer. "If you and Mrs. Bretton are *very* good to me, Polly – kind, you know, and attentive; if you pet me in a very nice manner, and make much of me, I may possibly be induced to wait an hour after breakfast and see whether this razor-edged wind settles. But, you see, you give me no breakfast; you offer me nothing: you let me starve."

"Quick! Please, Mrs. Bretton, and pour out the coffee," entreated Paulina, "whilst I take care of the Count de Bassompierre in other respects: since he grew into a Count, he has needed *so* much attention."

She separated and prepared a roll.

"There, papa, are your 'pistolets' charged," said she. "And there is some marmalade, just the same sort of marmalade we used to have at Bretton, and which you said was as good as if it had been conserved in Scotland –"

"And which your little ladyship used to beg for my boy – do you remember that?" interposed Mrs. Bretton. "Have you forgotten how you would come to my elbow and touch my sleeve with the whisper, 'Please, ma'am, something good for Graham – a little marmalade, or honey, or jam?'"

"No, mamma," broke in Dr. John, laughing, yet reddening; "it surely was not so: I could not have cared for these things."

"Did he or did he not, Paulina?"

"He liked them," asserted Paulina.

"Never blush for it, John," said Mr. Home, encouragingly. "I like them myself yet, and always did. And Polly showed her sense in catering for a friend's material comforts: it was I who put her into the way of such good manners – nor do I let her forget them. Polly, offer me a small slice of that tongue."

"There, papa: but remember you are only waited upon with this assiduity; on condition of being persuadable, and reconciling yourself to La Terrasse for the day."

"Mrs. Bretton," said the Count, "I want to get rid of my daughter – to send her to school. Do you know of any good school?"

"There is Lucy's place – Madame Beck's."

"Miss Snowe is in a school?"

"I am a teacher," I said, and was rather glad of the opportunity of saying this. For a little while I had been feeling as if placed in a false position. Mrs. Bretton and son knew my circumstances; but the Count and his daughter did not. They might choose to vary by some shades their hitherto cordial manner towards me, when aware of my grade in society. I spoke then readily: but a swarm of thoughts I had not anticipated nor invoked, rose dim at the words, making me sigh involuntarily. Mr. Home did not lift his eyes from his breakfast-plate for about two minutes, nor did he speak; perhaps he had not caught the words – perhaps he thought that on a confession of that nature, politeness would interdict comment: the Scotch are proverbially proud; and homely as was Mr. Home in look, simple in habits and tastes, I have all along intimated that he was not without his share of the national quality. Was his a pseudo pride? Was it real dignity? I leave the question undecided in its wide sense. Where it concerned me individually I can only answer: then, and always, he showed himself a true-hearted gentleman.

By nature he was a feeler and a thinker; over his emotions and his reflections spread a mellowing of melancholy; more than a mellowing: in trouble and bereavement it became a cloud. He did not know much about Lucy Snowe; what he knew, he did not very accurately comprehend: indeed his misconceptions of my character often made me smile; but he saw my walk in life lay rather on the shady side of the hill: he gave me credit for doing my endeavour to keep the course honestly straight; he would have helped me if he could: having no opportunity of helping, he still wished me well. When he did look at me, his eye was kind; when he did speak, his voice was benevolent.

"Yours," said he, "is an arduous calling. I wish you health and strength to win in it – success."

His fair little daughter did not take the information quite so composedly: she fixed on me a pair of eyes wide with wonder – almost with dismay.

"Are you a teacher?" cried she. Then, having paused on the unpalatable idea, "Well, I never knew what you were, nor ever thought of asking: for me, you were always Lucy Snowe."

"And what am I now?" I could not forbear inquiring.

"Yourself, of course. But do you really teach here, in Villette?"

"I really do."

"And do you like it?"

"Not always."

"And why do you go on with it?"

Her father looked at, and, I feared, was going to check her; but he only said, "Proceed, Polly, proceed with that catechism – prove yourself the little wiseacre you are. If Miss Snowe were to blush and look confused, I should have to bid you hold your tongue; and you and I would sit out the present meal in some disgrace; but she only smiles, so push her hard, multiply the cross-questions. Well, Miss Snowe, why do you go on with it?"

"Chiefly, I fear, for the sake of the money I get."

"Not then from motives of pure philanthropy? Polly and I were clinging to that hypothesis as the most lenient way of accounting for your eccentricity."

"No – no, sir. Rather for the roof of shelter I am thus enabled to keep over my head; and for the comfort of mind it gives me to think that while I can work for myself, I am spared the pain of being a burden to anybody."

"Papa, say what you will, I pity Lucy."

"Take up that pity, Miss de Bassompierre; take it up in both hands, as you might a little callow gosling squattering out of bounds without leave; put it back in the warm nest of a heart whence it issued, and receive in your ear this whisper. If my Polly ever came to know by experience the uncertain nature of this world's goods, I should like her to act as Lucy acts: to work for herself, that she might burden neither kith nor kin."

"Yes, papa," said she, pensively and tractably. "But poor Lucy! I thought she was a rich lady, and had rich friends."

"You thought like a little simpleton. *I* never thought so. When I had time to consider Lucy's manner and aspect, which was not often, I saw she was one who had to guard and not be guarded; to act and not be served: and this lot has, I imagine, helped her to an experience for which, if she live long enough to realize its full benefit, she may yet bless Providence. But this school," he pursued, changing his tone from grave to gay: "would Madame Beck admit my Polly, do you think, Miss Lucy?"

I said, there needed but to try Madame; it would soon be seen: she was fond of English pupils. "If you, sir," I added, "will but take Miss de Bassompierre in your carriage this very afternoon, I think I can answer for it that Rosine, the portress, will not be very slow in answering your ring; and Madame, I am sure, will put on her best pair of gloves to come into the salon to receive you."

"In that case," responded Mr. Home, "I see no sort of necessity there is for delay. Mrs. Hurst can send what she calls her young lady's 'things' after her; Polly can settle down to her horn-book before night; and you, Miss Lucy, I trust, will not disdain to cast an occasional eye upon her, and let me know, from time to time, how she gets on. I hope you approve of the arrangement, Countess de Bassompierre?"

The Countess hemmed and hesitated. "I thought," said she, "I thought I had finished my education –"

"That only proves how much we may be mistaken in our thoughts. I hold a far different opinion, as most of these will who have been auditors of your profound knowledge of life this morning. Ah, my little girl, thou hast much to learn; and papa ought to have taught thee more than he has done! Come, there is nothing for it but to try Madame Beck; and the weather seems settling, and I have finished my breakfast –"

"But, papa!"

"Well?"

"I see an obstacle."

"I don't at all."

"It is enormous, papa; it can never be got over; it is as large as you in your greatcoat, and the snowdrift on the top."

"And, like that snowdrift, capable of melting?"

"No! It is of too – too solid flesh: it is just your own self. Miss Lucy, warn Madame Beck not to listen to any overtures about taking me, because, in the end, it would turn out that she would have to take papa too: as he is so teasing, I will just tell tales about him. Mrs. Bretton and all of you listen: About five years ago, when I was twelve years old, he took it into his head that he was spoiling me; that I was growing unfitted for the world, and I don't know what, and nothing would serve or satisfy him, but I must go to school. I cried, and so on; but M. de Bassompierre proved hard-hearted, quite firm and flinty, and to school I went. What was the result? In the most admirable manner, papa came to school likewise: every other day he called to see me. Madame Aigredoux grumbled, but it was of no use; and so, at last, papa and I were both, in a manner, expelled. Lucy can just tell Madame Beck this little trait: it is only fair to let her know what she has to expect."

Mrs. Bretton asked Mr. Home what he had to say in answer to this statement. As he made no defence, judgment was given against him, and Paulina triumphed.

But she had other moods besides the arch and naïve. After breakfast; when the two elders withdrew – I suppose to talk over certain of Mrs. Bretton's business matters – and the Countess, Dr. Bretton, and I, were for a short time alone together – all the child left her; with us, more nearly her companions in age, she rose at once to the little lady: her very face seemed to alter; that play of feature, and candour of look, which, when she spoke to her father, made it quite dimpled and round, yielded to an aspect more thoughtful, and lines distincter and less *mobile*.

No doubt Graham noted the change as well as I. He stood for some minutes near the window, looking out at the snow; presently he approached the hearth, and entered into conversation, but not quite with his usual ease: fit topics did not seem to rise to his lips; he chose them fastidiously, hesitatingly, and consequently infelicitously: he spoke vaguely of Villette – its inhabitants, its notable sights and buildings. He was answered by Miss de Bassompierre in quite womanly sort; with intelligence, with a manner not indeed wholly disindividualized: a tone, a glance, a gesture, here and there, rather animated and quick than measured and stately, still recalled little Polly; but yet there was so fine and even a polish, so calm and courteous a grace, gilding and sustaining these peculiarities, that a less sensitive man than Graham would not have ventured to seize upon them as vantage points, leading to franker intimacy.

Yet while Dr. Bretton continued subdued, and, for him, sedate, he was still observant. Not one of those petty impulses and natural breaks escaped him. He did not miss one characteristic movement, one hesitation in language, or one lisp in utterance. At times, in speaking fast, she still lisped; but coloured whenever such lapse occurred, and in a painstaking, conscientious manner, quite as amusing as the slight error, repeated the word more distinctly.

Whenever she did this, Dr. Bretton smiled. Gradually, as they conversed, the restraint on each side slackened: might the conference have but been prolonged, I believe it would soon have become genial: already to Paulina's lip and cheek returned the wreathing, dimpling smile; she lisped once, and forgot to correct herself. And Dr. John, I know not how *he* changed, but change he did. He did not grow gayer – no raillery, no levity sparkled across his aspect – but his position seemed to become one of more pleasure to himself, and he spoke his augmented comfort in readier language, in tones more suave. Ten years ago this pair had always found abundance to say to each other; the intervening decade had not narrowed the experience or impoverished the intelligence of either: besides, there are certain natures of which the mutual influence is such, that the more they say, the more they have to say. For these out of association grows adhesion, and out of adhesion, amalgamation.

Graham, however, must go: his was a profession whose claims are neither to be ignored nor deferred. He left the room; but before he could leave the house there was a return. I am sure he came back – not for the paper, or card in his desk, which formed his ostensible errand – but to assure himself, by one more glance, that Paulina's aspect was really such as memory was bearing away: that he had not been viewing her somehow by a partial, artificial light, and making a fond mistake. No! He found the impression true – rather, indeed, he gained than lost by this return: he took away with him a parting look – shy, but very soft – as beautiful, as innocent, as any little fawn could lift out of its cover of fern, or any lamb from its meadow-bed.

Being left alone, Paulina and I kept silence for some time: we both took out some work, and plied a mute and diligent task. The white-wood workbox of old days was now replaced by one inlaid with precious mosaic, and furnished with implements of gold; the tiny and trembling fingers that could scarce guide the needle, though tiny still, were now swift and skilful: but there was the same busy knitting of the brow, the same little dainty mannerisms, the same quick turns and movements – now to replace a stray tress, and anon to shake from the silken skirt some imaginary atom of dust – some clinging fibre of thread.

That morning I was disposed for silence: the austere fury of the winter-day had on me an awing, hushing influence. That passion of January, so white and so bloodless, was not yet spent: the storm had raved itself hoarse, but seemed no nearer exhaustion. Had Ginevra Fanshawe been my companion in that drawing-room, she would not have suffered me to muse and listen undisturbed. The presence just gone from us would have been her theme; and how she would have rung the changes on one topic! How she would have pursued and pestered me with questions and surmises – worried and oppressed me with comments and confidences I did not want, and longed to avoid.

Paulina Mary cast once or twice towards me a quiet but penetrating glance of her dark, full eye; her lips half opened, as if to the impulse of coming utterance: but she saw and delicately respected my inclination for silence.

"This will not hold long," I thought to myself; for I was not accustomed to find in women or girls any power of self-control, or strength of self-denial. As far as I knew them, the chance of a gossip about their usually trivial secrets, their often very washy and paltry feelings, was a treat not to be readily foregone.

The little Countess promised an exception: she sewed till she was tired of sewing, and then she took a book.

As chance would have it, she had sought it in Dr. Bretton's own compartment of the bookcase; and it proved to be an old Bretton book – some illustrated work of natural history. Often had I seen her standing at Graham's side, resting that volume on his knee, and reading to his tuition; and, when the lesson was over, begging, as a treat, that he would tell her all about the pictures. I watched her keenly: here was a true test of that memory she had boasted; would her recollections now be faithful?

Faithful? It could not be doubted. As she turned the leaves, over her face passed gleam after gleam of expression, the least intelligent of which was a full greeting to the Past. And then she turned to the title-page, and looked at the name written in the schoolboy hand. She looked at it long; nor was she satisfied with merely looking: she gently passed over the characters the tips of her fingers, accompanying the action with an unconscious but tender smile, which converted the touch into a caress. Paulina loved the Past; but the peculiarity of this little scene was, that she *said* nothing: she could feel without pouring out her feelings in a flux of words.

She now occupied herself at the bookcase for nearly an hour; taking down volume after volume, and renewing her acquaintance with each. This done, she seated herself on a low stool, rested her cheek on her hand, and thought, and still was mute.

The sound of the front door opened below, a rush of cold wind, and her father's voice speaking to Mrs. Bretton in the hall, startled her at last. She sprang up: she was downstairs in one second.

"Papa! Papa! You are not going out?"

"My pet, I must go into town."

"But it is too – *too* cold, papa."

And then I heard M. de Bassompierre showing to her how he was well provided against the weather; and how he was going to have the carriage, and to be quite snugly sheltered; and, in short, proving that she need not fear for his comfort.

"But you will promise to come back here this evening, before it is quite dark; – you and Dr. Bretton, both, in the carriage? It is not fit to ride."

"Well, if I see the Doctor, I will tell him a lady has laid on him her commands to take care of his precious health and come home early under my escort."

"Yes, you must say a lady; and he will think it is his mother, and be obedient. And, papa, mind to come soon, for I *shall* watch and listen."

The door closed, and the carriage rolled softly through the snow; and back returned the Countess, pensive and anxious.

She *did* listen, and watch, when evening closed; but it was in stillest sort: walking the drawing-room with quite noiseless step. She checked at intervals her velvet march; inclined her ear, and consulted the night sounds: I should rather say, the night silence; for now, at last, the wind was fallen. The sky, relieved of its avalanche, lay naked and pale: through the barren boughs of the avenue we could see it well, and note also the polar splendour of the new-year moon – an orb white as a world of ice. Nor was it late when we saw also the return of the carriage.

Paulina had no dance of welcome for this evening. It was with a sort of gravity that she took immediate possession of her father, as he entered the room; but she at once made him her entire property, led him to the seat of her choice, and, while softly showering round him honeyed words of commendation for being so good and coming home so soon, you would have thought it was entirely by the power of her little hands he was put into his chair, and settled and arranged; for the strong man seemed to take pleasure in wholly yielding himself to this dominion-potent only by love.

Graham did not appear till some minutes after the Count. Paulina half turned when his step was heard: they spoke, but only a word or two; their fingers met a moment, but obviously with slight contact. Paulina remained beside her father; Graham threw himself into a seat on the other side of the room.

It was well that Mrs. Bretton and Mr. Home had a great deal to say to each other – almost an inexhaustible fund of discourse in old recollections; otherwise, I think, our party would have been but a still one that evening.

After tea, Paulina's quick needle and pretty golden thimble were busily plied by the lamp-light, but her tongue rested, and her eyes seemed reluctant to raise often their lids, so smooth and so full-fringed. Graham, too, must have been tired with his day's work: he listened dutifully to his elders and betters, said very little himself, and followed with his eye the gilded glance of Paulina's thimble; as if it had been some bright moth on the wing, or the golden head of some darting little yellow serpent.

Chapter Twenty-Six
A Burial

FROM THIS DATE my life did not want variety; I went out a good deal, with the entire consent of Madame Beck, who perfectly approved the grade of my acquaintance. That worthy directress had never from the first treated me otherwise than with respect; and when she found that I was liable to frequent invitations from a château and a great hotel, respect improved into distinction.

Not that she was fulsome about it: Madame, in all things worldly, was in nothing weak; there was measure and sense in her hottest pursuit of self-interest, calm and considerateness in her closest clutch of gain; without, then, laying herself open to my contempt as a time-server and a toadie, she marked with tact that she was pleased people connected with her establishment should frequent such associates as must cultivate and elevate, rather than those who might deteriorate and depress. She never praised either me or my friends; only once when she was sitting in the sun in the garden, a cup of coffee at her elbow and the Gazette in her hand, looking very comfortable, and I came up and asked leave of absence for the evening, she delivered herself in this gracious sort:

"*Oui, oui, ma bonne amie: je vous donne la permission de coeur et de gré. Votre travail dans ma maison a toujours été admirable, rempli de zèle et de discrétion: vous avez bien le droit de vous amuser. Sortez donc tant que vous voudrez. Quant à votre choix de connaissances, j'en suis contente; c'est sage, digne, laudable.*"

She closed her lips and resumed the Gazette.

The reader will not too gravely regard the little circumstance that about this time the triply-enclosed packet of five letters temporarily disappeared from my bureau. Blank dismay was naturally my first sensation on making the discovery; but in a moment I took heart of grace.

"Patience!" whispered I to myself. "Let me say nothing, but wait peaceably; they will come back again."

And they did come back: they had only been on a short visit to Madame's chamber; having passed their examination, they came back duly and truly: I found them all right the next day.

I wonder what she thought of my correspondence? What estimate did she form of Dr. John Bretton's epistolary powers? In what light did the often very pithy thoughts, the generally sound, and sometimes original opinions, set, without pretension, in an easily-flowing, spirited style, appear to her? How did she like that genial, half humorous vein, which to me gave such delight? What did she think of the few kind words scattered here and there – not thickly, as the diamonds were scattered in the valley of Sindbad, but sparely, as those gems lie in unfabled beds? Oh, Madame Beck! How seemed these things to you?

I think in Madame Beck's eyes the five letters found a certain favour. One day after she had *borrowed* them of me (in speaking of so suave a little woman, one ought to use suave terms), I caught her examining me with a steady contemplative gaze, a little puzzled, but not at all malevolent. It was during that brief space between lessons, when the pupils turned out into the court for a quarter of an hour's recreation; she and I remained in the first classe alone: when I met her eye, her thoughts forced themselves partially through her lips.

"*Il y a,*" said she, "*quelquechose de bien remarquable dans le caractère Anglais.*"

"How, Madame?"

She gave a little laugh, repeating the word 'how' in English.

"*Je ne saurais vous dire* 'how'; *mais, enfin, les Anglais ont des idées à eux, en amitié, en amour, en tout. Mais au moins il n'est pas besoin de les surveiller,*" she added, getting up and trotting away like the compact little pony she was.

"Then I hope," murmured I to myself, "you will graciously let alone my letters for the future."

Alas! Something came rushing into my eyes, dimming utterly their vision, blotting from sight the schoolroom, the garden, the bright winter sun, as I remembered that never more would letters, such as she had read, come to me. I had seen the last of them. That goodly river on whose banks I had sojourned, of whose waves a few reviving drops had trickled to my lips, was bending to another course: it was leaving my little hut and field forlorn and sand-dry, pouring its wealth of waters far away. The change was right, just, natural; not a word could be said: but I loved my Rhine, my Nile; I had almost worshipped my Ganges, and I grieved that the grand tide should roll estranged, should vanish like a false mirage. Though stoical, I was not quite a stoic; drops streamed fast on my hands, on my desk: I wept one sultry shower, heavy and brief.

But soon I said to myself, "The Hope I am bemoaning suffered and made me suffer much: it did not die till it was full time: following an agony so lingering, death ought to be welcome."

Welcome I endeavoured to make it. Indeed, long pain had made patience a habit. In the end I closed the eyes of my dead, covered its face, and composed its limbs with great calm.

The letters, however, must be put away, out of sight: people who have undergone bereavement always jealously gather together and lock away mementos: it is not supportable to be stabbed to the heart each moment by sharp revival of regret.

One vacant holiday afternoon (the Thursday) going to my treasure, with intent to consider its final disposal, I perceived – and this time with a strong impulse of displeasure – that it had been again tampered with: the packet was there, indeed, but the ribbon which secured it had been untied and retied; and by other symptoms I knew that my drawer had been visited.

This was a little too much. Madame Beck herself was the soul of discretion, besides having as strong a brain and sound a judgment as ever furnished a human head; that she should know the contents of my casket, was not pleasant, but might be borne. Little Jesuit inquisitress as she was, she could see things in a true light, and understand them in an unperverted sense; but the idea that she had ventured to communicate information, thus gained, to others; that she had, perhaps, amused herself with a companion over documents, in my eyes most sacred, shocked me cruelly. Yet, that such was the case I now saw reason to fear; I even guessed her confidant. Her kinsman, M. Paul Emanuel, had spent yesterday evening with her: she was much in the habit of consulting him, and of discussing with him matters she broached to no one else. This very morning, in class, that gentleman had favoured me with a glance which he seemed to have borrowed from Vashti, the actress; I had not at the moment comprehended that blue, yet lurid, flash out of his angry eye; but I read its meaning now. *He*, I believed, was not apt to regard what concerned me from a fair point of view, nor to judge me with tolerance and candour: I had always found him severe and suspicious: the thought that these letters, mere friendly letters as they were, had fallen once, and might fall again, into his hands, jarred my very soul.

What should I do to prevent this? In what corner of this strange house was it possible to find security or secrecy? Where could a key be a safeguard, or a padlock a barrier?

In the grenier? No, I did not like the grenier. Besides, most of the boxes and drawers there were mouldering, and did not lock. Rats, too, gnawed their way through the decayed wood; and mice made nests amongst the litter of their contents: my dear letters (most dear still, though Ichabod was written on their covers) might be consumed by vermin; certainly the writing would soon become obliterated by damp. No; the grenier would not do – but where then?

While pondering this problem, I sat in the dormitory window-seat. It was a fine frosty afternoon; the winter sun, already setting, gleamed pale on the tops of the garden-shrubs in the 'allée défendue'. One great old pear-tree – the nun's pear-tree – stood up a tall dryad skeleton, grey, gaunt, and stripped. A thought struck me – one of those queer fantastic thoughts that will sometimes strike solitary people. I put on my bonnet, cloak, and furs, and went out into the city.

Bending my steps to the old historical quarter of the town, whose hoax and overshadowed precincts I always sought by instinct in melancholy moods, I wandered on from street to street, till, having crossed a half deserted 'place' or square, I found myself before a sort of broker's shop; an ancient place, full of ancient things. What I wanted was a metal box which might be soldered, or a thick glass jar or bottle which might be stoppered or sealed hermetically. Amongst miscellaneous heaps, I found and purchased the latter article.

I then made a little roll of my letters, wrapped them in oiled silk, bound them with twine, and, having put them in the bottle, got the old Jew broker to stopper, seal, and make it air-tight. While obeying my directions, he glanced at me now and then suspiciously from under his frost-white eyelashes. I believe he thought there was some evil deed on hand. In all this I had a dreary something – not pleasure – but a sad, lonely satisfaction. The impulse under which I acted, the mood controlling me, were similar to the impulse and the mood which had induced me to visit the confessional. With quick walking I regained the pensionnat just at dark, and in time for dinner.

At seven o'clock the moon rose. At half-past seven, when the pupils and teachers were at study, and Madame Beck was with her mother and children in the salle-à-manger, when the half-boarders were all gone home, and Rosine had left the vestibule, and all was still – I shawled myself, and, taking the sealed jar, stole out through the first-classe door, into the berceau and thence into the 'allée défendue'.

Methusaleh, the pear-tree, stood at the further end of this walk, near my seat: he rose up, dim and grey, above the lower shrubs round him. Now Methusaleh, though so very old, was of sound timber still; only there was a hole, or rather a deep hollow, near his root. I knew there was such a hollow, hidden partly by ivy and creepers growing thick round; and there I meditated hiding my treasure. But I was not only going to hide a treasure – I meant also to bury a grief. That grief over which I had lately been weeping, as I wrapped it in its winding-sheet, must be interred.

Well, I cleared away the ivy, and found the hole; it was large enough to receive the jar, and I thrust it deep in. In a tool-shed at the bottom of the garden, lay the relics of building-materials, left by masons lately employed to repair a part of the premises. I fetched thence a slate and some mortar, put the slate on the hollow, secured it with cement, covered the hole with black mould, and, finally, replaced the ivy. This done, I rested, leaning against the tree; lingering, like any other mourner, beside a newly-sodded grave.

The air of the night was very still, but dim with a peculiar mist, which changed the moonlight into a luminous haze. In this air, or this mist, there was some quality – electrical, perhaps – which acted in strange sort upon me. I felt then as I had felt a year ago in England – on a night when the aurora borealis was streaming and sweeping round heaven, when, belated in lonely fields, I had paused to watch that mustering of an army with banners – that quivering of serried lances – that swift ascent of messengers from below the north star to the dark, high keystone of heaven's arch. I felt, not happy, far otherwise, but strong with reinforced strength.

If life be a war, it seemed my destiny to conduct it single-handed. I pondered now how to break up my winter-quarters – to leave an encampment where food and forage failed. Perhaps, to effect this change, another pitched battle must be fought with fortune; if so, I had a mind to the encounter: too poor to lose, God might destine me to gain. But what road was open? – What plan available?

On this question I was still pausing, when the moon, so dim hitherto, seemed to shine out somewhat brighter: a ray gleamed even white before me, and a shadow became distinct and marked. I looked more narrowly, to make out the cause of this well-defined contrast appearing a little suddenly in the obscure alley: whiter and blacker it grew on my eye: it took shape with instantaneous transformation. I stood about three yards from a tall, sable-robed, snowy-veiled woman.

Five minutes passed. I neither fled nor shrieked. She was there still.

I spoke. "Who are you? And why do you come to me?"

She stood mute. She had no face – no features: all below her brow was masked with a white cloth; but she had eyes, and they viewed me.

I felt, if not brave, yet a little desperate; and desperation will often suffice to fill the post and do the work of courage. I advanced one step. I stretched out my hand, for I meant to touch her. She seemed to recede. I drew nearer: her recession, still silent, became swift. A mass of shrubs, full-leaved evergreens, laurel and dense yew, intervened between me and what I followed. Having passed that obstacle, I looked and saw nothing. I waited. I said, – "If you have any errand to men, come back and deliver it." Nothing spoke or re-appeared.

This time there was no Dr. John to whom to have recourse: there was no one to whom I dared whisper the words, "I have again seen the nun."

* * *

Paulina Mary sought my frequent presence in the Rue Crécy. In the old Bretton days, though she had never professed herself fond of me, my society had soon become to her a sort of unconscious necessary. I used to notice that if I withdrew to my room, she would speedily come trotting after me, and opening the door and peeping in, say, with her little peremptory accent, – "Come down. Why do you sit here by yourself? You must come into the parlour."

In the same spirit she urged me now – "Leave the Rue Fossette," she said, "and come and live with us. Papa would give you far more than Madame Beck gives you."

Mr. Home himself offered me a handsome sum – thrice my present salary – if I would accept the office of companion to his daughter. I declined. I think I should have declined had I been poorer than I was, and with scantier fund of resource, more stinted narrowness of future prospect. I had not that vocation. I could teach; I could give lessons; but to be either a private governess or a companion was unnatural to me. Rather than fill the former post in any great house, I would deliberately have taken a housemaid's place, bought a strong pair of gloves, swept bedrooms and staircases, and cleaned stoves and locks, in peace and independence. Rather than be a companion, I would have made shirts and starved.

I was no bright lady's shadow – not Miss de Bassompierre's. Overcast enough it was my nature often to be; of a subdued habit I was: but the dimness and depression must both be voluntary – such as kept me docile at my desk, in the midst of my now well-accustomed pupils in Madame Beck's fist classe; or alone, at my own bedside, in her dormitory, or in the alley and seat which were called mine, in her garden: my qualifications were not convertible, nor adaptable; they could not be made the foil of any gem, the adjunct of any beauty, the appendage of any greatness in Christendom. Madame Beck and I, without assimilating, understood each other well. I was not *her* companion, nor her children's governess; she left me free: she tied me to nothing – not to herself – not even to her interests: once, when she had for a fortnight been called from home by a near relation's illness, and on her return, all anxious and full of care about her establishment, lest something in her absence should have gone wrong finding that matters had proceeded much as usual, and that there was no evidence of glaring neglect – she made each of the teachers a present, in acknowledgment of steadiness. To my bedside she came at twelve o'clock at night, and told me she had no present for me: "I must make fidelity advantageous to the St. Pierre," said she; "if I attempt to make it advantageous to you, there will arise misunderstanding between us – perhaps separation. One thing, however, I *can* do to please you – leave you alone with your liberty: *c'est-ce que je ferai.*" She kept her word. Every slight shackle she had ever laid on me, she, from that time, with quiet hand removed. Thus I had pleasure in voluntarily respecting her rules: gratification in devoting double time, in taking double pains with the pupils she committed to my charge.

As to Mary de Bassompierre, I visited her with pleasure, though I would not live with her. My visits soon taught me that it was unlikely even my occasional and voluntary society would long be indispensable to her. M. de Bassompierre, for his part, seemed impervious to this conjecture, blind to this possibility; unconscious as any child to the signs, the likelihoods, the fitful beginnings of what, when it drew to an end, he might not approve.

Whether or not he would cordially approve, I used to speculate. Difficult to say. He was much taken up with scientific interests; keen, intent, and somewhat oppugnant in what concerned his favourite pursuits, but unsuspicious and trustful in the ordinary affairs of life. From all I could gather, he seemed to regard his 'daughterling' as still but a child, and probably had not yet admitted the notion that others might look on her in a different light: he would speak of what should be done when 'Polly' was a woman, when she should be grown up; and 'Polly', standing beside his chair, would sometimes smile and take his honoured head between her little hands, and kiss his iron-grey locks; and, at other times, she would pout and toss her curls: but she never said, "Papa, I *am* grown up."

She had different moods for different people. With her father she really was still a child, or child-like, affectionate, merry, and playful. With me she was serious, and as womanly as thought and feeling could make her. With Mrs. Bretton she was docile and reliant, but not expansive. With Graham she was shy, at present very shy; at moments she tried to be cold; on occasion she endeavoured to shun him. His step made her start; his entrance hushed her; when he spoke, her answers failed of fluency; when he took leave, she remained self-vexed and disconcerted. Even her father noticed this demeanour in her.

"My little Polly," he said once, "you live too retired a life; if you grow to be a woman with these shy manners, you will hardly be fitted for society. You really make quite a stranger of Dr. Bretton: how is this? Don't you remember that, as a little girl, you used to be rather partial to him?"

"*Rather*, papa," echoed she, with her slightly dry, yet gentle and simple tone.

"And you don't like him now? What has he done?"

"Nothing. Y-e-s, I like him a little; but we are grown strange to each other."

"Then rub it off, Polly; rub the rust and the strangeness off. Talk away when he is here, and have no fear of him?"

"*He* does not talk much. Is he afraid of me, do you think, papa?"

"Oh, to be sure, what man would not be afraid of such a little silent lady?"

"Then tell him some day not to mind my being silent. Say that it is my way, and that I have no unfriendly intention."

"Your way, you little chatter-box? So far from being your way, it is only your whim!"

"Well, I'll improve, papa."

And very pretty was the grace with which, the next day, she tried to keep her word. I saw her make the effort to converse affably with Dr. John on general topics. The attention called into her guest's face a pleasurable glow; he met her with caution, and replied to her in his softest tones, as if there was a kind of gossamer happiness hanging in the air which he feared to disturb by drawing too deep a breath. Certainly, in her timid yet earnest advance to friendship, it could not be denied that there was a most exquisite and fairy charm.

When the Doctor was gone, she approached her father's chair.

"Did I keep my word, papa? Did I behave better?"

"My Polly behaved like a queen. I shall become quite proud of her if this improvement continues. By-and-by we shall see her receiving my guests with quite a calm, grand manner. Miss Lucy and I will have to look about us, and polish up all our best airs and graces lest we should be thrown into the shade. Still, Polly, there is a little flutter, a little tendency to stammer now and then, and even, to lisp as you lisped when you were six years old."

"No, papa," interrupted she indignantly, "that can't be true."

"I appeal to Miss Lucy. Did she not, in answering Dr. Bretton's question as to whether she had ever seen the palace of the Prince of Bois l'Etang, say, 'yeth', she had been there 'theveral' times?"

"Papa, you are satirical, you are méchant! I can pronounce all the letters of the alphabet as clearly as you can. But tell me this – you are very particular in making me be civil to Dr. Bretton, do you like him yourself?"

"To be sure: for old acquaintance sake I like him: then he is a very good son to his mother; besides being a kind-hearted fellow and clever in his profession: yes, the callant is well enough."

"*Callant*! Ah, Scotchman! Papa, is it the Edinburgh or the Aberdeen accent you have?"

"Both, my pet, both: and doubtless the Glaswegian into the bargain. It is that which enables me to speak French so well: a gude Scots tongue always succeeds well at the French."

"*The* French! Scotch again: incorrigible papa. You, too, need schooling."

"Well, Polly, you must persuade Miss Snowe to undertake both you and me; to make you steady and womanly, and me refined and classical."

The light in which M. de Bassompierre evidently regarded 'Miss Snowe', used to occasion me much inward edification. What contradictory attributes of character we sometimes find ascribed to us, according to the eye with which we are viewed! Madame Beck esteemed me learned and blue; Miss Fanshawe, caustic, ironic, and cynical; Mr. Home, a model teacher, the essence of the sedate and discreet: somewhat conventional, perhaps, too strict, limited, and scrupulous, but still the pink and pattern of governess-correctness; whilst another person, Professor Paul Emanuel, to wit, never lost an opportunity of intimating his opinion that mine was rather a fiery and rash nature – adventurous, indocile, and audacious. I smiled at them all. If anyone knew me it was little Paulina Mary.

As I would not be Paulina's nominal and paid companion, genial and harmonious as I began to find her intercourse, she persuaded me to join her in some study, as a regular and settled means of sustaining communication: she proposed the German language, which, like myself, she found difficult of mastery. We agreed to take our lessons in the Rue Crécy of the same mistress; this arrangement threw us together for some hours of every week. M. de Bassompierre seemed quite pleased: it perfectly met his approbation, that Madame Minerva Gravity should associate a portion of her leisure with that of his fair and dear child.

That other self-elected judge of mine, the professor in the Rue Fossette, discovering by some surreptitious spying means, that I was no longer so stationary as hitherto, but went out regularly at certain hours of certain days, took it upon himself to place me under surveillance. People said M. Emanuel had been brought up amongst Jesuits. I should more readily have accredited this report had his manoeuvres been better masked. As it was, I doubted it. Never was a more undisguised schemer, a franker, looser intriguer. He would analyze his own machinations: elaborately contrive plots, and forthwith indulge in explanatory boasts of their skill. I know not whether I was more amused or provoked, by his stepping up to me one morning and whispering solemnly that he "had his eye on me: *he* at least would discharge the duty of a friend, and not leave me entirely to my own devices. My proceedings seemed at present very unsettled: he did not know what to make of them: he thought his cousin Beck very much to blame in suffering this sort of fluttering inconsistency in a teacher attached to her house. What had a person devoted to a serious calling, that of education, to do with Counts and Countesses, hotels and châteaux? To him, I seemed altogether 'en l'air'. On his faith, he believed I went out six days in the seven."

I said, "Monsieur exaggerated. I certainly had enjoyed the advantage of a little change lately, but not before it had become necessary; and the privilege was by no means exercised in excess."

"Necessary! How was it necessary? I was well enough, he supposed? Change necessary! He would recommend me to look at the Catholic 'religieuses', and study *their* lives. *They* asked no change."

I am no judge of what expression crossed my face when he thus spoke, but it was one which provoked him: he accused me of being reckless, worldly, and epicurean; ambitious of greatness, and feverishly athirst for the pomps and vanities of life. It seems I had no 'dévouement', no 'récueillement' in my character; no spirit of grace, faith, sacrifice, or self-abasement. Feeling the inutility of answering these charges, I mutely continued the correction of a pile of English exercises.

"He could see in me nothing Christian: like many other Protestants, I revelled in the pride and self-will of paganism."

I slightly turned from him, nestling still closer under the wing of silence.

A vague sound grumbled between his teeth; it could not surely be a 'juron': he was too religious for that; but I am certain I heard the word 'sacré'. Grievous to relate, the same word was repeated, with the unequivocal addition of mille something, when I passed him about two hours afterwards in the corridor, prepared to go and take my German lesson in the Rue Crécy. Never was a better little man, in some points, than M. Paul: never, in others, a more waspish little despot.

* * *

Our German mistress, Fräulein Anna Braun, was a worthy, hearty woman, of about forty-five; she ought, perhaps, to have lived in the days of Queen Elizabeth, as she habitually consumed, for her first and second breakfasts, beer and beef: also, her direct and downright Deutsch nature seemed to suffer a sensation of cruel restraint from what she called our English reserve; though we thought we were very cordial with her: but we did not slap her on the shoulder, and if we consented to kiss her cheek, it was done quietly, and without any explosive smack. These omissions oppressed and depressed her considerably; still, on the whole, we got on very well. Accustomed to instruct foreign girls, who hardly ever will think and study for themselves – who have no idea of grappling with a difficulty, and overcoming it by dint of reflection or application – our progress, which in truth was very leisurely, seemed to astound her. In her eyes, we were a pair of glacial prodigies, cold, proud, and preternatural.

The young Countess *was* a little proud, a little fastidious: and perhaps, with her native delicacy and beauty, she had a right to these feelings; but I think it was a total mistake to ascribe them to me. I never evaded the morning salute, which Paulina would slip when she could; nor was a certain little manner of still disdain a weapon known in my armoury of defence; whereas, Paulina always kept it clear, fine, and bright, and any rough German sally called forth at once its steely glisten.

Honest Anna Braun, in some measure, felt this difference; and while she half-feared, half-worshipped Paulina, as a sort of dainty nymph – an Undine – she took refuge with me, as a being all mortal, and of easier mood.

A book we liked well to read and translate was Schiller's Ballads; Paulina soon learned to read them beautifully; the Fräulein would listen to her with a broad smile of pleasure, and say her voice sounded like music. She translated them, too, with a facile flow of language, and in a strain of kindred and poetic fervour: her cheek would flush, her lips tremblingly smile, her beauteous eyes kindle or melt as she went on. She learnt the best by heart, and would often recite them when we were alone together. One she liked well was 'Des Mädchens Klage': that is, she liked well to repeat the words, she found plaintive melody in the sound; the sense she would criticise. She murmured, as we sat over the fire one evening:

> *Du Heilige, rufe dein Kind zurück,*
> *Ich habe genossen das irdische Glück,*
> *Ich habe gelebt und geliebet!*

"Lived and loved!" said she, "is that the summit of earthly happiness, the end of life – to love? I don't think it is. It may be the extreme of mortal misery, it may be sheer waste of time, and fruitless torture of feeling. If Schiller had said to *be* loved, he might have come nearer the truth. Is not that another thing, Lucy, to be loved?"

"I suppose it may be: but why consider the subject? What is love to you? What do you know about it?"

She crimsoned, half in irritation, half in shame.

"Now, Lucy," she said, "I won't take that from you. It may be well for papa to look on me as a baby: I rather prefer that he should thus view me; but *you* know and shall learn to acknowledge that I am verging on my nineteenth year."

"No matter if it were your twenty-ninth; we will anticipate no feelings by discussion and conversation; we will not talk about love."

"Indeed, indeed!" said she – all in hurry and heat – "You may think to check and hold me in, as much as you please; but I *have* talked about it, and heard about it too; and a great deal and lately, and disagreeably and detrimentally: and in a way you wouldn't approve."

And the vexed, triumphant, pretty, naughty being laughed. I could not discern what she meant, and I would not ask her: I was nonplussed. Seeing, however, the utmost innocence in her countenance – combined with some transient perverseness and petulance – I said at last, –

"Who talks to you disagreeably and detrimentally on such matters? Who that has near access to you would dare to do it?"

"Lucy," replied she more softly, "it is a person who makes me miserable sometimes; and I wish she would keep away – I don't want her."

"But who, Paulina, can it be? You puzzle me much."

"It is – it is my cousin Ginevra. Every time she has leave to visit Mrs. Cholmondeley she calls here, and whenever she finds me alone she begins to talk about her admirers. Love, indeed! You should hear all she has to say about love."

"Oh, I have heard it," said I, quite coolly; "and on the whole, perhaps it is as well you should have heard it too: it is not to be regretted, it is all right. Yet, surely, Ginevra's mind cannot influence yours. You can look over both her head and her heart."

"She does influence me very much. She has the art of disturbing my happiness and unsettling my opinions. She hurts me through the feelings and people dearest to me."

"What does she say, Paulina? Give me some idea. There may be counteraction of the damage done."

"The people I have longest and most esteemed are degraded by her. She does not spare Mrs. Bretton – she does not spare...Graham."

"No, I daresay: and how does she mix up these with her sentiment and her...*love*? She does mix them, I suppose?"

"Lucy, she is insolent; and, I believe, false. You know Dr. Bretton. We both know him. He may be careless and proud; but when was he ever mean or slavish? Day after day she shows him to me kneeling at her feet, pursuing her like her shadow. She – repulsing him with insult, and he imploring her with infatuation. Lucy, is it true? Is any of it true?"

"It may be true that he once thought her handsome: does she give him out as still her suitor?"

"She says she might marry him any day: he only waits her consent."

"It is these tales which have caused that reserve in your manner towards Graham which your father noticed."

"They have certainly made me all doubtful about his character. As Ginevra speaks, they do not carry with them the sound of unmixed truth: I believe she exaggerates – perhaps invents – but I want to know how far."

"Suppose we bring Miss Fanshawe to some proof. Give her an opportunity of displaying the power she boasts."

"I could do that tomorrow. Papa has asked some gentlemen to dinner, all savants. Graham, who, papa is beginning to discover, is a savant, too – skilled, they say, in more than one branch of science – is among the number. Now I should be miserable to sit at table unsupported, amidst such a party. I could not talk to Messieurs A— and Z—, the Parisian Academicians: all my new credit for manner would be put in peril. You and Mrs. Bretton must come for my sake; Ginevra, at a word, will join you."

"Yes; then I will carry a message of invitation, and she shall have the chance of justifying her character for veracity."

Chapter Twenty-Seven
The Hôtel Crécy

THE MORROW turned out a more lively and busy day than we – or than I, at least – had anticipated. It seems it was the birthday of one of the young princes of Labassecour – the eldest, I think, the Duc de Dindonneau, and a general holiday was given in his honour at the schools, and especially at the principal 'Athénée', or college. The youth of that institution had also concocted, and were to present a loyal address; for which purpose they were to be assembled in the public building where the yearly examinations were conducted, and the prizes distributed. After the ceremony of presentation, an oration, or 'discours', was to follow from one of the professors.

Several of M. de Bassompierre's friends – the savants-being more or less connected with the Athénée, they were expected to attend on this occasion; together with the worshipful municipality of Villette, M. le Chevalier Staas, the burgomaster, and the parents and kinsfolk of the Athenians in general. M. de Bassompierre was engaged by his friends to accompany them; his fair daughter would, of course, be of the party, and she wrote a little note to Ginevra and myself, bidding us come early that we might join her.

As Miss Fanshawe and I were dressing in the dormitory of the Rue Fossette, she (Miss F.) suddenly burst into a laugh.

"What now?" I asked; for she had suspended the operation of arranging her attire, and was gazing at me.

"It seems so odd," she replied, with her usual half-honest half-insolent unreserve, "that you and I should now be so much on a level, visiting in the same sphere; having the same connections."

"Why, yes," said I; "I had not much respect for the connections you chiefly frequented awhile ago: Mrs. Cholmondeley and Co. would never have suited me at all."

"Who *are* you, Miss Snowe?" she inquired, in a tone of such undisguised and unsophisticated curiosity, as made me laugh in my turn.

"You used to call yourself a nursery governess; when you first came here you really had the care of the children in this house: I have seen you carry little Georgette in your arms, like a bonne – few governesses would have condescended so far – and now Madame Beck treats you with more courtesy than she treats the Parisienne, St. Pierre; and that proud chit, my cousin, makes you her bosom friend!"

"Wonderful!" I agreed, much amused at her mystification. "Who am I indeed? Perhaps a personage in disguise. Pity I don't look the character."

"I wonder you are not more flattered by all this," she went on; "you take it with strange composure. If you really are the nobody I once thought you, you must be a cool hand."

"The nobody you once thought me!" I repeated, and my face grew a little hot; but I would not be angry: of what importance was a school-girl's crude use of the terms nobody and somebody? I confined myself, therefore, to the remark that I had merely met with civility; and asked "what she saw in civility to throw the recipient into a fever of confusion?"

"One can't help wondering at some things," she persisted.

"Wondering at marvels of your own manufacture. Are you ready at last?"

"Yes; let me take your arm."

"I would rather not: we will walk side by side."

When she took my arm, she always leaned upon me her whole weight; and, as I was not a gentleman, or her lover, I did not like it.

"There, again!" she cried. "I thought, by offering to take your arm, to intimate approbation of your dress and general appearance: I meant it as a compliment."

"You did? You meant, in short, to express that you are not ashamed to be seen in the street with me? That if Mrs. Cholmondeley should be fondling her lapdog at some window, or Colonel de Hamal picking his teeth in a balcony, and should catch a glimpse of us, you would not quite blush for your companion?"

"Yes," said she, with that directness which was her best point – which gave an honest plainness to her very fibs when she told them – which was, in short, the salt, the sole preservative ingredient of a character otherwise not formed to keep.

I delegated the trouble of commenting on this 'yes' to my countenance; or rather, my under-lip voluntarily anticipated my tongue of course, reverence and solemnity were not the feelings expressed in the look I gave her.

"Scornful, sneering creature!" she went on, as we crossed a great square, and entered the quiet, pleasant park, our nearest way to the Rue Crécy. "Nobody in this world was ever such a Turk to me as you are!"

"You bring it on yourself: let me alone: have the sense to be quiet: I will let you alone."

"As if one *could* let you alone, when you are so peculiar and so mysterious!"

"The mystery and peculiarity being entirely the conception of your own brain – maggots – neither more nor less, be so good as to keep them out of my sight."

"But *are* you anybody?" persevered she, pushing her hand, in spite of me, under my arm; and that arm pressed itself with inhospitable closeness against my side, by way of keeping out the intruder.

"Yes," I said, "I am a rising character: once an old lady's companion, then a nursery-governess, now a school-teacher."

"Do – *do* tell me who you are? I'll not repeat it," she urged, adhering with ludicrous tenacity to the wise notion of an incognito she had got hold of; and she squeezed the arm of which she had now obtained full possession, and coaxed and conjured till I was obliged to pause in the park to laugh. Throughout our walk she rang the most fanciful changes on this theme; proving, by her obstinate credulity, or incredulity, her incapacity to conceive how any person not bolstered up by birth or wealth, not supported by some consciousness of name or connection, could maintain an attitude of reasonable integrity. As for me, it quite sufficed to my mental tranquillity that I was known where it imported that known I should be; the rest sat on me easily: pedigree, social position, and recondite intellectual acquisition, occupied about the same space and place in my interests and thoughts; they were my third-class lodgers – to whom could be assigned only the small sitting-room and the little back bedroom: even if the dining and drawing-rooms stood empty, I never confessed it to them, as thinking minor accommodations better suited to their circumstances. The world, I soon learned, held a different estimate: and I make no doubt, the world is very right in its view, yet believe also that I am not quite wrong in mine.

There are people whom a lowered position degrades morally, to whom loss of connection costs loss of self-respect: are not these justified in placing the highest value on that station and association which is their safeguard from debasement? If a man feels that he would become contemptible in his own eyes were it generally known that his ancestry were simple and not gentle, poor and not rich, workers and not capitalists, would it be right severely to blame him for keeping these fatal facts out of sight – for starting, trembling, quailing at the chance which threatens exposure? The longer we live, the more our experience widens; the less prone are we to judge our neighbour's conduct, to question the world's wisdom: wherever an accumulation of small defences is found, whether surrounding the prude's virtue or the man of the world's respectability, there, be sure, it is needed.

We reached the Hôtel Crécy; Paulina was ready; Mrs. Bretton was with her; and, under her escort and that of M. de Bassompierre, we were soon conducted to the place of assembly, and seated in good seats, at a convenient distance from the Tribune. The youth of the Athénée were marshalled before us, the municipality and their bourgmestre were in places of honour, the young princes, with their tutors, occupied a conspicuous position, and the body of the building was crowded with the aristocracy and first burghers of the town.

Concerning the identity of the professor by whom the 'discours' was to be delivered, I had as yet entertained neither care nor question. Some vague expectation I had that a savant would stand up and deliver a formal speech, half dogmatism to the Athenians, half flattery to the princes.

The Tribune was yet empty when we entered, but in ten minutes after it was filled; suddenly, in a second of time, a head, chest, and arms grew above the crimson desk. This head I knew: its colour, shape, port, expression, were familiar both to me and Miss Fanshawe; the blackness and closeness of cranium, the amplitude and paleness of brow, the blueness and fire of glance, were details so domesticated in the memory, and so knit with many a whimsical association, as almost by this their sudden apparition, to tickle fancy to a laugh. Indeed, I confess, for my part, I did laugh till I was warm; but then I bent my head, and made my handkerchief and a lowered veil the sole confidants of my mirth.

I think I was glad to see M. Paul; I think it was rather pleasant than otherwise, to behold him set up there, fierce and frank, dark and candid, testy and fearless, as when regnant on his estrade in class. His presence was such a surprise: I had not once thought of expecting him, though I knew he filled the chair of Belles Lettres in the college. With *him* in that Tribune, I felt sure that neither formalism nor flattery would be our doom; but for what was vouchsafed us, for what was poured suddenly, rapidly, continuously, on our heads – I own I was not prepared.

He spoke to the princes, the nobles, the magistrates, and the burghers, with just the same ease, with almost the same pointed, choleric earnestness, with which he was wont to harangue the three divisions of the Rue Fossette. The collegians he addressed, not as schoolboys, but as future citizens and embryo patriots. The times which have since come on Europe had not been foretold yet, and M. Emanuel's spirit seemed new to me. Who would have thought the flat and fat soil of Labassecour could yield political convictions and national feelings, such as were now strongly expressed? Of the bearing of his opinions I need here give no special indication; yet it may be permitted me to say that I believed the little man not more earnest than right in what he said: with all his fire he was severe and sensible; he trampled Utopian theories under his heel; he rejected wild dreams with scorn; – but when he looked in the face of tyranny – oh, then there opened a light in his eye worth seeing; and when he spoke of injustice, his voice gave no uncertain sound, but reminded me rather of the band-trumpet, ringing at twilight from the park.

I do not think his audience were generally susceptible of sharing his flame in its purity; but some of the college youth caught fire as he eloquently told them what should be their path and endeavour in their country's and in Europe's future. They gave him a long, loud, ringing cheer, as he concluded: with all his fierceness, he was their favourite professor.

As our party left the Hall, he stood at the entrance; he saw and knew me, and lifted his hat; he offered his hand in passing, and uttered the words *"Qu'en dites vous?"* – question eminently characteristic, and reminding me, even in this his moment of triumph, of that inquisitive restlessness, that absence of what I considered desirable self-control, which were amongst his faults. He should not have cared just then to ask what I thought, or what anybody thought, but he *did* care, and he was too natural to conceal, too impulsive to repress his wish. Well! If I blamed his over-eagerness, I liked his naiveté. I would have praised him: I had plenty of praise in my heart; but, alas! No words on my lips. Who *has* words at the right moment? I stammered some lame expressions; but was truly glad when other people, coming up with profuse congratulations, covered my deficiency by their redundancy.

A gentleman introduced him to M. de Bassompierre; and the Count, who had likewise been highly gratified, asked him to join his friends (for the most part M. Emanuel's likewise), and to dine with them at the Hôtel Crécy. He declined dinner, for he was a man always somewhat shy at meeting the advances of the wealthy: there was a strength of sturdy independence in the stringing of his sinews

– not obtrusive, but pleasant enough to discover as one advanced in knowledge of his character; he promised, however, to step in with his friend, M. A—, a French Academician, in the course of the evening.

At dinner that day, Ginevra and Paulina each looked, in her own way, very beautiful; the former, perhaps, boasted the advantage in material charms, but the latter shone pre-eminent for attractions more subtle and spiritual: for light and eloquence of eye, for grace of mien, for winning variety of expression. Ginevra's dress of deep crimson relieved well her light curls, and harmonized with her rose-like bloom. Paulina's attire – in fashion close, though faultlessly neat, but in texture clear and white – made the eye grateful for the delicate life of her complexion, for the soft animation of her countenance, for the tender depth of her eyes, for the brown shadow and bounteous flow of her hair – darker than that of her Saxon cousin, as were also her eyebrows, her eyelashes, her full irids, and large mobile pupils. Nature having traced all these details slightly, and with a careless hand, in Miss Fanshawe's case; and in Miss de Bassompierre's, wrought them to a high and delicate finish.

Paulina was awed by the savants, but not quite to mutism: she conversed modestly, diffidently; not without effort, but with so true a sweetness, so fine and penetrating a sense, that her father more than once suspended his own discourse to listen, and fixed on her an eye of proud delight. It was a polite Frenchman, M. Z—, a very learned, but quite a courtly man, who had drawn her into discourse. I was charmed with her French; it was faultless – the structure correct, the idioms true, the accent pure; Ginevra, who had lived half her life on the Continent, could do nothing like it; not that words ever failed Miss Fanshawe, but real accuracy and purity she neither possessed, nor in any number of years would acquire. Here, too, M. de Bassompierre was gratified; for, on the point of language, he was critical.

Another listener and observer there was; one who, detained by some exigency of his profession, had come in late to dinner. Both ladies were quietly scanned by Dr. Bretton, at the moment of taking his seat at the table; and that guarded survey was more than once renewed. His arrival roused Miss Fanshawe, who had hitherto appeared listless: she now became smiling and complacent, talked – though what she said was rarely to the purpose – or rather, was of a purpose somewhat mortifyingly below the standard of the occasion. Her light, disconnected prattle might have gratified Graham once; perhaps it pleased him still: perhaps it was only fancy which suggested the thought that, while his eye was filled and his ear fed, his taste, his keen zest, his lively intelligence, were not equally consulted and regaled. It is certain that, restless and exacting as seemed the demand on his attention, he yielded courteously all that was required: his manner showed neither pique nor coolness: Ginevra was his neighbour, and to her, during dinner, he almost exclusively confined his notice. She appeared satisfied, and passed to the drawing-room in very good spirits.

Yet, no sooner had we reached that place of refuge, than she again became flat and listless: throwing herself on a couch, she denounced both the 'discours' and the dinner as stupid affairs, and inquired of her cousin how she could hear such a set of prosaic 'gros-bonnets' as her father gathered about him. The moment the gentlemen were heard to move, her railings ceased: she started up, flew to the piano, and dashed at it with spirit. Dr. Bretton entering, one of the first, took up his station beside her. I thought he would not long maintain that post: there was a position near the hearth to which I expected to see him attracted: this position he only scanned with his eye; while *he* looked, others drew in. The grace and mind of Paulina charmed these thoughtful Frenchmen: the fineness of her beauty, the soft courtesy of her manner, her immature, but real and inbred tact, pleased their national taste; they clustered about her, not indeed to talk science; which would have rendered her dumb, but to touch on many subjects in letters, in arts, in actual life, on which it soon appeared that she had both read and reflected. I listened. I am sure that though Graham stood aloof, he listened too: his hearing as well as his vision was very fine, quick, discriminating. I knew he gathered the conversation; I felt that the mode in which it was sustained suited him exquisitely – pleased him almost to pain.

In Paulina there was more force, both of feeling and character; than most people thought – than Graham himself imagined – than she would ever show to those who did not wish to see it. To speak truth, reader, there is no excellent beauty, no accomplished grace, no reliable refinement, without strength as excellent, as complete, as trustworthy. As well might you look for good fruit and blossom on a rootless and sapless tree, as for charms that will endure in a feeble and relaxed nature. For a little while, the blooming semblance of beauty may flourish round weakness; but it cannot bear a blast: it soon fades, even in serenest sunshine. Graham would have started had any suggestive spirit whispered of the sinew and the stamina sustaining that delicate nature; but I who had known her as a child, knew or guessed by what a good and strong root her graces held to the firm soil of reality.

While Dr. Bretton listened, and waited an opening in the magic circle, his glance restlessly sweeping the room at intervals, lighted by chance on me, where I sat in a quiet nook not far from my godmother and M. de Bassompierre, who, as usual, were engaged in what Mr. Home called 'a two-handed crack': what the Count would have interpreted as a tête-à-tête. Graham smiled recognition, crossed the room, asked me how I was, told me I looked pale. I also had my own smile at my own thought: it was now about three months since Dr. John had spoken to me – a lapse of which he was not even conscious. He sat down, and became silent. His wish was rather to look than converse. Ginevra and Paulina were now opposite to him: he could gaze his fill: he surveyed both forms – studied both faces.

Several new guests, ladies as well as gentlemen, had entered the room since dinner, dropping in for the evening conversation; and amongst the gentlemen, I may incidentally observe, I had already noticed by glimpses, a severe, dark, professorial outline, hovering aloof in an inner saloon, seen only in vista. M. Emanuel knew many of the gentlemen present, but I think was a stranger to most of the ladies, excepting myself; in looking towards the hearth, he could not but see me, and naturally made a movement to approach; seeing, however, Dr. Bretton also, he changed his mind and held back. If that had been all, there would have been no cause for quarrel; but not satisfied with holding back, he puckered up his eyebrows, protruded his lip, and looked so ugly that I averted my eyes from the displeasing spectacle. M. Joseph Emanuel had arrived, as well as his austere brother, and at this very moment was relieving Ginevra at the piano. What a master-touch succeeded her school-girl jingle! In what grand, grateful tones the instrument acknowledged the hand of the true artist!

"Lucy," began Dr. Bretton, breaking silence and smiling, as Ginevra glided before him, casting a glance as she passed by, "Miss Fanshawe is certainly a fine girl."

Of course I assented.

"Is there," he pursued, "another in the room as lovely?"

"I think there is not another as handsome."

"I agree with you, Lucy: you and I do often agree in opinion, in taste, I think; or at least in judgment."

"Do we?" I said, somewhat doubtfully.

"I believe if you had been a boy, Lucy, instead of a girl – my mother's god-son instead of her god-daughter, we should have been good friends: our opinions would have melted into each other."

He had assumed a bantering air: a light, half-caressing, half-ironic, shone aslant in his eye. Ah, Graham! I have given more than one solitary moment to thoughts and calculations of your estimate of Lucy Snowe: was it always kind or just? Had Lucy been intrinsically the same but possessing the additional advantages of wealth and station, would your manner to her, your value for her, have been quite what they actually were? And yet by these questions I would not seriously infer blame. No; you might sadden and trouble me sometimes; but then mine was a soon-depressed, an easily-deranged temperament – it fell if a cloud crossed the sun. Perhaps before the eye of severe equity I should stand more at fault than you.

Trying, then, to keep down the unreasonable pain which thrilled my heart, on thus being made to feel that while Graham could devote to others the most grave and earnest, the manliest interest, he had no more than light raillery for Lucy, the friend of lang syne, I inquired calmly, – "On what points are we so closely in accordance?"

"We each have an observant faculty. You, perhaps, don't give me credit for the possession; yet I have it."

"But you were speaking of tastes: we may see the same objects, yet estimate them differently?"

"Let us bring it to the test. Of course, you cannot but render homage to the merits of Miss Fanshawe: now, what do you think of others in the room? – My mother, for instance; or the lions yonder, Messieurs A— and Z—; or, let us say, that pale little lady, Miss de Bassompierre?"

"You know what I think of your mother. I have not thought of Messieurs A— and Z—."

"And the other?"

"I think she is, as you say, a pale little lady – pale, certainly, just now, when she is fatigued with over-excitement."

"You don't remember her as a child?"

"I wonder, sometimes, whether you do."

"I had forgotten her; but it is noticeable, that circumstances, persons, even words and looks, that had slipped your memory, may, under certain conditions, certain aspects of your own or another's mind, revive."

"That is possible enough."

"Yet," he continued, "the revival is imperfect – needs confirmation, partakes so much of the dim character of a dream, or of the airy one of a fancy, that the testimony of a witness becomes necessary for corroboration. Were you not a guest at Bretton ten years ago, when Mr. Home brought his little girl, whom we then called 'little Polly', to stay with mamma?"

"I was there the night she came, and also the morning she went away."

"Rather a peculiar child, was she not? I wonder how I treated her. Was I fond of children in those days? Was there anything gracious or kindly about me – great, reckless, schoolboy as I was? But you don't recollect me, of course?"

"You have seen your own picture at La Terrasse. It is like you personally. In manner, you were almost the same yesterday as today."

"But, Lucy, how is that? Such an oracle really whets my curiosity. What am I today? What was I the yesterday of ten years back?"

"Gracious to whatever pleased you – unkindly or cruel to nothing."

"There you are wrong; I think I was almost a brute to *you*, for instance."

"A brute! No, Graham: I should never have patiently endured brutality."

"*This*, however, I *do* remember: quiet Lucy Snowe tasted nothing of my grace."

"As little of your cruelty."

"Why, had I been Nero himself, I could not have tormented a being inoffensive as a shadow."

I smiled; but I also hushed a groan. Oh! – I just wished he would let me alone – cease allusion to me. These epithets – these attributes I put from me. His 'quiet Lucy Snowe', his 'inoffensive shadow', I gave him back; not with scorn, but with extreme weariness: theirs was the coldness and the pressure of lead; let him whelm me with no such weight. Happily, he was soon on another theme.

"On what terms were 'little Polly' and I? Unless my recollections deceive me, we were not foes –"

"You speak very vaguely. Do you think little Polly's memory not more definite?"

"Oh! We don't talk of 'little Polly' *now*. Pray say, Miss de Bassompierre; and, of course, such a stately personage remembers nothing of Bretton. Look at her large eyes, Lucy; can they read a word in the page of memory? Are they the same which I used to direct to a horn-book? She does not know that I partly taught her to read."

"In the Bible on Sunday nights?"

"She has a calm, delicate, rather fine profile now: once what a little restless, anxious countenance was hers! What a thing is a child's preference – what a bubble! Would you believe it? That lady was fond of me!"

"I think she was in some measure fond of you," said I, moderately.

"You don't remember then? *I* had forgotten; but I remember *now*. She liked me the best of whatever there was at Bretton."

"You thought so."

"I quite well recall it. I wish I could tell her all I recall; or rather, I wish someone, you for instance, would go behind and whisper it all in her ear, and I could have the delight – here, as I sit – of watching her look under the intelligence. Could you manage that, think you, Lucy, and make me ever grateful?"

"Could I manage to make you ever grateful?" said I. "No, *I could not*." And I felt my fingers work and my hands interlock: I felt, too, an inward courage, warm and resistant. In this matter I was not disposed to gratify Dr. John: not at all. With now welcome force, I realized his entire misapprehension of my character and nature. He wanted always to give me a role not mine. Nature and I opposed him. He did not at all guess what I felt: he did not read my eyes, or face, or gestures; though, I doubt not, all spoke. Leaning towards me coaxingly, he said, softly, "*Do* content me, Lucy."

And I would have contented, or, at least, I would clearly have enlightened him, and taught him well never again to expect of me the part of officious soubrette in a love drama; when, following his, soft, eager, murmur, meeting almost his pleading, mellow – "*Do* content me, Lucy!" a sharp hiss pierced my ear on the other side.

"*Petite chatte, doucerette, coquette!*" sibillated the sudden boa-constrictor; "*Vous avez l'air bien triste, soumis, rêveur, mais vous ne l'êtes pas: c'est moi qui vous le dis: Sauvage! La flamme à l'âme, l'éclair aux yeux!*"

"*Oui; j'ai la flamme à l'âme, et je dois l'avoir!*" retorted I, turning in just wrath: but Professor Emanuel had hissed his insult and was gone.

The worst of the matter was, that Dr. Bretton, whose ears, as I have said, were quick and fine, caught every word of this apostrophe; he put his handkerchief to his face, and laughed till he shook.

"Well done, Lucy," cried he; "capital! *Petite chatte, petite coquette!* Oh, I must tell my mother! Is it true, Lucy, or half-true? I believe it is: you redden to the colour of Miss Fanshawe's gown. And really, by my word, now I examine him, that is the same little man who was so savage with you at the concert: the very same, and in his soul he is frantic at this moment because he sees me laughing. Oh! I must tease him."

And Graham, yielding to his bent for mischief, laughed, jested, and whispered on till I could bear no more, and my eyes filled.

Suddenly he was sobered: a vacant space appeared near Miss de Bassompierre; the circle surrounding her seemed about to dissolve. This movement was instantly caught by Graham's eye – ever-vigilant, even while laughing; he rose, took his courage in both hands, crossed the room, and made the advantage his own. Dr. John, throughout his whole life, was a man of luck – a man of success. And why? Because he had the eye to see his opportunity, the heart to prompt to well-timed action, the nerve to consummate a perfect work. And no tyrant-passion dragged him back; no enthusiasms, no foibles encumbered his way. How well he looked at this very moment! When Paulina looked up as he reached her side, her glance mingled at once with an encountering glance, animated, yet modest; his colour, as he spoke to her, became half a blush, half a glow. He stood in her presence brave and bashful: subdued and unobtrusive, yet decided in his purpose and devoted in his ardour. I gathered all this by one view. I did not prolong my observation – time failed me, had inclination served: the night wore late; Ginevra and I ought already to have been in the Rue Fossette. I rose, and bade goodnight to my godmother and M. de Bassompierre.

I know not whether Professor Emanuel had noticed my reluctant acceptance of Dr. Bretton's badinage, or whether he perceived that I was pained, and that, on the whole, the evening had not been one flow of exultant enjoyment for the volatile, pleasure-loving Mademoiselle Lucie; but, as I was leaving the room, he stepped up and inquired whether I had anyone to attend me to the Rue Fossette. The professor *now* spoke politely, and even deferentially, and he looked apologetic and repentant; but I could not recognise his civility at a word, nor meet his contrition with crude, premature oblivion.

Never hitherto had I felt seriously disposed to resent his brusqueries, or freeze before his fierceness; what he had said tonight, however, I considered unwarranted: my extreme disapprobation of the proceeding must be marked, however slightly. I merely said: "I am provided with attendance."

Which was true, as Ginevra and I were to be sent home in the carriage; and I passed him with the sliding obeisance with which he was wont to be saluted in classe by pupils crossing his estrade.

Having sought my shawl, I returned to the vestibule. M. Emanuel stood there as if waiting. He observed that the night was fine.

"Is it?" I said, with a tone and manner whose consummate chariness and frostiness I could not but applaud. It was so seldom I could properly act out my own resolution to be reserved and cool where I had been grieved or hurt, that I felt almost proud of this one successful effort. That "Is it?" sounded just like the manner of other people. I had heard hundreds of such little minced, docked, dry phrases, from the pursed-up coral lips of a score of self-possessed, self-sufficing misses and mesdemoiselles. That M. Paul would not stand any prolonged experience of this sort of dialogue I knew; but he certainly merited a sample of the curt and arid. I believe he thought so himself, for he took the dose quietly. He looked at my shawl and objected to its lightness. I decidedly told him it was as heavy as I wished. Receding aloof, and standing apart, I leaned on the banister of the stairs, folded my shawl about me, and fixed my eyes on a dreary religious painting darkening the wall.

Ginevra was long in coming: tedious seemed her loitering. M. Paul was still there; my ear expected from his lips an angry tone. He came nearer. "Now for another hiss!" thought I: had not the action been too uncivil I could have stopped my ears with my fingers in terror of the thrill. Nothing happens as we expect: listen for a coo or a murmur; it is then you will hear a cry of prey or pain. Await a piercing shriek, an angry threat, and welcome an amicable greeting, a low kind whisper. M. Paul spoke gently: "Friends," said he, "do not quarrel for a word. Tell me, was it I or *ce grand fat d'Anglais*" (so he profanely denominated Dr. Bretton), "who made your eyes so humid, and your cheeks so hot as they are even now?"

"I am not conscious of you, monsieur, or of any other having excited such emotion as you indicate," was my answer; and in giving it, I again surpassed my usual self, and achieved a neat, frosty falsehood.

"But what did I say?" he pursued; "Tell me: I was angry: I have forgotten my words; what were they?"

"Such as it is best to forget!" said I, still quite calm and chill.

"Then it was *my* words which wounded you? Consider them unsaid: permit my retractation; accord my pardon."

"I am not angry, Monsieur."

"Then you are worse than angry – grieved. Forgive me, Miss Lucy."

"M. Emanuel, I *do* forgive you."

"Let me hear you say, in the voice natural to you, and not in that alien tone, '*Mon ami, je vous pardonne.*'"

He made me smile. Who could help smiling at his wistfulness, his simplicity, his earnestness?

"*Bon!*" he cried. "*Voilà que le jour va poindre! Dites donc, mon ami.*"

"*Monsieur Paul, je vous pardonne.*"

"I will have no monsieur: speak the other word, or I shall not believe you sincere: another effort – *mon ami*, or else in English, – my friend!"

Now, 'my friend' had rather another sound and significancy than 'mon ami'; it did not breathe the same sense of domestic and intimate affection; 'mon ami' I could not say to M. Paul; 'my friend', I could, and did say without difficulty. This distinction existed not for him, however, and he was quite satisfied with the English phrase. He smiled. You should have seen him smile, reader; and you should have marked the difference between his countenance now, and that he wore half an hour ago. I cannot affirm that I had ever witnessed the smile of pleasure, or content, or kindness round M. Paul's lips, or in his eyes before. The ironic, the sarcastic, the disdainful, the passionately exultant, I had hundreds of times seen him express by what he called a smile, but any illuminated sign of milder or warmer feelings struck me as wholly new in his visage. It changed it as from a mask to a face: the deep lines left his features; the very complexion seemed clearer and fresher; that swart, sallow, southern darkness which spoke his Spanish blood, became displaced by a lighter hue. I know not that I have ever seen in any other human face an equal metamorphosis from a similar cause. He now took me to the carriage: at the same moment M. de Bassompierre came out with his niece.

In a pretty humour was Mistress Fanshawe; she had found the evening a grand failure: completely upset as to temper, she gave way to the most uncontrolled moroseness as soon as we were seated, and the carriage-door closed. Her invectives against Dr. Bretton had something venomous in them. Having found herself impotent either to charm or sting him, hatred was her only resource; and this hatred she expressed in terms so unmeasured and proportion so monstrous, that, after listening for a while with assumed stoicism, my outraged sense of justice at last and suddenly caught fire. An explosion ensued: for I could be passionate, too; especially with my present fair but faulty associate, who never failed to stir the worst dregs of me. It was well that the carriage-wheels made a tremendous rattle over the flinty Choseville pavement, for I can assure the reader there was neither dead silence nor calm discussion within the vehicle. Half in earnest, half in seeming, I made it my business to storm down Ginevra. She had set out rampant from the Rue Crécy; it was necessary to tame her before we reached the Rue Fossette: to this end it was indispensable to show up her sterling value and high deserts; and this must be done in language of which the fidelity and homeliness might challenge comparison with the compliments of a John Knox to a Mary Stuart. This was the right discipline for Ginevra; it suited her. I am quite sure she went to bed that night all the better and more settled in mind and mood, and slept all the more sweetly for having undergone a sound moral drubbing.

Volume Three

Chapter Twenty-Eight
The Watchguard

M. PAUL EMANUEL owned an acute sensitiveness to the annoyance of interruption, from whatsoever cause occurring, during his lessons: to pass through the classe under such circumstances was considered by the teachers and pupils of the school, individually and collectively, to be as much as a woman's or girl's life was worth.

Madame Beck herself, if forced to the enterprise, would 'skurry' through, retrenching her skirts, and carefully coasting the formidable estrade, like a ship dreading breakers. As to Rosine, the portress – on whom, every half-hour, devolved the fearful duty of fetching pupils out of the very heart of one or other of the divisions to take their music-lessons in the oratory, the great or little saloon, the salle-à-manger, or some other piano-station – she would, upon her second or third attempt, frequently become almost tongue-tied from excess of consternation – a sentiment inspired by the unspeakable looks levelled at her through a pair of dart-dealing spectacles.

One morning I was sitting in the carré, at work upon a piece of embroidery which one of the pupils had commenced but delayed to finish, and while my fingers wrought at the frame, my ears regaled themselves with listening to the crescendos and cadences of a voice haranguing in the neighbouring classe, in tones that waxed momentarily more unquiet, more ominously varied. There was a good strong partition-wall between me and the gathering storm, as well as a facile means of flight through the glass-door to the court, in case it swept this way; so I am afraid I derived more amusement than alarm from these thickening symptoms. Poor Rosine was not safe: four times that blessed morning had she made the passage of peril; and now, for the fifth time, it became her dangerous duty to snatch, as it were, a brand from the burning – a pupil from under M. Paul's nose.

"*Mon Dieu! Mon Dieu!*" cried she. "*Que vais-je devenir? Monsieur va me tuer, je suis sûre; car il est d'une colère!*"

Nerved by the courage of desperation, she opened the door.

"*Mademoiselle La Malle au piano!*" was her cry.

Ere she could make good her retreat, or quite close the door, this voice uttered itself:

"*Dès ce moment! – La classe est défendue. La première qui ouvrira cette porte, ou passera par cette division, sera pendue – fut-ce Madame Beck elle-même!*"

Ten minutes had not succeeded the promulgation of this decree when Rosine's French pantoufles were again heard shuffling along the corridor.

"Mademoiselle," said she, "I would not for a five-franc piece go into that classe again just now: Monsieur's lunettes are really terrible; and here is a commissionaire come with a message from the Athénée. I have told Madame Beck I dare not deliver it, and she says I am to charge you with it."

"Me? No, that is rather too bad! It is not in my line of duty. Come, come, Rosine! Bear your own burden. Be brave – charge once more!"

"I, Mademoiselle? – Impossible! Five times I have crossed him this day. Madame must really hire a gendarme for this service. *Ouf! Je n'en puis plus!*"

"Bah! You are only a coward. What is the message?"

"Precisely of the kind with which Monsieur least likes to be pestered: an urgent summons to go directly to the Athénée, as there is an official visitor – inspector – I know not what – arrived, and Monsieur *must* meet him: you know how he hates a *must*."

Yes, I knew well enough. The restive little man detested spur or curb: against whatever was urgent or obligatory, he was sure to revolt. However, I accepted the responsibility – not, certainly, without fear, but fear blent with other sentiments, curiosity, amongst them. I opened the door, I entered, I closed it behind me as quickly and quietly as a rather unsteady hand would permit; for to be slow or bustling, to rattle a latch, or leave a door gaping wide, were aggravations of crime often more disastrous in result than the main crime itself. There I stood then, and there he sat; his humour was visibly bad – almost at its worst; he had been giving a lesson in arithmetic – for he gave lessons on any and every subject that struck his fancy – and arithmetic being a dry subject, invariably disagreed with him: not a pupil but trembled when he spoke of figures. He sat, bent above his desk: to look up at the sound of an entrance, at the occurrence of a direct breach of his will and law, was an effort he could not for the moment bring himself to make. It was quite as well: I thus gained time to walk up the long classe; and it suited my idiosyncracy far better to encounter the near burst of anger like his, than to bear its menace at a distance.

At his estrade I paused, just in front; of course I was not worthy of immediate attention: he proceeded with his lesson. Disdain would not do: he must hear and he must answer my message.

Not being quite tall enough to lift my head over his desk, elevated upon the estrade, and thus suffering eclipse in my present position, I ventured to peep round, with the design, at first, of merely getting a better view of his face, which had struck me when I entered as bearing a close and picturesque resemblance to that of a black and sallow tiger. Twice did I enjoy this side-view with impunity, advancing and receding unseen; the third time my eye had scarce dawned beyond the obscuration of the desk, when it was caught and transfixed through its very pupil – transfixed by the 'lunettes'. Rosine was right; these utensils had in them a blank and immutable terror, beyond the mobile wrath of the wearer's own unglazed eyes.

I now found the advantage of proximity: these short-sighted 'lunettes' were useless for the inspection of a criminal under Monsieur's nose; accordingly, he doffed them, and he and I stood on more equal terms.

I am glad I was not really much afraid of him – that, indeed, close in his presence, I felt no terror at all; for upon his demanding cord and gibbet to execute the sentence recently pronounced, I was able to furnish him with a needleful of embroidering thread with such accommodating civility as could not but allay some portion at least of his surplus irritation. Of course I did not parade this courtesy before public view: I merely handed the thread round the angle of the desk, and attached it, ready noosed, to the barred back of the Professor's chair.

"*Que me voulez-vous?*" said he in a growl of which the music was wholly confined to his chest and throat, for he kept his teeth clenched; and seemed registering to himself an inward vow that nothing earthly should wring from him a smile.

My answer commenced uncompromisingly: "*Monsieur,*" I said, "*je veux l'impossible, des choses inouïes*"; and thinking it best not to mince matters, but to administer the 'douche' with decision, in a low but quick voice, I delivered the Athenian message, floridly exaggerating its urgency.

Of course, he would not hear a word of it. "He would not go; he would not leave his present class, let all the officials of Villette send for him. He would not put himself an inch out of his way at the bidding of king, cabinet, and chambers together."

I knew, however, that he *must* go; that, talk as he would, both his duty and interest commanded an immediate and literal compliance with the summons: I stood, therefore, waiting in silence, as if he had not yet spoken. He asked what more I wanted.

"Only Monsieur's answer to deliver to the commissionaire."

He waved an impatient negative.

I ventured to stretch my hand to the bonnet-grec which lay in grim repose on the window-sill. He followed this daring movement with his eye, no doubt in mixed pity and amazement at its presumption.

"Ah!" he muttered, "if it came to that – if Miss Lucy meddled with his bonnet-grec – she might just put it on herself, turn garçon for the occasion, and benevolently go to the Athénée in his stead."

With great respect, I laid the bonnet on the desk, where its tassel seemed to give me an awful nod.

"I'll write a note of apology – that will do!" said he, still bent on evasion.

Knowing well it would *not* do, I gently pushed the bonnet towards his hand. Thus impelled, it slid down the polished slope of the varnished and unbaized desk, carried before it the light steel-framed 'lunettes', and, fearful to relate, they fell to the estrade. A score of times ere now had I seen them fall and receive no damage – *this* time, as Lucy Snowe's hapless luck would have it, they so fell that each clear pebble became a shivered and shapeless star.

Now, indeed, dismay seized me – dismay and regret. I knew the value of these 'lunettes': M. Paul's sight was peculiar, not easily fitted, and these glasses suited him. I had heard him call them his treasures: as I picked them up, cracked and worthless, my hand trembled. Frightened through all my nerves I was to see the mischief I had done, but I think I was even more sorry than afraid. For some seconds I dared not look the bereaved Professor in the face; he was the first to speak.

"*Là!*" said he: "*Me voilà veuf de mes lunettes!* I think Mademoiselle Lucy will now confess that the cord and gallows are amply earned; she trembles in anticipation of her doom. *Ah, traitress! Traitress!* You are resolved to have me quite blind and helpless in your hands!"

I lifted my eyes: his face, instead of being irate, lowering, and furrowed, was overflowing with the smile, coloured with the bloom I had seen brightening it that evening at the Hotel Crécy. He was not angry – not even grieved. For the real injury he showed himself full of clemency; under the real provocation, patient as a saint. This event, which seemed so untoward – which I thought had ruined at once my chance of successful persuasion – proved my best help. Difficult of management so long as I had done him no harm, he became graciously pliant as soon as I stood in his presence a conscious and contrite offender.

Still gently railing at me as '*une forte femme – une Anglaise terrible – une petite casse-tout*' – he declared that he dared not but obey one who had given such an instance of her dangerous prowess; it was absolutely like the 'grand Empereur smashing the vase to inspire dismay'. So, at last, crowning himself with his bonnet-grec, and taking his ruined 'lunettes' from my hand with a clasp of kind pardon and encouragement, he made his bow, and went off to the Athénée in first-rate humour and spirits.

* * *

After all this amiability, the reader will be sorry for my sake to hear that I was quarrelling with M. Paul again before night; yet so it was, and I could not help it.

It was his occasional custom – and a very laudable, acceptable custom, too – to arrive of an evening, always à l'improviste, unannounced, burst in on the silent hour of study, establish a sudden despotism over us and our occupations, cause books to be put away, work-bags to be brought out, and, drawing forth a single thick volume, or a handful of pamphlets, substitute for the besotted 'lecture pieuse', drawled by a sleepy pupil, some tragedy made grand by grand reading, ardent by fiery action – some drama, whereof, for my part, I rarely studied the intrinsic merit; for M. Emanuel made it a vessel for an outpouring, and filled it with his native verve and passion like a cup with a vital brewage. Or else he would flash through our conventual darkness a reflex of a brighter world, show us a glimpse of the current literature of the day, read us passages from some enchanting tale, or the last witty feuilleton which had awakened laughter in the saloons of Paris; taking care always to expunge, with the severest hand, whether from tragedy, melodrama, tale, or essay, whatever passage, phrase, or word, could be deemed unsuited to an audience of 'jeunes filles'. I noticed more than once, that where retrenchment without substitute would have left unmeaning vacancy, or introduced weakness, he could, and did, improvise whole paragraphs, no less vigorous than irreproachable; the dialogue – the description – he engrafted was often far better than that he pruned away.

Well, on the evening in question, we were sitting silent as nuns in a 'retreat', the pupils studying, the teachers working. I remember my work; it was a slight matter of fancy, and it rather interested me; it had a purpose; I was not doing it merely to kill time; I meant it when finished as a gift; and the occasion of presentation being near, haste was requisite, and my fingers were busy.

We heard the sharp bell-peal which we all knew; then the rapid step familiar to each ear: the words "Voilà Monsieur!" had scarcely broken simultaneously from every lip, when the two-leaved door split (as split it always did for his admission – such a slow word as 'open' is inefficient to describe his movements), and he stood in the midst of us.

There were two study tables, both long and flanked with benches; over the centre of each hung a lamp; beneath this lamp, on either side the table, sat a teacher; the girls were arranged to the right hand and the left; the eldest and most studious nearest the lamps or tropics; the idlers and little ones towards the north and south poles. Monsieur's habit was politely to hand a chair to some teacher, generally Zélie St. Pierre, the senior mistress; then to take her vacated seat; and thus avail himself of the full beam of Cancer or Capricorn, which, owing to his near sight, he needed.

As usual, Zélie rose with alacrity, smiling to the whole extent of her mouth, and the full display of her upper and under rows of teeth – that strange smile which passes from ear to ear, and is marked only by a sharp thin curve, which fails to spread over the countenance, and neither dimples the cheek nor lights the eye. I suppose Monsieur did not see her, or he had taken a whim that he would not notice her, for he was as capricious as women are said to be; then his 'lunettes' (he had got another pair) served him as an excuse for all sorts of little oversights and shortcomings. Whatever might be his reason, he passed by Zélie, came to the other side of the table, and before I could start up to clear the way, whispered, "*Ne bougez pas*", and established himself between me and Miss Fanshawe, who always would be my neighbour, and have her elbow in my side, however often I declared to her, "Ginevra, I wish you were at Jericho."

It was easy to say, "*Ne bougez pas*"; but how could I help it? I must make him room, and I must request the pupils to recede that *I* might recede. It was very well for Ginevra to be gummed to me, 'keeping herself warm', as she said, on the winter evenings, and harassing my very heart with her fidgetings and pokings, obliging me, indeed, sometimes to put an artful pin in my girdle by way of protection against her elbow; but I suppose M. Emanuel was not to be subjected to the same kind of treatment, so I swept away my working materials, to clear space for his book, and withdrew myself to make room for his person; not, however, leaving more than a yard of interval, just what any reasonable man would have regarded as a convenient, respectful allowance of bench. But M. Emanuel never *was* reasonable; flint and tinder that he was! He struck and took fire directly.

"*Vous ne voulez pas de moi pour voisin,*" he growled: "*vous vous donnez des airs de caste; vous me traitez en paria*"; he scowled. "*Soit! Je vais arranger la chose!*" And he set to work.

"*Levez vous toutes, Mesdemoiselles!*" cried he.

The girls rose. He made them all file off to the other table. He then placed me at one extremity of the long bench, and having duly and carefully brought me my work-basket, silk, scissors, all my implements, he fixed himself quite at the other end.

At this arrangement, highly absurd as it was, not a soul in the room dared to laugh; luckless for the giggler would have been the giggle. As for me, I took it with entire coolness. There I sat, isolated and cut off from human intercourse; I sat and minded my work, and was quiet, and not at all unhappy.

"*Est ce assez de distance?*" he demanded.

"*Monsieur en est l'arbitre,*" said I.

"*Vous savez bien que non. C'est vous qui avez crée ce vide immense: moi je n'y ai pas mis la main.*"

And with this assertion he commenced the reading.

For his misfortune he had chosen a French translation of what he called "*un drame de Williams Shacskpire; le faux dieu,*" he further announced, "*de ces sots païens, les Anglais.*" How far otherwise he would have characterized him had his temper not been upset, I scarcely need intimate.

Of course, the translation being French, was very inefficient; nor did I make any particular effort to conceal the contempt which some of its forlorn lapses were calculated to excite. Not that it behoved or beseemed me to say anything: but one can occasionally *look* the opinion it is forbidden to embody in words. Monsieur's lunettes being on the alert, he gleaned up every stray look; I don't think he lost one: the consequence was, his eyes soon discarded a screen, that their blaze might sparkle free, and he waxed hotter at the north pole to which he had voluntarily exiled himself, than, considering the general temperature of the room, it would have been reasonable to become under the vertical ray of Cancer itself.

The reading over, it appeared problematic whether he would depart with his anger unexpressed, or whether he would give it vent. Suppression was not much in his habits; but still, what had been done to him definite enough to afford matter for overt reproof? I had not uttered a sound, and could not justly be deemed amenable to reprimand or penalty for having permitted a slightly freer action than usual to the muscles about my eyes and mouth.

The supper, consisting of bread, and milk diluted with tepid water, was brought in. In respectful consideration of the Professor's presence, the rolls and glasses were allowed to stand instead of being immediately handed round.

"Take your supper, ladies," said he, seeming to be occupied in making marginal notes to his 'Williams Shacskpire'. They took it. I also accepted a roll and glass, but being now more than ever interested in my work, I kept my seat of punishment, and wrought while I munched my bread and sipped my beverage, the whole with easy sang-froid; with a certain snugness of composure, indeed, scarcely in my habits, and pleasantly novel to my feelings. It seemed as if the presence of a nature so restless, chafing, thorny as that of M. Paul absorbed all feverish and unsettling influences like a magnet, and left me none but such as were placid and harmonious.

He rose. "Will he go away without saying another word?" Yes; he turned to the door.

No: he *re*-turned on his steps; but only, perhaps, to take his pencil-case, which had been left on the table.

He took it – shut the pencil in and out, broke its point against the wood, re-cut and pocketed it, and...walked promptly up to me.

The girls and teachers, gathered round the other table, were talking pretty freely: they always talked at meals; and, from the constant habit of speaking fast and loud at such times, did not now subdue their voices much.

M. Paul came and stood behind me. He asked at what I was working; and I said I was making a watchguard.

He asked, "For whom?" And I answered, "For a gentleman – one of my friends."

M. Paul stooped down and proceeded – as novel-writers say, and, as was literally true in his case – to 'hiss' into my ear some poignant words.

He said that, of all the women he knew, I was the one who could make herself the most consummately unpleasant: I was she with whom it was least possible to live on friendly terms. I had a '*caractère intraitable*', and perverse to a miracle. How I managed it, or what possessed me, he, for his part, did not know; but with whatever pacific and amicable intentions a person accosted me – crac! I turned concord to discord, good-will to enmity. He was sure, he – M. Paul

– wished me well enough; he had never done me any harm that he knew of; he might, at least, he supposed, claim a right to be regarded as a neutral acquaintance, guiltless of hostile sentiments: yet, how I behaved to him! With what pungent vivacities – what an impetus of mutiny – what a 'fougue' of injustice!

Here I could not avoid opening my eyes somewhat wide, and even slipping in a slight interjectional observation: "*Vivacities? Impetus? Fougue?* I didn't know...."

"*Chut! A l'instant!* There! There I went – *vive comme la poudre!*" He was sorry – he was very sorry: for my sake he grieved over the hapless peculiarity. This 'emportement', this 'chaleur' – generous, perhaps, but excessive – would yet, he feared, do me a mischief. It was a pity: I was not – he believed, in his soul – wholly without good qualities: and would I but hear reason, and be more sedate, more sober, less 'en l'air', less 'coquette', less taken by show, less prone to set an undue value on outside excellence – to make much of the attentions of people remarkable chiefly for so many feet of stature, '*des couleurs de poupée*', '*un nez plus ou moins bien fait*', and an enormous amount of fatuity – I might yet prove an useful, perhaps an exemplary character. But, as it was – and here, the little man's voice was for a minute choked.

I would have looked up at him, or held out my hand, or said a soothing word; but I was afraid, if I stirred, I should either laugh or cry; so odd, in all this, was the mixture of the touching and the absurd.

I thought he had nearly done: but no; he sat down that he might go on at his ease.

"While he, M. Paul, was on these painful topics, he would dare my anger for the sake of my good, and would venture to refer to a change he had noticed in my dress. He was free to confess that when he first knew me – or, rather, was in the habit of catching a passing glimpse of me from time to time – I satisfied him on this point: the gravity, the austere simplicity, obvious in this particular, were such as to inspire the highest hopes for my best interests. What fatal influence had impelled me lately to introduce flowers under the brim of my bonnet, to wear 'des cols brodés', and even to appear on one occasion in a *scarlet gown* – he might indeed conjecture, but, for the present, would not openly declare."

Again I interrupted, and this time not without an accent at once indignant and horror-struck.

"Scarlet, Monsieur Paul? It was not scarlet! It was pink, and pale pink to: and further subdued by black lace."

"Pink or scarlet, yellow or crimson, pea-green or sky-blue, it was all one: these were all flaunting, giddy colours; and as to the lace I talked of, *that* was but a '*colifichet de plus*'." And he sighed over my degeneracy. "He could not, he was sorry to say, be so particular on this theme as he could wish: not possessing the exact names of these 'babioles', he might run into small verbal errors which would not fail to lay him open to my sarcasm, and excite my unhappily sudden and passionate disposition. He would merely say, in general terms – and in these general terms he knew he was correct – that my costume had of late assumed '*des façons mondaines*', which it wounded him to see."

What 'façons mondaines' he discovered in my present winter merino and plain white collar, I own it puzzled me to guess: and when I asked him, he said it was all made with too much attention to effect – and besides, "had I not a bow of ribbon at my neck?"

"And if you condemn a bow of ribbon for a lady, Monsieur, you would necessarily disapprove of a thing like this for a gentleman?" – holding up my bright little chainlet of silk and gold. His sole reply was a groan – I suppose over my levity.

After sitting some minutes in silence, and watching the progress of the chain, at which I now wrought more assiduously than ever, he inquired: "Whether what he had just said would have the effect of making me entirely detest him?"

I hardly remember what answer I made, or how it came about; I don't think I spoke at all, but I know we managed to bid goodnight on friendly terms: and, even after M. Paul had reached the door, he turned back just to explain, "that he would not be understood to speak in entire condemnation of the scarlet dress" ("Pink! Pink!" I threw in); "that he had no intention to deny it the merit of *looking* rather well" (the fact was, M. Emanuel's taste in colours decidedly leaned to the brilliant); "only he wished to counsel me, whenever, I wore it, to do so in the same spirit as if its material were 'bure', and its hue 'gris de poussière'."

"And the flowers under my bonnet, Monsieur?" I asked. "They are very little ones –?"

"Keep them little, then," said he. "Permit them not to become full-blown."

"And the bow, Monsieur – the bit of ribbon?"

"Va pour le ruban!" was the propitious answer.

And so we settled it.

* * *

"Well done, Lucy Snowe!" cried I to myself; "You have come in for a pretty lecture – brought on yourself a 'rude savant', and all through your wicked fondness for worldly vanities! Who would have thought it? You deemed yourself a melancholy sober-sides enough! Miss Fanshawe there regards you as a second Diogenes. M. de Bassompierre, the other day, politely turned the conversation when it ran on the wild gifts of the actress Vashti, because, as he kindly said, 'Miss Snowe looked uncomfortable.' Dr. John Bretton knows you only as 'quiet Lucy' – 'a creature inoffensive as a shadow'; he has said, and you have heard him say it: 'Lucy's disadvantages spring from over-gravity in tastes and manner – want of colour in character and costume.' Such are your own and your friends' impressions; and behold! There starts up a little man, differing diametrically from all these, roundly charging you with being too airy and cheery – too volatile and versatile – too flowery and coloury. This harsh little man – this pitiless censor – gathers up all your poor scattered sins of vanity, your luckless chiffon of rose-colour, your small fringe of a wreath, your small scrap of ribbon, your silly bit of lace, and calls you to account for the lot, and for each item. You are well habituated to be passed by as a shadow in Life's sunshine: it is a new thing to see one testily lifting his hand to screen his eyes, because you tease him with an obtrusive ray."

Chapter Twenty-Nine
Monsieur's Fête

❦

I WAS UP the next morning an hour before daybreak, and finished my guard, kneeling on the dormitory floor beside the centre stand, for the benefit of such expiring glimmer as the night-lamp afforded in its last watch.

All my materials – my whole stock of beads and silk – were used up before the chain assumed the length and richness I wished; I had wrought it double, as I knew, by the rule of contraries, that to suit the particular taste whose gratification was in view, an effective appearance was quite indispensable. As a finish to the ornament, a little gold clasp was needed; fortunately I possessed it in the fastening of my sole necklace; I duly detached and re-attached it, then coiled compactly the completed guard; and enclosed it in a small box I had bought for its brilliancy, made of some tropic shell of the colour called 'nacarat', and decked with a little coronal of sparkling blue stones. Within the lid of the box, I carefully graved with my scissors' point certain initials.

* * *

The reader will, perhaps, remember the description of Madame Beck's fête; nor will he have forgotten that at each anniversary, a handsome present was subscribed for and offered by the school. The observance of this day was a distinction accorded to none but Madame, and, in a modified form, to her kinsman and counsellor, M. Emanuel. In the latter case it was an honour spontaneously awarded, not plotted and contrived beforehand, and offered an additional proof, amongst many others, of the estimation in which – despite his partialities, prejudices, and irritabilities – the professor of literature was held by his pupils. No article of value was offered to him: he distinctly gave it to be understood, that he would accept neither plate nor jewellery. Yet he liked a slight tribute; the cost, the money-value, did not touch him: a diamond ring, a gold snuff-box, presented, with pomp, would have pleased him less than a flower, or a drawing, offered simply and with sincere feelings. Such was his nature. He was a man, not wise in his generation, yet could he claim a filial sympathy with 'the dayspring on high'.

M. Paul's fête fell on the first of March and a Thursday. It proved a fine sunny day; and being likewise the morning on which it was customary to attend mass; being also otherwise distinguished by the half-holiday which permitted the privilege of walking out, shopping, or paying visits in the afternoon: these combined considerations induced a general smartness and freshness of dress. Clean collars were in vogue; the ordinary dingy woollen classe-dress was exchanged for something lighter and clearer. Mademoiselle Zélie St. Pierre, on this particular Thursday, even assumed a 'robe de soie', deemed in economical Labassecour an article of hazardous splendour and luxury; nay, it was remarked that she sent for a coiffeur to dress her hair that morning; there were pupils acute enough to discover that she had bedewed her handkerchief and her hands with a new and fashionable perfume. Poor Zélie! It was much her wont to declare about this time, that she was tired to death of a life of seclusion and labour; that she longed to have the means and leisure for relaxation; to have someone to work for her – a husband who would pay her debts (she was woefully encumbered with debt), supply her wardrobe, and leave her at liberty, as she said, to '*goûter un peu les plaisirs*'. It had long been rumoured that her eye was upon M. Emanuel. Monsieur Emanuel's eye was certainly often upon her. He would sit and watch her perseveringly for minutes together. I have seen him give her a quarter-of-an-hour's gaze, while the class was silently composing, and he sat throned on his estrade, unoccupied. Conscious always of this basilisk attention, she would writhe under it, half-flattered, half-puzzled, and Monsieur would follow her sensations, sometimes looking appallingly acute; for in some cases, he had the terrible unerring penetration of instinct, and pierced in its hiding-place the last lurking thought of the heart, and discerned under florid veilings the bare; barren places of the spirit: yes, and its perverted tendencies, and its hidden false curves – all that men and women would not have known – the twisted spine, the malformed limb that was born with them, and far worse, the stain or disfigurement they have perhaps brought on themselves. No calamity so accursed but M. Emanuel could pity and forgive, if it were acknowledged candidly; but where his questioning eyes met dishonest denial – where his ruthless researches found deceitful concealment – oh, then, he could be cruel, and I thought wicked! He would exultantly snatch the screen from poor shrinking wretches, passionately hurry them to the summit of the mount of exposure, and there show them all naked, all false – poor living lies – the spawn of that horrid Truth which cannot be looked on unveiled. He thought he did justice; for my part I doubt whether man has a right to do such justice on man: more than once in these his visitations, I have felt compelled to give tears to his victims, and not spared ire and keen reproach to himself. He deserved it; but it was difficult to shake him in his firm conviction that the work was righteous and needed.

Breakfast being over and mass attended, the school-bell rang and the rooms filled: a very pretty spectacle was presented in classe. Pupils and teachers sat neatly arrayed, orderly and expectant, each bearing in her hand the bouquet of felicitation – the prettiest spring-flowers all fresh, and filling the air with their fragrance: I only had no bouquet. I like to see flowers growing, but when they are gathered, they cease to please. I look on them as things rootless and perishable; their likeness to life makes me sad. I never offer flowers to those I love; I never wish to receive them from hands dear to me. Mademoiselle St. Pierre marked my empty hands – she could not believe I had been so remiss; with avidity her eye roved over and round me: surely I must have some solitary symbolic flower somewhere: some small knot of violets, something to win myself praise for taste, commendation for ingenuity. The unimaginative 'Anglaise' proved better than the Parisienne's fears: she sat literally unprovided, as bare of bloom or leaf as the winter tree. This ascertained, Zélie smiled, well pleased.

"How wisely you have acted to keep your money, Miss Lucie," she said: "silly I have gone and thrown away two francs on a bouquet of hot-house flowers!"

And she showed with pride her splendid nosegay.

But hush! A step: *the* step. It came prompt, as usual, but with a promptitude, we felt disposed to flatter ourselves, inspired by other feelings than mere excitability of nerve and vehemence of intent. We thought our Professor's 'foot-fall' (to speak romantically) had in it a friendly promise this morning; and so it had.

He entered in a mood which made him as good as a new sunbeam to the already well-lit first classe. The morning light playing amongst our plants and laughing on our walls, caught an added lustre from M. Paul's all-benignant salute. Like a true Frenchman (though I don't know why I should say so, for he was of strain neither French nor Labassecourien), he had dressed for the 'situation' and the occasion. Not by the vague folds, sinister and conspirator-like, of his soot-dark paletôt were the outlines of his person obscured; on the contrary, his figure (such as it was, I don't boast of it) was well set off by a civilized coat and a silken vest quite pretty to behold. The defiant and pagan bonnet-grec had vanished: bare-headed, he came upon us, carrying a Christian hat in his gloved hand. The little man looked well, very well; there was a clearness of amity in his blue eye, and a glow of good feeling on his dark complexion, which passed perfectly in the place of beauty: one really did not care to observe that his nose, though far from small, was of no particular shape, his cheek thin, his brow marked and square, his mouth no rose-bud: one accepted him as he was, and felt his presence the reverse of damping or insignificant.

He passed to his desk; he placed on the same his hat and gloves. *"Bon jour, mes amies,"* said he, in a tone that somehow made amends to some amongst us for many a sharp snap and savage snarl: not a jocund, good-fellow tone, still less an unctuous priestly, accent, but a voice he had belonging to himself – a voice used when his heart passed the words to his lips. That same heart did speak sometimes; though an irritable, it was not an ossified organ: in its core was a place, tender beyond a man's tenderness; a place that humbled him to little children, that bound him to girls and women to whom, rebel as he would, he could not disown his affinity, nor quite deny that, on the whole, he was better with them than with his own sex.

"We all wish Monsieur a good day, and present to him our congratulations on the anniversary of his fête," said Mademoiselle Zélie, constituting herself spokeswoman of the assembly; and advancing with no more twists of affectation than were with her indispensable to the achievement of motion, she laid her costly bouquet before him. He bowed over it.

The long train of offerings followed: all the pupils, sweeping past with the gliding step foreigners practise, left their tributes as they went by. Each girl so dexterously adjusted her separate gift, that when the last bouquet was laid on the desk, it formed the apex to a blooming pyramid – a pyramid blooming, spreading, and towering with such exuberance as, in the end, to eclipse the hero behind it. This ceremony over, seats were resumed, and we sat in dead silence, expectant of a speech.

I suppose five minutes might have elapsed, and the hush remained unbroken; ten – and there was no sound.

Many present began, doubtless, to wonder for what Monsieur waited; as well they might. Voiceless and viewless, stirless and wordless, he kept his station behind the pile of flowers.

At last there issued forth a voice, rather deep, as if it spoke out of a hollow:

"Est-ce là tout?"

Mademoiselle Zélie looked round.

"You have all presented your bouquets?" inquired she of the pupils.

Yes; they had all given their nosegays, from the eldest to the youngest, from the tallest to the most diminutive. The senior mistress signified as much.

"Est-ce là tout?" was reiterated in an intonation which, deep before, had now descended some notes lower.

"Monsieur," said Mademoiselle St. Pierre, rising, and this time speaking with her own sweet smile, "I have the honour to tell you that, with a single exception, every person in classe has offered her bouquet. For Meess Lucie, Monsieur will kindly make allowance; as a foreigner she probably did not know our customs, or did not appreciate their significance. Meess Lucie has regarded this ceremony as too frivolous to be honoured by her observance."

"Famous!" I muttered between my teeth: "you are no bad speaker, Zélie, when you begin."

The answer vouchsafed to Mademoiselle St Pierre from the estrade was given in the gesticulation of a hand from behind the pyramid. This manual action seemed to deprecate words, to enjoin silence.

A form, ere long, followed the hand. Monsieur emerged from his eclipse; and producing himself on the front of his estrade, and gazing straight and fixedly before him at a vast 'mappe-monde' covering the wall opposite, he demanded a third time, and now in really tragic tones –

"Est-ce là tout?"

I might yet have made all right, by stepping forwards and slipping into his hand the ruddy little shell-box I at that moment held tight in my own. It was what I had fully purposed to do; but, first, the comic side of Monsieur's behaviour had tempted me to delay, and now, Mademoiselle St. Pierre's affected interference provoked contumacity. The reader not having hitherto had any cause to ascribe to Miss Snowe's character the most distant pretensions to perfection, will be scarcely surprised to learn that she felt too perverse to defend herself from any imputation the Parisienne might choose to insinuate and besides, M. Paul was so tragic, and took my defection so seriously, he deserved to be vexed. I kept, then, both my box and my countenance, and sat insensate as any stone.

"It is well!" dropped at length from the lips of M. Paul; and having uttered this phrase, the shadow of some great paroxysm – the swell of wrath, scorn, resolve – passed over his brow, rippled his lips, and lined his cheeks. Gulping down all further comment, he launched into his customary 'discours'.

I can't at all remember what this 'discours' was; I did not listen to it: the gulping-down process, the abrupt dismissal of his mortification or vexation, had given me a sensation which half-counteracted the ludicrous effect of the reiterated "*Est-ce là tout?*"

Towards the close of the speech there came a pleasing diversion; my attention was again amusingly arrested.

Owing to some little accidental movement – I think I dropped my thimble on the floor, and in stooping to regain it, hit the crown of my head against the sharp corner of my desk; which casualties (exasperating to me, by rights, if to anybody) naturally made a slight bustle – M. Paul became irritated, and dismissing his forced equanimity, and casting to the winds that dignity and self-control with which he never cared long to encumber himself, he broke forth into the strain best calculated to give him ease.

I don't know how, in the progress of his 'discours', he had contrived to cross the Channel and land on British ground; but there I found him when I began to listen.

Casting a quick, cynical glance round the room – a glance which scathed, or was intended to scathe, as it crossed me – he fell with fury upon 'les Anglaises'.

Never have I heard English women handled as M. Paul that morning handled them: he spared nothing – neither their minds, morals, manners, nor personal appearance. I specially remember his abuse of their tall stature, their long necks, their thin arms, their slovenly dress, their pedantic education, their impious skepticism (!), their insufferable pride, their pretentious virtue: over which he ground his teeth malignantly, and looked as if, had he dared, he would have said singular things. Oh! He was spiteful, acrid, savage; and, as a natural consequence, detestably ugly.

"Little wicked venomous man!" thought I; "am I going to harass myself with fears of displeasing you, or hurting your feelings? No, indeed; you shall be indifferent to me, as the shabbiest bouquet in your pyramid."

I grieve to say I could not quite carry out this resolution. For some time the abuse of England and the English found and left me stolid: I bore it some fifteen minutes stoically enough; but this hissing cockatrice was determined to sting, and he said such things at last – fastening not only upon our women, but upon our greatest names and best men; sullying the shield of Britannia, and dabbling the union jack in mud – that I was stung. With vicious relish he brought up the most spicy current continental historical falsehoods – than which nothing can be conceived more offensive. Zélie, and the whole class, became one grin of vindictive delight; for it is curious to discover how these clowns of Labassecour secretly hate England. At last, I struck a sharp stroke on my desk, opened my lips, and let loose this cry:

"*Vive l'Angleterre, l'Histoire et les Héros! A bas la France, la Fiction et les Faquins!*"

The class was struck of a heap. I suppose they thought me mad. The Professor put up his handkerchief, and fiendishly smiled into its folds. Little monster of malice! He now thought he had got the victory, since he had made me angry. In a second he became good-humoured. With great blandness he resumed the subject of his flowers; talked poetically and symbolically of their sweetness, perfume, purity, etcetera; made Frenchified comparisons between the 'jeunes filles' and the sweet blossoms before him; paid Mademoiselle St. Pierre a very full-blown compliment on the superiority of her bouquet; and ended by announcing that the first really fine, mild, and balmy morning in spring, he intended to take the whole class out to breakfast in the country. "Such of the class, at least," he added, with emphasis, "as he could count amongst the number of his friends."

"*Donc je n'y serai pas,*" declared I, involuntarily.

"*Soit!*" was his response; and, gathering his flowers in his arms, he flashed out of classe; while I, consigning my work, scissors, thimble, and the neglected little box, to my desk, swept upstairs. I don't know whether *he* felt hot and angry, but I am free to confess that *I* did.

Yet with a strange evanescent anger, I had not sat an hour on the edge of my bed, picturing and repicturing his look, manner, words ere I smiled at the whole scene. A little pang of regret I underwent that the box had not been offered. I had meant to gratify him. Fate would not have it so.

In the course of the afternoon, remembering that desks in classe were by no means inviolate repositories, and thinking that it was as well to secure the box, on account of the initials in the lid, P.C.D.E., for Paul Carl (or Carlos) David Emanuel – such was his full name – these foreigners must always have a string of baptismals – I descended to the schoolroom.

It slept in holiday repose. The day pupils were all gone home, the boarders were out walking, the teachers, except the surveillante of the week, were in town, visiting or shopping; the suite of divisions was vacant; so was the grande salle, with its huge solemn globe hanging in the midst, its pair of many-branched chandeliers, and its horizontal grand piano closed, silent, enjoying its mid-week Sabbath. I rather wondered to find the first classe door ajar; this room being usually locked when empty, and being then inaccessible to any save Madame Beck and myself, who possessed a duplicate key. I wondered still more, on approaching, to hear a vague movement as of life – a step, a chair stirred, a sound like the opening of a desk.

"It is only Madame Beck doing inspection duty," was the conclusion following a moment's reflection. The partially-opened door gave opportunity for assurance on this point. I looked. Behold! Not the inspecting garb of Madame Beck – the shawl and the clean cap – but the coat, and the close-shorn, dark head of a man. This person occupied my chair; his olive hand held my desk open, his nose was lost to view amongst my papers. His back was towards me, but there could not be a moment's question about identity. Already was the attire of ceremony discarded: the cherished and ink-stained paletôt was resumed; the perverse bonnet-grec lay on the floor, as if just dropped from the hand, culpably busy.

Now I knew, and I had long known, that that hand of M. Emanuel's was on the most intimate terms with my desk; that it raised and lowered the lid, ransacked and arranged the contents, almost as familiarly as my own. The fact was not dubious, nor did he wish it to be so: he left signs of each visit palpable and unmistakable; hitherto, however, I had never caught him in the act: watch as I would, I could not detect the hours and moments of his coming. I saw the brownie's work in exercises left overnight full of faults, and found next morning carefully corrected: I profited by his capricious good-will in loans full welcome and refreshing. Between a sallow dictionary and worn-out grammar would magically grow a fresh interesting new work, or a classic, mellow and sweet in its ripe age. Out of my work-basket would laughingly peep a romance, under it would lurk the pamphlet, the magazine, whence last evening's reading had been extracted. Impossible to doubt the source whence these treasures flowed: had there been no other indication, one condemning and traitor peculiarity, common to them all, settled the question – *they smelt of cigars*. This was very shocking, of course: *I* thought so at first, and used to open the window with some bustle, to air my desk, and with fastidious finger and thumb, to hold the peccant brochures forth to the purifying breeze. I was cured of that formality suddenly. Monsieur caught me at it one day, understood the inference, instantly relieved my hand of its burden, and, in another moment, would have thrust the same into the glowing stove. It chanced to be a book, on the perusal of which I was bent; so for once I proved as decided and quicker than himself; recaptured the spoil, and – having saved this volume – never hazarded a second. With all this, I had never yet been able to arrest in his visits the freakish, friendly, cigar-loving phantom.

But now at last I had him: there he was – the very brownie himself; and there, curling from his lips, was the pale blue breath of his Indian darling: he was smoking into my desk: it might well betray him. Provoked at this particular, and yet pleased to surprise him – pleased, that is, with the mixed feeling of the housewife who discovers at last her strange elfin ally busy in the dairy at the untimely churn – I softly stole forward, stood behind him, bent with precaution over his shoulder.

My heart smote me to see that – after this morning's hostility, after my seeming remissness, after the puncture experienced by his feelings, and the ruffling undergone by his temper – he, all willing to forget and forgive, had brought me a couple of handsome volumes, of which the title and authorship were guarantees for interest. Now, as he sat bending above the desk, he was stirring up its contents; but with gentle and careful hand; disarranging indeed, but not harming. My heart smote me: as I bent over him, as he sat unconscious, doing me what good he could, and I daresay not feeling towards me unkindly, my morning's anger quite melted: I did not dislike Professor Emanuel.

I think he heard me breathe. He turned suddenly: his temperament was nervous, yet he never started, and seldom changed colour: there was something hardy about him.

"I thought you were gone into town with the other teachers," said he, taking a grim gripe of his self-possession, which half-escaped him – "It is as well you are not. Do you think I care for being caught? Not I. I often visit your desk."

"Monsieur, I know it."

"You find a brochure or tome now and then; but you don't read them, because they have passed under this?" – touching his cigar.

"They have, and are no better for the process; but I read them."

"Without pleasure?"

"Monsieur must not be contradicted."

"Do you like them, or any of them? – Are they acceptable?"

"Monsieur has seen me reading them a hundred times, and knows I have not so many recreations as to undervalue those he provides."

"I mean well; and, if you see that I mean well, and derive some little amusement from my efforts, why can we not be friends?"

"A fatalist would say – because we cannot."

"This morning," he continued, "I awoke in a bright mood, and came into classe happy; you spoiled my day."

"No, Monsieur, only an hour or two of it, and that unintentionally."

"Unintentionally! No. It was my fête-day; everybody wished me happiness but you. The little children of the third division gave each her knot of violets, lisped each her congratulation: you – nothing. Not a bud, leaf, whisper – not a glance. Was this unintentional?"

"I meant no harm."

"Then you really did not know our custom? You were unprepared? You would willingly have laid out a few centimes on a flower to give me pleasure, had you been aware that it was expected? Say so, and all is forgotten, and the pain soothed."

"I did know that it was expected: I *was* prepared; yet I laid out no centimes on flowers."

"It is well – you do right to be honest. I should almost have hated you had you flattered and lied. Better declare at once 'Paul Carl Emanuel – *je te déteste, mon garçon!*' – than smile an interest, look an affection, and be false and cold at heart. False and cold I don't think you are; but you have made a great mistake in life, that I believe; I think your judgment is warped – that you are indifferent where you ought to be grateful – and perhaps devoted and infatuated, where you ought to be cool as your name. Don't suppose that I wish you to have a passion for me, Mademoiselle; *Dieu vous en garde!* What do you start for? Because I said passion? Well, I say it again. There is such a word, and there is such a thing – though not within these walls, thank heaven! You are no child that one should not speak of what exists; but I only uttered the word – the thing, I assure you, is alien to my whole life and views. It died in the past – in the present it lies buried – its grave is deep-dug, well-heaped, and many winters old: in the future there will be a resurrection, as I believe to my souls consolation; but all will then be changed – form and feeling: the mortal will have put on immortality – it will rise, not for earth, but heaven. All I say to *you*, Miss Lucy Snowe, is – that you ought to treat Professor Paul Emanuel decently."

I could not, and did not contradict such a sentiment.

"Tell me," he pursued, "when it is *your* fête-day, and I will not grudge a few centimes for a small offering."

"You will be like me, Monsieur: this cost more than a few centimes, and I did not grudge its price." And taking from the open desk the little box, I put it into his hand.

"It lay ready in my lap this morning," I continued; "and if Monsieur had been rather more patient, and Mademoiselle St. Pierre less interfering – perhaps I should say, too, if *I* had been calmer and wiser – I should have given it then."

He looked at the box: I saw its clear warm tint and bright azure circlet pleased his eyes. I told him to open it.

"My initials!" said he, indicating the letters in the lid. "Who told you I was called Carl David?"

"A little bird, Monsieur."

"Does it fly from me to you? Then one can tie a message under its wing when needful."

He took out the chain – a trifle indeed as to value, but glossy with silk and sparkling with beads. He liked that too – admired it artlessly, like a child.

"For me?"

"Yes, for you."

"This is the thing you were working at last night?"

"The same."

"You finished it this morning?"

"I did."

"You commenced it with the intention that it should be mine?"

"Undoubtedly."

"And offered on my fête-day?"

"Yes."

"This purpose continued as you wove it?"

Again I assented.

"Then it is not necessary that I should cut out any portion – saying, this part is not mine: it was plaited under the idea and for the adornment of another?"

"By no means. It is neither necessary, nor would it be just."

"This object is *all* mine?"

"That object is yours entirely."

Straightway Monsieur opened his paletôt, arranged the guard splendidly across his chest, displaying as much and suppressing as little as he could: for he had no notion of concealing what he admired and thought decorative. As to the box, he pronounced it a superb bonbonnière – he was fond of bonbons, by the way – and as he always liked to share with others what pleased himself, he would give his 'dragées' as freely as he lent his books. Amongst the kind brownie's gifts left in my desk, I forgot to enumerate many a paper of chocolate comfits. His tastes in these matters were southern, and what we think infantine. His simple lunch consisted frequently of a 'brioche', which, as often as not, he shared with some child of the third division.

"A présent c'est un fait accompli," said he, re-adjusting his paletôt; and we had no more words on the subject. After looking over the two volumes he had brought, and cutting away some pages with his penknife (he generally pruned before lending his books, especially if they were novels, and sometimes I was a little provoked at the severity of his censorship, the retrenchments interrupting the narrative), he rose, politely touched his bonnet-grec, and bade me a civil good-day.

"We are friends now," thought I, "till the next time we quarrel."

We *might* have quarrelled again that very same evening, but, wonderful to relate, failed, for once, to make the most of our opportunity.

Contrary to all expectation, M. Paul arrived at the study-hour. Having seen so much of him in the morning, we did not look for his presence at night. No sooner were we seated at lessons, however, than he appeared. I own I was glad to see him, so glad that I could not help greeting his arrival with a smile; and when he made his way to the same seat about which so serious a misunderstanding had formerly arisen, I took good care not to make too much room for him; he watched with a jealous, side-long look, to see whether I shrank away, but I did not, though the bench was a little crowded. I was losing the early impulse to recoil from M. Paul. Habituated to the paletôt and bonnet-grec, the neighbourhood of these garments seemed no longer uncomfortable or very formidable. I did not now sit restrained, 'asphyxiée' (as he used to say) at his side; I stirred when I wished to stir, coughed when it was necessary, even yawned when I was tired – did, in short, what I pleased, blindly reliant upon his indulgence. Nor did my temerity, this evening at least, meet the punishment it perhaps merited; he was both indulgent and good-natured; not a cross glance shot from his eyes, not a hasty word left his lips. Till the very close of the evening, he did not indeed address me at all, yet I felt, somehow, that he was full of friendliness. Silence is of different kinds, and breathes different meanings; no words could inspire a pleasanter content than did M. Paul's worldless presence. When the tray came in, and the bustle of supper commenced, he just said, as he retired, that he wished me a good night and sweet dreams; and a good night and sweet dreams I had.

Chapter Thirty
M. Paul

YET THE READER is advised not to be in any hurry with his kindly conclusions, or to suppose, with an over-hasty charity, that from that day M. Paul became a changed character – easy to live with, and no longer apt to flash danger and discomfort round him.

No; he was naturally a little man of unreasonable moods. When over-wrought, which he often was, he became acutely irritable; and, besides, his veins were dark with a livid belladonna tincture, the essence of jealousy. I do not mean merely the tender jealousy of the heart, but that sterner, narrower sentiment whose seat is in the head.

I used to think, as I sat looking at M. Paul, while he was knitting his brow or protruding his lip over some exercise of mine, which had not as many faults as he wished (for he liked me to commit faults: a knot of blunders was sweet to him as a cluster of nuts), that he had points of resemblance to Napoleon Bonaparte. I think so still.

In a shameless disregard of magnanimity, he resembled the great Emperor. M. Paul would have quarrelled with twenty learned women, would have unblushingly carried on a system of petty bickering and recrimination with a whole capital of coteries, never troubling himself about loss or lack of dignity. He would have exiled fifty Madame de Staëls, if, they had annoyed, offended, outrivalled, or opposed him.

I well remember a hot episode of his with a certain Madame Panache – a lady temporarily employed by Madame Beck to give lessons in history. She was clever – that is, she knew a good deal; and, besides, thoroughly possessed the art of making the most of what she knew; of words and confidence she held unlimited command. Her personal appearance was far from destitute of advantages; I believe many people would have pronounced her 'a fine woman'; and yet there were points in her robust and ample attractions, as well as in her bustling and demonstrative presence, which, it appeared, the nice and capricious tastes of M. Paul could not away with. The sound of her voice, echoing through the carré, would put him into a strange taking; her long free step – almost stride – along the corridor, would often make him snatch up his papers and decamp on the instant.

With malicious intent he bethought himself, one day, to intrude on her class; as quick as lightning he gathered her method of instruction; it differed from a pet plan of his own. With little ceremony, and less courtesy, he pointed out what he termed her errors. Whether he expected submission and attention, I know not; he met an acrid opposition, accompanied by a round reprimand for his certainly unjustifiable interference.

Instead of withdrawing with dignity, as he might still have done, he threw down the gauntlet of defiance. Madame Panache, bellicose as a Penthesilea, picked it up in a minute. She snapped her fingers in the intermeddler's face; she rushed upon him with a storm of words. M. Emanuel was eloquent; but Madame Panache was voluble. A system of fierce antagonism ensued. Instead of laughing in his sleeve at his fair foe, with all her sore amour-propre and loud self-assertion, M. Paul detested her with intense seriousness; he honoured her with his earnest fury; he pursued her vindictively and implacably, refusing to rest peaceably in his bed, to derive due benefit from his meals, or even serenely to relish his cigar, till she was fairly rooted out of the establishment. The Professor conquered, but I cannot say that the laurels of this victory shadowed gracefully his temples. Once I ventured to hint as much. To my great surprise he allowed that I might be right, but averred that when brought into contact with either men or women of the coarse, self-complacent quality, whereof Madame Panache was a specimen, he had no control over his own passions; an unspeakable and active aversion impelled him to a war of extermination.

Three months afterwards, hearing that his vanquished foe had met with reverses, and was likely to be really distressed for want of employment, he forgot his hatred, and alike active in good and evil, he moved heaven and earth till he found her a place. Upon her coming to make up former differences, and thank him for his recent kindness, the old voice – a little loud – the old manner – a little forward – so acted upon him that in ten minutes he started up and bowed her, or rather himself, out of the room, in a transport of nervous irritation.

To pursue a somewhat audacious parallel, in a love of power, in an eager grasp after supremacy, M. Emanuel was like Bonaparte. He was a man not always to be submitted to. Sometimes it was needful to resist; it was right to stand still, to look up into his eyes and tell him that his requirements went beyond reason – that his absolutism verged on tyranny.

The dawnings, the first developments of peculiar talent appearing within his range, and under his rule, curiously excited, even disturbed him. He watched its struggle into life with a scowl; he held back his hand – perhaps said, "Come on if you have strength," but would not aid the birth.

When the pang and peril of the first conflict were over, when the breath of life was drawn, when he saw the lungs expand and contract, when he felt the heart beat and discovered life in the eye, he did not yet offer to foster.

"Prove yourself true ere I cherish you," was his ordinance; and how difficult he made that proof! What thorns and briers, what flints, he strewed in the path of feet not inured to rough travel! He watched tearlessly – ordeals that he exacted should be passed through – fearlessly. He followed footprints that, as they approached the bourne, were sometimes marked in blood – followed them grimly, holding the austerest police-watch over the pain-pressed pilgrim. And when at last he allowed a rest, before slumber might close the eyelids, he opened those same lids wide, with pitiless finger and thumb, and gazed deep through the pupil and the irids into the brain, into the heart, to search if Vanity, or Pride, or Falsehood, in any of its subtlest forms, was discoverable in the furthest recess of existence. If, at last, he let the neophyte sleep, it was but a moment; he woke him suddenly up to apply new tests: he sent him on irksome errands when he was staggering with weariness; he tried the temper, the sense, and the health; and it was only when every severest test had been applied and endured, when the most corrosive aquafortis had been used, and failed to tarnish the ore, that he admitted it genuine, and, still in clouded silence, stamped it with his deep brand of approval.

I speak not ignorant of these evils.

Till the date at which the last chapter closes, M. Paul had not been my professor – he had not given me lessons, but about that time, accidentally hearing me one day acknowledge an ignorance of some branch of education (I think it was arithmetic), which would have disgraced a charity-school boy, as he very truly remarked, he took me in hand, examined me first, found me, I need not say, abundantly deficient, gave me some books and appointed me some tasks.

He did this at first with pleasure, indeed with unconcealed exultation, condescending to say that he believed I was "*bonne et pas trop faible*" (i.e. well enough disposed, and not wholly destitute of parts), but, owing he supposed to adverse circumstances, "as yet in a state of wretchedly imperfect mental development."

The beginning of all effort has indeed with me been marked by a preternatural imbecility. I never could, even in forming a common acquaintance, assert or prove a claim to average quickness. A depressing and difficult passage has prefaced every new page I have turned in life.

So long as this passage lasted, M. Paul was very kind, very good, very forbearing; he saw the sharp pain inflicted, and felt the weighty humiliation imposed by my own sense of incapacity; and words can hardly do justice to his tenderness and helpfulness. His own eyes would moisten, when tears of shame and effort clouded mine; burdened as he was with work, he would steal half his brief space of recreation to give to me.

But, strange grief! When that heavy and overcast dawn began at last to yield to day; when my faculties began to struggle themselves, free, and my time of energy and fulfilment came; when I voluntarily doubled, trebled, quadrupled the tasks he set, to please him as I thought, his kindness became sternness; the light changed in his eyes from a beam to a spark; he fretted, he opposed, he curbed me imperiously; the more I did, the harder I worked, the less he seemed content. Sarcasms of which the severity amazed and puzzled me, harassed my ears; then flowed out the bitterest inuendoes against the 'pride of intellect'. I was vaguely threatened with I know not what doom, if I ever trespassed the limits proper to my sex, and conceived a contraband appetite for unfeminine knowledge. Alas! I had no such appetite. What I loved, it joyed me by any effort to content; but the noble hunger for science in the abstract – the godlike thirst after discovery – these feelings were known to me but by briefest flashes.

Yet, when M. Paul sneered at me, I wanted to possess them more fully; his injustice stirred in me ambitious wishes – it imparted a strong stimulus – it gave wings to aspiration.

In the beginning, before I had penetrated to motives, that uncomprehended sneer of his made my heart ache, but by-and-by it only warmed the blood in my veins, and sent added action to my pulses. Whatever my powers – feminine or the contrary – God had given them, and I felt resolute to be ashamed of no faculty of his bestowal.

The combat was very sharp for a time. I seemed to have lost M. Paul's affection; he treated me strangely. In his most unjust moments he would insinuate that I had deceived him when I appeared, what he called 'faible' – that is incompetent; he said I had feigned a false incapacity. Again, he would turn suddenly round and accuse me of the most far-fetched imitations and impossible plagiarisms, asserting that I had extracted the pith out of books I had not so much as heard of – and over the perusal of which I should infallibly have fallen down in a sleep as deep as that of Eutychus.

Once, upon his preferring such an accusation, I turned upon him – I rose against him. Gathering an armful of his books out of my desk, I filled my apron and poured them in a heap upon his estrade, at his feet.

"Take them away, M. Paul," I said, "and teach me no more. I never asked to be made learned, and you compel me to feel very profoundly that learning is not happiness."

And returning to my desk, I laid my head on my arms, nor would I speak to him for two days afterwards. He pained and chagrined me. His affection had been very sweet and dear – a pleasure new and incomparable: now that this seemed withdrawn, I cared not for his lessons.

The books, however, were not taken away; they were all restored with careful hand to their places, and he came as usual to teach me. He made his peace somehow – too readily, perhaps: I ought to have stood out longer, but when he looked kind and good, and held out his hand with amity, memory refused to reproduce with due force his oppressive moments. And then, reconcilement is always sweet!

On a certain morning a message came from my godmother, inviting me to attend some notable lecture to be delivered in the same public rooms before described. Dr. John had brought the message himself, and delivered it verbally to Rosine, who had not scrupled to follow the steps of M. Emanuel, then passing to the first classe, and, in his presence, stand 'carrément' before my desk, hand in apron-pocket, and rehearse the same, saucily and aloud, concluding with the words, "*Qu'il est vraiment beau, Mademoiselle, ce jeune docteur! Quels yeux – quel regard! Tenez! J'en ai le coeur tout ému!*"

When she was gone, my professor demanded of me why I suffered "*cette fille effrontée, cette créature sans pudeur,*" to address me in such terms.

I had no pacifying answer to give. The terms were precisely such as Rosine – a young lady in whose skull the organs of reverence and reserve were not largely developed – was in the constant habit of using. Besides, what she said about the young doctor was true enough. Graham *was* handsome; he had fine eyes and a thrilling glance. An observation to that effect actually formed itself into sound on my lips.

"*Elle ne dit que la vérité,*" I said.

"*Ah! Vous trouvez?*"

"*Mais, sans doute.*"

The lesson to which we had that day to submit was such as to make us very glad when it terminated. At its close, the released pupils rushed out, half-trembling, half-exultant. I, too, was going. A mandate to remain arrested me. I muttered that I wanted some fresh air sadly – the stove was in a glow, the classe over-heated. An inexorable voice merely recommended silence; and this salamander – for whom no room ever seemed too hot – sitting down between my desk and the stove – a situation in which he ought to have felt broiled, but did not – proceeded to confront me with – a Greek quotation!

In M. Emanuel's soul rankled a chronic suspicion that I knew both Greek and Latin. As monkeys are said to have the power of speech if they would but use it, and are reported to conceal this faculty in fear of its being turned to their detriment, so to me was ascribed a fund of knowledge which I was supposed criminally and craftily to conceal. The privileges of a 'classical education', it was insinuated, had been mine; on flowers of Hymettus I had revelled; a golden store, hived in memory, now silently sustained my efforts, and privily nurtured my wits.

A hundred expedients did M. Paul employ to surprise my secret – to wheedle, to threaten, to startle it out of me. Sometimes he placed Greek and Latin books in my way, and then watched me, as Joan of Arc's jailors tempted her with the warrior's accoutrements, and lay in wait for the issue. Again he quoted I know not what authors and passages, and while rolling out their sweet and sounding lines (the classic tones fell musically from his lips – for he had a good voice – remarkable for compass, modulation, and matchless expression), he would fix on me a vigilant, piercing, and often malicious eye. It was evident he sometimes expected great demonstrations; they never occurred, however; not comprehending, of course I could neither be charmed nor annoyed.

Baffled – almost angry – he still clung to his fixed idea; my susceptibilities were pronounced marble – my face a mask. It appeared as if he could not be brought to accept the homely truth, and take me for what I was: men, and women too, must have delusion of some sort; if not made ready to their hand, they will invent exaggeration for themselves.

At moments I *did* wish that his suspicions had been better founded. There were times when I would have given my right hand to possess the treasures he ascribed to me. He deserved condign punishment for his testy crotchets. I could have gloried in bringing home to him his worst apprehensions astoundingly realized. I could have exulted to burst on his vision, confront and confound his 'lunettes', one blaze of acquirements. Oh! Why did nobody undertake to make me clever while I was young enough to learn, that I might, by one grand, sudden, inhuman revelation – one cold, cruel, overwhelming triumph – have forever crushed the mocking spirit out of Paul Carl David Emanuel!

Alas! No such feat was in my power. Today, as usual, his quotations fell ineffectual: he soon shifted his ground.

'Women of intellect' was his next theme: here he was at home. A 'woman of intellect', it appeared, was a sort of 'lusus naturae', a luckless accident, a thing for which there was neither place nor use in creation, wanted neither as wife nor worker. Beauty anticipated her in the first office. He believed in his soul that lovely, placid, and passive feminine mediocrity was the only pillow on which manly thought and sense could find rest for its aching temples; and as to work, male mind alone could work to any good practical result – hein?

This 'hein?' was a note of interrogation intended to draw from me contradiction or objection. However, I only said – "*Cela ne me regarde pas: je ne m'en soucie pas;*" and presently added – "May I go, Monsieur? They have rung the bell for the second déjeuner" (i.e. luncheon).

"What of that? You are not hungry?"

"Indeed I was," I said; "I had had nothing since breakfast, at seven, and should have nothing till dinner, at five, if I missed this bell."

"Well, he was in the same plight, but I might share with him."

And he broke in two the 'brioche' intended for his own refreshment, and gave me half. Truly his bark was worse than his bite; but the really formidable attack was yet to come. While eating his cake, I could not forbear expressing my secret wish that I really knew all of which he accused me.

"Did I sincerely feel myself to be an ignoramus?" he asked, in a softened tone.

If I had replied meekly by an unqualified affirmative, I believe he would have stretched out his hand, and we should have been friends on the spot, but I answered –

"Not exactly. I am ignorant, Monsieur, in the knowledge you ascribe to me, but I *sometimes*, not *always*, feel a knowledge of my own."

"What did I mean?" he inquired, sharply.

Unable to answer this question in a breath, I evaded it by change of subject. He had now finished his half of the brioche feeling sure that on so trifling a fragment he could not have satisfied his appetite, as indeed I had not appeased mine, and inhaling the fragrance of baked apples afar from the refectory, I ventured to inquire whether he did not also perceive that agreeable odour. He confessed that he did. I said if he would let me out by the garden-door, and permit me just to run across the court, I would fetch him a plateful; and added that I believed they were excellent, as Goton had a very good method of baking, or rather stewing fruit, putting in a little spice, sugar, and a glass or two of vin blanc – might I go?

"*Petite gourmande!*" said he, smiling, "I have not forgotten how pleased you were with the pâté â la crème I once gave you, and you know very well, at this moment, that to fetch the apples for me will be the same as getting them for yourself. Go, then, but come back quickly."

And at last he liberated me on parole. My own plan was to go and return with speed and good faith, to put the plate in at the door, and then to vanish incontinent, leaving all consequences for future settlement.

That intolerably keen instinct of his seemed to have anticipated my scheme: he met me at the threshold, hurried me into the room, and fixed me in a minute in my former seat. Taking the plate of fruit from my hand, he divided the portion intended only for himself, and ordered me to eat my share. I complied with no good grace, and vexed, I suppose, by my reluctance, he opened a masked and dangerous battery. All he had yet said, I could count as mere sound and fury, signifying nothing: not so of the present attack.

It consisted in an unreasonable proposition with which he had before afflicted me: namely, that on the next public examination-day I should engage – foreigner as I was – to take my place on the first form of first-class pupils, and with them improvise a composition in French, on any subject any spectator might dictate, without benefit of grammar or lexicon.

I knew what the result of such an experiment would be. I, to whom nature had denied the impromptu faculty; who, in public, was by nature a cypher; whose time of mental activity, even when alone, was not under the meridian sun; who needed the fresh silence of morning, or the recluse peace of evening, to win from the Creative Impulse one evidence of his presence, one proof of his force; I, with whom that Impulse was the most intractable, the most capricious, the most maddening of masters (him before me always excepted) – a deity which sometimes, under circumstances – apparently propitious, would not speak when questioned, would not hear when appealed to, would not, when sought, be found; but would stand, all cold, all indurated, all granite, a dark Baal with carven lips and blank eye-balls, and breast like the stone face of a tomb; and again, suddenly, at some turn, some sound, some long-trembling sob of the wind, at some rushing past of an unseen stream of electricity, the irrational demon would wake unsolicited, would stir strangely alive, would rush from its pedestal like a perturbed Dagon, calling to its votary for a sacrifice, whatever the hour – to its victim for some blood, or some breath, whatever the circumstance or scene – rousing its priest, treacherously promising vaticination, perhaps filling its temple with a strange hum of oracles, but sure to give half the significance to fateful winds, and grudging to the desperate listener even a miserable remnant – yielding it sordidly, as though each word had been a drop of the deathless ichor of its own dark veins.

And this tyrant I was to compel into bondage, and make it improvise a theme, on a school estrade, between a Mathilde and a Coralie, under the eye of a Madame Beck, for the pleasure, and to the inspiration of a bourgeois of Labassecour!

Upon this argument M. Paul and I did battle more than once – strong battle, with confused noise of demand and rejection, exaction and repulse.

On this particular day I was soundly rated. 'The obstinacy of my whole sex', it seems, was concentrated in me; I had an 'orgueil de diable'. I feared to fail, forsooth! What did it matter whether I failed or not? Who was I that I should not fail, like my betters? It would do me good to fail. He wanted to see me worsted (I knew he did), and one minute he paused to take breath.

"Would I speak now, and be tractable?"

"Never would I be tractable in this matter. Law itself should not compel me. I would pay a fine, or undergo an imprisonment, rather than write for a show and to order, perched up on a platform."

"Could softer motives influence me? Would I yield for friendship's sake?"

"Not a whit, not a hair-breadth. No form of friendship under the sun had a right to exact such a concession. No true friendship would harass me thus."

He supposed then (with a sneer – M. Paul could sneer supremely, curling his lip, opening his nostrils, contracting his eyelids) – he supposed there was but one form of appeal to which I would listen, and of that form it was not for him to make use.

"Under certain persuasions, from certain quarters, *je vous vois d'ici*," said he, "eagerly subscribing to the sacrifice, passionately arming for the effort."

"Making a simpleton, a warning, and an example of myself, before a hundred and fifty of the 'papas' and 'mammas' of Villette."

And here, losing patience, I broke out afresh with a cry that I wanted to be liberated – to get out into the air – I was almost in a fever.

"*Chut!*" said the inexorable, "This was a mere pretext to run away; *he* was not hot, with the stove close at his back; how could I suffer, thoroughly screened by his person?"

"I did not understand his constitution. I knew nothing of the natural history of salamanders. For my own part, I was a phlegmatic islander, and sitting in an oven did not agree with me; at least, might I step to the well, and get a glass of water – the sweet apples had made me thirsty?"

"If that was all, he would do my errand."

He went to fetch the water. Of course, with a door only on the latch behind me, I lost not my opportunity. Ere his return, his half-worried prey had escaped.

Chapter Thirty-One
The Dryad

～～～

THE SPRING was advancing, and the weather had turned suddenly warm. This change of temperature brought with it for me, as probably for many others, temporary decrease of strength. Slight exertion at this time left me overcome with fatigue – sleepless nights entailed languid days.

One Sunday afternoon, having walked the distance of half a league to the Protestant church, I came back weary and exhausted; and taking refuge in my solitary sanctuary, the first classe, I was glad to sit down, and to make of my desk a pillow for my arms and head.

Awhile I listened to the lullaby of bees humming in the berceau, and watched, through the glass door and the tender, lightly-strewn spring foliage, Madame Beck and a gay party of friends, whom she had entertained that day at dinner after morning mass, walking in the centre-alley under orchard boughs dressed at this season in blossom, and wearing a colouring as pure and warm as mountain-snow at sun-rise.

My principal attraction towards this group of guests lay, I remember, in one figure – that of a handsome young girl whom I had seen before as a visitor at Madame Beck's, and of whom I had been vaguely told that she was a 'filleule', or god-daughter, of M. Emanuel's, and that between her mother, or aunt, or some other female relation of hers, and the Professor, had existed of old a special friendship. M. Paul was not of the holiday band today, but I had seen this young girl with him ere now, and as far as distant observation could enable me to judge, she seemed to enjoy him with the frank ease of a ward with an indulgent guardian. I had seen her run up to him, put her arm through his, and hang upon him. Once, when she did so, a curious sensation had struck through me – a disagreeable anticipatory sensation – one of the family of presentiments, I suppose – but I refused to analyze or dwell upon it. While watching this girl, Mademoiselle Sauveur by name, and following the gleam of her bright silk robe (she was always richly dressed, for she was said to be wealthy) through the flowers and the glancing leaves of tender emerald, my eyes became dazzled – they closed; my lassitude, the warmth of the day, the hum of bees and birds, all lulled me, and at last I slept.

Two hours stole over me. Ere I woke, the sun had declined out of sight behind the towering houses, the garden and the room were grey, bees had gone homeward, and the flowers were closing; the party of guests, too, had vanished; each alley was void.

On waking, I felt much at ease – not chill, as I ought to have been after sitting so still for at least two hours; my cheek and arms were not benumbed by pressure against the hard desk. No wonder. Instead of the bare wood on which I had laid them, I found a thick shawl, carefully folded, substituted for support, and another shawl (both taken from the corridor where such things hung) wrapped warmly round me.

Who had done this? Who was my friend? Which of the teachers? Which of the pupils? None, except St. Pierre, was inimical to me; but which of them had the art, the thought, the habit, of benefiting thus tenderly? Which of them had a step so quiet, a hand so gentle, but I should have heard or felt her, if she had approached or touched me in a day-sleep?

As to Ginevra Fanshawe, that bright young creature was not gentle at all, and would certainly have pulled me out of my chair, if she had meddled in the matter. I said at last: "It is Madame Beck's doing; she has come in, seen me asleep, and thought I might take cold. She considers me a useful machine, answering well the purpose for which it was hired; so would not have me needlessly injured. And now," methought, "I'll take a walk; the evening is fresh, and not very chill."

So I opened the glass door and stepped into the berceau.

I went to my own alley: had it been dark, or even dusk, I should have hardly ventured there, for I had not yet forgotten the curious illusion of vision (if illusion it were) experienced in that place some months ago. But a ray of the setting sun burnished still the grey crown of Jean Baptiste; nor had all the birds of the garden yet vanished into their nests amongst the tufted shrubs and thick wall-ivy. I paced up and down, thinking almost the same thoughts I had pondered that night when I buried my glass jar – how I should make some advance in life, take another step towards an independent position; for this train of reflection, though not lately pursued, had never by me been wholly abandoned; and whenever a certain eye was averted from me, and a certain countenance grew dark with unkindness and injustice, into that track of speculation did I at once strike; so that, little by little, I had laid half a plan.

"Living costs little," said I to myself, "in this economical town of Villette, where people are more sensible than I understand they are in dear old England – infinitely less worried about appearance, and less emulous of display – where nobody is in the least ashamed to be quite as homely and saving as he finds convenient. House-rent, in a prudently chosen situation, need not be high. When I shall have saved one thousand francs, I will take a tenement with one large room, and two or three smaller ones, furnish the first with a few benches and desks, a black tableau, an estrade for myself; upon it a chair and table, with a sponge and some white chalks; begin with taking day-pupils, and so work my way upwards. Madame Beck's commencement was – as I have often heard her say – from no higher starting-point, and where is she now? All these premises and this garden are hers, bought with her money; she has a competency already secured for old age, and a flourishing establishment under her direction, which will furnish a career for her children.

"Courage, Lucy Snowe! With self-denial and economy now, and steady exertion by-and-by, an object in life need not fail you. Venture not to complain that such an object is too selfish, too limited, and lacks interest; be content to labour for independence until you have proved, by winning that prize, your right to look higher. But afterwards, is there nothing more for me in life – no true home – nothing to be dearer to me than myself, and by its paramount preciousness, to draw from me better things than I care to culture for myself only? Nothing, at whose feet I can willingly lay down the whole burden of human egotism, and gloriously take up the nobler charge of labouring and living for others? I suppose, Lucy Snowe, the orb of your life is not to be so rounded: for you, the crescent-phase must suffice. Very good. I see a huge mass of my fellow-creatures in no better circumstances. I see that a great many men, and more women, hold their span of life on conditions of denial and privation. I find no reason why I should be of the few favoured. I believe in some blending of hope and sunshine sweetening the worst lots. I believe that this life is not all; neither the beginning nor the end. I believe while I tremble; I trust while I weep."

So this subject is done with. It is right to look our life-accounts bravely in the face now and then, and settle them honestly. And he is a poor self-swindler who lies to himself while he reckons the items, and sets down under the head – happiness that which is misery. Call anguish – anguish, and despair – despair; write both down in strong characters with a resolute pen: you will the better pay your debt to Doom. Falsify: insert 'privilege' where you should have written 'pain'; and see if your mighty creditor will allow the fraud to pass, or accept the coin with which you would cheat him. Offer to the strongest – if the darkest angel of God's host – water, when he has asked blood – will he take it? Not a whole pale sea for one red drop. I settled another account.

Pausing before Methusaleh – the giant and patriarch of the garden – and leaning my brow against his knotty trunk, my foot rested on the stone sealing the small sepulchre at his root; and I recalled the passage of feeling therein buried; I recalled Dr. John; my warm affection for him; my faith in his excellence; my delight in his grace. What was become of that curious one-sided friendship which was half marble and half life; only on one hand truth, and on the other perhaps a jest?

Was this feeling dead? I do not know, but it was buried. Sometimes I thought the tomb unquiet, and dreamed strangely of disturbed earth, and of hair, still golden, and living, obtruded through coffin-chinks.

Had I been too hasty? I used to ask myself; and this question would occur with a cruel sharpness after some brief chance interview with Dr. John. He had still such kind looks, such a warm hand; his voice still kept so pleasant a tone for my name; I never liked 'Lucy' so well as when he uttered it. But I learned in time that this benignity, this cordiality, this music, belonged in no shape to me: it was a part of himself; it was the honey of his temper; it was the balm of his mellow mood; he imparted it, as the ripe fruit rewards with sweetness the rifling bee; he diffused it about him, as sweet plants shed their perfume. Does the nectarine love either the bee or bird it feeds? Is the sweetbriar enamoured of the air?

"Goodnight, Dr. John; you are good, you are beautiful; but you are not mine. Goodnight, and God bless you!"

Thus I closed my musings. "Goodnight" left my lips in sound; I heard the words spoken, and then I heard an echo – quite close.

"Goodnight, Mademoiselle; or, rather, good-evening – the sun is scarce set; I hope you slept well?"

I started, but was only discomposed a moment; I knew the voice and speaker.

"Slept, Monsieur! When? Where?"

"You may well inquire when – where. It seems you turn day into night, and choose a desk for a pillow; rather hard lodging –?"

"It was softened for me, Monsieur, while I slept. That unseen, gift-bringing thing which haunts my desk, remembered me. No matter how I fell asleep; I awoke pillowed and covered."

"Did the shawls keep you warm?"

"Very warm. Do you ask thanks for them?"

"No. You looked pale in your slumbers: are you home-sick?"

"To be home-sick, one must have a home; which I have not."

"Then you have more need of a careful friend. I scarcely know anyone, Miss Lucy, who needs a friend more absolutely than you; your very faults imperatively require it. You want so much checking, regulating, and keeping down."

This idea of 'keeping down' never left M. Paul's head; the most habitual subjugation would, in my case, have failed to relieve him of it. No matter; what did it signify? I listened to him, and did not trouble myself to be too submissive; his occupation would have been gone had I left him nothing to 'keep down'.

"You need watching, and watching over," he pursued; "and it is well for you that I see this, and do my best to discharge both duties. I watch you and others pretty closely, pretty constantly, nearer and oftener than you or they think. Do you see that window with a light in it?"

He pointed to a lattice in one of the college boarding-houses.

"That," said he, "is a room I have hired, nominally for a study – virtually for a post of observation. There I sit and read for hours together: it is my way – my taste. My book is this garden; its contents are human nature – female human nature. I know you all by heart. Ah! I know you well – St. Pierre, the Parisienne – cette maîtresse-femme, my cousin Beck herself."

"It is not right, Monsieur."

"Comment? It is not right? By whose creed? Does some dogma of Calvin or Luther condemn it? What is that to me? I am no Protestant. My rich father (for, though I have known poverty, and once starved for a year in a garret in Rome – starved wretchedly, often on a meal a day, and sometimes not that – yet I was born to wealth) – my rich father was a good Catholic; and he gave me a priest and a Jesuit for a tutor. I retain his lessons; and to what discoveries, grand Dieu! Have they not aided me!"

"Discoveries made by stealth seem to me dishonourable discoveries."

"Puritaine! I doubt it not. Yet see how my Jesuit's system works. You know the St. Pierre?"

"Partially."

He laughed. "You say right – 'partially'; whereas I know her thoroughly; there is the difference. She played before me the amiable; offered me patte de velours; caressed, flattered, fawned on me.

Now, I am accessible to a woman's flattery – accessible against my reason. Though never pretty, she was – when I first knew her – young, or knew how to look young. Like all her countrywomen, she had the art of dressing – she had a certain cool, easy, social assurance, which spared me the pain of embarrassment –"

"Monsieur, that must have been unnecessary. I never saw you embarrassed in my life."

"Mademoiselle, you know little of me; I can be embarrassed as a petite pensionnaire; there is a fund of modesty and diffidence in my nature –"

"Monsieur, I never saw it."

"Mademoiselle, it is there. You ought to have seen it."

"Monsieur, I have observed you in public – on platforms, in tribunes, before titles and crowned heads – and you were as easy as you are in the third division."

"Mademoiselle, neither titles nor crowned heads excite my modesty; and publicity is very much my element. I like it well, and breathe in it quite freely; – but – but, in short, here is the sentiment brought into action, at this very moment; however, I disdain to be worsted by it. If, Mademoiselle, I were a marrying man (which I am not; and you may spare yourself the trouble of any sneer you may be contemplating at the thought), and found it necessary to ask a lady whether she could look upon me in the light of a future husband, then would it be proved that I am as I say – modest."

I quite believed him now; and, in believing, I honoured him with a sincerity of esteem which made my heart ache.

"As to the St. Pierre," he went on, recovering himself, for his voice had altered a little, "she once intended to be Madame Emanuel; and I don't know whither I might have been led, but for yonder little lattice with the light. Ah, magic lattice! What miracles of discovery hast thou wrought! Yes," he pursued, "I have seen her rancours, her vanities, her levities – not only here, but elsewhere: I have witnessed what bucklers me against all her arts: I am safe from poor Zélie."

"And my pupils," he presently recommenced, "those blondes jeunes filles – so mild and meek – I have seen the most reserved – romp like boys, the demurest – snatch grapes from the walls, shake pears from the trees. When the English teacher came, I saw her, marked her early preference for this alley, noticed her taste for seclusion, watched her well, long before she and I came to speaking terms; do you recollect my once coming silently and offering you a little knot of white violets when we were strangers?"

"I recollect it. I dried the violets, kept them, and have them still."

"It pleased me when you took them peacefully and promptly, without prudery – that sentiment which I ever dread to excite, and which, when it is revealed in eye or gesture, I vindictively detest. To return. Not only did *I* watch you; but often – especially at eventide – another guardian angel was noiselessly hovering near: night after night my cousin Beck has stolen down yonder steps, and glidingly pursued your movements when you did not see her."

"But, Monsieur, you could not from the distance of that window see what passed in this garden at night?"

"By moonlight I possibly might with a glass – I use a glass – but the garden itself is open to me. In the shed, at the bottom, there is a door leading into a court, which communicates with the college; of that door I possess the key, and thus come and go at pleasure. This afternoon I came through it, and found you asleep in classe; again this evening I have availed myself of the same entrance."

I could not help saying, "If you were a wicked, designing man, how terrible would all this be!"

His attention seemed incapable of being arrested by this view of the subject: he lit his cigar, and while he puffed it, leaning against a tree, and looking at me in a cool, amused way he had when his humour was tranquil, I thought proper to go on sermonizing him: he often lectured me by the hour together – I did not see why I should not speak my mind for once. So I told him my impressions concerning his Jesuit-system.

"The knowledge it brings you is bought too dear, Monsieur; this coming and going by stealth degrades your own dignity."

"My dignity!" he cried, laughing; "when did you ever see me trouble my head about my dignity? It is you, Miss Lucy, who are 'digne'. How often, in your high insular presence, have I taken a pleasure in trampling upon, what you are pleased to call, my dignity; tearing it, scattering it to the winds, in those mad transports you witness with such hauteur, and which I know you think very like the ravings of a third-rate London actor."

"Monsieur, I tell you every glance you cast from that lattice is a wrong done to the best part of your own nature. To study the human heart thus, is to banquet secretly and sacrilegiously on Eve's apples. I wish you were a Protestant."

Indifferent to the wish, he smoked on. After a space of smiling yet thoughtful silence, he said, rather suddenly – "I have seen other things."

"What other things?"

Taking the weed from his lips, he threw the remnant amongst the shrubs, where, for a moment, it lay glowing in the gloom.

"Look, at it," said he: "is not that spark like an eye watching you and me?"

He took a turn down the walk; presently returning, he went on: "I have seen, Miss Lucy, things to me unaccountable, that have made me watch all night for a solution, and I have not yet found it."

The tone was peculiar; my veins thrilled; he saw me shiver.

"Are you afraid? Whether is it of my words or that red jealous eye just winking itself out?"

"I am cold; the night grows dark and late, and the air is changed; it is time to go in."

"It is little past eight, but you shall go in soon. Answer me only this question."

Yet he paused ere he put it. The garden was truly growing dark; dusk had come on with clouds, and drops of rain began to patter through the trees. I hoped he would feel this, but, for the moment, he seemed too much absorbed to be sensible of the change.

"Mademoiselle, do you Protestants believe in the supernatural?"

"There is a difference of theory and belief on this point amongst Protestants as amongst other sects," I answered. "Why, Monsieur, do you ask such a question?"

"Why do you shrink and speak so faintly? Are you superstitious?"

"I am constitutionally nervous. I dislike the discussion of such subjects. I dislike it the more because –"

"You believe?"

"No: but it has happened to me to experience impressions –"

"Since you came here?"

"Yes; not many months ago."

"Here? – in this house?"

"Yes."

"*Bon!* I am glad of it. I knew it, somehow; before you told me. I was conscious of rapport between you and myself. You are patient, and I am choleric; you are quiet and pale, and I am tanned and fiery; you are a strict Protestant, and I am a sort of lay Jesuit: but we are alike – there is affinity between us. Do you see it, Mademoiselle, when you look in the glass? Do you observe that your forehead is shaped like mine – that your eyes are cut like mine? Do you hear that you have some of my tones of voice? Do you know that you have many of my looks? I perceive all this, and believe that you were born under my star. Yes, you were born under my star! Tremble! For where that is the case with mortals, the threads of their destinies are difficult to disentangle; knottings and catchings occur – sudden breaks leave damage in the web. But these 'impressions', as you say, with English caution. I, too, have had my 'impressions'."

"Monsieur, tell me them."

"I desire no better, and intend no less. You know the legend of this house and garden?"

"I know it. Yes. They say that hundreds of years ago a nun was buried here alive at the foot of this very tree, beneath the ground which now bears us."

"And that in former days a nun's ghost used to come and go here."

"Monsieur, what if it comes and goes here still?"

"Something comes and goes here: there is a shape frequenting this house by night, different to any forms that show themselves by day. I have indisputably seen a something, more than once; and to me its conventual weeds were a strange sight, saying more than they can do to any other living being. A nun!"

"Monsieur, I, too, have seen it."

"I anticipated that. Whether this nun be flesh and blood, or something that remains when blood is dried, and flesh is wasted, her business is as much with you as with me, probably. Well, I mean to make it out; it has baffled me so far, but I mean to follow up the mystery. I mean –"

Instead of telling what he meant, he raised his head suddenly; I made the same movement in the same instant; we both looked to one point – the high tree shadowing the great berceau, and resting some of its boughs on the roof of the first classe. There had been a strange and inexplicable sound from that quarter, as if the arms of that tree had swayed of their own motion, and its weight of foliage had rushed and crushed against the massive trunk. Yes; there scarce stirred a breeze, and that heavy tree was convulsed, whilst the feathery shrubs stood still. For some minutes amongst the wood and leafage a rending and heaving went on. Dark as it was, it seemed to me that something more solid than either night-shadow, or branch-shadow, blackened out of the boles. At last the struggle ceased. What birth succeeded this travail? What Dryad was born of these throes? We watched fixedly. A sudden bell rang in the house – the prayer-bell. Instantly into our alley there came, out of the berceau, an apparition, all black and white. With a sort of angry rush-close, close past our faces – swept swiftly the very *nun* herself! Never had I seen her so clearly. She looked tall of stature, and fierce of gesture. As she went, the wind rose sobbing; the rain poured wild and cold; the whole night seemed to feel her.

Chapter Thirty-Two
The First Letter

WHERE, it becomes time to inquire, was Paulina Mary? How fared my intercourse with the sumptuous Hôtel Crécy? That intercourse had, for an interval, been suspended by absence; M. and Miss de Bassompierre had been travelling, dividing some weeks between the provinces and capital of France. Chance apprised me of their return very shortly after it took place.

I was walking one mild afternoon on a quiet boulevard, wandering slowly on, enjoying the benign April sun, and some thoughts not unpleasing, when I saw before me a group of riders, stopping as if they had just encountered, and exchanging greetings in the midst of the broad, smooth, linden-bordered path; on one side a middle-aged gentleman and young lady, on the other – a young and handsome man. Very graceful was the lady's mien, choice her appointments, delicate and stately her whole aspect. Still, as I looked, I felt they were known to me, and, drawing a little nearer, I fully recognised them all: the Count Home de Bassompierre, his daughter, and Dr. Graham Bretton.

How animated was Graham's face! How true, how warm, yet how retiring the joy it expressed! This was the state of things, this the combination of circumstances, at once to attract and enchain, to subdue and excite Dr. John. The pearl he admired was in itself of great price and truest purity, but he was not the man who, in appreciating the gem, could forget its setting. Had he seen Paulina with the same youth, beauty, and grace, but on foot, alone, unguarded, and in simple attire, a dependent worker, a demi-grisette, he would have thought her a pretty little creature, and would have loved with his eye her movements and her mien, but it required other than this to conquer him as he was now vanquished, to bring him safe under dominion as now, without loss, and even with gain to his manly honour, one saw that he was reduced; there was about Dr. John all the man of the world; to satisfy himself did not suffice; society must approve – the world must admire what he did, or he counted his measures false and futile. In his victrix he required all that was here visible – the imprint of high cultivation, the consecration of a careful and authoritative protection, the adjuncts that Fashion decrees, Wealth purchases, and Taste adjusts; for these conditions his spirit stipulated ere it surrendered: they were here to the utmost fulfilled; and now, proud, impassioned, yet fearing, he did homage to Paulina as his sovereign. As for her, the smile of feeling, rather than of conscious power, slept soft in her eyes.

They parted. He passed me at speed, hardly feeling the earth he skimmed, and seeing nothing on either hand. He looked very handsome; mettle and purpose were roused in him fully.

"Papa, there is Lucy!" cried a musical, friendly voice. "Lucy, dear Lucy – *do* come here!"

I hastened to her. She threw back her veil, and stooped from her saddle to kiss me.

"I was coming to see you tomorrow," said she; "but now tomorrow you will come and see me."

She named the hour, and I promised compliance.

The morrow's evening found me with her – she and I shut into her own room. I had not seen her since that occasion when her claims were brought into comparison with those of Ginevra Fanshawe, and had so signally prevailed; she had much to tell me of her travels in the interval. A most animated, rapid speaker was she in such a tête-à-tête, a most lively describer; yet with her artless diction and clear soft voice, she never seemed to speak too fast or to say too much. My own attention I think would not soon have flagged, but by-and-by, she herself seemed to need some change of subject; she hastened to wind up her narrative briefly. Yet why she terminated with so concise an abridgment did not immediately appear; silence followed – a restless silence, not without symptoms of abstraction. Then, turning to me, in a diffident, half-appealing voice – "Lucy –"

"Well, I am at your side."

"Is my cousin Ginevra still at Madame Beck's?"

"Your cousin is still there; you must be longing to see her."

"No – not much."

"You want to invite her to spend another evening?"

"No…I suppose she still talks about being married?"

"Not to anyone you care for."

"But of course she still thinks of Dr. Bretton? She cannot have changed her mind on that point, because it was so fixed two months ago."

"Why, you know, it does not matter. You saw the terms on which they stood."

"There was a little misunderstanding that evening, certainly; does she seem unhappy?"

"Not she. To change the subject. Have you heard or seen nothing of, or from, Graham during your absence?"

"Papa had letters from him once or twice about business, I think. He undertook the management of some affair which required attention while we were away. Dr. Bretton seems to respect papa, and to have pleasure in obliging him."

"Yes: you met him yesterday on the boulevard; you would be able to judge from his aspect that his friends need not be painfully anxious about his health?"

"Papa seems to have thought with you. I could not help smiling. He is not particularly observant, you know, because he is often thinking of other things than what pass before his eyes; but he said, as Dr. Bretton rode away, 'Really it does a man good to see the spirit and energy of that boy.' He called Dr. Bretton a boy; I believe he almost thinks him so, just as he thinks me a little girl; he was not speaking to me, but dropped that remark to himself. Lucy…."

Again fell the appealing accent, and at the same instant she left her chair, and came and sat on the stool at my feet.

I liked her. It is not a declaration I have often made concerning my acquaintance, in the course of this book: the reader will bear with it for once. Intimate intercourse, close inspection, disclosed in Paulina only what was delicate, intelligent, and sincere; therefore my regard for her lay deep. An admiration more superficial might have been more demonstrative; mine, however, was quiet.

"What have you to ask of Lucy?" said I; "be brave, and speak out."

But there was no courage in her eye; as it met mine, it fell; and there was no coolness on her cheek – not a transient surface-blush, but a gathering inward excitement raised its tint and its temperature.

"Lucy, I *do* wish to know your thoughts of Dr. Bretton. Do, *do* give me your real opinion of his character, his disposition."

"His character stands high, and deservedly high."

"And his disposition? Tell me about his disposition," she urged; "you know him well."

"I know him pretty well."

"You know his home-side. You have seen him with his mother; speak of him as a son."

"He is a fine-hearted son; his mother's comfort and hope, her pride and pleasure."

She held my hand between hers, and at each favourable word gave it a little caressing stroke.

"In what other way is he good, Lucy?"

"Dr. Bretton is benevolent – humanely disposed towards all his race, Dr. Bretton would have benignity for the lowest savage, or the worst criminal."

"I heard some gentlemen, some of papa's friends, who were talking about him, say the same. They say many of the poor patients at the hospitals, who tremble before some pitiless and selfish surgeons, welcome him."

"They are right; I have witnessed as much. He once took me over a hospital; I saw how he was received: your father's friends are right."

The softest gratitude animated her eye as she lifted it a moment. She had yet more to say, but seemed hesitating about time and place. Dusk was beginning to reign; her parlour fire already glowed with twilight ruddiness; but I thought she wished the room dimmer, the hour later.

"How quiet and secluded we feel here!" I remarked, to reassure her.

"Do we? Yes; it is a still evening, and I shall not be called down to tea; papa is dining out."

Still holding my hand, she played with the fingers unconsciously, dressed them, now in her own rings, and now circled them with a twine of her beautiful hair; she patted the palm against her hot cheek, and at last, having cleared a voice that was naturally liquid as a lark's, she said:

"You must think it rather strange that I should talk so much about Dr. Bretton, ask so many questions, take such an interest, but –"

"Not at all strange; perfectly natural; you like him."

"And if I did," said she, with slight quickness, "is that a reason why I should talk? I suppose you think me weak, like my cousin Ginevra?"

"If I thought you one whit like Madame Ginevra, I would not sit here waiting for your communications. I would get up, walk at my ease about the room, and anticipate all you had to say by a round lecture. Go on."

"I mean to go on," retorted she; "what else do you suppose I mean to do?"

And she looked and spoke – the little Polly of Bretton – petulant, sensitive.

"If," said she, emphatically, "if I liked Dr. John till I was fit to die for liking him, that alone could not license me to be otherwise than dumb – dumb as the grave – dumb as you, Lucy Snowe – you know it – and you know you would despise me if I failed in self-control, and whined about some rickety liking that was all on my side."

"It is true I little respect women or girls who are loquacious either in boasting the triumphs, or bemoaning the mortifications, of feelings. But as to you, Paulina, speak, for I earnestly wish to hear you. Tell me all it will give you pleasure or relief to tell: I ask no more."

"Do you care for me, Lucy?"

"Yes, I do, Paulina."

"And I love you. I had an odd content in being with you even when I was a little, troublesome, disobedient girl; it was charming to me then to lavish on you my naughtiness and whims. Now you are acceptable to me, and I like to talk with and trust you. So listen, Lucy."

And she settled herself, resting against my arm – resting gently, not with honest Mistress Fanshawe's fatiguing and selfish weight.

"A few minutes since you asked whether we had not heard from Graham during our absence, and I said there were two letters for papa on business; this was true, but I did not tell you all."

"You evaded?"

"I shuffled and equivocated, you know. However, I am going to speak the truth now; it is getting darker; one can talk at one's ease. Papa often lets me open the letter-bag and give him out the contents. One morning, about three weeks ago, you don't know how surprised I was to find, amongst a dozen letters for M. de Bassompierre, a note addressed to Miss de Bassompierre. I spied it at once, amidst all the rest; the handwriting was not strange; it attracted me directly. I was going to say, 'Papa, here is another letter from Dr. Bretton'; but the 'Miss' struck me mute. I actually never received a letter from a gentleman before. Ought I to have shown it to papa, and let him open it and read it first? I could not for my life, Lucy. I know so well papa's ideas about me: he forgets my age; he thinks I am a mere school-girl; he is not aware that other people see I am grown up as tall as I shall be; so, with a curious mixture of feelings, some of them self-reproachful, and some so fluttering and strong, I cannot describe them, I gave papa his twelve letters – his herd of possessions – and kept back my one, my ewe-lamb. It lay in my lap during breakfast, looking up at me with an inexplicable meaning, making me feel myself a thing double-existent – a child to that dear papa, but no more a child to myself. After breakfast I carried my letter upstairs, and having secured myself by turning the key in the door, I began to study the outside of my treasure: it was some minutes before I could get over the direction and penetrate the seal; one does not take a strong place of this kind by instant storm – one sits down awhile before it, as beleaguers say. Graham's hand is like himself, Lucy, and so is his seal – all clear, firm, and rounded – no slovenly splash of wax – a full, solid, steady drop – a distinct impress; no pointed turns harshly pricking the optic nerve, but a clean, mellow, pleasant manuscript, that soothes you as you read. It is like his face – just like the chiselling of his features: do you know his autograph?"

"I have seen it: go on."

"The seal was too beautiful to be broken, so I cut it round with my scissors. On the point of reading the letter at last, I once more drew back voluntarily; it was too soon yet to drink that draught – the sparkle in the cup was so beautiful – I would watch it yet a minute. Then I remembered all at once that I had not said my prayers that morning. Having heard papa go down to breakfast a little earlier than usual, I had been afraid of keeping him waiting, and had hastened to join him as soon as dressed, thinking no harm to put off prayers till afterwards. Some people would say I ought to have served God first and then man; but I don't think heaven could be jealous of anything I might do for papa. I believe I am superstitious. A voice seemed now to say that another feeling than filial affection was in question – to urge me to pray before I dared to read what I so longed to read – to deny myself yet a moment, and remember first a great duty. I have had these impulses ever since I can remember. I put the letter down and said my prayers, adding, at the end, a strong entreaty that whatever happened, I might not be tempted or led to cause papa any sorrow, and might never, in caring for others, neglect him. The very thought of such a possibility, so pierced my heart that it made me cry. But still, Lucy, I felt that in time papa would have to be taught the truth, managed, and induced to hear reason.

"I read the letter. Lucy, life is said to be all disappointment. *I* was not disappointed. Ere I read, and while I read, my heart did more than throb – it trembled fast – every quiver seemed like the pant of an animal athirst, laid down at a well and drinking; and the well proved quite full, gloriously clear; it rose up munificently of its own impulse; I saw the sun through its gush, and not a mote, Lucy, no moss, no insect, no atom in the thrice-refined golden gurgle.

"Life," she went on, "is said to be full of pain to some. I have read biographies where the wayfarer seemed to journey on from suffering to suffering; where Hope flew before him fast, never alighting so near, or lingering so long, as to give his hand a chance of one realizing grasp. I have read of those who sowed in tears, and whose harvest, so far from being reaped in joy, perished by untimely blight, or was borne off by sudden whirlwind; and, alas! Some of these met the winter with empty garners, and died of utter want in the darkest and coldest of the year."

"Was it their fault, Paulina, that they of whom you speak thus died?"

"Not always their fault. Some of them were good endeavouring people. I am not endeavouring, nor actively good, yet God has caused me to grow in sun, due moisture, and safe protection, sheltered, fostered, taught, by my dear father; and now – now – another comes. Graham loves me."

For some minutes we both paused on this climax.

"Does your father know?" I inquired, in a low voice.

"Graham spoke with deep respect of papa, but implied that he dared not approach that quarter as yet; he must first prove his worth: he added that he must have some light respecting myself and my own feelings ere he ventured to risk a step in the matter elsewhere."

"How did you reply?"

"I replied briefly, but I did not repulse him. Yet I almost trembled for fear of making the answer too cordial: Graham's tastes are so fastidious. I wrote it three times – chastening and subduing the phrases at every rescript; at last, having confected it till it seemed to me to resemble a morsel of ice flavoured with ever so slight a zest of fruit or sugar, I ventured to seal and despatch it."

"Excellent, Paulina! Your instinct is fine; you understand Dr. Bretton."

"But how must I manage about papa? There I am still in pain."

"Do not manage at all. Wait now. Only maintain no further correspondence till your father knows all, and gives his sanction."

"Will he ever give it?"

"Time will show. Wait."

"Dr. Bretton wrote one other letter, deeply grateful for my calm, brief note; but I anticipated your advice, by saying, that while my sentiments continued the same, I could not, without my father's knowledge, write again."

"You acted as you ought to have done; so Dr. Bretton will feel: it will increase his pride in you, his love for you, if either be capable of increase. Paulina, that gentle hoar-frost of yours, surrounding so much pure, fine flame, is a priceless privilege of nature."

"You see I feel Graham's disposition," said she. "I feel that no delicacy can be too exquisite for his treatment."

"It is perfectly proved that you comprehend him, and then – whatever Dr. Bretton's disposition, were he one who expected to be more nearly met – you would still act truthfully, openly, tenderly, with your father."

"Lucy, I trust I shall thus act always. Oh, it will be pain to wake papa from his dream, and tell him I am no more a little girl!"

"Be in no hurry to do so, Paulina. Leave the revelation to Time and your kind Fate. I also have noticed the gentleness of her cares for you: doubt not she will benignantly order the circumstances, and fitly appoint the hour. Yes: I have thought over your life just as you have yourself thought it over; I have made comparisons like those to which you adverted. We know not the future, but the past has been propitious.

"As a child I feared for you; nothing that has life was ever more susceptible than your nature in infancy: under harshness or neglect, neither your outward nor your inward self would have ripened to what they now are. Much pain, much fear, much struggle, would have troubled the very lines of your features, broken their regularity, would have harassed your nerves into the fever of habitual irritation; you would have lost in health and cheerfulness, in grace and sweetness. Providence has protected and cultured you, not only for your own sake, but I believe for Graham's. His star, too, was fortunate: to develop fully the best of his nature, a companion like you was needed: there you are, ready. You must be united. I knew it the first day I saw you together at La Terrasse. In all that mutually concerns you and Graham there seems to me promise, plan, harmony. I do not think the sunny youth of either will prove the forerunner of stormy age. I think it is deemed good that you two should live in peace and be happy – not as angels, but as few are happy amongst mortals. Some lives *are* thus blessed: it is God's will: it is the attesting trace and lingering evidence of Eden. Other lives run from the first another course. Other travellers encounter weather fitful and gusty, wild and variable – breast adverse winds, are belated and overtaken by the early closing winter night. Neither can this happen without the sanction of God; and I know that, amidst His boundless works, is somewhere stored the secret of this last fate's justice: I know that His treasures contain the proof as the promise of its mercy."

Chapter Thirty-Three
M. Paul Keeps His Promise

ON THE FIRST OF MAY, we had all – i.e. the twenty boarders and the four teachers – notice to rise at five o'clock of the morning, to be dressed and ready by six, to put ourselves under the command of M. le Professeur Emanuel, who was to head our march forth from Villette, for it was on this day he proposed to fulfil his promise of taking us to breakfast in the country. I, indeed, as the reader may perhaps remember, had not had the honour of an invitation when this excursion was first projected – rather the contrary; but on my now making allusion to this fact, and wishing to know how it was to be, my ear received a pull, of which I did not venture to challenge the repetition by raising, further difficulties.

"Je vous conseille de vous faire prier," said M. Emanuel, imperially menacing the other ear. One Napoleonic compliment, however, was enough, so I made up my mind to be of the party.

The morning broke calm as summer, with singing of birds in the garden, and a light dew-mist that promised heat. We all said it would be warm, and we all felt pleasure in folding away heavy garments, and in assuming the attire suiting a sunny season. The clean fresh print dress, and the light straw bonnet, each made and trimmed as the French workwoman alone can make and trim, so as to unite the utterly unpretending with the perfectly becoming, was the rule of costume. Nobody flaunted in faded silk; nobody wore a second-hand best article.

At six the bell rang merrily, and we poured down the staircase, through the carré, along the corridor, into the vestibule. There stood our Professor, wearing, not his savage-looking paletôt and severe bonnet-grec, but a young-looking belted blouse and cheerful straw hat. He had for us all the kindest good-morrow, and most of us for him had a thanksgiving smile. We were marshalled in order and soon started.

The streets were yet quiet, and the boulevards were fresh and peaceful as fields. I believe we were very happy as we walked along. This chief of ours had the secret of giving a certain impetus to happiness when he would; just as, in an opposite mood, he could give a thrill to fear.

He did not lead nor follow us, but walked along the line, giving a word to everyone, talking much to his favourites, and not wholly neglecting even those he disliked. It was rather my wish, for a reason I had, to keep slightly aloof from notice, and being paired with Ginevra Fanshawe, bearing on my arm the dear pressure of that angel's not unsubstantial limb – (she continued in excellent case, and I can assure the reader it was no trifling business to bear the burden of her loveliness; many a time in the course of that warm day I wished to goodness there had been less of the charming commodity) – however, having her, as I said, I tried to make her useful by interposing her always between myself and M. Paul, shifting my place, according as I heard him coming up to the right hand or the left. My private motive for this manoeuvre might be traced to the circumstance of the new print dress I wore, being pink in colour – a fact which, under our present convoy, made me feel something as I have felt, when, clad in a shawl with a red border, necessitated to traverse a meadow where pastured a bull.

For awhile, the shifting system, together with some modifications in the arrangement of a black silk scarf, answered my purpose; but, by-and-by, he found out, that whether he came to this side or to that, Miss Fanshawe was still his neighbour. The course of acquaintance between Ginevra and him had never run so smooth that his temper did not undergo a certain crisping process whenever he heard her English accent: nothing in their dispositions fitted; they jarred if they came in contact; he held her empty and affected; she deemed him bearish, meddling, repellent.

At last, when he had changed his place for about the sixth time, finding still the same untoward result to the experiment – he thrust his head forward, settled his eyes on mine, and demanded with impatience, "*Qu'est-ce que c'est? Vous me jouez des tours?*"

The words were hardly out of his mouth, however, ere, with his customary quickness, he seized the root of this proceeding: in vain I shook out the long fringe, and spread forth the broad end of my scarf. "*A-b-b! C'est la robe rose!*" broke from his lips, affecting me very much like the sudden and irate low of some lord of the meadow.

"It is only cotton," I alleged, hurriedly; "and cheaper, and washes better than any other colour."

"*Et Mademoiselle Lucy est coquette comme dix Parisiennes,*" he answered. "*A-t-on jamais vu une Anglaise pareille. Regardez plutôt son chapeau, et ses gants, et ses brodequins!*" These articles of dress were just like what my companions wore; certainly not one whit smarter – perhaps rather plainer than most – but Monsieur had now got hold of his text, and I began to chafe under the expected sermon. It went off, however, as mildly as the menace of a storm sometimes passes on a summer day. I got but one flash of sheet lightning in the shape of a single bantering smile from his eyes; and then he said, "*Courage! – A vrai dire je ne suis pas fâché, peut-être même suis je content qu'on s'est fait si belle pour ma petite fête.*"

"*Mais ma robe n'est pas belle, Monsieur – elle n'est que propre.*"

"*J'aime la propreté,*" said he. In short, he was not to be dissatisfied; the sun of good humour was to triumph on this auspicious morning; it consumed scudding clouds ere they sullied its disk.

And now we were in the country, amongst what they called 'les bois et les petits sentiers'. These woods and lanes a month later would offer but a dusty and doubtful seclusion: now, however, in their May greenness and morning repose, they looked very pleasant.

We reached a certain well, planted round, in the taste of Labassecour, with an orderly circle of lime-trees: here a halt was called; on the green swell of ground surrounding this well, we were ordered to be seated, Monsieur taking his place in our midst, and suffering us to gather in a knot round him. Those who liked him more than they feared, came close, and these were chiefly little ones; those who feared more than they liked, kept somewhat aloof; those in whom much affection had given, even to what remained of fear, a pleasurable zest, observed the greatest distance.

He began to tell us a story. Well could he narrate: in such a diction as children love, and learned men emulate; a diction simple in its strength, and strong in its simplicity. There were beautiful touches in that little tale; sweet glimpses of feeling and hues of description that, while I listened, sunk into my mind, and since have never faded. He tinted a twilight scene – I hold it in memory still – such a picture I have never looked on from artist's pencil.

I have said, that, for myself, I had no impromptu faculty; and perhaps that very deficiency made me marvel the more at one who possessed it in perfection. M. Emanuel was not a man to write books; but I have heard him lavish, with careless, unconscious prodigality, such mental wealth as books seldom boast; his mind was indeed my library, and whenever it was opened to me, I entered bliss. Intellectually imperfect as I was, I could read little; there were few bound and printed volumes that did not weary me – whose perusal did not fag and blind – but his tomes of thought were collyrium to the spirit's eyes; over their contents, inward sight grew clear and strong. I used to think what a delight it would be for one who loved him better than he loved himself, to gather and store up those handfuls of gold-dust, so recklessly flung to heaven's reckless winds.

His story done, he approached the little knoll where I and Ginevra sat apart. In his usual mode of demanding an opinion (he had not reticence to wait till it was voluntarily offered) he asked, "Were you interested?"

According to my wonted undemonstrative fashion, I simply answered – "Yes."

"Was it good?"

"Very good."

"Yet I could not write that down," said he.

"Why not, Monsieur?"

"I hate the mechanical labour; I hate to stoop and sit still. I could dictate it, though, with pleasure, to an amanuensis who suited me. Would Mademoiselle Lucy write for me if I asked her?"

"Monsieur would be too quick; he would urge me, and be angry if my pen did not keep pace with his lips."

"Try some day; let us see the monster I can make of myself under the circumstances. But just now, there is no question of dictation; I mean to make you useful in another office. Do you see yonder farm-house?"

"Surrounded with trees? Yes."

"There we are to breakfast; and while the good fermière makes the café au lait in a caldron, you and five others, whom I shall select, will spread with butter half a hundred rolls."

Having formed his troop into line once more, he marched us straight on the farm, which, on seeing our force, surrendered without capitulation.

Clean knives and plates, and fresh butter being provided, half-a-dozen of us, chosen by our Professor, set to work under his directions, to prepare for breakfast a huge basket of rolls, with which the baker had been ordered to provision the farm, in anticipation of our coming. Coffee and chocolate were already made hot; cream and new-laid eggs were added to the treat, and M. Emanuel, always generous, would have given a large order for 'jambon' and 'confitures' in addition, but that some of us, who presumed perhaps upon our influence, insisted that it would be a most reckless waste of victual. He railed at us for our pains, terming us 'des ménagères avares'; but we let him talk, and managed the economy of the repast our own way.

With what a pleasant countenance he stood on the farm-kitchen hearth looking on! He was a man whom it made happy to see others happy; he liked to have movement, animation, abundance and enjoyment round him. We asked where he would sit. He told us, we knew well he was our slave, and we his tyrants, and that he dared not so much as choose a chair without our leave; so we set him the farmer's great chair at the head of the long table, and put him into it.

Well might we like him, with all his passions and hurricanes, when he could be so benignant and docile at times, as he was just now. Indeed, at the worst, it was only his nerves that were irritable, not his temper that was radically bad; soothe, comprehend, comfort him, and he was a lamb; he would not harm a fly. Only to the very stupid, perverse, or unsympathizing, was he in the slightest degree dangerous.

Mindful always of his religion, he made the youngest of the party say a little prayer before we began breakfast, crossing himself as devotedly as a woman. I had never seen him pray before, or make that pious sign; he did it so simply, with such child-like faith, I could not help smiling pleasurably as I watched; his eyes met my smile; he just stretched out his kind hand, saying, *"Donnez-moi la main!* I see we worship the same God, in the same spirit, though by different rites."

Most of M. Emanuel's brother Professors were emancipated free-thinkers; infidels, atheists; and many of them men whose lives would not bear scrutiny; he was more like a knight of old, religious in his way, and of spotless fame. Innocent childhood, beautiful youth were safe at his side. He had vivid passions, keen feelings, but his pure honour and his artless piety were the strong charm that kept the lions couchant.

That breakfast was a merry meal, and the merriment was not mere vacant clatter: M. Paul originated, led, controlled and heightened it; his social, lively temper played unfettered and unclouded; surrounded only by women and children there was nothing to cross and thwart him; he had his own way, and a pleasant way it was.

The meal over, the party were free to run and play in the meadows; a few stayed to help the farmer's wife to put away her earthenware. M. Paul called me from among these to come out and sit near him under a tree – whence he could view the troop gambolling, over a wide pasture – and read to him whilst he took his cigar. He sat on a rustic bench, and I at the tree-root. While I read (a pocket-classic – a

Corneille – I did not like it, but he did, finding therein beauties I never could be brought to perceive), he listened with a sweetness of calm the more impressive from the impetuosity of his general nature; the deepest happiness filled his blue eye and smoothed his broad forehead. I, too, was happy – happy with the bright day, happier with his presence, happiest with his kindness.

He asked, by-and-by, if I would not rather run to my companions than sit there? I said, no; I felt content to be where he was. He asked whether, if I were his sister, I should always be content to stay with a brother such as he. I said, I believed I should; and I felt it. Again, he inquired whether, if he were to leave Villette, and go far away, I should be sorry; and I dropped Corneille, and made no reply.

"*Petite soeur,*" said he; "how long could you remember me if we were separated?"

"That, Monsieur, I can never tell, because I do not know how long it will be before I shall cease to remember everything earthly."

"If I were to go beyond seas for two – three – five years, should you welcome me on my return?"

"Monsieur, how could I live in the interval?"

"*Pourtant j'ai été pour vous bien dur, bien exigeant.*"

I hid my face with the book, for it was covered with tears. I asked him why he talked so; and he said he would talk so no more, and cheered me again with the kindest encouragement. Still, the gentleness with which he treated me during the rest of the day, went somehow to my heart. It was too tender. It was mournful. I would rather he had been abrupt, whimsical, and irate as was his wont.

When hot noon arrived – for the day turned out as we had anticipated, glowing as June – our shepherd collected his sheep from the pasture, and proceeded to lead us all softly home. But we had a whole league to walk, thus far from Villette was the farm where he had breakfasted; the children, especially, were tired with their play; the spirits of most flagged at the prospect of this mid-day walk over chaussées flinty, glaring, and dusty. This state of things had been foreseen and provided for. Just beyond the boundary of the farm we met two spacious vehicles coming to fetch us – such conveyances as are hired out purposely for the accommodation of school-parties; here, with good management, room was found for all, and in another hour M. Paul made safe consignment of his charge at the Rue Fossette. It had been a pleasant day: it would have been perfect, but for the breathing of melancholy which had dimmed its sunshine a moment.

That tarnish was renewed the same evening.

Just about sunset, I saw M. Emanuel come out of the front-door, accompanied by Madame Beck. They paced the centre-alley for nearly an hour, talking earnestly: he – looking grave, yet restless; she – wearing an amazed, expostulatory, dissuasive air.

I wondered what was under discussion; and when Madame Beck re-entered the house as it darkened, leaving her kinsman Paul yet lingering in the garden, I said to myself – "He called me '*petite soeur*' this morning. If he were really my brother, how I should like to go to him just now, and ask what it is that presses on his mind. See how he leans against that tree, with his arms crossed and his brow bent. He wants consolation, I know: Madame does not console: she only remonstrates. What now –?"

Starting from quiescence to action, M. Paul came striding erect and quick down the garden. The carré doors were yet open: I thought he was probably going to water the orange-trees in the tubs, after his occasional custom; on reaching the court, however, he took an abrupt turn and made for the berceau and the first-classe glass door. There, in that first classe I was, thence I had been watching him; but there I could not find courage to await his approach. He had turned so suddenly, he strode so fast, he looked so strange; the coward within me grew pale, shrank and – not waiting to listen to reason, and hearing the shrubs crush and the gravel crunch to his advance – she was gone on the wings of panic.

Nor did I pause till I had taken sanctuary in the oratory, now empty. Listening there with beating pulses, and an unaccountable, undefined apprehension, I heard him pass through all the schoolrooms, clashing the doors impatiently as he went; I heard him invade the refectory which the 'lecture pieuse' was now holding under hallowed constraint; I heard him pronounce these words – "*Où est Mademoiselle Lucie?*"

And just as, summoning my courage, I was preparing to go down and do what, after all, I most wished to do in the world – viz., meet him – the wiry voice of St. Pierre replied glibly and falsely, "*Elle est au lit.*" And he passed, with the stamp of vexation, into the corridor. There Madame Beck met, captured, chid, convoyed to the street-door, and finally dismissed him.

As that street-door closed, a sudden amazement at my own perverse proceeding struck like a blow upon me. I felt from the first it was me he wanted – me he was seeking – and had not I wanted him too? What, then, had carried me away? What had rapt me beyond his reach? He had something to tell: he was going to tell me that something: my ear strained its nerve to hear it, and I had made the confidence impossible. Yearning to listen and console, while I thought audience and solace beyond hope's reach – no sooner did opportunity suddenly and fully arrive, than I evaded it as I would have evaded the levelled shaft of mortality.

Well, my insane inconsistency had its reward. Instead of the comfort, the certain satisfaction, I might have won – could I but have put choking panic down, and stood firm two minutes – here was dead blank, dark doubt, and drear suspense.

I took my wages to my pillow, and passed the night counting them.

Chapter Thirty-Four
Malevola

MADAME BECK called me on Thursday afternoon, and asked whether I had any occupation to hinder me from going into town and executing some little commissions for her at the shops.

Being disengaged, and placing myself at her service, I was presently furnished with a list of the wools, silks, embroidering thread, etcetera, wanted in the pupils' work, and having equipped myself in a manner suiting the threatening aspect of a cloudy and sultry day, I was just drawing the spring-bolt of the street-door, in act to issue forth, when Madame's voice again summoned me to the salle-à-manger.

"Pardon, Meess Lucie!" cried she, in the seeming haste of an impromptu thought, "I have just recollected one more errand for you, if your good-nature will not deem itself over-burdened?"

Of course I 'confounded myself' in asseverations to the contrary; and Madame, running into the little salon, brought thence a pretty basket, filled with fine hothouse fruit, rosy, perfect, and tempting, reposing amongst the dark green, wax-like leaves, and pale yellow stars of, I know not what, exotic plant.

"There," she said, "it is not heavy, and will not shame your neat toilette, as if it were a household, servant-like detail. Do me the favour to leave this little basket at the house of Madame Walravens, with my felicitations on her fête. She lives down in the old town, Numéro 3, Rue des Mages. I fear you will find the walk rather long, but you have the whole afternoon before you, and do not hurry; if you are not back in time for dinner, I will order a portion to be saved, or Goton, with whom you are a favourite, will have pleasure in tossing up some trifle, for your especial benefit. You shall not be forgotten, ma bonne Meess. And oh! Please!" (calling me back once more) "Be sure to insist on seeing Madame Walravens herself, and giving the basket into her own hands, in order that there may be no mistake, for she is rather a punctilious personage. *Adieu! Au revoir!*"

And at last I got away. The shop commissions took some time to execute, that choosing and matching of silks and wools being always a tedious business, but at last I got through my list. The patterns for the slippers, the bell-ropes, the cabas were selected – the slides and tassels for the purses chosen – the whole 'tripotage', in short, was off my mind; nothing but the fruit and the felicitations remained to be attended to.

I rather liked the prospect of a long walk, deep into the old and grim Basse-Ville; and I liked it no worse because the evening sky, over the city, was settling into a mass of black-blue metal, heated at the rim, and inflaming slowly to a heavy red.

I fear a high wind, because storm demands that exertion of strength and use of action I always yield with pain; but the sullen down-fall, the thick snow-descent, or dark rush of rain, ask only resignation – the quiet abandonment of garments and person to be, drenched. In return, it sweeps a great capital clean before you; it makes you a quiet path through broad, grand streets; it petrifies a living city as if by eastern enchantment; it transforms a Villette into a Tadmor. Let, then, the rains fall, and the floods descend – only I must first get rid of this basket of fruit.

An unknown clock from an unknown tower (Jean Baptiste's voice was now too distant to be audible) was tolling the third quarter past five, when I reached that street and house whereof Madame Beck had given me the address. It was no street at all; it seemed rather to be part of a square: it was quiet, grass grew between the broad grey flags, the houses were large and looked very old – behind them rose the appearance of trees, indicating gardens at the back. Antiquity brooded above this region, business was banished thence. Rich men had once possessed this quarter, and once grandeur had made her seat here. That church, whose dark, half-ruinous turrets overlooked the square, was the venerable and formerly opulent shrine of the Magi. But wealth and greatness had long since stretched their gilded pinions and fled hence, leaving these their ancient nests, perhaps to house Penury for a time, or perhaps to stand cold and empty, mouldering untenanted in the course of winters.

As I crossed this deserted 'place', on whose pavement drops almost as large as a five-franc piece were now slowly darkening, I saw, in its whole expanse, no symptom or evidence of life, except what was given in the figure of an infirm old priest, who went past, bending and propped on a staff – the type of eld and decay.

He had issued from the very house to which I was directed; and when I paused before the door just closed after him, and rang the bell, he turned to look at me. Nor did he soon avert his gaze; perhaps he thought me, with my basket of summer fruit, and my lack of the dignity age confers, an incongruous figure in such a scene. I know, had a young ruddy-faced bonne opened the door to admit me, I should have thought such a one little in harmony with her dwelling; but, when I found myself confronted by a very old woman, wearing a very antique peasant costume, a cap alike hideous and costly, with long flaps of native lace, a petticoat and jacket of cloth, and sabots more like little boats than shoes, it seemed all right, and soothingly in character.

The expression of her face was not quite so soothing as the cut of her costume; anything more cantankerous I have seldom seen; she would scarcely reply to my inquiry after Madame Walravens; I believe she would have snatched the basket of fruit from my hand, had not the old priest, hobbling up, checked her, and himself lent an ear to the message with which I was charged.

His apparent deafness rendered it a little difficult to make him fully understand that I must see Madame Walravens, and consign the fruit into her own hands. At last, however, he comprehended the fact that such were my orders, and that duty enjoined their literal fulfilment. Addressing the aged bonne, not in French, but in the aboriginal tongue of Labassecour, he persuaded her, at last, to let me cross the inhospitable threshold, and himself escorting me upstairs, I was ushered into a sort of salon, and there left.

The room was large, and had a fine old ceiling, and almost church-like windows of coloured-glass; but it was desolate, and in the shadow of a coming storm, looked strangely lowering. Within – opened a smaller room; there, however, the blind of the single casement was closed; through the deep gloom few details of furniture were apparent. These few I amused myself by puzzling to make out; and, in particular, I was attracted by the outline of a picture on the wall.

By-and-by the picture seemed to give way: to my bewilderment, it shook, it sunk, it rolled back into nothing; its vanishing left an opening arched, leading into an arched passage, with a mystic winding stair; both passage and stair were of cold stone, uncarpeted and unpainted. Down this donjon stair descended a tap, tap, like a stick; soon there fell on the steps a shadow, and last of all, I was aware of a substance.

Yet, was it actual substance, this appearance approaching me? This obstruction, partially darkening the arch?

It drew near, and I saw it well. I began to comprehend where I was. Well might this old square be named quarter of the Magi – well might the three towers, overlooking it, own for godfathers three mystic sages of a dead and dark art. Hoar enchantment here prevailed; a spell had opened for me elf-land – that cell-like room, that vanishing picture, that arch and passage, and stair of stone, were all parts of a fairy tale. Distincter even than these scenic details stood the chief figure – Cunegonde, the sorceress! Malevola, the evil fairy. How was she?

She might be three feet high, but she had no shape; her skinny hands rested upon each other, and pressed the gold knob of a wand-like ivory staff. Her face was large, set, not upon her shoulders, but before her breast; she seemed to have no neck; I should have said there were a hundred years in her features, and more perhaps in her eyes – her malign, unfriendly eyes, with thick grey brows above, and livid lids all round. How severely they viewed me, with a sort of dull displeasure!

This being wore a gown of brocade, dyed bright blue, full-tinted as the gentianella flower, and covered with satin foliage in a large pattern; over the gown a costly shawl, gorgeously bordered, and so large for her, that its many-coloured fringe swept the floor. But her chief points were her jewels: she had long, clear earrings, blazing with a lustre which could not be borrowed or false; she had rings on her skeleton hands, with thick gold hoops, and stones – purple, green, and blood-red. Hunchbacked, dwarfish, and doting, she was adorned like a barbarian queen.

"*Que me voulez-vous?*" said she, hoarsely, with the voice rather of male than of female old age; and, indeed, a silver beard bristled her chin.

I delivered my basket and my message.

"Is that all?" she demanded.

"It is all," said I.

"Truly, it was well worth while," she answered. "Return to Madame Beck, and tell her I can buy fruit when I want it, *et quant à ses félicitations, je m'en moque!*" And this courteous dame turned her back.

Just as she turned, a peal of thunder broke, and a flash of lightning blazed broad over salon and boudoir. The tale of magic seemed to proceed with due accompaniment of the elements. The wanderer, decoyed into the enchanted castle, heard rising, outside, the spell-wakened tempest.

What, in all this, was I to think of Madame Beck? She owned strange acquaintance; she offered messages and gifts at an unique shrine, and inauspicious seemed the bearing of the uncouth thing she worshipped. There went that sullen Sidonia, tottering and trembling like palsy incarnate, tapping her ivory staff on the mosaic parquet, and muttering venomously as she vanished.

Down washed the rain, deep lowered the welkin; the clouds, ruddy a while ago, had now, through all their blackness, turned deadly pale, as if in terror. Notwithstanding my late boast about not fearing a shower, I hardly liked to go out under this waterspout. Then the gleams of lightning were very fierce, the thunder crashed very near; this storm had gathered immediately above Villette; it seemed to have burst at the zenith; it rushed down prone; the forked, slant bolts pierced athwart vertical torrents; red zigzags interlaced a descent blanched as white metal: and all broke from a sky heavily black in its swollen abundance.

Leaving Madame Walravens' inhospitable salon, I betook myself to her cold staircase; there was a seat on the landing – there I waited. Somebody came gliding along the gallery just above; it was the old priest.

"Indeed Mademoiselle shall not sit there," said he. "It would displeasure our benefactor if he knew a stranger was so treated in this house."

And he begged me so earnestly to return to the salon, that, without discourtesy, I could not but comply. The smaller room was better furnished and more habitable than the larger; thither he introduced me. Partially withdrawing the blind, he disclosed what seemed more like an oratory than a boudoir, a very solemn little chamber, looking as if it were a place rather dedicated to relics and remembrance, than designed for present use and comfort.

The good father sat down, as if to keep me company; but instead of conversing, he took out a book, fastened on the page his eyes, and employed his lips in whispering – what sounded like a prayer or litany. A yellow electric light from the sky gilded his bald head; his figure remained in shade – deep and purple; he sat still as sculpture; he seemed to forget me for his prayers; he only looked up when a fiercer bolt, or a harsher, closer rattle told of nearing danger; even then, it was not in fear, but in seeming awe, he raised his eyes. I too was awe-struck; being, however, under no pressure of slavish terror, my thoughts and observations were free.

To speak truth, I was beginning to fancy that the old priest resembled that Père Silas, before whom I had kneeled in the church of the Béguinage. The idea was vague, for I had seen my confessor only in dusk and in profile, yet still I seemed to trace a likeness: I thought also I recognized the voice. While I watched him, he betrayed, by one lifted look, that he felt my scrutiny; I turned to note the room; that too had its half mystic interest.

Beside a cross of curiously carved old ivory, yellow with time, and sloped above a dark-red prie-dieu, furnished duly, with rich missal and ebon rosary – hung the picture whose dim outline had drawn my eyes before – the picture which moved, fell away with the wall and let in phantoms. Imperfectly seen, I had taken it for a Madonna; revealed by clearer light, it proved to be a woman's portrait in a nun's dress. The face, though not beautiful, was pleasing; pale, young, and shaded with the dejection of grief or ill health. I say again it was not beautiful; it was not even intellectual; its very amiability was the amiability of a weak frame, inactive passions, acquiescent habits: yet I looked long at that picture, and could not choose but look.

The old priest, who at first had seemed to me so deaf and infirm, must yet have retained his faculties in tolerable preservation; absorbed in his book as he appeared, without once lifting his head, or, as far as I knew, turning his eyes, he perceived the point towards which my attention was drawn, and, in a slow distinct voice, dropped, concerning it, these four observations:

"She was much beloved.

"She gave herself to God.

"She died young.

"She is still remembered, still wept."

"By that aged lady, Madame Walravens?" I inquired, fancying that I had discovered in the incurable grief of bereavement, a key to that same aged lady's desperate ill-humour.

The father shook his head with half a smile.

"No, no," said he; "a grand-dame's affection for her children's children may be great, and her sorrow for their loss, lively; but it is only the affianced lover, to whom Fate, Faith, and Death have trebly denied the bliss of union, who mourns what he has lost, as Justine Marie is still mourned."

I thought the father rather wished to be questioned, and therefore I inquired who had lost and who still mourned 'Justine Marie'. I got, in reply, quite a little romantic narrative, told not unimpressively, with the accompaniment of the now subsiding storm. I am bound to say it might have been made much more truly impressive, if there had been less French, Rousseau-like sentimentalizing and wire-drawing; and rather more healthful carelessness of effect. But the worthy father was obviously a Frenchman born and bred (I became more and more persuaded of his resemblance to my confessor) – he was a true son of Rome; when he did lift his eyes, he looked at me out of their corners, with more and sharper subtlety than, one would have thought, could survive the wear and tear of seventy years. Yet, I believe, he was a good old man.

The hero of his tale was some former pupil of his, whom he now called his benefactor, and who, it appears, had loved this pale Justine Marie, the daughter of rich parents, at a time when his own worldly prospects were such as to justify his aspiring to a well-dowered hand. The pupil's father – once a rich banker – had failed, died, and left behind him only debts and destitution. The son was then forbidden to think of Marie; especially that old witch of a grand-dame I had seen, Madame Walravens, opposed the match with all the violence of a temper which deformity made sometimes demoniac. The mild Marie had neither the treachery to be false, nor the force to be quite staunch to her lover; she gave up her first suitor, but, refusing to accept a second with a heavier purse, withdrew to a convent, and there died in her noviciate.

Lasting anguish, it seems, had taken possession of the faithful heart which worshipped her, and the truth of that love and grief had been shown in a manner which touched even me, as I listened.

Some years after Justine Marie's death, ruin had come on her house too: her father, by nominal calling a jeweller, but who also dealt a good deal on the Bourse, had been concerned in some financial transactions which entailed exposure and ruinous fines. He died of grief for the loss, and shame for the infamy. His old hunchbacked mother and his bereaved wife were left penniless, and might have died too of want; but their lost daughter's once-despised, yet most true-hearted suitor, hearing of the condition of these ladies, came with singular devotedness to the rescue. He took on their insolent pride the revenge of the purest charity – housing, caring for, befriending them, so as no son could have done it more tenderly and efficiently. The mother – on the whole a good woman – died blessing him; the strange, godless, loveless, misanthrope grandmother lived still, entirely supported by this self-sacrificing man. Her, who had been the bane of his life, blighting his hope, and awarding him, for love and domestic happiness, long mourning and cheerless solitude, he treated with the respect a good son might offer a kind mother. He had brought her to this house, "and," continued the priest, while genuine tears rose to his eyes, "here, too, he shelters me, his old tutor, and Agnes, a superannuated servant of his father's family. To our sustenance, and to other charities, I know he devotes three-parts of his income, keeping only the fourth to provide himself with bread and the most modest accommodations. By this arrangement he has rendered it impossible to himself ever to marry: he has given himself to God and to his angel-bride as much as if he were a priest, like me."

The father had wiped away his tears before he uttered these last words, and in pronouncing them, he for one instant raised his eyes to mine. I caught this glance, despite its veiled character; the momentary gleam shot a meaning which struck me.

These Romanists are strange beings. Such a one among them – whom you know no more than the last Inca of Peru, or the first Emperor of China – knows you and all your concerns; and has his reasons for saying to you so and so, when you simply thought the communication sprang impromptu from the instant's impulse: his plan in bringing it about that you shall come on such a day, to such a place, under such and such circumstances, when the whole arrangement seems to your crude apprehension the ordinance of chance, or the sequel of exigency. Madame Beck's suddenly-recollected message and present, my artless embassy to the Place of the Magi, the old priest accidentally descending the steps and crossing the square, his interposition on my behalf with the bonne who would have sent me away, his reappearance on the staircase, my introduction to this room, the portrait, the narrative so affably volunteered – all these little incidents, taken as they fell out, seemed each independent of its successor; a handful of loose beads: but threaded through by that quick-shot and crafty glance of a Jesuit-eye, they dropped pendent in a long string, like that rosary on the prie-dieu. Where lay the link of junction, where the little clasp of this monastic necklace? I saw or felt union, but could not yet find the spot, or detect the means of connection.

Perhaps the musing-fit into which I had by this time fallen, appeared somewhat suspicious in its abstraction; he gently interrupted: "Mademoiselle," said he, "I trust you have not far to go through these inundated streets?"

"More than half a league."

"You live –?"

"In the Rue Fossette."

"Not" (with animation), "not at the pensionnat of Madame Beck?"

"The same."

"*Donc*" (clapping his hands), "*donc, vous devez connaître mon noble élève, mon Paul?*"

"Monsieur Paul Emanuel, Professor of Literature?"

"He and none other."

A brief silence fell. The spring of junction seemed suddenly to have become palpable; I felt it yield to pressure.

"Was it of M. Paul you have been speaking?" I presently inquired. "Was he your pupil and the benefactor of Madame Walravens?"

"Yes, and of Agnes, the old servant: and moreover, (with a certain emphasis), he was and *is* the lover, true, constant and eternal, of that saint in heaven – Justine Marie."

"And who, father, are *you?*" I continued; and though I accentuated the question, its utterance was well nigh superfluous; I was ere this quite prepared for the answer which actually came.

"I, daughter, am Père Silas; that unworthy son of Holy Church whom you once honoured with a noble and touching confidence, showing me the core of a heart, and the inner shrine of a mind whereof, in solemn truth, I coveted the direction, in behalf of the only true faith. Nor have I for a day lost sight of you, nor for an hour failed to take in you a rooted interest. Passed under the discipline of Rome, moulded by her high training, inoculated with her salutary doctrines, inspired by the zeal she alone gives – I realize what then might be your spiritual rank, your practical value; and I envy Heresy her prey."

This struck me as a special state of things – I half-realized myself in that condition also; passed under discipline, moulded, trained, inoculated, and so on. "Not so," thought I, but I restrained deprecation, and sat quietly enough.

"I suppose M. Paul does not live here?" I resumed, pursuing a theme which I thought more to the purpose than any wild renegade dreams.

"No; he only comes occasionally to worship his beloved saint, to make his confession to me, and to pay his respects to her he calls his mother. His own lodging consists but of two rooms: he has no servant, and yet he will not suffer Madame Walravens to dispose of those splendid jewels with which you see her adorned, and in which she takes a puerile pride as the ornaments of her youth, and the last relics of her son the jeweller's wealth."

"How often," murmured I to myself, "has this man, this M. Emanuel, seemed to me to lack magnanimity in trifles, yet how great he is in great things!"

I own I did not reckon amongst the proofs of his greatness, either the act of confession, or the saint-worship.

"How long is it since that lady died?" I inquired, looking at Justine Marie.

"Twenty years. She was somewhat older than M. Emanuel; he was then very young, for he is not much beyond forty."

"Does he yet weep her?"

"His heart will weep her always: the essence of Emanuel's nature is – constancy."

This was said with marked emphasis.

And now the sun broke out pallid and waterish; the rain yet fell, but there was no more tempest: that hot firmament had cloven and poured out its lightnings. A longer delay would scarce leave daylight for my return, so I rose, thanked the father for his hospitality and his tale, was benignantly answered by a 'pax vobiscum', which I made kindly welcome, because it seemed uttered with a true benevolence; but I liked less the mystic phrase accompanying it.

"Daughter, you *shall* be what you *shall* be!" an oracle that made me shrug my shoulders as soon as I had got outside the door. Few of us know what we are to come to certainly, but for all that had happened yet, I had good hopes of living and dying a sober-minded Protestant: there was a hollowness within, and a flourish around 'Holy Church' which tempted me but moderately. I went on my way pondering many things. Whatever Romanism may be, there are good Romanists: this man, Emanuel, seemed of the best; touched with superstition, influenced by priestcraft, yet wondrous for fond faith, for pious devotion, for sacrifice of self, for charity unbounded. It remained to see how Rome, by her agents, handled such qualities; whether she cherished them for their own sake and for God's, or put them out to usury and made booty of the interest.

By the time I reached home, it was sundown. Goton had kindly saved me a portion of dinner, which indeed I needed. She called me into the little cabinet to partake of it, and there Madame Beck soon made her appearance, bringing me a glass of wine.

"Well," began she, chuckling, "and what sort of a reception did Madame Walravens give you? *Elle est drôle, n'est-ce pas?*"

I told her what had passed, delivering verbatim the courteous message with which I had been charged.

"*Oh la singulière petite bossue!*" laughed she. "*Et figurez-vous qu'elle me déteste, parcequ'elle me croit amoureuse de mon cousin Paul; ce petit dévot qui n'ose pas bouger, à moins que son confesseur ne lui donne la permission! Au reste*" (she went on), "if he wanted to marry ever so much – *soit moi, soit une autre* – he could not do it; he has too large a family already on his hands: Mère Walravens, Père

Silas, Dame Agnes, and a whole troop of nameless paupers. There never was a man like him for laying on himself burdens greater than he can bear, voluntarily incurring needless responsibilities. Besides, he harbours a romantic idea about some pale-faced Marie Justine – *personnage assez niaise à ce que je pense*" (such was Madame's irreverent remark), "who has been an angel in heaven, or elsewhere, this score of years, and to whom he means to go, free from all earthly ties, *pure comme un lis, à ce qu'il dit*. Oh, you would laugh could you but know half M. Emanuel's crotchets and eccentricities! But I hinder you from taking refreshment, ma bonne Meess, which you must need; eat your supper, drink your wine, *oubliez les anges, les bossues, et surtout, les Professeurs – et bon soir!*"

Chapter Thirty-Five
Fraternity

"OUBLIEZ LES PROFESSEURS." So said Madame Beck. Madame Beck was a wise woman, but she should not have uttered those words. To do so was a mistake. That night she should have left me calm – not excited, indifferent, not interested, isolated in my own estimation and that of others – not connected, even in idea, with this second person whom I was to forget.

Forget him? Ah! They took a sage plan to make me forget him – the wiseheads! They showed me how good he was; they made of my dear little man a stainless little hero. And then they had prated about his manner of loving. What means had I, before this day, of being certain whether he could love at all or not?

I had known him jealous, suspicious; I had seen about him certain tendernesses, fitfulnesses – a softness which came like a warm air, and a ruth which passed like early dew, dried in the heat of his irritabilities: *this* was all I had seen. And they, Père Silas and Modeste Maria Beck (that these two wrought in concert I could not doubt) opened up the adytum of his heart – showed me one grand love, the child of this southern nature's youth, born so strong and perfect, that it had laughed at Death himself, despised his mean rape of matter, clung to immortal spirit, and in victory and faith, had watched beside a tomb twenty years.

This had been done – not idly: this was not a mere hollow indulgence of sentiment; he had proven his fidelity by the consecration of his best energies to an unselfish purpose, and attested it by limitless personal sacrifices: for those once dear to her he prized – he had laid down vengeance, and taken up a cross.

Now, as for Justine Marie, I knew what she was as well as if I had seen her. I knew she was well enough; there were girls like her in Madame Beck's school – phlegmatics – pale, slow, inert, but kind-natured, neutral of evil, undistinguished for good.

If she wore angels' wings, I knew whose poet-fancy conferred them. If her forehead shone luminous with the reflex of a halo, I knew in the fire of whose irids that circlet of holy flame had generation.

Was I, then, to be frightened by Justine Marie? Was the picture of a pale dead nun to rise, an eternal barrier? And what of the charities which absorbed his worldly goods? What of his heart sworn to virginity?

Madame Beck – Père Silas – you should not have suggested these questions. They were at once the deepest puzzle, the strongest obstruction, and the keenest stimulus, I had ever felt. For a week of nights and days I fell asleep – I dreamt, and I woke upon these two questions. In the whole world there was no answer to them, except where one dark little man stood, sat, walked, lectured, under the head-piece of a bandit bonnet-grec, and within the girth of a sorry paletôt, much be-inked, and no little adust.

After that visit to the Rue des Mages, I *did* want to see him again. I felt as if – knowing what I now knew – his countenance would offer a page more lucid, more interesting than ever; I felt a longing to trace in it the imprint of that primitive devotedness, the signs of that half-knightly, half-saintly chivalry which the priest's narrative imputed to his nature. He had become my Christian hero: under that character I wanted to view him.

Nor was opportunity slow to favour; my new impressions underwent her test the next day. Yes: I was granted an interview with my 'Christian hero' – an interview not very heroic, or sentimental, or biblical, but lively enough in its way.

About three o'clock of the afternoon, the peace of the first classe – safely established, as it seemed, under the serene sway of Madame Beck, who, in *propria persona* was giving one of her orderly and useful lessons – this peace, I say, suffered a sudden fracture by the wild inburst of a paletôt.

Nobody at the moment was quieter than myself. Eased of responsibility by Madame Beck's presence, soothed by her uniform tones, pleased and edified with her clear exposition of the subject in hand (for she taught well), I sat bent over my desk, drawing – that is, copying an elaborate line engraving, tediously working up my copy to the finish of the original, for that was my practical notion of art; and, strange to say, I took extreme pleasure in the labour, and could even produce curiously finical Chinese facsimiles of steel or mezzotint plates – things about as valuable as so many achievements in worsted-work, but I thought pretty well of them in those days.

What was the matter? My drawing, my pencils, my precious copy, gathered into one crushed-up handful, perished from before my sight; I myself appeared to be shaken or emptied out of my chair, as a solitary and withered nutmeg might be emptied out of a spice-box by an excited cook. That chair and my desk, seized by the wild paletôt, one under each sleeve, were borne afar; in a second, I followed the furniture; in two minutes they and I were fixed in the centre of the grand salle – a vast adjoining room, seldom used save for dancing and choral singing-lessons – fixed with an emphasis which seemed to prohibit the remotest hope of our ever being permitted to stir thence again.

Having partially collected my scared wits, I found myself in the presence of two men, gentlemen, I suppose I should say – one dark, the other light – one having a stiff, half-military air, and wearing a braided surtout; the other partaking, in garb and bearing, more of the careless aspect of the student or artist class: both flourishing in full magnificence of moustaches, whiskers, and imperial. M. Emanuel stood a little apart from these; his countenance and eyes expressed strong choler; he held forth his hand with his tribune gesture.

"Mademoiselle," said he, "your business is to prove to these gentlemen that I am no liar. You will answer, to the best of your ability, such questions as they shall put. You will also write on such theme as they shall select. In their eyes, it appears, I hold the position of an unprincipled impostor. I write essays; and, with deliberate forgery, sign to them my pupils' names, and boast of them as their work. You will disprove this charge."

Grand ciel! Here was the show-trial, so long evaded, come on me like a thunder-clap. These two fine, braided, mustachioed, sneering personages, were none other than dandy professors of the college – Messieurs Boissec and Rochemorte – a pair of cold-blooded fops and pedants, sceptics, and scoffers. It seems that M. Paul had been rashly exhibiting something I had written – something, he had never once praised, or even mentioned, in my hearing, and which I deemed forgotten. The essay was not remarkable at all; it only *seemed* remarkable, compared with the average productions of foreign school-girls; in an English establishment it would have passed scarce noticed. Messieurs Boissec and Rochemorte had thought proper to question its genuineness, and insinuate a cheat; I was now to bear my testimony to the truth, and to be put to the torture of their examination.

A memorable scene ensued.

They began with classics. A dead blank. They went on to French history. I hardly knew Mérovée from Pharamond. They tried me in various 'ologies, and still only got a shake of the head, and an unchanging "Je n'en sais rien."

After an expressive pause, they proceeded to matters of general information, broaching one or two subjects which I knew pretty well, and on which I had often reflected. M. Emanuel, who had hitherto stood looking on, dark as the winter-solstice, brightened up somewhat; he thought I should now show myself at least no fool.

He learned his error. Though answers to the questions surged up fast, my mind filling like a rising well, ideas were there, but not words. I either *could* not, or *would* not speak – I am not sure which: partly, I think, my nerves had got wrong, and partly my humour was crossed.

I heard one of my examiners – he of the braided surtout – whisper to his co-professor, "*Est-elle donc idiote?*"

"Yes," I thought, "an idiot she is, and always will be, for such as you."

But I suffered – suffered cruelly; I saw the damps gather on M. Paul's brow, and his eye spoke a passionate yet sad reproach. He would not believe in my total lack of popular cleverness; he thought I *could* be prompt if I *would*.

At last, to relieve him, the professors, and myself, I stammered out:

"Gentlemen, you had better let me go; you will get no good of me; as you say, I am an idiot."

I wish I could have spoken with calm and dignity, or I wish my sense had sufficed to make me hold my tongue; that traitor tongue tripped, faltered. Beholding the judges cast on M. Emanuel a hard look of triumph, and hearing the distressed tremor of my own voice, out I burst in a fit of choking tears. The emotion was far more of anger than grief; had I been a man and strong, I could have challenged that pair on the spot – but it *was* emotion, and I would rather have been scourged than betrayed it.

The incapables! Could they not see at once the crude hand of a novice in that composition they called a forgery? The subject was classical. When M. Paul dictated the trait on which the essay was to turn, I heard it for the first time; the matter was new to me, and I had no material for its treatment. But I got books, read up the facts, laboriously constructed a skeleton out of the dry bones of the real, and then clothed them, and tried to breathe into them life, and in this last aim I had pleasure. With me it was a difficult and anxious time till my facts were found, selected, and properly jointed; nor could I rest from research and effort till I was satisfied of correct anatomy; the strength of my inward repugnance to the idea of flaw or falsity sometimes enabled me to shun egregious blunders; but the knowledge was not there in my head, ready and mellow; it had not been sown in Spring, grown in Summer, harvested in Autumn, and garnered through Winter; whatever I wanted I must go out and gather fresh; glean of wild herbs my lapful, and shred them green into the pot. Messieurs Boissec and Rochemorte did not perceive this. They mistook my work for the work of a ripe scholar.

They would not yet let me go: I must sit down and write before them. As I dipped my pen in the ink with a shaking hand, and surveyed the white paper with eyes half-blinded and overflowing, one of my judges began mincingly to apologize for the pain he caused.

"*Nous agissons dans l'intérêt de la vérité. Nous ne voulons pas vous blesser,*" said he.

Scorn gave me nerve. I only answered, –

"Dictate, Monsieur."

Rochemorte named this theme: "Human Justice."

Human Justice! What was I to make of it? Blank, cold abstraction, unsuggestive to me of one inspiring idea; and there stood M. Emanuel, sad as Saul, and stern as Joab, and there triumphed his accusers.

At these two I looked. I was gathering my courage to tell them that I would neither write nor speak another word for their satisfaction, that their theme did not suit, nor their presence inspire me, and that, notwithstanding, whoever threw the shadow of a doubt on M. Emanuel's honour, outraged that truth of which they had announced themselves the – champions: I *meant* to utter all this, I say, when suddenly, a light darted on memory.

Those two faces looking out of the forest of long hair, moustache, and whisker – those two cold yet bold, trustless yet presumptuous visages – were the same faces, the very same that, projected in full gaslight from behind the pillars of a portico, had half frightened me to death on the night of my desolate arrival in Villette. These, I felt morally certain, were the very heroes who had driven a friendless foreigner beyond her reckoning and her strength, chased her breathless over a whole quarter of the town.

"Pious mentors!" thought I. "Pure guides for youth! If 'Human Justice' were what she ought to be, you two would scarce hold your present post, or enjoy your present credit."

An idea once seized, I fell to work. 'Human Justice' rushed before me in novel guise, a red, random beldame, with arms akimbo. I saw her in her house, the den of confusion: servants called to her for orders or help which she did not give; beggars stood at her door waiting and starving unnoticed; a swarm of children, sick and quarrelsome, crawled round her feet, and yelled in her ears appeals for notice, sympathy, cure, redress. The honest woman cared for none of these things. She had a warm seat of her own by the fire, she had her own solace in a short black pipe, and a bottle of Mrs. Sweeny's soothing syrup; she smoked and she sipped, and she enjoyed her paradise; and whenever a cry of the suffering souls about her pierced her ears too keenly – my jolly dame seized the poker or the hearth-brush: if the offender was weak, wronged, and sickly, she effectually settled him: if he was strong, lively, and violent, she only menaced, then plunged her hand in her deep pouch, and flung a liberal shower of sugar-plums.

Such was the sketch of 'Human Justice', scratched hurriedly on paper, and placed at the service of Messrs. Boissec and Rochemorte. M. Emanuel read it over my shoulder. Waiting no comment, I curtsied to the trio, and withdrew.

After school that day, M. Paul and I again met. Of course the meeting did not at first run smooth; there was a crow to pluck with him; that forced examination could not be immediately digested. A crabbed dialogue terminated in my being called "*une petite moqueuse et sans-coeur*", and in Monsieur's temporary departure.

Not wishing him to go quite away, only desiring he should feel that such a transport as he had that day given way to, could not be indulged with perfect impunity, I was not sorry to see him, soon after, gardening in the berceau. He approached the glass door; I drew near also. We spoke of some flowers growing round it. By-and-by Monsieur laid down his spade; by-and-by he recommenced conversation, passed to other subjects, and at last touched a point of interest.

Conscious that his proceeding of that day was specially open to a charge of extravagance, M. Paul half apologized; he half regretted, too, the fitfulness of his moods at all times, yet he hinted that some allowance ought to be made for him. "But," said he, "I can hardly expect it at your hands, Miss Lucy; you know neither me, nor my position, nor my history."

His history. I took up the word at once; I pursued the idea.

"No, Monsieur," I rejoined. "Of course, as you say, I know neither your history, nor your position, nor your sacrifices, nor any of your sorrows, or trials, or affections, or fidelities. Oh, no! I know nothing about you; you are for me altogether a stranger."

"Hein?" he murmured, arching his brows in surprise.

"You know, Monsieur, I only see you in classe – stern, dogmatic, hasty, imperious. I only hear of you in town as active and wilful, quick to originate, hasty to lead, but slow to persuade, and hard to bend. A man like you, without ties, can have no attachments; without dependants, no duties. All we, with whom you come in contact, are machines, which you thrust here and there, inconsiderate of their feelings. You seek your recreations in public, by the light of the evening chandelier: this school and yonder college are your workshops, where you fabricate the ware called pupils. I don't so much as know where you live; it is natural to take it for granted that you have no home, and need none."

"I am judged," said he. "Your opinion of me is just what I thought it was. For you I am neither a man nor a Christian. You see me void of affection and religion, unattached by friend or family, unpiloted by principle or faith. It is well, Mademoiselle; such is our reward in this life."

"You are a philosopher, Monsieur; a cynic philosopher" (and I looked at his paletôt, of which he straightway brushed the dim sleeve with his hand), "despising the foibles of humanity – above its luxuries – independent of its comforts."

"*Et vous, Mademoiselle? Vous êtes proprette et douillette, et affreusement insensible, par-dessus le marché.*"

"But, in short, Monsieur, now I think of it, you *must* live somewhere? Do tell me where; and what establishment of servants do you keep?"

With a fearful projection of the under-lip, implying an impetus of scorn the most decided, he broke out –

"*Je vis dans un trou!* I inhabit a den, Miss – a cavern, where you would not put your dainty nose. Once, with base shame of speaking the whole truth, I talked about my 'study' in that college: know

now that this 'study' is my whole abode; my chamber is there and my drawing-room. As for my 'establishment of servants'" (mimicking my voice) "they number ten; les voilà."

And he grimly spread, close under my eyes, his ten fingers.

"I black my boots," pursued he savagely. "I brush my paletôt."

"No, Monsieur, it is too plain; you never do that," was my parenthesis.

"Je fais mon lit et mon ménage; I seek my dinner in a restaurant; my supper takes care of itself; I pass days laborious and loveless; nights long and lonely; I am ferocious, and bearded and monkish; and nothing now living in this world loves me, except some old hearts worn like my own, and some few beings, impoverished, suffering, poor in purse and in spirit, whom the kingdoms of this world own not, but to whom a will and testament not to be disputed has bequeathed the kingdom of heaven."

"Ah, Monsieur; but I know!"

"What do you know? Many things, I verily believe; yet not me, Lucy!"

"I know that you have a pleasant old house in a pleasant old square of the Basse-Ville – why don't you go and live there?"

"Hein?" muttered he again.

"I liked it much, Monsieur; with the steps ascending to the door, the grey flags in front, the nodding trees behind – real trees, not shrubs – trees dark, high, and of old growth. And the boudoir-oratoire – you should make that room your study; it is so quiet and solemn."

He eyed me closely; he half-smiled, half-coloured. "Where did you pick up all that? Who told you?" he asked.

"Nobody told me. Did I dream it, Monsieur, do you think?"

"Can I enter into your visions? Can I guess a woman's waking thoughts, much less her sleeping fantasies?"

"If I dreamt it, I saw in my dream human beings as well as a house. I saw a priest, old, bent, and grey, and a domestic – old, too, and picturesque; and a lady, splendid but strange; her head would scarce reach to my elbow – her magnificence might ransom a duke. She wore a gown bright as lapis-lazuli – a shawl worth a thousand francs: she was decked with ornaments so brilliant, I never saw any with such a beautiful sparkle; but her figure looked as if it had been broken in two and bent double; she seemed also to have outlived the common years of humanity, and to have attained those which are only labour and sorrow. She was become morose – almost malevolent; yet *somebody*, it appears, cared for her in her infirmities – somebody forgave her trespasses, hoping to have his trespasses forgiven. They lived together, these three people – the mistress, the chaplain, the servant – all old, all feeble, all sheltered under one kind wing."

He covered with his hand the upper part of his face, but did not conceal his mouth, where I saw hovering an expression I liked.

"I see you have entered into my secrets," said he, "but how was it done?"

So I told him how – the commission on which I had been sent, the storm which had detained me, the abruptness of the lady, the kindness of the priest.

"As I sat waiting for the rain to cease, Père Silas whiled away the time with a story," I said.

"A story! What story? Père Silas is no romancist."

"Shall I tell Monsieur the tale?"

"Yes: begin at the beginning. Let me hear some of Miss Lucy's French – her best or her worst – I don't much care which: let us have a good poignée of barbarisms, and a bounteous dose of the insular accent."

"Monsieur is not going to be gratified by a tale of ambitious proportions, and the spectacle of the narrator sticking fast in the midst. But I will tell him the title – the 'Priest's Pupil'."

"Bah!" said he, the swarthy flush again dyeing his dark cheek. "The good old father could not have chosen a worse subject; it is his weak point. But what of the 'Priest's Pupil?'"

"Oh! Many things."

"You may as well define *what* things. I mean to know."

"There was the pupil's youth, the pupil's manhood; – his avarice, his ingratitude, his implacability, his inconstancy. Such a bad pupil, Monsieur! – So thankless, cold-hearted, unchivalrous, unforgiving!"

"*Et puis?*" said he, taking a cigar.

"*Et puis,*" I pursued, "he underwent calamities which one did not pity – bore them in a spirit one did not admire – endured wrongs for which one felt no sympathy; finally took the unchristian revenge of heaping coals of fire on his adversary's head."

"You have not told me all," said he.

"Nearly all, I think: I have indicated the heads of Père Silas's chapters."

"You have forgotten one – that which touched on the pupil's lack of affection – on his hard, cold, monkish heart."

"True; I remember now. Père Silas *did* say that his vocation was almost that of a priest – that his life was considered consecrated."

"By what bonds or duties?"

"By the ties of the past and the charities of the present."

"You have, then, the whole situation?"

"I have now told Monsieur all that was told me."

Some meditative minutes passed.

"Now, Mademoiselle Lucy, look at me, and with that truth which I believe you never knowingly violate, answer me one question. Raise your eyes; rest them on mine; have no hesitation; fear not to trust me – I am a man to be trusted."

I raised my eyes.

"Knowing me thoroughly now – all my antecedents, all my responsibilities – having long known my faults, can you and I still be friends?"

"If Monsieur wants a friend in me, I shall be glad to have a friend in him."

"But a close friend I mean – intimate and real – kindred in all but blood. Will Miss Lucy be the sister of a very poor, fettered, burdened, encumbered man?"

I could not answer him in words, yet I suppose I *did* answer him; he took my hand, which found comfort, in the shelter of his. *His* friendship was not a doubtful, wavering benefit – a cold, distant hope – a sentiment so brittle as not to bear the weight of a finger: I at once felt (or *thought* I felt) its support like that of some rock.

"When I talk of friendship, I mean *true* friendship," he repeated emphatically; and I could hardly believe that words so earnest had blessed my ear; I hardly could credit the reality of that kind, anxious look he gave. If he *really* wished for my confidence and regard, and *really* would give me his – why, it seemed to me that life could offer nothing more or better. In that case, I was become strong and rich: in a moment I was made substantially happy. To ascertain the fact, to fix and seal it, I asked –

"Is Monsieur quite serious? Does he really think he needs me, and can take an interest in me as a sister?"

"Surely, surely," said he; "a lonely man like me, who has no sister, must be but too glad to find in some woman's heart a sister's pure affection."

"And dare I rely on Monsieur's regard? Dare I speak to him when I am so inclined?"

"My little sister must make her own experiments," said he; "I will give no promises. She must tease and try her wayward brother till she has drilled him into what she wishes. After all, he is no inductile material in some hands."

While he spoke, the tone of his voice, the light of his now affectionate eye, gave me such a pleasure as, certainly, I had never felt. I envied no girl her lover, no bride her bridegroom, no wife her husband; I was content with this my voluntary, self-offering friend. If he would but prove reliable, and he *looked* reliable, what, beyond his friendship, could I ever covet? But, if all melted like a dream, as once before had happened –?

"Qu'est-ce donc? What is it?" said he, as this thought threw its weight on my heart, its shadow on my countenance. I told him; and after a moment's pause, and a thoughtful smile, he showed me how an equal fear – lest I should weary of him, a man of moods so difficult and fitful – had haunted his mind for more than one day, or one month.

On hearing this, a quiet courage cheered me. I ventured a word of re-assurance. That word was not only tolerated; its repetition was courted. I grew quite happy – strangely happy – in making him secure, content, tranquil. Yesterday, I could not have believed that earth held, or life afforded, moments like the few I was now passing. Countless times it had been my lot to watch apprehended sorrow close darkly in; but to see unhoped-for happiness take form, find place, and grow more real as the seconds sped, was indeed a new experience.

"Lucy," said M. Paul, speaking low, and still holding my hand, "did you see a picture in the boudoir of the old house?"

"I did; a picture painted on a panel."

"The portrait of a nun?"

"Yes."

"You heard her history?"

"Yes."

"You remember what we saw that night in the berceau?"

"I shall never forget it."

"You did not connect the two ideas; that would be folly?"

"I thought of the apparition when I saw the portrait," said I; which was true enough.

"You did not, nor will you fancy," pursued he, "that a saint in heaven perturbs herself with rivalries of earth? Protestants are rarely superstitious; these morbid fancies will not beset *you?*"

"I know not what to think of this matter; but I believe a perfectly natural solution of this seeming mystery will one day be arrived at."

"Doubtless, doubtless. Besides, no good-living woman – much less a pure, happy spirit – would trouble amity like ours *n'est-il pas vrai?*"

Ere I could answer, Fifine Beck burst in, rosy and abrupt, calling out that I was wanted. Her mother was going into town to call on some English family, who had applied for a prospectus: my services were needed as interpreter. The interruption was not unseasonable: sufficient for the day is always the evil; for this hour, its good sufficed. Yet I should have liked to ask M. Paul whether the 'morbid fancies', against which he warned me, wrought in his own brain.

Chapter Thirty-Six
The Apple of Discord

BESIDES FIFINE BECK'S MOTHER, another power had a word to say to M. Paul and me, before that covenant of friendship could be ratified. We were under the surveillance of a sleepless eye: Rome watched jealously her son through that mystic lattice at which I had knelt once, and to which M. Emanuel drew nigh month by month – the sliding panel of the confessional.

"Why were you so glad to be friends with M. Paul?" asks the reader. "Had he not long been a friend to you? Had he not given proof on proof of a certain partiality in his feelings?"

Yes, he had; but still I liked to hear him say so earnestly – that he was my close, true friend; I liked his modest doubts, his tender deference – that trust which longed to rest, and was grateful when taught how. He had called me 'sister'. It was well. Yes; he might call me what he pleased, so long as he confided in me. I was willing to be his sister, on condition that he did not invite me to fill that relation to some future wife of his; and tacitly vowed as he was to celibacy, of this dilemma there seemed little danger.

Through most of the succeeding night I pondered that evening's interview. I wanted much the morning to break, and then listened for the bell to ring; and, after rising and dressing, I deemed prayers and breakfast slow, and all the hours lingering, till that arrived at last which brought me the lesson of literature. My wish was to get a more thorough comprehension of this fraternal alliance: to note with how much of the brother he would demean himself when we met again; to prove how much of the sister was in my own feelings; to discover whether I could summon a sister's courage, and he a brother's frankness.

He came. Life is so constructed, that the event does not, cannot, will not, match the expectation. That whole day he never accosted me. His lesson was given rather more quietly than usual, more mildly, and also more gravely. He was fatherly to his pupils, but he was not brotherly to me. Ere he left the classe, I expected a smile, if not a word; I got neither: to my portion fell one nod – hurried, shy.

This distance, I argued, is accidental – it is involuntary; patience, and it will vanish. It vanished not; it continued for days; it increased. I suppressed my surprise, and swallowed whatever other feelings began to surge.

Well might I ask when he offered fraternity – "Dare I rely on you?" Well might he, doubtless knowing himself, withhold all pledge. True, he had bid me make my own experiments – tease and try him. Vain injunction! Privilege nominal and unavailable! Some women might use it! Nothing in my powers or instinct placed me amongst this brave band. Left alone, I was passive; repulsed, I withdrew; forgotten – my lips would not utter, nor my eyes dart a reminder. It seemed there had been an error somewhere in my calculations, and I wanted for time to disclose it.

But the day came when, as usual, he was to give me a lesson. One evening in seven he had long generously bestowed on me, devoting it to the examination of what had been done in various studies during the past week, and to the preparation of work for the week in prospect. On these occasions my schoolroom was anywhere, wherever the pupils and the other teachers happened to be, or in their close vicinage, very often in the large second division, where it was easy to choose a quiet nook when the crowding day pupils were absent, and the few boarders gathered in a knot about the surveillante's estrade.

On the customary evening, hearing the customary hour strike, I collected my books and papers, my pen and ink, and sought the large division.

In classe there was no one, and it lay all in cool deep shadow; but through the open double doors was seen the carré, filled with pupils and with light; over hall and figures blushed the westering sun. It blushed so ruddily and vividly, that the hues of the walls and the variegated tints of the dresses seemed all fused in one warm glow. The girls were seated, working or studying; in the midst of their circle stood M. Emanuel, speaking good-humouredly to a teacher. His dark paletôt, his jetty hair, were tinged with many a reflex of crimson; his Spanish face, when he turned it momentarily, answered the sun's animated kiss with an animated smile. I took my place at a desk.

The orange-trees, and several plants, full and bright with bloom, basked also in the sun's laughing bounty; they had partaken it the whole day, and now asked water. M. Emanuel had a taste for gardening; he liked to tend and foster plants. I used to think that working amongst shrubs with a spade or a watering-pot soothed his nerves; it was a recreation to which he often had recourse; and now he looked to the orange-trees, the geraniums, the gorgeous cactuses, and revived them all with the refreshment their drought needed. His lips meantime sustained his precious cigar, that (for him) first necessary and prime luxury of life; its blue wreaths curled prettily enough amongst the flowers, and in the evening light. He spoke no more to the pupils, nor to the mistresses, but gave many an endearing word to a small spanieless (if one may coin a word), that nominally belonged to the house, but virtually owned him as master, being fonder of him than any inmate. A delicate, silky, loving, and lovable little doggie she was, trotting at his side, looking with expressive, attached eyes into his face; and whenever he dropped his bonnet-grec or his handkerchief, which he occasionally did in play, crouching beside it with the air of a miniature lion guarding a kingdom's flag.

There were many plants, and as the amateur gardener fetched all the water from the well in the court, with his own active hands, his work spun on to some length. The great school-clock ticked on. Another hour struck. The carré and the youthful group lost the illusion of sunset. Day was drooping. My lesson, I perceived, must tonight be very short; but the orange-trees, the cacti, the camelias were all served now. Was it my turn?

Alas! In the garden were more plants to be looked after – favourite rose-bushes, certain choice flowers; little Sylvie's glad bark and whine followed the receding paletôt down the alleys. I put up some of my books; I should not want them all; I sat and thought; and waited, involuntarily deprecating the creeping invasion of twilight.

Sylvie, gaily frisking, emerged into view once more, heralding the returning paletôt; the watering-pot was deposited beside the well; it had fulfilled its office; how glad I was! Monsieur washed his hands in a little stone bowl. There was no longer time for a lesson now; ere long the prayer-bell must ring; but still we should meet; he would speak; a chance would be offered of reading in his eyes the riddle of his shyness. His ablutions over, he stood, slowly re-arranging his cuffs, looking at the horn of a young moon, set pale in the opal sky, and glimmering faint on the oriel of Jean Baptiste. Sylvie watched the mood contemplative; its stillness irked her; she whined and jumped to break it. He looked down.

"Petite exigeante," said he; "you must not be forgotten one moment, it seems."

He stopped, lifted her in his arms, sauntered across the court, within a yard of the line of windows near one of which I sat: he sauntered lingeringly, fondling the spaniel in his bosom, calling her tender names in a tender voice. On the front-door steps he turned; once again he looked at the moon, at the grey cathedral, over the remoter spires and house-roofs fading into a blue sea of night-mist; he tasted the sweet breath of dusk, and noted the folded bloom of the garden; he suddenly looked round; a keen beam out of his eye rased the white façade of the classes, swept the long line of croisées. I think he bowed; if he did, I had no time to return the courtesy. In a moment he was gone; the moonlit threshold lay pale and shadowless before the closed front door.

Gathering in my arms all that was spread on the desk before me, I carried back the unused heap to its place in the third classe. The prayer-bell rang; I obeyed its summons.

The morrow would not restore him to the Rue Fossette, that day being devoted entirely to his college. I got through my teaching; I got over the intermediate hours; I saw evening approaching, and armed myself for its heavy ennuis. Whether it was worse to stay with my co-inmates, or to sit alone, I had not considered; I naturally took up the latter alternative; if there was a hope of comfort for any moment, the heart or head of no human being in this house could yield it; only under the lid of my desk could it harbour, nestling between the leaves of some book, gilding a pencil-point, the nib of a pen, or tinging the black fluid in that ink-glass. With a heavy heart I opened my desk-lid; with a weary hand I turned up its contents.

One by one, well-accustomed books, volumes sewn in familiar covers, were taken out and put back hopeless: they had no charm; they could not comfort. Is this something new, this pamphlet in lilac? I had not seen it before, and I re-arranged my desk this very day – this very afternoon; the tract must have been introduced within the last hour, while we were at dinner.

I opened it. What was it? What would it say to me?

It was neither tale nor poem, neither essay nor history; it neither sung, nor related, not discussed. It was a theological work; it preached and it persuaded.

I lent to it my ear very willingly, for, small as it was, it possessed its own spell, and bound my attention at once. It preached Romanism; it persuaded to conversion. The voice of that sly little book was a honeyed voice; its accents were all unction and balm. Here roared no utterance of Rome's thunders, no blasting of the breath of her displeasure. The Protestant was to turn Papist, not so much in fear of the heretic's hell, as on account of the comfort, the indulgence, the tenderness Holy Church offered: far be it from her to threaten or to coerce; her wish was to guide and win. *She* persecute? Oh dear no! Not on any account!

This meek volume was not addressed to the hardened and worldly; it was not even strong meat for the strong: it was milk for babes: the mild effluence of a mother's love towards her tenderest and her youngest; intended wholly and solely for those whose head is to be reached through the heart. Its appeal was not to intellect; it sought to win the affectionate through their affections, the sympathizing through their sympathies: St. Vincent de Paul, gathering his orphans about him, never spoke more sweetly.

I remember one capital inducement to apostacy was held out in the fact that the Catholic who had lost dear friends by death could enjoy the unspeakable solace of praying them out of purgatory. The writer did not touch on the firmer peace of those whose belief dispenses with purgatory altogether: but I thought of this; and, on the whole, preferred the latter doctrine as the most consolatory. The little book amused, and did not painfully displease me. It was a canting, sentimental, shallow little book, yet something about it cheered my gloom and made me smile; I was amused with the gambols of this unlicked wolf-cub muffled in the fleece, and mimicking the bleat of a guileless lamb. Portions of it reminded me of certain Wesleyan Methodist tracts I had once read when a child; they were flavoured with about the same seasoning of excitation to fanaticism. He that had written it was no bad man, and while perpetually betraying the trained cunning – the cloven hoof of his system – I should pause before accusing himself of insincerity. His judgment, however, wanted surgical props; it was rickety.

I smiled then over this dose of maternal tenderness, coming from the ruddy old lady of the Seven Hills; smiled, too, at my own disinclination, not to say disability, to meet these melting favours. Glancing at the title-page, I found the name of 'Père Silas'. A fly-leaf bore in small, but clear and well-known pencil characters: 'From P.C.D.E. to L—y'. And when I saw this I laughed: but not in my former spirit. I was revived.

A mortal bewilderment cleared suddenly from my head and vision; the solution of the Sphinx-riddle was won; the conjunction of those two names, Père Silas and Paul Emanuel, gave the key to all. The penitent had been with his director; permitted to withhold nothing; suffered to keep no corner of his heart sacred to God and to himself; the whole narrative of our late interview had been drawn from him; he had avowed the covenant of fraternity, and spoken of his adopted sister. How could such a covenant, such adoption, be sanctioned by the Church? Fraternal communion with a heretic! I seemed to hear Père Silas annulling the unholy pact; warning his penitent of its perils; entreating, enjoining reserve, nay, by the authority of his office, and in the name, and by the memory of all M. Emanuel held most dear and sacred, commanding the enforcement of that new system whose frost had pierced to the marrow of my bones.

These may not seem pleasant hypotheses; yet, by comparison, they were welcome. The vision of a ghostly troubler hovering in the background, was as nothing, matched with the fear of spontaneous change arising in M. Paul himself.

At this distance of time, I cannot be sure how far the above conjectures were self-suggested: or in what measure they owed their origin and confirmation to another quarter. Help was not wanting.

This evening there was no bright sunset: west and east were one cloud; no summer night-mist, blue, yet rose-tinged, softened the distance; a clammy fog from the marshes crept grey round Villette. Tonight the watering-pot might rest in its niche by the well: a small rain had been drizzling all the afternoon, and still it fell fast and quietly. This was no weather for rambling in the wet alleys, under the dripping trees; and I started to hear Sylvie's sudden bark in the garden – her bark of welcome. Surely she was not accompanied and yet this glad, quick bark was never uttered, save in homage to one presence.

Through the glass door and the arching berceau, I commanded the deep vista of the allée défendue: thither rushed Sylvie, glistening through its gloom like a white guelder-rose. She ran to and fro, whining, springing, harassing little birds amongst the bushes. I watched five minutes; no fulfilment followed the omen. I returned to my books; Sylvie's sharp bark suddenly ceased. Again I looked up. She was standing not many yards distant, wagging her white feathery tail as fast as the muscle would work, and intently watching the operations of a spade, plied fast by an indefatigable hand. There was M. Emanuel, bent over the soil, digging in the wet mould amongst the rain-laden and streaming shrubs, working as hard as if his day's pittance were yet to earn by the literal sweat of his brow.

In this sign I read a ruffled mood. He would dig thus in frozen snow on the coldest winter day, when urged inwardly by painful emotion, whether of nervous excitation, or, sad thoughts of self-reproach. He would dig by the hour, with knit brow and set teeth, nor once lift his head, or open his lips.

Sylvie watched till she was tired. Again scampering devious, bounding here, rushing there, snuffing and sniffing everywhere; she at last discovered me in classe. Instantly she flew barking at the panes, as if to urge me forth to share her pleasure or her master's toil; she had seen me occasionally walking in that alley with M. Paul; and I doubt not, considered it my duty to join him now, wet as it was.

She made such a bustle that M. Paul at last looked up, and of course perceived why, and at whom she barked. He whistled to call her off; she only barked the louder. She seemed quite bent upon having the glass door opened. Tired, I suppose, with her importunity, he threw down his spade, approached, and pushed the door ajar. Sylvie burst in all impetuous, sprang to my lap, and with her paws at my neck, and her little nose and tongue somewhat overpoweringly busy about my face, mouth, and eyes, flourished her bushy tail over the desk, and scattered books and papers far and wide.

M. Emanuel advanced to still the clamour and repair the disarrangement. Having gathered up the books, he captured Sylvie, and stowed her away under his paletôt, where she nestled as quiet as a mouse, her head just peeping forth. She was very tiny, and had the prettiest little innocent face, the silkiest long ears, the finest dark eyes in the world. I never saw her, but I thought of Paulina de Bassompierre: forgive the association, reader, it *would* occur.

M. Paul petted and patted her; the endearments she received were not to be wondered at; she invited affection by her beauty and her vivacious life.

While caressing the spaniel, his eye roved over the papers and books just replaced; it settled on the religious tract. His lips moved; he half checked the impulse to speak. What! Had he promised never to address me more? If so, his better nature pronounced the vow 'more honoured in the breach than in the observance', for with a second effort, he spoke. – "You have not yet read the brochure, I presume? It is not sufficiently inviting?"

I replied that I had read it.

He waited, as if wishing me to give an opinion upon it unasked. Unasked, however, I was in no mood to do or say anything. If any concessions were to be made – if any advances were demanded – that was the affair of the very docile pupil of Père Silas, not mine. His eye settled upon me gently: there was mildness at the moment in its blue ray – there was solicitude – a shade of pathos; there were meanings composite and contrasted – reproach melting into remorse. At the moment probably, he would have been glad to see something emotional in me. I could not show it. In another minute, however, I should have betrayed confusion, had I not bethought myself to take some quill-pens from my desk, and begin soberly to mend them.

I knew that action would give a turn to his mood. He never liked to see me mend pens; my knife was always dull-edged – my hand, too, was unskilful; I hacked and chipped. On this occasion I cut my own finger – half on purpose. I wanted to restore him to his natural state, to set him at his ease, to get him to chide.

"*Maladroit!*" he cried at last, "she will make mincemeat of her hands."

He put Sylvie down, making her lie quiet beside his bonnet-grec, and, depriving me of the pens and penknife, proceeded to slice, nib, and point with the accuracy and celerity of a machine.

"Did I like the little book?" he now inquired.

Suppressing a yawn, I said I hardly knew.

"Had it moved me?"

"I thought it had made me a little sleepy."

(After a pause:) "*Allons donc!* It was of no use taking that tone with him. Bad as I was – and he should be sorry to have to name all my faults at a breath – God and nature had given me '*trop de sensibilité et de sympathie*' not to be profoundly affected by an appeal so touching."

"Indeed!" I responded, rousing myself quickly, "I was not affected at all – not a whit."

And in proof, I drew from my pocket a perfectly dry handkerchief, still clean and in its folds.

Hereupon I was made the object of a string of strictures rather piquant than polite. I listened with zest. After those two days of unnatural silence, it was better than music to hear M. Paul haranguing again just in his old fashion. I listened, and meantime solaced myself and Sylvie with the contents of a bonbonnière, which M. Emanuel's gifts kept well supplied with chocolate comfits: It pleased him to see even a small matter from his hand duly appreciated. He looked at me and the spaniel while we shared the spoil; he put up his penknife. Touching my hand with the bundle of new-cut quills, he said: "*Dites donc, petite soeur* – speak frankly – what have you thought of me during the last two days?"

But of this question I would take no manner of notice; its purport made my eyes fill. I caressed Sylvie assiduously. M. Paul, leaning – over the desk, bent towards me: "I called myself your brother," he said: "I hardly know what I am – brother – friend – I cannot tell. I know I think of you – I feel I wish, you well – but I must check myself; you are to be feared. My best friends point out danger, and whisper caution."

"You do right to listen to your friends. By all means be cautious."

"It is your religion – your strange, self-reliant, invulnerable creed, whose influence seems to clothe you in, I know not what, unblessed panoply. You are good – Père Silas calls you good, and loves you – but your terrible, proud, earnest Protestantism, there is the danger. It expresses itself by your eye at times; and again, it gives you certain tones and certain gestures that make my flesh creep. You are not demonstrative, and yet, just now – when you handled that tract – my God! I thought Lucifer smiled."

"Certainly I don't respect that tract – what then?"

"Not respect that tract? But it is the pure essence of faith, love, charity! I thought it would touch you: in its gentleness, I trusted that it could not fail. I laid it in your desk with a prayer: I must indeed be a sinner: Heaven will not hear the petitions that come warmest from my heart. You scorn my little offering. *Oh, cela me fait mal!*"

"Monsieur, I don't scorn it – at least, not as your gift. Monsieur, sit down; listen to me. I am not a heathen, I am not hard-hearted, I am not unchristian, I am not dangerous, as they tell you; I would not trouble your faith; you believe in God and Christ and the Bible, and so do I."

"But *do* you believe in the Bible? Do you receive Revelation? What limits are there to the wild, careless daring of your country and sect. Père Silas dropped dark hints."

By dint of persuasion, I made him half-define these hints; they amounted to crafty Jesuit-slanders. That night M. Paul and I talked seriously and closely. He pleaded, he argued. *I* could not argue – a fortunate incapacity; it needed but triumphant, logical opposition to effect all the director wished to be effected; but I could talk in my own way – the way M. Paul was used to – and of which he could follow the meanderings and fill the hiatus, and pardon the strange stammerings, strange to him no longer. At ease with him, I could defend my creed and faith in my own fashion; in some degree I could lull his prejudices. He was not satisfied when he went away, hardly was he appeased; but he was made thoroughly to feel that Protestants were not necessarily the irreverent Pagans his director had insinuated; he was made to comprehend something of their mode of honouring the Light, the Life, the Word; he was enabled partly to perceive that, while their veneration for things venerable was not quite like that cultivated in his Church, it had its own, perhaps, deeper power – its own more solemn awe.

I found that Père Silas (himself, I must repeat, not a bad man, though the advocate of a bad cause) had darkly stigmatized Protestants in general, and myself by inference, with strange names, had ascribed to us strange 'isms'; Monsieur Emanuel revealed all this in his frank fashion, which knew not secretiveness, looking at me as he spoke with a kind, earnest fear, almost trembling lest there should be truth in the charges. Père Silas, it seems, had closely watched me, had ascertained that I went by turns, and indiscriminately, to the three Protestant Chapels of Villette – the French, German, and English – id est, the Presbyterian, Lutheran, Episcopalian. Such liberality argued in the father's eyes profound indifference – who tolerates all, he reasoned, can be attached to none. Now, it happened that I had often secretly wondered at the minute and unimportant character of the differences between these three sects – at the unity and identity of their vital doctrines: I saw nothing to hinder them from being one day fused into one grand Holy Alliance, and I respected them all, though I thought that in each there were faults of form, incumbrances, and trivialities. Just what I thought, that did I tell M. Emanuel, and explained to him that my own last appeal, the guide to which I looked, and the teacher which I owned, must always be the Bible itself, rather than any sect, of whatever name or nation.

He left me soothed, yet full of solicitude, breathing a wish, as strong as a prayer, that if I were wrong, Heaven would lead me right. I heard, poured forth on the threshold, some fervid murmurings to 'Marie, Reine du Ciel', some deep aspiration that *his* hope might yet be *mine*.

Strange! I had no such feverish wish to turn him from the faith of his fathers. I thought Romanism wrong, a great mixed image of gold and clay; but it seemed to me that *this* Romanist held the purer elements of his creed with an innocency of heart which God must love.

The preceding conversation passed between eight and nine o'clock of the evening, in a schoolroom of the quiet Rue Fossette, opening on a sequestered garden. Probably about the same, or a somewhat later hour of the succeeding evening, its echoes, collected by holy obedience, were breathed verbatim in an attent ear, at the panel of a confessional, in the hoary church of the Magi. It ensued that Père Silas paid a visit to Madame Beck, and stirred by I know not what mixture of motives, persuaded her to let him undertake for a time the Englishwoman's spiritual direction.

Hereupon I was put through a course of reading – that is, I just glanced at the books lent me; they were too little in my way to be thoroughly read, marked, learned, or inwardly digested. And besides, I had a book upstairs, under my pillow, whereof certain chapters satisfied my needs in the article of spiritual lore, furnishing such precept and example as, to my heart's core, I was convinced could not be improved on.

Then Père Silas showed me the fair side of Rome, her good works; and bade me judge the tree by its fruits.

In answer, I felt and I avowed that these works were *not* the fruits of Rome; they were but her abundant blossoming, but the fair promise she showed the world. That bloom, when set, savoured not of charity; the apple full formed was ignorance, abasement, and bigotry. Out of men's afflictions and affections were forged the rivets of their servitude. Poverty was fed and clothed, and sheltered, to bind it by obligation to 'the Church'; orphanage was reared and educated that it might grow up in the fold of 'the Church'; sickness was tended that it might die after the formula and in the ordinance of 'the Church'; and men were overwrought, and women most murderously sacrificed, and all laid down a world God made pleasant for his creatures' good, and took up a cross, monstrous in its galling weight, that they might serve Rome, prove her sanctity, confirm her power, and spread the reign of her tyrant 'Church'.

For man's good was little done; for God's glory, less. A thousand ways were opened with pain, with blood-sweats, with lavishing of life; mountains were cloven through their breasts, and rocks were split to their base; and all for what? That a Priesthood might march straight on and straight upward to an all-dominating eminence, whence they might at last stretch the sceptre of their Moloch 'Church'.

It will not be. God is not with Rome, and, were human sorrows still for the Son of God, would he not mourn over her cruelties and ambitions, as once he mourned over the crimes and woes of doomed Jerusalem!

Oh, lovers of power! Oh, mitred aspirants for this world's kingdoms! An hour will come, even to you, when it will be well for your hearts – pausing faint at each broken beat – that there is a Mercy beyond human compassions, a Love, stronger than this strong death which even you must face, and before it, fall; a Charity more potent than any sin, even yours; a Pity which redeems worlds – nay, absolves Priests.

* * *

My third temptation was held out in the pomp of Rome – the glory of her kingdom. I was taken to the churches on solemn occasions – days of fête and state; I was shown the Papal ritual and ceremonial. I looked at it.

Many people – men and women – no doubt far my superiors in a thousand ways, have felt this display impressive, have declared that though their Reason protested, their Imagination was subjugated. I cannot say the same. Neither full procession, nor high mass, nor swarming tapers, nor swinging censers, nor ecclesiastical millinery, nor celestial jewellery, touched my imagination a whit. What I saw struck me as tawdry, not grand; as grossly material, not poetically spiritual.

This I did not tell Père Silas; he was old, he looked venerable: through every abortive experiment, under every repeated disappointment, he remained personally kind to me, and I felt tender of hurting his feelings. But on the evening of a certain day when, from the balcony of a great house, I had been made to witness a huge mingled procession of the church and the army – priests with relics, and soldiers with weapons, an obese and aged archbishop, habited in cambric and lace, looking strangely like a grey daw in bird-of-paradise plumage, and a band of young girls fantastically robed and garlanded – *then* I spoke my mind to M. Paul.

"I did not like it," I told him; "I did not respect such ceremonies; I wished to see no more."

And having relieved my conscience by this declaration, I was able to go on, and, speaking more currently and clearly than my wont, to show him that I had a mind to keep to my reformed creed; the more I saw of Popery the closer I clung to Protestantism; doubtless there were errors in every church, but I now perceived by contrast how severely pure was my own, compared with her whose painted and meretricious face had been unveiled for my admiration. I told him how we kept fewer forms between us and God; retaining, indeed, no more than, perhaps, the nature of mankind in the mass rendered necessary for due observance. I told him I could not look on flowers and tinsel, on wax-lights and embroidery, at such times and under such circumstances as should be devoted to lifting the secret vision to Him whose home is Infinity, and His being – Eternity. That when I thought of sin and sorrow, of earthly corruption, mortal depravity, weighty temporal woe – I could not care for chanting priests or mumming officials; that when the pains of existence and the terrors of dissolution pressed before me – when the mighty hope and measureless doubt of the future arose in view – *then*, even the scientific strain, or the prayer in a language learned and dead, harassed: with hindrance a heart which only longed to cry – "God be merciful to me, a sinner!"

When I had so spoken, so declared my faith, and so widely severed myself, from him I addressed – then, at last, came a tone accordant, an echo responsive, one sweet chord of harmony in two conflicting spirits.

"Whatever say priests or controversialists," murmured M. Emanuel, "God is good, and loves all the sincere. Believe, then, what you can; believe it as you can; one prayer, at least, we have in common; I also cry – '*O Dieu, sois appaisé envers moi qui suis pécheur!*'"

He leaned on the back of my chair. After some thought he again spoke:

"How seem in the eyes of that God who made all firmaments, from whose nostrils issued whatever of life is here, or in the stars shining yonder – how seem the differences of man? But as Time is not for God, nor Space, so neither is Measure, nor Comparison. We abase ourselves in our littleness, and we do right; yet it may be that the constancy of one heart, the truth and faith of one mind according to the light He has appointed, import as much to Him as the just motion of satellites about their planets, of planets about their suns, of suns around that mighty unseen centre incomprehensible, irrealizable, with strange mental effort only divined.

"God guide us all! God bless you, Lucy!"

Chapter Thirty-Seven
Sunshine

IT WAS VERY WELL for Paulina to decline further correspondence with Graham till her father had sanctioned the intercourse. But Dr. Bretton could not live within a league of the Hôtel Crécy, and not contrive to visit there often. Both lovers meant at first, I believe, to be distant; they kept their intention so far as demonstrative courtship went, but in feeling they soon drew very near.

All that was best in Graham sought Paulina; whatever in him was noble, awoke, and grew in her presence. With his past admiration of Miss Fanshawe, I suppose his intellect had little to do, but his whole intellect, and his highest tastes, came in question now. These, like all his faculties, were active, eager for nutriment, and alive to gratification when it came. I cannot say that Paulina designedly led him to talk of books, or formally proposed to herself for a moment the task of winning him to reflection, or planned the improvement of his mind, or so much as fancied his mind could in any one respect be improved. She thought him very perfect; it was Graham himself, who, at first by the merest chance, mentioned some book he had been reading, and when in her response sounded a welcome harmony of sympathies, something pleasant to his soul, he talked on, more and better perhaps than he had ever talked before on such subjects. She listened with delight, and answered with animation. In each successive answer, Graham heard a music waxing finer and finer to his sense; in each he found a suggestive, persuasive, magic accent that opened a scarce-known treasure-house within, showed him unsuspected power in his own mind, and what was better, latent goodness in his heart. Each liked the way in which the other talked; the voice, the diction, the expression pleased; each keenly relished the flavour of the other's wit; they met each other's meaning with strange quickness, their thoughts often matched like carefully-chosen pearls. Graham had wealth of mirth by nature; Paulina possessed no such inherent flow of animal spirits – unstimulated, she inclined to be thoughtful and pensive – but now she seemed merry as a lark; in her lover's genial presence, she glanced like some soft glad light. How beautiful she grew in her happiness, I can hardly express, but I wondered to see her. As to that gentle ice of hers – that reserve on which she had depended; where was it now? Ah! Graham would not long bear it; he brought with him a generous influence that soon thawed the timid, self-imposed restriction.

Now were the old Bretton days talked over; perhaps brokenly at first, with a sort of smiling diffidence, then with opening candour and still growing confidence. Graham had made for himself a better opportunity than that he had wished me to give; he had earned independence of the collateral help that disobliging Lucy had refused; all his reminiscences of 'little Polly' found their proper expression in his own pleasant tones, by his own kind and handsome lips; how much better than if suggested by me.

More than once when we were alone, Paulina would tell me how wonderful and curious it was to discover the richness and accuracy of his memory in this matter. How, while he was looking at her, recollections would seem to be suddenly quickened in his mind. He reminded her that she had once gathered his head in her arms, caressed his leonine graces, and cried out, "Graham, I *do* like you!" He told her how she would set a footstool beside him, and climb by its aid to his knee. At this day he said he could recall the sensation of her little hands smoothing his cheek, or burying themselves in his thick mane. He remembered the touch of her small forefinger, placed half tremblingly, half curiously, in the cleft in his chin, the lisp, the look with which she would name it "a pretty dimple", then seek his eyes and question why they pierced so, telling him he had a "nice, strange face; far nicer, far stranger, than either his mamma or Lucy Snowe."

"Child as I was," remarked Paulina, "I wonder how I dared be so venturous. To me he seems now all sacred, his locks are inaccessible, and, Lucy, I feel a sort of fear, when I look at his firm, marble chin, at his straight Greek features. Women are called beautiful, Lucy; he is not like a woman, therefore I suppose he is not beautiful, but what is he, then? Do other people see him with my eyes? Do *you* admire him?"

"I'll tell you what I do, Paulina," was once my answer to her many questions. "*I never see him.* I looked at him twice or thrice about a year ago, before he recognised me, and then I shut my eyes; and if he were to cross their balls twelve times between each day's sunset and sunrise, except from memory, I should hardly know what shape had gone by."

"Lucy, what do you mean?" said she, under her breath.

"I mean that I value vision, and dread being struck stone blind."

It was best to answer her strongly at once, and to silence forever the tender, passionate confidences which left her lips sweet honey, and sometimes dropped in my ear – molten lead. To me, she commented no more on her lover's beauty.

Yet speak of him she would; sometimes shyly, in quiet, brief phrases; sometimes with a tenderness of cadence, and music of voice exquisite in itself; but which chafed me at times miserably; and then, I know, I gave her stern looks and words; but cloudless happiness had dazzled her native clear sight, and she only thought Lucy – fitful.

"Spartan girl! Proud Lucy!" she would say, smiling at me. "Graham says you are the most peculiar, capricious little woman he knows; but yet you are excellent; we both think so."

"You both think you know not what," said I. "Have the goodness to make me as little the subject of your mutual talk and thoughts as possible. I have my sort of life apart from yours."

"But ours, Lucy, is a beautiful life, or it will be; and you shall share it."

"I shall share no man's or woman's life in this world, as you understand sharing. I think I have one friend of my own, but am not sure; and till I *am* sure, I live solitary."

"But solitude is sadness."

"Yes; it is sadness. Life, however; has worse than that. Deeper than melancholy, lies heart-break."

"Lucy, I wonder if anybody will ever comprehend you altogether."

There is, in lovers, a certain infatuation of egotism; they will have a witness of their happiness, cost that witness what it may. Paulina had forbidden letters, yet Dr. Bretton wrote; she had resolved against correspondence, yet she answered, were it only to chide. She showed me these letters; with something of the spoiled child's wilfulness, and of the heiress's imperiousness, she *made* me read them. As I read Graham's, I scarce wondered at her exaction, and understood her pride: they were fine letters – manly and fond – modest and gallant. Hers must have appeared to him beautiful. They had not been written to show her talents; still less, I think, to express her love. On the contrary, it appeared that she had proposed to herself the task of hiding that feeling, and bridling her lover's ardour. But how could such letters serve such a purpose? Graham was become dear as her life; he drew her like a powerful magnet. For her there was influence unspeakable in all he uttered, wrote, thought, or looked. With this unconfessed confession, her letters glowed; it kindled them, from greeting to adieu.

"I wish papa knew; I *do* wish papa knew!" began now to be her anxious murmur. "I wish, and yet I fear. I can hardly keep Graham back from telling him. There is nothing I long for more than to have this affair settled – to speak out candidly; and yet I dread the crisis. I know, I am certain, papa will be angry at the first; I fear he will dislike me almost; it will seem to him an untoward business; it will be a surprise, a shock: I can hardly foresee its whole effect on him."

The fact was – her father, long calm, was beginning to be a little stirred: long blind on one point, an importunate light was beginning to trespass on his eye.

To *her*, he said nothing; but when she was not looking at, or perhaps thinking of him, I saw him gaze and meditate on her.

One evening – Paulina was in her dressing-room, writing, I believe, to Graham; she had left me in the library, reading – M. de Bassompierre came in; he sat down: I was about to withdraw; he requested me to remain – gently, yet in a manner which showed he wished compliance. He had taken his seat near the window, at a distance from me; he opened a desk; he took from it what looked like a memorandum-book; of this book he studied a certain entry for several minutes.

"Miss Snowe," said he, laying it down, "do you know my little girl's age?"

"About eighteen, is it not, sir?"

"It seems so. This old pocket-book tells me she was born on the 5th of May, in the year 18— , eighteen years ago. It is strange; I had lost the just reckoning of her age. I thought of her as twelve – fourteen – an indefinite date; but she seemed a child."

"She is about eighteen," I repeated. "She is grown up; she will be no taller."

"My little jewel!" said M. de Bassompierre, in a tone which penetrated like some of his daughter's accents.

He sat very thoughtful.

"Sir, don't grieve," I said; for I knew his feelings, utterly unspoken as they were.

"She is the only pearl I have," he said; "and now others will find out that she is pure and of price: they will covet her."

I made no answer. Graham Bretton had dined with us that day; he had shone both in converse and looks: I know not what pride of bloom embellished his aspect and mellowed his intercourse. Under the stimulus of a high hope, something had unfolded in his whole manner which compelled attention. I think he had purposed on that day to indicate the origin of his endeavours, and the aim of his ambition. M. de Bassompierre had found himself forced, in a manner, to descry the direction and catch the character of his homage. Slow in remarking, he was logical in reasoning: having once seized the thread, it had guided him through a long labyrinth.

"Where is she?" he asked.

"She is upstairs."

"What is she doing?"

"She is writing."

"She writes, does she? Does she receive letters?"

"None but such as she can show me. And – sir – she – *they* have long wanted to consult you."

"Pshaw! They don't think of me – an old father! I am in the way."

"Ah, M. de Bassompierre – not so – that can't be! But Paulina must speak for herself: and Dr. Bretton, too, must be his own advocate."

"It is a little late. Matters are advanced, it seems."

"Sir, till you approve, nothing is done – only they love each other."

"Only!" he echoed.

Invested by fate with the part of confidante and mediator, I was obliged to go on: "Hundreds of times has Dr. Bretton been on the point of appealing to you, sir; but, with all his high courage, he fears you mortally."

"He may well – he may well fear me. He has touched the best thing I have. Had he but let her alone, she would have remained a child for years yet. So. Are they engaged?"

"They could not become engaged without your permission."

"It is well for you, Miss Snowe, to talk and think with that propriety which always characterizes you; but this matter is a grief to me; my little girl was all I had: I have no more daughters and no son; Bretton might as well have looked elsewhere; there are scores of rich and pretty women who would not, I daresay, dislike him: he has looks, and conduct, and connection. Would nothing serve him but my Polly?"

"If he had never seen your 'Polly', others might and would have pleased him – your niece, Miss Fanshawe, for instance."

"Ah! I would have given him Ginevra with all my heart; but Polly! – I can't let him have her. No – I can't. He is not her equal," he affirmed, rather gruffly. "In what particular is he her match? They talk of fortune! I am not an avaricious or interested man, but the world thinks of these things – and Polly will be rich."

"Yes, that is known," said I: "all Villette knows her as an heiress."

"Do they talk of my little girl in that light?"

"They do, sir."

He fell into deep thought. I ventured to say, "Would you, sir, think anyone Paulina's match? Would you prefer any other to Dr. Bretton? Do you think higher rank or more wealth would make much difference in your feelings towards a future son-in-law?"

"You touch me there," said he.

"Look at the aristocracy of Villette – you would not like them, sir?"

"I should not – never a duc, baron, or vicomte of the lot."

"I am told many of these persons think about her, sir," I went on, gaining courage on finding that I met attention rather than repulse. "Other suitors will come, therefore, if Dr. Bretton is refused. Wherever you go, I suppose, aspirants will not be wanting. Independent of heiress-ship, it appears to me that Paulina charms most of those who see her."

"Does she? How? My little girl is not thought a beauty."

"Sir, Miss de Bassompierre is very beautiful."

"Nonsense! – Begging your pardon, Miss Snowe, but I think you are too partial. I like Polly: I like all her ways and all her looks – but then I am her father; and even I never thought about beauty. She is amusing, fairy-like, interesting to me; – you must be mistaken in supposing her handsome?"

"She attracts, sir: she would attract without the advantages of your wealth and position."

"My wealth and position! Are these any bait to Graham? If I thought so –"

"Dr. Bretton knows these points perfectly, as you may be sure, M. de Bassompierre, and values them as any gentleman would – as *you* would yourself, under the same circumstances – but they are not his baits. He loves your daughter very much; he feels her finest qualities, and they influence him worthily."

"What! Has my little pet 'fine qualities?'"

"Ah, sir! Did you observe her that evening when so many men of eminence and learning dined here?"

"I certainly was rather struck and surprised with her manner that day; its womanliness made me smile."

"And did you see those accomplished Frenchmen gather round her in the drawing-room?"

"I did; but I thought it was by way of relaxation – as one might amuse one's self with a pretty infant."

"Sir, she demeaned herself with distinction; and I heard the French gentlemen say she was '*pétrie d'esprit et de graces*'. Dr. Bretton thought the same."

"She is a good, dear child, that is certain; and I *do* believe she has some character. When I think of it, I was once ill; Polly nursed me; they thought I should die; she, I recollect, grew at once stronger and tenderer as I grew worse in health. And as I recovered, what a sunbeam she was in my sick-room! Yes; she played about my chair as noiselessly and as cheerful as light. And now she is sought in marriage! I don't want to part with her," said he, and he groaned.

"You have known Dr. and Mrs. Bretton so long," I suggested, "it would be less like separation to give her to him than to another."

He reflected rather gloomily.

"True. I have long known Louisa Bretton," he murmured. "She and I are indeed old, old friends; a sweet, kind girl she was when she was young. You talk of beauty, Miss Snowe! *She* was handsome, if you will – tall, straight, and blooming – not the mere child or elf my Polly seems to me: at eighteen,

Louisa had a carriage and stature fit for a princess. She is a comely and a good woman now. The lad is like her; I have always thought so, and favoured and wished him well. Now he repays me by this robbery! My little treasure used to love her old father dearly and truly. It is all over now, doubtless – I am an incumbrance."

The door opened – his 'little treasure' came in. She was dressed, so to speak, in evening beauty; that animation which sometimes comes with the close of day, warmed her eye and cheek; a tinge of summer crimson heightened her complexion; her curls fell full and long on her lily neck; her white dress suited the heat of June. Thinking me alone, she had brought in her hand the letter just written – brought it folded but unsealed. I was to read it. When she saw her father, her tripping step faltered a little, paused a moment – the colour in her cheek flowed rosy over her whole face.

"Polly," said M. de Bassompierre, in a low voice, with a grave smile, "do you blush at seeing papa? That is something new."

"I don't blush – I never *do* blush," affirmed she, while another eddy from the heart sent up its scarlet. "But I thought you were in the dining-room, and I wanted Lucy."

"You thought I was with John Graham Bretton, I suppose? But he has just been called out: he will be back soon, Polly. He can post your letter for you; it will save Matthieu a 'course', as he calls it."

"I don't post letters," said she, rather pettishly.

"What do you do with them, then? – Come here and tell me."

Both her mind and gesture seemed to hesitate a second – to say "Shall I come?" – but she approached.

"How long is it since you became a letter-writer, Polly? It only seems yesterday when you were at your pot-hooks, labouring away absolutely with both hands at the pen."

"Papa, they are not letters to send to the post in your letter-bag; they are only notes, which I give now and then into the person's hands, just to satisfy."

"The person! That means Miss Snowe, I suppose?"

"No, papa – not Lucy."

"Who then? Perhaps Mrs. Bretton?"

"No, papa – not Mrs. Bretton."

"Who, then, my little daughter? Tell papa the truth."

"Oh, papa!" she cried with earnestness, "I will – I *will* tell you the truth – all the truth; I am glad to tell you – glad, though I tremble."

She *did* tremble: growing excitement, kindling feeling, and also gathering courage, shook her.

"I hate to hide my actions from you, papa. I fear you and love you above everything but God. Read the letter; look at the address."

She laid it on his knee. He took it up and read it through; his hand shaking, his eyes glistening meantime.

He re-folded it, and viewed the writer with a strange, tender, mournful amaze.

"Can *she* write so – the little thing that stood at my knee but yesterday? Can she feel so?"

"Papa, is it wrong? Does it pain you?"

"There is nothing wrong in it, my innocent little Mary; but it pains me."

"But, papa, listen! You shall not be pained by me. I would give up everything – almost" (correcting herself); "I would die rather than make you unhappy; that would be too wicked!"

She shuddered.

"Does the letter not please you? Must it not go? Must it be torn? It shall, for your sake, if you order it."

"I order nothing."

"Order something, papa; express your wish; only don't hurt, don't grieve Graham. I cannot, *cannot* bear that. I love you, papa; but I love Graham too – because – because – it is impossible to help it."

"This splendid Graham is a young scamp, Polly – that is my present notion of him: it will surprise you to hear that, for my part, I do not love him one whit. Ah! Years ago I saw something in that lad's eye I never quite fathomed – something his mother has not – a depth which warned a man not to wade into that stream too far; now, suddenly, I find myself taken over the crown of the head."

"Papa, you don't – you have not fallen in; you are safe on the bank; you can do as you please; your power is despotic; you can shut me up in a convent, and break Graham's heart tomorrow, if you choose to be so cruel. Now, autocrat, now czar, will you do this?"

"Off with him to Siberia, red whiskers and all; I say, I don't like him, Polly, and I wonder that you should."

"Papa," said she, "do you know you are very naughty? I never saw you look so disagreeable, so unjust, so almost vindictive before. There is an expression in your face which does not belong to you."

"Off with him!" pursued Mr. Home, who certainly did look sorely crossed and annoyed – even a little bitter; "but, I suppose, if he went, Polly would pack a bundle and run after him; her heart is fairly won – won, and weaned from her old father."

"Papa, I say it is naughty, it is decidedly wrong, to talk in that way. I am *not* weaned from you, and no human being and no mortal influence *can* wean me."

"Be married, Polly! Espouse the red whiskers. Cease to be a daughter; go and be a wife!"

"Red whiskers! I wonder what you mean, papa. You should take care of prejudice. You sometimes say to me that all the Scotch, your countrymen, are the victims of prejudice. It is proved now, I think, when no distinction is to be made between red and deep nut-brown."

"Leave the prejudiced old Scotchman; go away."

She stood looking at him a minute. She wanted to show firmness, superiority to taunts; knowing her father's character, guessing his few foibles, she had expected the sort of scene which was now transpiring; it did not take her by surprise, and she desired to let it pass with dignity, reliant upon reaction. Her dignity stood her in no stead. Suddenly her soul melted in her eyes; she fell on his neck: "I won't leave you, papa; I'll never leave you. I won't pain you! I'll never pain you!" was her cry.

"My lamb! My treasure!" murmured the loving though rugged sire. He said no more for the moment; indeed, those two words were hoarse.

The room was now darkening. I heard a movement, a step without. Thinking it might be a servant coming with candles, I gently opened, to prevent intrusion. In the ante-room stood no servant: a tall gentleman was placing his hat on the table, drawing off his gloves slowly – lingering, waiting, it seemed to me. He called me neither by sign nor word; yet his eye said: "Lucy, come here." And I went.

Over his face a smile flowed, while he looked down on me: no temper, save his own, would have expressed by a smile the sort of agitation which now fevered him.

"M. de Bassompierre is there – is he not?" he inquired, pointing to the library.

"Yes."

"He noticed me at dinner? He understood me?"

"Yes, Graham."

"I am brought up for judgment, then, and so is *she*?"

"Mr. Home" (we now and always continued to term him Mr. Home at times) "is talking to his daughter."

"Ha! These are sharp moments, Lucy!"

He was quite stirred up; his young hand trembled; a vital (I was going to write *mortal*, but such words ill apply to one all living like him) – a vital suspense now held, now hurried, his breath: in all this trouble his smile never faded.

"Is he *very* angry, Lucy?"

"*She* is very faithful, Graham."

"What will be done unto me?"

"Graham, your star must be fortunate."

"Must it? Kind prophet! So cheered, I should be a faint heart indeed to quail. I think I find all women faithful, Lucy. I ought to love them, and I do. My mother is good; *she* is divine; and *you* are true as steel. Are you not?"

"Yes, Graham."

"Then give me thy hand, my little god-sister: it is a friendly little hand to me, and always has been. And now for the great venture. God be with the right. Lucy, say Amen!"

He turned, and waited till I said "Amen!" – which I did to please him: the old charm, in doing as he bid me, came back. I wished him success; and successful I knew he would be. He was born victor, as some are born vanquished.

"Follow me!" he said; and I followed him into Mr. Home's presence.

"Sir," he asked, "what is my sentence?"

The father looked at him: the daughter kept her face hid.

"Well, Bretton," said Mr. Home, "you have given me the usual reward of hospitality. I entertained you; you have taken my best. I was always glad to see you; you were glad to see the one precious thing I had. You spoke me fair; and, meantime, I will not say you *robbed* me, but I am bereaved, and what I have lost, *you*, it seems, have won."

"Sir, I cannot repent."

"Repent! Not you! You triumph, no doubt: John Graham, you descended partly from a Highlander and a chief, and there is a trace of the Celt in all you look, speak, and think. You have his cunning and his charm. The red – (Well then, Polly, the *fair*) hair, the tongue of guile, and brain of wile, are all come down by inheritance."

"Sir, I *feel* honest enough," said Graham; and a genuine English blush covered his face with its warm witness of sincerity. "And yet," he added, "I won't deny that in some respects you accuse me justly. In your presence I have always had a thought which I dared not show you. I did truly regard you as the possessor of the most valuable thing the world owns for me. I wished for it: I tried for it. Sir, I ask for it now."

"John, you ask much."

"Very much, sir. It must come from your generosity, as a gift; from your justice, as a reward. I can never earn it."

"Ay! Listen to the Highland tongue!" said Mr. Home. "Look up, Polly! Answer this 'braw wooer'; send him away!"

She looked up. She shyly glanced at her eager, handsome suitor. She gazed tenderly on her furrowed sire.

"Papa, I love you both," said she; "I can take care of you both. I need not send Graham away – he can live here; he will be no inconvenience," she alleged with that simplicity of phraseology which at times was wont to make both her father and Graham smile. They smiled now.

"He will be a prodigious inconvenience to me," still persisted Mr. Home. "I don't want him, Polly, he is too tall; he is in my way. Tell him to march."

"You will get used to him, papa. He seemed exceedingly tall to me at first – like a tower when I looked up at him; but, on the whole, I would rather not have him otherwise."

"I object to him altogether, Polly; I can do without a son-in-law. I should never have requested the best man in the land to stand to me in that relation. Dismiss this gentleman."

"But he has known you so long, papa, and suits you so well."

"Suits *me*, forsooth! Yes; he has pretended to make my opinions and tastes his own. He has humoured me for good reasons. I think, Polly, you and I will bid him goodbye."

"Till tomorrow only. Shake hands with Graham, papa."

"No: I think not: I am not friends with him. Don't think to coax me between you."

"Indeed, indeed, you *are* friends. Graham, stretch out your right hand. Papa, put out yours. Now, let them touch. Papa, don't be stiff; close your fingers; be pliant – there! But that is not a clasp – it is a grasp? Papa, you grasp like a vice. You crush Graham's hand to the bone; you hurt him!"

He must have hurt him; for he wore a massive ring, set round with brilliants, of which the sharp facets cut into Graham's flesh and drew blood: but pain only made Dr. John laugh, as anxiety had made him smile.

"Come with me into my study," at last said Mr. Home to the doctor. They went. Their intercourse was not long, but I suppose it was conclusive. The suitor had to undergo an interrogatory and a scrutiny on many things. Whether Dr. Bretton was at times guileful in look and language or not, there was a sound foundation below. His answers, I understood afterwards, evinced both wisdom and integrity. He had managed his affairs well. He had struggled through entanglements; his fortunes were in the way of retrieval; he proved himself in a position to marry.

Once more the father and lover appeared in the library. M. de Bassompierre shut the door; he pointed to his daughter.

"Take her," he said. "Take her, John Bretton: and may God deal with you as you deal with her!"

* * *

Not long after, perhaps a fortnight, I saw three persons, Count de Bassompierre, his daughter, and Dr. Graham Bretton, sitting on one seat, under a low-spreading and umbrageous tree, in the grounds of the palace at Bois l'Etang. They had come thither to enjoy a summer evening: outside the magnificent gates their carriage waited to take them home; the green sweeps of turf spread round them quiet and dim; the palace rose at a distance, white as a crag on Pentelicus; the evening star shone above it; a forest of flowering shrubs embalmed the climate of this spot; the hour was still and sweet; the scene, but for this group, was solitary.

Paulina sat between the two gentlemen: while they conversed, her little hands were busy at some work; I thought at first she was binding a nosegay. No; with the tiny pair of scissors, glittering in her lap, she had severed spoils from each manly head beside her, and was now occupied in plaiting together the grey lock and the golden wave. The plait woven – no silk-thread being at hand to bind it – a tress of her own hair was made to serve that purpose; she tied it like a knot, prisoned it in a locket, and laid it on her heart.

"Now," said she, "there is an amulet made, which has virtue to keep you two always friends. You can never quarrel so long as I wear this."

An amulet was indeed made, a spell framed which rendered enmity impossible. She was become a bond to both, an influence over each, a mutual concord. From them she drew her happiness, and what she borrowed, she, with interest, gave back.

"Is there, indeed, such happiness on earth?" I asked, as I watched the father, the daughter, the future husband, now united – all blessed and blessing.

Yes; it is so. Without any colouring of romance, or any exaggeration of fancy, it is so. Some real lives do – for some certain days or years – actually anticipate the happiness of Heaven; and, I believe, if such perfect happiness is once felt by good people (to the wicked it never comes), its sweet effect is never wholly lost. Whatever trials follow, whatever pains of sickness or shades of death, the glory precedent still shines through, cheering the keen anguish, and tinging the deep cloud.

I will go farther. I *do* believe there are some human beings so born, so reared, so guided from a soft cradle to a calm and late grave, that no excessive suffering penetrates their lot, and no tempestuous blackness overcasts their journey. And often, these are not pampered, selfish beings, but Nature's elect, harmonious and benign; men and women mild with charity, kind agents of God's kind attributes.

Let me not delay the happy truth. Graham Bretton and Paulina de Bassompierre were married, and such an agent did Dr. Bretton prove. He did not with time degenerate; his faults decayed, his virtues ripened; he rose in intellectual refinement, he won in moral profit: all dregs filtered away, the clear wine settled bright and tranquil. Bright, too, was the destiny of his sweet wife. She kept her husband's love, she aided in his progress – of his happiness she was the corner stone.

This pair was blessed indeed, for years brought them, with great prosperity, great goodness: they imparted with open hand, yet wisely. Doubtless they knew crosses, disappointments, difficulties; but these were well borne. More than once, too, they had to look on Him whose face flesh scarce can see and live: they had to pay their tribute to the King of Terrors. In the fulness of years, M. de Bassompierre was taken: in ripe old age departed Louisa Bretton. Once even there rose a cry in their halls, of Rachel weeping for her children; but others sprang healthy and blooming to replace the lost: Dr. Bretton saw himself live again in a son who inherited his looks and his disposition; he had stately daughters, too, like himself: these children he reared with a suave, yet a firm hand; they grew up according to inheritance and nurture.

In short, I do but speak the truth when I say that these two lives of Graham and Paulina were blessed, like that of Jacob's favoured son, with 'blessings of Heaven above, blessings of the deep that lies under'. It was so, for God saw that it was good.

Chapter Thirty-Eight
Cloud

BUT IT IS not so for all. What then? His will be done, as done it surely will be, whether we humble ourselves to resignation or not. The impulse of creation forwards it; the strength of powers, seen and unseen, has its fulfilment in charge. Proof of a life to come must be given. In fire and in blood, if needful, must that proof be written. In fire and in blood do we trace the record throughout nature. In fire and in blood does it cross our own experience. Sufferer, faint not through terror of this burning evidence. Tired wayfarer, gird up thy loins; look upward, march onward. Pilgrims and brother mourners, join in friendly company. Dark through the wilderness of this world stretches the way for most of us: equal and steady be our tread; be our cross our banner. For staff we have His promise, whose 'word is tried, whose way perfect': for present hope His providence, 'who gives the shield of salvation, whose gentleness makes great'; for final home His bosom, who 'dwells in the height of Heaven'; for crowning prize a glory, exceeding and eternal. Let us so run that we may obtain: let us endure hardness as good soldiers; let us finish our course, and keep the faith, reliant in the issue to come off more than conquerors: 'Art thou not from everlasting mine Holy One? *We Shall Not Die!*'

On a Thursday morning we were all assembled in classe, waiting for the lesson of literature. The hour was come; we expected the master.

The pupils of the first classe sat very still; the cleanly-written compositions prepared since the last lesson lay ready before them, neatly tied with ribbon, waiting to be gathered by the hand of the Professor as he made his rapid round of the desks. The month was July, the morning fine, the glass-door stood ajar, through it played a fresh breeze, and plants, growing at the lintel, waved, bent, looked in, seeming to whisper tidings.

M. Emanuel was not always quite punctual; we scarcely wondered at his being a little late, but we wondered when the door at last opened and, instead of him with his swiftness and his fire, there came quietly upon us the cautious Madame Beck.

She approached M. Paul's desk; she stood before it; she drew round her the light shawl covering her shoulders; beginning to speak in low, yet firm tones, and with a fixed gaze, she said, "This morning there will be no lesson of literature."

The second paragraph of her address followed, after about two minutes' pause.

"It is probable the lessons will be suspended for a week. I shall require at least that space of time to find an efficient substitute for M. Emanuel. Meanwhile, it shall be our study to fill the blanks usefully.

"Your Professor, ladies," she went on, "intends, if possible, duly to take leave of you. At the present moment he has not leisure for that ceremony. He is preparing for a long voyage. A very sudden and urgent summons of duty calls him to a great distance. He has decided to leave Europe for an indefinite time. Perhaps he may tell you more himself. Ladies, instead of the usual lesson with M. Emanuel, you will, this morning, read English with Mademoiselle Lucy."

She bent her head courteously, drew closer the folds of her shawl, and passed from the classe.

A great silence fell: then a murmur went round the room: I believe some pupils wept.

Some time elapsed. The noise, the whispering, the occasional sobbing increased. I became conscious of a relaxation of discipline, a sort of growing disorder, as if my girls felt that vigilance was withdrawn, and that surveillance had virtually left the classe. Habit and the sense of duty enabled me to rally quickly, to rise in my usual way, to speak in my usual tone, to enjoin, and finally to establish quiet. I made the English reading long and close. I kept them at it the whole morning. I remember feeling a sentiment of impatience towards the pupils who sobbed. Indeed, their emotion was not of much value: it was only an hysteric agitation. I told them so unsparingly. I half ridiculed them. I was severe. The truth was, I could not do with their tears, or that gasping sound; I could not bear it. A rather weak-minded, low-spirited pupil kept it up when the others had done; relentless necessity obliged and assisted me so to accost her, that she dared not carry on the demonstration, that she was forced to conquer the convulsion.

That girl would have had a right to hate me, except that, when school was over and her companions departing, I ordered her to stay, and when they were gone, I did what I had never done to one among them before – pressed her to my heart and kissed her cheek. But, this impulse yielded to, I speedily put her out of the classe, for, upon that poignant strain, she wept more bitterly than ever.

I filled with occupation every minute of that day, and should have liked to sit up all night if I might have kept a candle burning; the night, however, proved a bad time, and left bad effects, preparing me ill for the next day's ordeal of insufferable gossip. Of course this news fell under general discussion. Some little reserve had accompanied the first surprise: that soon wore off; every mouth opened; every tongue wagged; teachers, pupils, the very servants, mouthed the name of 'Emanuel'. He, whose connection with the school was contemporary with its commencement, thus suddenly to withdraw! All felt it strange.

They talked so much, so long, so often, that, out of the very multitude of their words and rumours, grew at last some intelligence. About the third day I heard it said that he was to sail in a week; then – that he was bound for the West Indies. I looked at Madame Beck's face, and into her eyes, for disproof or confirmation of this report; I perused her all over for information, but no part of her disclosed more than what was unperturbed and commonplace.

"This secession was an immense loss to her," she alleged. "She did not know how she should fill up the vacancy. She was so used to her kinsman, he had become her right hand; what should she do without him? She had opposed the step, but M. Paul had convinced her it was his duty."

She said all this in public, in classe, at the dinner-table, speaking audibly to Zélie St. Pierre.

"Why was it his duty?" I could have asked her that. I had impulses to take hold of her suddenly, as she calmly passed me in classe, to stretch out my hand and grasp her fast, and say, "Stop. Let us hear the conclusion of the whole matter. *Why* is it his duty to go into banishment?" But Madame always addressed some other teacher, and never looked at me, never seemed conscious I could have a care in the question.

The week wore on. Nothing more was said about M. Emanuel coming to bid us goodbye; and none seemed anxious for his coming; none questioned whether or not he would come; none betrayed torment lest he should depart silent and unseen; incessantly did they talk, and never, in all their talk, touched on this vital point. As to Madame, she of course could see him, and say to him as much as she pleased. What should *she* care whether or not he appeared in the schoolroom?

The week consumed. We were told that he was going on such a day, that his destination was 'Basseterre in Guadaloupe'. the business which called him abroad related to a friend's interests, not his own: I thought as much.

'Basseterre in Guadaloupe.' I had little sleep about this time, but whenever I *did* slumber, it followed infallibly that I was quickly roused with a start, while the words 'Basseterre', 'Guadaloupe', seemed pronounced over my pillow, or ran athwart the darkness round and before me, in zigzag characters of red or violet light.

For what I felt there was no help, and how could I help feeling? M. Emanuel had been very kind to me of late days; he had been growing hourly better and kinder. It was now a month since we had settled the theological difference, and in all that time there had been no quarrel. Nor had our peace been the cold daughter of divorce; we had not lived aloof; he had come oftener, he had talked with me more than before; he had spent hours with me, with temper soothed, with eye content, with manner home-like and mild. Kind subjects of conversation had grown between us; he had inquired into my plans of life, and I had communicated them; the school project pleased him; he made me repeat it more than once, though he called it an Alnaschar dream. The jar was over; the mutual understanding was settling and fixing; feelings of union and hope made themselves profoundly felt in the heart; affection and deep esteem and dawning trust had each fastened its bond.

What quiet lessons I had about this time! No more taunts on my 'intellect', no more menaces of grating public shows! How sweetly, for the jealous gibe, and the more jealous, half-passionate eulogy, were substituted a mute, indulgent help, a fond guidance, and a tender forbearance which forgave but never praised. There were times when he would sit for many minutes and not speak at all; and when dusk or duty brought separation, he would leave with words like these, "*Il est doux, le repos! Il est précieux le calme bonheur!*"

One evening, not ten short days since, he joined me whilst walking in my alley. He took my hand. I looked up in his face. I thought he meant to arrest my attention.

"*Bonne petite amie!*" said he, softly; "*douce consolatrice!*" But through his touch, and with his words, a new feeling and a strange thought found a course. Could it be that he was becoming more than friend or brother? Did his look speak a kindness beyond fraternity or amity?

His eloquent look had more to say, his hand drew me forward, his interpreting lips stirred. No. Not now. Here into the twilight alley broke an interruption: it came dual and ominous: we faced two bodeful forms – a woman's and a priest's – Madame Beck and Père Silas.

The aspect of the latter I shall never forget. On the first impulse it expressed a Jean-Jacques sensibility, stirred by the signs of affection just surprised; then, immediately, darkened over it the jaundice of ecclesiastical jealousy. He spoke to *me* with unction. He looked on his pupil with sternness. As to Madame Beck, she, of course, saw nothing – nothing; though her kinsman retained in her presence the hand of the heretic foreigner, not suffering withdrawal, but clasping it close and fast.

Following these incidents, that sudden announcement of departure had struck me at first as incredible. Indeed, it was only frequent repetition, and the credence of the hundred and fifty minds round me, which forced on me its full acceptance. As to that week of suspense, with its blank, yet burning days, which brought from him no word of explanation – I remember, but I cannot describe its passage.

The last day broke. Now would he visit us. Now he would come and speak his farewell, or he would vanish mute, and be seen by us nevermore.

This alternative seemed to be present in the mind of not a living creature in that school. All rose at the usual hour; all breakfasted as usual; all, without reference to, or apparent thought of their late Professor, betook themselves with wonted phlegm to their ordinary duties.

So oblivious was the house, so tame, so trained its proceedings, so inexpectant its aspect – I scarce knew how to breathe in an atmosphere thus stagnant, thus smothering. Would no one lend me a voice? Had no one a wish, no one a word, no one a prayer to which I could say – Amen?

I had seen them unanimous in demand for the merest trifle – a treat, a holiday, a lesson's remission; they could not, they *would* not now band to besiege Madame Beck, and insist on a last interview with a Master who had certainly been loved, at least by some – loved as *they* could love – but, oh! What *is* the love of the multitude?

I knew where he lived: I knew where he was to be heard of, or communicated with; the distance was scarce a stone's-throw: had it been in the next room – unsummoned, I could make no use of my knowledge. To follow, to seek out, to remind, to recall – for these things I had no faculty.

M. Emanuel might have passed within reach of my arm: had he passed silent and unnoticing, silent and stirless should I have suffered him to go by.

Morning wasted. Afternoon came, and I thought all was over. My heart trembled in its place. My blood was troubled in its current. I was quite sick, and hardly knew how to keep at my post – or do my work. Yet the little world round me plodded on indifferent; all seemed jocund, free of care, or fear, or thought: the very pupils who, seven days since, had wept hysterically at a startling piece of news, appeared quite to have forgotten the news, its import, and their emotion.

A little before five o'clock, the hour of dismissal, Madame Beck sent for me to her chamber, to read over and translate some English letter she had received, and to write for her the answer. Before settling to this work, I observed that she softly closed the two doors of her chamber; she even shut and fastened the casement, though it was a hot day, and free circulation of air was usually regarded by her as indispensable. Why this precaution? A keen suspicion, an almost fierce distrust, suggested such question. Did she want to exclude sound? What sound?

I listened as I had never listened before; I listened like the evening and winter-wolf, snuffing the snow, scenting prey, and hearing far off the traveller's tramp. Yet I could both listen and write. About the middle of the letter I heard – what checked my pen – a tread in the vestibule. No door-bell had rung; Rosine – acting doubtless by orders – had anticipated such réveillée. Madame saw me halt. She coughed, made a bustle, spoke louder. The tread had passed on to the classes.

"Proceed," said Madame; but my hand was fettered, my ear enchained, my thoughts were carried off captive.

The classes formed another building; the hall parted them from the dwelling-house: despite distance and partition, I heard the sudden stir of numbers, a whole division rising at once.

"They are putting away work," said Madame.

It was indeed the hour to put away work, but why that sudden hush – that instant quell of the tumult?

"Wait, Madame – I will see what it is."

And I put down my pen and left her. Left her? No: she would not be left: powerless to detain me, she rose and followed, close as my shadow. I turned on the last step of the stair.

"Are you coming, too?" I asked.

"Yes," said she; meeting my glance with a peculiar aspect – a look, clouded, yet resolute.

We proceeded then, not together, but she walked in my steps.

He was come. Entering the first classe, I saw him. There, once more appeared the form most familiar. I doubt not they had tried to keep him away, but he was come.

The girls stood in a semicircle; he was passing round, giving his farewells, pressing each hand, touching with his lips each cheek. This last ceremony, foreign custom permitted at such a parting – so solemn, to last so long.

I felt it hard that Madame Beck should dog me thus; following and watching me close; my neck and shoulder shrunk in fever under her breath; I became terribly goaded.

He was approaching; the semicircle was almost travelled round; he came to the last pupil; he turned. But Madame was before me; she had stepped out suddenly; she seemed to magnify her proportions and amplify her drapery; she eclipsed me; I was hid. She knew my weakness and deficiency; she could calculate the degree of moral paralysis – the total default of self-assertion – with which, in a crisis, I could be struck. She hastened to her kinsman, she broke upon him volubly, she mastered his attention, she hurried him to the door – the glass-door opening on the garden. I think he looked round; could I but have caught his eye, courage, I think, would have rushed in to aid feeling, and there would have been a charge, and, perhaps, a rescue; but already the room was all confusion, the semicircle broken into groups, my figure was lost among thirty more conspicuous. Madame had her will; yes, she got him away, and he had not seen me; he thought me absent. Five o'clock struck, the loud dismissal-bell rang, the school separated, the room emptied.

There seems, to my memory, an entire darkness and distraction in some certain minutes I then passed alone – a grief inexpressible over a loss unendurable. *What* should I do; oh! *What* should I do; when all my life's hope was thus torn by the roots out of my riven, outraged heart?

What I *should* have done, I know not, when a little child – the least child in the school – broke with its simplicity and its unconsciousness into the raging yet silent centre of that inward conflict.

"Mademoiselle," lisped the treble voice, "I am to give you that. M. Paul said I was to seek you all over the house, from the grenier to the cellar, and when I found you, to give you that."

And the child delivered a note; the little dove dropped on my knee, its olive leaf plucked off. I found neither address nor name, only these words:

> *It was not my intention to take leave of you when I said goodbye to the rest, but I hoped to see you in classe. I was disappointed. The interview is deferred. Be ready for me. Ere I sail, I must see you at leisure, and speak with you at length. Be ready; my moments are numbered, and, just now, monopolized; besides, I have a private business on hand which I will not share with any, nor communicate – even to you.*
> *Paul.*

'Be ready?' Then it must be this evening: was he not to go on the morrow? Yes; of that point I was certain. I had seen the date of his vessel's departure advertised. Oh! *I* would be ready, but could that longed-for meeting really be achieved? The time was so short, the schemers seemed so watchful, so active, so hostile; the way of access appeared strait as a gully, deep as a chasm – Apollyon straddled across it, breathing flames. Could my Greatheart overcome? Could my guide reach me?

Who might tell? Yet I began to take some courage, some comfort; it seemed to me that I felt a pulse of his heart beating yet true to the whole throb of mine.

I waited my champion. Apollyon came trailing his Hell behind him. I think if Eternity held torment, its form would not be fiery rack, nor its nature despair. I think that on a certain day amongst those days which never dawned, and will not set, an angel entered Hades – stood, shone, smiled, delivered a prophecy of conditional pardon, kindled a doubtful hope of bliss to come, not now, but at a day and hour unlooked for, revealed in his own glory and grandeur the height and compass of his promise: spoke thus – then towering, became a star, and vanished into his own Heaven. His legacy was suspense – a worse boon than despair.

All that evening I waited, trusting in the dove-sent olive-leaf, yet in the midst of my trust, terribly fearing. My fear pressed heavy. Cold and peculiar, I knew it for the partner of a rarely-belied presentiment. The first hours seemed long and slow; in spirit I clung to the flying skirts of the last. They passed like drift cloud – like the wrack scudding before a storm.

They passed. All the long, hot summer day burned away like a Yule-log; the crimson of its close perished; I was left bent among the cool blue shades, over the pale and ashen gleams of its night.

Prayers were over; it was bed-time; my co-inmates were all retired. I still remained in the gloomy first classe, forgetting, or at least disregarding, rules I had never forgotten or disregarded before.

How long I paced that classe I cannot tell; I must have been afoot many hours; mechanically had I moved aside benches and desks, and had made for myself a path down its length. There I walked, and there, when certain that the whole household were abed, and quite out of hearing – there, I at last wept. Reliant on Night, confiding in Solitude, I kept my tears sealed, my sobs chained, no longer; they heaved my heart; they tore their way. In this house, what grief could be sacred?

Soon after eleven o'clock – a very late hour in the Rue Fossette – the door unclosed, quietly but not stealthily; a lamp's flame invaded the moonlight; Madame Beck entered, with the same composed air, as if coming on an ordinary occasion, at an ordinary season. Instead of at once addressing me, she went to her desk, took her keys, and seemed to seek something: she loitered over this feigned search long, too long. She was calm, too calm; my mood scarce endured the pretence; driven beyond common range, two hours since I had left behind me wonted respects and fears. Led by a touch, and ruled by a word, under usual circumstances, no yoke could now be borne – no curb obeyed.

"It is more than time for retirement," said Madame; "the rule of the house has already been transgressed too long."

Madame met no answer: I did not check my walk; when she came in my way, I put her out of it.

"Let me persuade you to calm, Meess; let me lead you to your chamber," said she, trying to speak softly.

"No!" I said; "neither you nor another shall persuade or lead me."

"Your bed shall be warmed. Goton is sitting up still. She shall make you comfortable: she shall give you a sedative."

"Madame," I broke out, "you are a sensualist. Under all your serenity, your peace, and your decorum, you are an undenied sensualist. Make your own bed warm and soft; take sedatives and meats, and drinks spiced and sweet, as much as you will. If you have any sorrow or disappointment – and, perhaps, you have – nay, I *know* you have – seek your own palliatives, in your own chosen resources. Leave me, however. *Leave me*, I say!"

"I must send another to watch you, Meess: I must send Goton."

"I forbid it. Let me alone. Keep your hand off me, and my life, and my troubles. Oh, Madame! In *your* hand there is both chill and poison. You envenom and you paralyze."

"What have I done, Meess? You must not marry Paul. He cannot marry."

"Dog in the manger!" I said: for I knew she secretly wanted him, and had always wanted him. She called him 'insupportable': she railed at him for a 'dévot': she did not love, but she wanted to marry, that she might bind him to her interest. Deep into some of Madame's secrets I had entered – I know not how: by an intuition or an inspiration which came to me – I know not whence. In the course of living with her too, I had slowly learned, that, unless with an inferior, she must ever be a rival. She was *my* rival, heart and soul, though secretly, under the smoothest bearing, and utterly unknown to all save her and myself.

Two minutes I stood over Madame, feeling that the whole woman was in my power, because in some moods, such as the present – in some stimulated states of perception, like that of this instant – her habitual disguise, her mask and her domino, were to me a mere network reticulated with holes; and I saw underneath a being heartless, self-indulgent, and ignoble. She quietly retreated from me: meek and self-possessed, though very uneasy, she said, "If I would not be persuaded to take rest, she must reluctantly leave me." Which she did incontinent, perhaps even more glad to get away, than I was to see her vanish.

This was the sole flash-eliciting, truth-extorting, rencontre which ever occurred between me and Madame Beck: this short night-scene was never repeated. It did not one whit change her manner to me. I do not know that she revenged it. I do not know that she hated me the worse for my fell candour. I think she bucklered herself with the secret philosophy of her strong mind, and resolved to forget what it irked her to remember. I know that to the end of our mutual lives there occurred no repetition of, no allusion to, that fiery passage.

That night passed: all nights – even the starless night before dissolution – must wear away. About six o'clock, the hour which called up the household, I went out to the court, and washed my face in its cold, fresh well-water. Entering by the carré, a piece of mirror-glass, set in an oaken cabinet, repeated my image. It said I was changed: my cheeks and lips were sodden white, my eyes were glassy, and my eyelids swollen and purple.

On rejoining my companions, I knew they all looked at me – my heart seemed discovered to them: I believed myself self-betrayed. Hideously certain did it seem that the very youngest of the school must guess why and for whom I despaired.

'Isabelle', the child whom I had once nursed in sickness, approached me. Would she, too, mock me!

"*Que vous êtes pâle! Vous êtes donc bien malade, Mademoiselle!*" said she, putting her finger in her mouth, and staring with a wistful stupidity which at the moment seemed to me more beautiful than the keenest intelligence.

Isabelle did not long stand alone in the recommendation of ignorance: before the day was over, I gathered cause of gratitude towards the whole blind household. The multitude have something else to do than to read hearts and interpret dark sayings. Who wills, may keep his own counsel – be his own secret's sovereign. In the course of that day, proof met me on proof, not only that the cause of my present sorrow was unguessed, but that my whole inner life for the last six months was still mine only. It was not known – it had not been noted – that I held in peculiar value one life among all lives. Gossip had passed me by; curiosity had looked me over; both subtle influences, hovering always round, had never become centred upon me. A given organization may live in a full fever-hospital, and escape typhus. M. Emanuel had come and gone: I had been taught and sought; in season and out of season he had called me, and I had obeyed him: 'M. Paul wants Miss Lucy' – 'Miss Lucy is with M. Paul' – such had been the perpetual bulletin; and nobody commented, far less condemned. Nobody hinted, nobody jested. Madame Beck read the riddle: none else resolved it. What I now suffered was called illness – a headache: I accepted the baptism.

But what bodily illness was ever like this pain? This certainty that he was gone without a farewell – this cruel conviction that fate and pursuing furies – a woman's envy and a priest's bigotry – would suffer me to see him no more? What wonder that the second evening found me like the first – untamed, tortured, again pacing a solitary room in an unalterable passion of silent desolation?

Madame Beck did not herself summon me to bed that night – she did not come near me: she sent Ginevra Fanshawe – a more efficient agent for the purpose she could not have employed. Ginevra's first words – "Is your headache very bad tonight?" (for Ginevra, like the rest, thought I had a headache – an intolerable headache which made me frightfully white in the face, and insanely restless in the foot) – her first words, I say, inspired the impulse to flee anywhere, so that it were only out of reach. And soon, what followed – plaints about her own headaches – completed the business.

I went upstairs. Presently I was in my bed – my miserable bed – haunted with quick scorpions. I had not been laid down five minutes, when another emissary arrived: Goton came, bringing me something to drink. I was consumed with thirst – I drank eagerly; the beverage was sweet, but I tasted a drug.

"Madame says it will make you sleep, *chou-chou*," said Goton, as she received back the emptied cup.

Ah! The sedative had been administered. In fact, they had given me a strong opiate. I was to be held quiet for one night.

The household came to bed, the night-light was lit, the dormitory hushed. Sleep soon reigned: over those pillows, sleep won an easy supremacy: contented sovereign over heads and hearts which did not ache – he passed by the unquiet.

The drug wrought. I know not whether Madame had overcharged or under-charged the dose; its result was not that she intended. Instead of stupor, came excitement. I became alive to new thought – to reverie peculiar in colouring. A gathering call ran among the faculties, their bugles sang, their trumpets rang an untimely summons. Imagination was roused from her rest, and she came forth impetuous and venturous. With scorn she looked on Matter, her mate – "Rise!" she said. "Sluggard! This night I will have *my* will; nor shalt thou prevail."

"Look forth and view the night!" was her cry; and when I lifted the heavy blind from the casement close at hand – with her own royal gesture, she showed me a moon supreme, in an element deep and splendid.

To my gasping senses she made the glimmering gloom, the narrow limits, the oppressive heat of the dormitory, intolerable. She lured me to leave this den and follow her forth into dew, coolness, and glory.

She brought upon me a strange vision of Villette at midnight. Especially she showed the park, the summer-park, with its long alleys all silent, lone and safe; among these lay a huge stone basin – that basin I knew, and beside which I had often stood – deep-set in the tree-shadows, brimming with cool water, clear, with a green, leafy, rushy bed. What of all this? The park-gates were shut up, locked, sentinelled: the place could not be entered.

Could it not? A point worth considering; and while revolving it, I mechanically dressed. Utterly incapable of sleeping or lying still – excited from head to foot – what could I do better than dress?

The gates were locked, soldiers set before them: was there, then, no admission to the park?

The other day, in walking past, I had seen, without then attending to the circumstance, a gap in the paling – one stake broken down: I now saw this gap again in recollection – saw it very plainly – the narrow, irregular aperture visible between the stems of the lindens, planted orderly as a colonnade. A man could not have made his way through that aperture, nor could a stout woman, perhaps not Madame Beck; but I thought I might: I fancied I should like to try, and once within, at this hour the whole park would be mine – the moonlight, midnight park!

How soundly the dormitory slept! What deep slumbers! What quiet breathing! How very still the whole large house! What was the time? I felt restless to know. There stood a clock in the classe below: what hindered me from venturing down to consult it? By such a moon, its large white face and jet black figures must be vividly distinct.

As for hindrance to this step, there offered not so much as a creaking hinge or a clicking latch. On these hot July nights, close air could not be tolerated, and the chamber-door stood wide open. Will the dormitory-planks sustain my tread untraitorous? Yes. I know wherever a board is loose, and will avoid it. The oak staircase creaks somewhat as I descend, but not much: I am in the carré.

The great classe-doors are close shut: they are bolted. On the other hand, the entrance to the corridor stands open. The classes seem to my thought, great dreary jails, buried far back beyond thoroughfares, and for me, filled with spectral and intolerable Memories, laid miserable amongst their straw and their manacles. The corridor offers a cheerful vista, leading to the high vestibule which opens direct upon the street.

Hush! – The clock strikes. Ghostly deep as is the stillness of this convent, it is only eleven. While my ear follows to silence the hum of the last stroke, I catch faintly from the built-out capital, a sound like bells or like a band – a sound where sweetness, where victory, where mourning blend. Oh, to approach this music nearer, to listen to it alone by the rushy basin! Let me go – oh, let me go! What hinders, what does not aid freedom?

There, in the corridor, hangs my garden-costume, my large hat, my shawl. There is no lock on the huge, heavy, porte-cochère; there is no key to seek: it fastens with a sort of spring-bolt, not to be opened from the outside, but which, from within, may be noiselessly withdrawn. Can I manage it? It yields to my hand, yields with propitious facility. I wonder as that portal seems almost spontaneously to unclose – I wonder as I cross the threshold and step on the paved street, wonder at the strange ease with which this prison has been forced. It seems as if I had been pioneered invisibly, as if some dissolving force had gone before me: for myself, I have scarce made an effort.

Quiet Rue Fossette! I find on this pavement that wanderer-wooing summer night of which I mused; I see its moon over me; I feel its dew in the air. But here I cannot stay; I am still too near old haunts: so close under the dungeon, I can hear the prisoners moan. This solemn peace is not what I seek, it is not what I can bear: to me the face of that sky bears the aspect of a world's death. The park also will be calm – I know, a mortal serenity prevails everywhere – yet let me seek the park.

I took a route well known, and went up towards the palatial and royal Haute-Ville; thence the music I had heard certainly floated; it was hushed now, but it might re-waken. I went on: neither band nor bell music came to meet me; another sound replaced it, a sound like a strong tide, a great flow, deepening as I proceeded. Light broke, movement gathered, chimes pealed – to what was I coming? Entering on the level of a Grande Place, I found myself, with the suddenness of magic, plunged amidst a gay, living, joyous crowd.

Villette is one blaze, one broad illumination; the whole world seems abroad; moonlight and heaven are banished: the town, by her own flambeaux, beholds her own splendour – gay dresses, grand equipages, fine horses and gallant riders throng the bright streets. I see even scores of masks. It is a strange scene, stranger than dreams. But where is the park? – I ought to be near it. In the midst of this glare the park must be shadowy and calm – *there*, at least, are neither torches, lamps, nor crowd?

I was asking this question when an open carriage passed me filled with known faces. Through the deep throng it could pass but slowly; the spirited horses fretted in their curbed ardour. I saw the occupants of that carriage well: me they could not see, or, at least, not know, folded close in my large shawl, screened with my straw hat (in that motley crowd no dress was noticeably strange). I saw the Count de Bassompierre; I saw my godmother, handsomely apparelled, comely and cheerful; I saw, too, Paulina Mary, compassed with the triple halo of her beauty, her youth, and her happiness. In looking on her countenance of joy, and eyes of festal light, one scarce remembered to note the gala elegance of what she wore; I know only that the drapery floating about her was all white and light and bridal; seated opposite to her I saw Graham Bretton; it was in looking up at him her aspect had caught its lustre – the light repeated in *her* eyes beamed first out of his.

It gave me strange pleasure to follow these friends viewlessly, and I *did* follow them, as I thought, to the park. I watched them alight (carriages were inadmissible) amidst new and unanticipated splendours. Lo! The iron gateway, between the stone columns, was spanned by a flaming arch built of massed stars; and, following them cautiously beneath that arch, where were they, and where was I?

In a land of enchantment, a garden most gorgeous, a plain sprinkled with coloured meteors, a forest with sparks of purple and ruby and golden fire gemming the foliage; a region, not of trees and shadow, but of strangest architectural wealth – of altar and of temple, of pyramid, obelisk, and sphinx: incredible to say, the wonders and the symbols of Egypt teemed throughout the park of Villette.

No matter that in five minutes the secret was mine – the key of the mystery picked up, and its illusion unveiled – no matter that I quickly recognised the material of these solemn fragments – the timber, the paint, and the pasteboard – these inevitable discoveries failed to quite destroy the charm, or undermine the marvel of that night. No matter that I now seized the explanation of the whole great fête – a fête of which the conventual Rue Fossette had not tasted, though it had opened at dawn that morning, and was still in full vigour near midnight.

In past days there had been, said history, an awful crisis in the fate of Labassecour, involving I know not what peril to the rights and liberties of her gallant citizens. Rumours of wars there had been, if not wars themselves; a kind of struggling in the streets – a bustle – a running to and fro, some rearing of barricades, some burgher-rioting, some calling out of troops, much interchange of brickbats, and even a little of shot. Tradition held that patriots had fallen: in the old Basse-Ville was shown an enclosure, solemnly built in and set apart, holding, it was said, the sacred bones of martyrs. Be this as it may, a certain day in the year was still kept as a festival in honour of the said patriots and martyrs of somewhat apocryphal memory – the morning being given to a solemn Te Deum in St. Jean Baptiste, the evening devoted to spectacles, decorations, and illuminations, such as these I now saw.

While looking up at the image of a white ibis, fixed on a column – while fathoming the deep, torch-lit perspective of an avenue, at the close of which was couched a sphinx – I lost sight of the party which, from the middle of the great square, I had followed – or, rather, they vanished like a group of apparitions. On this whole scene was impressed a dream-like character: every shape was wavering, every movement floating, every voice echo-like – half-mocking, half-uncertain. Paulina and her friends being gone, I scarce could avouch that I had really seen them; nor did I miss them as guides through the chaos, far less regret them as protectors amidst the night.

That festal night would have been safe for a very child. Half the peasantry had come in from the outlying environs of Villette, and the decent burghers were all abroad and around, dressed in their best. My straw-hat passed amidst cap and jacket, short petticoat, and long calico mantle, without, perhaps, attracting a glance; I only took the precaution to bind down the broad leaf gipsy-wise, with a supplementary ribbon – and then I felt safe as if masked.

Safe I passed down the avenues – safe I mixed with the crowd where it was deepest. To be still was not in my power, nor quietly to observe. I took a revel of the scene; I drank the elastic night-air – the swell of sound, the dubious light, now flashing, now fading. As to Happiness or Hope, they and I had shaken hands, but just now – I scorned Despair.

My vague aim, as I went, was to find the stone-basin, with its clear depth and green lining: of that coolness and verdure I thought, with the passionate thirst of unconscious fever. Amidst the glare, and hurry, and throng, and noise, I still secretly and chiefly longed to come on that circular mirror of crystal, and surprise the moon glassing therein her pearly front.

I knew my route, yet it seemed as if I was hindered from pursuing it direct: now a sight, and now a sound, called me aside, luring me down this alley and down that. Already I saw the thick-planted trees which framed this tremulous and rippled glass, when, choiring out of a glade to the right, broke such a sound as I thought might be heard if Heaven were to open – such a sound, perhaps, as *was* heard above the plain of Bethlehem, on the night of glad tidings.

The song, the sweet music, rose afar, but rushing swiftly on fast-strengthening pinions – there swept through these shades so full a storm of harmonies that, had no tree been near against which to lean, I think I must have dropped. Voices were there, it seemed to me, unnumbered; instruments varied and countless – bugle, horn, and trumpet I knew. The effect was as a sea breaking into song with all its waves.

The swaying tide swept this way, and then it fell back, and I followed its retreat. It led me towards a Byzantine building – a sort of kiosk near the park's centre. Round about stood crowded thousands, gathered to a grand concert in the open air. What I had heard was, I think, a wild Jäger chorus; the night, the space, the scene, and my own mood, had but enhanced the sounds and their impression.

Here were assembled ladies, looking by this light most beautiful: some of their dresses were gauzy, and some had the sheen of satin, the flowers and the blond trembled, and the veils waved about their decorated bonnets, as that host-like chorus, with its greatly-gathering sound, sundered the air above them. Most of these ladies occupied the little light park-chairs, and behind and beside them stood guardian gentlemen. The outer ranks of the crowd were made up of citizens, plebeians and police.

In this outer rank I took my place. I rather liked to find myself the silent, unknown, consequently unaccosted neighbour of the short petticoat and the sabot; and only the distant gazer at the silk robe, the velvet mantle, and the plumed chapeau. Amidst so much life and joy, too, it suited me to be alone – quite alone. Having neither wish nor power to force my way through a mass so close-packed, my station was on the farthest confines, where, indeed, I might hear, but could see little.

"Mademoiselle is not well placed," said a voice at my elbow. Who dared accost *me*, a being in a mood so little social? I turned, rather to repel than to reply. I saw a man – a burgher – an entire stranger, as I deemed him for one moment, but the next, recognised in him a certain tradesman – a bookseller, whose shop furnished the Rue Fossette with its books and stationery; a man notorious in our pensionnat for the excessive brittleness of his temper, and frequent snappishness of his manner, even to us, his principal customers: but whom, for my solitary self, I had ever been disposed to like, and had always found civil, sometimes kind; once, in aiding me about some troublesome little exchange of foreign money, he had done me a service. He was an intelligent man; under his asperity, he was a good-hearted man; the thought had sometimes crossed me, that a part of his nature bore affinity to a part of M. Emanuel's (whom he knew well, and whom I had often seen sitting on Miret's counter, turning over the current month's publications); and it was in this affinity I read the explanation of that conciliatory feeling with which I instinctively regarded him.

Strange to say, this man knew me under my straw-hat and closely-folded shawl; and, though I deprecated the effort, he insisted on making a way for me through the crowd, and finding me a better situation. He carried his disinterested civility further; and, from some quarter, procured me a chair. Once and again, I have found that the most cross-grained are by no means the worst of mankind; nor the humblest in station, the least polished in feeling. This man, in his courtesy, seemed to find nothing strange in my being here alone; only a reason for extending to me, as far as he could, a retiring, yet efficient attention. Having secured me a place and a seat, he withdrew without asking a question, without obtruding a remark, without adding a superfluous word. No wonder that Professor Emanuel liked to take his cigar and his lounge, and to read his feuilleton in M. Miret's shop – the two must have suited.

I had not been seated five minutes, ere I became aware that chance and my worthy burgher friend had brought me once more within view of a familiar and domestic group. Right before me sat the Brettons and de Bassompierres. Within reach of my hand – had I chosen to extend it – sat a figure like a fairy-queen, whose array, lilies and their leaves seemed to have suggested; whatever was not spotless white, being forest-green. My godmother, too, sat so near, that, had I leaned forward, my breath might have stirred the ribbon of her bonnet. They were too near; having been just recognised by a comparative stranger, I felt uneasy at this close vicinage of intimate acquaintance.

It made me quite start when Mrs. Bretton, turning to Mr. Home, and speaking out of a kind impulse of memory, said – "I wonder what my steady little Lucy would say to all this if she were here? I wish we had brought her, she would have enjoyed it much."

"So she would, so she would, in her grave sensible fashion; it is a pity but we had asked her," rejoined the kind gentleman; and added, "I like to see her so quietly pleased; so little moved, yet so content."

Dear were they both to me, dear are they to this day in their remembered benevolence. Little knew they the rack of pain which had driven Lucy almost into fever, and brought her out, guideless and reckless, urged and drugged to the brink of frenzy. I had half a mind to bend over the elders' shoulders, and answer their goodness with the thanks of my eyes. M. de Bassompierre did not well know *me*, but I knew *him*, and honoured and admired his nature, with all its plain sincerity, its warm affection, and unconscious enthusiasm. Possibly I might have spoken, but just then Graham turned; he turned with one of his stately firm movements, so different from those, of a sharp-tempered under-sized man: there was behind him a throng, a hundred ranks deep; there were thousands to meet his eye and divide its scrutiny – why then did he concentrate all on me – oppressing me with the whole force of that full, blue, steadfast orb? Why, if he *would* look, did not one glance satisfy him? Why did he turn on his chair, rest his elbow on its back, and study me leisurely? He could not see my face, I held it down; surely, he *could* not recognise me: I stooped, I turned, I *would* not be known. He rose, by some means he contrived to approach, in two minutes he would have had my secret: my identity would have been grasped between his, never tyrannous, but always powerful hands. There was but one way to evade or to check him. I implied, by a sort of supplicatory gesture, that it was my prayer to be let alone; after that, had he persisted, he would perhaps have seen the spectacle of Lucy incensed: not all that was grand, or good, or kind in him (and Lucy felt the full amount) should have kept her quite tame, or absolutely inoffensive and shadowlike. He looked, but he desisted. He shook his handsome head, but he was mute. He resumed his seat, nor did he again turn or disturb me by a glance, except indeed for one single instant, when a look, rather solicitous than curious, stole my way – speaking what somehow stilled my heart like 'the south-wind quieting the earth'. Graham's thoughts of me were not entirely those of a frozen indifference, after all. I believe in that goodly mansion, his heart, he kept one little place under the sky-lights where Lucy might have entertainment, if she chose to call. It was not so handsome as the chambers where he lodged his male friends; it was not like the hall where he accommodated his philanthropy, or the library where he treasured his science, still less did it resemble the pavilion where his marriage feast was splendidly spread; yet, gradually, by long and equal kindness, he proved to me that he kept one little closet, over the door of which was written 'Lucy's Room'. I kept a place for him, too – a place of which I never took the measure, either by rule or compass: I think it was like the tent of Peri-Banou. All my life long I carried it folded in the hollow of my hand yet, released from that hold and constriction, I know not but its innate capacity for expanse might have magnified it into a tabernacle for a host.

Forbearing as he was tonight, I could not stay in this proximity; this dangerous place and seat must be given up: I watched my opportunity, rose, and stole away. He might think, he might even believe that Lucy was contained within that shawl, and sheltered under that hat; he never could be certain, for he did not see my face.

Surely the spirit of restlessness was by this time appeased? Had I not had enough of adventure? Did I not begin to flag, quail, and wish for safety under a roof? Not so. I still loathed my bed in the school dormitory more than words can express: I clung to whatever could distract thought. Somehow I felt, too, that the night's drama was but begun, that the prologue was scarce spoken: throughout this woody and turfy theatre reigned a shadow of mystery; actors and incidents unlooked-for, waited behind the scenes: I thought so foreboding told me as much.

Straying at random, obeying the push of every chance elbow, I was brought to a quarter where trees planted in clusters, or towering singly, broke up somewhat the dense packing of the crowd, and gave it a more scattered character. These confines were far from the music, and somewhat aloof even from the lamps, but there was sound enough to soothe, and with that full, high moon, lamps were scarce needed. Here had chiefly settled family-groups, burgher-parents; some of them, late as was the hour, actually surrounded by their children, with whom it had not been thought advisable to venture into the closer throng.

Three fine tall trees growing close, almost twined stem within stem, lifted a thick canopy of shade above a green knoll, crowned with a seat – a seat which might have held several, yet it seemed abandoned to one, the remaining members of the fortunate party in possession of this site standing dutifully round; yet, amongst this reverend circle was a lady, holding by the hand a little girl.

When I caught sight of this little girl, she was twisting herself round on her heel, swinging from her conductress's hand, flinging herself from side to side with wanton and fantastic gyrations. These perverse movements arrested my attention, they struck me as of a character fearfully familiar. On close inspection, no less so appeared the child's equipment; the lilac silk pelisse, the small swansdown boa, the white bonnet – the whole holiday toilette, in short, was the gala garb of a cherub but too well known, of that tadpole, Désirée Beck – and Désirée Beck it was – she, or an imp in her likeness.

I might have taken this discovery as a thunder-clap, but such hyperbole would have been premature; discovery was destined to rise more than one degree, ere it reached its climax.

On whose hand could the amiable Désirée swing thus selfishly, whose glove could she tear thus recklessly, whose arm thus strain with impunity, or on the borders of whose dress thus turn and trample insolently, if not the hand, glove, arm, and robe of her lady-mother? And there, in an Indian shawl and a pale-green crape bonnet – there, fresh, portly, blithe, and pleasant – there stood Madame Beck.

Curious! I had certainly deemed Madame in her bed, and Désirée in her crib, at this blessed minute, sleeping, both of them, the sleep of the just, within the sacred walls, amidst the profound seclusion of the Rue Fossette. Most certainly also they did not picture 'Meess Lucie' otherwise engaged; and here we all three were taking our 'ébats' in the fête-blazing park at midnight!

The fact was, Madame was only acting according to her quite justifiable wont. I remembered now I had heard it said among the teachers – though without at the time particularly noticing the gossip – that often, when we thought Madame in her chamber, sleeping, she was gone, full-dressed, to take her pleasure at operas, or plays, or balls. Madame had no sort of taste for a monastic life, and took care – largely, though discreetly – to season her existence with a relish of the world.

Half a dozen gentlemen of her friends stood about her. Amongst these, I was not slow to recognise two or three. There was her brother, M. Victor Kint; there was another person, moustached and with long hair – a calm, taciturn man, but whose traits bore a stamp and a semblance I could not mark unmoved. Amidst reserve and phlegm, amidst contrasts of character and of countenance, something there still was which recalled a face – mobile, fervent, feeling – a face changeable, now clouded, and now alight – a face from my world taken away, for my eyes lost, but where my best spring-hours of life had alternated in shadow and in glow; that face, where I had often seen movements so near the signs of genius – that why there did not shine fully out the undoubted fire, the thing, the spirit, and the secret itself – I could never tell. Yes – this Josef Emanuel – this man of peace – reminded me of his ardent brother.

Besides Messieurs Victor and Josef, I knew another of this party. This third person stood behind and in the shade, his attitude too was stooping, yet his dress and bald white head made him the most conspicuous figure of the group. He was an ecclesiastic: he was Père Silas. Do not fancy, reader, that there was any inconsistency in the priest's presence at this fête. This was not considered a show of Vanity Fair, but a commemoration of patriotic sacrifice. The Church patronised it, even with ostentation. There were troops of priests in the park that night.

Père Silas stooped over the seat with its single occupant, the rustic bench and that which sat upon it: a strange mass it was – bearing no shape, yet magnificent. You saw, indeed, the outline of a face, and features, but these were so cadaverous and so strangely placed, you could almost have fancied a head severed from its trunk, and flung at random on a pile of rich merchandise. The distant lamp-rays glanced on clear pendants, on broad rings; neither the chasteness of moonlight, nor the distance of the torches, could quite subdue the gorgeous dyes of the drapery. Hail, Madame Walravens! I think you looked more witch-like than ever. And presently the good lady proved that she was indeed no corpse or ghost, but a harsh and hardy old woman; for, upon some aggravation in the clamorous petition of Désirée Beck to her mother, to go to the kiosk and take sweetmeats, the hunchback suddenly fetched her a resounding rap with her gold-knobbed cane.

There, then, were Madame Walravens, Madame Beck, Père Silas – the whole conjuration, the secret junta. The sight of them thus assembled did me good. I cannot say that I felt weak before them, or abashed, or dismayed. They outnumbered me, and I was worsted and under their feet; but, as yet, I was not dead.

Chapter Thirty-Nine
Old and New Acquaintance

FASCINATED as by a basilisk with three heads, I could not leave this clique; the ground near them seemed to hold my feet. The canopy of entwined trees held out shadow, the night whispered a pledge of protection, and an officious lamp flashed just one beam to show me an obscure, safe seat, and then vanished. Let me now briefly tell the reader all that, during the past dark fortnight, I have been silently gathering from Rumour, respecting the origin and the object of M. Emanuel's departure. The tale is short, and not new: its alpha is Mammon, and its omega Interest.

If Madame Walravens was hideous as a Hindoo idol, she seemed also to possess, in the estimation of these her votaries, an idol's consequence. The fact was, she had been rich – very rich; and though, for the present, without the command of money, she was likely one day to be rich again. At Basseterre, in Guadaloupe, she possessed a large estate, received in dowry on her marriage sixty years ago, sequestered since her husband's failure; but now, it was supposed, cleared of claim, and, if duly looked after by a competent agent of integrity, considered capable of being made, in a few years, largely productive.

Père Silas took an interest in this prospective improvement for the sake of religion and the church, whereof Magliore Walravens was a devout daughter. Madame Beck, distantly related to the hunchback and knowing her to be without family of her own, had long brooded over contingencies with a mother's calculating forethought, and, harshly treated as she was by Madame Walravens, never ceased to court her for interest's sake. Madame Beck and the priest were thus, for money reasons, equally and sincerely interested in the nursing of the West Indian estate.

But the distance was great, and the climate hazardous. The competent and upright agent wanted, must be a devoted man. Just such a man had Madame Walravens retained for twenty years in her service, blighting his life, and then living on him, like an old fungus; such a man had Père Silas trained, taught, and bound to him by the ties of gratitude, habit, and belief. Such a man Madame Beck knew, and could in some measure influence. "My pupil," said Père Silas, "if he remains in Europe, runs risk of apostasy, for he has become entangled with a heretic." Madame Beck made also her private comment, and preferred in her own breast her secret reason for desiring expatriation. The thing she could not obtain, she desired not another to win: rather would she destroy it. As to Madame Walravens, she wanted her money and her land, and knew Paul, if he liked, could make the best and faithfullest steward: so the three self-seekers banded and beset the one unselfish. They reasoned, they appealed, they implored; on his mercy they cast themselves, into his hands they confidingly thrust their interests. They asked but two or three years of devotion – after that, he should live for himself: one of the number, perhaps, wished that in the meantime he might die.

No living being ever humbly laid his advantage at M. Emanuel's feet, or confidingly put it into his hands, that he spurned the trust or repulsed the repository. What might be his private pain or inward reluctance to leave Europe – what his calculations for his own future – none asked, or knew, or reported. All this was a blank to me. His conferences with his confessor I might guess; the part duty and religion were made to play in the persuasions used, I might conjecture. He was gone, and had made no sign. There my knowledge closed.

* * *

With my head bent, and my forehead resting on my hands, I sat amidst grouped tree-stems and branching brushwood. Whatever talk passed amongst my neighbours, I might hear, if I would; I was near enough; but for some time, there was scarce motive to attend. They gossiped about the dresses, the music, the illuminations, the fine night. I listened to hear them say, "It is calm weather for *his* voyage; the *Antigua*" (his ship) "will sail prosperously." No such remark fell; neither the *Antigua*, nor her course, nor her passenger were named.

Perhaps the light chat scarcely interested old Madame Walravens more than it did me; she appeared restless, turning her head now to this side, now that, looking through the trees, and among the crowd, as if expectant of an arrival and impatient of delay. "*Où sont-ils? Pourquoi ne viennent-ils?*" I heard her mutter more than once; and at last, as if determined to have an answer to her question – which hitherto none seemed to mind, she spoke aloud this phrase – a phrase brief enough, simple enough, but it sent a shock through me – "*Messieurs et mesdames,*" said she, "*où donc est Justine Marie?*"

"Justine Marie!" What was this? Justine Marie – the dead nun – where was she? Why, in her grave, Madame Walravens – what can you want with her? You shall go to her, but she shall not come to you.

Thus *I* should have answered, had the response lain with me, but nobody seemed to be of my mind; nobody seemed surprised, startled, or at a loss. The quietest commonplace answer met the strange, the dead-disturbing, the Witch-of-Endor query of the hunchback.

"Justine Marie," said one, "is coming; she is in the kiosk; she will be here presently."

Out of this question and reply sprang a change in the chat – chat it still remained, easy, desultory, familiar gossip. Hint, allusion, comment, went round the circle, but all so broken, so dependent on references to persons not named, or circumstances not defined, that listen as intently as I would – and I *did* listen *now* with a fated interest – I could make out no more than that some scheme was on foot, in which this ghostly Justine Marie – dead or alive – was concerned. This family-junta seemed grasping at her somehow, for some reason; there seemed question of a marriage, of a fortune – for whom I could not quite make out – perhaps for Victor Kint, perhaps for Josef Emanuel – both were bachelors. Once I thought the hints and jests rained upon a young fair-haired foreigner of the party, whom they called Heinrich Mühler. Amidst all the badinage, Madame Walravens still obtruded from time to time, hoarse, cross-grained speeches; her impatience being diverted only by an implacable surveillance of Désirée, who could not stir but the old woman menaced her with her staff.

"*La voilà!*" suddenly cried one of the gentlemen, "*Voilà Justine Marie qui arrive!*"

This moment was for me peculiar. I called up to memory the pictured nun on the panel; present to my mind was the sad love-story; I saw in thought the vision of the garret, the apparition of the alley, the strange birth of the berceau; I underwent a presentiment of discovery, a strong conviction of coming disclosure. Ah! When imagination once runs riot where do we stop? What winter tree so bare and branchless – what way-side, hedge-munching animal so humble, that Fancy, a passing cloud, and a struggling moonbeam, will not clothe it in spirituality, and make of it a phantom?

With solemn force pressed on my heart, the expectation of mystery breaking up: hitherto I had seen this spectre only through a glass darkly; now was I to behold it face to face. I leaned forward; I looked.

"She comes!" cried Josef Emanuel.

The circle opened as if opening to admit a new and welcome member. At this instant a torch chanced to be carried past; its blaze aided the pale moon in doing justice to the crisis, in lighting to perfection the dénouement pressing on. Surely those near me must have felt some little of the anxiety I felt, in degree so unmeted. Of that group the coolest must have "held his breath for a time!" As for me, my life stood still.

It is over. The moment and the nun are come. The crisis and the revelation are passed by.

The flambeau glares still within a yard, held up in a park-keeper's hand; its long eager tongue of flame almost licks the figure of the Expected – there – where she stands full in my sight. What is she like? What does she wear? How does she look? Who is she?

There are many masks in the park tonight, and as the hour wears late, so strange a feeling of revelry and mystery begins to spread abroad, that scarce would you discredit me, reader, were I to say that she is like the nun of the attic, that she wears black skirts and white head-clothes, that she looks the resurrection of the flesh, and that she is a risen ghost.

All falsities – all figments! We will not deal in this gear. Let us be honest, and cut, as heretofore, from the homely web of truth.

Homely, though, is an ill-chosen word. What I see is not precisely homely. A girl of Villette stands there – a girl fresh from her pensionnat. She is very comely, with the beauty indigenous to this country. She looks well-nourished, fair, and fat of flesh. Her cheeks are round, her eyes good; her hair is abundant. She is handsomely dressed. She is not alone; her escort consists of three persons – two being elderly; these she addresses as 'Mon Oncle' and 'Ma Tante'. She laughs, she chats; good-humoured, buxom, and blooming, she looks, at all points, the bourgeoise belle.

"So much for Justine Marie"; so much for ghosts and mystery: not that this last was solved – this girl certainly is not my nun: what I saw in the garret and garden must have been taller by a span.

We have looked at the city belle; we have cursorily glanced at the respectable old uncle and aunt. Have we a stray glance to give to the third member of this company? Can we spare him a moment's notice? We ought to distinguish him so far, reader; he has claims on us; we do not now meet him for the first time. I clasped my hands very hard, and I drew my breath very deep: I held in the cry, I devoured the ejaculation, I forbade the start, I spoke and I stirred no more than a stone; but I knew what I looked on; through the dimness left in my eyes by many nights' weeping, I knew him. They said he was to sail by the *Antigua*. Madame Beck said so. She lied, or she had uttered what was once truth, and failed to contradict it when it became false. The *Antigua* was gone, and there stood Paul Emanuel.

Was I glad? A huge load left me. Was it a fact to warrant joy? I know not. Ask first what were the circumstances attendant on this respite? How far did this delay concern *me?* Were there not those whom it might touch more nearly?

After all, who may this young girl, this Justine Marie, be? Not a stranger, reader; she is known to me by sight; she visits at the Rue Fossette: she is often of Madame Beck's Sunday parties. She is a relation of both the Becks and Walravens; she derives her baptismal name from the sainted nun who would have been her aunt had she lived; her patronymic is Sauveur; she is an heiress and an orphan, and M. Emanuel is her guardian; some say her godfather.

The family junta wish this heiress to be married to one of their band – which is it? Vital question – which is it?

I felt very glad now, that the drug administered in the sweet draught had filled me with a possession which made bed and chamber intolerable. I always, through my whole life, liked to penetrate to the real truth; I like seeking the goddess in her temple, and handling the veil, and daring the dread glance. O Titaness among deities! The covered outline of thine aspect sickens often through its uncertainty, but define to us one trait, show us one lineament, clear in awful sincerity; we may gasp in untold terror, but with that gasp we drink in a breath of thy divinity; our heart shakes, and its currents sway like rivers lifted by earthquake, but we have swallowed strength. To see and know the worst is to take from Fear her main advantage.

The Walravens' party, augmented in numbers, now became very gay. The gentlemen fetched refreshments from the kiosk, all sat down on the turf under the trees; they drank healths and sentiments; they laughed, they jested. M. Emanuel underwent some raillery, half good-humoured, half, I thought, malicious, especially on Madame Beck's part. I soon gathered that his voyage had been temporarily deferred of his own will, without the concurrence, even against the advice, of his friends; he had let the *Antigua* go, and had taken his berth in the *Paul et Virginie*, appointed to sail a fortnight later. It was his reason for this resolve which they teased him to assign, and which he would only vaguely indicate as 'the settlement of a little piece of business which he had set his heart upon.' What *was* this business? Nobody knew. Yes, there was one who seemed partly, at least, in his confidence; a meaning look passed between him and Justine Marie. "*La petite va m'aider – n'est-ce pas?*" said he. The answer was prompt enough, God knows?

"*Mais oui, je vous aiderai de tout mon coeur. Vous ferez de moi tout ce que vous voudrez, mon parrain.*"

And this dear 'parrain' took her hand and lifted it to his grateful lips. Upon which demonstration, I saw the light-complexioned young Teuton, Heinrich Mühler, grow restless, as if he did not like it. He even grumbled a few words, whereat M. Emanuel actually laughed in his face, and with the ruthless triumph of the assured conqueror, he drew his ward nearer to him.

M. Emanuel was indeed very joyous that night. He seemed not one whit subdued by the change of scene and action impending. He was the true life of the party; a little despotic, perhaps, determined to be chief in mirth, as well as in labour, yet from moment to moment proving indisputably his right of leadership. His was the wittiest word, the pleasantest anecdote, the frankest laugh. Restlessly active, after his manner, he multiplied himself to wait on all; but oh! I saw which was his favourite. I saw at whose feet he lay on the turf, I saw whom he folded carefully from the night air, whom he tended, watched, and cherished as the apple of his eye.

Still, hint and raillery flew thick, and still I gathered that while M. Paul should be absent, working for others, these others, not quite ungrateful, would guard for him the treasure he left in Europe. Let him bring them an Indian fortune: they would give him in return a young bride and a rich inheritance. As for the saintly consecration, the vow of constancy, that was forgotten: the blooming and charming Present prevailed over the Past; and, at length, his nun was indeed buried.

Thus it must be. The revelation was indeed come. Presentiment had not been mistaken in her impulse: there is a kind of presentiment which never *is* mistaken; it was I who had for a moment miscalculated; not seeing the true bearing of the oracle, I had thought she muttered of vision when, in truth, her prediction touched reality.

I might have paused longer upon what I saw; I might have deliberated ere I drew inferences. Some, perhaps, would have held the premises doubtful, the proofs insufficient; some slow sceptics would have incredulously examined ere they conclusively accepted the project of a marriage between a poor and unselfish man of forty, and his wealthy ward of eighteen; but far from me such shifts and palliatives, far from me such temporary evasion of the actual, such coward fleeing from the dread, the swift-footed, the all-overtaking Fact, such feeble suspense of submission to her the sole sovereign, such paltering and faltering resistance to the Power whose errand is to march conquering and to conquer, such traitor defection from the Truth.

No. I hastened to accept the whole plan. I extended my grasp and took it all in. I gathered it to me with a sort of rage of haste, and folded it round me, as the soldier struck on the field folds his colours about his breast. I invoked Conviction to nail upon me the certainty, abhorred while embraced, to fix it with the strongest spikes her strongest strokes could drive; and when the iron had entered well my soul, I stood up, as I thought, renovated.

In my infatuation, I said, "Truth, you are a good mistress to your faithful servants! While a Lie pressed me, how I suffered! Even when the Falsehood was still sweet, still flattering to the fancy, and warm to the feelings, it wasted me with hourly torment. The persuasion that affection was won could not be divorced from the dread that, by another turn of the wheel, it might be lost. Truth stripped away Falsehood, and Flattery, and Expectancy, and here I stand – free!"

Nothing remained now but to take my freedom to my chamber, to carry it with me to my bed and see what I could make of it. The play was not yet, indeed, quite played out. I might have waited and watched longer that love-scene under the trees, that sylvan courtship. Had there been nothing of love in the demonstration, my Fancy in this hour was so generous, so creative, she could have modelled for it the most salient lineaments, and given it the deepest life and highest colour of passion. But I *would* not look; I had fixed my resolve, but I would not violate my nature. And then – something tore me so cruelly under my shawl, something so dug into my side, a vulture so strong in beak and talon, I must be alone to grapple with it. I think I never felt jealousy till now. This was not like enduring the endearments of Dr. John and Paulina, against which while I sealed my eyes and my ears, while I withdrew thence my thoughts, my sense of harmony still acknowledged in it a charm. This was an outrage. The love born of beauty was not mine; I had nothing in common with it: I could not dare to meddle with it, but another love, venturing diffidently into life after long acquaintance, furnace-tried by pain, stamped by constancy, consolidated by affection's pure and durable alloy, submitted by intellect to intellect's own tests, and finally wrought up, by his own process, to his own unflawed completeness, this Love that laughed at Passion, his fast frenzies and his hot and hurried extinction, in *this* Love I had a vested interest; and whatever tended either to its culture or its destruction, I could not view impassibly.

I turned from the group of trees and the 'merrie companie' in its shade. Midnight was long past; the concert was over, the crowds were thinning. I followed the ebb. Leaving the radiant park and well-lit Haute-Ville (still well lit, this it seems was to be a 'nuit blanche' in Villette), I sought the dim lower quarter.

Dim I should not say, for the beauty of moonlight – forgotten in the park – here once more flowed in upon perception. High she rode, and calm and stainlessly she shone. The music and the mirth of the fête, the fire and bright hues of those lamps had out-done and out-shone her for an hour, but now, again, her glory and her silence triumphed. The rival lamps were dying: she held her course like a white fate. Drum, trumpet, bugle, had uttered their clangour, and were forgotten; with pencil-ray she wrote on heaven and on earth records for archives everlasting. She and those stars seemed to me at once the types and witnesses of truth all regnant. The night-sky lit her reign: like its slow-wheeling progress, advanced her victory – that onward movement which has been, and is, and will be from eternity to eternity.

These oil-twinkling streets are very still: I like them for their lowliness and peace. Homeward-bound burghers pass me now and then, but these companies are pedestrians, make little noise, and are soon gone. So well do I love Villette under her present aspect, not willingly would I re-enter under a roof, but that I am bent on pursuing my strange adventure to a successful close, and quietly regaining my bed in the great dormitory, before Madame Beck comes home.

Only one street lies between me and the Rue Fossette; as I enter it, for the first time, the sound of a carriage tears up the deep peace of this quarter. It comes this way – comes very fast. How loud sounds its rattle on the paved path! The street is narrow, and I keep carefully to the causeway. The carriage thunders past, but what do I see, or fancy I see, as it rushes by? Surely something white fluttered from that window – surely a hand waved a handkerchief. Was that signal meant for me? Am I known? Who could recognise me? That is not M. de Bassompierre's carriage, nor Mrs. Bretton's; and besides, neither the Hôtel Crécy nor the château of La Terrasse lies in that direction. Well, I have no time for conjecture; I must hurry home.

Gaining the Rue Fossette, reaching the pensionnat, all there was still; no fiacre had yet arrived with Madame and Désirée. I had left the great door ajar; should I find it thus? Perhaps the wind or some other accident may have thrown it to with sufficient force to start the spring-bolt? In that case, hopeless became admission; my adventure must issue in catastrophe. I lightly pushed the heavy leaf; would it yield?

Yes. As soundless, as unresisting, as if some propitious genius had waited on a sesame-charm, in the vestibule within. Entering with bated breath, quietly making all fast, shoelessly mounting the staircase, I sought the dormitory, and reached my couch.

* * *

Ay! I reached it, and once more drew a free inspiration. The next moment, I almost shrieked – almost, but not quite, thank Heaven!

Throughout the dormitory, throughout the house, there reigned at this hour the stillness of death. All slept, and in such hush, it seemed that none dreamed. Stretched on the nineteen beds lay nineteen forms, at full-length and motionless. On mine – the twentieth couch – nothing *ought* to have lain: I had left it void, and void should have found it. What, then; do I see between the half-drawn curtains? What dark, usurping shape, supine, long, and strange? Is it a robber who has made his way through the open street-door, and lies there in wait? It looks very black, I think it looks – not human. Can it be a wandering dog that has come in from the street and crept and nestled hither? Will it spring, will it leap out if I approach? Approach I must. Courage! One step! –

My head reeled, for by the faint night-lamp, I saw stretched on my bed the old phantom – the nun.

A cry at this moment might have ruined me. Be the spectacle what it might, I could afford neither consternation, scream, nor swoon. Besides, I was not overcome. Tempered by late incidents, my nerves disdained hysteria. Warm from illuminations, and music, and thronging thousands, thoroughly lashed up by a new scourge, I defied spectra. In a moment, without exclamation, I had rushed on the haunted couch; nothing leaped out, or sprung, or stirred; all the movement was mine, so was all the life, the reality, the substance, the force; as my instinct felt. I tore her up – the incubus! I held her on high – the goblin! I shook her loose – the mystery! And down she fell – down all around me – down in shreds and fragments – and I trode upon her.

Here again – behold the branchless tree, the unstabled Rosinante; the film of cloud, the flicker of moonshine. The long nun proved a long bolster dressed in a long black stole, and artfully invested with a white veil. The garments in very truth, strange as it may seem, were genuine nun's garments, and by some hand they had been disposed with a view to illusion. Whence came these vestments? Who contrived this artifice? These questions still remained. To the head-bandage was pinned a slip of paper: it bore in pencil these mocking words –

The nun of the attic bequeaths to Lucy Snowe her wardrobe. She will be seen in the Rue Fossette no more.

And what and who was she that had haunted me? She, I had actually seen three times. Not a woman of my acquaintance had the stature of that ghost. She was not of a female height. Not to any man I knew could the machination, for a moment, be attributed.

Still mystified beyond expression, but as thoroughly, as suddenly, relieved from all sense of the spectral and unearthly; scorning also to wear out my brain with the frct of a trivial though insoluble riddle, I just bundled together stole, veil, and bandages, thrust them beneath my pillow, lay down, listened till I heard the wheels of Madame's home-returning fiacre, then turned, and worn out by many nights' vigils, conquered, too, perhaps, by the now reacting narcotic, I deeply slept.

Chapter Forty
The Happy Pair

THE DAY SUCCEEDING this remarkable Midsummer night proved no common day. I do not mean that it brought signs in heaven above, or portents on the earth beneath; nor do I allude to meteorological phenomena, to storm, flood, or whirlwind. On the contrary: the sun rose jocund, with a July face. Morning decked her beauty with rubies, and so filled her lap with roses, that they fell from her in showers, making her path blush: the Hours woke fresh as nymphs, and emptying on the early hills their dew-vials, they stepped out dismantled of vapour: shadowless, azure, and glorious, they led the sun's steeds on a burning and unclouded course.

In short, it was as fine a day as the finest summer could boast; but I doubt whether I was not the sole inhabitant of the Rue Fossette, who cared or remembered to note this pleasant fact. Another thought busied all other heads; a thought, indeed, which had its share in my meditations; but this master consideration, not possessing for me so entire a novelty, so overwhelming a suddenness, especially so dense a mystery, as it offered to the majority of my co-speculators thereon, left me somewhat more open than the rest to any collateral observation or impression.

Still, while walking in the garden, feeling the sunshine, and marking the blooming and growing plants, I pondered the same subject the whole house discussed.

What subject?

Merely this. When matins came to be said, there was a place vacant in the first rank of boarders. When breakfast was served, there remained a coffee-cup unclaimed. When the housemaid made the beds, she found in one, a bolster laid lengthwise, clad in a cap and night-gown; and when Ginevra Fanshawe's music-mistress came early, as usual, to give the morning lesson, that accomplished and promising young person, her pupil, failed utterly to be forthcoming.

High and low was Miss Fanshawe sought; through length and breadth was the house ransacked; vainly; not a trace, not an indication, not so much as a scrap of a billet rewarded the search; the nymph was vanished, engulfed in the past night, like a shooting star swallowed up by darkness.

Deep was the dismay of surveillante teachers, deeper the horror of the defaulting directress. Never had I seen Madame Beck so pale or so appalled. Here was a blow struck at her tender part, her weak side; here was damage done to her interest. How, too, had the untoward event happened? By what outlet had the fugitive taken wing? Not a casement was found unfastened, not a pane of glass broken; all the doors were bolted secure. Never to this day has Madame Beck obtained satisfaction on this point, nor indeed has anybody else concerned, save and excepting one, Lucy Snowe, who could not forget how, to facilitate a certain enterprise, a certain great door had been drawn softly to its lintel, closed, indeed, but neither bolted nor secure. The thundering carriage-and-pair encountered were now likewise recalled, as well as that puzzling signal, the waved handkerchief.

From these premises, and one or two others, inaccessible to any but myself, I could draw but one inference. It was a case of elopement. Morally certain on this head, and seeing Madame Beck's profound embarrassment, I at last communicated my conviction. Having alluded to M. de Hamal's suit, I found, as I expected, that Madame Beck was perfectly au fait to that affair. She had long since discussed it with Mrs. Cholmondeley, and laid her own responsibility in the business on that lady's shoulders. To Mrs. Cholmondeley and M. de Bassompierre she now had recourse.

We found that the Hôtel Crécy was already alive to what had happened. Ginevra had written to her cousin Paulina, vaguely signifying hymeneal intentions; communications had been received from the family of de Hamal; M. de Bassompierre was on the track of the fugitives. He overtook them too late.

In the course of the week, the post brought me a note. I may as well transcribe it; it contains explanation on more than one point:

Dear Old Tim (short for Timon),

I am off you see – gone like a shot. Alfred and I intended to be married in this way almost from the first; we never meant to be spliced in the humdrum way of other people; Alfred has too much spirit for that, and so have I – Dieu merci! Do you know, Alfred, who used to call you 'the dragon', has seen so much of you during the last few months, that he begins to feel quite friendly towards you. He hopes you won't miss him now that he has gone; he begs to apologize for any little trouble he may have given you. He is afraid he rather inconvenienced you once when he came upon you in the grenier, just as you were reading a letter seemingly of the most special interest; but he could not resist the temptation to give you a start, you appeared so wonderfully taken up with your correspondent. En revanche, he says you once frightened him by rushing in for a dress or a shawl, or some other chiffon, at the moment when he had struck a light, and was going to take a quiet whiff of his cigar, while waiting for me.

Do you begin to comprehend by this time that M. le Comte de Hamal was the nun of the attic, and that he came to see your humble servant? I will tell you how he managed it. You know he has the entrée of the Athénée, where two or three of his nephews, the sons of his eldest sister, Madame de Melcy, are students. You know the court of the Athénée is on the other side of the high wall bounding your walk, the allée défendue. Alfred can climb as well as he can dance or fence: his amusement was to make the escalade of our pensionnat by mounting, first the wall; then – by the aid of that high tree overspreading the grand berceau, and resting some of its boughs on the roof of the lower buildings of our premises – he managed to scale the first classe and the grand salle. One night, by the way, he fell out of this tree, tore down some of the branches, nearly broke his own neck, and after all, in running away, got a terrible fright, and was nearly caught by two people, Madame Beck and M. Emanuel, he thinks, walking in the alley. From the grande salle the ascent is not difficult to the highest block of building, finishing in the great garret. The skylight, you know, is, day and night, left half open for air; by the skylight he entered. Nearly a year ago I chanced to tell him our legend of the nun; that suggested his romantic idea of the spectral disguise, which I think you must allow he has very cleverly carried out.

But for the nun's black gown and white veil, he would have been caught again and again both by you and that tiger-Jesuit, M. Paul. He thinks you both capital ghost-seers, and very brave. What I wonder at is, rather your secretiveness than your courage. How could you endure the visitations of that long spectre, time after time, without crying out, telling everybody, and rousing the whole house and neighbourhood?

Oh, and how did you like the nun as a bed-fellow? I dressed her up: didn't I do it well? Did you shriek when you saw her: I should have gone mad; but then you have such nerves! – Real iron and bend-leather! I believe you feel nothing. You haven't the same sensitiveness that a person of my constitution has. You seem to me insensible both to pain and fear and grief. You are a real old Diogenes.

Well, dear grandmother! And are you not mightily angry at my moonlight flitting and run away match? I assure you it is excellent fun, and I did it partly to spite that minx, Paulina, and that bear, Dr. John: to show them that, with all their airs, I could get married as well as they. M. de Bassompierre was at first in a strange fume with Alfred; he threatened a prosecution for 'détournement de mineur', and I know not what; he was so abominably in earnest, that I found myself forced to do a little bit of the melodramatic – go down on my knees, sob, cry, drench three pocket-handkerchiefs. Of course, 'mon oncle' soon gave in; indeed, where was the use of making a fuss? I am married, and that's all about it. He still says our marriage is not legal, because I am not of age, forsooth! As if that made any difference! I am just as much married as if I were a hundred. However, we are to be married again, and I am to have a trousseau, and Mrs. Cholmondeley is going to superintend it; and there are some hopes that M. de Bassompierre will give me a decent portion, which will be very convenient, as dear Alfred has nothing but his nobility, native and hereditary, and his pay. I only wish uncle would do things unconditionally, in a generous, gentleman-like fashion; he is so disagreeable as to make the dowry depend on Alfred's giving his written promise that he will never touch cards or dice from the day it is paid down. They accuse my angel of a tendency to play: I don't know anything about that, but I do know he is a dear, adorable creature.

I cannot sufficiently extol the genius with which de Hamal managed our flight. How clever in him to select the night of the fête, when Madame (for he knows her habits), as he said, would infallibly be absent at the concert in the park. I suppose you must have gone with her. I watched you rise and leave the dormitory about eleven o'clock. How you returned alone, and on foot, I cannot conjecture. That surely was you we met in the narrow old Rue St. Jean? Did you see me wave my handkerchief from the carriage window?

Adieu! Rejoice in my good luck: congratulate me on my supreme happiness, and believe me, dear cynic and misanthrope, yours, in the best of health and spirits,

   Ginevra Laura de Hamal, née Fanshawe.

P.S. – Remember, I am a countess now. Papa, mamma, and the girls at home, will be delighted to hear that. 'My daughter the Countess!' 'My sister the Countess!' Bravo! Sounds rather better than Mrs. John Bretton, hein?

* * *

In winding up Mistress Fanshawe's memoirs, the reader will no doubt expect to hear that she came finally to bitter expiation of her youthful levities. Of course, a large share of suffering lies in reserve for her future.

A few words will embody my farther knowledge respecting her.

I saw her towards the close of her honeymoon. She called on Madame Beck, and sent for me into the salon. She rushed into my arms laughing. She looked very blooming and beautiful: her curls were longer, her cheeks rosier than ever: her white bonnet and her Flanders veil, her orange-flowers and her bride's dress, became her mightily.

"I have got my portion!" she cried at once; (Ginevra ever stuck to the substantial; I always thought there was a good trading element in her composition, much as she scorned the 'bourgeoise';) "And uncle de Bassompierre is quite reconciled. I don't mind his calling Alfred a 'nincompoop' – that's only his coarse Scotch breeding; and I believe Paulina envies me, and Dr. John is wild with jealousy – fit to blow his brains out – and I'm so happy! I really think I've hardly anything left to wish for – unless it be a carriage and an hotel, and, oh! I – must introduce you to 'mon mari'. Alfred, come here!"

And Alfred appeared from the inner salon, where he was talking to Madame Beck, receiving the blended felicitations and reprimands of that lady. I was presented under my various names: the Dragon, Diogenes, and Timon. The young Colonel was very polite. He made me a prettily-turned, neatly-worded apology, about the ghost-visits, etc., concluding with saying that "the best excuse for all his iniquities stood there!" pointing to his bride.

And then the bride sent him back to Madame Beck, and she took me to herself, and proceeded literally to suffocate me with her unrestrained spirits, her girlish, giddy, wild nonsense. She showed her ring exultingly; she called herself Madame la Comtesse de Hamal, and asked how it sounded, a score of times. I said very little. I gave her only the crust and rind of my nature. No matter she expected of me nothing better – she knew me too well to look for compliments – my dry gibes pleased her well enough and the more impassible and prosaic my mien, the more merrily she laughed.

Soon after his marriage, M. de Hamal was persuaded to leave the army as the surest way of weaning him from certain unprofitable associates and habits; a post of attaché was procured for him, and he and his young wife went abroad. I thought she would forget me now, but she did not. For many years, she kept up a capricious, fitful sort of correspondence. During the first year or two, it was only of herself and Alfred she wrote; then, Alfred faded in the background; herself and a certain, newcomer prevailed; one Alfred Fanshawe de Bassompierre de Hamal began to reign in his father's stead. There were great boastings about this personage, extravagant amplifications upon miracles of precocity, mixed with vehement objurgations against the phlegmatic incredulity with which I received them. I didn't know 'what it was to be a mother'; 'unfeeling thing that I was, the sensibilities of the maternal heart were Greek and Hebrew to me,' and so on. In due course of nature this young gentleman took his degrees in teething, measles, hooping-cough: that was a terrible time for me – the mamma's letters became a perfect shout of affliction; never woman was so put upon by calamity: never human being stood in such need of sympathy. I was frightened at first, and wrote back pathetically; but I soon found out there was more cry than wool in the business, and relapsed into my natural cruel insensibility. As to the youthful sufferer, he weathered each storm like a hero. Five times was that youth 'in articulo mortis', and five times did he miraculously revive.

In the course of years there arose ominous murmurings against Alfred the First; M. de Bassompierre had to be appealed to, debts had to be paid, some of them of that dismal and dingy order called 'debts of honour'; ignoble plaints and difficulties became frequent. Under every cloud, no matter what its nature, Ginevra, as of old, called out lustily for sympathy and aid. She had no notion of meeting any distress single-handed. In some shape, from some quarter or other, she was pretty sure to obtain her will, and so she got on – fighting the battle of life by proxy, and, on the whole, suffering as little as any human being I have ever known.

Chapter Forty-One
Faubourg Clotilde

❧

MUST I, ere I close, render some account of that Freedom and Renovation which I won on the fête-night? Must I tell how I and the two stalwart companions I brought home from the illuminated park bore the test of intimate acquaintance?

I tried them the very next day. They had boasted their strength loudly when they reclaimed me from love and its bondage, but upon my demanding deeds, not words, some evidence of better comfort, some experience of a relieved life – Freedom excused himself, as for the present impoverished and disabled to assist; and Renovation never spoke; he had died in the night suddenly.

I had nothing left for it then but to trust secretly that conjecture might have hurried me too fast and too far, to sustain the oppressive hour by reminders of the distorting and discolouring magic of jealousy. After a short and vain struggle, I found myself brought back captive to the old rack of suspense, tied down and strained anew.

Shall I yet see him before he goes? Will he bear me in mind? Does he purpose to come? Will this day – will the next hour bring him? Or must I again assay that corroding pain of long attent – that rude agony of rupture at the close, that mute, mortal wrench, which, in at once uprooting hope and doubt, shakes life; while the hand that does the violence cannot be caressed to pity, because absence interposes her barrier!

It was the Feast of the Assumption; no school was held. The boarders and teachers, after attending mass in the morning, were gone a long walk into the country to take their goûter, or afternoon meal, at some farm-house. I did not go with them, for now but two days remained ere the *Paul et Virginie* must sail, and I was clinging to my last chance, as the living waif of a wreck clings to his last raft or cable.

There was some joiners' work to do in the first classe, some bench or desk to repair; holidays were often turned to account for the performance of these operations, which could not be executed when the rooms were filled with pupils. As I sat solitary, purposing to adjourn to the garden and leave the coast clear, but too listless to fulfil my own intent, I heard the workmen coming.

Foreign artisans and servants do everything by couples: I believe it would take two Labassecourien carpenters to drive a nail. While tying on my bonnet, which had hitherto hung by its ribbons from my idle hand, I vaguely and momentarily wondered to hear the step of but one 'ouvrier'. I noted, too – as captives in dungeons find sometimes dreary leisure to note the merest trifles – that this man wore shoes, and not sabots: I concluded that it must be the master-carpenter, coming to inspect before he sent his journeymen. I threw round me my scarf. He advanced; he opened the door; my back was towards it; I felt a little thrill – a curious sensation, too quick and transient to be analyzed. I turned, I stood in the supposed master-artisan's presence: looking towards the door-way, I saw it filled with a figure, and my eyes printed upon my brain the picture of M. Paul.

Hundreds of the prayers with which we weary Heaven bring to the suppliant no fulfilment. Once haply in life, one golden gift falls prone in the lap – one boon full and bright, perfect from Fruition's mint.

M. Emanuel wore the dress in which he probably purposed to travel – a surtout, guarded with velvet; I thought him prepared for instant departure, and yet I had understood that two days were yet to run before the ship sailed. He looked well and cheerful. He looked kind and benign: he came in with eagerness; he was close to me in one second; he was all amity. It might be his bridegroom mood which thus brightened him. Whatever the cause, I could not meet his sunshine with cloud. If this were my last moment with him, I would not waste it in forced, unnatural distance. I loved him well – too well not to smite out of my path even Jealousy herself, when she would have obstructed a kind farewell. A cordial word from his lips, or a gentle look from his eyes, would do me good, for all the span of life that remained to me; it would be comfort in the last strait of loneliness; I would take it – I would taste the elixir, and pride should not spill the cup.

The interview would be short, of course: he would say to me just what he had said to each of the assembled pupils; he would take and hold my hand two minutes; he would touch my cheek with his lips for the first, last, only time – and then – no more. Then, indeed, the final parting, then the wide separation, the great gulf I could not pass to go to him – across which, haply, he would not glance, to remember me.

He took my hand in one of his, with the other he put back my bonnet; he looked into my face, his luminous smile went out, his lips expressed something almost like the wordless language of a mother who finds a child greatly and unexpectedly changed, broken with illness, or worn out by want. A check supervened.

"Paul, Paul!" said a woman's hurried voice behind, "Paul, come into the salon; I have yet a great many things to say to you – conversation for the whole day – and so has Victor; and Josef is here. Come Paul, come to your friends."

Madame Beck, brought to the spot by vigilance or an inscrutable instinct, pressed so near, she almost thrust herself between me and M. Emanuel.

"Come, Paul!" she reiterated, her eye grazing me with its hard ray like a steel stylet. She pushed against her kinsman. I thought he receded; I thought he would go. Pierced deeper than I could endure, made now to feel what defied suppression, I cried –

"My heart will break!"

What I felt seemed literal heart-break; but the seal of another fountain yielded under the strain: one breath from M. Paul, the whisper, "Trust me!" lifted a load, opened an outlet. With many a deep sob, with thrilling, with icy shiver, with strong trembling, and yet with relief – I wept.

"Leave her to me; it is a crisis: I will give her a cordial, and it will pass," said the calm Madame Beck.

To be left to her and her cordial seemed to me something like being left to the poisoner and her bowl. When M. Paul answered deeply, harshly, and briefly – *"Laissez-moi!"* in the grim sound I felt a music strange, strong, but life-giving.

"Laissez-moi!" he repeated, his nostrils opening, and his facial muscles all quivering as he spoke.

"But this will never do," said Madame, with sternness. More sternly rejoined her kinsman –
"Sortez d'ici!"

"I will send for Père Silas: on the spot I will send for him," she threatened pertinaciously.

"Femme!" cried the Professor, not now in his deep tones, but in his highest and most excited key, *"Femme! Sortez à l'instant!"*

He was roused, and I loved him in his wrath with a passion beyond what I had yet felt.

"What you do is wrong," pursued Madame; "it is an act characteristic of men of your unreliable, imaginative temperament; a step impulsive, injudicious, inconsistent – a proceeding vexatious, and not estimable in the view of persons of steadier and more resolute character."

"You know not what I have of steady and resolute in me," said he, "but you shall see; the event shall teach you. Modeste," he continued less fiercely, "be gentle, be pitying, be a woman; look at this poor face, and relent. You know I am your friend, and the friend of your friends; in spite of your taunts, you well and deeply know I may be trusted. Of sacrificing myself I made no difficulty but my heart is pained by what I see; it *must* have and give solace. *Leave me!*"

This time, in the *'leave me'* there was an intonation so bitter and so imperative, I wondered that even Madame Beck herself could for one moment delay obedience; but she stood firm; she gazed upon him dauntless; she met his eye, forbidding and fixed as stone. She was opening her lips to retort; I saw over all M. Paul's face a quick rising light and fire; I can hardly tell how he managed the movement; it did not seem violent; it kept the form of courtesy; he gave his hand; it scarce touched her I thought; she ran, she whirled from the room; she was gone, and the door shut, in one second.

The flash of passion was all over very soon. He smiled as he told me to wipe my eyes; he waited quietly till I was calm, dropping from time to time a stilling, solacing word. Ere long I sat beside him once more myself – re-assured, not desperate, nor yet desolate; not friendless, not hopeless, not sick of life, and seeking death.

"It made you very sad then to lose your friend?" said he.

"It kills me to be forgotten, Monsieur," I said. "All these weary days I have not heard from you one word, and I was crushed with the possibility, growing to certainty, that you would depart without saying farewell!"

"Must I tell you what I told Modeste Beck – that you do not know me? Must I show and teach you my character? You *will* have proof that I can be a firm friend? Without clear proof this hand will not lie still in mine, it will not trust my shoulder as a safe stay? Good. The proof is ready. I come to justify myself."

"Say anything, teach anything, prove anything, Monsieur; I can listen now."

"Then, in the first place, you must go out with me a good distance into the town. I came on purpose to fetch you."

Without questioning his meaning, or sounding his plan, or offering the semblance of an objection, I re-tied my bonnet: I was ready.

The route he took was by the boulevards: he several times made me sit down on the seats stationed under the lime-trees; he did not ask if I was tired, but looked, and drew his own conclusions.

"All these weary days," said he, repeating my words, with a gentle, kindly mimicry of my voice and foreign accent, not new from his lips, and of which the playful banter never wounded, not even when coupled, as it often was, with the assertion, that however I might *write* his language, I *spoke* and always should speak it imperfectly and hesitatingly. "'All these weary days' I have not for one hour forgotten you. Faithful women err in this, that they think themselves the sole faithful of God's creatures. On a very fervent and living truth to myself, I, too, till lately scarce dared count, from any quarter; but – look at me."

I lifted my happy eyes: they *were* happy now, or they would have been no interpreters of my heart.

"Well," said he, after some seconds' scrutiny, "there is no denying that signature: Constancy wrote it: her pen is of iron. Was the record painful?"

"Severely painful," I said, with truth. "Withdraw her hand, Monsieur; I can bear its inscribing force no more."

"*Elle est toute pâle*," said he, speaking to himself; "*cette figure-là me fait mal.*"

"Ah! I am not pleasant to look at –?"

I could not help saying this; the words came unbidden: I never remember the time when I had not a haunting dread of what might be the degree of my outward deficiency; this dread pressed me at the moment with special force.

A great softness passed upon his countenance; his violet eyes grew suffused and glistening under their deep Spanish lashes: he started up; "Let us walk on."

"Do I displease your eyes *much*?" I took courage to urge: the point had its vital import for me.

He stopped, and gave me a short, strong answer; an answer which silenced, subdued, yet profoundly satisfied. Ever after that I knew what I was for *him*; and what I might be for the rest of the world, I ceased painfully to care. Was it weak to lay so much stress on an opinion about appearance? I fear it might be; I fear it was; but in that case I must avow no light share of weakness. I must own great fear of displeasing – a strong wish moderately to please M. Paul.

Whither we rambled, I scarce knew. Our walk was long, yet seemed short; the path was pleasant, the day lovely. M. Emanuel talked of his voyage – he thought of staying away three years. On his return from Guadaloupe, he looked forward to release from liabilities and a clear course; and what did I purpose doing in the interval of his absence? He asked. I had talked once, he reminded me, of trying to be independent and keeping a little school of my own: had I dropped the idea?

"Indeed, I had not: I was doing my best to save what would enable me to put it in practice."

"He did not like leaving me in the Rue Fossette; he feared I should miss him there too much – I should feel desolate – I should grow sad –?"

This was certain; but I promised to do my best to endure.

"Still," said he, speaking low, "there is another objection to your present residence. I should wish to write to you sometimes: it would not be well to have any uncertainty about the safe transmission of letters; and in the Rue Fossette – in short, our Catholic discipline in certain matters – though justifiable and expedient – might possibly, under peculiar circumstances, become liable to misapplication – perhaps abuse."

"But if you write," said I, "I *must* have your letters; and I *will* have them: ten directors, twenty directresses, shall not keep them from me. I am a Protestant: I will not bear that kind of discipline: Monsieur, I *will not.*"

"*Doucement – doucement*," rejoined he; "we will contrive a plan; we have our resources: *soyez tranquille.*"

So speaking, he paused.

We were now returning from the long walk. We had reached the middle of a clean Faubourg, where the houses were small, but looked pleasant. It was before the white door-step of a very neat abode that M. Paul had halted.

"I call here," said he.

He did not knock, but taking from his pocket a key, he opened and entered at once. Ushering me in, he shut the door behind us. No servant appeared. The vestibule was small, like the house, but freshly and tastefully painted; its vista closed in a French window with vines trained about the panes, tendrils, and green leaves kissing the glass. Silence reigned in this dwelling.

Opening an inner door, M. Paul disclosed a parlour, or salon – very tiny, but I thought, very pretty. Its delicate walls were tinged like a blush; its floor was waxed; a square of brilliant carpet covered its centre; its small round table shone like the mirror over its hearth; there was a little couch, a little chiffonnière, the half-open, crimson-silk door of which, showed porcelain on the shelves; there was a French clock, a lamp; there were ornaments in biscuit china; the recess of the single ample window was filled with a green stand, bearing three green flower-pots, each filled with a fine plant glowing in bloom; in one corner appeared a guéridon with a marble top, and upon it a work-box, and a glass filled with violets in water. The lattice of this room was open; the outer air breathing through, gave freshness, the sweet violets lent fragrance.

"Pretty, pretty place!" said I. M. Paul smiled to see me so pleased.

"Must we sit down here and wait?" I asked in a whisper, half awed by the deep pervading hush.

"We will first peep into one or two other nooks of this nutshell," he replied.

"Dare you take the freedom of going all over the house?" I inquired.

"Yes, I dare," said he, quietly.

He led the way. I was shown a little kitchen with a little stove and oven, with few but bright brasses, two chairs and a table. A small cupboard held a diminutive but commodious set of earthenware.

"There is a coffee service of china in the salon," said M. Paul, as I looked at the six green and white dinner-plates; the four dishes, the cups and jugs to match.

Conducted up the narrow but clean staircase, I was permitted a glimpse of two pretty cabinets of sleeping-rooms; finally, I was once more led below, and we halted with a certain ceremony before a larger door than had yet been opened.

Producing a second key, M. Emanuel adjusted it to the lock of this door. He opened, put me in before him.

"Voici!" he cried.

I found myself in a good-sized apartment, scrupulously clean, though bare, compared with those I had hitherto seen. The well-scoured boards were carpetless; it contained two rows of green benches and desks, with an alley down the centre, terminating in an estrade, a teacher's chair and table; behind them a tableau. On the walls hung two maps; in the windows flowered a few hardy plants; in short, here was a miniature classe – complete, neat, pleasant.

"It is a school then?" said I. "Who keeps it? I never heard of an establishment in this faubourg."

"Will you have the goodness to accept of a few prospectuses for distribution in behalf of a friend of mine?" asked he, taking from his surtout-pocket some quires of these documents, and putting them into my hand. I looked, I read – printed in fair characters:

Externat de demoiselles. Numéro 7, Faubourg Clotilde, Directrice, Mademoiselle Lucy Snowe.

* * *

And what did I say to M. Paul Emanuel?

Certain junctures of our lives must always be difficult of recall to memory. Certain points, crises, certain feelings, joys, griefs, and amazements, when reviewed, must strike us as things wildered and whirling, dim as a wheel fast spun.

I can no more remember the thoughts or the words of the ten minutes succeeding this disclosure, than I can retrace the experience of my earliest year of life: and yet the first thing distinct to me is the consciousness that I was speaking very fast, repeating over and over again:

"Did you do this, M. Paul? Is this your house? Did you furnish it? Did you get these papers printed? Do you mean me? Am I the directress? Is there another Lucy Snowe? Tell me: say something."

But he would not speak. His pleased silence, his laughing down-look, his attitude, are visible to me now.

"How is it? I must know all – *all*," I cried.

The packet of papers fell on the floor. He had extended his hand, and I had fastened thereon, oblivious of all else.

"Ah! You said I had forgotten you all these weary days," said he. "Poor old Emanuel! These are the thanks he gets for trudging about three mortal weeks from house-painter to upholsterer, from cabinet-maker to charwoman. Lucy and Lucy's cot, the sole thoughts in his head!"

I hardly knew what to do. I first caressed the soft velvet on his cuff, and then I stroked the hand it surrounded. It was his foresight, his goodness, his silent, strong, effective goodness, that overpowered me by their proved reality. It was the assurance of his sleepless interest which broke on me like a light from heaven; it was his – I will dare to say it – his fond, tender look, which now shook me indescribably. In the midst of all I forced myself to look at the practical.

"The trouble!" I cried, "and the cost! Had you money, M. Paul?"

"Plenty of money!" said he heartily. "The disposal of my large teaching connection put me in possession of a handsome sum with part of it I determined to give myself the richest treat that I *have* known or *shall* know. I like this. I have reckoned on this hour day and night lately. I would not come near you, because I would not forestall it. Reserve is neither my virtue nor my vice. If I had put myself into your power, and you had begun with your questions of look and lip – Where have you been, M. Paul? What have you been doing? What is your mystery? – My solitary first and last secret would presently have unravelled itself in your lap. Now," he pursued, "you shall live here and have a school; you shall employ yourself while I am away; you shall think of me sometimes; you shall mind your health and happiness for my sake, and when I come back –"

There he left a blank.

I promised to do all he told me. I promised to work hard and willingly. "I will be your faithful steward," I said; "I trust at your coming the account will be ready. Monsieur, monsieur, you are *too* good!"

In such inadequate language my feelings struggled for expression: they could not get it; speech, brittle and unmalleable, and cold as ice, dissolved or shivered in the effort. He watched me, still; he gently raised his hand to stroke my hair; it touched my lips in passing; I pressed it close, I paid it tribute. He was my king; royal for me had been that hand's bounty; to offer homage was both a joy and a duty.

* * *

The afternoon hours were over, and the stiller time of evening shaded the quiet faubourg. M. Paul claimed my hospitality; occupied and afoot since morning, he needed refreshment; he said I should offer him chocolate in my pretty gold and white china service. He went out and ordered what was needful from the restaurant; he placed the small guéridon and two chairs in the balcony outside the French window under the screening vines. With what shy joy I accepted my part as hostess, arranged the salver, served the benefactor-guest.

This balcony was in the rear of the house, the gardens of the faubourg were round us, fields extended beyond. The air was still, mild, and fresh. Above the poplars, the laurels, the cypresses, and the roses, looked up a moon so lovely and so halcyon, the heart trembled under her smile; a star shone subject beside her, with the unemulous ray of pure love. In a large garden near us, a jet rose from a well, and a pale statue leaned over the play of waters.

M. Paul talked to me. His voice was so modulated that it mixed harmonious with the silver whisper, the gush, the musical sigh, in which light breeze, fountain and foliage intoned their lulling vesper:

Happy hour – stay one moment! Droop those plumes, rest those wings; incline to mine that brow of Heaven! White Angel! Let thy light linger; leave its reflection on succeeding clouds; bequeath its cheer to that time which needs a ray in retrospect!

Our meal was simple: the chocolate, the rolls, the plate of fresh summer fruit, cherries and strawberries bedded in green leaves formed the whole: but it was what we both liked better than a feast, and I took a delight inexpressible in tending M. Paul. I asked him whether his friends, Père Silas and Madame Beck, knew what he had done – whether they had seen my house?

"*Mon amie*," said he, "none knows what I have done save you and myself: the pleasure is consecrated to us two, unshared and unprofaned. To speak truth, there has been to me in this matter a refinement of enjoyment I would not make vulgar by communication. Besides" (smiling) "I wanted to prove to Miss Lucy that I *could* keep a secret. How often has she taunted me with lack of dignified reserve and needful caution! How many times has she saucily insinuated that all my affairs are the secret of Polichinelle!"

This was true enough: I had not spared him on this point, nor perhaps on any other that was assailable. Magnificent-minded, grand-hearted, dear, faulty little man! You deserved candour, and from me always had it.

Continuing my queries, I asked to whom the house belonged, who was my landlord, the amount of my rent. He instantly gave me these particulars in writing; he had foreseen and prepared all things.

The house was not M. Paul's – that I guessed: he was hardly the man to become a proprietor; I more than suspected in him a lamentable absence of the saving faculty; he could get, but not keep; he needed a treasurer. The tenement, then, belonged to a citizen in the Basse-Ville – a man of substance, M. Paul said; he startled me by adding: "a friend of yours, Miss Lucy, a person who has a most respectful regard for you." And, to my pleasant surprise, I found the landlord was none other than M. Miret, the short-tempered and kind-hearted bookseller, who had so kindly found me a seat that eventful night in the park. It seems M. Miret was, in his station, rich, as well as much respected, and possessed several houses in this faubourg; the rent was moderate, scarce half of what it would have been for a house of equal size nearer the centre of Villette.

"And then," observed M. Paul, "should fortune not favour you, though I think she will, I have the satisfaction to think you are in good hands; M. Miret will not be extortionate: the first year's rent you have already in your savings; afterwards Miss Lucy must trust God, and herself. But now, what will you do for pupils?"

"I must distribute my prospectuses."

"Right! By way of losing no time, I gave one to M. Miret yesterday. Should you object to beginning with three petite bourgeoises, the Demoiselles Miret? They are at your service."

"Monsieur, you forget nothing; you are wonderful. Object? It would become me indeed to object! I suppose I hardly expect at the outset to number aristocrats in my little day-school; I care not if they never come. I shall be proud to receive M. Miret's daughters."

"Besides these," pursued he, "another pupil offers, who will come daily to take lessons in English; and as she is rich, she will pay handsomely. I mean my god-daughter and ward, Justine Marie Sauveur."

What is in a name? – what in three words? Till this moment I had listened with living joy – I had answered with gleeful quickness; a name froze me; three words struck me mute. The effect could not be hidden, and indeed I scarce tried to hide it.

"What now?" said M. Paul.

"Nothing."

"Nothing! Your countenance changes: your colour and your very eyes fade. Nothing! You must be ill; you have some suffering; tell me what."

I had nothing to tell.

He drew his chair nearer. He did not grow vexed, though I continued silent and icy. He tried to win a word; he entreated with perseverance, he waited with patience.

"Justine Marie is a good girl," said he, "docile and amiable; not quick – but you will like her."

"I think not. I think she must not come here."

Such was my speech.

"Do you wish to puzzle me? Do you know her? But, in truth, there *is* something. Again you are pale as that statue. Rely on Paul Carlos; tell him the grief."

His chair touched mine; his hand, quietly advanced, turned me towards him.

"Do you know Marie Justine?" said he again.

The name re-pronounced by his lips overcame me unaccountably. It did not prostrate – no, it stirred me up, running with haste and heat through my veins – recalling an hour of quick pain, many days and nights of heart-sickness. Near me as he now sat, strongly and closely as he had long twined his life in mine – far as had progressed, and near as was achieved our minds' and affections' assimilation – the very suggestion of interference, of heart-separation, could be heard only with a fermenting excitement, an impetuous throe, a disdainful resolve, an ire, a resistance of which no human eye or cheek could hide the flame, nor any truth-accustomed human tongue curb the cry.

"I want to tell you something," I said: "I want to tell you all."

"Speak, Lucy; come near; speak. Who prizes you, if I do not? Who is your friend, if not Emanuel? Speak!"

I spoke. All escaped from my lips. I lacked not words now; fast I narrated; fluent I told my tale; it streamed on my tongue. I went back to the night in the park; I mentioned the medicated draught – why it was given – its goading effect – how it had torn rest from under my head, shaken me from my couch, carried me abroad with the lure of a vivid yet solemn fancy – a summer-night solitude on turf, under trees, near a deep, cool lakelet. I told the scene realized; the crowd, the masques, the music, the lamps, the splendours, the guns booming afar, the bells sounding on high. All I had encountered I detailed, all I had recognised, heard, and seen; how I had beheld and watched himself: how I listened, how much heard, what conjectured; the whole history, in brief, summoned to his confidence, rushed thither, truthful, literal, ardent, bitter.

Still as I narrated, instead of checking, he incited me to proceed; he spurred me by the gesture, the smile, the half-word. Before I had half done, he held both my hands, he consulted my eyes with a most piercing glance: there was something in his face which tended neither to calm nor to put me down; he forgot his own doctrine, he forsook his own system of repression when I most challenged its exercise. I think I deserved strong reproof; but when have we our deserts? I merited severity; he looked indulgence. To my very self I seemed imperious and unreasonable, for I forbade Justine Marie my door and roof; he smiled, betraying delight. Warm, jealous, and haughty, I knew not till now that my nature had such a mood: he gathered me near his heart. I was full of faults; he took them and me all home. For the moment of utmost mutiny, he reserved the one deep spell of peace. These words caressed my ear:

"Lucy, take my love. One day share my life. Be my dearest, first on earth."

We walked back to the Rue Fossette by moonlight – such moonlight as fell on Eden – shining through the shades of the Great Garden, and haply gilding a path glorious for a step divine – a Presence nameless. Once in their lives some men and women go back to these first fresh days of our great Sire and Mother – taste that grand morning's dew – bathe in its sunrise.

In the course of the walk I was told how Justine Marie Sauveur had always been regarded with the affection proper to a daughter – how, with M. Paul's consent, she had been affianced for months to one Heinrich Mühler, a wealthy young German merchant, and was to be married in the course of a year. Some of M. Emanuel's relations and connections would, indeed, it seems, have liked him to marry her, with a view to securing her fortune in the family; but to himself the scheme was repugnant, and the idea totally inadmissible.

We reached Madame Beck's door. Jean Baptiste's clock tolled nine. At this hour, in this house, eighteen months since, had this man at my side bent before me, looked into my face and eyes, and arbitered my destiny. This very evening he had again stooped, gazed, and decreed. How different the look – how far otherwise the fate!

He deemed me born under his star: he seemed to have spread over me its beam like a banner. Once – unknown, and unloved, I held him harsh and strange; the low stature, the wiry make, the angles, the darkness, the manner, displeased me. Now, penetrated with his influence, and living by his affection, having his worth by intellect, and his goodness by heart – I preferred him before all humanity.

We parted: he gave me his pledge, and then his farewell. We parted: the next day – he sailed.

Chapter Forty-Two
Finis

❦

MAN CANNOT PROPHESY. Love is no oracle. Fear sometimes imagines a vain thing. Those years of absence! How had I sickened over their anticipation! The woe they must bring seemed certain as death. I knew the nature of their course: I never had doubt how it would harrow as it went. The juggernaut on his car towered there a grim load. Seeing him draw nigh, burying his broad wheels in the oppressed soil – I, the prostrate votary – felt beforehand the annihilating craunch.

Strange to say – strange, yet true, and owning many parallels in life's experience – that anticipatory craunch proved all – yes – nearly *all* the torture. The great Juggernaut, in his great chariot, drew on lofty, loud, and sullen. He passed quietly, like a shadow sweeping the sky, at noon. Nothing but a chilling dimness was seen or felt. I looked up. Chariot and demon charioteer were gone by; the votary still lived.

M. Emanuel was away three years. Reader, they were the three happiest years of my life. Do you scout the paradox? Listen. I commenced my school; I worked – I worked hard. I deemed myself the steward of his property, and determined, God willing, to render a good account. Pupils came – burghers at first – a higher class ere long. About the middle of the second year an unexpected chance threw into my hands an additional hundred pounds: one day I received from England a letter containing that sum. It came from Mr. Marchmont, the cousin and heir of my dear and dead mistress. He was just recovering from a dangerous illness; the money was a peace-offering to his conscience, reproaching him in the matter of, I know not what, papers or memoranda found after his kinswoman's death – naming or recommending Lucy Snowe. Mrs. Barrett had given him my address. How far his conscience had been sinned against, I never inquired. I asked no questions, but took the cash and made it useful.

With this hundred pounds I ventured to take the house adjoining mine. I would not leave that which M. Paul had chosen, in which he had left, and where he expected again to find me. My externat became a pensionnat; that also prospered.

The secret of my success did not lie so much in myself, in any endowment, any power of mine, as in a new state of circumstances, a wonderfully changed life, a relieved heart. The spring which moved my energies lay far away beyond seas, in an Indian isle. At parting, I had been left a legacy; such a thought for the present, such a hope for the future, such a motive for a persevering, a laborious, an enterprising, a patient and a brave course – I *could* not flag. Few things shook me now; few things had importance to vex, intimidate, or depress me: most things pleased – mere trifles had a charm.

Do not think that this genial flame sustained itself, or lived wholly on a bequeathed hope or a parting promise. A generous provider supplied bounteous fuel. I was spared all chill, all stint; I was not suffered to fear penury; I was not tried with suspense. By every vessel he wrote; he wrote as he gave and as he loved, in full-handed, full-hearted plenitude. He wrote because he liked to write; he did not abridge, because he cared not to abridge. He sat down, he took pen and paper, because he loved Lucy and had much to say to her; because he was faithful and thoughtful, because he was tender and true. There was no sham and no cheat, and no hollow unreal in him. Apology never dropped her slippery oil on his lips – never proffered, by his pen, her coward feints and paltry nullities: he would give neither a stone, nor an excuse – neither a scorpion; nor a disappointment; his letters were real food that nourished, living water that refreshed.

And was I grateful? God knows! I believe that scarce a living being so remembered, so sustained, dealt with in kind so constant, honourable and noble, could be otherwise than grateful to the death.

Adherent to his own religion (in him was not the stuff of which is made the facile apostate), he freely left me my pure faith. He did not tease nor tempt. He said:

"Remain a Protestant. My little English Puritan, I love Protestantism in you. I own its severe charm. There is something in its ritual I cannot receive myself, but it is the sole creed for 'Lucy'."

All Rome could not put into him bigotry, nor the Propaganda itself make him a real Jesuit. He was born honest, and not false – artless, and not cunning – a freeman, and not a slave. His tenderness had rendered him ductile in a priest's hands, his affection, his devotedness, his sincere pious enthusiasm blinded his kind eyes sometimes, made him abandon justice to himself to do the work of craft, and serve the ends of selfishness; but these are faults so rare to find, so costly to their owner to indulge, we scarce know whether they will not one day be reckoned amongst the jewels.

* * *

And now the three years are past: M. Emanuel's return is fixed. It is Autumn; he is to be with me ere the mists of November come. My school flourishes, my house is ready: I have made him a little library, filled its shelves with the books he left in my care: I have cultivated out of love for him (I was naturally no florist) the plants he preferred, and some of them are yet in bloom. I thought I loved him when he went away; I love him now in another degree: he is more my own.

The sun passes the equinox; the days shorten, the leaves grow sere; but – he is coming.

Frosts appear at night; November has sent his fogs in advance; the wind takes its autumn moan; but – he is coming.

The skies hang full and dark – a wrack sails from the west; the clouds cast themselves into strange forms – arches and broad radiations; there rise resplendent mornings – glorious, royal, purple as monarch in his state; the heavens are one flame; so wild are they, they rival battle at its thickest – so bloody, they shame Victory in her pride. I know some signs of the sky; I have noted them ever since childhood. God watch that sail! Oh! Guard it!

The wind shifts to the west. Peace, peace, Banshee – 'keening' at every window! It will rise – it will swell – it shrieks out long: wander as I may through the house this night, I cannot lull the blast. The advancing hours make it strong: by midnight, all sleepless watchers hear and fear a wild south-west storm. That storm roared frenzied, for seven days. It did not cease till the Atlantic was strewn with wrecks: it did not lull till the deeps had gorged their full of sustenance. Not till the destroying angel of tempest had achieved his perfect work, would he fold the wings whose waft was thunder – the tremor of whose plumes was storm.

Peace, be still! Oh! A thousand weepers, praying in agony on waiting shores, listened for that voice, but it was not uttered – not uttered till; when the hush came, some could not feel it: till, when the sun returned, his light was night to some!

Here pause: pause at once. There is enough said. Trouble no quiet, kind heart; leave sunny imaginations hope. Let it be theirs to conceive the delight of joy born again fresh out of great terror, the rapture of rescue from peril, the wondrous reprieve from dread, the fruition of return. Let them picture union and a happy succeeding life.

Madame Beck prospered all the days of her life; so did Père Silas; Madame Walravens fulfilled her ninetieth year before she died. Farewell.

Biographies

Emily and Charlotte Brontë

The intrigue surrounding Emily Brontë (1818–48) and Charlotte Brontë (1816–55), authors of some of the most well-known and loved British novels, still entices fans more than 150 years after their works' publication. As for many writers, childhood lay the groundwork for both Emily's and Charlotte's writing.

Early Lives of the Brontë Sisters

Emily and Charlotte and their four siblings (altogether five girls and one boy) grew up in Haworth, West Yorkshire, when the family moved there in 1820 for their father, Patrick (1777–1861), to take up the position of curate. At a young age, their mother, Maria (1783–1821), died of cancer, leaving the children under the care of Patrick and his sister, Elizabeth Branwell (1776–1842). The losses Emily and Charlotte were to suffer during childhood were not yet over. In 1824 four of the sisters, Maria (1814–25), Elizabeth (1815–25), Charlotte and Emily were sent away to the Clergy Daughters' School in Lancashire, a psychologically dark time that also resulted in the deaths the two elder sisters, Maria and Elizabeth – tuberculosis took them both in June 1825. Charlotte and Emily then returned home to their sister, Anne, and brother, Branwell, clearly marked by these formative experiences. The four siblings found mental relief by creating romantic, imaginary worlds, which they populated with complex characters and elaborate events, these exercises in fantasy equipping the Brontë sisters for later literary efforts. Their time at school, however brief, taught the sisters that life could be harsh and bleak, having a profound effect on Charlotte especially, as seen in her most famous novel, *Jane Eyre* (1847).

Emily's Writing Career

After trying her hand at teaching in 1838, an experience which left her tired and weak, Emily – accompanied by Charlotte and Anne – journeyed to Brussels to study French, German and literature under Constantin Heger. Of her sisters, Emily alone returned home to Haworth when her aunt died in 1842, and remained at Haworth to take care of her father.

It was not until 1846 that Emily first published any of her literary efforts, in the form of a book of poetry written by herself, Charlotte and Anne. Published under their male pseudonyms and entitled *Poems by Currer, Ellis and Acton Bell* to avoid being patronised from the largely male critics, the collection only sold two copies. However, Emily was not deterred and published *Wuthering Heights* in 1847 (first published as a three-volume set along with *Agnes Grey* by Anne Brontë). Unfortunately, Emily was unable to enjoy the later appreciation of her novel's genius, or to write further novels, as she died of tuberculosis on 19 December 1848, just months after Branwell passed on. She was interred in the family vault in the Church of St Michael in Haworth, which stand as an evocative reminder of a fascinating family.

Charlotte's Writing Career

It was at Haworth in the 1840s that Charlotte began to make her first steps into the world of professional writing. She worked on various pieces, and achieved her first publication – a book of poems, co-authored with Emily and Anne, though only two copies sold. Then, in 1847, Charlotte's first novel *Jane Eyre* was published. It was an instant sensation, and changed her life and reputation forever.

Charlotte wrote other novels, although *Jane Eyre* is by far her most popular. *Shirley* (1849) and *Villette* (1853) received moderate acclaim, as did *The Professor*, published posthumously in 1857. Brontë also started a novel called *Emma*, of which only around 20 pages were written. *Villette* shares several themes with *Jane Eyre*, especially regarding women struggling to live on their own terms, despite the straightjackets of gender conventions. But while Jane ends up happily married, *Villette* ends with the protagonist, Lucy Snowe, being independently secure yet without the man she loves. In *Shirley*, Brontë also wrestled with the theme of women's struggle for independence, but blended this into broader reflections on the nature of exploitation in industrial society.

After the publication of *Jane Eyre*, Charlotte's publisher persuaded her to reveal her true identity, whereupon she travelled to London regularly, becoming friends with authors Elizabeth Gaskell (1810–65), William Makepeace Thackeray (1811–63) and Harriet Martineau (1802–76), among others. Accounts of Charlotte's time in London, however, describe her as a serious, shy and quiet woman, not the dynamic personality expected by society. How this seemingly quiet, inexperienced country girl wrote works of such acute society commentary, emotion and passion remains an enduring mystery.

Charlotte married Arthur Bell Nichols, her father's curate – thought by many to be the basis for Rochester's character – in June 1854. Soon after their marriage, she fell pregnant but died from tuberculosis, along with her unborn child, aged 38. Charlotte was interred in the family vault in Haworth.

Alison Case (Foreword)

ALISON CASE is the author of *Nelly Dean*, a novel about the secret life of the housekeeper at Wuthering Heights (Borough Press). She is a Professor of Victorian Literature and chair of Women's, Gender, and Sexuality Studies at Williams College in Williamstown, MA, where she also lives. She has published two books and numerous articles about Victorian literature and the history of the novel. She is currently working on a novel based on Sanditon.

Original Publication

Wuthering Heights by Emily Brontë
Originally Published (under the pseudonym 'Ellis Bell')
by Thomas Cautley Newby, London, 1847

Villette by Charlotte Brontë
Originally Published (under the pseudonym 'Currer Bell')
by Smith, Elder & Co., London, 1853

New & Classic Writing

Other Romantic Fantasy titles from FLAME TREE PUBLISHING include

Jane Austen: Pride & Prejudice | Emma
Jane Austen: Sense & Sensibility | Mansfield Park
Brontë Sisters: Jane Eyre | The Tenant of Wildfell Hall

Flame Tree's Gothic Fantasy books offer a carefully curated series of new titles, each with combinations of original and classic writing:

Chilling Horror Short Stories
Chilling Ghost Short Stories
Science Fiction Short Stories
Murder Mayhem Short Stories
Crime & Mystery Short Stories
Swords & Steam Short Stories
Dystopia Utopia Short Stories
Supernatural Horror Short Stories
Lost Worlds Short Stories
Time Travel Short Stories
Heroic Fantasy Short Stories
Agents & Spies Short Stories
Pirates & Ghosts Short Stories

as well as new companion titles which offer rich collections of classic fiction from masters of the gothic fantasy genres:

H.G. Wells Short Stories
Lovecraft Short Stories
Edgar Allan Poe Collection
Sherlock Holmes Collection
Knights of the Round Table

Available from all good bookstores, worldwide, and online at
flametreepublishing.com